10649891

SelectEditions

SELECTED AND EDITED

SelectEditions

BY READER'S DIGEST

VOLUME 3 1998
THE READER'S DIGEST ASSOCIATION, INC.
PLEASANTVILLE, NEW YORK

READER'S DIGEST SELECT EDITIONS

Editor-in-Chief: Tanis H. Erdmann
Executive Editor: Marjorie Palmer
Volume Editor: Dana Adkins
Book Editors: Christopher W. Davis, Paula Marchese
Volume Copy Editor: Tatiana Ivanow
Copy Editors: Daphne Hougham, Alexandra C. Koppen, Charles Pendergast
Art Director: Angelo Perrone

CONTENTS

Win the lottery. Beat the odds and walk away with a one-hundred-million-dollar jackpot. Who hasn't had the dream?

Now, for one down-on-her-luck single mother, the dream is about to come true.

It's also about to land her in big trouble.

PART ONE

CHAPTER 1

JACKSON studied the shopping mall's long corridor, noting haggard mothers piloting loaded strollers and the senior citizens group walking the mall both for exercise and conversation. Dressed in a gray pin-striped suit, the stocky Jackson stared intently at the north entrance to the shopping mall. That would no doubt be the one she would use, since the bus stop was right in front. She had, Jackson knew, no other form of transportation. Her live-in boyfriend's truck was in the impoundment lot, the fourth time in as many months. It must be getting a little tedious for her, he thought. The bus stop was on the main road. She would have to walk about a mile to get there, but she often did that. What other choice did she have? The baby would be with her. She would never leave it with the boyfriend. Jackson was certain of that.

While his name always remained Jackson for all his business endeavors, next month his appearance would change dramatically from the hefty middle-aged man he was currently. Facial features would be altered; weight would be lost, height added or taken away. Male or female? Aged or youthful? Often the persona would be taken from people he knew, either wholly or with bits of thread from different ones, sewn together until the delicate quilt of fabrication was complete. In school, chemistry had been a favorite subject. Combining his love of acting with his acumen for science, Jackson had achieved a rare double major in drama and chemical engineering. The accomplishment was serving him very well. Indeed, if only his classmates could see him now.

In keeping with today's character—an overweight, middle-aged male—a bead of perspiration suddenly sprouted on Jackson's forehead. His lips curled into a smile. This physical reaction pleased him, aided as it was by the padding he was wearing to conceal his own wiry frame. But it was more than that. He took pride in totally becoming the person he was pretending to be.

He dabbed his forehead with a handkerchief and smoothed down the synthetic fibers of his neatly groomed wig. Then he pulled open the door to the space he had rented in the mall and went inside. The area was clean and orderly—in fact too much so, he thought. It lacked the look of a true working space. The receptionist seated at the desk in the foyer looked up at him. In accordance with his instructions, she didn't speak. She had no idea who he was or why she was here. As soon as Jackson's appointment showed up, she had been instructed to leave. Soon she would be on a bus out of town, her purse a little fatter for her troubles.

The phone beside her sat silent, the typewriter next to that, unused. Yes, absolutely, too well organized. Jackson put a piece of paper in the typewriter and gave several quick spins to the platen knob. He then walked past the small reception area to the interior office, where he sat behind a scuffed wooden desk. A small TV sat in one corner of the room. He leaned back in the chair and stroked his thin, dark mustache. It too was made of synthetic fiber and attached to his skin with spirit gum. A putty base highlighted and shadowed his own delicate and straight nose to make it appear bulky and slightly crooked. His straight teeth were covered with acrylic caps to give them an uneven appearance. These illusions would be remembered by even the most casual observer. Thus when they were removed, he in essence disappeared. What more could someone wholeheartedly engaged in illegal activities want?

Soon, if things went according to plan, it would all begin again.

He only had one question to ask LuAnn Tyler. Based upon his experience, he was reasonably certain of her answer, but one just never knew. He dearly hoped for her sake that she would give the right answer. If not? Well, the baby would never know its mother, because the baby would be an orphan.

THE brisk wind sailed down the dirt road between thick woods on either side. Some trees were dying, bent by wind and disease into what seemed painful shapes, but most were ramrod straight, with soaring, leafy branches. On the left side of the road was a half circle of open space consisting of mud interspersed with patches of new spring grass. Nestled into this clearing were rusted engine blocks, piles of trash, and a small mountain of beer cans. In the middle of that semicircular island rested a squat mobile trailer atop a crumbling cinder block foundation. The trailer was an eyesore in the middle of nowhere. Its occupants would have agreed with that description: The middle of nowhere applied to themselves as well.

Inside the trailer, LuAnn Tyler looked at herself in the small mirror perched atop the chest of drawers. She held her face at an angle because the battered piece of furniture listed to one side with a broken leg. Her looks were her only asset—that had been beaten into her head ever since she could remember—although she could have used some dental work. Never stepping foot inside a dentist's office had contributed to that situation.

No smarts, of course, her father had said over and over. No smarts—or no opportunity to use them? She had never broached the subject with Benny Tyler, dead now these past five years. Her mother, Joy, who had passed away almost three years ago, had never been happier than after her husband died. That should have completely dispelled Benny Tyler's opinions of LuAnn's mental ability, but little girls believed what their daddies told them.

She looked over to the wall where a clock hung. It was the only thing she had of her mother's—a family heirloom of sorts, as it had been given to Joy Tyler by her own mother on the day she married Benny. It had no intrinsic value, yet LuAnn treasured it. As a little girl, she had listened to its slow, methodical ticks far into the night, knowing that in the darkness the clock would always soothe her into sleep and greet her in the morning. As the years had gone by, its inner workings had worn down, so that it produced unique sounds. Before Joy died, she had told LuAnn to take it. And now LuAnn would keep it for her daughter.

She pulled her thick auburn hair straight back and tried a bun. Not satisfied with that look, she piled her thick tresses on top and secured them with a legion of bobby pins. At five feet ten inches tall she had to stoop to see herself in the mirror.

Every few seconds she looked over at the small bundle on the chair next to her. She smiled as she took in the droopy eyes and the chipmunk cheeks. Eight months and growing up fast. Her daughter had already started to crawl with the funny back-and-forth gyrations of infancy. Walking would soon replace that. LuAnn stopped smiling as she looked around. It wouldn't take Lisa long to navigate the boundaries of this place. The interior, despite LuAnn's efforts to keep it clean, resembled the exterior, largely due to the temperamental outbursts of the man sprawled on the bed. Duane Harvey had twitched once or twice since staggering into the house at four a.m. and climbing into bed, but otherwise he had remained motionless. She recalled fondly that on one night early in their relationship Duane had not come home drunk. Lisa had been the result. Tears glimmered for the briefest time in LuAnn's hazel eyes. She hadn't much time or sympathy for tears, particularly her own. At twenty years of age she'd already cried enough of them to last her until the end of her days, she figured.

She turned back to the mirror and pulled out all the bobby pins. She swept her hair back and then let her bangs fall forward over her forehead. It was a style she had worn in school, at least through the seventh grade, when she had joined many of her friends in dropping out and seeking work and the paycheck that came with it. Half of LuAnn's wages went to help her chronically unemployed parents. The other half went to pay for things her parents couldn't afford to give her, such as food and clothes.

She eyed Duane as she undid her tattered robe. Seeing no sign of life from him, she swiftly pulled on her underwear. As she grew up, her blossoming figure had been a true eye-opener for the local boys. LuAnn Tyler, the movie-star/supermodel-to-be. Residents of Rikersville, Georgia, had bestowed upon her that title, weighted down as it was with the highest of expectations. She was not long for their way of life, proclaimed the wrinkled, thick local women holding court on their broad, decaying porches. New York or maybe Los Angeles would beckon to LuAnn. Only she was still here, still in the very same town where she had lived all her life.

LuAnn studied the contents of her small closet. She owned only one dress that would be appropriate for her appointment—the short-sleeved navy blue with white trim. She remembered the day she bought it. A whole paycheck blown. *Sixty-five entire dollars.* That was two years ago, and she had never repeated that insane extravagance. She had stayed up late coloring in the nicks on her only pair of high heels. They were dark brown and didn't match the dress, but they would have to do. Flip-flops or sneakers, her only other choices, were not going to cut it today, although she would wear the sneakers on the mile-long trek to the bus stop.

LuAnn opened the zippered interior pocket of her purse and unfolded a piece of paper. She had written down the information during a phone call from a Mr. Jackson, a call she had almost not answered after pulling the midnight-to-seven shift as a waitress at the Number One Truck Stop.

When the call came, LuAnn had been sitting on the kitchen floor breast-feeding Lisa. The little girl's teeth were coming in, and LuAnn's nipples felt like they were on fire, but baby formula was too expensive and they were out of milk. At first LuAnn had no desire to answer the phone. Her job at the popular truck stop kept her running nonstop, with Lisa tucked safely under the counter in her baby seat. Luckily, the diner's manager liked LuAnn enough that the arrangement hadn't jeopardized her position.

They didn't get many calls. Mostly Duane's buddy looking for him to go drinking or strip a few cars that had broken down on the highway. But after the third ring, for some reason, LuAnn had plucked up the phone. The man had asked for her by name. And then he had offered her employment. She already had a job, she had told him. He asked what her salary was. She refused to answer at first, and then she told him. She wasn't sure why. Later she would think it was a premonition of things to come.

Because that's when he had mentioned the pay. One hundred dollars per weekday for a guaranteed two weeks. And they weren't full days. The man had said four hours tops per day. That wouldn't affect her job at the truck stop at all. The work, the man had said, involved getting her opinion on things. Sort of like a survey. Demographic analysis, he had termed it. A hundred dollars a day for giving her opinion—something she did for free about every minute of her life.

Too good to be true, really. She had thought that a number of times since his phone call. She was not nearly as dumb as her father had thought. In fact, housed behind her comely face was an intellect more powerful than the late Benny Tyler could have imagined, and it was coupled with a shrewdness that had allowed her to live by her wits for years now.

She looked over at Lisa. The little girl's eyes darted around the bedroom until they came to rest with glee upon her mother's face. LuAnn's eyes crinkled back at her little girl. She folded the piece of paper and put it back in her purse. Sliding a small box out of one of the drawers, she found enough change for bus fare. She swooped up Lisa and left the trailer.

THERE was a sharp knock on the door. The man stood up behind the desk. "Come in," he said, his voice firm and clear.

The door opened, and LuAnn stepped into the room. Her left hand clutched the handle of the baby carrier where Lisa lay. Over her right shoulder hung a large bag. The man observed the vein plunging down LuAnn's long, sinewy biceps until it connected with a maze of others in her muscular forearm. She was obviously strong physically. What about her character? Was it as strong?

"Are you Mr. Jackson?" LuAnn asked.

"I am." He held out his hand, and she shook it firmly. "Please sit down, Ms. Tyler." He seated himself.

LuAnn put Lisa and the bag down, pulled out a set of plastic keys, and handed them to her daughter to play with. She straightened back up and looked around curiously.

Jackson noted her scrutinizing the office. "Something wrong?" he asked.

"You got a funny office, is all."

"How do you mean?"

"Well, there's no clock, no calendar, and no phone. And the lady out front, she don't got a clue as to what's going on." LuAnn caught the stunned look on his face and bit her lip. Her mouth had gotten her in trouble before, and this was one job interview she couldn't afford to blow. "I don't mean nothing by it," she said quickly. "Just talking. Guess I'm a little nervous, is all."

Jackson smiled grimly. "You're very observant."

"Got two eyes like everybody else." LuAnn smiled prettily, falling back on the old reliable.

Jackson ignored her look. "You recall the terms of employment I gave to you over the phone?"

She snapped back to business. "One hundred dollars per day for two weeks. I work until seven in the morning right now. If it's all right, I'd like to come and do this job in the early afternoon. Around about two? And is it okay if I bring my little girl? She takes her nap then; she won't be no trouble at all." With an automatic motion LuAnn reached down and picked up the toy keys from the floor, where the little girl had flung them, and handed them back to Lisa.

Jackson stood up. "That's all fine. You're an only child, and your parents are dead, correct?" LuAnn jerked at the abrupt change in subject. She hesitated and then nodded, her eyes narrowing. "And you live with one Duane Harvey, currently unemployed, in a trailer in western Rikersville. Harvey is the father of your daughter, Lisa, age eight months. You quit school in the seventh grade and have held numerous dead-end jobs since. You are uncommonly bright and possess admirable survival skills. Nothing is more important to you than your daughter's well-being. You are desperate to change your life and just as desperate to leave Mr. Harvey far behind. Right now you are wondering how to accomplish this. You feel trapped, and well you should. You are most assuredly trapped, Ms. Tyler."

"How come you know all this 'bout me?" LuAnn demanded.

He came around the corner of the desk and perched on the edge. "It's in my best interest to know everything I can about someone with whom I'm about to do business."

"What does knowing about me have to do with my opinions and surveys and such?"

"Very simple. To know how to evaluate your opinion on things, I need to know intimate details about who you are, what you want, what you know. And don't know. I'm sorry if I offended you. I can be rather blunt; however, I didn't want to waste your time, Ms. Tyler. May I call you LuAnn?"

"That's my name," she said brusquely.

Jackson looked down at the desk, rubbing his hands slowly over its cracked surface. Then he looked at her. "Have you ever dreamed of being rich, LuAnn? So rich that you and your daughter could do anything in the world you wanted to do?"

"Who hasn't had that dream?"

Jackson stroked his chin for several seconds and then asked a question. "LuAnn, do you ever play the lottery?"

She was surprised by the inquiry but readily replied. "Now and then. Everybody around here does. It can get expensive, though. Duane plays every week, sometimes half his paycheck. Plays the same numbers every time. Says he saw them in a dream. I say he's dumber than dirt. Why?"

"Have you ever played the national lotto?"

"You mean the one for the whole country?"

Jackson nodded. "Yes, that's exactly the one I mean."

"Once in a while. But the odds are so big, I got a better chance of going for a stroll on the moon than I do of winning."

"You're right. In fact, the odds this month are approximately one in thirty million." Jackson licked his lips. "But what if I could better your chances of winning? What if I could lower your odds to one in one? Would you do it?"

LuAnn exploded. "Is this some kind of joke? What's this got to do with the job?"

"This is no joke, LuAnn."

She rose out of the chair. "You durn sure got something else on the burner, mister, and I don't want no parts of it. No parts! Hundred bucks a day or not," she said with disgust mingled with disappointment as her plans for the money she had hoped to earn rapidly faded away. She picked up Lisa and her bag and turned to leave.

Jackson's quiet tones rippled across her back. "I am guaranteeing that you will win, at minimum, fifty million dollars."

She stopped. Despite her brain's telling her to run as fast as she could out of the place, she found herself slowly turning to face him. *Had he said fifty million dollars? Lord Almighty!*

"I need an answer to my question. Do you want to be rich?"

"Are you a crazy man?" LuAnn switched Lisa's carrier from her right to her left hand. "There is no way in hell that you can guarantee me something like that. So I'm just gonna walk on out of here and call the nuthouse to come get you."

In response Jackson looked at his watch and walked over to turn on the TV. "In one minute the national daily drawing will be held. It's *only* a one-million-dollar payoff; however, it will illustrate a point." LuAnn looked at the screen. She watched as the lottery drawing began and the ball machines fired up. Jackson glanced at her. "The winning numbers will be eight, four, seven, eleven, nine, and six, in that order." He pulled a pen and paper from his pocket, wrote the numbers down, and handed the paper to LuAnn.

She almost laughed, and a loud snort did escape her mouth. It stopped just as quickly when the first number announced was eight. In rapid succession the four, seven, eleven, nine, and six balls were kicked out. Her face pale, LuAnn stared at the paper.

Jackson turned off the TV. "Perhaps now we can get back to my offer."

LuAnn looked at the TV. She saw no special wires that could

have aided him in predicting the outcome. No VCR. It was just plugged into the wall. She looked back at him. "How did you do that?" The words came out in a hushed, fearful tone.

"Just answer my question, please."

She took a deep breath, tried to calm her twitching nerves. "You're asking me to do something wrong. I'm telling you flat out that I won't. I ain't got much, but I'm no criminal."

"Who says it's anything wrong?"

"Excuse me, but guaranteeing to win the lottery sure sounds like a fix to me. You think I'm stupid?"

"I actually have a high opinion of your intelligence. However, someone has to win that money, LuAnn. Why not you?"

"Because it's wrong." She turned and gripped the doorknob.

This was the moment Jackson had been waiting for. His voice rose. "So Lisa grows up in a trailer in the woods. Your little girl will be extraordinarily beautiful if she takes after her mother. She reaches a certain age, young men get interested, she drops out of school, a baby comes along, the cycle starts anew. Like your mother?" He paused. "Like you?" LuAnn turned around, her eyes glimmering. Jackson eyed her sympathetically. "It's inevitable, Lu-Ann. You'll live in poverty and you'll die in poverty and your little girl will do the same. I'm offering you a way out."

LuAnn leaned up against the door. She felt her heart beating erratically. "Why me? Why'd you come knocking on my door?"

"Fair question, but not one I'm prepared to answer."

"So what if I play along and I still don't win?"

"Then what have you lost?"

"The two bucks it costs to play, that's what! It might not sound like much to you, but that's bus fare for almost a week!"

Jackson pulled two singles from his pocket and handed them to her. "Then consider that risk eliminated."

"I want to know what's in it for you. I'm a little old to believe in good fairies." LuAnn's eyes were clear and focused now.

"Again, a good question, but one that only becomes applicable if and when you agree to participate. You're right, however. I'm not doing this out of the goodness of my heart." A tiny smile escaped his lips. "It's a business transaction."

LuAnn slid the money into her bag. "If you need my answer right this very minute, it's a big, fat no."

"I will give you some time to think about it." He wrote a toll-free phone number on a piece of paper and walked over to her. "But not too much time. The monthly lottery drawing takes place in four days. I have to have your answer by ten a.m. the day after tomorrow. This number will reach me anywhere."

"And if I still say no in two days, which I probably will?"

Jackson shrugged. "Then someone else will win the lottery, Lu-Ann." He put the paper in her hand. "Remember, one minute past ten a.m., and the offer to you is gone. Forever." Jackson of course did not mention the fact that if LuAnn said no, he would have her immediately killed. As she passed through the doorway, he added, "Thank you for coming, LuAnn. And have a nice day."

"What makes me think your name ain't Jackson?" she said, giving him a piercing stare.

"I hope to hear from you, LuAnn. I like to see good things happen to deserving people." He shut the door softly behind her.

INSTEAD of taking the bus home, LuAnn took Lisa to her friend Wanda's house. She needed time to think and could not bear going back to the trailer where Duane Harvey lurked, awaiting their return in what she was certain would be a foul temper.

That evening she called in sick to work and spent a sleepless night staring at the full moon while her mind examined Jackson's proposal. If she actually won the lottery, the man had said she could have anything she wanted. Anything! The thought made her want to scream with joy. Would she travel the world? She had never been outside Rikersville, which was best known for its annual fair and reeking slaughterhouses. She could count on one hand the times when she had ridden in an elevator.

The only catch was that Jackson's proposal resonated with illegality, with fraud. That was a big catch. What if she went along and was caught? She could go to prison. Then what would happen to Lisa? She suddenly felt miserable. Like most people, she had dreamed often of the pot of gold. In her dreams, though, it had not been attached to a ball and chain. She finally decided not to make a decision until she had some more information.

CHAPTER 2

THE next morning LuAnn went to the public library. It had been years since she'd been there, but she remembered from her school days that the library kept different newspapers on microfilm. She located microfilm for a major newspaper in a file cabinet and checked the boxes housing the spools until she found the dates corresponding to the last six months. LuAnn sat down at one of the terminals and inserted the first spool into the machine. With Lisa perched on her lap, she scanned the front page. It didn't take long to locate the story: LOTTERY WINNER NETS FORTY-FIVE MILLION DOLLARS. She pulled a blanket from her bag, set it on the floor with some toys, and put Lisa down before turning back to the headline. The U.S. lotto drawing was held on the fifteenth of each month. The dates she was looking at were for the sixteenth through the twentieth. She flipped to the next month.

Two hours later she had completed her review of the past five winners: Judy Davis, twenty-seven, a welfare mother with three young children; Herman Rudy, fifty-eight, a truck driver on disability with massive medical bills; Wanda Tripp, sixty-six, widowed and subsisting on four hundred dollars a month from Social Security; Randy Stith, thirty-one, a widower, who had been laid off from his assembly-line job; and Bobbie Jo Reynolds, thirty-three, a waitress.

LuAnn slumped back in her seat. *And LuAnn Tyler, twenty years old, single mother, uneducated, no prospects, no future.* She would fit in perfectly with this group. Jackson's face appeared in her thoughts.

Someone has to win. Why not you? She felt herself beginning to slide over the top of an imaginary dam. What was awaiting her in the deep waters below she was not sure. She looked at Lisa. She could not shake the image of her little girl growing into a woman in a trailer with no way to escape while the young wolves circled.

IT WAS eight o'clock in the morning on *the day*. LuAnn had just completed her regular shift at the diner. She and Lisa had taken the bus as usual. When they got off, LuAnn looked ahead to the gently rolling fields, and her manner grew both somber and expectant. She walked slowly through the arched gateway and past the sign proclaiming her entrance into the Heavenly Meadows Cemetery. Her long, slender feet carried her automatically to section 14, plot 6. She laid Lisa's carrier down on the stone bench near her mother's grave and lifted out the little girl. Kneeling in the dewy grass, she brushed some twigs and dirt off the bronze marker. Her mother, Joy, had not lived all that long—thirty-seven years. It had seemed both brief and an eternity for Joy Tyler; that LuAnn knew. The years with Benny had not been pleasant.

"This is where your grandma is, Lisa." LuAnn held up her daughter and pointed at the recessed ground. "She can't talk to us, but if you close your eyes tight as a baby bird's and listen real hard, you can kinda hear her. She's letting you know what she thinks about things." LuAnn rose and sat on the bench with Lisa on her lap. The silence of the deserted cemetery was peaceful, and she closed her eyes tight as a baby bird's and listened as hard as she could.

LuAnn came here often to lay flowers at her mother's final resting-place and to talk. She thought she actually did communicate with her mother. Euphoria or deep sadness sometimes overtook her here, and she felt it was her mother reaching out to her. Today LuAnn had hoped for something to speak to her, to let her know what to do. But nothing was happening. She was preparing to leave when a feeling she had never experienced before came over her. Her eyes were drawn to another plot about five hundred yards away. Something was pulling her there, and she had no doubt what it was. LuAnn

clutched Lisa tightly and made her way down the winding asphalt
walkway. As she drew nearer to the spot, the sky seemed to turn
dark. The wind whistled around the weathered testaments to the
dead. Her hair blowing straight back, LuAnn finally stopped and
looked down. The bronze marker was similar to her mother's, and
the last name on it was identical: BENJAMIN HERBERT TYLER. As Lu-
Ann looked at her father's name, the intense feeling she had not
realized beside her mother's grave suddenly overtook her. She could
almost see wisps of gauzy membrane swirling above the grave like
a spiderweb picked up by the wind. She had not closed her eyes
tight like a baby bird's. She had not even been listening particularly
hard. Yet the immortal speech of Benny Tyler had reached his only
child. *Take the money, little girl. Daddy says take it. Use what little
brain you've got. Do it for Big Daddy.*

She turned and ran. Gripping Lisa to her chest, LuAnn snatched
up the baby carrier and flew past the gates of the cemetery. Her
long legs ate up the ground with a stride that was both machinelike
in its precision and wonderfully animalistic in its grace.

Her chest was burning. She slowed down. Lisa was bawling now,
and LuAnn finally stopped and hugged her baby hard, whispering
soothing words into the little girl's ear while she made slow, wide circles on the long dirt road until the cries finally stopped.

LuAnn walked the rest of the way home. Benny Tyler's words
had made up her mind. She would pack what she could from the
trailer and send somebody back for the rest. She would stay with
her friend Beth for a while. Beth had offered before. She had an old
house, but it had a lot of rooms, and her only companions were a
pair of cats that Beth swore were crazier than she was. LuAnn
would take Lisa into the classroom with her if need be, but she was
going to get her GED and then maybe take some classes at the community college. Mr. Jackson could find somebody else to take her
place. All these answers to her dilemmas had come roaring in upon
her so fast she could barely keep her head from exploding off her
shoulders with relief. Her mother had spoken to her in a round-
about manner perhaps, but the magic had been worked.

LuAnn slowed as she neared the trailer. There was a car parked out front. A shiny black convertible, big and wide, with white sidewalls. Duane's battered Ford pickup was in the impoundment lot. None of his cronies drove anything like this crazy machine. What was going on? She examined the vehicle. The seats were covered in white leather. The keys hung in the ignition. A phone rested in a device attached to the hump between the front seat and the dashboard.

LuAnn moved quickly up the trailer steps. "Duane?" She slammed the door loudly. There was no answer. LuAnn put an agitated Lisa down in her baby carrier and moved through the trailer. "Duane, are you here?" She went into the bedroom, but he wasn't there. Her eyes were riveted by her clock on the wall. It took her an instant to stuff it into her bag. She wasn't going to leave it with Duane. She exited the bedroom and moved down the hall. She stopped to calm Lisa and placed her bag next to the baby.

LuAnn finally saw Duane lying on the raggedy couch. A grease-stained bucket of chicken wings was on the coffee table. Whether this was breakfast or the remnants of dinner from last night she didn't know. "Hey, Duane, didn't you hear me?"

He turned his head slowly. She scowled. Drunk again. She started forward. "Duane, we got to talk. And you ain't going to like it, but that's too bad becau—" She got no further as a big hand clamped over her mouth. A thick arm encircled her waist, pinning her arms to her sides. As her panicked eyes swept the room, she noted for the first time that the front of Duane's shirt was a mass of splotchy crimson. As she watched in horror, he fell off the couch with a small groan and then didn't move again.

The hand shot to her throat and pushed her chin up so hard she thought her neck was going to snap. She saw the other hand holding a blade that descended toward her neck. He had made a mistake, though. With one hand bracing her chin and the other holding the knife, he had left her arms free. Perhaps he thought she would be paralyzed with fear. She was far from it. Her foot crunched backward against his knee at the same moment her bony elbow sunk into his flabby gut, hitting the diaphragm.

The force of her blow caused his hand to jerk, and the knife slashed her jaw. The man dropped to the floor, coughing, and the knife clattered to the carpet. LuAnn hurtled toward the front door, but her attacker snagged a leg as she passed by, and she tumbled to the floor a few feet from him. He clamped thick fingers around her ankle and dragged her toward him. He was twice her size. She knew she had no chance against him strengthwise, so instead of resisting, she threw herself toward him, screaming as loudly as she could. The scream and her sudden leap startled him. Off-balance, he let go of her leg. In the next second LuAnn planted her index fingers in both his eyes. Howling, the man fell back against the wall but then ricocheted off like a bouncing ball and slammed blindly into her. They both pitched over the couch. LuAnn's hand seized an object on the way down. She couldn't see exactly what it was, but it was solid and hard and that's all she cared about as she swung with all her might and smashed it against his head right before she hit the floor.

The telephone had shattered into pieces upon impact with the man's thick skull. Seemingly unconscious, her attacker lay facedown on the floor as blood poured from his head wound. After a moment LuAnn sat up. Her arm tingled where she had hit the coffee table, and her shirt was ripped and bloody. She wiped her face and touched the cut; it was jagged and painful. Although the big man was clearly still breathing, LuAnn wasn't sure about Duane. She crawled over and felt for his pulse. If it was there, she couldn't find it. "Oh, Lord, Duane, what have you done?" LuAnn eyed the remnants of the phone. There was no way to call an ambulance, although she should probably go and fetch the police. Find out who the other man was, why he had cut up Duane and tried to kill her.

When LuAnn rose to leave, she noticed the small pile of plastic bags that had been hidden behind the bucket of chicken. They had fallen off the table in the scuffle. LuAnn picked one up. Inside was a small amount of white powder. Drugs.

Then she heard the whimpering. Oh, no, where was Lisa? But there was another sound. LuAnn jerked around and looked down. The big man was starting to rise. He was coming for her! She dropped the bag and raced to the hallway. Using her good arm to snatch up Lisa, LuAnn bolted through the front door. She ran past the convertible, stopped, and turned back. The dangling keys glimmered temptingly in the sunlight. She hesitated for only an instant; then she and Lisa were in the car. LuAnn gunned the motor and fishtailed out onto the road. Duane must have started selling drugs. Only he had apparently gotten greedy and kept a little too much for himself. The idiot! She had to call the police. If Duane was alive, she couldn't just leave him to die.

As LuAnn turned onto the main highway, she looked over at Lisa. The little girl sat wide-eyed in her baby carrier. LuAnn settled her injured arm over her daughter, biting back the pain this simple movement caused her. Then her eyes alighted on the cellular phone. She pulled off the road, snatched it up, and started to dial 911. But she put down the phone as it dawned on her that she could be implicated in all of this. Despite his starting to move, the guy could have slumped back down dead, for all she knew. She would have killed him in self-defense. She knew that, but would anyone else? A drug dealer. She was driving his car. She tore down the road.

Would the police believe she knew nothing about Duane's selling drugs? Somehow Duane had kept it from her, but who would accept that as the truth? She didn't believe it herself. This reality swept over her like a fire raging through a paper house. There seemed to be no escape. But maybe there was. Her gaze locked on the dashboard clock. It was five minutes past ten. *Gone. Forever,* Jackson had said. She pulled off the road and slumped over the steering wheel in her misery. What would happen to Lisa while she was in prison?

She slowly raised her head and looked across the street, wiping her eyes to make out the image—a bank branch, squat, solid, all-brick. As her eyes drifted to the front of the bank, her state of mind suddenly changed. The bank clock showed four minutes *before* ten. She snatched up the phone, digging frantically in her pocket for the slip of paper with the number on it. The line rang only once before being answered.

"I was beginning to wonder about you, LuAnn," Jackson said.

She forced herself to breathe normally. "I guess the time just got away from me. So what now?"

"Aren't you forgetting something?"

"What?"

"I made you an offer, LuAnn. In order to have a legal arrangement, I need an acceptance from you."

"I accept."

"Fine. Now go purchase a lottery ticket."

"What numbers do I play?"

"That doesn't matter."

"I don't understand. I thought you were gonna tell me what numbers to play. The winning numbers."

"There is no need for you to understand anything, LuAnn." Jackson's voice had risen a notch. "Once you have the ticket, call me back with the numbers. I'll take care of the rest."

"So when do I get the money?"

"There will be a press conference—"

"Press conference!"

Jackson sounded exasperated. "Haven't you ever watched one of these things? The winner attends a press conference in New York. It's televised across the country. You'll have your photo taken holding a ceremonial check. It's terrific PR for the Lottery Commission."

"Do I have to do it? I don't want to be on TV."

"Well, I'm afraid you don't have a choice. You'll be at least fifty million dollars richer. For that kind of money the Lottery Commission expects you to be able to handle *one* press conference. And frankly, they are right."

LuAnn let out a deep breath. "When do I get the money?"

"It will be transferred into an account of your designation."

"But I don't have any account. I've never had enough money to open an account."

"I'll take care of all of that. The only thing you have to do is win. Go to New York with Lisa, hold that big check, smile, and then spend the rest of your life on the beach."

"How do I get to New York?"

"You'll take a bus to the train station in Atlanta. That's on Amtrak's Crescent line. It's a long ride, about eighteen hours or so; however, a good part of it will be while you're sleeping. You can leave for New York right after the lottery drawing takes place."

The prone figures of Duane and the man who had tried to kill her flashed across LuAnn's mind. "Can I take the train today?"

"I don't I want you in New York that quickly."

"Please?"

"Hold on for one minute." Jackson clicked off. When he clicked back on, he said, "The Crescent pulls into Atlanta at seven fifteen this evening and arrives in New York at one thirty tomorrow afternoon. Atlanta is only a couple hours' bus ride from where you are. You're going to need money for the ticket and additional funds for travel-related incidentals. There's a Western Union office near the station. I'll wire you five thousand dollars there." LuAnn gulped at the amount. "You just have to show identification—"

"I don't have any."

"A driver's license or passport is all they need."

LuAnn almost laughed. "Passport? You don't need a passport to go from the Piggly Wiggly to the Wal-Mart, do you? And I don't have a driver's license either."

"Well, you can't get the money without identification."

A sudden thought struck LuAnn. She put down the phone and quickly searched the car's interior. The brown leather bag she pulled from underneath the front seat didn't disappoint her. There was enough cash in there to buy the train. "A woman I work with, her husband left her some money when he passed on. I can ask her for a loan," she said. "I won't need no ID for cash, will I?"

"Money is king, LuAnn. I'm sure Amtrak will accommodate you. Just don't use your real name and wear something to hide your face so you won't be recognized. Now go buy the lottery ticket and call me back."

LuAnn put down the phone. She had to ditch the car. The only question was where. An idea hit her, and she did a U-turn. Within twenty minutes she was pulling up in front of the trailer, cold dread pouring over her as she once again felt the man's hands around her throat. She pulled a diaper wipe out of Lisa's bag and rubbed the car's surfaces that she had touched. Then she climbed out, stuffing as much cash from the leather bag as she could under the liner of Lisa's baby seat. She pulled her torn shirt together and, holding Lisa with her good arm, made her way down the dirt road.

From within the trailer, a pair of dark eyes watched LuAnn's hasty departure. The man's dark leather jacket was zipped halfway up, the butt of a 9-millimeter sticking out of the inside pocket. He stepped over the two men on the floor, careful to avoid the pools of blood. He had happened along at an opportune time. He was left with the spoils of a battle he had not even had to fight. As he scooped up the drug packets, he noted the torn fabric on the floor. It was from the woman's shirt. He put it in his pocket. She must have walked right into the middle of this, he deduced. Fat man got the little man, and LuAnn somehow got the fat man. His admiration for her increased as he noted the man's bulk.

As if he sensed this observation, the fat man stirred. The other man stooped down, used a cloth to snatch up the knife, and then plunged it repeatedly into the man's side. Next he flipped over Duane and tried to determine if his chest was moving. Just to be safe, the man used several carefully aimed thrusts to make certain Duane Harvey joined the fat man in the hereafter.

In a few seconds he was through the front door. His car was parked off a dirt trail that snaked through the woods. When he climbed into his car, his car phone was ringing. He picked it up.

"Your duties are at an end," Jackson said. "The hunt has been called off."

Anthony Romanello debated whether to tell Jackson about the two bodies in the trailer and then decided not to. He might have stumbled onto something interesting. "I saw the little lady tearing out of here on foot. But she doesn't look like she has the resources to go very far," Romanello said.

Jackson chuckled. "I think money will be the least of her worries." Then the line went dead.

Romanello pondered the matter for a moment. His work was at an end. But there was something screwy going on here. Sending him down to the sticks to kill some hick chick. And then being told not to. And there was Jackson's passing reference to money. Dollars always held Romanello's interest. He made up his mind and put the car in gear. He was going to follow LuAnn Tyler.

LuAnn stopped at a gas station rest room and cleaned up as best as she could. She pulled a Band-Aid out of Lisa's diaper bag and covered the wound on her jaw. Then LuAnn bought her lottery ticket at a 7-Eleven. She called Jackson from a nearby pay phone and gave him the ten digits from her ticket.

"Read them to me once more," he said. She read them again, and he read them back to her. "Good," he said. "Very good. Now get on the train. Someone will meet you at Penn Station." He paused. "I trust you did not include Duane in the travel plans."

LuAnn swallowed hard as she thought back to the bloodstains on Duane's shirt. "Duane won't be coming," she said.

THE bus dropped LuAnn and Lisa at the train station in Atlanta. After her phone call to Jackson she had stopped at the Wal-Mart to purchase some essentials for herself and Lisa, which were in a bag slung over her shoulder. Her own torn shirt had been replaced with a new one. A cowboy hat and a pair of sunglasses hid her face. She went to the ticket counter to purchase her train ticket. And that's when LuAnn made a big mistake.

"Name, please," the agent said.

LuAnn was fiddling with a fussing Lisa and thus answered automatically, "LuAnn Tyler." She caught her breath as soon as she said it. She looked at the clerk, who was busily typing the information into her computer. LuAnn couldn't change it now without making her suspicious. She hoped the slip would not come back to haunt her. The woman recommended the sleeping car, since LuAnn was traveling with a baby. The sales agent raised an eyebrow when Lu-Ann pulled some bills from under Lisa's baby seat to pay for the ticket. LuAnn observed the woman's look, thought quickly, and smiled at her. "My rainy day money. Figured I'd use it while the weather's nice. Go up to New York and see the sights."

The woman looked behind LuAnn. "Where's your luggage?"

"Oh, I like to travel light. Besides, we got family up there." Lu-Ann turned and walked toward the departure area.

The woman stared after her as another person appeared in front of her window. "One-way ticket to New York City, please," Anthony Romanello said politely, and then stole a sideways glance in LuAnn's direction. He had watched through the plate glass of the 7-Eleven as LuAnn had purchased her lottery ticket. Next he had observed her make the phone call from the pay phone. The fact that she was now on her way to New York was convenient, because he happened to live there. It could be she was simply running from the bodies in the trailer. Or it could be more. He took the train ticket and headed toward the platform.

THE train had been delayed at several points along the route, and it was nearly three thirty in the afternoon when LuAnn and Lisa emerged into the frenzy of Penn Station. LuAnn had never seen this many people in one place in all her life. Jackson said someone would be here, but how could anyone find her in all this chaos?

She jerked slightly as a man brushed against her. LuAnn looked up into dark brown eyes, with a silvery mustache resting below a broad, flattened nose. In his early fifties, he had the battered face that marked him as an ex-boxer.

"Miss Tyler?" His voice was low but clear. "Mr. Jackson sent me to pick you up."

LuAnn put out her hand. "Call me LuAnn. What's your name?"

The man started for an instant. "That's not important. Please follow me. I have a car waiting." He started to walk away.

"I like to know people's names," LuAnn said, not budging.

He came back. "Okay, you can call me Charlie. How's that?"

"That's fine, Charlie. I guess you work for Mr. Jackson. Do you use your real names with each other?"

He didn't answer as he led her toward the exit. "You want me to carry the little girl? That thing looks heavy."

"I've got it okay."

They exited the train station, and Charlie opened the door of a stretch limo for LuAnn. She gawked for a minute at the luxurious vehicle before climbing in. Charlie sat across from her.

"We'll be at the hotel in about twenty minutes. You want something to eat or drink in the meantime?" he asked.

"I am kinda hungry, but I don't want you to have to stop."

"We don't have to stop." He reached into a refrigerator and pulled out soda, beer, and some sandwiches. Then he unlocked a section of the limo's interior paneling, and a table materialized. "I knew you were bringing the baby, so I had the limo stocked with milk, bottles, and stuff like that."

LuAnn made up a bottle for Lisa, cradled her against one arm, and fed her with one hand while she devoured a sandwich with the other. Charlie watched the tender way she handled her daughter. "She's cute. What's her name?"

"Lisa. Lisa Marie. You know, after Elvis's daughter."

"You look a little young to be a fan of the King."

"I don't really listen to that kind of music. But my momma was a big fan. I did it for her. She died before Lisa was born."

"Oh, sorry." Charlie fell silent for a moment. "Well, what kind of music do you like?"

"Classical. I don't really know nothing about that kinda music. I just like the way it makes me feel, sorta clean and graceful."

Charlie grinned. "I never thought about it that way. Jazz is my thing. I actually play a little horn myself. Outside of New Orleans, New York has some of the best jazz clubs around. A couple of them not too far from the hotel."

"Which hotel are we going to?" she asked.

"Waldorf-Astoria. The Towers."

LuAnn finished her sandwich. "Do you know why I'm here?"

Charlie settled a keen gaze upon her. "Let's just say I know enough not to ask too many questions." He smiled curtly.

Before they climbed out of the limo, Charlie pulled out a black trench coat and matching wide-brimmed hat and asked LuAnn to put them on. "For obvious reasons we don't want you to be observed right now. You can ditch the cowboy hat." LuAnn put on the coat and hat, cinching the belt up tight. "I'll check you in. Your suite is under the name of Linda Freeman, an American business executive traveling with her daughter."

"Business executive? I hope nobody asks me no questions."

"Don't worry. Nobody will."

The suite Charlie escorted her to after he checked her in was mammoth. LuAnn looked around in wonder at the elegant furnishings and almost fell over when she saw the opulent bathroom.

She walked over to the window and drew back the curtains. A slice of the New York City skyline confronted her. "I ain't never seen so many buildings in all my life. How in the world do people tell 'em apart? They all look the same to me."

Charlie shook his head. "You know, you're real funny. If I didn't know better, I'd think you were the biggest hick in the world."

LuAnn looked down. "I am the biggest hick in the world. At least the biggest one you'll probably ever see."

He caught her look. "Hey, I didn't mean anything by it. You grow up here, you get an attitude about things. You know what I mean?" He paused for a minute while he watched LuAnn go over and stroke Lisa's face. Then he headed to the door. "I'll be back tomorrow morning. In the meantime you get hungry or anything, order up room service. Just sign the bill as Linda Freeman. Here's some tip money." Charlie took a wad of bills from his pocket and handed them to her. "Generally, keep a low profile. Don't go walking around the hotel or stuff like that."

"Don't worry. I know I don't sound like no executive person." LuAnn tried to sound flippant, although her low self-esteem was as plain as the hurt tones in Charlie's response.

"That's not it, LuAnn. I didn't mean . . ." He shrugged. "Look, I barely finished high school, and I did okay for myself. So neither one of us could pass as a Harvard grad. Who cares?" He touched her shoulder. "Get a good night's sleep. Tomorrow we'll go out and see some of the sights. How about that?"

She brightened. "Going out would be nice."

"It's supposed to be chilly tomorrow, so dress warmly."

LuAnn suddenly looked down at her wrinkled shirt and jeans. "Uh, these are all the clothes I have. I, uh, I left home kind of quick." She looked embarrassed.

Charlie sized her up quickly. "You're about five ten, right? Size eight?" LuAnn nodded. "I'll bring some clothes with me tomorrow. I'll get some things for Lisa too."

"Thanks, Charlie. I really appreciate it."

After he left, LuAnn gave Lisa a bath in the oversize tub and dressed her in her pajamas. After laying the little girl on the bed and propping pillows on either side of her so she wouldn't roll off, LuAnn debated whether to give the tub a try as well. That's when the phone rang. She picked it up. "Hello?"

"Miss Freeman?"

"Sorry, you've—" LuAnn mentally kicked herself. "Yes, this is Miss Freeman," she said quickly, trying to sound professional.

"A little faster next time, LuAnn," Jackson said. "How are things? Are you being taken care of?"

"Sure am. Charlie's wonderful."

"Charlie? Yes, of course. Do you have pen and paper?"

LuAnn took a sheet of paper and a pen from a desk by the window. Jackson continued. "At six p.m. tomorrow the winning ticket will be announced. You can watch it on TV from your hotel room. Officially, you have thirty days to claim the money, so there's no problem there. By the way, that's why I wanted you to wait before coming. It would not look good if people were aware you arrived in New York *before* the winning number was announced. You'll have to remain incognito until we're ready to present you as the winner."

LuAnn scribbled down notes as fast as she could. "I'm sorry, but I really couldn't wait, Mr. Jackson," she said.

"It doesn't matter, LuAnn. In a few days you'll be far away from New York."

"Where exactly will I be?"

"You tell me. Europe? Asia? South America?"

LuAnn thought for a moment. "Do I have to decide now?"

"Of course not. But if you want to leave after the press conference, the sooner you let me know the better, particularly since you don't have a passport or any other identification documents. These will have to be prepared."

"Can you have them put another name on the passport? I mean, with my picture but with a different name?"

Jackson said slowly, "Why would you want that, LuAnn?"

"Well, because of Duane. When he finds out I won all this money, he's gonna try to find me. I thought it'd be best if I disappeared. Start over again fresh. New name and everything. Of course, if it's too hard for you . . ." LuAnn held her breath.

"It's not," Jackson snapped. "It's quite simple, in fact, when you have the right connections, as I do. Well, I suppose you haven't thought of the name you want, have you?" She surprised him by rattling one off immediately, as well as the place the fictitious person was from. "It seems you've been thinking about doing this for a while. Perhaps with or without the lottery money. True?"

"You got secrets, Mr. Jackson. Why not me too?"

"Very well, LuAnn. Your request is certainly unprecedented, but I'll take care of it." She heard him sigh. "Why am I suddenly worried that I will regret having selected you for this little adventure?" Something in his tone caused LuAnn to shudder.

THE next morning Charlie arrived with several bags from Bloomingdale's and Baby Gap. During the next hour LuAnn tried on several outfits that made her tingle all over. "Thanks, Charlie. You got the size just right." After putting on a cream-colored jacket over a pleated black skirt, she dressed Lisa in the latest Baby Gap fashions and put her in her baby carrier. She turned to Charlie. "You ready?"

"Not just yet." He opened the door to the suite and looked back at her. "Close your eyes." LuAnn looked strangely at him. "Go on, just do it," he said, grinning.

She obeyed. A few seconds later he said, "Okay, open them."

When she did, she was staring at a brand-new and very expensive baby carriage. "Oh, Charlie."

"You keep lugging that thing around," he said, pointing at the baby carrier, "your hands are going to scrape the ground."

LuAnn gave him a big hug, loaded Lisa in, and they were off.

"YOU sure didn't buy much, LuAnn." Charlie surveyed the few bags on the chaise longue in her hotel room.

"I just like looking. That was fun enough. Besides, I flat-out can't believe the prices up here."

"But I would've paid for it," Charlie protested.

"I don't want you spending money on me, Charlie."

Charlie sat down in a chair and stared at her. "LuAnn, it's not my money. I told you I'm on an expense account. Whatever you wanted, you could have."

"Is that what Mr. Jackson said?"

"Something like that. Let's just call it an advance on your future winnings." He grinned.

"Have you done this before? I mean, looked after people that . . . Mr. Jackson has met with?"

"I've worked with him for a while, yeah. I've never met him in person. We communicate solely over the phone. He pays me well. And baby-sitting people in fancy hotels isn't such a bad life." Charlie added with a big smile, "I've never looked after anybody I had this much fun with, though."

LuAnn knelt down beside the baby carriage and handed Charlie a gift-wrapped package from the storage bin underneath.

Charlie's mouth gaped in surprise. "What's this?"

"I got you a present. It's from me and Lisa. I was looking for something for you, and she started pointing and squealing at it."

"LuAnn, you didn't have to—"

"I know that," she said quickly. "That's why it's called a gift. You're not supposed to have to."

While Charlie pulled off the wrapping paper, LuAnn picked up

Lisa from the baby carriage. They both watched Charlie as he took off the box top and lifted out a dark green fedora.

"I saw you trying it on at the store. I thought you looked real nice in it. But then you put it back. I could tell you didn't want to."

"LuAnn, this thing cost a lot of money."

"I had some saved up. I hope you like it."

"I love it, thank you." He gave her a hug and then took one of Lisa's dimpled fists in his. He gave it a gentle, formal shake. "And thank you, little lady. Excellent taste." He slid it over his head, checked himself out in the mirror, and smiled. "Not bad." Then he took it off and sat back down. "I've never gotten a gift from the people I've looked after."

LuAnn quickly picked up on the opening. "So how'd you come to be doing this kind of work?"

"I take it you'd like to hear my life story?" Charlie settled back in the chair. He pointed to his face. "Bet you didn't guess I used to ply my skills in the boxing ring." He grinned. "Mostly I was a sparring partner—a punching bag for up-and-comers. After that I took up semipro football. I coached a little, got married, floated around here and there, never finding anything that fit, you know?"

LuAnn said, "I know that feeling real good."

"Then my career path took a big turn."

"What happened?"

"I spent some time as a guest of the U.S. government." LuAnn looked at him curiously, not getting his meaning. "I was in a federal prison, LuAnn."

She looked astonished. "What'd you do, Charlie?"

"Income tax evasion. The prosecutor called it fraud. And he was right. I just got tired of paying it. There was never enough to live on, let alone giving a chunk to the government. That little mistake cost me three years and my marriage."

"I'm sorry, Charlie."

He shrugged. "Probably the best thing that ever happened to me. Gave me time to think about what I wanted to do with my life. When I got out, I went to work for my lawyer, sort of as an in-house investigator. He knew I was an honest, reliable sort despite my conviction. It was a good gig. I enjoyed the work."

"So how'd you hook up with Mr. Jackson?"

Charlie looked uncomfortable. "Let's just say he happened to call one day. I was in a little trouble. Nothing serious, but I was still on parole, and it could've cost me some serious time inside. He offered to help me out, and I accepted that offer."

"Kind of like I did," said LuAnn, an edge to her voice. "His offers can be kind of hard to refuse."

He glanced at her, his eyes suddenly weary. "Yeah."

CHAPTER 3

"WE SHOULD'VE watched it from the hotel." Charlie sounded nervous. "Jackson would kill me if he knew we were here." "Here" was the headquarters of the United States National Lottery Commission, located in a needle-thin skyscraper on Park Avenue. The huge auditorium was filled with people. Network news correspondents were scattered throughout, microphones clamped in their fists.

Near the front of the stage LuAnn cradled Lisa against her chest. She wore a baseball cap turned backward. Her memorable figure was hidden under the full-length trench coat. "I had to come, Charlie. It just wouldn't be the same watching it on TV."

LuAnn looked at the stage, where the lottery machine was set up on a table. It comprised ten large tubes, each one rising above an attached bin of Ping-Pong balls. Every ball had a number painted on it. After the machine was activated, air would circulate the balls until one made its way through the tiny hatch and popped into the tube. Then the next bin would activate. Down the line it would go until all ten winning numbers were revealed.

People were nervously looking at their lottery tickets; many held at least a dozen in their hands. LuAnn had no need to look at her ticket.

She had memorized the numbers: 0810080521, which represented her birthday and Lisa's, and LuAnn's age on her next birthday.

A man walked onto the stage. The crowd hushed. LuAnn had half expected to see Jackson, but the man was younger and far better-looking. LuAnn wondered if he was in on it. A blond woman in a short skirt joined the man and stood next to the sophisticated-looking machine. The man welcomed everyone to the drawing, and then, staring dramatically out at the crowd, he announced that the official jackpot was a record-setting one hundred million dollars! A collective gasp went up from the crowd at the mention of the gigantic sum. Even LuAnn's mouth dropped open.

It was indeed the largest jackpot ever, and one incredibly fortunate person was about to win it, the lottery man declared with a beaming smile. He gestured to the woman, who hit the power switch on the side of the machine. LuAnn watched as the balls in the first bin started bouncing around. Despite Charlie's presence beside her, she suddenly felt that being here was crazy. How could Jackson or anyone else control what those gyrating balls would do?

She clutched Lisa tightly, and one of her hands drifted over and clasped Charlie's fingers. She felt her heart race. A ball squirted through the opening and was caught in the first tube. It was the number zero. It was shown on a large screen suspended over the stage. In a few seconds the second bin too had produced a winner: the number eight. In quick succession six more of the balls popped through. The tally now stood at 08100805. LuAnn mouthed the familiar numbers. Sweat appeared on her forehead, and her legs began to give way. Somehow Jackson had done it. She watched, completely mesmerized, as the ninth bin of balls started bouncing. Finally the number two ball kicked out and was held in tube number nine. There were no hopeful faces left in the crowd. Except for one.

The last bin fired up, and the number one ball quickly fought its way against the hatch of the last tube. Then, like a pricked balloon hemorrhaging air, it slid back down to the bottom and was replaced near the hatch by a suddenly energetic number four ball. With sharp, jerky motions it grew closer and closer to the open pathway leading into the final tube, although it appeared to be repeatedly repelled from the opening. The blood drained from LuAnn's face. She squeezed Charlie's fingers so tightly he almost yelled out in pain.

Charlie's own heart was racing. He had never known Jackson to fail, but, well, you never knew. He moved his free hand up and felt under his shirt for the thick silver crucifix he had worn for as long as he could remember. He rubbed it for good luck.

Ever so slowly the two balls, as though choreographed, again swapped places. After a momentary collision the number one ball finally shot through the opening into the tenth and final tube.

It was all LuAnn could do not to scream out loud from pure relief, rather than from the excitement of having just become one hundred million dollars richer. She and Charlie looked at each other, their eyes wide, faces drenched with perspiration. Charlie inclined his head toward her as if to say, "You won, didn't you?" LuAnn nodded slightly. Charlie led her out of the room, and in a couple of minutes they were walking down the street in the direction of the hotel. It was a beautiful, brisk night.

LuAnn sucked in the sweet, chilly air and gave Lisa a tender kiss on the cheek. She suddenly elbowed Charlie in the side, a mischievous grin on her face. "Last one to the hotel pays for dinner." She took off like a blue streak, the trench coat billowing out like a parachute in her wake. Even as she left him in the dust, Charlie could hear her shrieks of joy. He grinned, then bolted after her.

Neither one would have been so happy had they seen the man watching from across the street. Romanello had figured that tailing LuAnn might result in some interesting developments. But even he had to admit his expectations had been exceeded.

"YOU'RE certain that's where you want to go, LuAnn?"

LuAnn spoke earnestly into the phone. "Yes, sir, Mr. Jackson. I've always wanted to go to Sweden. My momma's people came from there. Is it much trouble?"

"Everything is trouble, LuAnn. It's just a matter of degrees."

She looked over at Charlie, who was holding Lisa and playing with her. She smiled at him. "You look real good doing that," she said.

"What's that?" Jackson asked.

"I'm sorry. I was talking to Charlie."

"Put him on."

LuAnn swapped the phone for Lisa. Charlie spoke in low tones into the phone, his back to her. Then he hung up. "Everything okay?" she asked.

"Sure, everything's A-OK. You have to see the lottery people this afternoon to present the winning ticket. They'll validate it and issue you an official receipt. Then we'll go to another hotel, where you can check in as LuAnn Tyler. You ready to be filthy rich, lady?"

She took a deep breath before answering. "I'm ready."

LUANN emerged from the Lottery Commission building, walked down the street, and turned a corner, where she met Charlie at a prearranged spot. He had kept Lisa for her.

"She's been watching everything going by. She's a real alert kid," he said, putting Lisa back in her carriage. "So how'd it go?"

"They treated me real special. One woman asked me if I wanted to hire her as my personal assistant." She laughed.

"You better get used to that. What time's the press conference?"

"Tomorrow at six o'clock, they said."

"Here." Charlie handed her her new passport. She solemnly looked at the name inside. The small blue book represented a gateway to another world, a world she would soon be embracing. "Fill it up, LuAnn. See the whole damned planet. You and Lisa."

She looked up at him. "Why don't you come with us, Charlie?"

He stared at her. "What?"

LuAnn spoke hurriedly. "I got all this money now. And I never been anywhere before, and, well, I'd like you to come."

"That's a very generous offer, LuAnn," he said. "But it's a big commitment to make to someone you don't really know."

"I know all I need to," she said stubbornly. "I know you're a good person. And Lisa took to you like nobody's business. That counts for a lot in my book."

"Why don't we both think on it, LuAnn. Then we'll talk."

She shrugged. "I ain't proposing marriage to you, Charlie, if that's what you think."

"Good thing, since I'm almost old enough to be your grandfather." He smiled at her.

"But I really like having you with me. I know I can count on you. You're my friend, ain't you?"

There was a catch in his throat when Charlie answered, "Yes." He coughed and assumed a more businesslike tone. "Let's get you checked in at the new hotel. We'll talk about this again after the press conference, LuAnn. Promise."

CHARLIE got LuAnn and Lisa settled in their new hotel suite and then left to run some errands. LuAnn had just put Lisa down for a nap when there was a knock at the door.

"Room service," the voice said. LuAnn squinted through the peephole on the door. The man standing there was dressed in a bellman's uniform.

"I didn't order anything," she said.

"It's a note and package for you, ma'am."

"Who from?"

"I don't know. A man in the lobby asked me to give it to you."

LuAnn opened the door slightly. She stuck out her arm, and the bellman put the package in it. She immediately closed the door, tore open the envelope, and unfolded the letter.

> LuAnn, how's Duane feeling? And the other guy, what'd you hit him with anyway? Dead as a doornail. Sure hope the police don't find out you were there. Let's chat in one hour. Take a cab to the Empire State Building. Leave the big guy and the kid at home.

LuAnn ripped off the brown packing paper, and a newspaper fell out—the Atlanta *Journal and Constitution*. It had a page marked with a yellow piece of paper. She opened to that page, and her eyes fed voraciously on the story. Two men dead. Drugs involved. Lu-

Ann read quickly, then stopped searching when she found her name. The police were looking for her right now, although the paper didn't say she had been charged with any crime.

LuAnn sat down and tried to compose herself. But another knock on the door almost made her jump out of her chair. "LuAnn?"

She took a deep breath. "Charlie?"

"Who else?"

"Just a minute." LuAnn jumped up, hastily ripped the article out of the paper, and stuffed it in her pocket. She slid the letter and the rest of the newspaper under the couch. Then she unlocked the door, and Charlie entered carrying two large suitcases.

He grinned at her surprised look. "You can't go on your big trip without the proper baggage. One bag is already packed with things for Lisa. I had a lady friend of mine do it. We'll have to do some more shopping to fill up the other one, though."

LuAnn nervously fingered the article in her pocket. Her heart seemed to be climbing into her throat, but she managed to thank Charlie and give him a hug. When she looked at him, her face was calm. "I want to get my hair done, Charlie. With the press conference going on across the whole country, I'd like to look good."

"Sure. Let's look up a fancy one in the phone book—"

"There's one in the lobby," LuAnn said hurriedly. "I saw it, coming in. It looked real nice."

"Even better, then."

"Could you watch Lisa for me?"

"We can come down and hang out with you."

"Charlie, men don't come to the beauty parlor and watch. That's for us females to keep secret. If you knew how much trouble it takes to get us all pretty, it wouldn't be as special. But you got a job to do."

"What's that?"

"You can ooh and aah when I get back and tell me how beautiful I look."

Charlie grinned. "I think I can handle that one."

"I don't know how long I'll be. I might not be able to get in right away. There's a bottle in the refrigerator for Lisa for when she gets hungry." LuAnn opened the door, trying to hide her anxiety. "I'll be back as soon as I can."

"Take your time. I've got nothing else on the agenda. A beer and cable TV"—he went over and lifted Lisa out of the baby carriage— "and the company of this little lady, and I'm a happy man."

LuAnn stepped from the cab and looked up at the towering presence of the Empire State Building. She felt an arm slide around hers. "This way. We can talk." The voice was smooth, comforting, and made every hair on her neck stiffen.

She pulled her arm free and looked at him. Tall and broad-shouldered, he was clean-shaven, his hair thick and dark, matching the eyebrows. "What do you want?" LuAnn asked.

"There's a deli across the street. I suggest we go there."

"Why should I?"

"We have some things to discuss." Romanello looked around. "Do you want everybody here to know our business?"

LuAnn looked at the passersby, then stalked toward the deli.

Inside they found an isolated booth. Romanello ordered coffee, then looked at LuAnn. "Anything interest you on the menu?"

"Nothing." She glared back at him. After the waitress departed, LuAnn asked, "What's your name?"

He looked startled. "Why?"

"Just make up one. That's what everybody else seems to do."

"What are you talking—" He stopped and considered for a moment. "All right. Call me Rainbow."

"Rainbow? You don't look like no rainbow I've ever seen."

"See, that's where you're wrong." His eyes gleamed. "Rainbows have pots of gold at the end, and you're my pot of gold, LuAnn."

"I ain't never been good at games, Mr. Rainbow, so why don't you say whatever it is you want to say and be done with it."

Romanello waited for a moment as the waitress returned with his coffee. After she left, he leaned across the table. "I was at your trailer, LuAnn. I saw the bodies."

She flinched. "What were you doing there?"

He sat back. "Just happened by."

"You're full of it and you know it."

"Maybe. The point is, I saw you drive up to the trailer in that car. I saw you pull a wad of cash out of your kid's baby seat at the train station. I saw you make a number of phone calls."

"So what? I'm not allowed to make phone calls?"

"The trailer had two dead bodies and a bunch of drugs in it."

LuAnn's eyes narrowed. *Was Rainbow a policeman sent to get her to confess?* "I don't know what you're talking about." She dug her hand into her pocket and pulled out the article. "Here, take this back and go scare somebody else."

Romanello put the paper in his pocket. When his hand returned to view, LuAnn could barely keep from trembling as she saw the torn piece of bloody shirt. "Recognize this, LuAnn?"

She struggled to maintain her composure. "Looks like a shirt with some stains on it. So what?"

He smiled at her. "So like I said, you're my pot of gold."

"I ain't got any money," she said quickly.

He almost laughed. "Why are you in New York, LuAnn?"

She rubbed her hands nervously across the table. "Okay, maybe I knew what happened in that trailer. But I didn't do nothing wrong. I had to get out, though, because I knew it might look real bad for me. New York seemed as good as anyplace."

"What are you going to do with all the money, LuAnn?"

She nearly crossed her eyes. "What money?"

"Let's see," he said, "what's the going price for blackmail these days? Ten percent? Twenty percent? Fifty percent? Even at half, you're still talking millions in your bank account."

"You're crazy, mister." LuAnn stood up. "I've gotta go."

"Don't be a fool, LuAnn. I saw you buy the lottery ticket. I was at the lottery drawing. I saw the big smile on your face, the way you ran down the street whooping and hollering. You walk out of here, and I'm going to call that Podunk County sheriff and tell him everything I saw. And then I'm going to send him this piece of shirt. When I tell him you just won the lottery and maybe he should grab you before you disappear, then you can kiss your new life good-bye."

"I didn't do nothing wrong."

"No, what you did was stupid, LuAnn. You ran. And when you run, the cops figure you're guilty. So what's it gonna be?"

Slowly, inch by inch, she sat back down. "I can't pay you half."

His face darkened. "Don't be greedy, lady."

"It's got nothing to do with that. I can pay you. I just don't know how much. But before I agree to anything, I want you to answer one question for me, and I want the truth or you can just go and call the cops. I don't care."

He eyed her cautiously. "What's the question?"

LuAnn leaned across the table. "What were you doing in that trailer? Did it have to do with the drugs Duane was dealing?"

Romanello was already shaking his head. "I didn't know anything about the drugs. Duane was already dead. Maybe he was skimming off the top and the other guy cut him up. Who knows?"

"What happened to the other guy?"

"You were the one who hit him, weren't you? Like I said in the note, dead as a doornail."

"You haven't answered my question. And unless you answer it, you ain't getting one red cent from me."

Romanello hesitated, but then his greed won out over his better judgment. "I went there to kill you," he said simply.

"Why?" LuAnn demanded fiercely.

"I don't ask questions. I just do what I'm paid to do."

"Who told you to kill me?"

He shrugged. "I don't know. I got a phone call. I got the money up front. Through the mail."

"I'm still alive."

"That's right. But only because I got called off."

"When?"

"I was in your trailer. I saw you get out of the car and take off. I went to my car and got the call then. Around ten fifteen."

LuAnn sat back as the truth dawned on her: Jackson. So that's how he took care of those who refused to go along.

WHEN ROMANELLO AND LUANN exited the deli, she climbed into a cab and headed back to her hotel, where, to follow through on her cover story to Charlie, she would spend the next several hours at the beauty salon. Romanello walked down the street in the opposite direction, silently whistling to himself. The arrangements he had made with LuAnn weren't foolproof, but his gut told him she would honor their deal. If the first installment wasn't in his account two days from now, he would be on the phone to the Rikersville police. She would pay. He was sure of that.

Romanello took the subway to his apartment. When he got home, he turned the key in his door, closed and locked it. He was about to take off his jacket when he heard a sound behind him.

Jackson emerged from the shadows of the living room. Dressed immaculately, he looked at Romanello behind a pair of dark glasses.

"Who the hell are you, and how did you get in here?"

Jackson slipped off the glasses. "As soon as I hung up with you, I knew my little slip over the phone would prove to be serious. I made mention of LuAnn Tyler and money, and money, as you well know, makes people do strange things."

"What exactly are you talking about?"

"Mr. Romanello, you were hired to perform a job for me. Once that task was called off, your participation in my affairs was at an end. Or was *supposed* to be at an end."

"They were at an end. I didn't kill the lady."

Jackson ticked the points off with his fingers. "You followed the woman back to New York. You sent her a note. You met with her, and while I wasn't privy to the conversation itself, from the looks of things the subject matter wasn't pleasant."

"How do you know all that?"

"There really isn't much I don't know, Mr. Romanello." Jackson put the glasses back on. "You disobeyed my instructions and, in doing so, jeopardized my plans. I have decided upon the appropriate punishment. A punishment that I fully intend to mete out now." Twin darts shot out from a stun gun in Jackson's hand and hit Romanello dead center in the chest. Jackson continued to squeeze the trigger, sending 120,000 volts of electricity along the thin metal cords attached to the darts. Romanello went down as though poleaxed.

"This will incapacitate you for at least fifteen minutes, more than ample for my purposes." Jackson knelt beside Romanello, gingerly pulled the two darts free, and packed the apparatus back in his pocket. He opened Romanello's shirt. "Quite hairy, Mr. Romanello. A medical examiner will never pick up on the small holes in your chest." With no physical sensation in his limbs, Romanello thought he had suffered a stroke. He could still see, however, and he watched in horror as Jackson methodically checked the hypodermic needle in his hand.

"It's mostly an innocuous saline solution," Jackson said as though he were addressing a science class. "I say mostly, because it also contains prostaglandin, a substance produced naturally in the body. Normal levels are measured in micrograms. I'm about to give you a dose several thousand times that. When this dose hits your heart, it will cause the coronary arteries to constrict, triggering what doctors term a myocardial infarction, also known as a heart attack. Since prostaglandin occurs naturally in the body, it's also naturally metabolized by the body. There will be no suspiciously high traces left for a medical examiner to detect." Jackson plunged the needle into Romanello's jugular. "They will find you here, a young, strapping man felled in his prime by natural causes." He smiled and gently patted Romanello on the head.

From his bag Jackson extracted a razor blade. "Now, a sharp-eyed medical examiner might pick up on the hypodermic's entry site." Using the razor, he nicked Romanello's skin at the precise place the needle had gone in. A drop of blood floated to the surface of the skin. Jackson replaced the razor in the bag and pulled out a Band-Aid. He pressed it across the fresh cut.

He was about to stand up when he noted the edge of the newspaper article sticking out from Romanello's jacket pocket. He plucked it out and read the story of the two murders, drugs, Lu-Ann's disappearance, and the police's search for her. His features became grim. That explained a lot. Romanello was blackmailing her.

Had Jackson discovered this information a day earlier, he would've executed LuAnn Tyler on the spot. Now he could not do that, and he hated the loss of control. She had already been confirmed as the winning ticket holder. He folded the paper and put it in his pocket. Like it or not, he was wedded to LuAnn Tyler. However, he would take control back. He would tell her exactly what to do, and if she didn't follow his instructions precisely, he would kill her.

CHAPTER 4

CHARLIE glanced around the crowded auditorium. He would've liked to be up on the stage with LuAnn, giving her moral support. However, he had to remain in the background. Raising suspicion was not part of his job description. He would see LuAnn after the press conference, when he would have to tell her whether he would accompany her or not. The problem was he hadn't made up his mind yet. If he went, he knew that he would enjoy LuAnn and Lisa's company, with an added plus of being a father figure for the little girl. But what would happen after the first few years?

It was inevitable that beautiful LuAnn, with her new wealth and the refinement that would come from those riches, would be the target of dozens of the world's most eligible men. She would marry one of them. And what about Charlie? At some point he would be compelled to leave them. It wasn't like he was family or anything. And when that time came, it would be painful. After spending only a few days with them, he felt a bond with LuAnn and Lisa that he had not formed in ten years of marriage with his ex-wife. Could he calmly walk away from Lisa and her mother without suffering a broken heart? He shook his head. What a tough guy he had turned out to be. He barely knew these simple people from the South, yet he was now engulfed in a life-churning decision, the consequences of which he was extrapolating years into the future.

He knew he could be LuAnn's friend for the rest of his life, but he didn't know if he could do it close-up every day with the knowledge that it might end abruptly. It came down to pure envy, he decided. Envy of the guy who would eventually win her love, a love that he was sure would last forever, at least on her side. And heaven help the poor man who betrayed her. She was a hellcat—that was easy to see. A firecracker with a heart of gold.

Charlie stopped his musings and looked up at the stage as the cameras started clicking away and LuAnn appeared. She wore a pale blue knee-length dress with matching shoes, her hair and makeup impeccable. Tall, queenly, and calm, she walked gracefully into the crowd's field of vision. Charlie shook his head in wonder. She had just made his decision that much harder.

SHERIFF Roy Waymer nearly spit his mouthful of beer clear across the room as he watched LuAnn Tyler waving at him from the TV. He looked over at his wife, Doris, whose eyes were boring into the twenty-seven-inch screen.

"You been looking for her all over the county, and there she is right there in New York City!" Doris exclaimed. "The gall of that girl. And she just won all that money." Doris said this bitterly. Twenty-four torn-up lottery tickets resided in her trash can.

Waymer wrestled his considerable girth out of his La-Z-Boy and headed toward the telephone. "I didn't take her to be heading up to no New York. I mean, the girl ain't even got a car. I thought she'd just hightail it over to some friend's house."

"Well, it sure looks like she slipped right out on you." Doris pointed at LuAnn on the TV.

"Well, Mother," he said to his wife, "we don't exactly have the manpower of the FBI down here. With Freddie out with his back, I only got two uniformed officers on duty." He picked up the phone. "I'll contact the police up in New York to pick her up."

"Think they'll do that?"

"Mother, she's a possible suspect in a double murder investigation," he said importantly.

Doris looked at him anxiously. "You think LuAnn killed Duane and that other boy?"

Waymer held the phone up to his ear and shrugged. "She'd been in a fight. More than one person saw her with a bandage on her face that day."

"Drugs was behind it, that's for sure," Doris said. "I betcha LuAnn was the brains behind it all. She's sharp, all right. We all know that. And she was always too good for us. She didn't belong here. She wanted to get out, but she didn't have no way. Drug money— that was her way. You mark my words, Roy."

Sheriff Waymer didn't answer. He was trying to get through to the NYPD.

WHEN the press conference was over, LuAnn was escorted off the stage. She quickly changed into slacks and a blouse, piled her long hair under a cowboy hat, and picked up Lisa, who was being watched by someone from the in-house lottery staff. She checked her watch. Barely twenty minutes had passed since she had been introduced to the world as the new lottery winner. She expected that Sheriff Roy Waymer would be contacting the New York police by now. Everyone from LuAnn's hometown watched the lottery drawing. The timing would be very tight.

A BLACK stretch limo confronted LuAnn as she left the building. The chauffeur tipped his cap to her and held open the door. She got in and settled Lisa in the seat next to her.

"Good work, LuAnn. Your performance was flawless," Jackson said as the limo proceeded down the street.

LuAnn jerked around and stared into the dark recesses of the limo's far corner. All the interior lights were off except for one directly over her head. She felt as though she were back onstage. She could barely make out his shape as his voice drifted out to her. "Frankly, I was concerned that you would make a fool of yourself. Nothing against you, of course. Anyone thrust into a strange situation is more apt to fail than not, wouldn't you agree?"

"I've had a lot of practice."

Jackson leaned forward slightly. "Practice with what?"

LuAnn stared toward the darkened corner. "Strange situations."

"You know, LuAnn, you really do amaze me sometimes. In limited instances your perspicacity rivals my own, and I don't say that lightly." He opened a briefcase and pulled out several pieces of paper. "It's time to discuss the conditions."

"We need to talk about something first."

Jackson cocked his head. "Really? And what might that be?"

LuAnn let out a deep breath. She had wondered whether Jackson needed to know about the man calling himself Rainbow. Then she decided he would find out anyway. Better it be from her. "A man came and talked to me yesterday. He wanted money from me."

Jackson laughed. "LuAnn, everybody will want money from you."

"No, it's not like that. He wanted half my winnings."

"That's absurd."

"No, it ain't. He had some information about me. . . ." LuAnn paused. "Can I have something to drink?" A gloved finger came out of the darkness and pointed to a door built into one side of the limo. LuAnn opened it and pulled out a Coke. She took a long drink, wiped her lips, and continued. "Something happened to me right before I called to accept your offer."

"Would that be the two dead bodies in your trailer? The drugs there? The fact that the police are looking for you?" She didn't answer at first, the astonishment clear on her face.

"I didn't have nothing to do with those drugs. And that man was trying to kill me. I was just protecting myself."

"I should have realized when you wanted to leave town so quickly, change your name, all that, that there was something up." He shook his head sadly. "My poor LuAnn. I guess I would've left town quickly too, confronted with those circumstances. And who would have thought it of Duane. Drugs! How terrible. But I tell you what. Out of the goodness of my heart I won't hold it against you this time. However"—here Jackson's tone became starkly forceful—"don't ever try to hide anything from me again."

"But this man—"

Jackson spoke impatiently. "That's taken care of. You certainly won't be giving any money to him."

She stared into the darkness, amazement again spreading across her face. "But how could you have done that?"

"People are always saying that about me. How could I have done that?" Jackson spoke in a hushed voice. "I can do anything, LuAnn. Don't you know that by now?"

"The man said he was sent to kill me but got called off."

"How terribly peculiar."

"I figure he got called off right after I called you."

"Life is chock full of coincidences, isn't it?" Jackson's tone had become mocking.

LuAnn's features took on a glint of ferocity. "I get bit, I bite back. Real hard. Just so we understand each other, Mr. Jackson."

"I think we understand each other perfectly, LuAnn." She heard papers rustling. "However, this complicates matters."

"What do you mean?"

"Taxes, LuAnn. On one hundred million dollars you will owe roughly fifty million dollars in state and federal income tax. The law states the tax must be paid over ten years in equal installments. That comes to five million dollars per year. In addition to that, any money you earn from the principal amount is taxable. And I must tell you, I have plans for that principal—rather grand plans. You will make a great deal more money in the coming years; however, it will almost all be taxable income. That ordinarily would not present a problem, since law-abiding citizens who are not on the run from the police can file their tax returns, pay their fair share, and live quite nicely. You can no longer do that. If my people filed your tax return under the name LuAnn Tyler with your current address, don't you think the police might come knocking on your door?"

"Well, can't I pay tax under my new name?"

"Ah, potentially a brilliant solution; however, the IRS tends to get quite curious when the very first tax return filed by someone barely out of her teens has so many zeros on it."

"So what do we do?"

When Jackson next spoke, his tone made LuAnn tighten her grip on Lisa. "You will do exactly as I tell you. You are ticketed on a flight out of the country. You will never return to the United States. This little mess in Georgia has bestowed upon you a life on the move. Forever, I'm afraid. Do you understand?"

LuAnn said stubbornly, "I don't like people telling me what to do."

"Is that right? Well, then why don't you take your chances on getting out of the country by yourself? Would you like to do that?"

"I can take care of myself."

"That's not the point. You made a deal with me, LuAnn. A deal I expect you to honor. I can stop the limo right here, toss you and the child out, and phone the police to come and pick you up. It's your choice. Decide. Now!"

LuAnn looked desperately around the interior of the limo. Her eyes finally settled on Lisa. Her daughter looked up at her with big, soft eyes; there was complete faith there. LuAnn let out a deep breath. What choice did she really have? "All right."

Jackson again rustled the papers he held. "Now, we have a number of documents for you to sign, but let me discuss the terms first. You have just won one hundred million dollars. That money has been placed into an escrow account set up by the Lottery Commission under your name. By the way, I have obtained a Social Security number for you under your new name. Once you execute these papers, my people will be able to transfer the funds out of that account and into one over which I will have complete control."

"But how do I get to the money?" LuAnn protested.

"Patience, LuAnn. All will be explained. The money will be invested as I see fit and for my own account. However, from those investments you will be guaranteed a minimum return of twenty-five percent per annum, which comes to twenty-five million dollars per year." He held up a cautionary finger. "Understand that that is income from principal. The one hundred million is never touched. I will control that principal for ten years and invest it however I choose. After ten years you will receive the full one hundred million dollars back. Any yearly income you've earned over the ten years is yours to keep. We will invest that for you as well, free of charge. Under any reasonable projection you will be worth hundreds of millions of dollars at the end of the ten-year period." Jackson's eyes sparkled. "It sure beats a hundred dollars a day, doesn't it, LuAnn?" He laughed heartily. "To start you off, I'll advance you five million dollars. That should keep you until the investment earnings come rolling in." From out of the darkness he extended the documents and a pen to her. "They're clearly marked where your signature is required." LuAnn hesitated. "Is there a problem?" Jackson asked sharply.

She shook her head and quickly signed the documents.

"Your bags are in the trunk. I have your plane tickets and hotel reservations with me. I have planned your itinerary for twelve months, and I have honored your request to travel to Sweden, the land of your maternal ancestors. I've put together an intricate cover story for you. In sum, you left the States as a young girl. You married a wealthy foreign national. The money will be all his, as far as the IRS is concerned. The funds will be kept only in foreign banks and offshore accounts. U.S. banks have stringent reporting requirements to the IRS. None of your money will ever ever be kept in the United States." LuAnn reached out for the tickets. "Not yet, LuAnn. We have some steps to take. The police," he said pointedly. "Don't be surprised if New York's finest are stationed at every airport, bus, and train station right this very minute. Since you're a felon fleeing across state lines, they've probably called the FBI in as well."

As Jackson was talking, LuAnn felt the limo stop. She heard a slow, clanking sound, as though a door were being raised. When it stopped, the limo pulled through, then came to a halt.

He patted the seat. "Now I need you to sit next to me. Close your eyes and give me your hand so I can guide you," Jackson said, his hand reaching out of the darkness.

"Why do I have to close my eyes?"

"Indulge me, LuAnn. I can't resist a little drama in life."

LuAnn took his hand and closed her eyes. He settled her down beside him. She could feel a light shine down on her features. She jerked as she felt scissors cut into her hair. "I would advise you not to do that again," Jackson said. "It's hard enough to do this in such a small space. I wouldn't want to do you serious damage." He continued cutting until her hair stopped just above her ears. A wet substance was run through the remaining strands, and then it quickly hardened. Jackson used a styling brush to manipulate the strands into place. Next he clamped a portable mirror to the edge of the limo's console. Jackson applied a malleable substance to her nose, kneading and pressing until a satisfactory shape was created. "Your nose is long and straight, LuAnn. However, a little putty, a little shadowing, and we have a thick, crooked piece of cartilage that isn't nearly as becoming. However, it's only temporary." Using subtle shadowing, he made LuAnn's eyes seem closer together and made her chin seem less prominent with the aid of powders and creams.

She felt him examining the wound on her jaw. "Nasty cut. Souvenir from your trailer experience?" When LuAnn didn't answer, he said, "This will require stitching. Even with that, it probably will scar. Don't worry. After I'm done, it will be invisible. But eventually you may want plastic surgery." He chuckled and added, "In my professional opinion." Next Jackson painted her lips. "A little thin, LuAnn. You may want to consider collagen."

It was all LuAnn could do not to jump up and run screaming from him. It was as though he were some mad scientist bringing her back from the dead.

"I'm stippling in freckles now along the nose and cheeks." Finally Jackson guided her back to her seat. "There's a small mirror in the compartment next to you," he informed her.

LuAnn pulled out the mirror and held it up in front of her face. She gasped. Looking back at her was a redheaded woman, with short, spiky hair and an abundance of freckles. Her lips were a deep red and made her mouth look huge. Her nose was much broader and bore a distinctive curve to the right. She was completely unrecognizable to herself.

Jackson tossed something onto her lap. She looked down. It was a passport. She opened it. The photo staring back at her was the same woman she had looked at in the mirror.

"Wonderful work, wouldn't you say?" Jackson said.

As LuAnn looked up, he hit a switch and a light illuminated him. Or rather her, as LuAnn received a second jolt. Sitting across from her was the double of the woman she had just become. The same short red hair, crooked nose, everything. The only difference was LuAnn had on slacks and her twin was wearing a dress.

Jackson quietly clapped his hands together. "I've impersonated women before, but I believe this is the first time I've impersonated an impersonation. That photo is of me, by the way. Taken this morning." He smiled at her shocked look. "No need to applaud. However, I do think that considering it was done in an underground parking garage, it does deserve some degree of acclaim."

The limo started moving again, and in little more than half an hour they arrived at JFK. Before the driver opened the door, Jackson looked sharply at LuAnn. "Don't put on your hat or your glasses, as that suggests attempting to hide one's features. Remember rule number one: When trying to hide, make yourself as obvious as possible. Put yourself right out in the open. Seeing adult twins together is fairly rare, but while people—the police included—will notice us, there will be no suspicion. The police will be looking for one woman. When they see two, and twins at that, even with a child, they'll discount us entirely." He reached across for Lisa. LuAnn blocked his hand. "LuAnn, I am trying to get you and this little girl safely out of the country. We will shortly be walking through a squadron of police and FBI agents. Believe me, I have no interest in keeping your daughter, but I do need her for a very specific reason."

Finally LuAnn let go. They climbed out of the limo. In high heels Jackson was a little taller than LuAnn, but she had to admit his lean build looked good in the stylish clothing. He put a black coat on over his dark dress. "Come on," he said to LuAnn. She stiffened at the new tone of his voice. Now he also *sounded* like her.

"Where's Charlie?" LuAnn asked as they entered the terminal a few minutes later, a chubby skycap with the bags in tow.

"I'm afraid Charlie's duties with you are at an end."

"Oh."

"Don't worry. You're in much better hands," Jackson said.

LuAnn swallowed quickly as she eyed the quartet of police officers scrutinizing each of the patrons at the crowded airport. They passed by the officers, who did indeed stare at them. Then, just as Jackson had predicted, they lost interest in them and focused on other persons coming into the terminal.

Jackson and LuAnn stopped near the international flight check-in for British Airways. "I'll check in for you while you wait by that snack bar." Jackson pointed across the broad aisle of the terminal. "Give me your passport, the one I just gave you." LuAnn did so and watched as Jackson, the skycap behind him, swung Lisa's baby carrier in one hand as he sauntered over to the ticket counter. Jackson had even picked up that mannerism of hers. LuAnn shook her head in awe.

Jackson was in the short first-class line, and it moved quickly. He rejoined LuAnn in a few minutes. "So far, so good. Now, I wouldn't recommend changing your appearance for several months. Once things die down and your hair grows out, you can use the passport I originally made up for you."

From the corner of his eye Jackson watched as two men and a woman dressed in suits moved down the aisle, their eyes sweeping the area. LuAnn glanced in their direction. She spied in one of their hands a picture of her. She froze. "Those are FBI agents," Jackson said quietly. "But remember, you don't look anything like that photo. It's as if you're invisible." His confident tones assuaged her fears. Jackson moved forward. "Your flight leaves in twenty minutes. Follow me." They went through security and down to the departure gate and sat in the waiting area.

Jackson handed her the new passport, along with a small packet. "There's cash, credit cards, and an international driver's license in there, all in your new name." He took a moment to grip her by the hand and even patted her shoulder. "Good luck. If you find yourself in difficulty at any time, here is a phone number that will reach me anywhere in the world day or night. I will tell you, though, that unless there is a problem, you and I will never meet or speak to each other again." He handed her a card with the number on it.

LuAnn looked down at it, hoping she would never have to use it. If she never saw Jackson again, it would be all right with her. When she looked up, he had disappeared into the crowd.

She sighed. She was already tired of running, and now she was about to start a lifetime of just that. LuAnn opened her passport and stared at the strange photo and the name underneath it: Catherine Savage from Charlottesville, Virginia. Her mother had been born in Charlottesville, and LuAnn thought it appropriate that her new identity should call that city her hometown as well. Her new name had been well thought out too. A savage she was and a savage she would remain despite an enormous fortune at her command. She looked at the photo again, and her skin tingled as she remembered that it was Jackson staring back at her. She closed the passport and put it away.

Since first-class passengers could board at their leisure, LuAnn walked down to the Jetway. The flight attendant greeted her warmly. "Right this way, Ms. Savage. Beautiful little girl." LuAnn was escorted to her seat. She looked around the lavish space in awe and noted the built-in TV and phone at each seat. She had never been on a plane before. This was quite a princely way to experience it for the first time. The darkness was rapidly gathering as the other passengers entered the first-class compartment.

Twenty minutes after the plane had lifted into the air, LuAnn had put on her headphones and was gently swaying to some classical music. She jerked upright when a hand fell upon her shoulder and Charlie's voice filtered down to her. He wore the hat she had bought him. His smile was big and genuine, but there was nervousness evident in his body language. LuAnn took off the headphones.

"Good gosh," he whispered. "If I hadn't recognized Lisa, I would've passed right by you. What the hell happened?"

"A long story." She gripped his wrist tightly. "Does this mean you're finally gonna tell me your real name, Charlie?"

A LIGHT RAIN STARTED TO FALL shortly after the 747 had lifted off. Walking down the street in midtown Manhattan, an old man in a black trench coat seemed not to notice the inclement weather. Jackson's appearance had changed drastically since his last encounter with LuAnn. He had aged at least forty years. Heavy pouches hung under his eyes, a fringe of white hair circled the back of his bald head. He looked up into the cloudy sky. The plane would be over Nova Scotia now as it traveled its convex path to Europe.

And she had not gone alone. Charlie had gone off with her. Jackson had stayed behind after dropping off LuAnn and watched him board the aircraft. Godspeed to you both, he said under his breath. And heaven help you if you ever betray me.

He pulled his collar up and ambled down the street, thinking intently. It was now time to plan for next month's winner.

PART TWO
Ten Years Later

CHAPTER 5

THE small private jet landed at the airstrip at Charlottesville-Albemarle Airport and taxied to a halt. Three people quickly exited the plane and climbed into a waiting limousine, which immediately drove off, heading south on Route 29.

Inside the limo, the woman took off her glasses and laid her arm across the young girl's shoulder. Then LuAnn Tyler slumped back against the seat and took a deep breath. Home. Finally they were back in the United States. She had thought about little else for some time now. She glanced at the man who sat in the rear-facing seat. His thick fingers drummed a somber rhythm across the car's window. Charlie was concerned, but he managed a reassuring grin. He put his hands in his lap and cocked his head at her. "You scared?"

LuAnn nodded and then looked down at ten-year-old Lisa, who had slumped over her mother's lap and fallen into an exhausted sleep. The trip had been a long one. "How about you?" she asked.

Charlie shrugged. He scrutinized Lisa to make sure she was sleeping. Satisfied, he undid his seat belt, sat down next to LuAnn, and spoke softly. "Jackson doesn't know we've come back."

She whispered back. "We don't know that, Charlie."

"If he knew, do you think he'd have let us get this far? We took about as circuitous a route as anybody could take. Five plane changes, four countries, we zigzagged halfway across the world to get here. And even if he does know, he's not going to care. It's been ten years. The deal's expired." Charlie lay back against the seat.

LuAnn gently rubbed his shoulder. "You're right. It's not like I'm going to announce to the whole world that I'm around again. We're going to live a nice, quiet life."

"In considerable luxury. You saw the photos of the house."

LuAnn nodded. "It looks beautiful."

"An old estate. Been on the market for a long time, but with an asking price of six million bucks, can't say I'm surprised. We got a deal at three point five mil. Of course, we dumped another million into renovation."

"And secluded?"

"Very. Almost three hundred acres. I never saw so much green grass. It's got a three-stall horse barn and a pool. Lisa will love that. Plenty of room for a tennis court. The works. And there's dense forest all around. Look at it as a hardwood moat. I've already started shopping around for a firm to construct a security fence."

"My name's not on the ownership papers?"

"Catherine Savage appears nowhere. Deed was transferred into the name of the corporation I had set up."

"I wish I could have changed my name again, just in case he's on the lookout for it."

"Your cover story as Catherine Savage is complicated enough without adding another layer to it."

"I know." She sighed. "Lisa's enrolled in private school?"

Charlie nodded. "St. Anne's-Belfield. Pretty exclusive, but Lisa's educational qualifications are outstanding. She speaks multiple languages, been all over the world."

"I don't know. Maybe I should have hired a private tutor."

"Come on, LuAnn, you've been doing that ever since she could walk. She needs to be around other kids. It'll be good for her and for you too. You know what they say about time away."

She suddenly smiled at him slyly. "Are you feeling claustrophobic with us, Charlie?"

"You bet I am. I'm gonna start staying out late. Might even take up some hobbies like golf or something." He grinned at LuAnn to show her he was only joking.

"It's been a good ten years, hasn't it?" Her voice was anxious.

"Wouldn't trade 'em for anything," he said.

LuAnn laid her head against his shoulder. The last ten years had been good to her only if you defined good as being constantly on the move, fearful of discovery, and having pangs of guilt every time she bought something, because of how she had come by the money. As the limo drove on, she closed her eyes and tried to rest. She would need it. Her second new life was about to commence.

THOMAS Donovan sat staring at his computer screen in the frenetic newsroom of the Washington *Tribune*. Journalistic awards dotted the walls of his cluttered cubicle, including a Pulitzer he had won before he was thirty. Now in his early fifties, Donovan still possessed the drive and fervor of his youth.

A shadow fell across his desk. "Mr. Donovan?"

Donovan looked up at a kid from the mailroom. "Yeah?"

"This just came in for you. I think it's some research you requested." Donovan took the packet and dug into it with obvious zeal. The lottery story he was working on had so much potential. The national lottery took in billions of dollars each year. The government maintained that the poor didn't spend a disproportionate share of their income on the game, but Donovan knew for a fact that millions of people who played were borderline poverty-level, squandering food stamps and anything else they could get their hands on to purchase the chance at an easy life, even though the odds were so astronomically high as to be farcical. But that wasn't all. Donovan had turned up an astonishing seventy-five percent bankruptcy rate for the winners. Nine out of every twelve winners each year subsequently had declared bankruptcy. His angle had to do with financial-management companies and other scheming types getting hold of these poor people and basically ripping them off.

The government was just as much to blame, Donovan felt, because rather than take taxes out automatically from lottery prizes, it left the winners to structure their own payment of taxes. When winners weren't astute enough to set up sophisticated accounting systems, the tax boys came after them and took every last dime they had, under the guise of penalties and interest, leaving them poorer than when they started. The public thought that lottery money was earmarked for education and highway maintenance, but much of it ended up in other places. Lottery officials received fat paychecks. Politicians supporting the lottery saw large funds flow to their states. It all stank, and Donovan felt it was high time the truth came out.

He focused on the packet of documents. He had tested his theory on the bankruptcy rate going back five years. The documents he was holding went back another seven years. As he paged through year after year of lottery winners, the bankruptcy ratio stayed at nine out of twelve a year. Astonishing. His instincts had been dead-on.

Then he abruptly stopped and stared at one page. It was a list of lottery winners from exactly ten years ago. Herman Rudy, Bobbie Jo Reynolds, LuAnn Tyler—the list went on, twelve winners in a row. Not one had declared bankruptcy. Yet every twelve-month period except this one had resulted in nine bankruptcies.

Donovan had some sources to check, and he wanted to do it in more privacy than the crowded newsroom allowed. He threw the file in his battered briefcase and left the office. In non-rush-hour traffic he reached his small apartment in Virginia in twenty minutes. Twice divorced and with no children, Donovan led a life focused solely on his work. He had a relationship slowly percolating with Alicia Crane, a well-known Washington socialite from a wealthy family. He had never been fully comfortable moving in her circles; however, Alicia was devoted to him, and, truth be known, flitting around the edges of her luxurious existence wasn't so bad.

He settled into his home office, picked up the phone, and dialed the number of a source at the Internal Revenue Service. Donovan gave that person the names of the twelve consecutive lottery winners who had not declared bankruptcy. Two hours later he got a call back. Eleven of the lottery winners had filed tax returns each year. One had not. In fact, this person had outright disappeared. Donovan had a vague recollection of why. Two murders—her boyfriend in rural Georgia and another man. Drugs had been involved. The woman had disappeared after winning a hundred million dollars, and the money had disappeared with her. With her lottery winnings she could easily have switched identities on her run from the murder charge and invented a new life for herself.

Donovan smiled. He might have a way of discovering LuAnn Tyler's new identity. At least he could try.

The next day he phoned the sheriff in Rikersville, Georgia, Lu-Ann's hometown. Roy Waymer had died five years ago. Ironically, the current sheriff was Billy Harvey, Duane's uncle. Harvey was very talkative when the subject of LuAnn came up.

"She got Duane killed," he said angrily. "She got him involved in those drugs sure as I'm talking to you."

"Have you heard from her over the last ten years?"

Harvey paused for a moment. "Well, she sent some money to Duane's folks. They didn't ask for it, I can tell you that."

"Did they keep it?"

"Well, they're on in years and poorer'n dirt. You don't just turn your back on that kind of money."

"How much are we talking about?"

"Two hundred thousand dollars."

Donovan whistled softly. "Did you try to trace the money?"

"I wasn't sheriff then, but Roy Waymer did. He even had some local FBI boys over to help, but they never turned up a durn thing."

"Anything else?"

"Yeah. You ever talk to her, you tell her the Harvey family ain't forgot, not even after all these years. That murder warrant is still outstanding. We get her back to Georgia, she'll spend some nice quality time with us. I'm talking twenty to life."

"I'll let her know, Sheriff, thanks. Oh, could you send me a copy of the file? Autopsy reports, forensics, the works." He gave Harvey the *Trib*'s FedEx number and address, then hung up.

Donovan spent the next week exploring every crevice of LuAnn's life. From copies of her parents' death notices in the Rikersville *Gazette,* he learned that her mother had been born in Charlottesville, Virginia. From conversations with the NYPD and the FBI in New York, he discovered that the police had thrown their net over the bus and train stations and the airports a half hour after LuAnn had appeared on national television, but there had been no sign of the woman. That had greatly puzzled the FBI, who wanted to know how a twenty-year-old woman with a seventh-grade education from rural Georgia—carrying a baby, no less—had waltzed right through their net. Donovan's gut told him that LuAnn had left the country. If she had gotten on a plane, then he had something to work with.

JACKSON sat in a chair in the darkened living room of a luxurious apartment in a building overlooking New York's Central Park. Approaching forty years of age, he was still lean in build, although the years had etched fine lines around his eyes and mouth. He rose and moved slowly through the apartment. The furnishings were eclectic: European antiques mixed with Oriental art and sculpture.

He entered his makeup room and workshop. Recessed lighting covered the ceiling. Multiple mirrors ringed the room. Two reclining leather chairs sat in front of the largest mirrors. Wigs and hairpieces lined one wall. Customized cabinets housed latex caps, acrylic teeth, and other synthetic materials and putties. One massive storage unit contained absorbent cotton; acetone; spirit gum; powders; brushes; cake makeup; modeling clay; collodion to make scars and pockmarks; crepe hair to make beards, mustaches, and eyebrows; and hundreds of other substances designed to reshape one's appearance. There were three racks of clothing of all descriptions and, in a specially built case, over fifty sets of identification documents that allowed Jackson to travel as a man or a woman.

Jackson sat down and stared into a mirror. He didn't see his reflection staring back at him. Instead, he saw a blank countenance, one to be manipulated, painted, and massaged into someone else. Why be limited to one physical identity one's whole life, he thought, when there was so much more out there to experience? Go anywhere, do anything. He had told that to all twelve of his lottery winners. And they had all bought it, completely and absolutely, for he had been dead right.

Over the last ten years he had earned hundreds of millions of dollars for each of them and billions for himself. Ironically, Jackson had grown up in affluent circumstances, and his family had been old money. His parents were long dead. Jackson's father had been both arrogant and insecure. A politician and insider in Washington, the old man had taken his family connections as far as he could until the escalator had stopped moving upward. And then he had spent the family money in a futile attempt to regain that upward momentum. And then the money was gone. Jackson, the eldest child, had often taken the brunt of the old man's wrath over the years. Upon turning eighteen, Jackson discovered that the large trust fund his grandfather had set up for him had been raided illegally so many times by his father that there wasn't anything left. The continuing rage and physical abuse the old man had wielded after Jackson had confronted him with this discovery had psychologically damaged the son. The physical bruises eventually healed, but Jackson's inner rage seemed to grow exponentially each year.

It might seem trite to others. Lost your fortune? So what. But Jackson had counted on that money to free him from his father's tyranny. Instead Jackson had gotten an empty bank account and the hate-filled blows of a madman. And Jackson had taken it. Up to a point. But then he hadn't taken it anymore.

His father had died unexpectedly. Parents killed their small children every day, never with good reason. Children killed their parents only rarely, usually with excellent purpose. An early chemical experiment, administered through his father's Scotch, the rupturing of a brain aneurysm the result. As with any occupation, one had to start somewhere.

The elder son had been compelled to go out and earn the family fortune back. A scholarship to a prestigious university and graduation at the top of his class had been followed by his careful nurturing of old family contacts, for those embers could not die out if Jackson's long-range plan was to succeed. Over the years he had mastered a variety of skills that allowed him to pursue his dream of wealth and power. And he did it while remaining completely invisible from scrutiny. Despite his love of acting, he did not crave the spotlight as his politician father had. And so he built his invisible empire, albeit in a profoundly illegal manner.

He smiled at this thought as he continued to move through the apartment. Jackson had a younger brother and sister. Like their father, his brother expected the world to offer up its best for nothing of comparable value in return. Jackson had given him enough money to live comfortably. If he ran through it, there would be no more. His sister was another matter. Jackson cared deeply for her, although she had adored the old man with the blind faith a daughter often shows to her father. Jackson had set her up in grand style but never visited her. He had no desire to lie to her about what he did for a living.

Still, Jackson had done right by his family. He was not his father. He had allowed himself one reminder of the old man, the name he used in all his dealings: Jackson. His father's name was Jack. And he would always be Jack's son.

He stopped at a window and looked out at a spectacular evening in New York. The apartment was the same one he had grown up in, although he had gutted it after purchasing it, ostensibly to modernize and make it suitable for his particular needs. The more subtle motivation had been to obliterate the past.

Jackson entered and exited his penthouse by private elevator. No one was ever allowed in. All mail and other deliveries were left at the front desk. Jackson had created a disguise for his real identity and used it whenever he left his apartment. Horace Parker, the elderly doorman, was the same one who had tipped his cap to the shy, bookish boy all those years ago. Jackson's family had left New York when he was a teenager, so the aged Parker had accepted Jackson's altered appearance as simply maturation. Now with the fake image firmly in people's minds, Jackson was confident no one could ever identify him. For Jackson, hearing his given name from Horace Parker was both comforting and troubling. Juggling so many identities was not easy, and Jackson occasionally found himself not responding to his real name.

With his limitless capital he had made the world his playpen. His funds had propelled enterprises as diverse as his identities, from guerrilla activities in third world countries to the cornering of precious metal markets in the industrialized world. He had exhibited a benevolent side as well, and large sums of money had been funneled to deserving causes across the globe. Always he demanded and received ultimate control, however invisible it was.

He entered a smaller room, filled from floor to ceiling with computers. The flat screens told him how his many worldwide interests were doing. Everything from futures markets to late-breaking news stories was analyzed here by him. He craved information, absorbed it like a three-year-old learning a foreign language.

Jackson went into another, larger room that housed his mementos from past projects. He pulled out a scrapbook and opened it. Inside were photographs of and background information on his twelve precious pieces of gold—the winners who had allowed him to recoup his family's fortune. He flipped idly through the pages. He had handpicked them carefully, culling them from welfare rolls and bankruptcy filings, searching for desperate people who would do anything to change their fortunes.

The lottery had been remarkably easy to fix. It was often that way. People just assumed institutions like that were above corruption. They must have forgotten that government lotteries had been banned in the last century because of widespread corruption. History did tend to repeat itself. If Jackson had learned one thing over the years, it was that nothing, absolutely nothing, was above corruption so long as human beings were involved, because, in truth, most people were not above the lure of money.

As he perused one page of the scrapbook, he felt an emotion he almost never experienced: uncertainty. Jackson stared at the truly remarkable countenance of LuAnn Tyler. Of the twelve lottery winners she had been by far the most memorable. There was danger in that woman, danger and a definite volatility that drew Jackson like a magnet. He had not seen or spoken to her in ten years; however, rarely a week went by that he did not think of her. At first he had kept a watchful eye on her movements, but as the years went by and she continued to move from country to country in accordance with his wishes, his diligence had lessened. The last he had heard she was in New Zealand. She would never return to the United States. Of that he was certain.

DONOVAN sat at his dining-room table, the pages he had taken out of his briefcase in front of him. It had taken two months to accumulate the information he was now sifting through.

Initially, his task seemed destined for failure through sheer numbers. On the day LuAnn Tyler had disappeared, there had been two hundred scheduled international passenger flights at JFK. Donovan had whittled down the parameters of his search to include women between the ages of twenty and thirty traveling between the hours of seven p.m. and one a.m. The press conference had lasted until six thirty, and Donovan doubted she could have made a seven-o'clock flight, but he wasn't taking any chances. That meant checking sixty flights and about fifteen thousand passengers. However, while most airlines kept active records of passengers going back five years, only the FBI could get passenger records from ten years ago.

Through a contact at the Bureau, Donovan had been able to pursue his request. He had given his FBI contact the precise parameters of his search, including the fact that the person he was seeking had probably been traveling under a newly issued passport and with a baby. Only three people satisfied those very narrow criteria. From a national credit-check agency he had been able to obtain Social Security numbers for all three people and their last known addresses. He had checked those against the records from the airlines. Two of the women had moved, which wasn't surprising given their ages ten years ago; in the interim they had probably moved on to careers and marriages. One had not. Catherine Savage was still listed as living in Virginia. Donovan had called directory assistance in Virginia, but no number came up for that name and address.

Then Donovan had taken more serious steps, filling out IRS form 2848, "Power of Attorney and Declaration of Representative"— a relatively simple form but one that carried extraordinary power. With it Donovan could obtain all sorts of confidential tax documents on the person he was investigating. A little falsification of signature was involved, but his motives were pure and thus his conscience clear. On the form he had listed the woman's name and last known address, put in her Social Security number, listed himself as her representative for tax purposes, and mailed it off.

With subdued excitement Donovan was now devouring the contents of the package from the IRS. Catherine Savage was an awfully wealthy woman, and her tax return from the prior year, at a full forty pages, reflected that wealth. He had requested returns for three years, but the IRS had sent only one for the simple reason that she had filed only one return. The mystery behind that had been cleared up quickly because Donovan, as Catherine Savage's tax representative, had been able to contact the IRS and ask virtually any question he wanted about the taxpayer.

Donovan looked at his notes from the conversation with the IRS agent. Catherine Savage had been born in Charlottesville, Virginia, and had left the country as a young girl. Living in France, she had met and married a wealthy German businessman. The man had died two years ago, and his fortune had passed to his young widow. Now, as a U.S. citizen with control of her own money, she had begun paying income taxes to her homeland.

Donovan leaned back in his chair. The agent had provided him with another piece of news. The IRS had recently received a change of address for Catherine Savage. She was now in the United States. In fact, she had returned to the town of her birth, Charlottesville, Virginia—the same town where LuAnn Tyler's mother had been born. That was too much of a coincidence for Donovan. He was certain LuAnn Tyler had come home. It was time they met.

CHAPTER 6

SITTING in his pickup truck parked on the side of the road, Matt Riggs surveyed the area through a pair of field binoculars. The half mile of winding asphalt private road running to his right formed a T-intersection with the road he was on; beyond that sat a grand country estate with beautiful vistas of the nearby mountains. The tree-filled, steeply graded land was, to his experienced eye, impenetrable, which made him wonder why the owner wanted an expensive perimeter security fence. The estate already had the best of nature's own protection.

Riggs shrugged and pulled on his coat. The chilly wind buffeted him as he stepped from his truck. He put a hand through his unkempt dark brown hair, working the kinks out of his muscular frame. It would take about an hour to walk the front location of the fence. Plans called for the fence to be seven feet high, with electronic sensors spaced randomly across its frame. A video camera, intercom system, and a locking mechanism on the front gates would ensure that nothing could open them without the permission of the owner, whom he had never met. All the negotiations had been handled through an intermediary. He reasoned that someone who could afford a fence such as this probably had better things to do than sit down and chat with a lowly general contractor. Not that he was complaining. This single job would guarantee his best year ever.

Binoculars dangling around his neck, he trudged down the road until he found a narrow pathway into the woods.

THE BMW pulled out from the garage and headed down the drive. The road going down was lined on either side with four-board oak fencing painted a pristine white. At seven in the morning the stillness of the day remained unbroken. These early morning drives had become a soothing ritual for LuAnn. She glanced back at the house in her rearview mirror. Constructed of Pennsylvania stone and weathered brick, with a row of white columns bracketing a deep front porch, it was elegantly refined despite its imposing size.

As the car passed down the drive and out of sight of the house, LuAnn turned her eyes back to the road and suddenly hit the brake. A man was waving at her, flagging her down. She stopped. He came up to the driver's-side window and motioned for her to open it. Out of the corner of her eye she saw a black Honda parked on a grass strip bordering the road. She eyed him with deep suspicion but hit the button, and the window descended slightly. His appearance was innocent enough—middle-aged and slight of build, with a beard laced around the edges with gray. "Can I help you?" she asked.

"I think I'm lost. Is this the old Brillstein estate?"

LuAnn shook her head. "We recently moved in, but that's not the name of the owners before us. It's called Wicken's Hunt. Who are you looking for?"

The man's face filled her window. "Maybe you know her. LuAnn Tyler from Georgia." LuAnn sucked in a mouthful of air. There was no hiding the astonishment on her face. Thomas Donovan leaned even closer. "LuAnn, I'd like to talk to you—"

She hit the accelerator, and Donovan had to jump back to avoid having his feet crushed by the car tires. "Hey!" he screamed after her. The car was almost out of sight. Donovan, his face ashen, ran to his car, started it up, and roared off down the road.

Donovan had decided the direct approach would be best. He had watched the house for a week, noted her pattern of early morning drives, and chosen today to make contact. Despite being almost run over, he had the satisfaction of knowing he had been right. Throwing the question at her out of the blue like that was the only sure way to get the truth. And now he had it. Catherine Savage was LuAnn Tyler. Her looks had changed considerably from the photos taken ten years ago. Except for the look on her face and her abrupt departure, Donovan wouldn't have known it was her.

He focused on the road, glimpsing the gray BMW far ahead. But on the curvy mountain road his smaller and more agile Honda was gaining. He didn't like playing the daredevil role, but he had to make her understand what he was trying to do.

MATT Riggs studied the terrain. The most difficult part of the job would be getting the heavy equipment up here. He was about to pull the property survey out of his jacket to study it in more detail when there was an explosion of sound. He whipped the binoculars up to his eyes. Through the trees he spied two cars hurtling down the road where the estate was situated, their respective engines at full throttle. The car in front was a big BMW sedan. The car behind was smaller. What Riggs saw next made him turn and run as fast as he could back to his truck. The look of raw fear on the woman's face in the Bimmer and the grim countenance of the man chasing her were all he needed to kick-start every instinct he had ever gained from his former life. He gunned the engine and pulled onto the road.

Suddenly the two cars appeared in front of him on the main road. The Bimmer took the turn almost on two wheels before stabilizing, the other car right behind it. However, now on a straightaway, the three hundred plus horses of the BMW quickly opened a gap between the woman and her pursuer. That wouldn't last, Riggs knew, because a curve qualifying for deadman's status was fast approaching. He hoped the woman knew it; if she didn't, he would be watching the BMW sail off the road. He punched the gas and gained on what he now saw was a black Honda. The man apparently had all of his attention focused on the BMW, because when Riggs passed him on the left, the man didn't even look over until Riggs cut in front of him and slowed to twenty miles an hour. Up ahead Riggs saw the woman glance back in her rearview mirror as the truck and Honda fought a pitched battle for supremacy of the road. Like the coils of a sidewinder, the truck and the Honda swayed back and forth across the narrow roadway as the driver of the Honda tried mightily to pass. But in his past career Riggs had done his share of dangerous, high-speed driving, and he expertly matched the other man maneuver for maneuver. A minute later they rounded the almost V-shaped curve, a wall of sheer jutting rock on the left and an almost vertical drop to the right. Riggs breathed a sigh of relief when they were once again on straight road.

He reached across to his glove compartment and pulled out his portable phone. He was about to punch in 911 when the Honda rammed his truck from behind. The phone flew out of his hand and smashed into pieces against the dashboard. Riggs clenched the wheel, shifted into low gear, and slowed down even more as the Honda repeatedly smashed into him. What he was hoping would happen did, as the Honda's front bumper and the truck's heavy-duty rear one locked together. Riggs peered into the rearview mirror and saw the man's hand slide over to his glove compartment. Riggs wasn't going to wait around to see whether a weapon emerged. He stopped the truck, slammed into reverse, and the two vehicles roared backward down the road. The man in the Honda gripped the steering wheel in a panic. Riggs slowed as he came to the curve, cleared it, then shot forward again. As he came to the straightaway, he cut the wheel sharply to the left and slammed the Honda into the rocky side of the road. The collision uncoupled the two vehicles. The driver appeared unhurt. Riggs threw the truck into drive and disappeared down the road. He looked back for several minutes, but he didn't see the Honda. Either it had been disabled or the driver had decided not to pursue his reckless actions further.

With no sign of the BMW and his damaged bumper clanking loudly, Riggs slowed down and pulled off the road. He plucked a pen from his shirt pocket and wrote the license plate numbers of the Honda and BMW on a pad of paper he kept affixed to his dashboard. He had a pretty good idea who was in the Bimmer.

Someone who lived in the big house. The same big house he had been hired to surround with a state-of-the-art security fence. Now the owner's request started to make a lot more sense.

THE BMW had pulled off on a side road. The driver's door was open, the motor running. Arms clutched tightly around her sides, LuAnn walked in tight, frenetic circles in the middle of the road. Anger, confusion, and frustration raced across her features.

Now thirty years old, she still carried the impulsive energy and sleek animal movements of her youth. The years had grafted onto her a more complete, mature beauty. Her body was leaner, making her appear even taller. Her hair now was far more blond than auburn and cut in a sophisticated manner that highlighted her more defined facial features. Her teeth were now perfect, having benefitted from years of dentistry. However, she had not followed Jackson's advice regarding the knife wound to her jaw. She had had it stitched but let the scar remain. Every time she looked in the mirror, it was a stark reminder of where she had come from, how she had gotten here. She would never cover it over with surgery. She wanted to be reminded of the unpleasantness, the pain.

For a few moments her thoughts centered on the man in the truck. Was he a good Samaritan, or was he something else? She took one long, deep breath and wondered for the hundredth time if she had made a grievous mistake returning to the United States.

RIGGS drove his battered truck up the private road. Going to the house, he figured, was the quickest way to find a phone and perhaps also to seek an explanation for this morning's events. He rounded a curve, and the mansion, which stood three stories tall, suddenly appeared in front of him. His truck resembled a plain, squat tug bearing down on the *QE2*. He parked in the wraparound drive. As he walked up to the front door, a voice spoke to him from an intercom in the wall. "Can I help you?" It was a man's voice.

"Matthew Riggs. My company was hired to build the privacy fence on the property's perimeter. I'd like to use a telephone."

"I'm sorry. That's not possible."

"Well, it should be possible, since I just crashed my truck into a car that was chasing a gray BMW that I'm pretty sure came from this house. I want to make sure that the woman driving the car is okay. She looked pretty scared the last time I saw her."

The front door opened. The elderly man facing him matched the six-foot-one Riggs in height but was far broader across the shoulders and chest. "What are you talking about?"

Riggs pointed toward the road. "I was out doing a survey of the property line when this BMW comes bolting down the road, a woman driving and, from what I could see, scared to death. Another car, a black Honda Accord, was right on her butt."

"The woman—is she all right?"

"As far as I know. I got in between them and took the Honda out. Banged up my truck in the process."

"We'll take care of the truck. Where's the woman?"

"I'm not here to complain about the truck, mister—"

"Charlie. Call me Charlie." The man extended his hand, which Riggs shook. As he took his hand back, Riggs observed the indentations in his fingers caused by the other man's viselike grip.

"I go by Matt. Like I said, she got away, and as far as I know, she's fine. But I still wanted to call it in."

"Call it in?"

"The police. The guy in the Honda was breaking at least several laws that I know of, including a couple of felonies."

"You a cop?"

Had Charlie's face darkened, or was that his imagination? Riggs wondered. "Something like that. A long while back. I got the license plate numbers of both cars. I'm assuming the BMW belongs to this house and the woman."

Charlie hesitated, then nodded. "She's the owner."

"And the Honda?"

"Never seen it before."

A sound reached Riggs's ears. A second later he turned and watched the BMW pull up behind his truck. LuAnn got out of the car, glanced at the truck for a moment; then she strode up the steps, passing over Riggs to focus on Charlie.

"This guy said you ran into some trouble," said Charlie, pointing at Riggs.

"Matt Riggs." Riggs extended his hand. The impression of exceptional beauty he had gotten through his binoculars was magnified up close. The hair was long, with golden highlights. The face and complexion were flawless except for the scar along her jawline. He noted the lean, elegant body. But from the smallish hips and waist there grew a breadth of shoulders that suggested exceptional physical strength. When her hand closed around his, he nearly gasped. The grip was almost indistinguishable from Charlie's.

"I hope you're okay," said Riggs. "I got the plate number of the Honda. I was going to call it in to the cops, but my cell phone broke when the guy hit me. I got a good look at him. We should be able to nail him if we act fast enough."

LuAnn looked confused. "What are you talking about?"

Riggs blinked. "The car that was chasing you."

LuAnn looked over at Charlie. "I saw a truck and a car driving erratically, but I didn't stop to ask questions. It was none of my business." She turned to Riggs. "However, since you are on my property, I think it is my business to know why you're here."

Charlie piped in. "He's the guy building the security fence."

LuAnn eyed Riggs steadily. "Then I would strongly suggest you concentrate on that."

Riggs's face flushed. He started to say something, then decided against it. "Have a good day, ma'am." He turned and headed back to his truck. LuAnn passed by Charlie and walked quickly into the house. As Riggs climbed into his truck, a car pulled up the drive. An older woman was driving. The back seat of the car was stacked with groceries. The woman was Sally Beecham, LuAnn's live-in housekeeper. She glanced at Riggs and, as was her custom, pulled around to the side garage. The door from the garage led directly into the kitchen, and Beecham was an efficient person who detested wasted effort. As Riggs pulled off, he glanced back up at the massive house. With so many windows staring back at him, he didn't catch the one framing LuAnn Tyler, arms folded across her chest, looking resolutely at him, a mixture of worry and guilt on her face.

A FIRE blazed in the hearth of the spacious two-story library, which had floor-to-ceiling maple bookcases on three walls and inviting, overstuffed furniture. LuAnn sat on a leather sofa, her legs drawn up under her. Charlie sat down next to her. "Are you gonna tell me what happened or not?" When LuAnn didn't answer, Charlie gripped one of her hands. "Your hands are like ice." He rose and stoked the fire, then looked at her expectantly. "I can't help you if you don't tell me what's wrong, LuAnn."

Over the last ten years a lasting bond had been built between the two. From the time Charlie had touched her shoulder as the 747 climbed into the skies, until they had arrived back in America, they had been inseparable. Though his given name was Robert, he had taken Charlie as his accepted name. It wasn't far from the truth, as his middle name was Charles. He was her closest friend and confidant—really her only one, since there were things she could not even tell her daughter.

As he sat back down, Charlie winced in pain. He was aware that he was slowing down. The difference in years between the two was now more pronounced than ever. Even with that, he would do anything for her, would face any danger, confront any enemy she had with every ounce of strength he had left.

It was the look in Charlie's eyes as LuAnn read these very thoughts that made her finally tell him what the man in the Honda had done that morning. When she finished, she was perceptibly shaking. "I've got strong nerves, Charlie, you know that, but they have their limits," she said. "I was just starting to feel comfortable here. Jackson hasn't shown up, Lisa loves school, and this place is so beautiful."

"What about the other guy? Riggs. Is his story true?"

LuAnn stood up and paced the room. She ran her hand along a row of finely bound novels resting on the shelves. She had read just about every book in the room. Ten years of private tutoring had produced a polished, cosmopolitan woman far removed from the one who had run from that trailer, from those bodies. Now those bloody images would not budge from her mind. "Yes. He jumped right into the middle of it. He did help me, and I would've liked to have thanked him. But I couldn't exactly do that, could I?"

Charlie rubbed his chin as he pondered the situation. "You know, legally the statute of limitations has expired on the lottery scam. The guy can't really hurt you there."

"What about the murder charge? There's no statute of limitations on that. I did kill the man, Charlie. I did it in self-defense, but who would believe me now?" LuAnn trembled. Going to jail was not her biggest concern. She sat back down. "My daddy probably never said one word to me that was true. I swore to myself that I would never ever lie to any child of mine. And you know what? Everything I've told Lisa is a lie. If this man has found out my past and brings it out into the open, then Lisa will know that her mother told her more lies than my daddy probably ever thought of, and I'll lose my little girl as certain as the sun comes up." LuAnn shuddered, and her eyes held a fatalistic look. "If I lose Lisa, I won't have any reason to be anymore. Despite all this." She swept her arms around the room. "No reason at all." LuAnn rubbed her forehead.

Charlie finally broke the silence. "Riggs got the license plate number. On both cars." He added, "Riggs is an ex-cop, LuAnn."

Her head in her hands, LuAnn looked at him.

"Don't worry. He runs your plate, he gets nothing except Catherine Savage with this address. Your identity has no holes in it."

"I think we have a very big hole, Charlie. The guy in the Honda."

Charlie conceded the point with a nod of his head. "Right, but I'm talking about Riggs. Your end with him is okay."

"But if he tracks the other guy down, maybe talks to him?"

"Then maybe we got a big problem," Charlie said.

"You think Riggs might do that?"

"I don't know. I do know that he didn't buy your story about not knowing you were being chased. Under the circumstances, I don't blame you for not acknowledging it, but an ex-cop? He's got to be suspicious. I don't think we can count on him letting it lie."

LuAnn flipped the hair out of her eyes. "So what do we do?"

Charlie gently took one of her hands. "You do nothing. You let old Charlie see what he can find out."

MATT Riggs walked quickly up the steps of the old Victorian he had meticulously restored over the last year. He went inside to his home office and placed a phone call to an old friend in Washington, D.C. The Honda had D.C. tags. Riggs was pretty sure it was either a rental or stolen. The BMW would be another matter. At least he would find out the woman's name. Neither the man calling himself Charlie nor the woman had mentioned it.

A half hour later he had his answers. The Honda was a rental. Tom Jones was the name of the lessee. Real clever, Riggs thought. The address would be just as phony. Then he stared down at the woman's name he had written on a piece of paper. Catherine Savage. Age: thirty. Social Security number had checked out. Unmarried. Excellent credit. No red flags at all. And yet . . .

He looked at her age again. Thirty years old. He thought back to the house. How does a woman that young afford three hundred acres of prime Virginia real estate? Or was it Charlie who had the bucks? They weren't husband and wife—that was clear. It could be she had inherited family money or was the rich widow of some old duffer. Recalling her face, he could easily see that. A lot of men would shower her with everything they had.

So what now? He looked out the window of his office at the beauty of the surrounding trees with their vibrant fall colors. Things were going well for him. An unhappy past behind him; a thriving business in a place he loved. He held the piece of paper with her name on it up to eye level. Despite having no material incentive to care at all about her, Riggs's curiosity was at a high pitch.

"YOU about ready, honey?" LuAnn peeked in the door and gazed fondly at the young girl who was finishing dressing.

Lisa looked around at her mother. "Almost."

A few minutes later Charlie met them downstairs. "My, don't we look pretty this morning," he said to Lisa. "Go get your coat. I'll be out front in the car." After Lisa had gone, Charlie turned a serious face to LuAnn. "I'll check some things out after I drop Lisa off."

"You think you can find this guy?"

Charlie shrugged as he buttoned up his overcoat. "Maybe."

LuAnn nodded. "What about Riggs?"

"I'll save him for later. I go knock on his door now, he might get more suspicious than he already is."

LuAnn watched the two climb into Charlie's Range Rover and drive off. Deep in thought, she pulled on a heavy coat, walked through the house and out the back. She passed the Olympic-size pool. The tennis court would probably go in next year. LuAnn cared little for either activity. But Lisa was an avid swimmer and tennis player, and upon arriving at Wicken's Hunt, she had pressed eagerly for a tennis court.

The one activity LuAnn had picked up in her travels was what she was heading to do right now. The horse barn was about five hundred yards behind the main house. Her long strides took her there quickly. She pulled the gear from the tack room and saddled her horse, Joy, named for her mother. One reason she and Charlie had decided upon the property was its myriad of riding trails. She started off at a good pace and soon left the house behind. The morning's briskness helped clear LuAnn's head, let her think about things.

Many times she had thought about going back to Georgia and telling the truth, but she had never managed to do it. Although she had killed in self-defense, the words of the person calling himself Rainbow continually came back to her. She had run. Thus the police would assume the worst. Added to that was the fact that she had done something that was absolutely wrong. The horse she was riding, the clothes she was wearing, the home she was living in—all had been paid for with what amounted to stolen dollars. Her day-to-day existence vacillated between fear of total collapse of the flimsy veneer shrouding her true identity and immense guilt for what she had done. But if she lived for anything, it was to ensure that Lisa's life would not be harmed by her mother's past or future actions.

Lisa believed her father to have been a wealthy European financier who had died when she was very young, leaving her mother one of the richest women in the world. And one of the most generous. Half of LuAnn's yearly income had been donated anonymously to a number of charities. She was determined to do as much good as she could with the money to atone, at least in part, for the manner in which she had acquired it. Even with all that, the money came in far faster than she could dispose of it.

After an invigorating ride through the countryside LuAnn was making her way back to the horse barn, when the face of Matthew Riggs sprang up before her. He had risked his life for her, and the best she could do was accuse him of lying. She pondered a moment, then urged Joy into a gallop.

Back at the house, LuAnn went straight to Charlie's office. Flipping through his card file, she found the one she wanted and plucked it out. LuAnn showered, changed into a black skirt and sweater, threw on a full-length coat, and went down to the garage. She didn't know whether what she was planning would help or hurt matters, but ever one to choose action over passivity, she couldn't change her ways now. Besides, it was her problem, not anyone else's. Eventually she would have to deal with it.

CHAPTER 7

JACKSON was in his makeup room when his business phone rang. He snatched it up. "Yes?"

"I think we might have a problem here," the voice said.

"I'm listening." Jackson sat down.

"Two days ago we wired income from the last quarter to Catherine Savage's account in the Caymans. To Banque International, just like always. Subsequently I got a call from Banque's wire department confirming that they had wired all the monies from Savage's accounts to Citibank in New York."

New York! Trying to absorb this stunning news, Jackson asked, "Why would they call you if it was her account?"

"They shouldn't have. I think the guy at the wire desk is new. He must have seen my name and phone number on the paperwork and figured I was a principal on the receiving account instead of being on the other end of the transaction."

"Thank you." Jackson hung up the phone. None of LuAnn's money was ever supposed to end up in the United States. Money in the United States was traceable. He picked up his phone again and dialed a number.

"Yes, sir?" the voice asked.

"The taxpayer's name is Catherine Savage," Jackson said. "Find out whether she has filed a U.S. tax return or any other documents with the IRS. I need this information within the hour."

Forty-five minutes later Jackson's phone rang. The voice was crisp. "Catherine Savage filed an income tax return last year. She also recently filed a change of address form with the IRS."

"Give it to me." Jackson wrote the Charlottesville, Virginia, address down on a piece of paper and put it in his pocket.

"One more thing," the voice said. "My source pulled up a recent filing of form 2848 in connection with Savage's tax account. It gives a third party power of attorney to represent the taxpayer."

"Who was the requesting party?"

"A fellow named Thomas Jones. According to the file, he's already received information on her account, including her change of address and last year's income tax return. I was able to get a facsimile of the 2848 form he filed. I can send it to you right now."

"Do so."

Jackson hung up and a minute later had the fax in his hands. He looked at Catherine Savage's signature on the form. He pulled out the originals of the documents LuAnn had signed ten years earlier. The signatures weren't even close. A forgery. Whoever the man was, he had filed this document without the woman's knowledge.

Jackson sat down in a chair and studied the wall as his mind moved in ever expanding circles of thought. LuAnn had come back to the United States despite his explicit instructions to the contrary. She had disobeyed him. And now someone else was interested in her. For what reason? Where was this person? Probably the same place Jackson was about to head to: Charlottesville, Virginia.

LuAnn stopped her car in front of the house. She didn't see the pickup truck anywhere. She was about to leave, but the simple beauty of Matt Riggs's home made her get out of the BMW and go up the plank steps. The graceful lines of the old structure, the obvious care and skill that had gone into rehabbing it, made her eager to explore the place, even if its owner was absent.

She knocked at the front door, but there was no answer. She hesitated, then tried the doorknob. It turned easily in her hand. Entering the man's home without his knowledge might only compound matters. However, she might be able to obtain some useful information about him, something she could use to extricate herself from this potential disaster.

She pushed open the front door. The living-room furnishings were simple but of excellent quality. LuAnn moved through the other rooms, stopping to admire the man's handiwork here and there. She reached his office and peered inside. Moving to his desk, she saw the paper on which Riggs had jotted down information about her. Then she glanced at the notation on the Honda. Riggs's sources were obviously more than a little sophisticated. That was troubling. LuAnn jerked her head up to look out the broad window into the backyard. There was a barnlike structure there. The door was open. She went outside, crept over to the barn door, and peered in. An overhead light illuminated the area. Shelving on two walls held wood supplies and tools. LuAnn eyed a staircase at the rear. In former times it would have led to a hayloft. Riggs, however, had no animals. She wondered what it housed now.

She took the steps slowly and found a small study and observation area. There were bookcases, a beat-up leather chair, and an ancient potbellied stove. A telescope pointed out a huge window in the rear of the barn. As LuAnn looked through the window, her heart started to pound. Riggs's truck was behind the barn.

As she turned to run down the stairs, she found herself staring down the barrel of a 12-gauge shotgun.

When Riggs saw who it was, he slowly lowered the weapon. "What the hell are you doing here?" She tried to move past him, but Riggs grabbed her arm. She just as quickly pulled it free.

"You scared me to death," she said. "Is this how you usually welcome company into your home?"

"Company usually comes in through the front door and only after I've opened it."

LuAnn looked around the space, then returned her gaze to his angry features. "This is a nice place to come and think. How would you like to build me something like this at my house?"

Riggs leaned against the wall. "I would think you'd want to see my work on the fence before you hired me for something else, Ms. Savage." She feigned surprise at the sound of her name but apparently not enough to satisfy Riggs. "So did you find anything else of interest in my office besides my homework on you?"

Slightly unnerved, LuAnn brushed a strand of hair out of her face. "Look, Mr. Riggs—"

"My friends call me Matt. We're not friends, but I'll allow you the privilege," he said coolly.

"I'd rather call you Matthew. I don't want to break any rules."

Riggs looked startled for a moment. "Whatever."

"Charlie said you were a cop."

"I never said so."

"Well, were you?"

"What I was really isn't any of your business. And you still haven't told me what you're doing here."

"What happened this morning is a little more complicated than it appears." She paused and looked up at him, her eyes searching his. "I appreciate what you did. You helped me, and you didn't have to. I came here to thank you." Riggs relaxed a little. "I also came to ask you to forget about it. If you get involved, it might make things more difficult for me."

Riggs rubbed his chin. "You know, the guy banged my truck up. So I already feel like I'm involved."

LuAnn moved closer. "It would mean a lot to me if you would just drop it." Her eyes seemed to widen with each word.

Riggs felt himself drawing closer to her, although he hadn't physically budged an inch. "I'll tell you what. Unless the guy gives me any more trouble, I'll forget it ever happened."

LuAnn's tensed shoulders slumped in relief. "Thank you."

She moved past him toward the stairs. The scent of her perfume drifted through his nostrils. His skin started to tingle. It had been a long time since that had happened.

"Your home is beautiful," she said. "Did you do it all yourself?"

"Most of it. I'm pretty handy."

"Why don't you come by tomorrow, and we can talk about you doing some more work for me?"

"Ms. Savage—"

"Around noon? I can have some lunch ready."

Riggs gave her a searching look and then shrugged. "I can make that." As she started down the stairs, he called after her. "That guy in the Honda. Don't assume he's going to give up."

She glanced back at him. "I never assume anything anymore, Matthew."

"WELL, it's a good cause, John, and she likes to help good causes." Charlie leaned back in his chair and sipped the hot coffee. He was in the dining room of the Boar's Head Inn, a little west of the University of Virginia. Two plates held the remnants of breakfast. The man across from him beamed.

"I can't tell you how much it means to the community." Wearing a costly double-breasted suit, John Pemberton was one of the area's most successful and well-connected real estate agents. He also sat on the boards of numerous charities and local committees. The man knew virtually everything that happened in the area, which was precisely the reason Charlie had asked him to breakfast. Further, the commission on the sale of LuAnn's home had landed six figures in Pemberton's pocket, and he was thus an eternal friend. Now a sheepish grin appeared on his handsome face. "We are hoping to actually *meet* Ms. Savage at some point."

"Absolutely, John, absolutely. It'll just take some time. She's a very private person."

"Of course. And speaking of privacy, I understand Matt Riggs is putting in a security fence for you." Noting Charlie's surprised look, Pemberton smiled. "Despite its cosmopolitan appearance, Charlottesville really is a small town. Very little happens that isn't known by most people soon thereafter."

At those words Charlie's spirits plummeted. Had Riggs already told someone? With an effort he shook off the thought. "Right. Well, the guy had some terrific references."

"He does very good work. In the five years he's been here, I've never heard a bad word said about him."

"Where'd he come from?"

"Washington, D.C."

"So he was a builder up there, then?"

"No. He got his general contractor's license after he got here." Pemberton looked around the dining area. When he spoke next, it was with a lowered voice. "Rumor has it that before Riggs moved to Charlottesville, he held some important position in Washington." He paused for effect. "In the intelligence community."

Charlie tried hard to appear calm. "In intelligence? Like a spy?"

Pemberton threw up his hands. "Who knows? He only talks about his past in vague terms. Still, he's an exceptional builder. He'll do good work for you." Pemberton laughed. "Just so long as he doesn't start snooping around. You know, if he was a spy, those habits probably die hard. I've led a pretty squeaky-clean life, but everybody has skeletons in their closet, don't you think?"

Charlie cleared his throat before answering. "Some more than others." He leaned forward, his hands clasped in front of him on the table. "John, I've got a small favor to ask of you."

Pemberton's smile broadened. "Consider it done, Charlie."

"A man came by the house the other day asking for a donation to a charitable foundation he said he headed. He wasn't local, and it all seemed a little suspicious. You know what I'm saying?"

"Absolutely."

"Someone in Ms. Savage's position has to be careful. There are a lot of scams out there. This guy said he'd be in the area for a while and asked for a follow-up meeting. I thought it probable that he was renting someplace hereabouts, instead of sacking out at a hotel. That gets expensive if you're living scam to scam."

"And you want to know if I can find out where he's staying?"

"Exactly. I want to know who I'm dealing with."

"Give me a description of the man."

Charlie did so, then laid some cash on the table for the meal and stood up. "We really appreciate it, John."

THOMAS Donovan scanned the streets of Georgetown for a parking spot. He was driving another rental car, a late-model Chrysler. He had not turned in the Honda, because he did not want to have to explain the damaged bumper. Donovan finally snagged a spot on a side street not far from where he was heading. A light rain began to fall as he walked toward an elite neighborhood of towering brick-and-clapboard residences. He stopped at a three-story town house sitting behind a waist-high brick wall topped by black wrought-iron fencing. He inserted a key into the gate's lock and went up the side-walk. Another key allowed him entry through the front door.

A housekeeper took his wet coat. "I'll tell the missus you're here, Mr. Donovan." He nodded and moved past her into the drawing room, where he warmed himself in front of the fire before mixing a drink from the stock housed behind a cabinet in the corner.

A woman appeared, moved quickly to him, and gave him a deep kiss. "I missed you," she said.

He led her over to the large sofa. Their knees touched as they sat close together. Alicia Crane was petite, in her mid-thirties, with delicate features and long ash-colored hair. Her dress was costly, as was the jewelry clinging to her wrists and ears. Her cheek trembled slightly as he stroked it. "I missed you too, Alicia. A lot."

"I don't like it when you have to be away."

"Well, it's part of the job." He smiled at her. "But you're making that job a lot more difficult to do." He *was* attracted to Alicia Crane. While not the brightest star in the universe, she was a good person, without the pretenses and airs that her level of wealth usually stamped on its possessors.

"Will you have to leave again soon? I was thinking we could go down to the islands. It's so beautiful this time of year."

"That sounds wonderful, but I'm afraid it'll have to keep. I have to leave tomorrow."

Her disappointment shone through on her face. "Oh, I see."

He tucked one hand under her chin and stared into her eyes. "Alicia, I had a breakthrough today. It was a risk on my part, but it paid off." He remembered from that morning the haunted look in LuAnn Tyler's eyes.

"That's wonderful, Thomas. But I hope you didn't place yourself in danger. What would I do if anything happened to you?"

He sat back as he contemplated his daredevil morning. "I can take care of myself. But I'll promise you something. After I break this story, we're going to take a long vacation. Someplace warm. Just you and me. How's that sound?"

She laid her head against his shoulder. "Wonderful."

"YOU invited him for lunch?" Charlie stared at LuAnn with a mixture of anger and frustration on his face. "Would you mind telling me why you did that? I told you I would handle it."

They were in Charlie's office. He sat in front of the mahogany desk, while LuAnn was perched on the edge of his chair.

Defiance was all over her features. "I couldn't just sit around and do nothing. I figured if I could get to Riggs before he had a chance to do anything, apologize and then get him to drop it, we'd be free and clear."

Charlie shook his head and put an arm around her waist. "Lu-

Ann, I had a conversation with John Pemberton this morning. He's going to try to track down the guy in the Honda for us."

LuAnn stood up. "You didn't tell him—"

"I concocted a cover story. I also talked to him about Riggs. Pemberton thinks he was a government spy."

"A spy? Like the CIA?"

"Who the hell knows? It's not like the guy's gonna advertise what outfit he was with."

LuAnn shuddered, remembering the info Riggs had gathered on her so quickly. Now it made sense. "Well, having him for lunch is one way to learn more about him. Sounds like he's got some secrets too," she said. "When is Pemberton supposed to get back to you?"

"No set time. Could be tonight, could be next week."

"Let me know when you hear from him."

"You'll be the first to know, milady."

She turned to leave.

"Oh, am I invited to this lunch tomorrow?" Charlie asked.

LuAnn glanced back and studied his face. Was there a touch of jealousy there? "I was kind of counting on it, Charlie."

RIGGS had put on a pair of chinos, and the collar of his button-down shirt peeked out from under his patterned sweater. He had driven over in a Jeep Cherokee he had borrowed while his pickup was in the shop having its bumper repaired. He smoothed down his freshly washed hair and walked up the steps of the mansion.

The door was answered by a maid, who escorted Riggs to the library. His attention fell upon the photos lining the fireplace mantel, photos of Charlie and a little girl who strongly resembled Catherine Savage, but none of Catherine Savage. He turned when the double doors to the library opened. His first real encounter with the woman, in his reconfigured hayloft, had not prepared him for his second. The golden hair tumbled down the stylishly flared shoulders of a black, one-piece dress. She wore matching black, low-heel shoes. The image of a sleek, muscular panther held fast in his mind. Curiously, the small scar on her jaw heightened her attraction.

"I'm glad you could make it," she said, moving briskly forward and extending a hand, which Riggs shook. "Lunch will be ready in a few minutes. Would you like something to drink beforehand?"

"I'm okay." He pointed at the photos. "Is that your daughter? Or younger sister?"

She blushed, then settled herself on the couch before answering. "My daughter, Lisa. She's ten."

"You must have had her very young, then," Riggs said.

"Younger than I probably should have, but I wouldn't give her back for anything in the world. Do you have children?"

Riggs shook his head quickly. "Never been that lucky."

LuAnn had noted the absence of a wedding ring, but she assumed a man who worked with his hands all day might not wear it for safety reasons. "Your wife—"

"I'm divorced." He put his hands in his pockets. "You?"

"Widowed."

"I'm sorry."

She shrugged. "It was a long time ago," she said simply.

"Ms. Savage—"

"Call me Catherine." She smiled impishly. "All my friends do."

He sat down next to her. "I take it your late husband did very well for himself. Or maybe you did. I don't want to sound politically incorrect." Riggs grinned. "Either that, or one of you won the lottery."

LuAnn's hand tightened on the edge of the couch. "My husband left me very well-off." She managed to say this with a casual air. "And you? Have you lived here all your life?"

"I moved here about five years ago from D.C. Apprenticed with a local builder, who taught me the trade. When he died, I set up my own shop."

"I take it you like what you do."

"It can be a hassle sometimes, but I like putting things together. And I've been lucky. Business has been steady."

"I'm glad your career change has worked out."

He sat back, digesting her words, then chuckled. "Let me guess. You heard I was either a CIA spy or an assassin."

"Actually, I hadn't heard the assassin angle."

They exchanged brief smiles.

LuAnn looked at her watch. "Lunch should be just about ready. I thought after we eat, you could look at a site where I'm thinking of having you build a studio." She stood up, and Riggs did too. He appeared relieved that this particular conversation was over.

"SO WHAT'RE we looking at timewise on the fence, Matt?" Charlie asked. He and Riggs were on the rear terrace overlooking the grounds. Lunch was over, and LuAnn had gone to pick up Lisa from school. She had asked Riggs to remain until she returned so they could talk about the studio construction.

"I figure a week to dig all the postholes. Two weeks clearing land and assembling and installing the fencing. Another week to install the gate and security systems. One month total. That's about what I estimated in the contract."

Charlie looked him over. "I know, but sometimes what you put on paper doesn't work exactly that way in reality."

"That pretty much sums up the construction business," Riggs said. "But we'll get it in before the frost, and the lay of the land isn't as bad as I originally thought." He paused and eyed Charlie. "After yesterday I wish I could have put it in today. I'm sure you do too."

It was an invitation for discussion, and Charlie didn't disappoint Riggs. "Catherine told me about your little discussion yesterday."

"I assumed she would. She shouldn't go sneaking around people's houses, though. That's not always a healthy thing to do."

"That's exactly what I told her. I know it might be hard to see, but she's rather headstrong."

The two men exchanged knowing chuckles.

"I do appreciate your agreeing not to pursue it," Charlie said.

"I told her if the guy didn't bother me, I wouldn't bother him."

"Fair enough."

"So any luck finding the guy in the Honda?" Riggs asked.

"I'm working on it. Got some inquiries going."

"If you find him, what do you plan on doing about it?"

Charlie looked over at him. "What would you do?"

"Depends on his intentions."

"Exactly. So until I find him and determine what his intentions are, I don't know what I'm going to do." There was a slight trace of hostility in Charlie's tone.

The men fell silent until they heard the sounds of LuAnn and Lisa approaching. In person Lisa Savage resembled her mother even more than in the photo. "This is Mr. Riggs, Lisa."

Riggs put out his hand. "Call me Matt, Lisa. Pleased to meet you."

She squeezed his hand in return. "Pleased to meet you, Matt."

"That's quite a grip." He glanced up at LuAnn and Charlie. "That particular attribute must run in the family." Lisa smiled.

"Matthew is going to build a studio for me, Lisa. Out there somewhere." LuAnn pointed toward the rear grounds.

Lisa looked up at the house in undisguised wonderment. "Isn't our house big enough?" All the adults burst into laughter, and finally Lisa joined in too. "What's the studio for?" Lisa asked.

"Well, maybe it'll be kind of a surprise," LuAnn said. "But I might let you use it sometimes." Lisa grinned broadly at the news. "Now run along, and I'll see you after I finish up with Matthew. Miss Sally has a snack ready for you."

LuAnn and Riggs walked through the rear grounds. Charlie had begged off. He had some things to do, he said. After Riggs had walked the property, he pointed to a clearing that had an unobstructed view of the mountains. "That looks like a nice spot. Actually, with this much land, you have a number of potential locations. By the way, if I knew what you were going to use the place for, I could make a more informed choice for the site."

"I want it set up like yours. Two stories. The first floor could be a workshop for some of my hobbies—that is, when I get around to having some hobbies. On the second level I want a woodstove, a telescope, comfortable furniture. When could you start?"

"Not any time this year, Catherine."

"You're that busy?"

"It's got nothing to do with that. The ground will be freezing soon, and I don't like to pour footers after that. Weather can get real nasty up here. This is definitely a next-spring project."

"Oh." LuAnn was deeply disappointed. Would they even be here next spring?

They walked back to the house, and Charlie met them at the rear entrance. There was a suppressed excitement in his manner, and the darting glances he gave LuAnn told her why: Pemberton had found where the man in the Honda was staying. While not showing it, Riggs picked up on the subtle undercurrents.

After he left, Charlie and LuAnn went into Charlie's study and closed the door. "Where is the guy?" she asked.

"He's our neighbor."

"What?"

"A little rental cottage. About four miles from here up Highway 22. Used to be a big estate up there, but now there's just the caretaker's cottage. Remember, we took a drive there a while back?"

"I remember exactly. You could walk or ride it through the back trails. I've done it."

Charlie unlocked a drawer of his desk and pulled out his .38.

"What are you going to do?" LuAnn said fiercely.

"I'm going to go check it out."

"I'm going with you."

"No, LuAnn. Something happens, the last thing we need is you in the middle of it." He touched her cheek gently. "I want you and Lisa safe."

She watched him open the door. "Charlie, please be careful."

He looked back. "LuAnn, you know I'm always careful."

As soon as Charlie hit the main road, Riggs started to follow him in the Cherokee. Riggs had thought it a fifty-fifty possibility that something was going to happen as soon as he left. A friend of Riggs's had mentioned seeing Pemberton and Charlie having breakfast the day before. That was smart on Charlie's part and, indeed, was probably the path Riggs would have taken to track down the man in the Honda. That and Charlie's excited manner had been enough to convince Riggs that something was up. He kept the Range Rover just in sight as it turned north onto Highway 22. On the seat next to him was his shotgun.

CHARLIE pulled the Range Rover underneath a cover of trees. He could see the cottage up ahead. He got out and threaded his way through the thick trees, stopping first at a small shed located behind the cottage. Rubbing away the dirt and grime on the window, he was able to make out the black Honda inside.

Charlie waited about ten minutes. The cottage appeared unoccupied, but the car in the shed belied that appearance. Charlie moved forward cautiously. He glanced around but did not notice Riggs crouched behind a stand of holly bushes to the left of the house.

Riggs lowered his binoculars and surveyed the area. Like Charlie, he had detected no movement or sound coming from the cottage, but that didn't mean anything. The guy could be in there just waiting for Charlie to put in an appearance. Shoot first and ask questions later. Riggs gripped his shotgun and waited.

The front door was locked. Charlie knocked, but there was no answer. He looked at the lock and pulled two items from his coat pocket—a straight pick and a tension tool. Within seconds his federal-pen degree had worked its magic, and he had picked the lock.

Inside, a hallway ran from front to back, splitting the cottage in half. The kitchen was in the back on the left; the small dining room fronted that. On his right was a modest living room. Plain wooden stairs made their way to bedrooms on the second floor. Charlie observed little of this because his attention was riveted on the dining room. He stared in amazement at a computer, fax, and stacks of file boxes. His eyes swept to a bulletin board with news photos affixed to it. LuAnn's face was prominent among the various photos. The whole story was there—the murders, LuAnn's winning the lottery, her disappearance. He made his way around the room, carefully lifting papers, examining the file boxes, searching for anything that would identify the man staying here; however, there was nothing. Charlie thought about turning on the computer, but his skills with that technology were nil. He was about to begin a search of the rest of the house, when a solitary box in the far corner caught his eye.

Lifting off the top, Charlie's eyes started to twitch uncontrollably. His legs made a serious threat of giving out on him.

A single piece of paper stared back at him, names listed neatly on it. LuAnn's name was there, along with those of other past lottery winners—Herman Rudy, Wanda Tripp, Bobbie Jo Reynolds. Most of them Charlie had personally escorted, like LuAnn. All, he knew, had won their fortunes with Jackson's help. Charlie placed a shaking hand on the windowsill. He had been prepared to find evidence of the man's knowing all about the murders and LuAnn's involvement. He had not been prepared to learn that the lottery scam had been uncovered. How? How could the guy have found out? Who the hell was he? Charlie put the box top back, turned, and headed out the door. He swiftly climbed into the Range Rover and drove off.

As RIGGS watched Charlie drive off, he caught only a glimpse of the man's face. However, it was enough to tell him that something was up. And that what was up was all bad. After the Range Rover disappeared, Riggs turned and stared at the cottage. Should he make an attempt as well to search the place? It might answer a lot of questions. He had almost decided to flip a coin, when he saw a Chrysler drive up to the cottage. A man was hunched over the steering wheel, but Riggs had no trouble recognizing him. Thinking quickly, Riggs hurried to the Cherokee. If he wanted to investigate the cottage, he'd have to return later.

THERE was a haunted look in Charlie's features as he faced LuAnn in his study. "He knows about the murders and the lottery scam. I saw some names. A list of them, in fact. Yours was on there." He paused and LuAnn braced herself. "Herman Rudy. Wanda Tripp. They were on there too. I escorted them all in New York."

A painful weariness laced LuAnn's words. "We have to go, Charlie. We have to pack up and go. Tonight."

He considered the request. "I've been thinking about that.

We can run, like we've done before. But there's a difference now."

LuAnn's response was immediate. "He knows about the lottery fix, *and* he knows LuAnn Tyler and Catherine Savage are one and the same. Our cover isn't going to work anymore." She started pacing around the room. "What does he want, Charlie?"

He shook his head. "I don't know. Maybe money."

"But he hasn't tried to blackmail us. He hasn't asked for anything. I wish I knew why." She was lost in thought for a moment.

Charlie sighed deeply. "So what do we do now?"

"Wait," was finally the answer from LuAnn's lips. "But make arrangements for us to leave the country on a moment's notice."

CHAPTER 8

"THANK you for meeting on such short notice, Mr. Pemberton."

"John. Please call me John, Mr. Conklin." Pemberton shook the other man's hand, and they sat down in Pemberton's office.

"I go by Harry," the other man said.

Without seeming to do so, Pemberton looked Harry Conklin over. In his sixties, expensive clothing, air of assurance. Pemberton swiftly calculated his potential commission.

"I understand that you specialize in the upper-end market around here," Conklin said.

"That's correct. Know every property worth knowing about."

Conklin assumed a comfortable look. "Let me tell you a little about myself. I make my living on Wall Street, and it's a good living if I do say so myself. But it's also a young man's game, and I'm not a young man anymore. I'm looking to get out of New York and simplify my life. And this place is about as beautiful as they come."

"Absolutely right," Pemberton chimed in.

"Now, I do a lot of entertaining, so it would have to be a substantial place. But I want privacy as well. Something elegant. A friend told me that a property named Wicken's Hunt might fit that bill."

Pemberton made a clicking sound with his tongue. "Wicken's Hunt," he repeated, looking depressed. "A beautiful place. Unfortunately, it's no longer on the market. I sold it myself about two years ago, although the people have only been in it for several months. There was a lot of renovation work to do."

Conklin looked at him slyly, eyebrows cocked. "Think they might want to sell?"

Pemberton's mind raced through the possibilities. Flipping a property like that within two years? What a wonderful impact on his wallet. "Anything's possible. I've gotten to know them—well, one of them—fairly well. Just had breakfast with him, in fact."

"So it's a couple, then, old like me, I guess. Wicken's Hunt isn't exactly a starter home."

"Actually, they're not a couple. And the man—Charlie Thomas—is older, but the property doesn't belong to him. It belongs to her."

Conklin leaned forward. "To her?"

Pemberton looked around for a moment, got up and shut the door to his office, and then sat back down. "You understand I'm telling you this in confidence."

An hour later the men shook hands, and Conklin took his leave.

BACK at the country inn where he was staying, Harry Conklin walked into the bathroom and closed the door. Fifteen minutes later the door opened and Jackson emerged, the remnants of Harry Conklin bundled in a plastic bag. His conversation with Pemberton had been very enlightening. The real estate agent had related everything he knew about Catherine Savage, the owner of Wicken's Hunt. He had even mentioned a friend of his who, while driving to work one morning, had happened to witness a high-speed car chase between Catherine Savage and a man using the obviously false name of Tom Jones. At Charlie's request, Pemberton had located the man. He was staying in a cottage barely ten minutes from Wicken's Hunt.

Jackson sat on the bed and opened a large, detailed map of the Charlottesville area, committing to memory the directions Pemberton had given him to the cottage. Then he closed his eyes, deep in thought. Pemberton had mentioned another man. A local contractor hired by LuAnn to install a security fence around her property had apparently also been involved in the car chase. According to Pemberton, Matt Riggs had not always been a contractor. It was Pemberton's opinion that Riggs had worked for the government in some secret capacity. Who was he? Jackson had wondered, and had asked Pemberton for a precise description of the man.

RIGGS had given it a day before he went back to the cottage. He went armed, and he went at night. The Chrysler was nowhere to be seen. He shone his flashlight in the window of the shed. The Honda was still there. Riggs went up to the front door and wondered for the hundredth time if he should just leave this business alone. Dangerous things seemed to happen around Catherine Savage. Still, he could not stop his hand from carefully turning the doorknob. The door swung open, and he moved forward slowly.

Riggs was reasonably certain that the place was empty. He shone his flashlight around the room. There was a light switch on the wall, but he wasn't about to use it. In what had been the dining room he discerned dust patterns on the floor that showed certain objects had been removed. He moved into the kitchen, where he lifted the phone. There was no dial tone. He went back into the dining room. As Riggs's eyes swept the room, they passed right over the figure dressed all in black standing just inside the half-opened closet door.

Jackson gripped the handle of his knife tightly. This was not the man who had leased the cottage. He was long gone. This man had come to reconnoiter the place as well. Riggs, it must be, Jackson concluded. He had done some preliminary checking on Riggs's background after his discussion with Pemberton. The fact that there was little to find out had intrigued him greatly. When Riggs passed within a few feet of him, Jackson contemplated killing him with the razor-sharp knife. But as quickly as the homicidal impulse flared through his system, it passed. Killing Riggs would further no purpose. Jackson's hand gripping the knife relaxed. Riggs would live another day. If there was a next time, Jackson decided, the outcome might be different. He didn't like people meddling in his business.

JACKSON watched from a window as Riggs left the cottage and headed for his Cherokee. From the floor of the closet Jackson picked up what looked like a doctor's bag. He moved to the dining room and unpacked the contents of a fingerprint kit. Jackson then went over to the light switch and hit it from various angles with a handheld laser. Several latent prints sprang to life under the beam. Jackson dusted the area with a fiberglass brush dipped in black powder. The kitchen counter, telephone, and doorknobs were subjected to the same process. Jackson smiled. Riggs's real identity would not be a mystery much longer. Using pressure-wound tape, he lifted the prints from each area, transferred them to index cards, and placed them in separate plastic-lined containers. It took him only a few minutes to repack his kit, and then he left the cottage.

"I LIKE Mr. Riggs, Mom."

"Well, you don't really know him, do you?" LuAnn sat on the edge of her daughter's bed.

"I have good instincts about these things."

Mother and daughter exchanged smiles. "Really? Well, maybe you can share some of your insights with me."

"Seriously, is he going to come back soon?"

LuAnn took a deep breath. "Lisa, we may have to go away soon."

Lisa's hopeful smile faded away at this abrupt change of subjects. "Go away? Where?"

"I'm not sure yet. Uncle Charlie and I are talking about it."

"Were you going to include me in those discussions?"

The unfamiliar tone in her daughter's voice startled LuAnn. "What are you talking about?"

"How many times have we moved in the last six years? Eight? It's not fair." Lisa's face colored, and her voice shook.

LuAnn swept an arm around her shoulders. "I know it's hard on you, baby."

"I'm not a baby, Mom. Not anymore. And I'd really like to know what we're running from."

LuAnn stiffened, her eyes searching Lisa's. "We're not running from anything. What would we possibly be running from?"

"I was hoping you would tell me. I like it here. I don't want to leave, and unless you can give me a really good explanation why we have to, I'm not going."

"Lisa, you're ten years old. Even though you're very intelligent and mature, you're still only a child. So where I go, you go."

Lisa turned her face away. "Do I have a big trust fund?"

"Yes. Why?"

"Because when I turn eighteen, I'm going to have my own home, and I'm going to stay there until I die. And I don't want you to ever visit me." Lisa lay down in the bed and put the covers up almost over her head. "And right now I'd like to be alone."

LuAnn started to say something, then thought better of it. Biting her lip, she raced to her room, where she collapsed on the bed. It was unraveling. She could feel it, like a big ball of twine tossed down the stairs. She rose, went into the bathroom, and started the shower. She pulled off her clothes and stepped under the steaming water. Closing her eyes, LuAnn tried to tell herself that it would be okay, that in the morning Lisa's love for her mother would remain undiminished. After a few minutes LuAnn let the soothing water envelop her.

When she opened her eyes, another image invaded her thoughts. Matthew Riggs. He was a very attractive man. Strong, honest, courageous. And there was secrecy in his background too. But she wasn't looking for a relationship. How could she? How could she even contemplate partnering with someone? She'd be afraid to speak for fear of letting a secret scurry free. With all that, the image of Matt Riggs remained fixed in her head. She closed her eyes again, and a large tear made its way down her face. The last man she had slept with was Duane Harvey, over ten long years ago.

She cut off the water, then toweled off and went into the bedroom. Among the costly furnishings there was a familiar object—the clock her mother had given her. As it ticked away, LuAnn's nerves began to reassemble themselves. It skipped every third beat, but it was like listening to an old friend. She pulled on a pair of panties and went into the bathroom to dry her hair, when Lisa's words came back to her. She couldn't let that resentment and anger fester all night. She had to talk to her daughter again. Or at least try to. She went back into the bedroom to put on her robe.

"Hello, LuAnn."

So stunned was LuAnn that she had to reach out and grip the doorjamb or she would've sagged to the floor.

"It's been a long time." Jackson stepped away from the window and sat down on the edge of the bed.

"What do you want?" LuAnn forced the words to come out.

"We have much to discuss, and I would suggest you do so in the comfort of some clothing." He stared pointedly at her.

LuAnn found it extremely difficult to take her eyes off him. Being half naked in front of the man was far less disturbing than having to turn her back on him. Finally she threw open her closet door, pulled out a knee-length robe, and put it on. She turned back around. Jackson's eyes were roaming the parameters of her boudoir, resting briefly on the clock on the wall. Then he scrutinized her altered appearance. "Very good. The look is chic and sophisticated. Congratulations." He motioned LuAnn to sit at a small writing desk situated against one wall. She did so. "Now let's talk. I understand you had a visitor. A man chased you in a car."

"How do you know that?" LuAnn said angrily.

"You just won't accept the fact that you can't conceal information from me. Like the fact that you have reentered the United States against my most explicit instructions."

"The ten years are up. You cannot run my life."

Jackson stood up. "First things first. This man following you discovered your identity, in part, through your tax records. Do you have any reason to think that he knows about the lottery?"

LuAnn hesitated a second. "No."

"You're lying. Tell me the truth, or I'll kill everyone in this house." This abrupt threat made her suck in her breath.

"He has a list. A list with twelve names on it. Mine, Herman Rudy, Bobbie Jo Reynolds, and some others."

Jackson assimilated this information. "And the man Riggs?"

"What about him?"

"He has a mysterious past, and he just happens to be around when you need assistance. That worries me."

"I don't think it was anything other than a coincidence. He was hired to do a job for me. It was perfectly natural he would be nearby when the other man started chasing me."

Jackson shook his head. "I don't like it. I saw him tonight." LuAnn stiffened perceptibly. "At the cottage. I was this close to him." He spread his hands about two feet apart. "I contemplated killing him on the spot."

LuAnn's face turned white. "There's no reason to do that."

"You have no way of knowing that. I'm going to check him out, and if I find anything in his background to suggest trouble, then I will eliminate him. It's that simple."

"Let me get that information for you."

"What?" Jackson looked startled.

"Riggs likes me. He's already helped me. It would be natural for me to show my gratitude. Get to know him better."

"No. I don't like it."

"Riggs is a nobody. Why trouble yourself with him?"

Jackson studied her for a moment. "All right, LuAnn, you do that. However, any information you obtain better be reported to me in a timely fashion, or I will take matters into my own hands. Clear?"

LuAnn let out a deep breath. "Clear."

"The other man, of course, I must find. It shouldn't be too terribly difficult."

"Don't do that." The memory of Mr. Rainbow came flooding back to LuAnn. She did not want another death on her conscience. "If he shows up again, we're just going to leave the country."

"You obviously do not fully understand the situation," Jackson said. "Were you the only one he was onto, then perhaps your simplistic solution might resolve the matter, at least temporarily. However, the man has a list of eleven other people with whom I worked."

"But he can't prove anything. And even if he could, they'll never be able to trace anything to you."

Jackson took a moment to rub his left hand along the bedspread. "Beautiful needlework here," he commented. "Indian, isn't it?"

Distracted by his query, LuAnn was suddenly staring down the barrel of a 9-millimeter, a suppressor attached to its muzzle.

"One potential solution could involve my killing all twelve of you. That would certainly qualify as a startling dead end for our inquisitive friend. Remember that the ten-year period is up. The lottery's principal amount has already been returned to a Swiss account in your name. I would strongly advise against transferring that money into the United States." He pulled a slip of paper from his pocket and put it down on her bed. "Here are the authorization codes and other account information that will enable you to access it. The funds are untraceable. There you have it. As agreed. However, now I really don't have any incentive to keep you around, do I?" He advanced toward her. She backed up against the wall.

"The most prudent action on my part would be to kill you. Right now. In fact, what the hell." He pointed the gun at her head and pulled the trigger. LuAnn jerked back, her eyes slamming shut.

When she reopened them, Jackson was studying her reaction. She was shaking terribly; her heart was thumping around inside her; she couldn't catch her breath.

Jackson shook his head. "Your nerves don't seem to be as strong, LuAnn, as when we were last together. And nerves, or a lack thereof, really are the whole ball of wax." He looked at the pistol for a moment, slipped off the safety, and continued speaking calmly. "I'm not going to kill you, at least not yet. Not even after you've disobeyed me, jeopardized everything. Would you like to know why?"

LuAnn remained planted against the wall, afraid to move.

He took her silence for assent. "Because in very large measure you are my creation. Would you be living in this house without me? Of course not. In killing you, I would in effect be killing part of myself. That I am loath to do. Nevertheless, please keep in mind that a wild animal, when trapped, will ultimately sacrifice a limb in order to escape and survive. Don't think that I am not capable of that sacrifice. If you do, you're a fool. I sincerely hope that we are able to extricate you from this little problem, and I'm counting on you to do your part." Jackson's tone became businesslike. "You will report to me any further contact with our mysterious stranger. The number I gave you ten years ago will still reach me. Whatever additional instructions I give you, you will follow precisely. Understood?" She nodded. "I'm serious, LuAnn. If you disobey me again, I will kill you. Now go into the bathroom and compose yourself."

She started to turn away. "Oh, LuAnn?" She looked back.

"Keep in mind that if we fail to contain this problem and I have to eliminate you, there will be no reason to stop there." He glanced ominously in the direction of the doorway leading to the hallway, where barely twenty feet away Lisa lay sleeping.

LuAnn ran into the bathroom, locking the door after her. She gripped the cold marble of the vanity, every limb shaking. She understood clearly the personal jeopardy she was in, but that was far from her greatest fear. The fact that Jackson might set his murderous sights on Lisa made her nearly delirious with terror.

Curiously, it was with this thought that LuAnn's features grew deadly still in their own right. If Jackson ever came after Lisa, then either he would die or LuAnn would. There would be no other possibilities. She unlocked the door and was certain what she would find when she returned to the bedroom.

Nothing. Jackson was gone.

LuAnn hurried down the hallway to check on Lisa. The little girl's steady breathing told her mother that she was asleep. Next LuAnn made her way to Charlie's bedroom and gently roused him from sleep. "I just had a visitor."

"What? Who?"

"We should've known he'd find out," she said wearily.

Charlie sat straight up in bed. "Good God! Jackson was here? How did he find us?"

"I don't know, but he knows everything." She told him about the visit, including the fact that Jackson seemed very suspicious about Riggs and talked about killing him. Then LuAnn took Charlie's hand. "I want you to take Lisa away."

"There's no way I'm leaving you alone with that guy."

"Yes, you will, Charlie, because you know I'm right. By myself I'm okay. But if he were to get hold of Lisa . . ." She didn't need to finish the thought.

"Why don't you go with her and let me handle it here?"

LuAnn shook her head. "That won't work. If I leave, Jackson will come looking. So long as I'm around, he's not going to stray too far. In the meantime you two can get away."

"I don't like it. I don't want to abandon you, LuAnn. Not now."

She put her arms around his burly shoulders. "You're not abandoning me. You're going to be taking care of the most precious thing I have—" She broke off.

Finally Charlie said, "Okay. When do you want us to leave?"

"Right now. I'll go get Lisa ready while you pack."

"Where do we go?"

"You pick the place. Call when you get there."

"And what about you? What are you going to do?"

"Whatever it takes to make sure we all survive this."

"And Riggs?"

LuAnn looked squarely at him. "Especially Riggs."

"I HATE this, Mom. I hate it." Lisa stomped around the room in her pajamas as LuAnn hurriedly packed her daughter's bags.

"I'm sorry, Lisa, but you just have to trust me on this."

"Trust, ha. That's a funny one coming from you."

"I don't need that kind of talk right now, young lady."

"And I don't need this." Lisa sat down on the bed and stubbornly crossed her arms. "We're having a party at school tomorrow. Can't it at least wait until after that?"

LuAnn slammed the suitcase shut. "No, Lisa, it can't."

"When are you going to stop dragging me all over the place?"

LuAnn ran a shaky hand through her hair and sat down next to her daughter, putting an arm around Lisa's quaking form. She sensed the pain coursing through the small body. Could the truth hurt her daughter any worse than this? LuAnn spoke slowly. "I promise that very soon I will tell you everything. All right?"

"But why—"

LuAnn put her hand gently across her daughter's mouth, silencing her. "When I do, it will shock you. You may be sorry I'm your mother, but however you feel, I want you to know that I did what I thought was best for you at the time. I was very young, and I didn't have anyone to help me make my decision." She cupped Lisa's chin with her hand and tilted her daughter's face up to hers. Lisa's eyes were now filled with tears. "I don't want you to go away, but I will die before I'd let anything happen to you. So would Uncle Charlie."

"Mom, you're scaring me."

LuAnn gripped Lisa with both hands. "I love you, Lisa. More than I've ever loved anything in my whole life."

"I don't want anything to happen to you." Lisa touched her mother's face. "Mom, will you be okay?"

LuAnn managed a reassuring smile. "Mommy'll be just fine."

THE next morning LuAnn rose early after a mostly sleepless night. Saying good-bye to her daughter had been the most wrenching thing she had ever done, yet a huge wave of relief had swept over her when she had watched the Range Rover disappear down the road.

She brewed a pot of coffee in the small kitchenette next to her dressing room. Then she put on a silk robe, and holding a cup of steaming coffee in one hand, she stepped through a pair of French doors out onto a balcony that opened off her third-floor bedroom. She perched on the marble railing and looked out over her property. What she saw almost caused her to fall off the balcony.

Matthew Riggs was kneeling in the grass near the spot where she wanted her studio to be built. LuAnn watched in amazement as he unrolled a set of blueprints and eyed the land. She could make out stakes planted at various points. LuAnn jumped down from the railing, raced through her bedroom, not even pausing to put on shoes.

She took the stairs two at a time and unlocked the back door. Sprinting across the dewy grass in her bare feet, she reached the spot where Riggs had been and looked around. Where had he gone?

"Morning."

LuAnn whirled around as he emerged from a stand of trees. "What are you doing?" she asked in an amazed tone.

"You always run around outside like that? You're going to catch pneumonia." He stared at her and then discreetly looked away as the emerging sun's rays made her thin robe almost transparent.

"I don't usually see someone on my property at the crack of dawn putting stakes into the ground."

"Just following orders. You wanted me to build you a studio."

"You said there wasn't enough time before winter set in."

"Well, you admired mine so much, I had the brilliant idea of using those diagrams for this one. That'll save a lot of time." He paused and looked at her as she stood there shivering, then took off his heavy coat and draped it around her shoulders. "You know you really shouldn't be outside in your bare feet."

"You don't have to do this, Matthew. I think I've intruded on your time and patience enough."

"I don't really mind, Catherine. There are a lot worse things than hanging out with a woman like you."

LuAnn blushed, biting nervously at her bottom lip, while Riggs shoved his hands in his pockets and stared off at nothing. The pair emulated two teens nervously feeling each other out on a first date.

"How about some breakfast?" she finally said.

"I already ate, but thanks."

"Coffee?" She was balancing on one bare foot and then the other as the cold ate at her skin.

Riggs watched her movements, then said, "I'll take you up on that one." He turned around and bent down. "Climb on."

"Excuse me?"

"Climb on." He patted his back. "Just pretend I'm a horse."

LuAnn didn't budge. "I don't think so."

Riggs turned and looked at her. "Come on. I'm not kidding about the pneumonia. Besides, I do this with billionaires all the time."

LuAnn laughed, pulled his coat on all the way, and hoisted herself up piggyback-style, wrapping her arms around his neck. Halfway there she jabbed him playfully in the sides with her knees.

"What was that for?"

"I'm pretending, just like you said. So giddyap."

"Don't push it," he groused back, and then smiled.

RIGGS sipped a cup of coffee in the kitchen while LuAnn munched on a piece of buttered toast. She rose and fixed herself another cup of coffee and freshened his.

Riggs couldn't help staring when her back was turned. The clingy robe was making him think about things he probably shouldn't be. He finally looked away, his face hot. "Everybody else still sleeping?"

"Charlie and Lisa went on a little vacation."

"Without you?"

LuAnn sat down and spoke casually. "I had some things to take care of. I might have to go to Europe soon. If I do, I'll meet up with them there. Italy is beautiful this time of year. Ever been?"

"The only Rome I've been to is in New York."

"In your past life?"

"My past life is really not all that exciting. I have a hunch your secrets are a lot more interesting than mine."

LuAnn tried to look surprised. "I don't have any secrets."

He put down his cup. "I can't believe you can actually say that with a straight face. Who was the guy in the Honda?" LuAnn stood up and abruptly turned away from him. "Catherine, I'm trying to help you." He rose and put a hand on her shoulder, turning her to face him. "I know you're scared. And I also know you've got stronger nerves and more spirit than just about anybody I've run across, so I'm assuming whatever you're facing is pretty bad. And I want to help you if you'll let me." He cupped her chin with his hand. "I'm playing straight with you, Catherine. I really am."

She winced slightly as he said her name. Her *fake* name. She finally reached up and lightly caressed his fingers with her own. "I know you are, Matthew. I know." She looked up at him, and their eyes did not budge from each other as their fingers exchanged touches that were suddenly electrifying both their bodies.

Riggs swallowed hard and pulled LuAnn against him. She moaned as Riggs kissed her neck; then LuAnn wrapped her arms around his head as he hoisted her up in the air.

Following her whispered directions, he lunged blindly along the hallway to the small first-floor guest bedroom. Riggs pushed open the door. LuAnn jerked away from him and sprawled on the bed. Riggs's heavy work boots hit the hardwood floor with a loud thump, and his pants followed immediately. She jerked his shirt off, popping several buttons in the process. They didn't bother with the bedcovers, although Riggs did manage to back-kick the door closed before he fell into her arms.

JACKSON sat at a table in his large suite at the country inn and studied the laptop's small screen. The night before, he had checked out as Harry Conklin and checked back in under another name. He became uncomfortable staying in one character too long. Besides, he had met with Pemberton as Conklin, and he didn't want to run into the man again. Now a baseball cap covered his head, and his blondish gray hair was tied in a ponytail that sprouted out the back of the cap. He looked like an aging hippie.

Two hours earlier Jackson had scanned one set of fingerprints lifted from the cottage into his hard drive and transmitted them via modem to one of his information contacts. Now he smiled as his computer screen filled up with data. A digitized photo of a man accompanied the personal details. Thomas J. Donovan. The name was actually familiar to Jackson. Donovan was a journalist at the Washington *Tribune*. About a year ago he had done an in-depth piece on Jackson's father's career as a United States Senator. Jackson had condemned it as a fluff piece that came nowhere near to addressing the personal side of his father and his monstrous behavior.

Jackson sat back and mused for a moment. Donovan was undoubtedly onto an enormous story, and he would not stop until he achieved his goal. Or until someone stopped him. It was an inter-esting challenge. Simply killing the man might make people suspi-cious. Also Donovan might have told others of his investigations. Jackson had a sudden thought. What if Donovan didn't get what he wanted from LuAnn and attempted to contact the other lottery winners? Jackson took out his Rolodex and started making calls. Compared to LuAnn, the other eleven were sheep. What he told them to do they did. Now, if Donovan bit, the trap would spring.

Jackson opened his briefcase. He pulled out some photos he had taken with a long-range lens his first day in Charlottesville. Sally Beecham, in her forties, was LuAnn's live-in housekeeper. Her suite was on the first floor of the mansion. He studied the next two pho-tos. The two young Hispanic women constituted the cleaning staff. Jackson had watched each of these people intently. A handheld sound wand had picked up their voices. Possibly, none of the infor-mation he had painstakingly gathered about Catherine Savage's daily world would ever come into play. But on the chance that it might, he would be ready. He put the photos back in his briefcase.

LuAnn watched Riggs, who lay dozing next to her. A grin spread over her face. She stroked his shoulder. With this movement he stirred and looked over at her. A boyish smile cracked his face.

"What?" she asked, her eyes impish.

"I'm trying to remember how many times I said, 'Oh, baby.' "

LuAnn said, "I think it was more often than I said, 'Yes, yes,' but that was only because I couldn't catch my breath." She nestled on Riggs's chest. "You know, if you come over every day to work on the studio, we might make this a regular thing." She smiled and then almost immediately caught herself. What was the chance of that happening? The impact of this thought was crushing. She quickly moved away from him and started to get up.

Riggs could hardly miss this dramatic transformation.

"Was it something I didn't say?"

She pulled the bedspread off the bed and draped it around her. "I've got a lot to do today."

Riggs sat up. "Well, excuse me. I didn't mean to get in the way of your schedule. I guess I had the six a.m. to seven a.m. slot. Who's up next? The Kiwanis Club?"

"Hey, I don't deserve that."

Riggs started to pull on his clothes. "Okay. It's just that I'm having trouble switching gears as fast as you. Going nonstop from the most intensive passion I can ever remember to discussing the day's workload sort of rubbed me the wrong way."

LuAnn looked down. "That's how it was for me too, Matthew," she said quietly. "I'm embarrassed to tell you how long it's been." She paused and then said almost to herself, "Years."

He looked at her incredulously. "You've gotta be kidding." She didn't answer, and he was reluctant to break the silence. The ringing phone did.

LuAnn picked it up, hoping it was Charlie and not Jackson. "Hello?"

It turned out to be neither. "We're going to talk, Ms. Tyler, and we're going to do it today," Thomas Donovan said.

"Who is this?" LuAnn demanded. Riggs looked over at her.

"We met briefly the other day when you were out driving."

"How did you get this number? It's unlisted."

"Ms. Tyler, no information is safe if you know where to look."

"What do you want?"

"Like I said, I want to talk." Riggs went to the phone and held the receiver with her. LuAnn tried to push him off, but Riggs held firm. "You're sitting on a story of immense importance, and I want to know what it is. If you talk to me, I'll give you forty-eight hours to leave the country before I go public. If you don't, then I go public with everything I have as soon as I get off the phone. Murder doesn't have a statute of limitations, LuAnn."

Riggs stared at LuAnn, wide-eyed. "Where?" she asked.

"Michie's Tavern," Donovan said. "I'm sure you know where that is. One o'clock. And don't bring anyone with you, or the deal is off and I call the sheriff in Georgia. Do you understand?"

LuAnn ripped the phone free from Riggs and slammed it down.

Riggs faced her. "Would you like to fill me in? Who are you sup-posed to have murdered? Somebody in Georgia?"

LuAnn pushed past him, her face crimson from the abrupt re-vealing of this secret. Riggs grabbed her arm roughly. "Dammit, tell me what's going on." She snapped around and, quick as a ferret, connected her right fist flush with his chin, causing his head to snap back and hit hard against the wall.

When he came to, Riggs was lying on the bed. LuAnn sat next to him holding a cold compress to his bruised chin. "I'm sorry, Matthew. I didn't mean to do that. I just—"

He rubbed his head in disbelief. "I can't believe you knocked me out. I'm not a chauvinist, but I can't believe a woman just flattened my butt with one punch." Riggs sat up. "Next time we're having an argument and you're thinking about popping me, just let me know and I'll surrender on the spot. Deal?"

She touched his face gently and kissed him on the forehead. "I'm not going to hit you anymore."

Riggs looked at the phone. "Are you going to meet him?"

"I don't have a choice—that I can see."

"I'm going with you."

LuAnn shook her head. "You heard him."

Riggs sighed. "I don't believe you murdered anyone."

LuAnn took a deep breath and decided to tell him. "I didn't murder him. It was self-defense. The man I was living with ten years ago was involved in drugs. I guess he was skimming off the top, and I walked right into the middle of it."

"So you killed your boyfriend?"

"No. The man who killed my boyfriend."

"And the police—"

"I didn't stay around long enough to find out what they were going to do."

Riggs looked around the room. "Drugs. Is that where all this came from?"

LuAnn almost laughed. "No. Drug money didn't have anything to do with this."

Riggs wanted desperately to ask what did, but he sensed that she had divulged enough for now. Instead he watched in frustration as LuAnn slowly got up and started to leave the room, the bedspread dragging behind her. "LuAnn? That's your real name?"

She turned to look at him and nodded faintly. "LuAnn Tyler." She frowned, looked down, and then walked out of the room.

CHAPTER 9

WEARING a long black leather coat, LuAnn stood outside an aged wooden building that was part of Michie's Tavern, a historic structure built in the 1700s. It was lunchtime, and the place was filled with people. Inside, a fire blazed in the hearth, and LuAnn, who had arrived early to check things out, had soaked in the warmth from the flames before deciding to wait for Donovan outside. She looked up when the man walked toward her.

"Let's go," he said.

LuAnn looked at him. "Go where?"

"You follow me in your car. If I see anyone following us, then I pick up my cell phone and you go to prison."

"I'm not following you anywhere," LuAnn said. "You said you wanted to meet. Well, I'm here. You picked the place."

"That I did." Donovan looked at a line of people making their way into the tavern. "But I had in mind a little more privacy than this."

"I'll tell you what. We'll go for a drive in my car." LuAnn stared at him ominously and spoke in low tones. "But don't try anything, because if you do, I *will* hurt you." Donovan snorted for a moment and then just as quickly stopped as he stared into her eyes. An involuntary shiver swept over him. He followed her to her car.

LuANN got on Interstate 64 and put the BMW on cruise control. Donovan turned to her. "You know, you threatened me back there with bodily injury. Maybe you did kill that guy in the trailer."

"I didn't *murder* anyone."

When Donovan spoke next, his tone was softer. "I didn't track you down, LuAnn, in order to destroy your life."

She glanced at him. "Then what did you track me down for?"

"Tell me what did happen in that trailer. I've read the newspaper accounts. I'd like to hear your version."

LuAnn let out a deep sigh. "Duane was dealing drugs. I didn't know about it. I just wanted to get out of that life. I went to the trailer to tell him so. Duane was cut up badly. A man grabbed me, tried to cut my throat. I hit him with the telephone, and he died."

Donovan looked puzzled. "You hit him with the phone?"

"Really hard. I guess I cracked his skull."

Donovan rubbed his chin thoughtfully. "The man didn't die from that. He was stabbed to death."

The BMW almost ran off the road before LuAnn regained control. She stared over at him. "What?" she gasped.

"I've seen the autopsy reports. He did have a wound on his head, but he died from multiple stab wounds. No doubt about it."

It didn't take LuAnn long to realize the truth. *Rainbow.* Rainbow had killed him. And then lied to her. She shook her head. "All these years I believed that I had killed him."

"That's a horrible thing to carry around inside. I'm glad I could clear your conscience."

"The police can't still be interested in all this," LuAnn said.

"That's where you've run into some incredibly bad luck. Duane Harvey's uncle is the sheriff in Rikersville now."

"Billy Harvey is sheriff?" LuAnn said in astonishment. "He's one of the biggest crooks down there."

"Probably figured the best way to avoid trouble with the police was to become the police. According to him, the family has never gotten over poor Duane's death. Bottom line is, he's not going to rest until you're brought in for trial. His theory is that you're the one who was involved in the drug dealing because you wanted to escape Duane and the boring life. Duane died trying to protect you;

then you murdered the other guy, who allegedly was your partner."

"That's a bunch of lies."

Donovan shrugged. "You know it is. I know it is. But the people deciding that will be a jury of your peers down in Rikersville, Georgia." He appraised her expensive clothing. "I wouldn't recommend wearing that outfit to the trial. It might rub people the wrong way. Duane being flower food and all these last ten years while you were living the high life and doing a pretty good impersonation of Jackie O., it wouldn't sit well with folks down there."

"Tell me something I don't know." She paused. "So that's your deal? If I don't talk, you're going to throw me to Billy Harvey?"

Donovan said, "I don't really care about all that stuff."

LuAnn stared across at him. "What do you care about?"

"The lottery." He leaned toward her. "How'd you win it?"

"I bought a ticket. How else do you win it?"

"I don't mean that. Let me fill you in on something. I went back through years' worth of lottery winners. There's a constant rate of bankruptcy declared by all those winners. Nine out of twelve every year. You can set your clock by it. Then I run across twelve consecutive winners who somehow managed to avoid the big B, and you're smack in the middle of them. How is that possible?"

She glanced over at him. "How should I know? I've got good money managers. Maybe they do too."

"You haven't paid taxes on your income nine out of the last ten years. I guess that helps."

"So call up the IRS and report me."

"That's not the story I'm looking for."

"Story?"

"That's right. I forgot to fill you in on the reason I came to visit you. My name's Thomas Donovan. I'm a journalist for the Washington *Trib*. A while back I decided to do a story on the national lottery. While I'm researching it, I find this interesting coincidence about all the lottery winners from your year. So I track you down, and here I am. What I want is simple: the truth."

"And if I don't tell you, I end up in a Georgia prison?"

"I'm not going to blackmail you," Donovan said. "I don't operate that way. If Sheriff Billy catches up to you, it's not going to be with my help. Personally I hope he never does."

"Thank you."

"But if you don't tell me the truth, I'll find it out someplace else. And when I write that story, if you haven't told me your side of things, I can't guarantee how flatteringly I can portray you. If you talk to me, your side will be heard. So what'll it be?"

She didn't speak for several minutes, her eyes staring down the road. Finally she looked over at him. "I want to tell you the truth." She took a deep breath. "But I can't."

"Why not?"

"You're already in a great deal of danger. If I talk to you, that danger turns to an absolute certainty that you're going to die. I want you to leave the country. I'll pay. You pick a place."

"Is that your way of dealing with problems? Send them off to Europe? Sorry, but I've got a life right here."

"That's just it. If you stay, you're not going to have a life."

"You're really going to have to do better than that. If you'd work with me, we could really accomplish something here. Just talk to me. Trust me."

"I'm not telling you anything. And I'm doing it to keep you safe."

"If you work with me, we both win."

"I don't consider being murdered winning. Do you? If I tell you what I know, it's like I'm putting a pistol against your head and pulling the trigger myself."

Donovan sighed. "Then why don't you take me back to my car. You grew up dirt-poor, raised a kid by yourself, and then got this incredible break. I thought you might care."

LuAnn started speaking in a very low voice, as though she were afraid of being overheard. "Mr. Donovan, someone is looking for you right this very minute. He told me he's going to kill you because you might know too much. And he will. Unless you leave right now, he'll find you for sure, and when he does, it won't be pretty. This person can do anything. Anything."

Donovan snorted, and then his face froze as the answer finally hit him. "Including making a poor woman from Georgia rich?" Donovan saw LuAnn jerk slightly as he said the words. His eyes widened. "That's it, isn't it? You said this man can do anything. He made you the lottery winner, didn't he?"

"Mr. Donovan, please."

"Good God, the national lottery was fixed."

"Mr. Donovan, you have got to let this drop."

"No way, LuAnn. This elaborate cover story you had in Europe. Your perfect money managers. This guy set all of it up, didn't he?" He turned sideways in his seat. "You're not the only one, are you? The other eleven nonbankrupts? Maybe more. Am I right?"

LuAnn was shaking her head hard. "Please stop."

"He didn't do it for free. He must've gotten some of your winnings. But how did he fix it? It can't be just one guy." Donovan fired questions left and right. "Who, what, when, why, how?" He gripped her shoulder. "Okay, I'll accept that this is one dangerous individual. But don't discount the power of the press, LuAnn. It's toppled crooks bigger than this guy. We can do it if we work together." When she didn't respond, Donovan let go of her shoulder. "All I'm asking is that you think about it, LuAnn."

When they returned to his car, Donovan got out. "This number will reach me." He handed her a card. LuAnn didn't take it.

"I don't want to know how to reach you. You'll be safer that way."

Donovan insisted on giving her the card. Then he got in his car and drove off. LuAnn watched him go, trying to calm her shaken nerves. Jackson was going to kill the man unless she did something. But what could she do? For one thing, she wasn't going to tell Jackson about her meeting with Donovan. However, as she drove away, she had no inkling that beneath her seat a small transmitter had been affixed to the floorboard. Her entire conversation with Donovan had just been heard, not by Jackson but by someone else.

RIGGS turned off the receiving unit, and the sounds of LuAnn's BMW coming through his earphones vanished. He took off the headphones, sat back in his chair, and let out a long breath. Riggs eyed the phone, hesitated, then picked it up. The number he was calling had been given to him five years ago for emergencies. Well, Riggs decided as he punched in the numbers, this qualified as such.

An automated voice came on the line. Riggs left a series of numbers and then his name. He put down the phone. One minute later it rang. He picked it up. "That was fast," Riggs said.

"That number gets our attention. You in trouble?"

"Not directly. But I need to check on something."

"Person, place, or thing?"

"Person."

"I'm ready. Who is it?"

Riggs hesitated. He knew his inquiry would eventually bring federal agents to Charlottesville. Riggs took a silent breath and hoped he was doing the right thing. "I need to find out about someone named LuAnn Tyler."

LUANN'S car phone buzzed as she was driving back home.

"Hello?"

The voice on the other end of the line made her breathe easier.

"Charlie, how's Lisa?"

His tone was low. "Fine. We're both okay."

"Where is she?"

"Crashed on the bed. We drove all night, and she didn't sleep much, just stared out the car window."

"Where are you?"

"At a motel on the outskirts of Gettysburg, Pennsylvania. We had to stop. I was falling asleep at the wheel."

"Any sign that you've been followed?"

"I've varied my route and checked every car that looks even remotely familiar. No one's onto us. How's it on your end? You hook up with Riggs?"

LuAnn blushed. "You could say that." She paused and then told Charlie about her meeting with Donovan.

"I don't like it that you're all alone in this," Charlie said.

"I'm holding my own. Look, I've got to go. Give me the number there." Charlie did so.

They said good-bye; then she hung up the phone.

LuAnn had been home for only a few minutes when something drew her attention to the window. She watched as a figure made its way down the tree line toward the main road. The steps were animal-like in their stealth and precision. She felt no fear as she watched Jackson move down the hillside. LuAnn knew she was now his main focus. And to be the main focus of the man was akin to treading on the very edge of the grave. Was Lisa truly safe, beyond his reach? The answer to that was so obvious that it hit her like a hard slap in the face. She ran upstairs. Whether she was making the right decision or not, she didn't care. She needed help. LuAnn unlocked a box in her closet and placed a loaded .44 magnum in her purse. Then she headed for the garage.

The BMW pulled into the front drive. LuAnn got out and walked up the wide steps of the Victorian. Riggs heard her coming. He was just finishing up his phone call, the paper in front of him covered with notes. He opened the door to her knock.

"How'd it go?" he asked.

LuAnn drifted into the living room and settled down on the couch. She shrugged. "Not all that well, really." Her voice was listless. Riggs sat down in the chair opposite her.

"Tell me about it."

"Why? Why would I want to get you involved in all this?"

He paused and briefly considered what he was about to say. He could walk away from this. She was obviously giving him the opportunity to do so. He could just say "You're right" and escort her to the door and out of his life. As he looked at her, so tired, so alone, he spoke quietly and intensely. "The lottery was fixed, wasn't it?"

LuAnn jolted upright for an instant, but then she let out an almost simultaneous breath of relief. "Yes." With that one word she felt as though the last ten years of her life had suddenly evaporated.

It was a cleansing feeling. "How'd you figure it out?" she asked.

"I had some help."

LuAnn tensed and slowly rose. Had she just made the biggest mistake of her life?

Riggs sensed her sudden change. He calmly said, "Nobody else knows. I pulled pieces of information from different sources and took a wild stab." He hesitated, then added, "I also bugged your car. I heard your entire conversation with Donovan."

"Who are you?" LuAnn hissed, staring at him.

"I'm someone very much like you," was Riggs's surprising reply. He stood and put his hands in his pockets. "My past is a secret; my present is all made up. A lie. But for a good reason." He raised his eyebrows. "Like you." LuAnn trembled for an instant. Her legs felt weak, and she abruptly sat down on the floor. Riggs swiftly knelt beside her, taking her hand in his. "We don't have a lot of time, so I'm not going to sugarcoat things. I made some inquiries about you. I did it discreetly, but it's going to have ripple effects nonetheless." He looked at her intently. "Are you ready to hear this?"

LuAnn swallowed hard and nodded.

"The FBI has been interested in you ever since you fled the country. The case has been dormant for a while, but that's not going to last. Do you know how the lottery was rigged?" LuAnn shook her head. "Is it a group, an organization behind it?" he continued.

"No. It's one person as far as I know."

"What can you tell me about this person?"

"He calls himself Jackson." As the name passed over her lips, LuAnn closed her eyes and imagined for an instant what Jackson would do to her if he had any idea what she was revealing. "He's here. He was in my garden forty-five minutes ago."

"What?"

"I'm not sure what he was up to, but I'm assuming he's laying the groundwork for whatever plan he's about to implement."

"What sort of plan?"

"He's going to kill Donovan, for starters. Then he'll probably come after us." LuAnn put her face in her hands.

"Well, you won't be seeing him again."

"You're wrong there, Matthew. I have to meet with him."

"LuAnn, you don't—"

"Jackson suddenly appeared in my bedroom last night. We had quite a lengthy discussion. He was going to check you out. He was going to look into your background, and if he found anything worrisome, he said he would kill you. But I told him I'd check you out instead. I didn't want anything to happen to you. Not because of me."

Riggs spread his hands wide. "So why? Why the lottery fix? Did you give him some of your winnings?"

"All of it." Riggs looked blankly at her. LuAnn said, "He had control of the money for ten years. That period just ended. He invested it and paid me income from those investments."

"He had a hundred million to invest. How much did you earn each year?"

"Around forty million."

Riggs gaped at her. "That's a forty percent return."

"I know. And Jackson made a lot more than that, I'm certain."

"What happened at the end of ten years?"

"I got the hundred million back."

Riggs rubbed his brow. "And if there were twelve of you at, say, an average of seventy million dollars each, this guy had almost one billion dollars to invest."

She saw worry lines on his face. "What are you thinking?"

"Another thing that's had the FBI's dander up. For years they've been aware that tremendous amounts of money have been funneled into lots of activities across the globe—some legit, others not. At first they thought it was drug-cartel money. That didn't turn out to be the case. They picked up threads here and there, but the leads always fizzled. Someone with that much money can cover himself really well. Maybe that someone is Jackson."

"You're sure the feds don't know about the lottery?"

Riggs looked uneasy. "If they do, they didn't learn it from me."

"But if they've figured it out for themselves, then we have Jackson *and* the federal government coming for us. Right?"

Riggs stared her directly in the eye. "Right."

They looked at each other, similar thoughts running through their minds. Two people against all of this. "I need to go now," Lu-Ann said. "I'm pretty certain that Jackson's been following my movements closely. He'll know we've seen each other. He may know I've met with Donovan. If I don't report back to him right away, it won't be pretty."

Riggs gripped her shoulders tightly. "LuAnn, this guy is a psycho, but he must be brilliant as well. That makes him even more dangerous. I say we bring in the troops, set the guy up, and take him."

"And what about me? You heard Donovan. The folks in Georgia want to lynch me."

"You could probably work a deal with the authorities," he said lamely. "The feds could—" Riggs broke off as he realized nothing could be guaranteed. "Okay, but listen, why can't you report back to the guy over the phone? You don't need to see him in person."

LuAnn considered this for a minute. "I'll try," was all she could promise. She stood up to her full height and gazed down at him. She looked strong, rangy, confident. "Despite having zillions of dollars and traveling all over the world, I'm still just a dumb girl from Georgia, but you might be a little surprised at what I can do when I set my mind to it." Lisa's face was conjured up in her thoughts. "And I've got a lot to lose. Too much. So I'm not going to lose."

GEORGE Masters stared down at a file intently. He was sitting in his office at the Hoover Building in Washington. Masters had been with the FBI for over twenty-five years, ten of which had been spent in the New York office. Now he was staring down at a very familiar name: LuAnn Tyler. Masters had been part of the federal investigation of Tyler's disappearance, and although the investigation had been officially closed years ago, he had never lost interest, mainly because none of it made sense. Now recent events had ignited that spark of interest into a full flame. Matthew Riggs had inquired about LuAnn Tyler. Masters knew Riggs, or who Riggs used to be, very well. If someone like Riggs was interested in Tyler, so was Masters.

After failing to prevent Tyler's escape from New York, Masters and his team had spent considerable time reconstructing the days leading up to her disappearance. He had figured that she would have either driven up from Georgia to New York or taken the train. At the train station in Atlanta he had hit the jackpot. LuAnn Tyler had taken the Amtrak Crescent to New York City on the day the authorities believed the murders were committed. That had gotten Masters's curiosity up.

Now that he was once again focused on LuAnn Tyler, Masters had instructed his men to go over NYPD records looking for any unusual events occurring around the time of LuAnn's disappearance. His men had just discovered that a man named Anthony Romanello had been found dead in his New York apartment the night before the press conference announcing LuAnn as the lottery winner. The discovery of a dead body in New York was hardly news; however, Romanello had a long arrest record and was suspected of being a hired assassin. He and a woman matching LuAnn Tyler's description had been seen at a restaurant shortly before Romanello had died. And then came the kicker: Found on Romanello's person was a receipt for a train ticket. He had been in Georgia and returned to New York on the same train as LuAnn. Was there a connection?

But the thing was, Romanello and Tyler had taken the train to New York City *before* LuAnn had won the lottery. Had she been running from a possible murder charge and coincidentally chosen New York in which to hide and then just happened to win a hundred million bucks? If so, she must be the luckiest person in the world. George Masters did not believe anyone could be that lucky. It must have been planned well in advance. And that meant one thing. LuAnn Tyler knew she was going to win the lottery.

The implications of this last thought sent a shudder through the grim-faced agent. He couldn't believe he hadn't seen that possibility ten years ago, but he had been looking for a potential murderer and nothing else. He drew solace from the fact that ten years ago he didn't have the Romanello angle to chew on. Masters picked up his phone. "Get me the director," he instructed.

JACKSON WAS AGAIN IN HIS SUITE staring at his laptop. He knew LuAnn had met with Riggs. Jackson would give her another few hours to call. He had not tapped her phone line, an oversight that he decided was not worth remedying at this point. She had caught him a little off guard by sending Lisa away so quickly. The associate he had retained to track LuAnn's movements had been compelled to follow Charlie and Lisa. Thus Jackson did not know that LuAnn and Donovan had already met.

He had contemplated sending for more people so that all bases would be covered, but too many strangers lurking around town would probably raise suspicion. He wanted to avoid that if possible. Particularly because there was a wild card out there he was unsure of: Matt Riggs. He had transmitted Riggs's fingerprints to his information source and was awaiting a reply.

Jackson's mouth sagged as the information spread over the screen. The owner of the fingerprints was not Matthew Riggs. For a moment Jackson wondered if he could have lifted someone else's prints in the cottage by mistake. But that was impossible; he had seen the exact area the man had touched. He dialed a number and spoke at length on the phone. When he hung up, he stared again at the screen.

Daniel Buckman: Deceased. Now it all made sense.

IT WAS less than three minutes after LuAnn left that Riggs received a telephone call. The message was terse.

"Someone just made an unauthorized access of your fingerprint file. Exercise extreme care. We're checking it out right now."

Riggs slammed down the phone and grabbed his receiving unit. From his desk drawer he pulled out two pistols and an ankle holster. The larger pistol he put in his pocket, and the smaller one he inserted in the holster he belted around his ankle. He hoped LuAnn hadn't found and removed the transmitter in her car.

FROM her car phone LuAnn called the number Jackson had given her. He buzzed her back less than a minute later.

"We need to talk," he said.

"I'm reporting back to you, like you said."

"I'm sure you are. I trust you have a good deal to tell me. But in person."

"Why?"

"Why not?" he fired back. "And I have some information that might be of interest to you."

"About what?"

"No, about whom. Matt Riggs. Like his real name, his real background, and why you should be cautious in dealing with him."

"You can tell me that over the phone."

"LuAnn, perhaps you didn't hear me. I said you're going to meet me in person."

"Why should I?"

"I'll give you a wonderful reason. If you don't, I'll find Riggs and kill him in the next half hour. If you call to warn him, I'll go to your daughter's school and slaughter everyone there."

LuAnn, pale and trembling at this verbal onslaught, knew that he meant every insane word. "Where and when?"

"Let's meet in thirty minutes at the cottage where our inquisitive friend was nesting. You know where it is, don't you?"

LuAnn thought back to her conversation with Charlie. She knew she could find the place. "I'll be there," she said.

Jackson hung up the phone and felt for a short-handled throwing knife hidden in his jacket.

Ten miles away LuAnn slipped off the safety on her .44.

DUSK was gathering as LuAnn drove down the treelined dirt road. The cottage was up ahead. She saw no car. She knew that meant nothing. Jackson seemed to appear and disappear whenever he pleased. She pulled the BMW to a stop in front of the ramshackle structure and climbed out. He was already there, she was certain. It was as though the man carried a scent detectable only to her. It smelled like the grave, moldy and dank. LuAnn entered the cottage.

"You're early." Jackson stepped from the shadows. His face was the same one from each of their face-to-face encounters. He liked to be consistent. Jackson wore a leather jacket and jeans. He folded his arms and leaned against the wall, his lips pursed. "You can start delivering your report," he ordered.

LuAnn kept her hands in her jacket, one fist closed around her pistol. She shifted slightly so that her back was against a wall, and she spoke in short bursts. "I met with Donovan. He's the man who was following me. Thomas Donovan." LuAnn assumed Jackson had already run down his identity. She had decided to tell Jackson mostly the truth and to lie only at critical junctures. "He's a reporter with the Washington *Tribune*. He's doing a story on the lottery. Twelve of the winners from ten years ago." She nodded toward Jackson. "You know the ones. They've all flourished financially."

"So?"

"So Donovan wanted to know how, since so many of the other winners have gone belly-up. A very consistent percentage, he said. So your twelve sort of stuck out." LuAnn read the smallest of self-doubts in his features. That was comforting to her.

"What did you tell him?"

"I told him I had an excellent investment firm. I gave him the name of the firm you used. I assume they're legitimate."

"Very," Jackson replied. "At least on the surface. And he knew about your situation in Georgia?"

"That's what drew him to me initially, I would imagine." LuAnn drew in a breath of relief as she saw Jackson nod slightly at this remark. "He thought I would confess to some big conspiracy, I guess."

"Did he mention any theories, like the lottery being fixed?"

To hesitate now would be disastrous, LuAnn knew, so she plunged ahead. "No. Although he thought he had a big story. I told him to talk directly to the investment firm, that I had nothing to hide. That seemed to take the wind out of his sails."

"How did you leave it?"

"He thanked me for meeting with him, even apologized for troubling me."

Jackson clapped his hands. "I love a good performance, and I think you handled the situation very well, LuAnn."

"I had a good teacher."

"What?"

"Ten years ago. The airport, where you impersonated an impersonation. You told me the best way to hide is to stick out. I used the same principle. Be overly open, cooperative, and honest, and even suspicious people tend to rethink things."

"I am honored that you remembered all that."

A little ego stroking went a long way with most men, LuAnn knew, and Jackson was no exception. In an understatement of mammoth proportions LuAnn said, "You're a little hard to forget. Now tell me about Riggs."

"Well, let's start with his real name. Daniel Buckman."

"Buckman? Why would he have a different name?"

"Funny question coming from you. Why do people change their names, LuAnn?"

"Because they have something to hide."

"Precisely."

"Was he a spy?"

Jackson laughed. "Not quite. Actually, he's not anything. He's dead."

"Dead?" LuAnn's body froze. *Had Jackson killed Matthew?*

"I obtained his fingerprints, had them run through a database, and the computer told me that he's dead."

"The computer's wrong."

"The computer only relays what it's been told. Someone wanted it to appear that Riggs was dead in case anyone came looking." When LuAnn didn't respond, Jackson said, "Have you ever heard of the Witness Protection and Relocation Program?"

"No. Should I?"

"You've lived abroad for so long, I suppose not. It's run by the government to protect persons testifying against dangerous criminals or organizations. They get new identities, new lives."

"Riggs—Buckman—was a witness? To what?"

Jackson shrugged. "Who knows? Who cares? What I'm telling you is that Riggs is a criminal. Or was a criminal. Probably drugs. Maybe

Mafia informant. Witness Protection isn't used for purse snatchers."

LuAnn settled back against the wall to keep herself from falling. *Riggs was a criminal.*

Jackson continued. "I hope you haven't confided anything to him. There's no telling what his agenda might be."

"I haven't," LuAnn managed to say.

"So what can you tell me about the man?"

"Not as much as you just told me. He doesn't know any more than he did before. He's not pushing the issue. From what you just said, I'm sure he doesn't want to draw attention to himself."

"True. That's very good for us."

LuAnn blurted out, "Look, the ten years is up. You've made your money. I say we call it a day. In thirty-six hours I can be on the other side of the world. You go your way, I'll go mine."

"You'll leave right away?"

"Just give me time to pack my bags."

Jackson rubbed his chin as he considered this proposal. "You disobeyed me. Tell me why I shouldn't kill you right now."

She had been prepared for that question. "Because Donovan might find it a little peculiar that right after he talks to me, I end up a corpse. You really want that kind of trouble?"

Jackson motioned to the door. "Go pack."

LuAnn looked at him. "You first."

"Let's leave together."

They went to the door in unison. Just when Jackson put his hand on the doorknob, the door burst open and Riggs stood there, his gun leveled on Jackson. Before he could fire, Jackson pulled LuAnn in front of him, his hand edging downward.

"Matthew, don't," LuAnn cried out.

Riggs shot her a glance. "LuAnn—"

LuAnn sensed rather than saw Jackson cock his arm to hurl the knife. Her hand shot out, partially colliding with Jackson's forearm. The next instant Riggs was grunting in pain, the knife sticking out of his arm. He dropped to the floor. LuAnn pulled her gun out of her pocket and whipped around, trying to draw a bead on Jackson. At the same time, Jackson pulled her backward against him.

Their combined momentum sent Jackson and LuAnn crashing through a glass window. She landed on top of him as they hit the porch hard. LuAnn's pistol squirted free from her hand. Each felt the strength of the other as they wrestled amid the slippery shards of glass, trying to gain some footage. Locked together, they both rose slowly. She noted the blood pouring from a grisly wound on Jackson's hand. His grip couldn't be a hundred percent. With a sudden burst of strength LuAnn tore free from him, seized him by his shirtfront, and threw him face first against the side of the cottage, where he slumped down, momentarily stunned by the impact. LuAnn propelled herself forward, straddled his back, gripped his chin with both hands, and pulled it backward, trying to crack his spine. As Jackson screamed in pain, her hands suddenly slipped and she fell backward. She got up, then froze as she looked down. In her hands was Jackson's face.

Jackson staggered up. For the first time, LuAnn was staring at his real face. Jackson touched his face, felt his own skin, his own hair. Now she could identify him. She had to die. The same thought occurred to LuAnn. She dove for the gun at the same time Jackson pounced on her. They slid together along the porch.

"Get off her!" Riggs screamed. LuAnn turned to see him standing at the window, his shirt red, the gun in his shaky hands. Jackson leaped over the porch railing. Riggs fired an instant too late, bullets striking the porch instead of flesh. Riggs groaned and dropped to his knees, disappearing from LuAnn's line of sight.

"Matthew!" LuAnn sprang to the window. Meanwhile, Jackson had disappeared into the woods.

LuAnn raced through the door, pulling off her jacket as she did so. She was next to Riggs in an instant. Using her teeth, she tore her jacket sleeve into strips. Next she ripped open his shirtsleeve and exposed the wound. She tried to stanch the bleeding with the cloths but couldn't. She searched under Riggs's armpit and applied pressure with her finger at a certain spot. The flow of blood finally stopped. As gently as she could LuAnn pulled the knife free while

Riggs's fingers dug into her arm. "Matthew, hold your finger right here." She guided his finger to the pressure point under his arm. "I've got a first-aid kit in my car. I'll dress it as best as I can. Then we need to get you to a doctor."

LuAnn retrieved her gun from the porch, and they hustled out to the BMW, where LuAnn dressed the wound. As she cut the last piece of tape off with her teeth and wound it around the gauze, Riggs looked at her. "Where did you learn to do this stuff?"

LuAnn grunted. "The first time I ever saw a doctor was when Lisa was born. You live in the boonies with no money, you have to learn to do this just to survive."

When they got to an urgent-care center off Route 29, Riggs went in alone while LuAnn waited for him in the car. She locked the doors and then slumped against the seat. Riggs had come to her rescue; for that she could hardly fault him. But right before that she had Jackson convinced that everything was okay. Another minute and they would've been home free. It was possible that she could explain Riggs's sudden and armed presence. He had been concerned for her safety and had followed her. But Riggs had done something she couldn't explain away. In front of Jackson, Riggs had called her LuAnn. That one word had destroyed everything. Now Jackson knew she had lied to him about what Riggs knew. She had no doubt what the punishment for that would be.

JACKSON pressed a cloth against his palm. He had badly cut his hand going through the glass. Damn the woman. Riggs would've been dead if she hadn't hit Jackson's arm a millisecond before he had released the knife. LuAnn had confided in Riggs—that was clear. He knew her real name. If she had lied about Riggs, she had probably lied about Donovan. Jackson had to assume that the reporter was closing in on the truth. He had to be stopped as well.

Jackson's portable phone rang. He picked it up, listened, conveyed some instructions, and when he hung up, a deep look of satisfaction graced his true features. The timing couldn't have been better. His trap had just been sprung.

CHAPTER 10

THE Bell Ranger helicopter landed in a grassy field where three black sedans bearing government plates were waiting. George Masters alighted from the chopper, another agent, Lou Berman, right at his elbow. They climbed into one of the cars and started off.

Twenty minutes later the procession stopped in front of Riggs's home. Car doors swung open, and serious-looking men, weapons out and ready, swarmed the house and barn.

Masters strode up to the front door. When his knocks were not answered, he motioned to one of his men. The burly agent planted one foot against the lock, and the door flew open. They searched the house thoroughly, then converged in Riggs's office. Masters sat down at the desk, his eyes alighting on Riggs's notes on LuAnn Tyler and someone named Catherine Savage. Masters looked up at Berman. "Tyler disappears, and Catherine Savage reappears. That's the cover. Find out Savage's address pronto."

Berman nodded and pulled out a portable phone.

Masters ran his eyes around Riggs's office, wondering how he fit into all this. Earlier that day Masters had been at the White House with the President, the Attorney General, and the director of the FBI. As Masters had outlined his theory, he had watched their faces go sickly pale. A scandal of horrific proportions. The government lottery fixed. The American people would believe their own government had done it to them. How could they not? The President had announced his support for the lottery, even appeared in a TV commercial touting it. If it came out that the game was fixed, there would be a tremendous bloodletting, and everyone from the President on down was going to take a major hit. So Masters had been given explicit instructions. Bring in LuAnn Tyler at any cost and by any means possible. And he intended to do just that.

"HOW'S IT feel?"

Riggs climbed into the car. His right arm was in a sling. "Well, they gave me enough painkillers to where I'm not sure I can feel anything. So tell me, how badly did I screw things up for you?"

"Matthew, I'm not blaming you."

"I know. But I thought you were walking into a trap."

She stared over at him. "And why's that?"

"Right after you left, I got a call."

"Is that right? What did it have to do with me?"

He sighed. "For starters, my real name's not Matthew Riggs."

"Well, at least we're even on that score."

He said with a forced grin, "Daniel Buckman." He held out his hand. "My friends call me Dan."

LuAnn didn't take it. "You're Matthew to me. Do your friends also know that technically you're dead and that you're in the Witness Protection Program?"

Riggs slowly withdrew his hand. "I was betting it was Jackson who tapped into my file. That's why I followed you. If he knew about me, I didn't know how he'd react. I thought he might kill you."

"That's always a possibility with the man." She slid her hands nervously over the steering wheel. "Jackson said you were a criminal. So what'd you do?"

"You believe everything that guy says to you?"

"Are you saying you're not in Witness Protection?"

"No, but the program isn't just for bad guys." Riggs leaned over and pulled out the listening device from under LuAnn's seat. "I told you I bugged your car." He held up the sophisticated device. "They almost never give out equipment like this to felons." LuAnn looked at him, her eyes wide. Riggs continued. "Until five years ago I was a special agent with the FBI. I worked undercover, infiltrating gangs operating in Mexico and along the Texas border. These guys did everything from extortion to drugs to murder for hire. When we busted the case open, I was the prosecution's lead witness. We knocked out the entire operation, sent a bunch of them to prison for life. But the big bosses in Colombia didn't like my depriving them of four hundred million a year. I knew how badly they'd want me. So I asked to disappear."

"And?"

"And the Bureau turned me down. They said I was too valuable in the field. They did have the courtesy to set me up in another town. After I relocated, I got married. Her name was Julie."

LuAnn said very quietly, "Was?"

Riggs shook his head. "Ambush on the Pacific Coast Highway. Car went over a cliff, with a hundred bullet holes in it. Julie was killed by the gunfire. I took two slugs; somehow neither hit any vitals. I was thrown clear of the car, landed on a ledge."

"Oh, I'm so sorry, Matthew."

"Guys like me, we probably shouldn't get married. It wasn't something I was looking for. It just happened. You know, you meet, you fall in love, you want to get married. If I had resisted that impulse, Julie would still be alive and teaching first grade." He looked down at his hands. "Anyway, that was when the brilliant higher-ups at the Bureau decided I just might want to retire and change my identity. Officially, I died in the ambush."

LuAnn took his hand in a firm grip. He squeezed back and said, "It's tough wiping out so many years of your life. Trying not to think about people and places, things that were important to you for so long. Always afraid you're going to slip up."

She raised her hand up and stroked his face. "I never realized how much we had in common," she said. They kissed, and then their bodies instinctively embraced and held tightly, like two pieces from a mold, joined at last.

When they pulled away, Riggs checked the parking lot, refocusing on the present situation. "Let's get to your house, pack what you need. Then we'll go to mine. I left some notes about you on my desk. I don't want to leave a trail for anyone."

RIGGS sat on LuAnn's bed while she stuffed some things in a small travel bag. "You're sure Lisa and Charlie are okay?" he asked.

"As sure as I can be. They're far away from here."

Riggs went over to the window overlooking the front drive. What he saw coming up the driveway made his knees buckle. He snatched LuAnn by the hand, and they raced down the stairs.

THE black sedans stopped in front of the house, and the men quickly scrambled out. George Masters laid a hand on the BMW's hood. "It's warm. She's here somewhere. Find her." The men fanned out and surrounded the house.

LUANN and Riggs entered the horse barn. While LuAnn readied Joy, Riggs pulled a pair of binoculars off the wall and went outside. Setting up in some thick bushes that hid the horse barn from the house, Riggs focused the binoculars. He jerked back. It was five years since he had seen the man. George Masters hadn't changed much. Riggs hustled back to the horse barn, where LuAnn was sliding a bridle on Joy. "You ready?" she asked Riggs.

"Better be. As soon as they find the house empty, they're going to check the grounds."

LuAnn planted a wooden crate next to Joy, swung up, and reached out a hand for Riggs. "Step on the crate and hold on tight to me." Riggs managed to struggle up and planted his good arm around LuAnn's waist.

"I'll go as slow as I can, but it's going to jostle you a lot regardless," she said.

"I'll take a little pain rather than explain things to the FBI."

As they started off on the trail, LuAnn said, "So that's who it was? Your old friends?"

Riggs nodded. "One used to be a friend anyway. George Masters. He's the guy who said I was too valuable in the field, who wouldn't let me enter Witness Protection until my wife was dead."

"Matthew, there's no reason you should be running from them. You haven't done anything wrong. What if I'm caught and you're with me?"

"Well, we just won't get caught." He winced as pain shot through his right arm. "First thing we need is a car."

"I've got another one at the house. Fat lot of good that'll do us."

"Wait a minute. We do have a car."

"Where?"

"We've got to get to the cottage pronto."

WHEN they arrived at the cottage, Riggs opened the doors to the shed and went inside. In the darkness LuAnn couldn't see what he was doing. Then she heard a motor turn over and start running. A moment later Donovan's black Honda, torn-up front bumper and all, appeared in the doorway. Riggs pulled it to a stop outside and got out. "What do you want to do with the horse?"

"I'll put her in the shed and call somebody to come get her." LuAnn swung down and led Joy inside the shed. She noted a watering trough and two bales of hay in the back. "It's perfect. The tenant before Donovan must have used this as a stable."

Lifting off the saddle and slipping off the bridle, LuAnn tethered Joy to a hook on the wall with a piece of rope she found. She scrounged up a bucket and, using water from the outside tap, filled up the watering trough and laid out the hay in front of Joy. LuAnn shut the doors and climbed into the driver's seat of the Honda while Riggs eased in the other side.

There was no key in the ignition. LuAnn glanced under the steering column and saw a bundle of exposed wires. "They teach hotwiring at the FBI?"

"You learn a lot of things going through life."

She put the car in gear. "Tell me about it."

They were silent for a moment, and then Riggs stirred. "We may only have one shot at getting out of this relatively intact."

"And what's that?"

"The FBI can be accommodating to people who cooperate."

"But Matthew—"

He broke in. "But they can be absolutely forgiving to people who give them what they really want."

"Are you suggesting what I think you are?"

"All we need to do is deliver Jackson to them."

"That's good to hear. For a minute there I thought it might be something difficult."

They drove off in the Honda.

IT WAS ten o'clock in the morning. Donovan stared through a pair of binoculars at a large southern colonial home in McLean, Virginia, one of the most affluent locales in the United States. You had to have substantial wealth for a place like this.

As Donovan watched, a brand-new Mercedes approached the gates to the property. Through the binoculars he eyed the woman driving. In her forties now, she still matched her lottery photo from ten years ago. He glanced at his watch. He had gotten here early to scope things out. He checked his gun to make sure it was fully loaded. He had taken LuAnn Tyler's warning seriously. He would've been a fool to think there weren't some serious forces behind all this. Donovan waited a few more minutes, then pulled up to the gates and spoke into an intercom. The gates opened, and a minute later he was standing inside the foyer. "Ms. Reynolds?"

Bobbie Jo Reynolds nodded. She was dressed in a way Donovan would describe as put together. You wouldn't have suspected that ten years ago she had been hustling tables. She was now a respected member of the Washington social community. He suddenly wondered if she knew Alicia Crane.

After failing to get anywhere with LuAnn, Donovan had contacted the eleven other lottery winners. Reynolds was the only one who had agreed to speak with him. Five of the winners had hung up on him. The others hadn't called back after he had left messages.

Reynolds escorted him into the living room, which was filled with costly antiques. She sat down in a wing chair and motioned Donovan to the settee across from her. "Would you like some coffee?" Her hands were nervously clasping and unclasping.

"I'm fine." He slipped a tape recorder from his pocket. "Ms. Reynolds, do you mind if I call you Bobbie Jo?"

"I go by Roberta," she said primly.

Reynolds reminded Donovan so much of Alicia he was tempted

to ask if they knew each other. He decided to pass on that impulse. "All right, Roberta, I want to talk about the past."

"You mentioned that on the phone. The lottery." She swept a shaky hand through her hair. "I won it ten years ago. That's hardly news now, Mr. Donovan."

"Call me Tom."

"I would prefer not."

"Fine, Roberta, but talk to me. You knew you were going to win the lottery, didn't you?"

She looked startled. "I . . . I . . . ."

Donovan persisted. "The story's going to come out, Roberta. It's only a matter of time. The question is, Do you want to cooperate and maybe get out of this whole thing relatively unscathed, or do you want to go down with everybody? I'll offer you a deal. Tell me all you know, I go and write my story, and you do whatever you want to do until the story hits. Like disappear."

Reynolds took a deep breath. "What do you want to know?"

Donovan turned on the recorder. "Was the lottery fixed?" She nodded. "I need an audible response, Roberta."

"Yes."

"How?"

"It had to do with chemicals." Reynolds pulled a handkerchief from her pocket and wiped at a cluster of tears in her eyes.

As Donovan watched her, he figured she was near the breaking point. "I'm no scientist, Roberta. Give it to me simply."

Reynolds gripped the handkerchief tightly. "All but one ball—the one with the winning number—was sprayed with some chemical. And the passageway through which the ball traveled was sprayed with something. I can't explain it exactly, but it made certain that only the one ball that wasn't sprayed went through."

Donovan stared at her in amazement. "Do the other winners know about this? How it was done? And by whom?"

"No, none of the winners knew."

Donovan studied the recorder as he reflected on her words. "But that's not exactly right, because you knew how the lottery was fixed,

Roberta. You just told me. Come on, give me the whole truth."

The crunching blow to his upper torso sent Donovan over the top of the settee. He landed hard on the oak floor. His breath gone, he could feel shattered ribs floating inside him. Reynolds hovered over him. "The truth is, only the *person* who came up with the scheme knew how it was done." The feminine hair and face came off, and Jackson stared down at the injured man.

Donovan's hand slipped down to his pocket, fumbling for his gun. His limbs would barely respond.

"You're obviously not feeling well. Let me help you." Jackson knelt down and, using the handkerchief, pulled the gun out of Donovan's pocket. He kicked Donovan viciously in the head, and the reporter's eyes closed. Jackson pulled plastic locking binds from his pocket and quickly secured Donovan.

He took off the rest of the disguise, packed it in his bag pulled from under the couch, and went up the stairs two at a time. He opened the bedroom door at the far end of the hallway. Bobbie Jo Reynolds lay on the bed, her arms and legs tied, tape over her mouth. She looked up at Jackson, her body twitching in fear.

He sat down next to her. "Thank you for following my directions so precisely. You gave the staff the day off and made the appointment with Mr. Donovan just as I requested." He patted her hand. "I knew I could count on you." He looked at her with soft, comforting eyes until her trembling subsided. He unloosened her straps and gently removed the tape. "Mr. Donovan and I will be gone soon. Stay here until we leave. Do you understand?"

She nodded in a jerky motion, rubbing her wrists.

Jackson stood up, pointed Donovan's gun at her, and squeezed the trigger. He watched for a moment as blood spread over the sheets.

Jackson then went back downstairs, pulled out his makeup kit, and spent the next thirty minutes hovering over Donovan. When the reporter finally came to, his head was splitting, but at least he was still alive. His heart almost stopped when he found himself staring up at . . . Thomas Donovan. The person even had his coat and hat on.

Jackson knelt down. "You look surprised, but I assure you I'm very adept at this. Powders, creams, latex, spirit gum, putty." He grabbed Donovan under his armpits and lifted him to the couch.

"I need to get to a doctor." Donovan managed to get the words out through blood-caked lips.

"I'm afraid that's not going to happen. But I will take a couple of minutes to explain some things to you. I believe I owe you that. You were quite ingenious to figure out the bankruptcy angle. That, I admit, had never occurred to me."

Donovan coughed. "How'd you pick up my trail?"

"I knew LuAnn would tell you basically nothing. What would you do next? Ferret out the others. I alerted all my other winners that you might call. Ten of them I instructed to blow you off. I told Bobbie Jo—excuse me, Roberta—to meet with you."

"Where is she?"

"Not relevant." Jackson smiled. "Now to continue. The substance applied to nine of the ten balls was a clear acrylic, a solution of poly-dimethyl siloxane. It builds up a powerful static charge and increases the size of the ball by approximately one thousandth of an inch without measurably changing the weight. They do weigh the balls, you know, to ensure that all are of equal weight. In each bin the ball with the winning number had no chemicals applied. Each passage-way through which the winning ball must travel was given a small trace of the polydimethyl siloxane solution as well. Under those conditions the nine balls with the static charge could not enter a passageway coated with the same substance. Thus they could not be part of the winning combination. Only the uncoated ball could."

"How'd you get the access?" Donovan was starting to slur his words as his injuries took their toll.

Jackson's smile broadened. "I gained employment as a technician at the company that provided and maintained the ball machines. No one really cared about the geeky little techie. It was like I wasn't even there. I sprayed the balls with what everyone thought was a so-lution to get rid of dust. All I had to do was hold the winning ball in my hand while I did so. The solution dries immediately. I surrep-titiously drop the winning ball back into the bin, and I'm all set."

Jackson put on a pair of thick gloves. "I think that covers every-thing." He placed both hands around the sides of Donovan's head and gave it an abrupt twist. The sound of bone cracking was un-mistakable. Jackson lifted the dead man over his shoulder. He car-ried him down to the garage, opened the front door of the Mercedes, and pressed Donovan's fingers against the steering wheel, dash, and clock. Finally, Jackson clinched the dead man's hand around the gun he had used to kill Bobbie Jo Reynolds. Wrap-ping the body in a blanket, Jackson loaded it in the trunk of the Mercedes. He retrieved his bag and Donovan's recorder from the house, and in a few minutes the car had left the quiet neighborhood. Jackson stopped by the side of the road, rolled down the window, and hurled the gun into the woods. He would wait until nightfall, and then a certain local incinerator he had found on an earlier visit would prove to be Thomas Donovan's final resting-place.

As he drove on, Jackson thought briefly of how he would deal with LuAnn Tyler and Riggs. He would focus his undivided attention on the matter shortly, but first he had something else to take care of.

JACKSON entered Donovan's apartment and took a moment to survey the premises. A journalist kept records, and those records were what Jackson had come for. He soon found them. He stacked the record boxes in the middle of the small foyer.

He was preparing to leave when he noted the answering machine in the living room. The red light was blinking. He hit the PLAYBACK button. The voice on the message made Jackson bend his head low to catch every single word. Alicia Crane sounded nervous and scared. "Where are you, Thomas?" she implored. "You haven't called. What you're working on is too dangerous. Please, please call me." Jackson rewound the tape and listened to Alicia's voice again. He hit another button on the machine. Finally, he picked up the boxes and left the apartment.

LuAnn looked at the Lincoln Memorial as she drove the Honda over the Memorial Bridge. The water of the Potomac River was dark and choppy. "I can't believe I'm doing this," she said as they drove along.

"Trust me, LuAnn. I know what I'm doing. There are two things I know: how to build things and how the Bureau works. This is the only way to do it. You run, they'll eventually find you."

"I got away before," she said confidently.

"You had some help and a better head start. You'd never get out of the country now." He looked out the window. "Here we are." She pulled over to an open spot at the curb. Riggs got out. "You remember the plan?"

LuAnn nodded.

"Good. See you soon."

As Riggs walked down the street to a pay phone, LuAnn looked up at the large, ugly building. The J. EDGAR HOOVER BUILDING was stenciled on its façade, home of the Federal Bureau of Investigation. These people were looking for her everywhere, and here she was parked ten feet from their headquarters. Putting the car in gear, LuAnn shivered and tried to keep her nerves in check. She hoped that Matthew knew what he was doing.

RIGGS made the phone call. Within a few minutes he was inside the Hoover Building, waiting in a conference room. He almost cracked a smile. He had come home, in a manner of speaking.

The door opened, and two men dressed in white shirts and similar ties entered. George Masters extended his hand. He was large, nearly bald, but his figure was trim. Lou Berman sported a severe crew cut and a grim demeanor.

"It's been a long time, Dan."

Riggs shook his hand. "It's Matt now. Dan's dead, remember, George?"

George Masters cleared his throat nervously and motioned Riggs to sit down at the conference table. After they were all seated, Masters inclined his head toward the other man. "Lou Berman. He's heading up the investigation we discussed over the phone." Berman nodded curtly at Riggs. "Dan"—Masters paused, correcting himself—"Matt was one of the best undercover agents we ever had."

"Sacrificed a lot in the name of justice, didn't I, George?" Riggs looked over at Berman. "George here will tell you I stayed in the ball game one inning too many. Right, George?"

"Goes with the territory, Matt."

"That's easy to say if you haven't watched your wife get her brains blown out because of what her husband did for a living. How's your wife, George? Three kids too, right? Having kids and a wife must be nice."

"Okay, Matt. I get your point. I'm sorry."

Riggs swallowed hard. He was feeling far more emotion than he had expected. "It would've meant a lot more if you had said it five years ago, George."

Riggs's stare was so intense that Masters finally had to look down. When he looked up, he eyed the sling. "Accident?"

"The construction business can be very hazardous. I'm here to strike a deal, George. A mutually satisfactory deal."

Berman's eyes darted all over Riggs's face. "Why should we deal? LuAnn Tyler's a criminal."

"Who says she's a criminal?"

"The state of Georgia."

"Have you really looked at that case? My sources—"

"Your sources?" Berman almost laughed.

"My sources say it's a load of crap."

Masters said, "I've looked at it, Matt. It probably is." He glowered over at Berman. "And even if it isn't, it's Georgia's problem, not ours."

Berman refused to give it up. "She's also a tax evader. She won a hundred million bucks and then disappeared for ten years."

"I thought you were an FBI agent, not an accountant," Riggs shot back.

"Let's settle down, guys," Masters said.

Riggs leaned forward. "Anyway, I thought you'd be more interested in the person behind LuAnn Tyler. The invisible guy with billions of dollars running around the planet causing havoc, making your lives miserable. Now, do you want to get to him, or do you want to talk to LuAnn Tyler about her itemized deductions?"

"What are you suggesting?"

Riggs sat back. "Just like old times, George. We reel in the big fish and let the little one go. We deliver the man, and LuAnn Tyler walks. And I mean from everything—federal, taxes, and the state of Georgia."

"We can't guarantee that, Matt," Masters said. "The boys at the IRS go their own way."

"Well, maybe she pays some money. But no jail. You have to make the murder charge go away."

Masters spoke slowly. "Supposing we go along, what's the connection between Tyler and this other person?"

"He had to get the money from somewhere."

Masters's eyes flickered. "The lottery? Was it compromised?"

Riggs tapped his fingers on the table. "Maybe."

"Listen, Matt, if the lottery was fixed, then this situation has to be handled very delicately."

Riggs chuckled. "Translation: If it ever gets out to the public, half the guys in Washington will be looking through the want ads. So what you're suggesting is a major cover-up."

Masters banged his fist on the table. "Do you realize what would happen if it becomes public that the lottery was fixed? It would almost be like the country defaulting on its debt. It cannot be allowed to happen. It *will not* be allowed to happen."

"So what's your suggestion, George?"

Masters rapidly calmed down. "You bring in Tyler. We question her, get her cooperation. We bring in the people—"

"Person, George," Riggs interrupted. "There's just one of him, but let me tell you, he's a very special one."

"Okay, so with Tyler's help we nail him."

"And what happens to LuAnn Tyler?"

Masters spread his hands helplessly. "Come on, Matt, she's got a state murder warrant out. She hasn't paid taxes for almost a decade. I have to assume she was in on the lottery scam. That all adds up to a few lifetimes in prison, but I'll settle for just one."

Riggs stared over at Masters. "If you think the woman's going to waltz in here so she can risk her life in order to bring this guy down and then be rewarded by spending the rest of her life in prison, then your brains are gone. Let me fill you in on something. It's called who's got the leverage. You call up the state of Georgia and tell them LuAnn Tyler is no longer wanted for murder there or for anything else. If she's got a parking ticket outstanding, it's wiped out. Then you call up the IRS and you tell them she'll pay what she owes, but they can forget jail time. As far as being involved in any lottery scam, if the statute of limitations hasn't already expired, then that goes away too."

"Or?" Masters said quietly, his eyes fixed on Riggs.

"Or we go public, George. If she's going to prison for life, then she's going to have to have some hobbies to fill up her days. I'm thinking appearances on *60 Minutes, Prime Time Live,* maybe even *Oprah.* She can just talk her little heart out about the lottery being fixed, how the President and the FBI wanted to cover it up, and how they were stupid enough to let a master criminal walk away so a young woman who grew up dirt-poor could be put in prison for doing something all of us would've done in an instant!" Riggs and Masters locked eyes. "What do you say, George? Is it a deal? Or do I go and phone Oprah?"

Slowly, almost imperceptibly, Masters nodded.

"I'd really love to hear you *say* it, George."

Berman started to cut in, but Masters stared him into silence. "Yes, it's a deal," Masters said. "No jail."

"Georgia too?"

"Georgia too."

"Good. Now get the director and the Attorney General in here because I want to hear the same things from them."

"You don't trust my word?"

"Let's just say your track record hasn't inspired my confidence." Riggs nodded at the phone. "Make the call."

It took some schedule juggling, but within thirty minutes the director of the FBI and the Attorney General of the United States were sitting across from Riggs. Riggs presented the same deal to them, and he extracted the same promises. Then Riggs rose. "Thank you for your cooperation."

Berman got up too. "All right. If we're working together now, bring Tyler in. We can wire her, get a team together, and go get this one man crime wave."

"Uh-uh, Lou. The deal was *I'd* bring him in, not the FBI."

Berman looked ready to explode. "Listen, you—"

"Shut up, Lou!" The FBI director's eyes bored into him. Then he looked at Riggs. "You really think you can pull this off?"

Riggs smiled. "Have I ever let you guys down before?" He walked across the room to the door, but the big-voiced Attorney General had a final question. "Was the lottery fixed, Mr. Riggs?"

Riggs looked back at her. "You bet it was. And you want to know the kicker? It looks like the United States lottery was used to finance the plans of one of the most dangerous psychopaths I've personally ever seen. I truly hope this never makes it onto the six-o'clock news." His eyes took in the steadily rising panic in each of their faces. "Have a good day." Riggs left the room and closed the door behind him.

WALKING down the street, Riggs looked at his watch. The clock housing was actually a sophisticated recording device; the tiny perforations in the leather strap were the speaker component. At least his deal with the government was recorded somewhere other than in his memory. With operations like this he shouldn't put too much faith in anyone.

He entered a convenience store and bought a newspaper. On the front page were two photos. One person he knew. With a press badge dangling around his neck, Thomas Donovan looked like he had just climbed off a plane from covering some major news event on the other side of the world. The woman in the photo next to his was identified as Roberta Reynolds. The story said her brutal murder had robbed Washington of a great benefactor. One line in the article recounted the source of her wealth: a sixty-five-million-dollar lottery win ten years earlier.

She had been murdered—allegedly, the story reported, by one Thomas Donovan. A message from Donovan requesting an interview was on the dead woman's answering machine. The pistol apparently used to slaughter Roberta Reynolds had been found about a mile from her home, along with her Mercedes, with Donovan's prints all over both. There was an APB out on Donovan, and the police were confident they would soon apprehend him.

Riggs folded up the newspaper. He knew the police were completely wrong. Donovan hadn't killed Reynolds. And it was highly likely he was dead as well. Riggs took a deep breath and thought about how he would break the news to LuAnn.

WHILE Riggs had been dealing with the FBI, LuAnn had driven to a pay phone. She left the Honda running because she didn't share Riggs's skill at hot-wiring automobiles. She dialed a certain phone number. It rang several times; then a voice answered. She could barely recognize it, the connection was so bad.

"Charlie?"

"LuAnn?"

"Where are you?"

"On the road. From Pennsylvania we headed through West Virginia, then into Kentucky, skirted Tennessee, and now we're floating back toward Virginia. Hang on. Someone wants to talk to you."

"Mom?"

"Hello, baby."

"Are you okay?"

"I'm fine, sweetie. I told you Mommy would be fine."

"I miss you. Can we come home soon?"

Home? Where was home now? "I think so, baby. Mommy's working really hard on that right now."

"I love you."

"Oh, sweetie, I love you too. Lisa?"

"Yes?"

"I mean to keep my promise to you. I'm going to tell you every-thing. The truth. Okay?"

The voice was small, a little scared. "All right, Mom. Here's Un-cle Charlie."

Charlie came back on the phone, and LuAnn filled him in on the latest events, including Riggs's plan and his real background.

Charlie could barely contain himself. "Are you crazy? You let Riggs, an ex–FBI agent, walk into the Hoover Building and cut a deal for you. How do you know he's not selling you down the river right now?"

"I trust him."

Charlie was silent for a minute. From everything LuAnn had just told him, Riggs probably was going to bat for her. Charlie thought he knew why. The man was in love with her. Was LuAnn in love with him? Why shouldn't she be? And where did that leave him? The fact was, Charlie wanted Riggs out of their lives. But Charlie loved LuAnn. And he loved Lisa. He had always put his own inter-ests behind theirs. "I'll go with your instincts, LuAnn," he finally said. "Just keep your eyes open."

"I will, Charlie, and thanks."

LuAnn hung up the phone. She would be meeting Riggs soon if everything went according to plan.

CHAPTER 11

THE burly man looked around at the other pricey homes in the Georgetown neighborhood. Fiftyish, with pale skin and a neatly trimmed mustache, he rang the bell next to the front door.

Alicia Crane opened the door, looking anxious. "Yes?"

"Alicia Crane?"

"Yes."

The man flashed his identification. "Hank Rollins, homicide detective, Fairfax County, Virginia. Are you an acquaintance of Thomas Donovan?"

Alicia bit her lip on the inside. "Yes."

Rollins rubbed his hands together. "Ma'am, I've got some questions to ask you. We can either do it down at the station, or you can ask me in before I freeze to death. It's your call."

Alicia let him in. "Of course. I'm sorry." In the living room, he settled on the sofa, and she asked if he wanted coffee.

"That'd be great, yes, ma'am."

As soon as she left the room, Rollins lurched to his feet and looked around. One item commanded his immediate attention—a photo of Donovan, his arm around Alicia Crane. They both looked extremely happy. Rollins was holding the photo when Alicia walked back in carrying a tray with two cups of coffee, some cream, and two blue packets of Equal. She lowered the tray to the coffee table. "I couldn't find the sugar. The housekeeper ran an errand. She'll be back in about an hour, and I don't usually—" Her eyes caught the photo. "May I have that?" she asked.

Rollins quickly passed the photo over and returned to his seat. "I'll get to the point, Ms. Crane. You've read the paper, I assume?"

"You mean that pack of lies." Her eyes flashed for an instant. "Thomas wouldn't hurt anyone."

Rollins picked up a cup of coffee and stirred some cream into it. He tasted the result and then poured the contents of an Equal pack into the cup. "But he did go visit Roberta Reynolds."

Alicia crossed her arms and glared at him. "Did he?"

"He never mentioned it to you that he was going to meet with her?"

"He told me nothing."

Rollins pondered this for a moment. "Ma'am, I listened to your voice on Donovan's answering machine. That voice told me two things. First, you were scared for him; second, you knew exactly why you were scared for him. Now I've already talked to someone at the *Trib*. He told me Donovan was working on a story about lottery winners. And Roberta Reynolds was one of those winners. I'm not a reporter, but when you're talking that kind of money, maybe somebody would have a motive for murder."

Alicia closed and opened her eyes several times. Rollins waited patiently while she went through her decision-making process. Finally she said, "The lottery was fixed."

"Fixed?"

"Thomas called two days ago and told me. He made me promise not to breathe a word to anyone." She clutched the hem of her skirt in her anxiety. "And now I'm just so worried about him. He was supposed to call again, but never did."

"Did he tell you who fixed the lottery?"

"No, but he mentioned a man. Someone very dangerous. I'm sure this person had something to do with that woman's death."

Rollins stared sadly at her and took a big gulp of the hot coffee.

"I told Thomas to go to the police with what he knew."

Rollins sat forward. "Did he?"

She shook her head fiercely. "Dammit, no!" A huge breath escaped her lungs. "I pleaded with him to. If someone had fixed the lottery— I mean, people would kill for all that money. You're a policeman. Aren't I right about that?"

"I know people who'd cut your heart out for a couple of singles," was Rollins's chilling reply. He looked down at his empty coffee cup. "Got any more?"

Alicia started. "What? Oh, yes. I just made a fresh pot." She left the room. When Alicia came back a couple of minutes later balancing the wooden tray, her eyes were focused on the filled cup, trying not to spill it. As she looked up, her eyes widened in disbelief, and she dropped the tray on the floor. "Peter?"

The remnants of Detective Rollins—wig, mustache, facial mask—were on the wing chair. Jackson, or Peter Crane, Alicia Crane's elder brother, was looking back at her, his features infinitely troubled. Donovan's observation that Bobbie Jo Reynolds had looked like Alicia Crane was right on the mark. However, it had been Peter Crane's alias, Jackson, disguised as Bobbie Jo Reynolds, who looked like Alicia Crane. The family resemblance was remarkable.

"Hello, Alicia."

She stared at the discarded disguise. "What is all this? I almost had a heart attack. Why were you asking me all those questions?"

"I didn't mean to upset you," said Jackson. "But I needed to know what Donovan had told you." He encircled her waist with one of his arms and guided her over to the sofa.

She jerked away. "Thomas? How do you know about Thomas? I haven't spoken to you in three years."

"Has it been that long?" he said evasively. "You don't need anything, do you? You just had to ask."

"Your checks come like clockwork," she said a bit bitterly. "I don't need any more money. It would have been nice to have seen you once in a while. I know you're busy, but we are family."

"I know." He looked down for a moment. "I always said I would take care of you. And I always will. Family is family."

"Speaking of, I spoke with Roger the other day."

"And how is our decadent, undeserving younger brother?"

"He needed money, like always."

"I hope you didn't send him any. I gave him enough to last a lifetime. All he has to do is stay within a reasonable budget."

She looked at him a little nervously. "I sent him some money. I just couldn't let him be thrown out on the street."

"Why not?"

"He wouldn't survive. He's not strong like Father."

Jackson held his tongue at the mention of their father. The years had not cleared up his sister's blindness in that regard. "Forget it. I'm not going to waste my time discussing Roger. When did you meet Donovan?"

"Almost a year ago. He did a piece on Father, a wonderful testimonial." Jackson shook his head. She would view it that way: the exact opposite of the truth. "So I called Thomas up to thank him. We had lunch and then dinner, and, well, it's been wonderful. Thomas is a noble man with a noble purpose in life."

"Like Father?" Jackson's mouth curled into a smirk.

"Very much like him," she said indignantly.

"It's truly a small world." He shook his head at the irony.

"Why do you say that?"

Jackson stood up and spread his arms to show the sweep of the room. "Alicia, where do you think all this came from?"

"Why, from the family money, of course."

"The family money? That was gone. Has been for years."

"What are you talking about? I know that Father ran into some financial difficulty, but he recovered. He always did."

Jackson looked at her with contempt. "He recovered nothing, Alicia. He was a fake and a loser."

She jumped up and slapped his face. "How dare you! Everything you have is because of him."

Jackson slowly rubbed his skin where she had hit him. His real skin was pale, smooth, as though he had lived his life in a temple like a Buddhist monk, which in one sense he had. "Ten years ago *I* fixed the national lottery," he said quietly, his dark eyes glittery as he stared at her small, stunned face. "Everything you have came from that money. From me. Not dear old Dad."

Alicia's lips began trembling. "Where is Thomas?"

"He was no good for you, Alicia. No good at all. An opportunist. I'm sure he loved all this. All that I had given you."

"*Was? Was* no good? What have you done to him?"

Jackson stared at her, searching her features for some redeeming quality. From afar he had long held idyllic visions of his only sister. Face to face with her, though, he found that image was unsustainable. "I killed him, Alicia."

She stood there frozen for an instant, then started toppling to the floor. He grabbed her and laid her on the couch. The tears stained her cheeks. "You'll have to leave the country, Alicia. I erased your phone message to Donovan, so the police won't have that to go on. However, your relationship must be well known to others. The police will come calling. You have no experience in these matters, and they will get the truth from you quite easily. I'll make the arrangements. How about New Zealand? Or perhaps Austria. We had lovely times there as children."

"Stop it! Stop it, you animal."

He turned to find her on her feet. "Alicia—"

"I'm not going anywhere." She hit him with her fists as violently as she could. They did no physical damage to him; however, the blows conjured up the memory of violent confrontations with his father. "I loved Thomas," Alicia shrieked in his face.

Jackson focused his eyes upon her. "I loved someone too," he said. "Someone who should have loved me back but didn't." Despite the years of pain, Jack's son still held long-buried feelings for the old man. Feelings that he had never dwelt upon or vocalized until now. The resurgence of this emotional maelstrom had a violent impact on him. He grabbed her by the shoulders and threw her roughly on the sofa. "You're leaving the country. Do you understand?"

"Peter—" She looked at his eyes and suddenly shivered to the depths of her soul as terror replaced her anger. She hastily changed course and spoke as calmly as she could. "Yes, Peter, I understand. I . . . I'll pack tonight."

Jackson's face took on a level of despair as his fingers clutched a large throw pillow on the sofa.

Her chin trembled uncontrollably as she watched the pillow come toward her. "Peter. Please. Please don't."

His words were stated very precisely. "My name is Jackson, Alicia. Peter Crane doesn't live here anymore." With a sudden pounce he pushed her flat against the couch, the pillow completely covering her face. She fought hard, kicking, scratching, but she was so small, so weak; he barely felt her fighting for her life. Soon it was over. The violent movements diminished, then stopped altogether.

He removed the pillow and looked down at her one last time. There was a peace there, a serenity that was heartening to him, as though what he had just done wasn't all that terrible. It needn't have ended this way. Now all the family he had left was the useless Roger. It should have been him lying there, not his cherished Alicia. He froze for an instant as an idea occurred to him. Perhaps his brother could play a supporting role in this production.

Jackson gathered up the elements of his disguise and methodically reapplied them, all the time making darting glances at his dead sister. *I am sorry, Alicia. It shouldn't have come to this.* This unexpected turn of events had come closer than anything he could remember to completely immobilizing him. Above all else Jackson cherished complete control, and it suddenly had been stripped from him. As he looked down at his hands, the instruments of his sister's death, his mind focused on the one person he clearly saw as responsible for all of this: LuAnn Tyler.

RIGGS slumped on a bench on the Mall and stared up at the Washington Monument while the cold wind whipped up and down the flat, open space that stretched from the Lincoln Memorial to the Capitol. The sky was overcast; it would be raining soon. You could smell it in the air. A hand touched his neck, and LuAnn settled in beside him, slipping her arm through his.

"Let's find a warm place where I can fill you in on developments and we can discuss our plan of attack," he said. "Sound good?"

"I'm all yours."

They ditched the Honda, which was acting up, and rented a sedan. After driving to the outskirts of western Fairfax County, they stopped for lunch at a nearly empty restaurant. On the drive out Riggs filled LuAnn in on the meeting at the Hoover Building. They walked past the bar area and sat at a table in the corner. LuAnn absently watched the bartender tinker with the TV to better the reception of a daytime soap he was watching. They ordered their food, and then Riggs pulled out the newspaper. He didn't say a word until LuAnn had read the entire story.

"You think Jackson killed Donovan?" she asked.

Riggs nodded grimly. LuAnn let her head rest in her hands. Riggs gently touched her. "Hey, LuAnn, you tried to warn the guy. There was nothing else you could do."

"I could have said no to Jackson ten years ago."

"If you had, he would've done you right then and there."

LuAnn wiped her eyes with her sleeve. "So now I've got this great deal with the FBI, and to finalize it, all we need to do is drop a net over Lucifer. Would you care to tell me how we'll do that?"

Riggs put away the paper. "If we can find out who he really is, then we might be in business." Riggs paused as their food came. After the waitress left, he picked up his sandwich and talked in between bites. "You don't remember anything about the guy? I mean anything that could help us find out who he is?"

"He was always disguised."

"The financial documents he sent you?"

"They were from a firm in Switzerland. I've got some back at the house, which I guess I can't get to. Even with our deal?"

"I wouldn't advise that, LuAnn. The feds run across you now, they might forget all about our little deal. How about Charlie? Would he have any ideas?"

"I wouldn't bet on it. Charlie told me he'd never even met Jackson face to face. It was always over the phone."

Riggs looked down for a moment, trying to think. When he looked back up at LuAnn, he was about to say something, but the look on her face froze the words in his mouth. "LuAnn?"

"Oh, no!" Her voice was filled with panic.

"What is it?" She didn't answer him. She was looking at something over his shoulder. He whirled around, expecting to see Jackson coming for them, foot-long knives in either hand. He scanned the restaurant; then his eyes settled on the TV, where a special news report was being broadcast. A woman's face spread across the screen. Two hours ago Alicia Crane, prominent Washingtonian, had been found dead in her home by her housekeeper. Evidence suggested that she had been murdered. Riggs's eyes widened as the broadcaster mentioned that Thomas Donovan, prime suspect in the Roberta Reynolds murder, had been dating Alicia Crane.

LuAnn could not pull her eyes away from that face. She had seen those eyes staring at her from the front porch of the cottage. *His real face.* She raised a shaky finger toward the screen. "That's Jackson," she said, her voice breaking. "Dressed up like a woman."

Riggs looked at the screen. That couldn't be Jackson, he thought. He turned back to LuAnn. "How do you know?"

"At the cottage, when we fought, his face—plastic, rubber, whatever—came off. I saw his real face. That face."

Riggs's first thought was the correct one. Family? The connection to Donovan couldn't be a coincidence, could it? He raced to the phone.

"WHERE are you?" Masters demanded.

"Just listen." Riggs recounted the news story.

"You think he's related to Alicia Crane?" Masters asked.

"Could be. Brother, maybe. I don't know."

"We'll check her family. Shouldn't be too hard to do. Her father was a U.S. Senator. If she has brothers, cousins, whatever, we bring 'em in for questioning."

"Be careful, George. The guy may have just killed a relative. I'd hate to see what he'd do to a non–family member."

THE doorman, Horace Parker, looked around with intense curiosity as the small army of men in FBI windbreakers swept into the private elevator that went to the penthouse. They looked deadly serious and had the weaponry to prove it. Parker went outside and looked up and down the street. A cab pulled up, and out stepped Jackson. Parker immediately went over to him. The doorman had known Jackson for most of his life. To earn extra money, he had baby-sat him and his younger brother, Roger. When the Cranes had fallen on hard times, they had left New York. Peter Crane, though, had come back and bought the penthouse. Apparently, he had done awfully well for himself.

"Good evening, Horace," Jackson said cordially.

"Evening, Mr. Crane," Parker said, tipping his cap. Jackson started past him. "Sir, there's some men in your apartment. FBI. Guns and everything. I think they're waiting for you to get home."

Jackson's reply was calm. "Thank you for the information, Horace. Simply a misunderstanding." He put out his hand, which Parker took. Jackson immediately turned and walked away. When Parker opened his hand, there was a wad of hundred-dollar bills there.

He put the cash in his pocket and took up his position by the door.

Jackson went down the street and called his brother. He told Roger to meet him in front of the St. James Theatre immediately. Jackson wasn't sure how the police had found out his identity, but he couldn't be sure they wouldn't wind up at Roger's apartment at any minute. Then he called the pilot of his private jet.

THE FBI did converge on Roger Crane's apartment but a little too late. Yet they were far more intrigued by what they discovered at Peter Crane's penthouse: Jackson's makeup and archive rooms and his computerized control center. While FBI technicians collected evidence, George Masters studied Jackson's scrapbook of lottery winners. Looking at the page on LuAnn Tyler, he now understood why she had done what she had. For a number of reasons Masters was starting to feel immense guilt.

IT WAS nearing midnight when Riggs and LuAnn stopped at a motel. After checking in, Riggs phoned George Masters. The FBI agent had just returned from New York, and he detailed to Riggs what had happened since they last spoke. Riggs hung up the phone and looked over at a very anxious LuAnn.

"What happened? What did he say?"

Riggs shook his head. "As expected. Jackson wasn't there, but they found enough evidence to keep him in prison for the rest of his life. Including a scrapbook on all the lottery winners."

"So he *was* related to Alicia Crane."

Riggs nodded grimly. "Her older brother, Peter."

LuAnn was wide-eyed. "Then he murdered his own sister."

"Looks that way."

She shuddered. "Where do you think he is?"

Riggs shrugged. "There are a million places he could go."

LuAnn let out a deep breath. "Until Jackson's caught, my life's not worth spit. Or yours. Or Charlie's." Her lips trembled. "Or Lisa's." She suddenly jumped up and grabbed the phone.

"What are you doing?" Riggs asked.

"I need to see my daughter. I need to know she's safe."

"Wait a minute. What are you going to tell her and Charlie?"

"That we can meet up somewhere. I want her near me. Nothing's going to happen to her without it happening to me first."

"LuAnn, look—"

"This subject isn't open for discussion."

"All right, all right, I hear you. Where are they now?"

"The last I heard, they were heading back to Virginia."

"What's Charlie driving?"

"The Range Rover."

"Terrific. It'll hold all of us. We'll meet them tomorrow wherever they are. We'll leave the rental and head out. Go somewhere and wait for the FBI to do its thing. Call Charlie while I take a shower."

When Riggs got out of the shower, he looked at LuAnn. "You reach them?"

"They're at a motel outside Danville, Virginia. I said we'd be there at one o'clock tomorrow."

"Sounds good."

They slid into bed, and Riggs wrapped his good arm around her slim waist. His 9-millimeter was under his pillow, a chair wedged under the door lock. He had unscrewed a lightbulb, broken it, and sprinkled the remains in front of the door. It anything was to happen, he wanted as much warning as he could get. Still, as he lay next to her, he was uneasy.

She sensed this and turned to face him. "You're not sorry you got involved in all this, are you?"

He pulled her closer to him. "Why in the world would I be?"

"Well, let me list some things for you. You've been stabbed. A madman is trying his best to kill us. You stuck your neck out with the FBI for me, and your cover is blown. That cover it?"

Riggs stroked her hair and figured he might as well say it now. He might not get another chance. "You left out the part about me falling in love with you." Her breath caught. She tried to say something but couldn't. He filled in the silence. "I know it's probably the world's worst timing, but I just wanted you to know."

"Oh, Matthew," she finally managed to say. Her voice was trembling; everything about her was. Her lips searched out and found his in the darkness.

CHARLIE rubbed the sleep from his eyes and pulled himself up from the couch. His knees were aching more than usual. He went into the adjoining room and checked on Lisa. She was sleeping soundly. The ringing phone startled him. He checked his watch. Almost two a.m. He snatched up the receiver.

"Charlie? Matt Riggs," a voice said.

"Riggs? Where's LuAnn? Is she okay?"

"She's more than okay. They caught him. They caught Jackson." His tone was one of unbridled joy.

"Hallelujah! Where?"

"In Charlottesville. The FBI had a team of agents at the airport, and he and his brother walked right into it. I guess he was coming to pay LuAnn back. The FBI wants LuAnn to come to Washington in the morning to give a deposition. That's why I called. I want you and Lisa to meet us in Washington. At the Hoover Building. If you leave now, you can meet us for breakfast."

"We'll be there. Where's LuAnn?"

"She's on the other phone talking to the FBI. Tell Lisa that her mother loves her and can't wait to see her."

"You got it." He hung up and started to pack. He figured he'd load the car before waking Lisa. Might as well let her sleep as long as possible. When she heard the news about her mother, further sleep would not be possible for the little girl. It looked like Riggs had come through after all.

His heart lighter than it had been in years, Charlie, a bag under each arm, opened the front door. He immediately froze. A man was standing in the doorway, his face covered by a black ski mask, a pistol in his hand. With a scream of rage Charlie threw a bag at him, knocking the gun free. Next Charlie grabbed the man by the mask and hurled him into the room, where he slammed against a wall and went down. Before the man could get up, Charlie was on top of him, hammering him with lefts and rights, his boxing skills coming back as though he'd never left the ring. The man slumped down, groaning. Charlie turned his head as he felt a second presence in the room. "Hello, Charlie."

As soon as he recognized the voice, Charlie leaped for him, surprising Jackson with his quickness. The twin darts from the stun gun hit Charlie in the chest, but not before his massive fist collided with Jackson's chin, knocking him back against the door. However, Jackson continued to squeeze the trigger, sending the massive electrical current into Charlie's body. Charlie was on his knees, trying to propel himself forward, but his body refused to follow his orders. As he slowly sank to the floor, he stared at a terrified Lisa standing in the bedroom doorway. He tried to scream to her to run, but all that came out was a whisper. He watched in horror as Jackson flew over to Lisa and pressed something against her mouth. The girl struggled, but it was no use. As her nostrils sucked in the chloroform, she was soon on the floor next to Charlie. Jackson wiped the blood from his face and roughly pulled his associate up. "Take her to the car."

Charlie watched helplessly as the man carried the unconscious Lisa out. Jackson knelt down next to him. Speaking in a voice that exactly impersonated Riggs, he said, "They caught Jackson. They caught him." Then Jackson laughed out loud.

Charlie didn't say anything. He just lay there as Jackson pulled a knife from his coat. He packed the stun gun away but left the darts. He wasn't worried about leaving evidence behind this time. "You sided with the wrong person." As Jackson said this, he ripped open the shirtsleeve up to Charlie's shoulder.

As slowly as he could, Charlie tried to flex his legs. He grimaced a little. It hurt, but at least he could feel something down there. What Jackson didn't know was that one of the darts had hit Charlie's thick crucifix before entering his chest, so the voltage rocking his body was far less than Jackson had counted on it to be.

"The stun charge will last fifteen minutes," Jackson lectured him. "The cut I'm about to inflict upon you will take about ten minutes to cause you to bleed to death. You won't feel anything physically. Mentally, well, it might be rather unnerving, watching yourself bleed to death." As he spoke, Jackson made a deep gash in Charlie's upper arm. As Charlie's blood started to pour out, Jackson rose. "Good-bye, Charlie. I'll tell LuAnn you said hello. Right before I kill her." He smiled and left the room.

Inch by agonizing inch Charlie brought his massive hands up until they closed around the darts. He pulled with all his strength, and little by little they came loose. That didn't lessen the numbness, but it felt good nonetheless. With what little control he had over his limbs, he slid over to the wall backward and inched his torso up to a sitting position. His legs were on fire, the equivalent of a million burning needles stuck in them, and his body was covered in blood, but he managed to thrust himself upward. Keeping himself pressed against the wall for support, he made it to the closet. He gripped a wooden suit hanger in one hand and ripped off the slender stem that normally kept trousers in place. Pushing off from the wall, he propelled himself into the bedroom. Using his teeth and one of his hands, he shredded the bedsheet into strips, working more quickly now as his limbs returned to a semblance of normalcy. He wound a long strip above the cut and then used the thin piece of wood to torque down on it. The rude tourniquet worked its lifesaving magic, and the flow of blood halted. Charlie knocked the phone receiver off the hook and punched in 911 before he lost consciousness.

LUANN sat bolt upright in bed, feeling as if every nerve were on fire. Her breath came in big chunks, her heart pounding.

Riggs sat up and wrapped an arm around her. "What is it?"

"Something's happened to Lisa. He's got her. He's got my baby. Oh, God, he was touching her. I saw it."

"LuAnn, nothing's wrong with Lisa. You had a nightmare."

She jumped up and started tossing things off the table next to the bed. "Where's the phone?" As soon as she said it, she uncovered it. Her fingers punched in the cell phone number. She waited for an answer. "They're not answering."

"So? Charlie probably turned off the phone. Do you know what time it is?"

"He wouldn't turn off the phone." She redialed, with the same result. "Something's happened. Something's wrong."

Riggs went over to her. "LuAnn, listen to me. Lisa is fine. You had a nightmare." He put his arm around her. "We're going to see them tomorrow, and everything is going to be fine. Okay?"

He continued to murmur in her ear, and his soothing tones finally reached her. She let him draw her back to bed, and they climbed in. As he settled back to sleep, however, LuAnn stared at the ceiling, silently praying that it really had been only a nightmare. However, something deep within her kept telling her it wasn't.

CHAPTER 12

THE two FBI agents stationed at the road leading up to LuAnn's home sipped hot coffee and enjoyed the late morning calm. At eleven o'clock a car approached their checkpoint and stopped. The window came down on the driver's side. Sally Beecham looked expectantly at one of the agents, and he waved her through. When she had gone out two hours before to run some errands, she had been very nervous. The FBI had made it clear that she wasn't in trouble, and as she passed by this time, she looked more comfortable.

The next vehicle that came down the road and stopped drew special attention. The older man driving the van explained that he was the groundskeeper. The younger man in the passenger seat was his assistant. They produced ID, which the agents checked thoroughly. The agents opened the back of the van, and it was indeed filled with tools. They let the van through.

LuAnn and Riggs were standing in the parking lot of the motel outside Danville, Virginia. Riggs had talked to the manager. The police had been summoned the night before. The man in room 112 had been stabbed and badly injured. A medevac helicopter had air-lifted him out. The manager was not aware of a young girl being with the man.

LuAnn closed her eyes. She knew what had happened. The thought of Jackson touching Lisa, hurting her, all because of what LuAnn had done or hadn't done was totally incapacitating.

Riggs watched as LuAnn began pacing. "We need information, Matthew. Right now."

Riggs took her hand. "Come on." They went into the motel of-fice, and Riggs phoned Masters. He explained the situation.

"Hold on," Masters said. When he came back on the line, his tone was low and nervous. "The medevac took the man who was stabbed at the motel to the UVA trauma center in Charlottesville. He was unconscious. Lost a lot of blood. As of early this morning they weren't sure he was going to make it."

"Was there any mention of a ten-year-old girl with him?"

"I asked. The report said that the man came to for a few seconds and started shouting a name."

"Lisa?"

Riggs heard Masters clear his throat. "Yes. It's her daughter, isn't it? This guy's got her, doesn't he?" Masters asked.

"Looks like it," Riggs managed to get out.

Masters spoke forcefully. "You two could be next, Matt. Think about it. We can protect you both. You have got to come in."

"I don't know."

"Look, you can go back to her house. I've got the entrance under twenty-four-hour guard. If she agrees to go there, I'll fill the place up with agents."

"Hold on, George." Riggs held the phone against his chest and looked at LuAnn. His eyes told her all she needed to know.

"Charlie?"

"Unconscious. A medevac helicopter flew him to the trauma cen-ter at UVA hospital."

"He's in Charlottesville?" she asked.

Riggs nodded. "It's only a short hop from Danville by air, and the trauma unit there is top-notch. He'll get the best care. Jackson probably has Lisa." He moved on quickly. "LuAnn, the FBI wants us to come in. So they can protect us—"

She snatched the phone out of his hand and screamed into it. "I don't want protection. He's got my daughter, and I'm going to find her. I'm going to get her back. You hear me?"

"I'm assuming this is LuAnn Tyler—" Masters began.

"You just stay out of the way. He'll kill her sure as hell if he even *thinks* you're around."

"Ms. Tyler, you can't be sure he hasn't already done something to her."

Her reply was surprising both for its content and its intensity. "I know he hasn't hurt her. Not yet. I know exactly what he wants, and it's not Lisa. You just stay out of the way, FBI man. If my daughter dies because you got in the way, there won't be anyplace on this earth that I won't find you."

Sitting at his desk in the heavily guarded Hoover Building, George Masters actually shivered as he listened to those words. The next sound he heard was the phone slamming down.

THE medical facility at the University of Virginia was a teaching component of the medical school, as well as a highly regarded public hospital with a level-one trauma center. LuAnn and Riggs raced down the corridor. Charlie was in a private room. LuAnn pushed open the door and went in. Riggs was right behind her.

LuAnn stared across at Charlie lying in the bed. As if he sensed her presence, he looked over, and a smile spread across his face. LuAnn took his big hand in hers. "Thank heavens you're okay."

Charlie was about to say something when the door opened and a middle-aged man in a white coat popped his head in. "Just making rounds, folks." He carried a clipboard. "Dr. Reese," he said, introducing himself. He checked Charlie's vital signs while he spoke. "It's lucky Charlie's so good with a tourniquet."

"So he's going to be okay?" LuAnn asked anxiously.

"Oh, yes. He's in no danger. We replaced the blood he lost; the wound is all stitched up. All he needs is some rest."

Charlie half sat up. "I feel fine. When can I check out?"

"We'll give you a couple of days to get back on your feet." Charlie was clearly not pleased with that answer. "I'll be back in the morning," Reese said.

As soon as he was gone, Charlie sat all the way up. "Any word on Lisa?" LuAnn closed her eyes and looked down. Tears slid out from under her eyelids. Charlie looked over at Riggs.

"We think he has her, Charlie," said Riggs.

"I *know* he has her. He hasn't contacted you, LuAnn?"

"I'm going to contact him," LuAnn said, opening her eyes. "But I had to come see you first. They said you might not make it." Her voice shook, and her hand gripped his tighter.

"It'd take a lot more than one cut to send yours truly into oblivion." He paused, struggling with what he was about to say. "I'm sorry, LuAnn. That bastard's got her, and it's my fault. He called in the middle of the night, impersonated Riggs's voice. Said the FBI had Jackson. I should've suspected something, but he sounded just like Riggs."

LuAnn leaned over and hugged him. "Lisa will be okay, Charlie." She sounded more confident than she felt. "He wants me."

"Well, you can't just walk in there and give yourself to him," Charlie said. He started to get up.

"What the hell are you doing?" she said sharply.

"Getting dressed."

"Excuse me. Didn't you hear the doctor?"

"I'm old; my hearing's going. And so am I. Going, that is."

"Charlie—"

"Look," he said angrily as he stumbled trying to get his pants on. LuAnn gripped his good arm. "I'm not going to lie here in this bed while that man has Lisa."

LuAnn nodded in understanding and helped him get his pants on. "You're a big old ornery bear. You know that?"

"I've got one good arm. Just let me get it around that guy's neck."

Riggs held up his own injured arm. "Well, between us we have two good arms. I owe the guy too."

Before long the three of them were in the car. It was pouring rain and already dark when LuAnn pulled into a gas station. She took a slip of paper from her pocket. "I'm going to call him."

"And then what?" Riggs asked.

"I'll let him tell me," she replied.

"You know what he'll say," Charlie rejoined. "He'll set up a meeting, just you and him. And if you go, he'll kill you."

"And if I don't go, he'll kill Lisa."

"He'll kill her anyway," Riggs said hotly.

She looked over at him. "Not if I get him first."

"LuAnn, I have a lot of confidence in you," Riggs said, "but this guy is something else again."

"He's right, LuAnn," Charlie added.

"Thanks for the vote of confidence, guys." She pulled the portable phone out of her bag and punched in the number, then looked at both of them. "But remember, I've got *two* good arms."

Riggs and Charlie watched as LuAnn spoke into the receiver, leaving the number of the cell phone. She hung up and waited. Barely three minutes had passed before the phone rang.

Before Jackson could say anything, LuAnn said, "When and where?"

"No greeting? No small talk? Where are your manners?"

"I want to talk to Lisa. Right now."

"Sorry about Charlie," Jackson said.

She wasn't about to tell him that Charlie was sitting right behind her wanting nothing more than to wring the life out of him. "I want to talk to Lisa!"

"You can talk to her, but how will you know it's not me mimicking her voice? 'Mommy, Mommy,' I could say. 'Come help me.' I could say all those things. So if you want to talk to her, you can, but it will prove nothing. Would you still like to talk to her?"

"Yes," LuAnn said pleadingly.

"Just a minute. Now where have I put that child?"

Riggs was doing his best to listen in. Exasperated, LuAnn finally opened the door and got out of the car. She strained to hear any sound in the background.

"Mom, Mom, is that you?"

"Honey, baby, it's Mom. Oh, sweetie, I'm so sorry."

"Oh, excuse me, LuAnn, that's still me," Jackson said. "Oh, Mom, Mommy, are you there?" he said again, mimicking Lisa's voice precisely. LuAnn was too stunned to say anything. The next voice she heard was Jackson's real one as he said forcefully, "I'll let you talk to her, really talk to her, but when you're done, I will tell you exactly what to do. If you deviate from my instructions . . ."

He didn't finish. He didn't have to. They both sat there on the phone, not saying anything, just listening to each other's breathing.

"Do you understand?"

"Yes." As soon as she said the word, she heard it. A sound in the background that made her both smile and grimace. She looked at her watch. Five o'clock. Her eyes took on a gleam of hope.

The next minute she was talking to Lisa, quickly asking her questions only her little girl would know the answer to. And then Jackson came back on the line and gave her the instructions. He ended the call by saying with daunting finality, "See you soon."

She got back in the car and spoke with a calmness that astonished the two men. "I'm to call him tomorrow at ten a.m. He'll give me the meeting place then. He'll let Lisa go if I come alone."

"So it's you for Lisa," Riggs said.

"That's the way it's going to be." She looked at both of them before putting the car in gear and driving off.

She had one more card to play. But Charlie and Riggs weren't going to be invited to the game. They had already sacrificed too much for her. Jackson had nearly killed both men, and she wasn't about to give the man another try on either. It was now up to her to save her daughter, and that, she felt, was the way it should be. She had been self-reliant most of her life, and, truth be known, that was the way she liked it. And there was something else: She knew where Jackson and Lisa were.

THE RAIN HAD FINALLY SLACKENED off, but the showers were far from over. LuAnn had tacked up a blanket over the shattered window of the cottage. Charlie and Riggs had pulled mattresses down from the upstairs bedroom. They had decided the cottage was the best place to spend the night.

Exhausted, both men soon began snoring deeply. LuAnn looked at her watch; it was after midnight. She made sure her gun was loaded, then climbed through the window to avoid the squeaky front door. Ignoring the car, she went to the shed. Joy was still there. LuAnn had forgotten to call anyone to come get the horse. She saddled the animal and swung onto Joy's back. Easing her out of the shed, they made it to the woods with scarcely any noise. When she reached the edge of her property, she dismounted and led Joy back to the horse barn. Then she carefully made her way to the side of the house. Peering around the corner, she noticed Sally Beecham's car out front. That puzzled her. She shrugged and went around to the rear door.

The sound she had heard in the background during Jackson's call was what had brought her here—the unique sounds of the old clock passed down to her from her mother. It had proved to be the most valuable possession she had. Jackson had called from her house, and LuAnn was convinced that Lisa was there now.

LuAnn inserted her key in the lock and slowly opened the door. She paused for a minute; the gun she held made quick, darting movements all around. Hearing nothing, she moved down the hallway and then froze. She heard voices. LuAnn slowly let out her breath as the music from a commercial came on. Someone was watching TV. A glint of light came from the doorway of Sally Beecham's bedroom. LuAnn listened for a few seconds more, then edged the door inward, pointing her gun through the opening. The room was dark, the only light coming from the TV. What she saw next made her freeze again. Sally Beecham was directly in front of her, watching TV. Or was she? She was sitting so still that LuAnn couldn't tell if she was alive or not.

LuAnn's movements had made some noise. Sally Beecham was

now staring her with horror in her eyes. She started to say something, but LuAnn put a finger up to her lips and whispered, "Shh. There's someone here." Sally looked confused. "Have you seen anyone?" LuAnn asked. Sally shook her head.

And that's when it hit LuAnn, and her face went pale. Sally never parked in front of the house. She always parked in the garage, which led into the kitchen. LuAnn's hand tightened on the gun. She looked at the face again. It was hard to tell in the dark light, but she wasn't taking any chances. "I'll tell you what, Sally. I want you to get in the kitchen pantry, and I'm going to lock you in. Just to be safe." LuAnn watched as a hand started to move behind the woman's back. LuAnn thrust the gun forward. "And we're going to do it now, or I'll shoot you right here. Pull out the gun, butt first."

When the pistol emerged, LuAnn motioned to the floor. The gun clunked when it hit the hardwood.

As the person moved in front of LuAnn, she quickly reached out and pulled the wig off, revealing the man. He had short, dark hair. He jerked around for an instant, but LuAnn shoved the gun in his ear. "Move, Mr. Jackson! Or should I say Mr. Crane?"

When they reached the kitchen, LuAnn shoved him inside the pantry and locked the door from the outside. Then she flew up the carpeted stairs. She reached her bedroom door, slid her hand around the doorknob, took a deep breath, and turned it.

A BOLT of lightning cut across the sky, followed by a deafening clap of thunder. At the same instant, the blanket was blown off the window and rain started coming in. Riggs woke. He looked around and saw the open window, the wind and rain coming through. He glanced over at Charlie, who was still sleeping. Then it hit him. He staggered up. "LuAnn? LuAnn?" His cries roused Charlie. In a minute they had searched the small cottage.

"She's not here," he screamed to Charlie.

They went outside. The car was still there. Riggs looked over at the shed. The doors were open. He raced over and looked down at the mud in front of the empty shed. Even in the darkness he could make out the hoofprints. He followed the tracks to the edge of the woods. Charlie ran up beside him.

"Joy was in the shed," he told Charlie. "It looks like LuAnn's gone back to the house. Why? The FBI is guarding the place. What would be there that she'd take that sort of risk?"

Charlie went pale, and he staggered slightly.

"What is it, Charlie?"

"Jackson once told LuAnn that if you want to hide something, put it out in plain sight because no one would see it."

Now it was Riggs's turn to go pale as the truth hit him. They raced to the car. As the sedan flew down the road, Riggs picked up the portable phone. He dialed the local FBI and was shocked to hear Masters's voice come on the line. "He's here, George. Crane's at Wicken's Hunt. Bring everything you got."

AS THE bedroom door swung open, LuAnn darted into the room. Smack in the center was Lisa, her body bound to a chair. The next sound LuAnn heard was the labored ticking of that beautiful clock. She ran to her daughter, hugged her. And then a loop of thick cord was around LuAnn's neck, was pulled tight, and her breath was suddenly gone. Her gun fell to the floor. Lisa screamed in agonizing silence, a tape stretched across her mouth. She kicked at her chair, trying to topple it over, trying to reach her mother.

Jackson had watched from the darkness next to the dresser as LuAnn had sailed toward Lisa, oblivious to his presence in the room. Then he had struck. The cord had a piece of wood attached to it, and Jackson was winding it tighter and tighter. LuAnn's face was turning blue, her senses were slipping away as the cord dug into her neck.

He whispered into her ear. "Ticktock, LuAnn. Ticktock of the little clock. Like a magnet, it led you right to me. I told you I find out everything about someone I do business with. I visited your trailer in Rikersville. I listened to the rather unique sounds of that time-piece. And then I saw it on the wall of the bedroom the night I visited you. Your little cheap family heirloom." He laughed. "Now don't forget your daughter. There she is." He hit a light switch and swung her around violently so she could see Lisa reaching for her. "She'll watch you die, LuAnn. And then it will be her turn. You cost me a family member. Someone I loved. How does it feel to be responsible for her death?" He yanked on the cord harder and harder. "Die, LuAnn. Do it for me," he hissed.

LuAnn's eyes were close to erupting out of their sockets now, her lungs almost dead. As she listened to those taunting words, she was swept back to a graveyard, to a small brass marker in the ground. Exactly where she was heading. *Do it for Big Daddy, LuAnn. It's so easy. Come and see Big Daddy.* From the corner of her blood-filled right eye she could barely see Lisa reaching for her across a chasm that was barely seconds from becoming eternal. At that very moment and from a place so deep that LuAnn never even knew she possessed it, there came a powerful rush of strength. With a shriek she jerked upright and then bent forward, lifting an astonished Jackson completely off the floor. She clamped her arms around his legs so that she was carrying him piggyback-style. Then she exploded backward, slamming Jackson into the heavy dresser against the wall. The sharp wooden edge caught him dead on the spine.

He screamed in pain and dropped the cord. Feeling the rope go lax, LuAnn whipped her torso forward, and Jackson went flying over her shoulders, crashing into a mirror hanging on the wall. LuAnn staggered drunkenly around the room, sucking in air. She reached up to her throat and pulled off the cord.

Jackson struggled to stand up. With a scream LuAnn pounced and pinned him to the floor. Her legs clamped against his, immobilizing them. Her hands encircled his throat. He looked into her eyes and knew he could never break her choke hold. His fingers closed around a bit of glass from the shattered mirror. He swung it upward, catching her in the arm and cutting through her clothing and into her skin. She didn't release her grip. He cut her again and again, but she was beyond pain. She would not let go.

Finally, with the last bit of strength he had, his fingers felt under her arm, and he pressed as hard as he could. Suddenly LuAnn's arms went dead as Jackson found the pressure point, and her grip was abruptly broken. In an instant he had pushed her off and sprinted across the room. LuAnn watched in horror as he grabbed Lisa's chair and dragged it over to the window. She got to her feet, flying toward them, knowing exactly what he was going to do. He was lifting the chair and Lisa with it, when LuAnn dove for it, her hand closing around her daughter's leg as the chair smashed against the window that overlooked the brick patio, almost thirty feet below. LuAnn and Lisa crashed to the floor amid the shattered glass.

Jackson tried to snatch up LuAnn's gun, but she landed a powerful right hand squarely against his chin. He went down to the floor. In the distance they heard sirens. Jackson swore under his breath, picked himself up, and raced through the doorway.

LuAnn let him go. Crying in relief, she gently pulled off the tape and undid the ropes holding Lisa. Mother and daughter held each other tightly. LuAnn pushed her face in Lisa's hair; her nose drank in every wonderful smell of her little girl. Then LuAnn stood and picked up her gun and fired two shots out the window.

RIGGS and Charlie and the FBI agents were engaged in an animated discussion at the entrance to the private road when they heard the shots. Riggs threw the car in gear and roared up the road. The FBI agents ran to their car.

JACKSON looked in Sally Beecham's bedroom. Empty. He spied the gun on the floor and snatched it up. Then he heard the pounding. He raced to the kitchen and unlocked the pantry door. Roger Crane, squinting and quivering, stumbled out. "She had a gun, Peter. She put me in here. I—I did exactly as you told me."

"Thank you, Roger. Tell Alicia I said hello." He lifted the pistol and fired point-blank at his brother. Then he was out the door.

As RIGGS and Charlie jumped out of their car, they saw Jackson and sprinted after him. Riggs was first, with Charlie right behind. When the lawmen pulled up, they ran to the house.

LuAnn met them on the stairs. "Where are Matthew and Charlie?" she asked.

The men looked at each other. "I saw somebody running into the woods," one of them answered.

That's when they heard it—the drone of a helicopter as it landed on the front lawn. The group raced outside; LuAnn and Lisa reached the helicopter first. George Masters climbed out, followed by a team of FBI agents. He looked at LuAnn. "LuAnn Tyler?" She nodded. Masters looked at Lisa. "Your daughter?"

"Yes," LuAnn said.

"Thank God." He let out a deep sigh of relief and held out his hand. "George Masters. FBI. I came into town to interview Charlie Thomas. When I got to the hospital, he was gone."

"We've got to go after Jackson—I mean, Crane. He went into the woods," LuAnn said. "Matthew and Charlie went after him. But I can't leave Lisa without knowing she'll be completely safe."

Masters looked from mother to daughter, spitting images of each other. "We'll transport her to the FBI office here in Charlottesville in this helicopter. I'll put her in the center of a room with a half-dozen heavily armed FBI agents. That good enough?" He smiled weakly.

A grateful look crossed her face. "Yes. Thanks."

"I've got children too, LuAnn."

She gave Lisa one more hug, then turned and raced for the woods, a swarm of FBI agents right behind her. As fleet of foot as she was, and knowing the terrain, she soon left them far behind.

RIGGS could hear the feet flying in front of him. Charlie had dropped back a bit, but Riggs heard his heavy breathing not far behind. The woods were wreathed in darkness, and the rain continued to pour down. Riggs slipped the safety off his gun, then halted abruptly as the sounds ahead of him stopped. He heard the sound behind him an instant too late as a foot slammed into his back, sending him lunging forward and then down. He hit the wet ground hard, slid across the grass, and slammed against a tree, his gun smacking against the trunk. The impact caused his wounded arm to start bleeding again. When he flipped over on his back, he saw a man flying at him, the foot poised to deliver another crunching blow. Then Charlie blindsided Jackson, and the two men went sprawling.

An incensed Charlie pounded Jackson with his fists and then cocked his arm back to deliver a knockout punch. Quick as an eel Jackson made a direct hit on Charlie's wound, a blow that made him scream and double over. Charlie fell off Jackson and lay on the ground groaning. "I should've slit your throat at the motel," Jackson spat down at him. He was about to deliver a crushing kick to Charlie's head when he heard Riggs scream at him.

"Get away from him before I blow your head off!"

When Jackson looked over, Riggs's gun was pointed directly at him. Jackson stepped away from Charlie. "Finally we meet. Riggs the criminal. How about discussing a financial arrangement that will make you very rich?" Jackson said.

"I'm not a criminal. I was an FBI agent who testified against a cartel. That's why I was in Witness Protection."

Jackson circled closer to Riggs. "Ex-FBI? Well, then at least I'm certain you won't shoot me down in cold blood."

"That's where you're wrong," Riggs said. He pulled the trigger, but the gun didn't fire. The impact with the tree had jammed it.

Jackson instantly drew his own gun and pointed it at Riggs, who dropped the useless pistol and backed up as Jackson advanced. He stopped retreating when his foot felt nothing but air. He looked behind him: a sheer drop. Down below was fast-moving water, the swift, powerful thrust of a swollen creek that cut a jagged path across LuAnn's property.

Jackson fired. The bullet hit in front of Riggs's feet, and he stepped back a half inch, teetering on the edge. "Let's see how well you swim with no arms." The next shot hit Riggs's good arm. He doubled over and clutched it, trying to maintain his balance.

Jackson sneered. "Take the bullet or jump. It's your choice."

Riggs had only an instant. As he crouched over, the arm that had just been hit slid up the length of his sling. What Riggs was about to do had saved his life while working undercover. It would not save his life this time, but it would save several others, including one that he cared about more than his own: LuAnn's. His hand closed around the butt of a compact gun taped inside his sling. Its muzzle was pointed at Jackson, who was only a few feet away.

"Riggs!" Charlie screamed.

Jackson didn't take his eyes off Riggs. "You're next, Charlie."

Riggs fired and hit Jackson in the face. The gun fell from an astonished Jackson's hand. Riggs kept pulling the trigger until the firing pin banged empty. And all the time Jackson's countenance held a look of supreme disbelief as blood mixed with fake hair and skin; creams and powders mutated into a dull crimson. The total effect was eerie, as though the man were dissolving. Jackson dropped to his knees, then fell face forward to the ground and did not move again. His last performance.

That's when Riggs went fully over the edge, as the multiple kicks from the pistol completely unsettled his balance. He heard Charlie scream his name one more time, and then he hit the water and went under. Charlie scrambled over and was about to plunge in, when a body hurtled by him and went over the edge.

LuAnn broke the surface of the water cleanly and almost instantly reappeared. She scanned the rapidly moving water that was already pulling her downstream. "Matthew!" she screamed. Nothing. She dove under. Twenty seconds later she resurfaced.

"LuAnn!" Charlie yelled. On the bank, he stumbled through the thick trees and heavy underbrush, trying to keep up.

She ignored his cries and went under again. When she broke the surface this time, she was gripping Riggs around the chest as the current swept them along. He gagged and spit up water as his lungs struggled to function. She tried to swim crosscurrent but was making little progress. She was freezing. In another minute hypothermia could well incapacitate her. Riggs was sheer dead weight, and she felt her strength fading. She scissored her legs around his upper torso, angling just enough that his face was above the water's surface.

She looked desperately around for some way out. Her eyes fell upon a thick branch suspended out over the water. It would be close. She readied herself, gauging the distance and height. She tensed her legs around Riggs and then made her lunge. Her hands closed around the branch and held. She raised herself up. She and Riggs were now partially out of the water. She looked down and saw him staring at her, his breath coming in short gasps. Then she watched horrified as he started to unwrap her legs from around him. "Matthew, don't! Please!"

Through blue lips he said, "We're not going to both die, Lu-Ann." He pushed her legs again, and she was now fighting him and the current and the weary ache in her limbs. For the first time in her life her strength failed her, and her grip was broken. She started to plummet downward. The thick arm that clamped around her body ended her fall, and the next thing she felt was herself and Riggs being lifted completely out of the water.

Straddling a tree trunk, Charlie, bad arm and all, grunted and grimaced and finally pulled them safely to a narrow dirt bank, where they all three collapsed. LuAnn's legs were still locked in a death grip around Riggs. She lay back, her head on Charlie's chest, which was heaving mightily from his efforts. LuAnn slid her right hand down to Riggs, who took it, laying it against his cheek. Her left hand went up and gripped Charlie's shoulder. He covered her hand with his. None of them said a word.

"WELL, it's all done," Riggs said, hanging up the phone. They were in his home office—LuAnn, Charlie, and Lisa. A gentle snow was falling outside. Christmas was rapidly closing in.

"So what's the bottom line?" LuAnn asked.

LuAnn and Charlie were healed. Riggs was out of his sling, and the cast he had had to wear to mend the bone Jackson's bullet had broken had recently been removed as well.

"Not great. The IRS finished its calculations of the back taxes you owed. With penalties and interest compounded, it came to all the cash you had, all the investments you had, and all the property you had, including Wicken's Hunt." He managed a grin. "You were actually short sixty-five cents, so I threw it in at no charge."

Charlie snorted. "I can't believe it. After all she's been through. She broke up Crane's criminal syndicate; the FBI look like heroes; they confiscated his property—billions of bucks into the Treasury— and she winds up with nothing. It's not fair!"

LuAnn put a hand on a seething Charlie's shoulder. "It's okay, Charlie. I didn't deserve any of that money. And I wanted to pay what I owed. I just want to be LuAnn Tyler again. I told Matthew that. But I didn't murder anyone. All the charges against me are gone, right?" She looked at Riggs for confirmation.

"That's right. Federal, state, everything. Free as a bird."

"Yeah, and poor as a church mouse," Charlie added.

"Can't the IRS come back on me later for more money?"

"No, but even if they did, you don't have any more money."

Lisa looked at him. "Maybe we can move in here, Mom." She added quickly, "I mean for a little while." LuAnn smiled at Lisa. Telling her daughter the truth had been the hardest thing she had ever had to do, but Lisa had taken the news admirably. Now at least their relationship could take on a semblance of normalcy.

Riggs looked at LuAnn. "I was thinking along those lines myself. Can you excuse us for a minute?" he asked Charlie and Lisa.

He took LuAnn by the arm, and they left the room.

Charlie and Lisa watched them go and exchanged smiles.

RIGGS sat LuAnn down by the fireplace and stood in front of her. "I'd love for all of you to move in here. But—"

"But what?" she asked.

"I was thinking about a more permanent arrangement. I mean, I earn a good living, and, well, now that you don't have all that money . . ." She cocked her head at him. "I just never wanted you to think I was after you because of your wealth. It was like this big roadblock I couldn't get around. But now that you're not rich, I just want you to know . . ." He was unable to continue, suddenly terrified at the deep waters he had ventured into.

"I love you, Matthew," LuAnn said simply.

Riggs's features relaxed. He didn't look terrified anymore. In fact, he couldn't remember ever being this happy before. "I love you too, LuAnn Tyler."

"Have you ever been to Switzerland?" she asked.

He looked surprised. "No. Why?"

"I always thought about honeymooning there. It's so romantic, so beautiful. Especially at Christmastime."

Riggs looked troubled. "Well, sweetie, I work hard, but small-town general contractors don't make enough money to do those sorts of things. I'm sorry." He licked his lips nervously.

In response LuAnn opened her purse and took out a slip of paper. On it was an account number at a bank in Switzerland. The account had been opened with one hundred million dollars: Jackson's return of her principal. It was all there, just waiting. It cranked out six million a year in interest alone. She would retain her lottery prize after all. And she wasn't feeling any guilt about it this time around. Right now, in fact, it seemed like she had earned it. She had spent the last ten years trying to be someone she wasn't. It had been a life of great wealth and great misery. Now she was going to spend the rest of her life being who she really was and enjoying it. She had a beautiful, healthy daughter and two men who loved her. No more running, no more hiding for LuAnn Tyler. She was truly blessed.

She smiled at him, stroked his face. "You know what, Matthew?"

"What?"

Right before she kissed him she said, "I think we'll be just fine."

EPORT

Nora
Roberts

Miranda Jones has it all: brains, beauty, and a brilliant career in the art world.

But her heart is locked up as tightly as a masterpiece in a museum. What would it take to open it?

It would take a thief.

HOMEPORT
Chapter One

THE damp, snapping wind iced the bones through to the marrow. Snow from a storm earlier in the week was piled in irregular hills along the side of the road. The sky was bitter blue. Stern trees with black, empty branches rose out of winter-browned grass and shook their limbs like fists against the cold.

That was March in Maine.

Miranda pumped the heater up to full, programmed her CD player to Puccini's *La Bohème,* and drove with the music soaring.

She was coming home. After a ten-day lecture tour, bumping from hotel to college campus to airport and back to hotel, Miranda was more than ready for home. Her relief might have had something to do with the fact that she hated giving lectures, suffered miserably every time she had to face those rows of eager faces. But shyness and stage fright weren't allowed to interfere with duty.

She was Dr. Miranda Jones, a Jones of Jones Point, Maine.

The city had been founded by the first Charles Jones to make his mark in the New World. The Joneses were required to make their marks, to maintain their position as the leading family of Jones Point.

A woman who stood nearly six feet tall and had hair the color of a Tonka toy fire engine rarely went unnoticed. Even when Miranda wasn't in charge, she looked as if she was. Her face was pure New

England, with a long, straight nose and cheekbones that could have chipped ice. Her mouth was wide and most often set in a serious line. Her eyes were Fourth of July blue and most often sober.

But now, as she turned onto the coast road, both her mouth and her eyes smiled. Beyond the cliffs the sea was choppy and steel gray. She loved the moods of it, its power to soothe or thrill.

The road climbed as the land narrowed, with the water creeping in on both sides. The crooked spit of land rose, its topmost point humped like an arthritic knuckle and graced by the old Victorian house that looked over sea and land. Beyond it, where the ground tumbled down again toward the water, was the white spear of the lighthouse that guarded the coast.

The big stone house had been her refuge as a child because of the woman who lived in it. Amelia Jones had bucked the Jones tradition and had lived as she chose, said what she thought, and always had a place in her heart for her two grandchildren.

Miranda had adored her. The only true grief she'd ever known was when Amelia had died in her sleep eight winters ago. She'd left the house, the tidy portfolio she'd cleverly put together over the years, and her art collection to Miranda and her brother. To her son, Miranda's father, she left her wishes that he be half the man she'd hoped before they met again. To her daughter-in-law she left a strand of pearls, because it was the only thing that Elizabeth had ever fully approved of.

Miranda reached the end of the coast road and turned into the long, curving drive. The house that topped it had survived years and gales. Now, Miranda thought with a little twist of guilt, it was surviving benign neglect. Neither she nor Andrew seemed to find the time to arrange for painters or lawn care. Still, she thought it lovely, rather like an old woman not afraid to act her age. Long terraces and narrow balconies offered views in every direction. Grand old oaks rose high, and a thick stand of pines broke the wind on the north side.

She and her brother shared the space compatibly enough—or had until Andrew's drinking became more habitual. But she wasn't going to think about that. She enjoyed having him close, liked as well as loved him.

She stepped out of the car, then leaned in to retrieve her laptop and briefcase. Shouldering both, she walked back to the trunk and popped it open.

Her hair blew into her face, causing her to huff out an irritated breath. The half sigh ended in a choked gasp as her hair was grabbed in one hard yank to snap her head back. The point of a knife pressed cold and sharp against the pulse in her throat.

Fear screamed in her head and shrieked toward her throat. Before she could release it, she was twisted around, shoved hard against the car, so that the pain in her hip blurred her vision and turned her legs to jelly.

His face was hideous—pasty white and scarred. It took her several seconds to see it was a mask. He was big. Six four or five, she noted, struggling to pay attention. Two hundred and fifty or sixty pounds, wide at the shoulders, short at the neck.

Brown eyes, muddy brown. It was all she could see through the slits in the rubber fright mask he wore. And the eyes were flat and dispassionate as a shark's as he tipped the point of the knife, slid it over her throat to delicately slice the skin. A thin line of blood trickled down to the collar of her coat.

"Please." The word bubbled out as she instinctively shoved at the wrist of his knife hand. "Please don't. I'll give you money." Please let it be money he wants, she thought frantically.

She gasped as he tossed her aside like a bundle of rags. She fell hard on her hands and knees on the gravel drive, felt the burn of small, nasty cuts on her palms.

He picked up her purse, her briefcase, then leaned down and jammed the knife into a rear tire. When he yanked it free and took a step in her direction, she began to crawl toward the house. She waited for him to strike again, to plunge the blade into her back. When she reached the steps, she turned. And saw she was alone.

She dragged herself up the steps. She had to get inside, lock the door before he came back. Her hand slid off the knob, once, twice.

Locked. For a moment she simply curled there shivering with shock.

Move, she ordered herself. You have to move. Using the knob for support, she pulled herself to her feet. Her legs threatened to buckle, her left knee was screaming, but she darted off the porch in a kind of drunken lope, searched frantically for her purse before she remembered he'd taken it.

She yanked open the car door and fumbled with the glove compartment. Even as her fingers closed over her spare keys, a sound had her whirling around wildly. There was nothing there but the wind sweeping through the bare black branches of trees.

Breath whistling, she took off for the house in a limping run and all but wailed with relief when the key slid home in the lock.

She stumbled inside, slammed the door, turned the locks. Her ears were ringing. Gritting her teeth, she took one step forward, then another as the foyer seemed to tilt gently right and left.

She was nearly to the base of the stairs when she realized it wasn't her ears ringing, but the telephone. Mechanically she walked through the haze into the parlor and picked up the phone.

"Hello?" Her voice sounded far away. "Yes. . . . Yes, I understand. I'll be there. I have . . ." Shaking her head to clear it, Miranda struggled to remember what she needed to say. "I have some things to take care of first. . . . No, I'll leave as soon as I can."

Hysteria bubbled up inside her. "I'm already packed," she said, and laughed.

She was still laughing when she hung up the phone. Laughing when she slid bonelessly into a chair, and didn't realize when she tucked herself into a small defensive ball that the laughter had turned to sobs.

SHE had both hands wrapped tight around a cup of hot tea. It was a comfort to hold it. She'd been clear and precise when she'd reported the crime. She'd spoken to the police officers who had come to the house. But now that she was alone again, she couldn't seem to keep a single solid thought in her mind for more than ten seconds.

"Miranda!" The shout was followed by the bang of the front door slamming. Andrew rushed in, took one horrified study of his sister's face. "Oh, honey." He hurried to her and crouched at her feet. His coloring was like his sister's, though his hair was a darker red, almost mahogany.

"I'm all right. Just some bruises." But she trembled.

He saw the tears in the knees of her trousers, the dried blood on the wool. His eyes, a quieter blue than hers, abruptly went dark with horror. "Did he . . . Did he rape you?"

"No. No. It was nothing like that. He stole my purse. He just wanted money. I'm sorry I had the police call you."

"It's all right." He took the cup from her hands, set it aside. "I'm so sorry. Come on, I'll take you to the hospital."

"I don't need the hospital. It's just bumps and bruises." She drew a deep breath. He could infuriate her and had disappointed her. But in all of her life he'd been the only one to stick with her, to be there.

"I should have been here." He rose and sat beside her.

"You can't be everywhere, Andrew. No one could have predicted that I'd be mugged in our own front yard."

"They said he had a knife."

"Yeah." Gingerly she lifted a hand to the shallow cut on her throat. "One look at it, and my mind just froze."

"I should have been here," he said again.

"You're here now." She leaned into him, closed her eyes. And that, it seemed, was enough to steady her. "Mother called."

"What?"

"The phone was ringing when I got into the house." She rubbed at her temple. "I have to go to Florence tomorrow."

"Don't be ridiculous. You're hurt. You're shaken. How can she ask you to get on a plane right after you've been mugged?"

"I didn't tell her." She only shrugged. "I wasn't thinking. In any case, the summons was loud and clear."

"You're going to bed. I'll call her." He sucked in his breath as a man might when faced with an ugly chore. "I'll explain."

"My hero." She kissed his cheek. "No, I'll go. A hot bath, some aspirin, and I'll be fine. And after this little adventure, I could use a distraction. She has a bronze she wants me to test. She wants an archaeometrist, and she wants one quickly."

"She's got archaeometrists on staff at Standjo."

"Exactly." Miranda's smile was thin and bright. "So if she's sending for me, it's big. She wants to keep it in the family. Elizabeth Standford-Jones, director of Standjo, Florence, is sending for an expert on Italian Renaissance bronzes. I don't intend to disappoint her."

AS SHE tried to soak out the aches in a hot tub, Miranda decided she'd hire a car to take her to the airport tomorrow night. The way her knee was throbbing, driving could be a problem even if she could replace her tire quickly. She sat straight up, sloshing water to the tub's rim. Her passport, her driver's license. He'd taken her briefcase and her purse—he'd taken all her identification documents.

Angrily she yanked the chain plug out of the drain of the clawfoot tub. The burst of energy had her getting to her feet before her wrenched knee buckled under her. Biting back a yelp, she braced a hand against the wall and sat on the lip of the tub.

The tears wanted to come, but tears wouldn't help her get back her papers. She used her hands to lift her legs out of the tub, one at a time. Clutching the sink for support, she stood and took stock of herself in the full-length mirror on the back of the door.

Her hip was black-and-blue and stunningly painful. Her knees were scraped and raw, the left one unattractively red and swollen. But it was the long, shallow slice on her throat that had her head going light. Fascinated and appalled, she lifted her fingers to it. Just a breath from the jugular, she thought. Just a breath from death.

She wrapped herself in her robe. As she was struggling to belt it, a movement outside the window had her head jerking up. With her teeth gritted, she eased closer to the window, looked out.

It was Andrew, she saw with relief. He'd turned the floodlights on, and she could see something glinting in his hand, something he swung as he strode along over the yard.

Puzzled, she pressed her face against the window. A golf club? What was he doing marching across the snowy lawn with a golf club?

Then she knew, and love flooded into her. He was guarding her.
Then she saw him stop, pull something from his pocket.
And she watched him take a long swig from a bottle.

IT WAS the pain in her knee that woke her. Miranda fumbled on
the light, shook out pills from the bottle she'd put on her bedside
table. She glanced at her clock, saw it was after three. Might as well
face the music. With the time difference, Elizabeth would be at her
desk. Miranda picked up the phone and put the call through.

"Miranda, I was about to call to leave a message at your hotel for
your arrival."

"I'm going to be delayed. I—"

"Delayed?" The word was like an ice chip, frigid and sharp. "I've
guaranteed the government that we would begin tests today."

"I'm going to send John Carter. I—"

"I didn't send for John Carter. I sent for you."

"I had every intention of being there, but my passport and other
identification were stolen yesterday. This being Friday, I doubt I can
have new documents before sometime next week."

"Even in a relatively quiet place like Jones Point, it's foolishly
careless not to lock your car."

"The documents weren't in my car. They were on me. I'll let you
know as soon as they're replaced and I've rescheduled. I apologize
for the delay. Good-bye, Mother."

It gave her perverse satisfaction to hang up before Elizabeth
could say another word.

IN HER elegant and spacious office three thousand miles away,
Elizabeth stared at the phone with a mixture of annoyance and
confusion.

"Is there a problem?"

Distracted, Elizabeth glanced over at her former daughter-in-law,
Elise Warfield. The marriage between Elise and Andrew hadn't
worked, but her professional and personal relationship with Elise
hadn't been damaged by the divorce.

"Yes. Miranda's been delayed. Her passport and other identification were stolen."

"Oh, that's dreadful." Elise got to her feet. Just over five two, with a sleek cap of ebony hair, large green eyes, and milky white skin, she resembled an efficient and sexy fairy. "She was robbed?"

"I didn't get the details." Elizabeth's lips tightened briefly.

"I know you want to begin testing today. I can shift some of my work and start myself."

Elizabeth rose and turned to her window. She always thought more clearly when she looked out over the city. Florence was her home, had been her home since the first time she'd seen it at eighteen, a young college student with a desperate love for art and a secret thirst for adventure.

She'd fallen hopelessly in love with the city, with its red rooftops and majestic domes, its twisting streets and bustling piazzas. And she'd fallen in love with a young sculptor. Her parents had snapped her back to Boston the moment they'd learned of the affair. And that, of course, had been the end of that.

She shook herself, annoyed that her mind had drifted there.

Now she was the head of one of the largest and most respected research facilities for art in the world. Standjo might be one of the arms of the Jones organization, but it was hers. Her name came first and, here, so did she.

She stood framed in the window, a trim, attractive woman of fifty-eight. Her hair was a quiet ash-blond. Her impeccable taste was reflected in the perfectly cut Valentino suit she wore. Her eyes were a ruthlessly intelligent blue. The image was one of a cool, fashionable, professional woman of wealth and position.

She would never have settled for less. No, she thought, she would never settle for less than the absolute best.

"We'll wait for her," she said, and turned back to Elise. "It's her field, her specialty. I'll contact the minister personally and explain the short delay."

Elise smiled at her. "You're the boss."

"Oh, John Carter will be coming in tomorrow. He'll be working on Miranda's team. Feel free to assign him another project in the meantime."

"We can always use him in the lab. I'll take care of it."

"Thank you, Elise."

When she was alone, Elizabeth sat at her desk again. Miranda would head the project. It would be a Standjo operation, with a Jones at the helm. That was what she had planned, what she expected. And it was what she would have.

SHE was five days late, so Miranda moved fast, pushing through the towering medieval doors of Standjo, Florence, and striding across the gleaming white marble lobby.

She'd dressed strategically for the day, selecting a royal-blue silk suit, military in style. When you were to meet with the director of one of the top archaeometry laboratories in the world, your appearance was important. Even if that director was your mother. Especially, Miranda thought, if that director was your mother.

She stepped into the elevator and ran a hand over the sophisticated French twist that had taken her entirely too much time and trouble to create. When the doors opened again, she stepped out into the quiet, elegant lobby of what she thought of as the inner sanctum.

"Buon giorno," Miranda said as she approached the receptionist's desk.

"Ah. Dottoressa Jones. Un momento."

The receptionist gave her the go-ahead, and Miranda walked through the double glass doors and down the cool white hallway that led to the office of the *Signora Direttrice.* She knocked. One was always expected to knock on any door of Elizabeth's. The responding *"Entri"* came immediately.

Elizabeth was at her desk. They faced each other, appraising swiftly. Elizabeth spoke first. "How was your trip?"

"Uneventful." Miranda stood straight as a cadet at inspection.

"Would you like some coffee? Something cold?"

"No, thank you."

Elizabeth rose. "The Fiesole Bronze is a priority. You'll have full use of the labs and the assistance of any members of the team you choose." Elizabeth inclined her head. "What happened to your leg? You're limping a bit."

"I was mugged, remember?"

"You said you'd been robbed. You didn't say you'd been injured."

"You didn't ask. The priority was the loss of my documents and the delay that caused. That much was made very clear."

"I assumed—" Elizabeth cut herself off. "Why don't you sit down while I give you some background?"

Miranda sat and crossed her legs.

"The man who discovered the bronze—"

"The plumber."

"Yes. Carlo Rinaldi. He claims to have found the piece hidden under a broken step in the cellar of the Villa della Donna Oscura." Elizabeth's New England spine was straight as a ruler. "The fact that he smuggled it out of the villa in his toolbox, then took five days reporting it to the proper channels caused some initial concern."

"There was no damage? You've examined it?"

"I have. I'd rather not make any comments until you've seen it yourself."

"Well then"—Miranda cocked her head—"let's have a look."

In answer, Elizabeth walked over to a cabinet and, opening the door, revealed a small steel safe. With one coral-tipped finger she punched in a code. Opening the reinforced door, she took out a metal box. After setting it on her desk, she opened the lid and took out a bundle wrapped in faded velvet. "We'll date the cloth as well, and the wood from the step."

Miranda rose and stepped forward slowly when Elizabeth set the bundle on her spotless white blotter. "There are no documents, correct?" she said.

"None so far. You know the history of the villa."

"Yes, of course. It was once the home of Julietta Buenodarni, a mistress of Lorenzo the Magnificent known as the Dark Lady. At one time or another every light of the Renaissance in or around Florence was welcomed into her home."

"So, you understand the possibilities."

"I don't deal in possibilities," Miranda said curtly.

"Exactly. That's why you're here."

Gently Miranda brushed a finger over the tattered velvet. "Is it?"

"I wanted the best, and I also demand discretion. If news of this find leaks, the speculation will be wild. The government wants no publicity until the tests are complete. We require an objective eye, someone who believes in facts, not romance."

"There's no room for romance in science," Miranda murmured, and carefully unwrapped the velvet. Her heart gave one hard thud against her ribs when the bronze lay naked. Her skilled eye recognized the brilliance of the workmanship, the glory of it. But she frowned, instinctively burying admiration under skepticism.

"It's beautifully conceived and executed—certainly the style falls within the realm of the Renaissance." She slipped her glasses out of the case in her pocket, put them on before she lifted the bronze. She judged the weight, turning it slowly.

The proportions were perfect. The smallest details—toenails, each tendril of hair, the definition of calf muscles—were stunningly depicted. Her long, curvy body was arched back, the arms lifted up—not in supplication, in triumph. The face wasn't delicate, but stunning, the eyes half closed as if in pleasure. She was balanced on the balls of her feet, like a woman about to leap into a warm, scented pool. Or a lover's arms.

The patina indicated age, but Miranda knew patinas could be created. The style of the artist was unmistakable, but styles could be mimicked.

"It's the Dark Lady," she said. "Julietta Buenodarni. There's no doubt about that. I've seen this face often enough in paintings and sculpture of the period. But I've never seen nor heard of this bronze."

Her eyes narrowed as she slowly turned the bronze in her hands. Idly she scraped a bit at the blue-green patina with her thumbnail. The surface corrosion was visibly thick, but she needed more, much more.

"I'll start right away."

THE WALLS OF THE STANDJO lab were a pale hospital green, the floor spotlessly white. Each station was militarily neat, fitted with microscopes, computer terminals, vials or tubes or sample bags. Conversation was muted and minimal. Elizabeth expected a tight ship, and her former daughter-in-law knew how to run one.

"It's been some time since you were here," Elizabeth began. "But Elise will refresh your memory as to the setup."

Elise turned from a microscope and started toward them. "Miranda, welcome to Florence."

"It's nice to be back. How are you?"

"Fine. Busy." She flashed a hundred-watt smile and took Miranda's hand. "How's Drew?"

"Not quite so fine—but busy. I need a lab coat, a microscope, a computer. I'll want to take photos and X rays, of course."

"There you are." John Carter loped his way over. Miranda's lab manager looked endearingly rumpled in the midst of ruthless efficiency and style. His tie, with silly grinning cows grazing, was already askew, and there were smudges on the lenses of his glasses.

"You okay?" He patted her arm in three bouncing strokes, then asked, "How's the knee? Andrew told me the guy who mugged you tossed you around."

"Tossed you around?" Elise looked over quickly. "We didn't know you were hurt."

"He held a knife to her throat," Carter announced.

"A knife." Elise put a hand to her own throat. "That's horrible."

"It's all right," Miranda said. "He just wanted money." She met her mother's eyes. "He's cost us enough valuable time."

Elizabeth decided the time for sympathy had passed. "Then I'll let Elise set you up. Here are your ID and security cards." She handed Miranda an envelope, then glanced at her wristwatch. "I have another meeting shortly. I hope to have a preliminary report by end of day."

"You will," Miranda murmured as her mother walked away.

Elise gestured. "I have an office set up for you. You're authorized to pick your team from any of the 'A' security staff."

"Miranda!" There was a wealth of pleasure in the word, and it was delivered with the heavy and exotic tones of Italy. Miranda turned and had her hand taken and lavishly kissed.

"Giovanni! You don't change." Indeed the chemistry technician was as outrageously handsome as Miranda remembered. Dark and sleek, with eyes like melted chocolate and a smile that radiated charm. He stood an inch or so below her and still managed to make her feel feminine and tiny. Besides being beautiful to look at, Giovanni Beredonno was a genius.

"But you change, *bella donna.* You're even more lovely. But what is this about being hurt? Do you want me to go break someone in half for you?" He kissed her gently, one cheek, then the other.

"Can I get back to you on that?"

"Giovanni, Miranda has work."

"Yes, yes." He brushed off Elise's disapproving words with a careless gesture. "I know—a big project, very hush-hush." He wiggled his expressive eyebrows. "So, *bellissima,* can you use me?"

"You're first on my list."

"I think Richard Hawthorne would be helpful to you." Elise tapped the shoulder of a man hunkered over a computer keyboard.

"Dr. Hawthorne." Miranda watched the balding man blink owlishly through his glasses, then fumble them off. There was something familiar about him, and she struggled to place him.

"Dr. Jones." His chin was short, but his smile was sweet as a boy's. "It's nice to see you again. We're, ah, happy to have you here."

"Thank you." Oh, yes, she remembered. He'd done a stint at the institute a few years earlier. "Elise has an office for me. Could you join us for a moment? I'd like to show you what I have."

"I'd be delighted."

"It's not large," Elise apologized to Miranda as she ushered them through a door. "I've set it up with what I thought you'd need."

Miranda took a quick scan. The computer station appeared efficient and neat. A wide white counter held microscopes, the small hand tools of her trade, and a tape recorder. There was no window, but there was a chair, a phone, and the pencils were sharpened. It would do, she thought, very well.

She set the metal box on the counter. Carefully she removed the wrapped bronze. "I'd like your opinion, Dr. Hawthorne."

"Of course. I'd be delighted."

Miranda began to unwrap the velvet. "Ah." Giovanni let out a sigh as she set the bronze on the counter. *"Bella, molto bella."*

"A fine execution." Richard pushed his glasses back into place and squinted at the bronze. "Simple. Fluid. Wonderful form and details. It's the Dark Lady of the Medicis. Renaissance, unquestionably. I wouldn't say the model was used to represent a mythical or religious figure, but herself."

"Yes," Miranda agreed. "I would say the artist knew her personally. I need to search for documents. Your help would be invaluable."

"I'd be happy to help."

"If she spent any amount of time in the environment in which she was found, the corrosion growth would have been affected. I'll want the results of that, of course," she said to Giovanni.

"You'll run relative comparisons, thermoluminescence."

"Yes. We'll also be testing the cloth and the wood from the stair tread. But the documentation will make it all more conclusive."

Miranda leaned a hip on the corner of the small desk. "I need any and all information on the Villa della Donna Oscura. She was found in the cellar there, secreted under the bottom tread of the stairs. I'll have a report on the details we know at this point for the three of you. The three of you only," she added. "Security is one of the director's top concerns."

Richard nodded. "I'll start right away."

Miranda turned to the bronze. "Let's see what she's made of."

A FEW hours later Miranda eased back in her chair. The bronze stood before her, smiling slyly. There were no signs of materials that weren't used in the Renaissance in the sliver of patina and metal she'd extracted. The bronze had a clay core, just as a piece of that era should have. The early testing of the corrosion levels indicated late fifteenth century.

Jet lag was threatening, but she refused to acknowledge it. She hammered out a preliminary report, E-mailed it to her mother, and then took the bronze for the thermoluminescence test.

Ionizing radiation would trap electrons in higher-energy states in the clay core of a bronze. When heated, the crystals in the clay would give off bursts of light. Miranda took the measurements of those bursts. She increased the radiation and heated the clay again to measure how susceptible it was to electron trapping. The next step was to test the radiation levels from the location where the bronze had been discovered. She tested dirt samples and the wood. Late fifteenth century. She had no doubt of it.

The Medicis were in control of Florence, Miranda mused. The Renaissance was moving from its early glory, when the architect Brunelleschi, the sculptor Donatello, and the painter Masaccio revolutionized the conception and the functions of art. Then came the next generation and the dawn of the sixteenth century—Leonardo, Michelangelo, Raphael, nonconformists searching for pure originality.

She knew the artist. Knew in her heart, her gut. There was nothing he had created that she hadn't studied as intensely and completely as a woman studies the face of her lover. But the lab wasn't the place for heart, she reminded herself, or gut instinct. She would run all the tests again. And a third time.

And she'd find the answers.

SUNRISE over the rooftops and domes of Florence was a magnificent moment. The sky turned from black velvet to pearl gray. The silhouettes of the long, slender pines that dotted the Tuscan hillsides blurred as the light shifted, wavered, then bloomed.

Miranda dressed quickly, facing away from the stunning canvas that was quietly painting itself outside her hotel room, her mind on work. Her early arrival would guarantee her a few hours of solitude.

She held her ID up to the glass door for the heavy-eyed guard.

"*Grazie*," she murmured as he unlocked the door.

She used her key card to access the correct floor, then entered her code at the security post outside the lab. Once she hit the switches, banks of fluorescent lights blinked on. Within moments she had coffee brewing, her computer booted, and was transcribing her notes from the evening before.

She had retested the samples and was studying her computer screen when Giovanni hunted her down with a fresh cup of coffee and a sugared roll.

"Tell me what you see," she demanded, and continued to study the colors and shapes on the screen.

"I see a woman who doesn't know how to relax." He laid his hands on her shoulders, rubbed gently. "Miranda, you've been here a week now and haven't taken an hour to yourself."

"The imaging, Giovanni."

"Ah." Still massaging, he shifted so that their heads were close. "The corrosion is thick on the surface, and it grows downward, deep into the metal, which would be typical of a bronze of four hundred years."

"We need to pinpoint the rate of growth."

"Never easy," he said. "And *The Dark Lady* was in a damp basement. The corrosion would have grown quickly there."

"I'm taking that into account."

"The cloth is no more than a hundred years old."

"A hundred?" Miranda turned to face him. "You're certain?"

"Yes. Eighty to a hundred years. Here, eat your breakfast."

"Um." She took the roll absently and bit in. "Eighty years ago. World War One. Valuables are often hidden during wartime."

"True enough."

"But where was she before that? Why have we never heard of her? This isn't the work of an amateur, Giovanni. It's the work of a master. I need to know more about that villa, more about the woman. Who did she leave her possessions to? Who lived in the villa immediately after she died? Did she have children?"

"I'm a chemist," he said with a smile. "Not a historian. For this you want Richard."

"Is he in yet?"

"He is ever punctual. Wait." He took her arm before she could hurry away. "Have dinner with me tonight."

"Giovanni, I'm too busy to go out to dinner."

"You're working too hard and not taking care of yourself."

"I promise I'll order an enormous meal from room service while I work at the hotel tonight."

She touched her lips to his cheek just as the door opened. Elise lifted a brow, mouth tight in disapproval.

"I'm sorry to interrupt. Miranda, the director would like you to come to her office at four thirty for a discussion of your progress."

"Of course. Elise, do you know if Richard's free?"

"We're all at your disposal."

"That's exactly what I was telling her." Obviously immune to frost, Giovanni grinned, then slipped out of the room.

"Miranda"—Elise shut the door at her back—"I hope you won't be offended, but I feel I should warn you that Giovanni . . ."

Miranda smiled at Elise's obvious discomfort. "Giovanni?"

"He's brilliant at his work, but on a personal level he's a womanizer. I nearly fell for it myself when I first transferred here. I was feeling so low and unhappy."

"Were you?"

Elise straightened her slim shoulders. "Divorcing your brother was a painful and difficult decision. I loved Drew, but he—" Her voice broke, and she shook her head fiercely.

Miranda felt a hard tug of shame. "I'm sorry. Andrew's been so miserable, and it was easier for me to blame you. I don't imagine the breakup of a marriage is ever one person's fault."

"I don't think either of us were very good at marriage. It seemed kinder to end it than to go on pretending."

"Like my parents?"

Elise's eyes widened. "Oh, Miranda, I didn't mean—"

"It's all right. My parents haven't lived under the same roof in more than twenty-five years, but neither of them bothers to end it. Andrew may be hurt, but all in all I prefer your way. Shall I apologize for all the nasty thoughts I've had about you in the last year or so?"

"Not necessary. We were colleagues, then relatives, but never really made it to friends. I'd like to think we could at least be friendly."

"I don't have many friends. It would be foolish of me to refuse the offer of one."

Elise opened the door again. "I don't have many friends either," she said quietly. "It's nice to have you."

Touched, Miranda stared after her, then gathered her computer printouts and samples to lock them in the safe.

She found Richard nearly buried in books.

"Find anything I can use?" Miranda asked him.

"The villa was completed in 1489. Lorenzo de' Medici commissioned the architect, but the deed was held by Julietta Buenodarni. Her name comes up from time to time. But there's not much detail. The first mentions of her begin in 1487. Indications are she was a member of the Medici household, potentially a young cousin of Clarice Orsini."

"So, Lorenzo took his wife's cousin for his mistress."

"Lorenzo moved her into the villa in 1489. By all accounts she was as devoted to the arts as he, and used her power and influence to gather the stars of the era under her roof. She died in 1530, during the siege of Florence."

"Interesting." Again, Miranda thought, a time when valuables might have been secreted away. "Children?"

"I haven't found anything on children."

"Give me a few of those books. I'll help you look."

ELIZABETH scanned the paperwork with sharp eyes. Miranda had been very careful with every step of every test. But it was still possible to see where she was leaning. "You believe it's genuine."

"Testing so far indicates it was cast in the last decade of the fifteenth century," Miranda said. "You have copies of the computer-generated photos, the chemical tests."

"Who took them?"

"I did."

"And the thermoluminescence process. Who conducted it?"

"I did."

"And the dating by style is also yours," Elizabeth said. "The bulk of the documentation is from your own research. You supervised the chemical tests, testing the patina and metal personally."

"Isn't that why you brought me here?"

"Yes. But I also provided you with a team of experts. I expected you to make more use of them."

"If I run the tests myself, I have more control," Miranda said. "This is my field. I've authenticated five pieces from this era."

Wearily Elizabeth leaned back. "No one is questioning your skill. I'm commenting on your lack of teamwork, and I'm concerned that you formed your opinion the moment you saw the bronze."

"I recognized the style, the era, and the artist." As did you, Miranda thought furiously. "However," she continued coolly, "I conducted every standard test, then retested and documented the results. From these I can form an opinion that the bronze is a depiction of Julietta Buenodarni, cast circa 1493, and the work of a young Michelangelo Buonarroti."

"To my knowledge there is no documentation of a bronze of this artist that supports this piece as his work."

"Then the documentation has yet to be found, or it never existed. *The Dark Lady* exists. The age is right. The style is right. He would have been about eighteen when this was cast. He'd already carved *Madonna of the Stairs* and *Battle of the Centaurs*."

"There is no argument that the bronze is superior work and of his style. This does not, however, prove it is his work."

"He lived in the Medici Palace, was treated like Lorenzo's son," Miranda said. "He knew her. There *is* documentation that they were acquainted. She was often used as a model. It would be more unusual if he hadn't used her. After a careful and objective study of the piece, it's my conclusion that the bronze is the work of Michelangelo."

Elizabeth folded her hands. "I won't argue with the results of your testing. With your conclusions, however, I hold reservations. You're to say nothing of this to any of the staff and nothing at all outside the lab. If any rumors leak to the press, it would be disastrous."

"I'm hardly going to call the newspapers and announce I've authenticated a lost Michelangelo. But I have. I know it."

"Nothing would please me more, I promise you. But in the meantime, this must be kept quiet."

"I'm not in this for glory."

"We're all in this for glory," Elizabeth corrected. "If your theory proves out, you'll have plenty of it. If it doesn't, you'll damage your reputation and mine and that of this facility. That, Miranda, I won't allow. Continue the document search."

"I intend to." Miranda turned on her heel and stalked out.

AT THREE a.m., when the phone rang, Miranda was in bed, surrounded by books and papers. The two-toned shrill jerked her out of a colorful dream. Disoriented, she blinked against the glare of the lights she'd left burning and groped for the phone.

"Miranda, come to my house as soon as possible."

"What? Mother? It's three in the morning."

"I'm perfectly aware of the time. As is the assistant minister who was awakened some twenty minutes ago by a reporter who demanded to know the details of the lost bronze by Michelangelo. I'll expect you within thirty minutes."

Miranda made it in twenty.

Elizabeth's home was an elegant two-story dwelling with ivory walls and a red-tiled roof. It was roomy, as Miranda recalled, but it would have occurred to neither mother nor daughter to share the space while Miranda was in Florence.

The door was wrenched open before she could knock. Elizabeth stood there, perfectly groomed, in a peach-colored robe.

"What happened?" Miranda demanded.

"That's precisely my question." Straight as a general, Elizabeth turned and strode into the front parlor. Lamps blazed, shooting shine from polished wood. "The reporter, of course, refused to reveal his source. But he had quite a bit of information."

"Could the plumber have talked to a reporter?"

"The plumber couldn't have provided him with photos of the bronze, with test results."

"Test results." Because her knees were suddenly loose, Miranda sat. "My tests? But how . . ." It hit home then, the look in her mother's eyes. She rose. "You think I called a reporter?"

Elizabeth merely studied Miranda's furious face. "Did you?"

Miranda saw the opinion had already been formed. "You can go straight to hell. And take your precious lab with you. It's always meant more to you than your own flesh and blood."

"My precious lab has provided you with training and employment. Now, because of haste and ego, my professional integrity is in question and your reputation may very well be ruined. The bronze is being transferred to another facility today. We've been fired."

"It doesn't matter." Though her stomach was jumping, Miranda spoke calmly. "Let them transfer her. Any reputable lab will only verify my findings."

"That's precisely the kind of arrogance that put us in this position." Elizabeth's eyes fired such icy temper that Miranda didn't notice the strain or dark circles under them. "I expect you to avoid the press. You will leave Italy today. You will not return to the lab or contact anyone who works there. If you don't agree, I'll be forced to terminate your position at the museum."

"You don't run the New England Institute of Art History anymore, and neither does father. Andrew and I do."

"If you want that situation to continue, you'll do what I say."

Miranda spoke quietly. "I'll never forgive you for this."

She turned and walked out. She didn't look back.

Chapter Two

ANDREW Jones was thinking of marriage and failure as he sipped Jack Daniel's. He was well aware that everyone who knew him thought it was long past time for him to turn the page on his divorce and move on. But he didn't feel like moving on. Not when it was so comforting to wallow.

Marriage had been an enormous step for him, one he'd considered carefully. No one on the Jones side of the family had ever made a successful run at marriage. He and Miranda called it the Jones curse.

His grandmother had never had a good word to say about the man she'd lived with for thirty-odd years. It was hard to blame her, as he had been infamous for his affection for young blondes.

Andrew's father, Charles, preferred digs to home fires and had spent most of his son's childhood away from home, brushing ancient dirt from ancient bones. When he was in residence, he'd agreed with everything his wife said and blinked owlishly at his children as if he'd forgotten how they came to be in his line of sight.

Not that Dr. Elizabeth Standford-Jones had cared, Andrew thought as he brooded over what he'd intended to be one friendly drink at Annie's Place. She'd left the child rearing to servants and ignored her husband as sublimely as he had ignored her.

"I'll take another, Annie."

"No, you won't."

Andrew shifted on his stool, sighed gustily. He'd known Annie McLean most of his life and knew how to get around her.

In the sweet summer when they were seventeen, they'd tumbled together onto a rough blanket over rougher sand and had made love by the crashing waves of the Atlantic. He supposed the stumbling sex—a first for both of them—had as much to do with the beer they'd consumed and the foolishness of youth as the licks of heat they'd sparked off each other. And neither of them could have known what that one night would do to both of them.

"Come on, Annie, one more won't hurt."

At five six and a hundred and thirty well-toned pounds, Annie McLean gave the impression of no-nonsense competence. Her wheat-colored hair was worn short. Her nose was splattered with freckles. She could, and had, tossed grown men out of her bar with her own work-roughened hands. She ran a clean place, knew her regulars, and knew when to draw another draft, when to switch to coffee, and when to demand car keys and call cabs.

She looked at Andrew and shook her head. "Andrew, go home. Make yourself a meal."

"I'm not hungry." He smiled, putting his dimples to work. "It's cold and rainy out. I just want a little something to warm the blood."

"Fine." She filled a mug from the coffeepot. "This is hot."

Annie's Place was hers because she'd sunk every penny of her savings from her days of cocktail waitressing into the bar—every penny her slick-talking ex hadn't run off with—and had begged and borrowed the rest. Not many had believed she could succeed, a twenty-six-year-old woman whose only business experience had come from serving mugs of beer and counting tips.

Six years later, and Annie's Place was a Jones Point standard.

Andrew had believed, she remembered with a tug of guilt as she saw him stomp out of the bar. He'd lent her money when the banks wouldn't. He'd listened to her dreams when others had ignored them. He figured he owed her, she thought now. And he was a decent man who paid his debts.

But he couldn't erase the night fifteen years before when, lost in love, they'd created a life—one that had flickered only briefly.

He couldn't make her forget the look on his face when she'd told him she was pregnant. And his voice—flat, impersonal—when he'd offered to marry her. Paying a debt, she thought now. And by offering to do what most would consider the honorable thing, he'd broken her heart.

Losing the baby only two weeks later was fate, she supposed. But she'd loved what had been growing inside her, just as she'd loved Andrew. Once the baby was gone, she'd stopped loving. That, she knew, had been as much a relief to Andrew as it had been to her.

The hum of friendship, she thought, was a lot easier to dance to than the pluck of heartstrings.

WOMEN were the bane of his existence, Andrew decided as he unlocked his car and climbed behind the wheel. Always telling you what to do, how to do it, and how you were doing it wrong.

He was better off burying himself in work at the institute by day and blurring the edges with whiskey at night. Nobody got hurt that way. Especially him.

He saw lights winking as he drove up to the house. Miranda. He hadn't expected his sister home from Florence, not for days yet.

When he was inside the foyer, he could hear the funereal tones of Mozart's *Requiem* coming from the parlor. If Miranda was playing that, he knew the trip hadn't gone well.

He found her curled up in a chair in front of the fire.

"You're back early," he said.

"Looks that way." She studied him. At least he was still marginally sober.

He sat down across from her. "So, what's the deal?"

"She had a project for me. An incredible project. A bronze was discovered in the cellar of the Villa della Donna Oscura. The bronze was of Julietta Buenodarni, the Dark Lady herself—no mistaking that face. Elizabeth wanted me to do the tests."

"So you ran them?"

"I did, and I ran them again and again." Some of the excitement leaked through as she leaned forward. "Late fifteenth century."

"That's wonderful. Why aren't you celebrating?"

"There's more." She took a deep breath. "It's a Michelangelo. I'd have proven it without a doubt if she'd given me more time."

"Why didn't she?"

Miranda got up to jab at the fire with a poker. "Someone leaked it to the press, and the government got nervous. They fired Standjo, and she fired me. She accused me of leaking it." Furious, she whirled back. "I would never have done that."

"No, of course not."

"Now I've lost the project. Not only won't I get credit but the only way I'll see that piece again is in a museum."

"You can bet that when the bronze is authenticated and announced, she'll find a way to get Standjo's name in it. And when she does, you'll just have to make sure yours isn't left out."

"It's not the same."

He rose and wandered over to the liquor cabinet. "You saw Elise?"

"Yes. She looks just fine. She asked how you were."

"And you told her I was just dandy."

Miranda watched him pour the first drink. "I didn't tell her you were turning into a brooding, self-destructive drunk. Andrew, you have to stop this. It's a waste, and it's stupid. And frankly, though I like her, she's not worth it. No one's worth it."

"I loved her," he murmured, watching the liquor swirl before he drank. "I gave her the best I had."

"Marriages fail all the time. People get over it."

He studied the liquor, watching the light flicker through the glass. "Maybe if they didn't get over it so easily, marriages wouldn't fail so often." He lifted his glass and drank deeply.

FROM the warm comfort of his rented Mercedes he watched the Land Rover turn into the parking lot beside the New England Institute of Art History.

She made quite a picture, he mused, watching her climb out. About six feet of female and most of it wrapped in a steel-gray coat that owed more to warmth than fashion. Her hair was a sexy stoplight red that escaped in untidy curls from a black ski cap, and she moved with precision and purpose. She was, he thought with a slow smile, a hard woman not to notice.

He'd been sitting there for nearly an hour now, entertaining himself with arias from *Carmen, La Bohème, The Marriage of Figaro,* loitering long enough to see her arrive.

An early riser, he decided, who liked her work well enough to face it on a cold, snowy morning before the city stirred. He appreciated a person who enjoyed their work. Lord knows, he loved his.

But what to do about Dr. Miranda Jones?

He could work around her, or he could use her. Either way, he would get the job done. But using her would be so much more entertaining. Since this would be his last job, it seemed only fair it include some entertainment in addition to thrill and profit.

He thought it would be worth his while to get to know Miranda Jones, to indulge himself with her. Before he stole from her.

He saw the light flick on in a window on the third floor of the sprawling granite building. Straight to work, he mused.

It was about time he got to work himself. He started the car and drove away to dress for the next part of his day.

THE New England Institute of Art History had been built by Miranda's great-grandfather. But it was her grandfather Andrew Jones who had expanded it to its full potential. He'd always had an interest in the arts and had even fancied himself a painter. He'd been at least good enough to convince a number of healthy young models to take off their clothes and pose for him.

The gray granite building, with its towering columns, its wings and squared-off archways, spread over a full block. The original structure had been a museum, but Andrew had wanted more. He'd seen the institute as a showcase for art and for artists, as an arena where art was displayed, restored, taught, and analyzed. So he had erected the graceful and somewhat fanciful additions.

There were classrooms with high, light-filled windows, laboratories, storerooms, and a beehive of offices. Gallery space had been more than tripled. Students who wished to study there were taken on merit. Those who could afford to pay paid dearly for the privilege. Those who couldn't were subsidized.

The museum galleries were the finest in Maine, and the work represented there had been carefully acquired over the years, beginning with Charles's and then Andrew's own collections.

The public areas swept the main floor, gallery spilling into gallery through wide archways. Classrooms and studios jammed the second level. The labs occupied the lower level.

Miranda moved to the table under her office window to brew coffee. As she switched the pot on, her fax line rang. She opened her blinds, went to the machine, and took out the page.

Welcome home, Miranda. Did you enjoy Florence? Too bad your trip was cut so rudely short.
Prepare for the fall. It's going to be a hard jolt.
I've waited so long. I've watched so patiently.
I'm watching still, and the wait's almost over.

There was no name, no return number. The tone taunting and eerily threatening. But why, and who?

Her mother? Surely a woman of Elizabeth's power, personality, and position wouldn't stoop to cryptic and anonymous messages.

It was more likely a disgruntled employee or a student who was unhappy with a grade. This was only meant to unsettle her, and she wouldn't allow it to work. But rather than discarding it, she slipped it into her bottom drawer and turned the key in the lock.

"Miranda?" A quick rap on the door jolted her.

"Yes, come in." Her assistant, Lori, was punctual, as always.

"I saw your car. I didn't know you were coming back today."

"No, it was . . . unscheduled."

"So how was Florence?" Lori moved briskly around the room, checking for messages, adjusting the blinds.

"Warm, sunny."

"Sounds wonderful." Lori sat and perched her notebook on her knee. She was a pretty blonde with an edge of efficiency sharp as a honed razor. "It's nice to have you back," she said.

"Thanks. It's nice to *be* back. I've got a lot to catch up on."

The routine was so soothing, Miranda forgot everything but the matters at hand for the next two hours. Leaving Lori to set up appointments and meetings, she went to check in with Andrew.

His domain was in the opposite wing, closer to the public areas. The galleries, acquisitions, and displays were his province.

Miranda stepped through the door of her brother's outer office. Inside was a sturdy Victorian desk, two viciously straight-backed chairs, gray filing cabinets, and the woman who guarded it all.

"Good morning, Ms. Purdue. Is my brother in?"

Andrew's assistant was somewhere on the downside of fifty. She wore her streaky salt-and-pepper hair in a knot and was never without a starched blouse, dark blazer, and skirt.

"Good morning, Dr. Jones. He just stepped downstairs to greet a guest. He should be back momentarily. Would you care to wait?"

"No. It's nothing. I'll see him later." She turned when she heard male voices echo up the stairs.

"Miranda, this is handy." Andrew beamed at her as he reached the top of the stairs. "Saves me from calling your office. I'd like you to meet Ryan Boldari, of the Boldari Gallery."

He stepped forward, took Miranda's hand, and brought it smoothly to his lips. "How nice to meet you finally."

He had a face that could have been reproduced with rich bold strokes on one of the institute's paintings. The dark, wild good looks were only marginally tamed by an impeccably cut gray suit and perfectly knotted silk tie. His hair was black as ink and gloriously wavy. His skin was dusky gold, taut over strong bones, and marred intriguingly by a small crescent-shaped scar at the far tip of his left eyebrow. His eyes held hers and were a dark, rich brown.

She heard a ping, a single and cheerful snapping sound, inside her head as her heart bumped twice.

"Welcome to the institute, Mr. Boldari."

"I'm delighted to be here." He kept her hand in his because it appeared to fluster her.

"Why don't we step into my office?" Andrew gestured toward his office door. "Miranda, got a minute?"

"Actually, I was just—"

"I'd appreciate a few moments of your time, Dr. Jones." Ryan shifted his hand to her elbow. "I have a proposition I believe you'll be interested in. You know the work of Giorgio Vasari?"

Trapped, she allowed herself to be guided into Andrew's office. "Of course—Late Renaissance, a Mannerist."

"Ryan has three Vasaris." Andrew gestured toward chairs.

"Really?" Miranda took a seat.

"Yes." Ryan settled himself into a chair. "Don't you find his work a bit self-conscious? Overripe?"

"That is typical of mannerism," Miranda countered. "Vasari is an important artist of that time and style."

"Agreed." Ryan merely smiled. "On a personal level I prefer the style of the Early and High Renaissance, but business is business." He waved a hand—he had strong, graceful hands, Miranda noted.

It embarrassed her to have—for a second or two—imagined the

feel of them on her skin. When she deliberately shifted her gaze from his hands, it collided with his. He smiled again, with a definite gleam in his eyes. In defense her voice turned chilly. "And what business do you have with the institute?"

He wondered how she looked in those wire-framed glasses that were hooked into the neck of her sweater. Scholarly sexy.

Andrew leaned back in his chair. "Ryan's interested in our Cellini Madonna."

Miranda arched a brow. "It's one of our prizes."

"Yes, I've seen it. Glorious. Your brother and I discussed a trade."

"The Cellini." Miranda's gaze whipped to her brother. "Andrew."

"Not permanent," Ryan said quickly. "A three-month exchange. I'm planning on doing a Cellini exhibit in our New York gallery. In exchange I'm willing to loan the institute all three of my Vasaris for the same span of time."

"You could do the three-styles-of-the-Renaissance exhibit you've muttered about for years," Andrew pointed out.

It was one of her dreams, a full-scale exhibit showcasing art, artifacts, history, documents—all on display, precisely as she chose. She kept her hands neatly folded to stop herself from pumping a triumphant fist in the air.

"Yes, I suppose I could. The Vasaris have been authenticated?"

Ryan inclined his head. "Yes, of course. I'll see that you get copies of the documents before we draft the agreement. And you'll do the same for me, on the Cellini."

"My assistant can have them messengered to your hotel today. I'll leave you to work out the details."

But when she rose, he rose with her and took her hand again. "I wonder if I can impose on you to show me around a bit. Andrew tells me that the labs and restoration facilities are your milieu. I'd very much like to see them."

"I—"

Before she could excuse herself, Andrew gave her a none-too-subtle jab in the ribs. "You couldn't be in better hands, Ryan."

"My galleries are for the display of art," he began, keeping Miranda's hand casually in his as they strode down to the lower level. "I know next to nothing about the science of it. Do you ever find yourself at odds merging the two?"

"No. Without one there wouldn't be the other." She drew a careful breath. The man made her nervous, nervous enough to show. "The institute was built to celebrate both. As a scientist who studies art, I appreciate that."

He was an observant man and noted carefully the flow of space between wings, the position of the stairs, offices, storerooms, windows. And of course, the security cameras.

At the end of a corridor she turned right, then stopped to slide her key card into a slot beside a gray metal door. A buzzer sounded; locks clicked. Ryan flicked a mild glance upward at the camera.

She led him into an area much like that at Standjo, Florence, where technicians worked at computers and microscopes.

"We're primarily an institute for art, but as my father's interests are in archaeology, we do quite a bit of testing and dating in that area. It's not my field. Now this . . ." She walked over to a microscope. "Take a look," she invited. "Tell me what you see."

Miranda nearly bumped into him as he moved closer. She shifted aside immediately, but not before noting that he had a good two inches on her in height. And that glint in his eyes of amused awareness took his face a step beyond sensual and straight into sexy. She heard the ping again.

He bent over, adjusted his focus. "Color, shape—rather like a Pollack painting." He straightened. "What am I looking at?"

"A scraping from a Bronzino we're restoring. The paint is unquestionably sixteenth century."

"How do you know this is sixteenth-century paint?"

"Do you want a science lesson, Mr. Boldari?"

"Ryan. Then I can say your name. Miranda's such a lovely name." His voice was like warm cream over whiskey and made her itchy. "And I might actually enjoy that science lesson. Have dinner with me. We can discuss art and science, and I can tell you about the Vasaris. We'll call it business if it makes you more at ease."

"I'm not ill at ease."

"I'll pick you up at seven."

SHE didn't know why she'd agreed to dinner. Although, when she thought back, she hadn't actually agreed. Which didn't explain why she was getting dressed to go out.

He was an associate, she reminded herself. The Boldari Gallery had a reputation for elegance and exclusivity. The single time she'd visited it in New York, she'd been impressed with the understated grandeur of the building almost as much as the art itself. It would hardly hurt the institute for her to help forge a relationship with one of the most glamorous galleries in the country.

It was only a matter of pride and professional courtesy that she chose to be particular about her appearance this evening. The first time she'd seen him, she'd resembled a scruffy student. Tonight he would see she was a mature, sophisticated woman.

She'd selected a black dress in thin, soft wool scooped low at the bodice. The sleeves were long and snug, the skirt narrow and fluid to the ankles. She added an excellent reproduction of a Byzantine cross that rested in the hollow of her breasts.

She yanked her hair up, jamming in pins at random. The result was, if she said so herself, carelessly sexy.

She grabbed her purse, then headed downstairs.

Andrew was in the front parlor, already into his second whiskey. He lowered the glass when she walked in. "Well. Wow."

"Andrew, you're such a poet. Do I look fat in this?"

"There's never a correct answer to that question. Or if there is, no man has ever found it. Therefore, I abstain. Where is he taking you?"

"I didn't ask."

"The roads are still pretty crappy."

"It's March in Maine. Of course the roads are crappy. Don't go big brother on me, Andrew." She patted his cheek. "That must be Ryan," she added when the doorbell rang.

It was a punch to the gut, Ryan thought, when Miranda opened the door and stood framed in it. "You look like something Titian would have painted." He took her hand, stepped in, and brushed his lips over her cheeks—one, then the other, European style.

"Thank you. Andrew's in the parlor. Would you like to come in for a moment?"

"Yes, I would." And he followed her into the parlor.

"Hello, Andrew." He offered his hand. "I'm stealing your sister away for the evening, unless you'd like to join us."

Andrew shook his head. "I appreciate it, but I've got some plans. You two enjoy yourselves."

"I'll just get my coat."

Andrew saw them off, then dragged his own coat out of the closet. His plans had changed. He no longer felt like drinking alone. He preferred getting drunk in company.

MIRANDA slid into the back of the limo. "Do you always travel this way?"

"No." Ryan slipped in beside her, took a single white rose out of a bud vase and offered it. "But I had a yen for champagne I couldn't indulge if I was driving." He lifted an already-opened bottle of Cristal from an ice bucket and poured her a flute.

"Business dinners rarely start with roses and champagne."

"They should"—he poured his own glass, tapped it to hers— "when they include women with arresting looks. To the beginning of an entertaining relationship."

"Association," she corrected, and sipped. "I've been in your New York gallery."

"Really? And what did you think of it?"

"Intimate. Glamorous."

"I'm flattered. Our gallery in San Francisco is airier, more light and space. We focus on modern art there. My brother Michael has an eye for it."

"So Boldari is a family enterprise."

"Yes. Like yours."

"How did you become involved with art?"

"My parents are artists. For the most part they teach, but my mother's watercolors are glorious. My father sculpts, complicated metal structures no one but Michael seems to understand. It was a huge disappointment to them that none of their six children had a talent for creating art."

"Six." Miranda blinked.

"My mother's Irish, my father Italian." Ryan grinned. "I have two brothers, three sisters, and I'm the oldest of the lot. You have the most fascinating hair." He twirled a loose lock around his finger.

"It's red and unmanageable, and if I wouldn't look like a six-foot azalea, I'd chop it off short."

"It was the first thing I noticed about you. Then it was your eyes. You're made up of bold colors and shapes."

"Like modern art?"

He chuckled. "No. Too much classic practicality for that. I like your looks," he said when the limo pulled to the curb and stopped. When the door opened, he took her hand to help her out. His mouth nearly grazed her ear. "Let's see if we like each other's company."

SHE couldn't say when she started to relax. Perhaps it was sometime during her third glass of champagne. She had to admit he was smooth—maybe a tad too smooth, but it worked.

And he listened. She couldn't remember the last time she'd spent an evening talking about her work and why she loved it. "It's the discovery, the study of a piece of art—finding its history, its personality."

"Dissecting it?"

"In a way, yes." It was so pleasant to sit like this, in the cozy warmth of the restaurant, with a fire blazing nearby and the cold dark sea just outside the window. "All the parts of it that can be studied and analyzed to give the answers."

"Don't you feel, in the end, the answer is simply the art itself?"

"Without the history and the analysis it's just a painting."

"When something's beautiful, it's enough. If I was to analyze your face, I'd take your eyes, the bold blue of them, the intelligence in them, the hint of sadness. Your mouth, soft, wide, reluctant to smile. Your cheekbones, sharp, aristocratic. Separate the features, study, analyze. I'd still come to the conclusion that you're a stunning woman. And I can do that by just sitting back and appreciating the whole."

She toyed with her scrod, struggling not to be overly flattered. "That was clever."

"I'm a clever man, and you don't trust me."

Her gaze lifted to his again. "I don't know you."

"What else can I tell you? I come from a big, loud, ethnic family, grew up in New York. I've never married, which displeases my mother—enough that I once considered it briefly."

She arched a brow. "And rejected it?"

"At that particular time, with that particular woman. We lacked a spark." He leaned closer. "Do you believe in sparks, Miranda?"

Sparks, she imagined, were cousins to pings. "I believe they fuel initial attraction, but sparks die out."

"You're cynical," he decided. "I'm a romantic. You analyze, and I appreciate. That's an interesting combination, don't you think?"

"I don't understand romantics. They make decisions based on feelings rather than fact."

"But we have so much more fun than cynics." And he, he realized, was much more attracted to her than he'd anticipated.

"Dessert? Coffee?" he asked her.

"No, I couldn't. It was a lovely meal."

Still watching her, he signaled for the bill. "Why don't we take a walk? You can show me the waterfront."

WHEN they strolled in the icy wind, the limo followed them at a crawl, a fact that both amused and staggered her. However much wealth she'd come from, no Jones would ever hire a limo to pace them as they walked. "You've never been here before?" she said.

"No. Your family's lived here for generations?"

"Yes. There have always been Joneses in Jones Point."

"Is that why you live here?" His gloved fingers tangled with hers, leather sliding over leather. "Because it's expected?"

"No. It's where I come from, where I am." It was difficult to explain, even to herself, how deep her roots were sunk in that rocky

New England soil. "I enjoy traveling, but this is where I want to be when it's time to come home."

"Tell me about Jones Point."

"The city shows best in the spring. But in dead winter it can be a postcard. The pond freezes in the park, and people ice-skate."

"Do you?" He slipped an arm around her shoulder to block her from the edge of the wind. "Skate?"

"Yes." Her blood simmered. "It's excellent exercise."

He laughed and, just beyond the circle of light tossed out by a streetlamp, turned her to him. "So it's for exercise, not for fun."

"I enjoy it." Her pulse was beginning to jump. "It's too cold to stand."

"Then why don't we consider this an exercise in sharing body heat." He hadn't intended to kiss her—eventually yes, of course, but not this soon. Still, the moment simply called for it.

He was a man who believed in practicing until he was skilled in a matter he enjoyed. He was very skilled in the matter of women and warmed her lips with his until hers softened, parted.

His mouth was firm and persuasive, his body long and hard. She found herself leaning into him. Her mind went blank with pleasure.

"Let's try that again," he said.

This time his mouth was rough and hot, plundering hers until her head roared with sounds like the sea below the cliffs of her home.

He knew what it was to want. He'd wanted a great deal in his life. Wanting her was acceptable, even expected. But wanting her now, this forcibly, was dangerous. Growing attached to a pawn was a certain way to lose the game. He never lost.

He held her away. "I should take you home."

"Yes." She wanted to steady herself. "It's getting late."

"Another minute," he murmured, "it would have been too late."

Taking her hand, he led her to the waiting limo.

SHE sang in the shower. It was something she never did. But this morning she belted out "Making Whoopee." She had no idea she even knew the lyrics.

She was still humming when she dried off.

Bending from the waist, she wrapped a towel around her mass of hair, swinging her hips as she did so. The members of the art council would have been shocked to see the cool Dr. Jones bumping and grinding around her efficient bathroom.

She giggled at the thought of it, a sound so unprecedented she had to stop and catch her breath. She realized with a kind of jolt that she was happy. Really happy.

She left for work in the chilly dark, and was still singing.

ANDREW awoke with the mother of all hangovers.

It was Annie's fault, he decided. She'd gotten just annoyed enough with him the night before to let him drink himself blind. He'd counted on her to cut him off, as she usually did. But no, she'd kept slapping those drinks in front of him every time he'd called for one. He dimly remembered her shoving him into a cab and saying something about hoping he was sick as three dogs.

She'd gotten her wish, he thought as he stumbled downstairs. If he felt any worse, he'd be dead. Never again, he promised himself. Even as he vowed, the slick longing for just one glass to steady his hands shuddered through him.

He refused it. If he took a drink at seven a.m., he'd be an alcoholic. At seven p.m., now, it was fine. He could wait twelve hours.

He sat at the long trestle table in the kitchen, laid his head down, and prayed for oblivion. He'd nearly dozed off when the back door opened, letting in a frigid blast of air and an angry woman.

"Look at you. Half naked, unshaven, bloodshot, and smelly." Annie set a grocery bag on the counter and scowled at him. "Go take a shower while I fix your breakfast."

She took a handful of his hair and dragged his head up.

"What are you doing here, Annie? Go away."

"I sold you the liquor." She let his hair go, and his head fell back onto the table with a thunk that made him howl. "You made me mad, so I let you keep drinking. So I'm going to fix you a decent breakfast, see that you get yourself cleaned up and go to work.

Now go take a shower. You smell like the floor of a second-class bar."

"Okay, okay." With what dignity he could muster in his boxer shorts, he rose.

Annie waited until she heard him shuffle away, then closed her eyes and leaned on the counter. He'd looked so pathetic she'd wanted to cuddle him.

She heard the pipes clunk as he ran the shower. He was like this house, she thought, a little threadbare, a little damaged, but surprisingly sturdy under it all. He just couldn't see that Elise, for all her brains and beauty, hadn't been right for him. He needed tending.

That she could do, Annie decided.

The kitchen was full of homey scents when he came back. He cleared his throat. "Smells great."

"Sit down," she told him without turning.

"I'm sorry, Annie."

"No need to apologize to me. You should apologize to yourself. That's who's being hurt here."

"I'm sorry anyway." He looked down at the bowl she put in front of him. "Oatmeal?"

"It'll stick to you, coat your stomach." Annie added a plate of hot toasted bread. "Eat."

"Yes, ma'am." He took the first bite. "Thanks."

When she saw he was making headway and his color was no longer sickly gray, she sat across from him. Friends stood by friends, she thought. And they were honest with each other.

She reached out, touched his hand. "Andrew, you've got to stop doing this to yourself."

Annoyed, he jerked his shoulders. "Nothing wrong with getting drunk now and then."

"There is when you're an alcoholic."

"I'm not."

"I run a bar, and I was married to a drunk. I know the signs. You and I were both half drunk the night we . . ." It hurt to say it.

"Jeez, Annie. We were just kids."

"We were old enough to make a baby between us." No matter

what it cost, she would get at least part of it out. "We were stupid, and we were irresponsible. I've accepted that. But it taught me what you can lose, what it can do if you don't stay in control. You're not in control, Andrew."

"One night fifteen years ago doesn't have anything to do with now." The minute the words were out, he regretted it. "I didn't mean it like that, Annie. Not that it didn't matter. I just—"

"Don't." Her voice was cool and distant. "I only brought it up because you were seventeen then, but you already had a drinking problem. You've managed to get through most of your life without letting it take over. Now you've crossed the line, and you have to take back the controls. I'm telling you this as a friend." She rose. "Don't come in my place anymore. I won't serve you."

"Come on, Annie."

"You can come for conversation, but don't come for a drink, because I won't give it to you."

She turned, picked up her coat, and hurried out.

Chapter Three

RYAN wandered the South Gallery. The Joneses knew their business, he mused. The displays were elegantly arranged. The guards were unobtrusive, but there were plenty of them. He noted their stations and judged by one uniform's surreptitious glance at his watch that they were nearing change of shift.

He appeared to wander aimlessly, but in his mind he counted off paces. From the doorway to the camera in the southwest corner, from the camera to the archway, from the archway to the next camera, and from there to his goal.

He lingered no longer in front of the display case than any art lover might when studying the rare beauty of a fifteenth-century bronze. The bronze *David* was a small jewel—young, cocky, slender, his sling whipped back at that historic moment of truth. Though the artist was unknown, the plaque indicated it was assumed to be the work of one of Leonardo's students.

Ryan was already feeling a little sorry that he would cause Miranda some inconvenience. But, after all, she was insured.

If he was choosing for himself, he'd have taken the Cellini or perhaps the Titian woman who reminded him of Miranda. But the pocket-size bronze was his client's choice.

He'd spent a productive hour or two, after taking Miranda home and changing out of his dinner suit, in the crawl space beneath the institute. There, as he'd known, was the wiring for the building's security system. Alarms, cameras, sensors. All he'd needed was his laptop and a little time to reset the main to his personal specifications.

Now, with his hands in his pockets, he studied a portrait of the Annunciation. Once he had the small mechanism in hand, he ran his thumb over the controls until he felt the proper button. The camera was directly to his right. He smiled when he saw the tiny red light on the camera blink out. In his other pocket he started a stopwatch. And waited.

He judged nearly two minutes passed before the nearest guard's walkie-talkie beeped. Ryan clicked the stopwatch again, unjammed the camera with his other hand.

He left the gallery and stepped outside to use his cell phone.

"Dr. Jones's office. May I help you?"

"Is Dr. Jones available? Ryan Boldari calling."

"One moment, Mr. Boldari."

"Ryan?" Her voice sounded slightly breathless.

"I've just wandered through your galleries." Best that she know, as it was likely they'd be reviewing tapes the following day. "I wanted to tell you I believe my Vasaris are going to have a wonderful temporary home. You should come to New York and see where your Cellini will be staying." He hadn't meant to say that.

"I might do that. Would you like to come up?"

"I would, but I have some appointments. I wondered if you'd have lunch with me tomorrow. How about noon?"

He heard papers rustle. Checking her calendar, he thought. "Yes, noon's fine. Um, the documentation on your Vasaris just came across my desk. You work quickly."

"Beautiful women shouldn't have to wait. I'll see you tomorrow." He broke the connection and suffered a very rare sensation. He recognized it as guilt, only because he couldn't actually recall experiencing it before. Certainly not when it came to women or work.

"Can't be helped," he said softly. As he strode toward the parking lot, he took out his stopwatch. One hundred and ten seconds. Time enough. More than time enough.

He glanced up toward the window where he knew Miranda's office to be. There'd be time for that too. But professional obligations came first.

Ryan spent the next several hours in his suite. He ordered up a quick lunch from room service and spread out his notes. He had the blueprints for the institute on the conference table. The schematics of the security system were on the screen of his laptop.

The Boldari galleries were completely aboveboard and earned a nice, comfortable profit. But they had been built on funds he'd accumulated over the years, beginning as a nimble-fingered, fast-thinking boy on the streets of New York.

Some people were born artists; others were born accountants. Ryan had been born a thief.

Initially he'd picked pockets because, after all, art teachers weren't raking in dough and there had been a lot of mouths to feed in the Boldari household. Later he shifted into second-story work because, well, he was good at it.

For more than a decade he had specialized in art. He had a feel for art, a love of it, and in his heart considered it public domain. If he slipped a painting out of the Smithsonian—and he had—he was simply providing a service to an individual, for which he was well paid. And with his fee he acquired more art to put on display at his galleries for public view and enjoyment.

It seemed to balance things out nicely.

Since he had a flair for electronics and gadgets, why shouldn't he put them to use along with his God-given gift for larceny?

Turning to his laptop, he logged in the measurements he'd taken in the South Gallery. Camera positions were highlighted in red. With a few keystrokes, he requested the machine to calculate the angles, the distance, and the best approach.

As a matter of habit he checked the batteries in his pocket jammer. If he worked with a partner, one could work the computer in the crawl space to bypass locks. He worked alone and needed the jammer for the cameras.

Locks were a relatively simple matter. After spending two nights on the scene, he'd earmarked the side door and had forged a key card. The security code itself had come courtesy of Andrew. The numbers and sequence had been written on a piece of paper behind Andrew's driver's license. It had taken Ryan seconds to lift the wallet, find the numbers, and memorize them, and nothing more than a friendly pat on the back to slide the wallet back into Andrew's pocket.

Ryan figured he would see a profit of eighty-five thousand. Nice work if you can get it, he thought, and tried not to regret that this was his last adventure. He'd given his word on that, and he never went back on a promise. Not to family.

He checked the time, noted he had eight hours before curtain. That left him time for a workout and a short nap. He believed in being alert in mind and body before breaking and entering.

JUST past six Miranda sat alone in her office to compose a letter, when the phone rang. "New England Institute. Dr. Jones."

"Miranda, thank God I caught you. It's Giovanni."

"Giovanni?" She scanned her desk clock, calculated time. "It's after midnight there. Is something wrong?"

"Everything's wrong. It's a disaster. The bronze, the Fiesole Bronze. It's a fake."

"That's ridiculous." She sat straight up, her voice snapping out. "Of course it's not a fake. Who says so?"

"The results came back from Rome. I saw them myself. The bronze was probably cast no more than months ago, if that. The formula was right for the metal, the patina was perfect, but the corrosion levels were all wrong. I don't know how we missed it, Miranda. Your mother asked me who took the X rays, who programmed the computer, who ran the radiation tests. *Cara,* I'm sorry."

"I understand." She was numb now, her mind clouding. "It's my responsibility. I took the tests. I wrote the reports."

"I hate to ask, Miranda, but your mother can't know I spoke with you. She intends to contact you in the morning herself."

"Don't worry, I won't mention your name. I can't talk now. I need to think."

"All right. I'm sorry, so sorry."

Slowly she replaced the receiver and sat, still as a stone. A fake? It couldn't be. Her heart thudded painfully. There had to be a mistake, but she hadn't made it. Because if she had, no one would trust her again. She wouldn't even trust herself.

She closed her eyes, laid her head back.

That was how Andrew found her twenty minutes later. She was as pale as water. "Hey, are you sick?"

"Andrew . . . *The Dark Lady*. It's fake."

He sat on the edge of the desk. "How do you know?"

"Giovanni—he just called. He wasn't supposed to. If Mother finds out, she could fire him for it."

"Are you sure his information's accurate?"

"I don't see how." She crossed her arms over her chest, digging her fingers into her biceps. "I followed procedure. I documented the results. But I wanted it, Andrew. Maybe I wanted it too much."

She pushed away from the desk now and began to pace. "I need to see my data again, and the results. I need to see the retest. I need to see *The Dark Lady*."

"You'll need to talk to Elizabeth."

"I know." She stopped, turned to the window, but saw only the dark. "When the results are made public, I'll be either a fool or a fraud. She was right about that. It'll affect Standjo, her, me." She turned back to face him. "It's going to affect the institute."

"We can handle it." He put his hands on her shoulder. "We'll stand together, just like always."

THE MIDNIGHT WIND WAS bitter as a scorned woman and just as bad-tempered. Ryan didn't mind it. He found it invigorating as he walked the three blocks from where he'd parked his car.

How he would miss this. The planning stage was over, and so was that aspect of his life. Now the execution was approaching, his last. He saw the institute up ahead. It pleased him that his last job would be to break into such a proud and dignified old building.

He crossed to the south side of the structure. His long coat gave him the illusion of bulk, a fedora shadowed his face, and his hair was now a dignified steel gray. Anyone taking notice would see a slightly overweight middle-aged businessman, carrying a briefcase.

Two yards from the door he took his jammer out of his pocket and aimed it at the camera. He saw the red light blink off. The slot accepted his forged key card. Recalling the code from memory, he logged it in and was inside the anteroom within forty-five seconds. He reset the camera, then closed the door, relocked it.

He hung his coat neatly beside the staff's soft-drink machine. His black doeskin gloves went into the pocket. Beneath them he wore surgical gloves. He covered his silver hair with a black cap.

With his eyes adjusted to the dark, he moved to the next door. It had a good lock that required his picks, his penlight, and approximately thirty seconds of his time. He smiled at the music of tumblers clicking, then slipped through and into the hallway.

The first camera was at the end of the corridor, where it split left and right. A shadow among shadows, he slid along the wall beneath it, out of range, and took the left fork. Using his measurements and excellent night vision, he moved to the corner of the gallery, aimed his jammer, and shut down the bothersome camera.

In one part of his brain he counted off seconds. The rest of him moved fast. By the time he crouched in front of the display, his glass cutter was in hand. He made a neat circle, slightly larger than his fist, suctioned it off with barely a tickle of sound, and set it neatly on the top of the cabinet. He wasted no time in admiring his take or taking more than he'd come for. That was for amateurs. He simply reached in, picked up the bronze, and tucked it into the pouch on his belt.

Because he appreciated order and irony, he fitted the circle of glass back into place, then cat-footed it back to the corner. He turned the camera on again and started back the way he came.

By his count it had taken him seventy-five seconds.

When he reached the anteroom, he transferred the bronze to the briefcase. He switched hats, stripped off the surgical gloves, and rolled them neatly into his pocket. He bundled into his coat, keyed himself out, and locked up tidily behind him.

Smooth, slick, and neat, he thought. A good way to end a career.

AT SIX thirty a.m. Miranda was standing beside her brother and a security guard in the South Gallery, staring down at the perfect circle in the glass and the empty space behind it.

Andrew heaved a sigh. "I'll want to review the security tapes for the last twenty-four hours."

"Yes, sir," the guard replied. "So far we've found nothing else missing, but the night chief reported a small problem with two of the cameras. This camera"—he gestured up—"blanked for about a hundred seconds yesterday morning. No one thought much of it. Last night, at about midnight, the camera on the south entrance failed for just under a minute. There were high winds, and the glitch was attributed to weather. This interior camera also went off, for about eighty seconds between midnight and one."

"I see." Andrew stuck his hands in his pockets. "Opinion?"

"My take would be the burglar's a pro. He knew what he was after and didn't mess around."

"He waltzes in," Miranda said with barely suppressed fury, "takes what he wants, then waltzes out."

"Yes, ma'am."

"Will you go out in the lobby and wait for the police, please?" They waited until his footsteps receded.

"I'll have to call Florence." Andrew smiled weakly. "Our little incident might push your problem to the back burner for a while."

Miranda snorted. "If I thought that would happen, I might have stolen the damn thing myself."

"Dr. Jones." A man stepped into the room, his cheeks red with cold, his eyes of pale green narrowly focused under heavy graying brows. "And Dr. Jones. Detective Cook." He held up a gold shield. "Word is you've lost something."

BY NINE o'clock Miranda's head was pounding violently. She had her door closed and was allowing herself ten minutes to indulge in despair and self-pity. But she'd only managed five when her intercom buzzed. "Miranda, I'm sorry. Dr. Standford-Jones is on line one."

She drew a deep breath, straightened her spine. "Thank you, Lori." She punched line one. "Hello, Mother."

"The testing on the Fiesole Bronze has been completed," Elizabeth said without preamble. "Your findings were inaccurate. The bronze is nothing more than a clever attempt to mimic Renaissance style and materials."

"I want to see the results of the second test."

"That is not an option. My priority at this point is to prevent this damage from spreading. Your reputation—and, as a result, my own—is under attack. There are some who believe you purposely doctored tests and results in order to take credit for a find."

"Is that what you believe?"

The hesitation spoke more clearly than the words that followed. "I believe you allowed ambition, haste, and enthusiasm to cloud judgment, logic, and efficiency. I'm sure the media will attempt to contact you over the next few days. You'll be unavailable for comment."

"I have plenty of comments."

"Which you'll keep to yourself. It would be best if you took a leave of absence."

"Would it?" Her hand was starting to tremble. "That's a passive admission of guilt, and I won't do it. I want to see those results." She glanced over in irritation as her fax rang and whined.

"The matter is closed. Transfer me to Andrew's office."

"Oh, I'll be delighted to. He has some news for you." Furious, she jabbed the HOLD button, then buzzed Lori. "Transfer this call to Andrew," she ordered.

She took a deep breath. To distract herself, she walked over and snagged the page from the fax tray.

And her blood iced over.

What's left for you now, Miranda, now that your reputation is in tatters? Nothing. That's all you were, a reputation, a name, a chestful of degrees. Now you're just pitiful. Now you have nothing. Now I have everything.

"Who are you? Who the hell are you?"

It doesn't matter, she told herself. She wouldn't let these mean, petty messages affect her. But she slipped the fax into the drawer with the other, and locked it.

Squaring her shoulders, she marched out of her office.

Detective Cook stood by Lori's desk. "Another moment of your time, Dr. Jones."

"Of course." She composed her features and gestured. "Please come in and sit down. Lori, hold my calls please. Can I get you coffee, Detective?"

"No, thanks." He settled into a chair, took out his notebook. "Dr. Jones—Dr. Andrew Jones—tells me that the piece that was taken was insured for five hundred thousand dollars. Isn't that a lot for a little piece like that?"

"The artist was believed to be a student of Leonardo da Vinci. It was an excellent study of David, circa 1524." She'd tested it herself. And no one had questioned her findings. "Five hundred thousand is well within the range should the piece have been auctioned or sold to a collector."

"Just for my notes would you go over your evening for me?"

"Andrew and I both worked until around seven. I sent my assistant home just after six. I had a long-distance call shortly after."

"From?"

"Florence, Italy. An associate of mine. Andrew dropped by here a bit after that, and we left together. We share the house our grandmother left us. We had a little dinner. I went upstairs around nine."

"And your brother was at home all night."

She had no idea. "Yes, he was. I woke him right after I got the call from security at around six o'clock this morning."

"That little bronze . . . You've got pieces in that gallery worth a lot more, I'd guess. Funny he only took that one piece."

"Yes," she said evenly. "I thought the same myself. How would you explain that, Detective?"

He smiled. "I'd have to say he wanted it." He rose, tucked his notebook away. "That should do it for now. We'll be interviewing your staff, and it's likely I'll need to talk to you again."

"We're more than willing to cooperate." She rose and walked him to the door. When she opened it, she saw Ryan in the outer office.

"Miranda"—he came straight to her, took both of her hands— "I just heard. How much was taken?"

"I— Ryan, this is Detective Cook. He's in charge. Detective, this is Ryan Boldari, an associate."

"Detective." Ryan could have spotted him as a cop from six blocks at a dead run in the opposite direction.

"Mr. Boldari. You work here?"

"No. I own galleries in New York and San Francisco. I'm here on business. Miranda, what can I do to help?"

"There's nothing. I don't know." She battled back tears.

"You should sit down. You're upset."

"Mr. Boldari?" Cook held up a finger as Ryan nudged Miranda back into her office. "What are the names of your galleries?"

"Boldari," he said with an arch of brow. "The Boldari Gallery." He took out a business card. "Excuse me, Detective." It gave him a quiet satisfaction to shut the door in Cook's face. "Sit down, Miranda. Tell me what happened."

She did as he asked, finishing with some spirit. "He had to be a stupid thief. He could have cleaned out that display without much more time and effort."

Ryan reminded himself not to be offended. "Apparently he was selective, but stupid? Difficult to believe a stupid man could get past your security with such ease."

"Well, he might know electronics, but he doesn't know art."

Unable to sit, she rose and flipped on her coffeepot. "The *David* was hardly the best piece we have. I'm just angry he got in."

"As I would be." He walked over to kiss the top of her head. "I'm sure the police will find him."

"Oh, lunch," she remembered. "I won't be able to make it."

"Don't give it a thought. We'll reschedule for my next trip."

"Next trip?"

"I have to leave this evening. I'd hoped to stay another day or two . . . for personal reasons. But I need to get back tonight."

"Oh." She hadn't thought it possible to be any more unhappy. "I'm sorry you can't stay longer. This problem isn't going to change your mind about the exchange, is it?"

"Miranda." He lifted her hands to his lips. Sad eyes, he thought, were so compelling. "Don't be foolish. The Vasaris will be in your hands within the month. Now say good-bye."

She began to, but he stopped her mouth with his. Indulged himself by sliding past her initial resistance, like the thief he was. Their lives separated here, but he wanted to take something with him.

He studied her face. "Good-bye, Miranda," he said with more regret than was comfortable. And left her, certain she would deal with the small inconvenience he'd caused in her life.

By THE time Andrew got off the phone with his mother, he would have betrayed his country for three fingers of Jack Daniel's. She was going to contact their father in Utah. His intercom buzzed.

"Dr. Jones," said Ms. Purdue, "Detective Cook would like to speak with you again as soon as possible. He's downstairs."

He found Cook in the anteroom perusing the offerings of the snack machine. "Is this how you find this thief?" Andrew demanded. "By munching on potato chips?"

"Actually, I'm going for the pretzels. I'm cutting down on fat grams. Why don't we sit here?" He gestured to one of the little tables.

"My sister often works late, alone, in this building, Detective. If she hadn't felt ill last night, I might have lost something a great deal more valuable to me than a bronze."

"I understand your concern. I got family myself." Cook turned to the coffee machine. "How do you take it?"

"Black," Andrew muttered. "Just black."

Cook set the coffee on the table and sat. "Let me relieve your mind a bit, Dr. Jones. Typically a B and E man—especially a smart one—isn't looking to hurt anyone. He won't even carry a weapon, because if he does, that adds years onto his time if he's caught. If your sister had been here, he'd have avoided her."

"You don't know my sister."

"A strong lady, your sister?"

"She's had to be. But she was mugged recently, right in front of our house."

Cook pursed his lips. "When was this?"

"A couple of weeks ago, I guess." He dug fingers through his hair. "He knocked her down, took her purse, her briefcase. They never caught him."

A mugging and a burglary in less than a month. Same victim? It was, Cook decided, interesting. "You say your sister wasn't well last night. What was wrong with her?"

"A problem in Florence," he said briefly. "Some difficulty with our mother. It upset her."

"Your mother's in Italy?"

"She lives there. She heads Standjo, an offshoot of the institute."

"So there's friction between your mother and your sister."

Andrew's eyes went hard. "My family relationships aren't police business."

"Just trying to get the whole picture. This is a family organization, after all. There's no sign of forced entry."

Andrew nearly spilled his coffee. "Excuse me?"

Cook wagged a finger to the exterior and interior doors. "Both doors were locked. You need a key card and a code, correct?"

"Yes. Only department heads can use this entrance."

"I'll need a list of department heads."

"Of course. You think it's someone who works here."

"I don't think anything." He smiled. "It's just procedure."

TECHNOLOGY NEVER FAILED to delight and amaze Cook.

This particular Sunday he'd come to the station house on a whim. He'd run a computer check, searching for like crimes. Now he had a pattern in front of him. He had six likes over a period of ten years.

New York, Chicago, San Francisco, Boston, Kansas City, Atlanta. A museum or gallery in each of those cities had reported a break-in and the loss of one item. And no arrest had been made.

Slick, he thought. The guy was slick. Could be he enlisted a guard as an inside source. It was something to check out.

It wouldn't hurt to see where the Joneses had been during the dates of the other thefts.

COMING back to the house from the health club, where she had tried to sweat out her depression, Miranda found Andrew nursing a hangover. She was on her way upstairs when the doorbell chimed.

"Let me take your jacket, Detective Cook," she heard Andrew say. Cook? On a Sunday afternoon?

Andrew led Cook into the parlor. Miranda entered and offered him a polite smile. "Do you have news for us?"

"Nothing solid, Dr. Jones. Just a loose end or two."

"Let's sit down. What can we do for you?"

"I wonder if you could tell me where you were, where both of you were, last November. First week."

"Last November." It was such an odd question. Andrew scratched his head over it. "I was here in Jones Point. I didn't do any traveling last fall. Why is that important, Detective?"

"Just clearing up details. Were you here as well, Dr. Jones?"

"I was in D.C. for a few days. Some consult work at the Smithsonian. I'd have to get my desk calendar to be sure."

"Would you mind?" He smiled apologetically.

"All right." She couldn't see the point, but she couldn't see the harm either. "It's up in my office."

When she left the room, Cook asked, "You do much traveling?"

"The institute keeps me pretty close to home. Miranda's the frequent flier. She does a lot of consulting."

"According to my records," Miranda said as she came back in, "I was in Washington from November third through the seventh. I stayed at The Four Seasons."

And the burglary in San Francisco had occurred in the early hours of the fifth, Cook recalled. "Would you have where you were in June in that book? Say the third week."

"Of course." She flipped back to June. "I was at the institute the entire month. Summer classes. You taught a couple yourself, didn't you, Andrew?"

"Yeah. Oriental Art of the Twelfth Century. We can easily get the exact dates for you, Detective."

"Fine. Appreciate it."

"We'll cooperate." Miranda's voice was brisk. "But I think we have the right to know what avenues you're investigating."

"No problem. I'm checking out a series of burglaries that match the profile of yours." He rose. "I appreciate your time." He turned away, turned back. "I wonder if I could borrow that datebook of yours, Dr. Jones."

Miranda hesitated but held the slim leather book out to him. "You're welcome to it."

"I'll have mine messengered over to you," Andrew said.

"That would be a big help."

"I'll show you out," Miranda said.

She shut the door loudly at Cook's back and, fuming, stalked back into the parlor. It didn't surprise her to see Andrew pouring himself a drink. "The man thinks we're thieves. He thinks we're bouncing around the country breaking into museums."

"Would be kind of fun, wouldn't it?"

"This isn't a game, Andrew. We're under investigation. The press is bound to get ahold of some of this."

"Miranda"—he spoke softly—"I'm sorry. You're right."

"I'm going to make a pot roast," she announced as she walked toward the kitchen.

"A pot roast." His mood lifted dramatically. "With the little potatoes and carrots?"

"You peel the potatoes. Keep me company, Andrew." She wanted to get him away from the bottle. "I don't want to be alone."

"Sure." He set the glass down. It was empty anyway. And slipped an arm over her shoulders.

THE pot roast had done its work, Miranda thought as she prepared for bed. Good, solid meat and potatoes, conversation with Andrew. Maybe he'd had more wine with dinner than she liked, but at least he hadn't been alone.

She climbed into bed, then picked up her volume of bedtime reading. By midnight she was dreamlessly asleep.

Deeply enough that she didn't hear the door open, close again. She didn't hear the footsteps cross the room toward the bed.

She awoke with a jolt, a gloved hand hard over her mouth, another clamped firmly at her throat, and a man's voice softly threatening in her ear.

"I could strangle you."

THE THIEF
Chapter Four

HER mind simply froze.

"Lie still and keep quiet," he hissed. "However much I'd like to hurt you, I won't. You won't scream, will you?" His fingers gentled on her throat, with a shivering caress of thumb. "It'd bruise your Yankee pride."

She muttered something against his gloved hand. He removed it, but kept the other on her throat. "What do you want?"

"I want to kick your excellent behind from here to Chicago. You screwed up, Dr. Jones."

"I don't know what you're talking about. Let go of me. I won't scream." She wouldn't, because Andrew might hear and might come roaring in. And whoever was currently pinning her to the bed was probably armed.

In response, he sat on the bed beside her and, still holding her in place, reached out for the switch on the bedside lamp. She blinked rapidly against the flash of light, then stared wide-eyed.

He was dressed in black—snug jeans, boots, a turtleneck, and bomber jacket. His face was as strikingly handsome as ever, but his eyes weren't warm and appealing as she remembered. They were hot, impatient, and unmistakably dangerous.

"Ryan," she managed. "What are you doing here?"

"Trying to clean up the mess you made."

"I see." Perhaps he'd had some sort of breakdown. It was vital to remain calm. She nudged his hand away from her throat and sat up, primly tugging at the collar of her pajamas. "How did you get in?"

"The way I usually get into houses that aren't my own. I picked your locks. You really ought to have better."

"You picked the locks?" She blinked. "You broke in?"

"That's right." He toyed with the hair that tumbled over her shoulder. He was absolutely crazy about her hair. "It's what I do."

"But you're a businessman. You're an art patron. You're— Why, you're not Ryan Boldari at all, are you?"

"I certainly am." For the first time, that wicked smile flashed. "And have been since my sainted mother named me thirty-two years ago in Brooklyn. Up to my association with you, that name has stood for something." The smile vanished into a snarl. "Reliability, perfection. The bronze was a fake."

"The bronze?" The blood drained out of her face. "How do you know about the bronze?"

"I know about it because I stole it. Or maybe you're thinking of the bronze in Florence. I got wind of that yesterday—after my client reamed me out for passing him a forgery. A forgery!" He sprang off the bed and began to pace the room. "Over twenty years without a blemish, and now this. And all because I trusted you."

"Trusted me." She shoved up to her knees. "You stole from me!"

"So what? What I took's worth maybe a hundred bucks as a paperweight." He stepped close again. "How many other pieces are you passing off in that museum of yours?"

She was off the bed like a bullet. At five eleven she was no fly-weight, and Ryan got the full impact of her well-toned body and well-oiled temper. He shifted his body to break her fall—a gesture he instantly regretted as they hit the floor. He rolled over and pinned her flat.

"You stole from me." She bucked, wriggled. "You used me. You came on to me." Oh, and that was the worst of it.

"The last was a side benefit." He clamped her wrists with his hands. "You're very attractive. It was no trouble at all."

"You're a thief. You're nothing but a common thief."

"I'm a really good thief. Now we can sit down and work this out, or we can lie here and keep wrestling. But I'm going to warn you that even in those incredibly ugly pajamas, you're an appealing handful. Up to you, Miranda."

She went very still. "Get off me."

"Okay." He eased off, then rocked up to his feet. Though he offered her a hand, she slapped it away and pushed herself up.

She snatched her robe from the foot of the bed. "What are you going to do now? Shoot me, then clean out the house?"

"I don't shoot people. I'm a thief, not a thug."

"Then you're remarkably stupid. The moment you're gone, I'm going to call Detective Cook." She tugged on the robe.

The robe, he decided, was as amazingly unattractive as the pajamas. "If you call the cops, you'd have to explain why the stolen item was insured for six figures and was worth pocket change."

"You're lying. I authenticated that piece myself."

"Yeah, and the Fiesole Bronze was cast by Michelangelo." He smirked at her. "Now sit down. Listen. You owe me, Miranda."

"I—" She almost choked. "I *owe* you?"

"I had a spotless record. Every time I took on a job, I satisfied the client. And this was my last one, damn it. I had to refund my client's fee." He spoke calmly. "I want the Donatello."

"Excuse me. You want what?"

"The small Venus that was in the display with your forged David. I want you to give it to me, and if it's authentic, we'll consider this matter closed."

"You're out of your mind."

"If you don't, I'll arrange for the *David* to find its way on the market again. When the insurance company recovers it and has it tested, your incompetence will be uncovered. That, on top of your recent disaster in Florence, would put a snug cap on your career."

"Don't blackmail me. The bronze is not a fake," Miranda said.

"Just can't admit you made a mistake, can you?"

"I couldn't have made a mistake. Not that kind of a mistake." Hot tears rose inside her like a tide.

"Hold on. Let's not get emotional."

"I'm not going to cry. I'm not going to cry," she repeated.

"This is business, Miranda. Let's keep it on that level, and we'll both be happier."

"Business." The absurdity of the statement had stemmed the tide of tears. "All right, Mr. Boldari. You say the bronze is a fake. I say it's not. You say I won't report this to the police. I say I will. What are you going to do about it?"

He studied her a moment. "Okay, get dressed."

"Why?"

"We'll go to the lab. You can test it again, in front of me, satisfy the first level of business." He gestured toward the leather bag he'd set just inside the door. "I brought it with me, with the idea of ramming it down your throat. But reason prevailed."

"I'm not taking you into the institute."

"You're a logical woman. Be logical. I have the bronze and your reputation in my hands. You want a chance of getting the first back and salvaging the second. I'm giving it to you. That's the deal, Dr. Jones. Be smart. Take the deal."

She needed to know, didn't she? To be sure. And once she was sure, she would toss him to the police before he could blink those pretty eyes of his.

IT WASN'T POSSIBLE THAT SHE was driving through the chilly Maine night with a thief, intending to break into her own lab and conduct clandestine tests on a stolen bronze. She hit the brakes and swung her car to the shoulder of the road. "I can't do this. It's ridiculous, not to mention illegal. I'm calling the police."

"Fine." Ryan shrugged as she reached for her car phone. "You do that. Then you can explain to the insurance company how you expected them to pay you five hundred grand for a fake."

"It's not a fake," she said between her teeth.

"Prove it." His grin flashed in the dark. "Call your security. Tell them you and your brother are coming in to do some work in the lab. Go on, Miranda. You want to know the truth, don't you?" He leaned over, kissed her lightly.

She elbowed him aside and jabbed in the number. The cameras would be on, she thought. He'd never pass as Andrew. Her security chief would call the police, and Ryan Boldari would be cuffed and penned and out of her life.

"This is Dr. Miranda Jones. My brother and I are on our way in." She disconnected, sniffed. She had him now, she decided, and he'd turned the key himself. "They're expecting me and will switch off the alarm when I get there."

He stretched out his legs as she pulled onto the road again. "I'm doing this for you, you know."

"I can't tell you how much I appreciate it."

"No thanks necessary." Grinning, he unhooked his seat belt and turned to reach into the back seat for the bag he'd tossed there. He took out a ski cap and pulled it down low over his head. Next came a long black scarf of cashmere that he wrapped around his neck and over the lower part of his face.

"You'll go in, head to the lab like you would normally. Andrew's a little taller than I am." He unrolled a long, dark coat. "Shouldn't matter. They'll see what they expect to see. People always do."

When she got out of the car, she had to admit he was right. She might have taken him for Andrew herself. The body language, the gait, the slight hunch in the shoulders were perfect.

She yanked her card through the slot with one irritable flick of the wrist. After a pause she punched in her code.

Ryan opened the doors himself, laying one brotherly hand on her shoulder, guiding her down the corridors, down the stairs, to the lab doors. Again she keyed them in.

He turned on the lights. "Run your tests," he said, peeling off his coat. He kept his gloves on to take out the bronze and hand it to her.

He watched her take a pair of wire-rimmed glasses out of a drawer and slip them on. He'd been right about that, he mused. The sexy scholar. Tucking that thought away, he made himself comfortable while she took the bronze to a workstation.

Miranda's brows were knitted as she finally straightened from the microscope. "This bronze is a forgery," she said.

"Well, well, Dr. Jones," he murmured, "you surprise me."

"This is not the bronze I authenticated three years ago. I don't know what you thought you could prove, bringing me this forgery, taking us through this ridiculous charade."

"That's the bronze I took from the South Gallery," he said evenly. "I stole it in good faith."

"Oh, for God's sake. I'm calling security."

He grabbed her arm. "Maybe it was an honest mistake, but—"

"I didn't make a mistake." Her voice shook. "I can prove it. I have the records for the tests on the original bronze."

He shook his head and followed her into a room lined with file cabinets. "The weight was wrong," she said, fumbling with keys to unlock a drawer. "It was too heavy but— Where is the file?" She slammed the drawer shut, unlocked another, then another. "It's not here. The files aren't here. They're missing." Fighting for calm, she closed the drawer. "You took them."

"To what purpose?" he asked with what he considered saintly patience. "Look, if I could get in here and take a fake, I could have taken anything I wanted."

"I have to think." Logical, be logical, she ordered herself.

He'd stolen the bronze, and the bronze was fake. What was the point in stealing a fake, then bringing it back? None. If it had been genuine, why would he be here? He wouldn't. Logic, when properly applied, was amazingly simple.

"Someone beat you to it," she said quietly. "Someone beat you to it and replaced it with a forgery."

She turned to him, seeing by the considering look on his face that he was likely reaching the same conclusion.

"Well, Dr. Jones"—he angled his head to study her—"what are we going to do about it?"

MIRANDA decided to accept that it was a day for abnormal behavior when she found herself sitting in a truck stop off Route 1 at six a.m. with a pot of coffee, two thick brown mugs, and a pair of laminated menus.

"What are we doing here?"

"Having breakfast." He kicked back and studied the menu.

She took a deep breath. "I don't have time to sit in some truck stop trading witticisms with a thief."

"So far you haven't been that witty. Are you going to run into anyone you know here?"

"Of course not."

"Exactly. We need to eat, and we need to talk." He shot a smile at their waitress when she came over, pad in hand. "I'll go for the half-stack of hotcakes, eggs over easy, and side of bacon, please."

"You got it, cap'n. How 'bout you, honey?"

"I . . ." Resigned, Miranda scanned the menu in search of something nonlethal. "Just, um, oatmeal. Do you have skim milk for that?"

"I'll see what I can do and be back to you in a jiff."

"Okay, let's outline our situation," Ryan continued. "Three years ago you acquired a small bronze statue of David. My research indicates this came through your father, from a private dig outside of Rome. You authenticated it."

"Your research is correct."

"Who worked with you?"

"Andrew. My father was in and out of the lab, checking the progress. John Carter," she added. "He's lab manager."

"So he'd have had access to it. Who else?"

"Almost anyone working in the lab during that period."

"We'll assume that anyone who worked in the lab had access to the files. You'll need to get a list of names from personnel."

"Will I really?"

"You want to find it? Whoever replaced the statue had to have access to the original to make the copy. The simplest way to do that would be to make a silicone mold, a wax reproduction from that. You'd need the original to make the mold."

"This isn't skim milk," she complained, frowning at the little pitcher the waitress had brought with the oatmeal.

"Live dangerously." He dashed salt on his eggs. "Here's how I see it. Someone in the lab at that time saw the way your tests were leaning. It's a nice little piece, one a collector would pay a fair price for. So this person—maybe he has debts or he's angry at your family—makes the mold some night. If he doesn't know how to cast it himself, he certainly knows someone who does. More, he knows how to make the bronze appear to be, on the surface, several centuries old. When it's done, he switches the pieces just before it's moved to display. Nobody's the wiser. How long was the bronze in the lab?"

"I don't know for sure. Two weeks, maybe three."

"More than enough." Ryan gestured with a slice of bacon before biting it. "If I were you, I'd run tests on some of my other pieces."

"Others?"

"Don't look so devastated, darling. I'm going to help you."

"Help me." She pressed her fingers to her eyes. "Why?"

"Because I want that bronze. I guaranteed it to my client."

She dropped her hands. "You're going to help me get it back so you can steal it again?"

"I've got a vested interest. Finish your breakfast. We've got work to do." He picked up his coffee and grinned at her. "Partner."

PARTNER. The word made her shudder. Perhaps she was too tired to think clearly, but at the moment she couldn't see her way to recovering her property without him. He'd used her, she remembered, as she unlocked the front door of her house. Now she would use him. Then she would see that he spent the next twenty years of his life taking group showers in a federal institution.

"Andrew's left for work by now." Ryan noted by his watch it was eight fifteen. "Give your assistant a call. Tell her you're not going to make it in today." He moved into the parlor and made himself at home by stacking kindling for a fire. "Tell her to get copies of personnel records for the lab, going back three years. Have her shoot them to your computer here."

Within seconds the kindling was crackling. He chose two logs and placed them on the fire with the efficiency of an Eagle Scout.

When he rose, turned, her smile was as sharp as an unsheathed blade. "Is there anything else I can do?"

"Honey, somebody's got to be in charge. I know a lot more about larceny than you do. Make the call, and let's get to work."

By nine thirty she was in her home office, calling up data on her desktop. They sat hip to hip at her desk, scanning names.

"Looks like you had an unusually large turnover about eighteen months ago," he pointed out.

"Yes. My mother revamped her lab in Florence. Several staff members transferred there."

"I'm surprised you didn't."

She shot the file to the printer. A hard copy would mean she didn't have to sit next to him. "It wasn't an option. Andrew and I run the institute. My mother runs Standjo."

"I see. Some friction between you and Mama?"

"My family relationships are none of your concern."

"How about your father? Are you Daddy's little girl?"

She laughed before she could stop herself, then rose to retrieve the printout. "I've never been anyone's little girl."

"That's too bad," he said, and meant it.

"My family isn't the issue here." She sat on the raspberry-colored love seat and tried to concentrate on the names.

"They could be. Yours is a family-run business. Maybe someone took a shot at your family by taking the bronze."

"Your Italian's showing," she said dryly.

"The Irish are every bit as interested in revenge, darling. Tell me about the people on the list."

"John Carter. Lab manager. Got his doctorate from Duke. He's worked at the institute for sixteen years. Married, two children. His wife's a lawyer. Money isn't a problem for them." She stifled a yawn and snuggled down into the cushions.

"Take a nap, Miranda."

"I'm all right. Who's next? Oh, Elise. My brother's ex-wife."

"Ugly divorce?"

"I don't imagine they're ever pretty. She was John's assistant here. Now she's lab manager for my mother."

"What did she want? Snazzy clothes, a big, fancy house?"

"She wanted Andrew's attention," Miranda mumbled and pillowed her head on her hands. "She wanted him to stay sober. It's the Jones curse. We're relationship-jinxed. I have to rest my eyes."

"Sure, go ahead."

He went back to studying the list and added three names: Andrew Jones, Charles Jones, and Elizabeth Standford-Jones.

He rose, took the chenille throw from the back of the love seat, and tossed it over her. While she slept, he made a call to New York. There was no point in having a brother who was a genius with computers if you didn't use him once in a while.

"Patrick? It's Ryan. I've got a little hacker job. Interested?" He laughed. "Yeah, it pays."

MIRANDA awoke with a jolt. The buzzer on the front door sounded repeatedly. She tossed back the throw and hurried out of the room.

It was surprising enough to see Ryan at the front door. But it was a shock to see her father standing on the doorstep.

"Father, I didn't know you were coming to Maine."

"Just got in." He was a tall man, trim, browned by the sun. His hair was full and thick and shiny as polished steel. It matched his trim beard and mustache and suited his narrow face. His eyes—the same deep blue as his daughter's—studied Ryan.

"I see you have company. I hope I'm not intruding."

Ryan offered a hand. "Dr. Jones, what a pleasure. Rodney J. Pettebone. I'm an associate of your daughter's—and a friend, I hope. Just in from London." Drawing Charles neatly inside, he continued, "Miranda's been kind enough to give me a bit of her time while I'm here. Miranda, dear." He held out a hand and gave a ridiculously adoring smile. Then to Charles he said, "Can I take your coat, Dr. Jones?"

She wasn't sure which baffled her more, the puppy dog smile or the upper-crust British accent that was rolling off his tongue.

"Yes, thank you. Miranda, I was just at the institute. I was told you weren't feeling well today."

"We've been caught, darling." Ryan took her hand, squeezing it hard. "I'm sure your father will understand."

"No," Miranda said definitely, "he won't."

"It's completely my fault, Dr. Jones." He kissed Miranda's fingers lovingly. "I persuaded your daughter to take the day off."

"I see." Obvious disapproval flickered in Charles's eyes.

"I was about to make some tea," Miranda said. "If you'll excuse us, Father. Rodney, you'll give me a hand, won't you?"

"Love to." He beamed a smile.

"Have you lost your mind?" she hissed as she slammed through the kitchen door. "You gave my father the impression we were spending the day playing patty-cake." She grabbed the kettle from the stove and took it to the sink.

"Patty-cake." He wrapped his arms around her. He didn't even mind the elbow in the ribs. "You're so cute, Miranda."

"I am not cute, and I am not happy with this ridiculous lie." Teeth clenched, she warmed the teapot. "Why a British twit, for heaven's sake?"

"I thought he might be your type." He reached into a cupboard. "I'll get two cups. Rodney perceives your father wants to have a private chat with you."

"Coward," she muttered as he left and went up the back stairs.

She arranged the pot and the cups and saucers on the tray and carried it out to the parlor, where her father sat in front of the fireplace. He was so handsome. When she'd been young, she'd thought he looked like a picture out of a fairy tale. Not a prince, but a wizard—wise and dignified. She'd so desperately wanted him to love her. To give her piggyback rides and cuddle her in his lap. Instead, she'd had to settle for a mild and often absent kind of affection.

She sighed. "I asked Rodney to give us a few minutes alone," she began. "I imagine you want to talk about the burglary." She set the tray down, settled into a chair, and poured as she had been taught. Hands steady, she held out his cup.

"It's very upsetting, Miranda. I've had to leave my project at a very key time to come here. Obviously our security is not at an acceptable level. Your brother is responsible for that."

"This isn't Andrew's fault. He's doing a marvelous job. Class attendance is up. Gate receipts have increased. The quality of our acquisitions over the past five years has been astonishing."

Oh, and it galled so to have to defend and justify when the man across from her had walked away from the responsibilities of the institute as easily as he had the responsibilities of family.

"And now we have our first theft in more than a generation. It can't be overlooked, Miranda."

"No, but the improvements we've made can be overlooked."

"No one's faulting your enthusiasm." He waved it aside. "However, this must be dealt with. And with your misstep in Florence added to it, it leaves us in a difficult position. I can tell you, your mother is very displeased. If the press hadn't been notified—"

"I never talked to the press." She rose now, unable to sit, unable to pretend she was calm. "I *never* discussed *The Dark Lady* with anyone outside of the lab. Why would I?"

He paused a moment, set his teacup aside. He hated confrontations. "I believe you. It hardly changes the situation, however. The publicity must be downplayed. Through circumstances you're at the center of the storm, so to speak."

He stood up. "Starting today, you're to take a month's personal leave. You may clear up any pending business, but it would be best if you do that from here, within the next forty-eight hours."

"You might as well paint a G for guilty on my forehead."

"You're overreacting, as usual."

Tears swam into her eyes. "And you're walking away, as usual."

"I'll be at the Regency until tomorrow if you need to reach me."

"I've never been able to reach you," she said. "I'll get your coat."

He followed her into the foyer. "You should do a little traveling. Perhaps your, ah, young man would join you."

"My what?" She took his coat out of the closet, then glanced up the stairs and began to laugh. "Oh, sure. I bet old Rodney would just love to go traveling with me."

She waved her father out of the house, then sat on the bottom step and laughed like a loon—until she started to weep.

A MAN who had three sisters knew all about women's tears. There were the lovely ones that could slide down a cheek like small liquid diamonds and reduce a man to begging. There were hot, angry ones that induced a wise man to run for cover. And there were those that were hidden so deep in the heart that when they broke loose, they were a deluge of pain beyond any man's comfort.

So he let her be, let her curl into herself on the bottom step while those heart-born tears raged. All he could do was give her privacy.

When those harsh, ripping sobs quieted, he went to the hall closet and held out a jacket. "Here. Let's get some air."

"I'd prefer to be alone."

"You've been alone long enough." He grabbed his own jacket, shrugged it on, then pulled her to her feet and out the front door.

The air was bracing, the sun strong enough to sting her sore eyes. Humiliation was beginning to seep through.

"This is a great spot," he said conversationally. "Privacy, a great view, the smell of the sea. Did you grow up here?"

"No." Her head felt stuffy from the weeping. She wanted to go back inside, take some aspirin, lie down. But he pulled her along the cliff path. "It was my grandmother's."

"Makes more sense. I couldn't see your father choosing to live here as an adult. Wouldn't suit him at all."

"You don't know my father."

"Sure I do." The wind whipped, circling them as they climbed smooth, rounded rocks. "He's pompous. He's arrogant. He didn't hear you," he added when they'd reached the ledge that speared out over the sea, "because he doesn't know how to listen."

"Obviously you do." She jerked her hand from his. "I don't know why it should surprise me that someone who steals for a living should eavesdrop on a private conversation."

"I don't know either. But the point is, you've been left to twist in the wind. What are you going to do about it? Show them what you're made of. The institute isn't the only place you can shine."

"Do you think there's any major museum or lab that would have me after this? The Fiesole Bronze has ruined me."

Defeated, she sat on the rocks. "The minute I saw it, understood what the project was, I was totally entrenched in it. I'd authenticate it, I'd prove how smart I was, and my mother would applaud with sentimental enthusiasm and pride." She dropped her head on her knees. "That's pathetic."

"No, it's not. I still remember the opening of my New York gallery. The moment my parents walked inside. My father in his good suit—the one he always wore to weddings and funerals—and my mother in a new dress. I remember the look on their faces. Sentimental enthusiasm and pride. It mattered to me."

She looked out to sea and sighed. "If I could just go back and see where I went wrong." She pressed her fingers to her eyes. "Test it again like I did the *David*." Slowly she lowered her hands. "Like the *David*. Oh, my God!" She sprang to her feet so quickly, for one wild moment Ryan feared she meant to jump.

"Hold on." He took a firm hold of her hand as he got to his feet. "You're a little too close to the edge to suit me."

"It's like the *David*." She grabbed his jacket. "Someone switched it. What the lab in Rome had was a forgery, but it wasn't the same bronze. It was a copy."

"That's a pretty big leap, Dr. Jones."

"It fits. It makes sense. I wasn't thinking clearly. When you're told you're wrong often enough, you believe it. Even when you aren't wrong." She began walking back toward the house, letting the wind clear her head. "I'd have gone on believing it if it hadn't been for the *David*."

"Good thing I stole it."

She slanted a look at him. He was matching his pace to hers. "Apparently. Why did you steal that particular piece?"

"I told you. I had a client."

"Who?"

"Really, Miranda, some things are sacred. And he would hardly have commissioned me to steal a forgery."

"I still believe whoever replaced the *David* replaced *The Dark Lady*. And I'd be able to solidify that conclusion if I was able to examine both pieces and compare them."

"Okay."

"Okay, what?"

"Let's do it."

She stopped. "Do what?"

"Compare them. We have one. It's just a matter of getting the other."

"Don't be ridiculous. I'm not flying to Italy, breaking into a government facility, and stealing a worthless copy." She saw the gleam in his eye. "Why would you bother?"

"If you're right, it would bring me a step closer to the original *David*. I have my reputation to salvage too." And if *The Dark Lady* was real, he'd be a step closer to that as well. What a marvelous addition she would make to his private collection.

"I'm not breaking the law."

"You already are. You're standing here with me, fully aware I'm holding stolen property. You're an accessory after the fact." He gave her a friendly kiss on top of the head.

He checked his watch. "You go up and pack. I need to call my cousin Joey."

Her head was reeling. "Your cousin Joey?"

"He's a travel agent. He'll get us on the first flight out. We should be in New York in time for dinner. Don't forget your passport—and your laptop. We'll want to finish going through those personnel files."

IT WAS nearly six before Andrew managed to get home. He'd tried to call Miranda half a dozen times but had only reached their answering machine. He wasn't certain what shape he'd find her in—manic with temper or desolate with hurt.

But all he found was a note on the refrigerator.

Andrew,

I'm sure you're aware I've been ordered to take a leave of absence from the institute. I'm sorry to leave you in the lurch at a time like this. I'll be gone for a couple of weeks. Please, don't worry. I'll be in touch when I can.

Love,
Miranda

"I DON'T see why we didn't just fly to Florence," Miranda said as Ryan took the wheel of a natty little BMW and navigated out of La Guardia Airport. "If we're going to do something this insane, there's no point in taking a detour."

"It isn't a detour. It's a scheduled stop. I need my things."

"You could have bought clothes in Italy."

"I probably will. If the Italians dressed the world, it would be a much more attractive place. However, there are certain things I need that can't be bought in the retail market."

"Your burglary tools," she muttered. "Well, there's no reason to go to Brooklyn."

"Sure there is. I miss my mother's cooking. You're going to love her linguine. And I have a couple of things to straighten out, family-wise, before I go to Italy. My sister's going to want shoes. She's addicted to Ferragamo."

"You steal shoes for your sister?"

"Please. I'm not a shoplifter."

"There's no reason for *me* to go to Brooklyn. Why don't you just drop me off at whatever hotel I'm staying in?"

"You're not staying in a hotel. You're staying with me."

Her eyes narrowed. "I certainly am not."

"We're joined at the hip until this is finished. Your conscience is going to kick in from time to time and tempt you to call a cop and confess all." He reached over to pat her hand. "Just consider me the bad angel on your shoulder, kicking the good angel in the face whenever he starts spouting about honesty and truth."

"I have no intention of sleeping with you."

"Now you've done it." The laughter in his voice put her teeth on edge. "It's been my lifelong dream, and now it's crushed."

"I despise you," she hissed, then stared out the side window and ignored him for the rest of the drive.

SHE didn't know what she'd expected, but it hadn't been the pretty two-level house with yellow trim in a quiet neighborhood and a big brown dog sleeping in the yard.

"Come on, Mama's likely got some antipasto ready."

The dog uncurled itself, let out one bark that echoed like a cannon blast, then jumped lovingly on Ryan.

"Not afraid of dogs, are you?"

"No. I like them," she replied as Ryan pushed open the front door. Through it emerged the sound of the evening news, voices raised in bitter argument, the delicious aroma of roasted garlic and spices, and a large spotted cat.

"Home, sweet home," Ryan said, and pulled her into the melee.

"If you can't behave like a decent human being, I don't want you to speak to any of my friends ever again."

"All I did was mention that if she had some basic plastic surgery, she would improve her sex life."

"You're a pig, Patrick."

"I'm trying to hear the news here. Take it outside."

"This," Miranda said, "is obviously a bad time."

"No, this is normal," Ryan assured her.

"Hey, Ry!"

The man—boy, really, Miranda noted—with a grin nearly as lethal as Ryan's, took a few gangly strides and punched Ryan in the shoulder. A sign, Miranda assumed, of affection.

With equal affection Ryan caught him in a headlock for the introduction. "My baby brother, Patrick. Miranda Jones."

Before she could answer, the young woman Patrick had been arguing with stepped up. She gave Miranda a long, measuring look as she slipped her arms proprietarily around Ryan. "Hello, Miranda. I'm Colleen." She had the onyx-and-gold good looks of the Boldaris and a sharp, assessing gleam in her eyes.

"It's nice to meet you both," Miranda said.

"You gonna leave the girl at the door, or you bringing her in so I can get a look at her?" This boomed out of the living room.

"I'm bringing her in, Papa."

Giorgio Boldari rose out of his easy chair and politely muted the television. Ryan hadn't gotten his build from his father, Miranda decided. The man who studied her was short and stocky and sported a graying mustache over his unsmiling lips.

No one spoke. Miranda's ears began to buzz with nerves.

"You're not Italian, are you?" he asked at length.

"No, I'm not."

Giorgio pursed his lips, let his gaze skim over her face. "Hair like that, you probably got some Irish in you."

"My father's mother was a Riley."

He smiled then. "This one's got a classy look to her, Ry. Get the girl some wine, Colleen." He enveloped Ryan in a fierce bear hug. "You should stay home more."

"I'm working on it. Mama in the kitchen?"

"Yeah, yeah. Maureen! Ryan's here with his girl. She's a looker."

The house was cluttered, full of light and art. She saw Ryan had been right about his mother's watercolors. The three dreamy New York street scenes on the wall were lovely.

"Welcome to the Boldaris'." Ryan took two glasses off the tray Colleen had brought in and handed Miranda one. "Your life may never be the same." She was beginning to believe him.

Even as she took the first sip, a woman hurried into the room, wiping her hands on an apron. Maureen Boldari was a good three inches taller than her husband, slim as a willow, and possessed of striking black Irish looks. Her vivid blue eyes sparkled with pleasure as she opened her arms.

"There's my boy. Come kiss your mama."

Ryan obeyed, lifting her off her feet as he did so, making her let loose a rich, hearty laugh. "Patrick, Colleen, stop that bickering before I give the pair of you the back of my hand. Giorgio, turn that television off. Ryan, introduce me to your young lady."

"Yes, ma'am. Maureen Boldari, the love of my life, meet Dr. Miranda Jones. Pretty, isn't she, Mama?"

"Yes, she is. Welcome to our home, Miranda."

"It's very kind of you to have me, Mrs. Boldari."

"Good manners," Maureen said with a brisk nod. "Ryan, show Miranda where she can freshen up."

Ryan led her out of the living room, down a hall, into a small pink-and-white powder room.

She grabbed his shirt. "You told them we were involved."

"We are involved."

"You know what I mean. Your girl? That's ridiculous."

"I didn't tell them you were my girl. I'm thirty-two. They want me married and making babies. They assume."

"It's deceitful. Not that such niceties as honesty matter to you."

"I'm always honest with my family."

"Undoubtedly your mother is very proud of her son the thief."

"Of course she is. I don't lie to my mother. Now hurry up in there, will you?" He gave her a nudge into the powder room. "I'm hungry."

He wasn't hungry for long. There was enough food to feed a small and starving third world army and enough wine to float a battleship. Conversation never lagged. In fact, if you didn't heave your words out fast and furiously, there was no room for them. Ryan had been right about one thing. Miranda loved his mother's linguine.

She was brought up to date on the family. Michael, the second son, ran Boldari Gallery, San Francisco. He was married to his college sweetheart and had two children.

"You like children?" Maureen asked her.

"Um, yes."

"Center your life, children do. Celebrate the love that brings a man and woman together." Maureen passed a basket of bread to Miranda. "Take my Mary Jo." And Miranda was treated to the virtues of the eldest daughter, who owned a boutique in Manhattan *and* had three children. Then there was Bridgit, who'd taken a sabbatical from a publishing career to stay at home with her baby daughter.

"All my children went to college. Patrick's a freshman. He knows all about computers."

"Really." It seemed a safer topic. "It's a fascinating field."

"It's like playing games for a living," Patrick replied. "Oh, Ry, I've got some of the data you asked me to access."

"Great."

"What data?" Colleen narrowed her eyes suspiciously at Ryan.

"Colleen"—Maureen's voice was mild, with honed steel beneath— "we have company. Help me clear the table."

"We're going to discuss this," Colleen said between her teeth, but rose obediently to clear plates.

"Let me help." Miranda started to rise and was waved back.

"Guests don't clear. You sit."

"Don't worry about Colleen," Patrick said the moment she was out of earshot. "We'll handle her."

"Shut up, Patrick." Though Ryan smiled over at Miranda, she caught a glint of discomfort in his eyes. "I don't think we mentioned what Colleen does."

"No, you didn't."

"She's a cop." With a sigh, Ryan rose. "I'll give them a hand with the coffee."

"Oh, wonderful." Blindly Miranda reached for her wine.

SHE kept out of the way, obeying the house rules by retiring to the living room after dessert. Since Giorgio was busy grilling her on why she wasn't married, her mind was well engaged. No one seemed bothered by the angry words coming out of the kitchen.

Colleen stormed out. "You promised, Ry. You gave your word."

"I'm keeping it." Obviously frustrated, he dragged a hand through his hair. "I'm just finishing what I started, baby."

"What does she have to do with it?" She jabbed a finger at Miranda.

"Colleen, it's not polite to point," Giorgio told her.

Tossing something uncomplimentary in Italian over her shoulder, Colleen strode out of the house.

"Damn it." Ryan blew out a breath, offered Miranda an apologetic smile. "Be right back."

"Um, I'll go see if Mrs. Boldari needs any help after all." Miranda escaped into what she hoped was some area of sanity.

The kitchen was big and airy, with bright counters and a sparkling white floor. Dozens of crayon pictures crowded the front of the refrigerator. There was a bowl of fresh fruit on the table. Normality, Miranda decided.

"I hoped you'd bend your rule and let me give you a hand."

"Sit." Maureen gestured to the table. "Have coffee. I should wallop them both for making a scene in front of company. My kids." She turned to an efficient home cappuccino maker and began to fix a cup. "They got passion. Take after their father."

"Do you think so? I see a lot of you in Ryan."

It was exactly the right thing to say. Maureen's eyes turned warm and loving. "The firstborn. No matter how many you have, there's only one first. You'll know, one day."

"Hmmm." Miranda declined to comment.

"Colleen, she's mad at Ryan," Maureen continued as she set the cup in front of Miranda. "He'll charm her out of it."

"I'm sure he will. He's very charming."

"Girls always chased after him. But my Ryan's very particular. He's got his eye on you."

It was time, Miranda decided, to put the record straight. "Mrs. Boldari, we're just business associates."

"You think so?" Maureen said placidly, and turned back to load the dishwasher. "He doesn't look good enough to you?"

"He looks very good, but—"

"He doesn't kiss you?"

"He . . . I . . ." She filled her mouth with hot coffee to shut it up.

"I thought so. I'd worry about that boy if he didn't kiss a woman who looks like you. But maybe you don't like the way he kisses. It matters. A man doesn't get your blood up with his kisses, you aren't going to have a happy relationship. Sex is important. Anybody who says different never had good sex."

"Oh, my," Miranda said. "I haven't had sex with Ryan."

"Why not?"

Miranda couldn't believe she was having this conversation. "I don't just have sex with every attractive man I meet."

"Good. I don't want my boy going around with easy women."

She had no comment for that. She glanced up with relief as Ryan and his sister came into the kitchen.

As expected, he'd charmed Colleen out of her snit. The two of them were smiling. Colleen sent Miranda a friendly look. "Sorry about that. Just a few things we needed to straighten out."

"No problem."

"So"—Colleen sat at the table—"do you have any solid feeling for who might have stolen the original bronze?"

Miranda just blinked at her. "Excuse me?"

"Ryan filled me in. Maybe I can help you sort it out."

Maureen glanced around. "Somebody steal something from your lady?"

"I did," Ryan said easily. "It turned out to be a forgery. We're straightening it out."

"Good."

"Wait. Wait just a minute." Miranda lifted both hands. "You're telling me you know your son's a thief?"

Maureen neatly wiped her hands. "Of course I know."

"I told you she knew," Ryan pointed out.

"And you"—she pointed at Colleen—"you're a police officer. Your brother steals. How do you resolve the two?"

"He's retiring." Colleen lifted her shoulders.

"I don't understand." She pressed her hands to her head. "You're his mother. How can you encourage him to break the law?"

"Encourage?" Maureen gave that rich laugh again. "Who had to encourage him? When God gives you a gift, it's a sin not to use it."

Miranda closed her eyes a moment. "You're saying that God gave Ryan a talent and that it would be a sin for him not to break into buildings and steal?"

"Don't argue," Ryan murmured. "You'll just give yourself a headache."

"Do you know what he does with this gift? He buys this house for his family because the old neighborhood isn't safe anymore. He sees that his brothers and sisters get a college education. God gave him a gift," Maureen said again, and rested her hand on Ryan's shoulder. "You going to argue with God?"

RYAN was right. She did have a headache. She nursed it with silence during the drive to Manhattan. She wasn't sure which baffled her more, the stand Maureen had taken to defend her son or the warm hugs she'd been given before they'd left.

"I don't understand your life," Miranda began as he escorted her through the elegant lobby of his building.

"That's all right. I don't understand yours either." He stepped into an elevator and used a key to access the top floor.

"Your mother wanted to know why I wasn't having sex with you."

"I wonder the same thing." The elevator opened into a spacious living area done in bold blues and greens. Wide terrace windows offered a pricey view of New York. He'd obviously indulged himself in his affection for the finer things. Art deco lamps, Chippendale tables, Baccarat crystal. She wondered how much of it he'd stolen.

"All purchased legitimately," he said, reading her perfectly.

Art on the walls ranged from a misty Corot to a soft, lovely watercolor of what she recognized as the Irish countryside.

"Your mother's work."

"Yes. She's good, isn't she? She likes you."

With a sigh, Miranda wandered to the window. Her own mother

had never hugged her that way. She wondered how, despite it all, his family had seemed so much more blissfully normal than her own.

Ryan put down her bags and crossed to her. "You're tense," he murmured after he began kneading her shoulders. "I'd hoped an evening with my family would relax you."

"How does anyone relax with all that energy around them?" She arched back against his hands before she could stop herself. "You must have had an interesting childhood."

"I had a terrific childhood." He bent down to nibble at her neck. "Don't."

"I was about to work my way around . . . here." He turned her, covered her mouth with his, and stole her breath.

His mother had said kisses should get the blood up. Hers was up.

"Don't," she said again weakly.

"Let me touch you." As he asked, his hands ran up her sides.

Oh, yes. Touch me. "No." It was a shock to hear herself say it. "If we're going to finish this arrangement successfully, it has to be on a business level. And only that level."

"Your tongue ever get frostbite when you use that tone? Okay, Dr. Jones, it's all business. I'll show you your room."

He picked up her suitcases and carried them up a fluid curve of metal stairs. Then, setting her bags down just inside a door, he nodded. "You should find this comfortable enough. Sleep well." He shut the door in her face.

Her eyes widened when she heard the click of a lock. In one leap she was at the door. "You can't lock me in here."

"Just to make sure you stay where I put you until tomorrow."

He walked away whistling while she pounded and promised vengeance.

MIRANDA showered quickly in the morning. She wanted to be completely dressed before she saw him. There would be, she determined, no cozy little breakfast chat in pajamas.

Of course, he had to let her out first.

"Let me out of here, Boldari," she called as she rapped on the door. She rattled the knob. It turned smoothly under her hand.

She stepped out, glanced cautiously down the hallway. Doors to a library, bedroom, and office were open. She headed downstairs. He wasn't in the living room or kitchen. But there was a half pot of coffee left on WARM. He wasn't in the apartment at all.

She snatched up the phone. There was no dial tone. She dashed back out into the living room and jabbed the button on the elevator. It didn't make a sound. Snarling, she turned to the door, found it locked. He'd simply expanded the perimeters of her cage.

IT WAS after one before she heard the quiet hum of the elevator. She hadn't whiled away the morning. She'd taken the opportunity to go over every inch of his living quarters. She'd pawed through his closet without guilt. She'd riffled through his drawers. The desks— bedroom, library, and office—had all been annoyingly locked. The caffeine she'd continued to drink had her system jumping.

She was ready for him when he walked through the elevator door. "How dare you lock me in this way. I'm not a prisoner."

"Just a precaution." He took off his coat and hung it up. "I had a few errands I had to run. I hope you made yourself at home."

"I'm leaving."

He waited until she was at the base of the stairs. "*The Dark Lady* is being held in a storeroom at the Bargello."

She stopped, as he'd known she would. "How do you know?"

"It's my business to know. With or without you I'm going to Italy and liberating her. I can find another archaeometrist. You walk out, you're all the way out."

"You'll never get it out of the Bargello."

"Oh, yes, I will. You can have a pass at her once I do, or you can run back to Maine and wait for your parents to decide you're not grounded anymore. In or out, Dr. Jones. Time's wasting."

It was here, she realized, where she passed the point of no return. "If you perform a miracle and actually get inside the Bargello, you take nothing but the bronze. It isn't a shopping spree."

"Agreed."

"If we do end up in possession of the bronze, I'm in charge of it."

"You're the scientist," he said with a smile. She was welcome to the copy, he thought. He wanted the original.

"In." Her breath exploded out. "God help me."

"Good. Now"—he opened his briefcase, tossed items onto the table—"these are for you."

She picked up the dark blue book. "This isn't my passport."

"It is now."

"This isn't my name. How did you get this picture? This is the photo in my passport."

"Exactly."

"No, *my* passport. And my driver's license," she continued, snatching it up. "You stole my wallet."

"Borrowed certain items in your wallet," he corrected.

"You came in my room while I was sleeping and took my things. That's despicable."

"No, it was necessary. It would have been despicable if I'd climbed into bed with you. Fun, but despicable."

She tossed the passport down. "I'm not Abigail O'Connell."

"Mrs. Abigail O'Connell. We're on our second honeymoon. And I think I'll call you Abby. I'm Kevin O'Connell, your devoted spouse. I'm a stockbroker. You're in advertising. We've been married for five years, and we're considering starting a family."

"It's illegal to enter a foreign country with false identification."

He roared with laughter. "You're wonderful. Seriously. Now I need a detailed drawing of the bronze. I need to be able to recognize her quickly." He took a pad and pencil from a drawer. "As precise as you can."

She sat and, with a speed and skill that had his brows lifted, put the image of the bronze on paper. The face, that sly and sensuous smile, the fingers lifted high, the fluid arch of the body.

"Gorgeous. Absolutely gorgeous," he murmured.

She set her pencil down and rose. "The drawing's accurate. If you're lucky enough to stumble across it, you'll recognize her."

"Luck has very little to do with it." Idly he flicked a fingertip down her cheek. "You look a bit like her. It would be interesting to see you with that cagey, self-aware smile on your face. You don't smile very often, Miranda."

"I haven't had much to smile about lately."

"I think we can change that. Oh, one last thing." He pulled a small jeweler's box out of his pocket. "By the power invested in me," he said, plucking a ring out of the box and taking her hand.

It wasn't possible to look down and not be dazzled when he shoved it onto her finger. The wedding band was studded with brilliant square-cut diamonds, four in all, that sparkled like ice.

"I suppose it's stolen."

"You wound me. I've got a friend who runs a place in the diamond district. I got it wholesale. I need to pack."

She worried the ring on her finger while he started up the stairs. It was absurd, but she wished the ring hadn't fit quite so perfectly. "Ryan? Can you really do this?"

He sent her a wink over his shoulder. "Watch me."

He knew immediately she'd been into his things. She'd been neat, but not neat enough. He shook his head. She wouldn't have found anything he hadn't wanted her to find.

He opened his closet, pressed a hidden mechanism, and stepped into his private room. He would need his picks, the pocket electronics of his trade. The coil of thin, flexible rope. Spirit gum, hair color, two pairs of glasses. These he packed in the false bottom of his suitcase. He added the expected choices a man on a romantic vacation to Italy would take, filling the case and a garment bag.

In his office he locked his current identification in the safe behind the complete volumes of Edgar Allan Poe and on impulse took out the plain gold band he kept there. It had been his grandfather's wedding ring. Though he'd had occasion to wear a wedding ring as cover before, he'd never used this one.

The intercom buzzed, announcing the car, as he carried his suitcases and laptop downstairs. Miranda had already brought her things down.

Ryan lifted his brows. "All set?"

She drew a deep breath. This, she thought, was it. "Let's get going. I hate to rush at the airport."

He smiled at her. "That's my girl," he said, and bent down to pick up one of her cases.

"I can carry my own things. And I'm not your girl."

With a shrug he stepped back. "After you, Dr. Jones."

Chapter Five

THERE'S only one bedroom." Miranda saw nothing of the lovely suite but the single bedroom with its king-size bed.

In the parlor Ryan opened the double doors and stepped out onto an enormous terrace, where the air was ripe with spring and the Italian sun shone cheerfully on the soft red rooftops.

"Check this view. You could live out here."

"Good." She stepped out. "Why don't you plan to do just that? There's only one bed in the only one bedroom."

"We're married." He draped an arm over her shoulders and added a friendly squeeze. "Relax, Miranda. A view like this makes up for a long plane flight, doesn't it?"

"The view isn't my first priority."

"Let's unpack. Then I've got some shopping to do."

"I'm not spending the day in Ferragamo's for your sister."

"That won't take long, and I'll need trinkets for the rest of the family."

"Look, Boldari, I think we have a higher priority than gathering souvenirs for your family."

He infuriated her by leaning over and kissing the tip of her nose. "Don't worry, darling. I'll buy you something too."

ENJOYING the press of tourists and bargain hunters who swarmed the Ponte Vecchio, over the placid Arno, he bought gold chains, marcasite earrings, and Florentine-style brooches for his sisters.

"Stand here long enough," he told Miranda as she waited impatiently, "you can hear every language in the world."

"Have we stood here long enough?"

He slipped an arm around her shoulders, shaking his head. "Don't you ever let yourself fall into the moment, Dr. Jones? It's Florence. We're standing on the oldest of the city's bridges. The sun's shining. Take a breath and drink it in."

He bought three pairs of shoes in Ferragamo's cathedral to footwear. She bought nothing—not even a gorgeous pair of gray leather pumps that had caught her eye. "What now?" she asked.

"Can't come to Florence without buying some art."

They entered a shop crowded with marble and bronze reproductions. He nodded at a statue of Venus. "What do you think?"

"It's adequate, not particularly good, but if one of your relatives is looking for some lawn art, it would do well enough."

"Yeah, I think she'll do well enough." He aimed a delighted smile toward the clerk. Throughout the shopping spree he'd spoken Italian fluidly. Now he slaughtered the most basic of phrases.

The clerk beamed at him. Ryan tugged Miranda closer. "It'll look great in the sunroom, won't it, Abby?"

Her answer was a "Hmmm."

When the deal was made and the statue wrapped, Ryan hefted the bag and put an arm around Miranda. "Let's get some of that ice cream, Abby."

"I don't need any ice cream." They stepped outside again.

"We've got one more stop to make."

"Look, my feet hurt. I'll just meet you back at the hotel."

"And miss all the fun? We're going to the Bargello."

"Now? We're going to do it now?"

"We'll check the place out, get a feel for things, take some pictures." He winked. "Case the joint, as they say in the movies."

"Case the joint," she murmured.

"Where are the security cameras? How far is it across the courtyard? When do the guards change shift?"

She imagined they looked exactly like American tourists—cameras, shopping bags, and guidebooks. He bought her an ice-cream cone as they walked. She licked at the tart, frothy lemon ice.

"Fabulous, isn't it?" He paused, studying the magnificent cathedral that dominated the city. "Go stand over there."

"Why?"

"So we can get our picture taken, honey." He snagged a couple of tourists, who happily agreed to take a picture of them.

"This is ridiculous," Miranda muttered as she found herself posing with Ryan's arm around her waist.

"It's for my mother," he said, then impulsively kissed her.

A flock of pigeons swarmed up with a rush of wings. She had no time to resist. His mouth was warm, firm. The quiet sound she made had nothing to do with protest. The hand she lifted to his face had everything to do with holding him there. The sun was white, the air full of sound. And her heart trembled on the edge of something extraordinary.

"Sorry," Ryan said. "I guess I fell into the moment."

And leaving her there with her knees trembling, he retrieved his camera. He held out a hand. "Let's go."

With a nod she fell into step with him.

Inside the old palace, he dug out his video camera. "Look at this guy—he's knocked back a few, huh?" He aimed the camera at Michelangelo's bronze of the drunken Bacchus, then began to pan the room. "Wait until Jack and Sally see these." He swung the camera toward a doorway, where a guard sat. "Wander around," he said under his breath. "Look awed and middle-class."

After an hour Miranda began to suspect that a great deal of criminal activity involved the tedious. They went into every room, capturing every inch on camera. "Haven't you got enough?"

"Nearly. Go flirt with that guard." Ryan lowered the camera and undid the top two buttons on Miranda's blouse.

"What do you think you're doing?"

"Making sure his attention's focused on you. Ask him some questions and bat your eyes. In five minutes ask him where the bathroom is, then head there. Meet me in the courtyard in ten."

"All right." Her stomach tilted down toward her shaky knees as she approached the guard. "Ah . . . *scusi,*" she began. *"Per favore."* She watched the guard's eyes dip to the opening of her blouse. She swallowed hard, then spread her hands helplessly. "English?"

"Sì, signora, a little."

"Oh, wonderful." She experimented with fluttering lashes and saw that such pitiful ploys actually worked. "I wonder if you could tell me anything about . . ." She chose a sculpture at random.

Ryan waited until he saw the guard's focus fix on Miranda, then took a thin pick out of his pocket and went to work on a side door. It was easy enough, even dealing with it behind his back.

He kept one eye on the security camera, biding his time until a group of art lovers shuffled in front of him. Before they'd gone by, he was through the door, closing it softly behind him.

He took one long breath of appreciation, tugged on the gloves he'd tucked in his pocket, then flexed his fingers.

Several pieces caught his eye, including a sad-eyed Madonna. But he was looking for another type of lady altogether.

SHE waited the ten minutes, then fifteen. By twenty she was wringing her hands and imagining what an Italian prison would be like.

Then she saw him, strolling across the courtyard like a man without a care in the world. Her relief was so great that she threw her arms around him. "Where have you been? I—"

He kissed her to stop her babbling. "Let's go get a drink."

"Where did you go?" she demanded. "I fiddled around with the guard as long as I could. When I looked around, you were gone."

"I wanted to see what was behind door number three. The interior doors are child's play," he said as they walked.

"How could you take a chance like that, breaking into an off-limits area with a guard not three yards away?"

"Usually that's the best time." He glanced in a shopwindow as they passed. "I found our lady," he said casually.

"It's irresponsible, foolish, and . . . What?"

"I found her." His grin flashed like the Tuscan sun. "I'm thirsty."

He pulled her toward a wide awning in front of a bustling trattoria and maneuvered her to an empty table.

"You're out of your mind. Buying souvenirs, wandering around the Bargello as if you've never been there before. And now—"

His hand closed hard over hers as he leaned across the table. "Now, we're just going to sit here awhile, and you're not going to give me any trouble."

"I—"

"No trouble at all." He glanced up at the waiter and requested a bottle of local wine and a selection of cheeses.

"I'm not tolerating your feeble attempts at bullying me."

"Sweetheart, I've got the lady. She's sitting under the table."

"Under the— Are you telling me that you walked into a museum in broad daylight and walked out with the bronze?"

"I'm good. I told you."

"But you said we had to check the place out, to get the feel."

He kissed her fingers. "I lied." He kept her hand in his, kept his eyes dreamily on hers while the waiter set their wine and cheese on the table. Recognizing lovers, he left them alone.

Ryan poured wine for both of them, sampled, and approved. "The wine from this region is exceptional. Aren't you going to try it?"

Still staring at him, she lifted her glass and downed the contents. She was now an accessory to theft.

"If you're going to drink like that, you better soak some of it up." He sliced off some cheese, offered it. "Here."

"You knew going in that you were going to do this?"

"I knew going in that if the opportunity presented itself, I'd make the switch."

"What switch?"

"The bronze we bought earlier. I put that in her place. Odds are no one's going to notice it's the wrong bronze for a bit. If our luck holds, we'll be back in the States by that time anyway."

IT WAS surreal, sitting in the hotel room and holding *The Dark Lady* in her hands. She set it on the table beside the *David*.

"She's gorgeous," Ryan commented as he puffed on his slim Cuban cigar. "Your sketch of her was very accurate. But you'd be a better artist if you put some heart into your work."

"I'm not an artist. I'm a scientist. This isn't the bronze I tested."

He lifted a brow. "How do you know?"

"I took scrapings. Here, and here." She used a fingertip to point. "There's no sign of them on this piece. I need my equipment and my notes to verify, but this isn't the bronze I worked on."

Ryan tapped his cigar in an ashtray. "Let's verify it. You're going to want to change. Basic black works best for an entertaining evening of breaking and entering. I'll arrange for transportation."

She moistened her lips. "We're going into Standjo?"

"That's the plan."

He was using her was all she could think in the bedroom. She was about to break into her family's business. How would she stop him if he decided to do more than run a few basic tests?

She could hear him talking on the phone in the parlor and took her time changing into a black shirt and slacks. She needed her own plan, needed to enlist someone she could trust.

"I've got to run down to the desk," he called out. "Snap it up in there. I'll only be a minute, and I need to change too."

The minute she heard the door shut, she made the call.

"Giovanni, it's Miranda."

"Miranda? Where are you? Your brother's been—"

"I'm in Florence," she interrupted. "I need to see you right away. Meet me in Santa Maria Novella. Ten minutes. Please, it's vital." She hung up, then covered the bronzes in bubble wrap and stuffed them back into their bag. She grabbed the bag and her purse and ran.

The church, with its beguiling patterns of green and white marble, was a short walk from the hotel. Miranda walked into its cool, dim interior and found a seat near the left of the chancel.

She heard the rapid footsteps and tensed. He'd found her. Oh, God. She jumped up, whirled, and nearly wept with relief. "Giovanni." She stepped forward and wrapped her arms around him.

"Bella." He returned the embrace. "Why do you ask me to meet

you like a spy"—he glanced at the high altar—"and in church?"

"It's quiet. It's safe. Sanctuary," she said with a weak smile as she drew back. "I want to explain, but I don't know how much time I have. He knows I'm gone by now, and he'll be looking for me."

"Who knows?"

"Too complicated. Sit down a minute." Her voice was a whisper, as suited churches and conspiracies. "Giovanni, the bronze—*The Dark Lady*—it was a forgery."

"Miranda, to be a forgery makes it necessary to have something to forge. The bronze was a fake, a bad joke."

"It was genuine. You saw the test results."

He took her hands. "*Sì,* but . . ."

"Do you think I doctored them?"

"I think there were mistakes. We moved too fast, all of us."

"That bronze was real. This one is a forgery." She reached down and brought the wrapped bronze to the top of the bag. "It's the one they tested."

"*Dio mio!* How did you get it? It was being held in the Bargello."

"That's not important. What is important is this is not the bronze we worked on. You'll be able to see that for yourself once you have it in the lab."

"In the lab? Miranda, what madness is this?"

"This is sanity. I'm barred from Standjo. The records are there. The equipment is there. I need your help. There's a bronze *David* in this bag as well. It's a forgery. I've tested it. But I want you to take them both in and run what tests you can. You'll compare the results of the Fiesole Bronze with the ones that were run on the original. I can't trust anyone but you."

She squeezed his hands, knowing she played on his friendship. But the tears that swam into her eyes were genuine. "It's my reputation, Giovanni. It's my work. It's my life. For friendship. For me."

"I'll do what you ask."

Her heart swelled with gratitude. "Tonight, right away."

"The sooner it's done, the better. The lab, it's closed for a few days, so no one will know."

"Closed. Why?"

He smiled for the first time. "Tomorrow, my lovely pagan, is Good Friday." And this was not the way he'd intended to spend his holiday weekend. "Where will I reach you when it's done?"

"I'll reach you." She leaned forward to touch her lips to his. "*Grazie, Giovanni. Mille grazie.* I'll never be able to repay you."

"An explanation when it's done would be a fine start."

"A full one, I promise. Take good care of them." She nudged the bag toward him with her foot. "Wait a minute or two before you leave, just in case." She kissed him again, then left.

She didn't see the figure standing in the dimness, turned as if to contemplate the faded frescoes of Dante's *Inferno*. She didn't feel the fury or the threat.

She stepped outside and walked in the opposite direction of the hotel, toward the river. It wouldn't do, she thought, to have Ryan find her before she and Giovanni had plenty of distance between them.

She reached the river, watched the dying sun sprinkle its last lights on the water. When the roar of an engine sounded behind her, she knew he'd found her. She'd known he would.

"Get on."

She glanced back, saw his furious face. He was all in black now and astride a blue motorbike. He looked dangerous and absurdly sexy. Since the alternative was to run like a coward, she walked to the curb, swung a leg over to sit behind him, and gripped the back of the seat for balance.

But when he took off like a bullet, survival instinct took over and had her wrapping her arms tightly around him.

AFTER taking the narrow, winding streets with a reckless and risky speed that suited his mood, Ryan jerked the bike to a halt in the Piazzale Michelangelo. It was nearly empty, with a broody storm gathering in the western sky.

"Off," he ordered, and waited for her to pry her hands from their death grip around his waist. He swung off himself, then dragged her to the wall, where Florence spread like an old jewel below, and held her there, body against body. "I want the bronzes, Miranda. Damn it, I trusted you."

Her eyes fired back. "You mean you couldn't lock me into the suite the way you did in your apartment."

He put his arms around her so that they looked like desperate lovers too involved with each other to notice storm or city.

"You're hurting me."

"Not yet I'm not. You had to give them to someone."

Thunder grumbled, rolled closer.

"They're safe. I made arrangements. If I run the tests, it could be claimed I slanted them. We'd be no better off. It was your job to get the bronze. It's mine to determine how to prove it's a forgery."

"You gave them to someone from Standjo."

"I gave them to someone I trust. He'll do the work. And tomorrow I'll contact him and get the results."

"Follow this logic: The bronze is a forgery; therefore someone at Standjo made the copy, someone who knows what the tests would show."

"He wouldn't do that. His work's important to him."

"Mine's important to me. Let's go."

"Where?"

He was already dragging her across the plaza to the bike when the first fat drops of rain fell. "To the lab, sweetheart. Now get on, or I leave you here and take care of business myself."

She got on.

A half block from Standjo he parked the bike and removed pouches from the saddlebags. "Do what you're told and carry this." He shoved one of the bags into her hands. "We'll go in the back. We'll cross directly over the photo lab to the stairs."

"How do you know the setup?"

"I do my research. I've got blueprints of the whole facility." He pulled out a pair of surgical gloves. "Put these on." He pulled on his own gloves as he spoke. "There are no guards. It's all electronic, so it's unlikely we'd run into anyone but your good pal over a holiday weekend."

He approached the door, setting down his bag to prepare to work. Then his eyes narrowed as he studied the fixture beside the door. "Alarm's off," he murmured. "Your friend's careless, Dr. Jones."

"I suppose he didn't think it necessary."

"Um-hmm. Door's locked, though. We'll fix that."

He had to work by feel alone. The pounding of the rain prevented him from hearing that faint and satisfying click of tumblers, but the sturdy lock surrendered degree by degree.

"Bring the bag," he told her when he pulled the door open.

He used his penlight to guide them to the stairs. "You explain to your friend that I'm helping you out. That is, if he's here."

"He said he'd be here. He promised me."

"Then he must like to work in the dark." He shone his light straight ahead. "That's your lab, right?"

"Yes." Her brows drew together. It was black as pitch. "He's probably in the chem lab. That's his field."

"We'll check that out in a minute. Meanwhile, we'll just see if your notes are still in your office."

The door was unlocked, which gave him an unhappy feeling. He shut off his flashlight. "Stay behind me."

He eased through the door. For several seconds he listened and, hearing nothing, reached over to turn on the lights.

"Oh, my God." She gripped his shoulder.

It looked as if someone had indulged in a vicious tantrum. Computers were smashed; glass from test tubes littered the floor; the stench of chemicals was in the air.

"I don't understand this. What's the point of this?"

"Looks to me, Dr. Jones, like your friend's come and gone."

"Giovanni would never do this." She pushed past Ryan to kick her way through the rubble. "It had to be vandals."

"Let's get out of here."

"I have to check the other sections, see how extensive the damage is. If they got to the chem lab—"

She broke off, shoving her way through the mess with the terrible idea of a gang of hoods with a volatile supply of stolen chemicals.

He started after her. When he caught up, she was standing in an open doorway, staring, swaying.

Giovanni had kept his promise, and he wasn't going anywhere. He lay on his back, his head resting in a dark, glossy pool. His eyes, open and dull, were fixed on *The Dark Lady,* who lay with him, her graceful hands and smiling face covered with blood.

Ryan jerked Miranda back, forced her around so that she stared into his eyes instead of at what lay in the room beyond.

"I . . . Giovanni." Her pupils had dilated with shock, so that her eyes were as black and lifeless as a doll's.

"Hold it together, Miranda. Our fingerprints are all over that bronze. Do you understand? We've been set up here."

There was a roaring in her ears. "Giovanni's dead."

"Yeah, he is. Now stand right here." He propped her against the wall. He stepped into the room, picked up the bronze, stuffed it into his bag, and did a quick search. The *David* had been heaved into a corner. Very smart, Ryan thought as he pushed it into the bag. Very tidy. Leave both pieces and tie it right around Miranda's neck like a noose.

She was shaking, and her skin was the color of paste.

"We've got to get out of here," he said roughly.

"I can't leave him."

Rather than wasting time arguing, he caught her up in a fireman's carry. She didn't struggle, only hung limply. When they were out on the street, he dumped her onto her feet and shook her hard. "You don't fall apart until we're out of here. Put it on ice, Miranda."

He pulled her around the building and down the street. She slid onto the bike behind him, held on, so that he could feel the jumping skip of her heart against his back as he drove through the rain.

HE DROVE to the hotel, taking narrow side streets at random to be certain they weren't being followed. Once there, he kept an arm around her waist until they were inside the suite. Her teeth were starting to chatter.

He locked the door, added the safety latch before taking her into the bedroom. "Get out of the wet clothes, into a robe. You're in shock. You need to get warm and dry."

She stumbled into the bathroom. When the door clicked shut, he resisted the urge to open it again and be certain she wasn't in a heap on the floor.

He stripped off his wet clothes and pulled on slacks and a shirt.

"Miranda?" With his hands in his pockets he frowned at the door. Modesty be damned, he decided, and pushed it open.

She'd put on a robe and stood in the center of the room, her arms wrapped tight around her body as she rocked herself. She sent Ryan one look of unspeakable misery. "Giovanni."

"Okay, all right." He put his arms around her, cradled her head on his shoulder. "You did fine. It's okay to fall apart now."

"Who could have done that?"

"We'll figure it out step by step. But your mind has to be clear. I need your brain. I need your logic."

"I keep seeing him, lying there. He was my friend. He . . ." And the full horror struck her. "Oh, Ryan, I killed him."

"No." He pulled her back. "Whoever bashed in his head killed him. You get over that, Miranda, because it's not going to help."

"He's dead because I asked him to help me."

"Dry your hair while I order some food. We've got a lot to talk about."

She dried her hair and slipped into white cotton pajamas, then wrapped the robe over them. She would eat, because she needed to be strong and clearheaded if she was going to avenge Giovanni. Whatever it took, however long it took, she would see that whoever had killed him would pay for it.

When she came out of the bedroom, she saw that Ryan had ordered the waiter to set up the meal on the terrace. The rain had stopped, and the air was fresh.

"What are we eating?" She managed what passed for a smile.

"Minestrone to start, then a couple of Florentine steaks. It'll help."

She took a chair and sampled the soup. It stuck like paste in her throat, but the heat of it thawed some of the ice in her belly.

He uncovered the steaks. "Tell me about Giovanni."

"He's— He was brilliant. A chemist. He was born here in Florence and joined Standjo about ten years ago. He did some time in the lab at the institute. That's where I worked with him initially." She rubbed at her temple. "He was a lovely man, sweet and funny. He was single. He enjoyed women."

"Were you lovers?"

She winced but shook her head. "No. We were friends. It was Giovanni who called me to tell me the bronze had been discredited."

"Today was the first time you talked to him about the bronze being a copy?"

"Yes. I called him at the lab when you went downstairs. He came right away. It couldn't have been more than fifteen minutes."

Enough time, Ryan mused, for him to have told someone of the call. The wrong someone. "What did you tell him?"

"Almost everything." She stopped pushing her steak around on her plate. "I asked him to take the bronzes into the lab to run tests, to do a comparison. I said I'd contact him. I didn't give him the hotel."

Ryan lit a cigar. "That may very well be why we're sitting here enjoying the moonlight."

"What do you mean?"

"Put your brain to work, Dr. Jones. The murder weapon and the *David* were left on the scene. What connects the two? You do."

"Killing Giovanni to implicate me." It was too cold, too hideous to be contemplated. And too logical to ignore.

"He'd have begun to wonder himself after the tests. He'd take another look at your notes, your results."

"That's why the lab was trashed," she murmured. "We'll never find my documentation now."

"Taken or destroyed," Ryan agreed. "Your friend was in the way. And Miranda, so are you. You know what they say about killing? The first one's tough. After that it's just business."

"If that means you want to end our deal, I won't blame you."

He leaned back, drawing on the cigar. "I finish what I start."

She raised her wineglass in a half salute. "So do I."

STANDING ON THE TERRACE IN the strong morning light, Miranda gazed out at the city. The end of Giovanni's life had irrevocably changed hers. There was an urgency to grab hold, to take time, to savor details. To feel alive.

"Miranda."

She saw Ryan standing in the doorway. "It's a beautiful morning. Spring, rebirth. I don't think I really appreciated that before."

He crossed the terrace, laid a hand over hers on the parapet. She saw the look in his eye. "Oh, no. What now? What happened?"

"The man who discovered the bronze—the plumber, Carlo Rinaldi. He's dead. Hit-and-run, last night. I just heard it on the news."

"It could have been an accident. Why would anyone kill him? He isn't connected to the lab. He can't know anything."

"He was a loose end, Miranda, and loose ends get snipped."

"Was there anything in the news about Giovanni?"

"No, but there will be. Get dressed. We're going out."

Thirty minutes later they were at a phone booth and Ryan was doing something he'd avoided all of his life. He was calling the cops. He used a nervous whisper and colloquial Italian to report a body at Standjo and hung up. "That should do it." He swung onto the bike. "Now we're going to your mother's."

"My mother's? Why? Are you crazy?"

"We'll give the cops enough time to find the body, for her to hear about it. What do you figure she'll do when she does?"

"She'll go straight to the lab."

"That's what I'm counting on. Put this on." He pulled out a cap. "The neighbors will spot that hair of yours a mile away."

HE WALKED right up to the front door, slipped out his picks, and had defeated the locks in little more time than if he'd used a key.

"You make me wonder why anyone bothers. Why not just leave the doors and windows open?"

"My sentiments exactly. Where's her office?"

"Second floor, to the left."

"Let's try it." As they climbed up a set of stairs, he said, "Any paperwork dealing with your tests that were kept at the lab are a loss. There's a chance she might have copies here."

"Why would she?"

"Because you're her daughter."

"It wouldn't matter to her."

"Maybe, maybe not."

Ryan found the office feminine, but not fussy. He began tipping forward the backs of paintings. "Here is the safe, behind this very nice Renoir print. I'll deal with this. You go through the desk."

She hesitated, but shoved aside the conditioning of a lifetime and dived in. "Copies of contracts," she murmured, "and reports. Oh." Her fingers froze. "The Fiesole Bronze. She has a file."

"Take it. We'll look through it later." He listened to the last tumbler click into place. "Now I have you, my little beauty. Very nice," he murmured, opening a velvet case and examining a double rope of pearls. "Heirlooms—they'd suit you."

"Put those back."

"I'm not stealing them. I don't do jewelry. Look at this." He pulled out a thin plastic holder. "Look familiar?"

"The X rays." She was away from the desk and grabbing for them in two heartbeats. "The computer printouts. Look. The corrosion level. It's there. It's real. I didn't make a mistake." She felt swamped with emotion.

"I never thought you did."

"Liar. You broke into my bedroom and threatened to strangle me."

"I said I could strangle you. That was before I knew you. Tidy up, honey. We've got enough to keep us busy for a while."

THEY spent the next several hours in the hotel, with Miranda going over her reports and Ryan huddled at his laptop computer.

"It's all here. Every test I did, every result."

"Take a look at this." He motioned her over. "These are the names I come up with. People who had access to both bronzes."

She rose and read over his shoulder. She was there, her mother, her father, Andrew, Giovanni, Elise, Carter, Hawthorne.

"Andrew didn't have access to *The Dark Lady*."

A tendril of her hair tickled his cheek.

"He's connected to you, your mother, and Elise. Close enough. I want to know how accurate it is."

She sniffed. "It's fairly complete, and insulting."

"Was Hawthorne's wife with him in Florence?"

"No. Richard's divorced." Her eyes locked on his. Her heart did a quick cartwheel. "Why does it matter?"

"Because people tell their lovers and spouses all kinds of confidential things. Sex," he murmured, and wrapped that loose tendril around his finger, "is a great communicator." One little tug, he thought, and her mouth would be on his. "We need a break."

"A break? What did you have in mind?"

"Let's put this away and go have a meal. What would you like for your last night in Florence?"

"The last night?"

"Things might get sticky here. We're better off working on home ground. Now—fast, fancy, or rowdy?"

"I think I'd like rowdy for a change."

"Excellent choice. I know just the place."

IT WAS loud. It was crowded. Tables were pushed together so that diners—friends and strangers alike—ate elbow to elbow.

They were wedged into a corner by a round man with a stained apron, who took Ryan's order for a bottle of local red. At Miranda's left was an American couple. They shared a basket of bread while Ryan engaged them in conversation. By the time the wine was set on the table, Miranda knew they were from New York and had been together for ten years. It was, they said, their anniversary trip.

"It's our second honeymoon." Ryan picked up Miranda's hand and kissed it. "Right, Abby, darling?"

She stared at him, then responded to his kick under the table. "Oh, yes. We couldn't afford a honeymoon when we were first married. Now we're treating ourselves before kids come along." Stunned at herself, she gulped down wine while Ryan beamed at her.

Less than an hour later Miranda wanted more wine. "It's a wonderful place." She grinned tipsily at him. "I love it here."

"Yes, I can see that." He nudged the bottle farther out of her reach. "Let's try the zabaglione and cappuccino."

"I'd rather have more wine."

"Not a good idea."

"Why not?" She drained her glass. She snagged the bottle. Eyes narrowed, she poured until the wine was precisely a half inch from the rim of the glass. "See that—steady as a rock. Dr. Jones is always steady." She leaned forward conspiratorially. "But Abby's a lush."

"Kevin is more than a little concerned that she's going to pass out at the table, so that he has to carry her home."

"Nah. Dr. Jones wouldn't permit that. Too embarrassing. Let's walk down by the river. Abby'll let you kiss her."

"That's an interesting offer, but I think we'd better get you home." He quickly dug out more than enough lire to cover the tab. "Let's take that walk, honey."

"Okay." She popped up, then had to brace a hand against the wall. "Oh, my, there's quite a bit of gravity in here."

He scooped an arm around her waist and pulled her through the restaurant, laughing as she called cheerful good-byes.

"You're a handful, Dr. Jones." He guided her along the uneven sidewalk.

"I'm sharing a hotel suite with a thief, and I broke into my mother's house. Coulda robbed her blind."

"You only had to ask. Left turn. Almost there."

"Maybe you could teach me how to pick locks. Wouldya?"

"Oh, yeah, that's going to happen." He steered her toward the front entrance of the hotel.

"I could seduce it out of you." She turned, plowing into him at the edge of the elegant lobby, and she crushed her mouth against his before he could gain his balance.

"Miranda . . ."

"That's Abby to you, pal," she murmured as the desk clerk discreetly averted his eyes. "So how about it?"

"Let's talk upstairs." He dragged her into the elevator.

"Don't want to talk." She plastered herself against him. "I've wanted you ever since I saw you and heard the ping."

"Ping?" He was becoming breathless, trying to unwind her from around him.

"I hear pings with you. My head's just full of pings right now. Kiss me again, Ryan. You know you want to."

"Cut it out." A little desperately he shoved at her hands before they could unbutton his shirt. "You're hammered."

"What do you care?"

"There are rules," he muttered. One of them, he thought, needed a cold shower.

"Oh, now there're rules." Laughing, she tugged his shirt free of his slacks as he fought to shoot the key into the lock. His eyes were crossed when they stumbled inside together.

She released him only long enough to fuse her mouth to his. "I want you. Oh, I want you."

The little beam of sanity that remained in his mind was growing dimmer. "You're going to hate both of us in the morning."

"So what?" She shook back her hair. "This is now."

Their gazes remained locked as he carried her through the doorway into the bedroom. "Then let's see how long now can last. And remember, Dr. Jones. You asked for it."

THE *Dark Lady* stood under a single beam of light. The one who studied her sat in the dark.

Murder had not been planned. If all had gone correctly, violence would not have been necessary. The blame for the loss of two lives lay with the theft of the *David*. Who could have anticipated it?

But murder was not as abhorrent as one would think. That, too, brought power. Nothing and no one could substantiate the existence of *The Dark Lady* and be permitted to exist. That was simple fact. It would be taken care of; it would be dealt with. When the time was right, it would end. With Miranda.

It was a pity such a bright and clever mind had to be destroyed.

Reputation alone would have sufficed once. Now everything had to be taken. There was no room for sentiment.

An accident perhaps, though suicide would be best. It would take some thought, some planning. It would take . . . A smile spread as slyly as that on the glorious face of the bronze. It would take patience.

Chapter Six

SPRING was drifting over Maine. There was a softness in the air that hadn't been there even a week before. On its hill the old house stood with its back to the sea, its windows going gold in the setting sun. It was good to be home.

Miranda stepped inside and found Andrew in the den, keeping company with a bottle of Jack Daniel's. He got to his feet, swaying a little. "Where've you been?" He caught her up in a sloppy hug. "I've been worried about you. Nobody knew where you'd gone."

Though she hugged him back, her intention of telling him everything wavered. How much could a drunk be trusted?

"I'm on leave," she reminded him. "I went away for a few days. I ran into Ryan Boldari in New York. He's back in Maine now. He's going to stay here for a few days."

"Here?"

"Yes. I— We're involved."

"You're— Oh." He ran his tongue around his teeth and tried to think. "Okay. That was . . . quick."

"Not really. We have a lot in common." She didn't want to dwell on that. "Has there been any progress in the investigation?"

"We hit a snag. We can't find the documentation on the *David*."

She ran a nervous hand over her hair and prepared to continue the deception. "Can't find it? It should be in the files."

He poured a drink. "It's not there. I've looked. Insurance company's balking until they have documents, and our mother is threatening to come in and see why we're so inept."

"Please, Andrew." She walked over and took the glass out of his hand. "I can't talk to you when you're drunk."

He smiled, dimples popping into his cheeks. "I'm not drunk."

"Yes, you are. You need to get into a program."

The dimples faded. "What I need is a little cooperation and support." Irked, he snatched the glass back and took a long gulp.

As she stared at him, her chest tightened. "I love you, Andrew, and you're killing yourself in front of my eyes."

"Fine. I'll kill myself in private." He grabbed the bottle and strode out.

He slammed the door of his bedroom, sat in a chair, and drank straight from the bottle. He was entitled to relax, wasn't he? He got his work done. He did his job, so why did he have to get grief for having a couple of drinks? It wasn't that he had to drink. He could quit whenever he wanted. He'd quit drinking all right. Tomorrow, he thought with a chuckle as he lifted the bottle.

He saw headlights cut across the room. Company's coming. Probably Boldari. He grinned.

Miranda had a boyfriend. It had been a long time since he'd been able to tease his sister over something as interesting as a man. He got to his feet and stumbled toward the door. He had to show that slick New Yorker that little Miranda had herself a big brother looking out for her. He lurched down the hall and, grabbing the banister at the top of the steps, looked down.

There was his baby sister, right at the foot of the steps, in a hot lip lock with New York. "Hey!" he called out, gesturing with the bottle. "Whatcha doing with my sister, Mr. New York?"

"Hello, Andrew."

"You sleeping with my sister, you bastard?"

"Not at the moment." He kept his arm around Miranda.

"Well, I wanna talk to you, buddy." Andrew started down, made it halfway on his feet, and tumbled the rest.

Miranda leaped forward, kneeling beside his sprawled body. There was blood on his face. "Oh, Andrew."

"I'm all right," he muttered. "Just took a little spill's all."

"Steps are a tricky thing," Ryan said. He crouched beside Miranda. "Why don't we get you back up them, clean you up?"

Ryan glanced over at Miranda. She'd gone pale. "Come on, Andrew." He hauled Andrew to his feet as Miranda got to hers. But when she started to go up the stairs with them, Ryan shook his head. "No women. This is a guy thing. Right, Andrew?"

"Damn right." Boozily he made Ryan his best friend. "Women are the root of all evil. I had one for a while. She dumped me."

"Who needs her?" Ryan steered him into the bathroom.

It took the best part of an hour to pour Andrew into bed. When Ryan came downstairs, he couldn't find Miranda in the house. He grabbed a jacket and headed outside.

She was on the cliffs, her face turned to the sea. He studied her silhouette—alone, tall, slender. He didn't think he'd ever seen anyone lonelier. He climbed up to her, draped the jacket over her shoulders.

"That's the second time you've had to deal with an embarrassingly drunk Jones," she said. "I don't know if I could have handled Andrew tonight by myself. But I would have preferred it."

"That's too bad." Annoyed, he spun her around to face him. "Because I was here, and I'm going to be here for a while."

"Until we find the bronzes."

"That's right. And if I'm not done with you by then"—he cupped her face and kissed her—"you'll have to deal with it."

She turned away, stared at the steady circling beam from the lighthouse. He would be the one to run when it was done, she thought.

"Everything that's happened since I met you is foreign to me. Two men are dead. My reputation's in ruins. I've broken the law, and I'm having an affair with a criminal."

"But you haven't been bored, have you?"

She let out a weak laugh. "No. I don't know what to do next."

"I can help you with that." He took her hand and began to walk.

"I need to put everything in order." She glanced back toward the house. "I should check on Andrew first, then organize."

"Andrew's asleep, and organizing takes a clear, focused mind. You've got too much on yours."

"Excuse me, but organization is my life. I can organize three projects, outline a lecture, and teach a class at the same time."

"You're a frightening woman, Dr. Jones. I've never been inside a lighthouse." He studied it as they approached. "How old is it?"

"It was built in 1853, but my grandfather had the interior revamped in the '40s with the idea of using it as his art studio. According to my grandmother, he used it for illicit affairs."

"Good old Grandpa." Ryan took a Leatherman knife kit out of his pocket, chose his tool, and went to work on the lock.

"Don't. I have a key in the house if you want to see the inside."

"This is more fun and quicker. See?"

He opened the door. "Damp," he said, and took out his penlight to shine it around the large lower room. "Yet cozy."

The walls were paneled with old-fashioned knotty pine. A small fireplace was built into the far side.

"So, is this where Grandpa entertained his ladies?" He walked around, pleased when he spotted both an oil lamp and candles. He lit them, appreciating the eerie glow they gave the room. "Spooky." He grinned at her. "Come on."

"What are you doing?"

"Going up." He was already climbing the metal tight-winder stairs to the pilot room.

"Don't touch anything." She scurried after him. "It's all automated now."

The modern equipment hummed along as the great lights circled overhead. The room was round, with a narrow ledge circling outside. The iron rails were rusted, but he found them charming. When he stepped out, the wind slapped at him like an insulted woman. The sea raged, sliced by the light, churning under it, through it.

"Fabulous. I would have brought my women here too. Romantic, sexy, and just a little scary," he said, glancing back at her.

He stepped back inside and closed out the wind. "Cold?"

"A little." She hugged herself. "It's very damp in here."

"You're going to have rot if you don't deal with that. That would be a crime. I'm an expert on crime." He put his hands on her arms, rubbing to warm her with friction. "The sea sounds different from in here. Mysterious, almost threatening. The ghosts of shipwrecked sailors haunting the shore, moaning for mercy." He slipped his arms around her.

"You hear the wind," she corrected, but he'd managed to draw a shudder out of her. "Seen enough?"

"Not nearly." He lowered his mouth on hers. "But I intend to."

She tried to wiggle free. "Boldari, if you think you can seduce me inside a damp and dusty lighthouse, you're delusional."

"Is that a dare?"

"No. It's a fact. There's a perfectly good bedroom in the house, several in fact. They're warm, convenient, and have excellent mattresses. This isn't the place for—"

"It was good enough for Grandpa," he reminded her. When his mouth came back to hers, she answered the demand with her own.

They lowered to a floor that was layered with dust, that was hard and cold, and drew together as gently as a couple on a feather bed.

THE next day, Easter Sunday, Miranda was in her office at the house, working on her computer, when her fax phone rang. She walked over as the message slid into the tray.

Did you enjoy Florence, Miranda? I know where you go. I know what you do. I'm right there, inside your mind, all the time. You killed Giovanni. His blood's on your hands.

Miranda pressed her fingers to her eyes, waiting for the fury and fear to fade. When it had, she calmly picked up the paper and put it neatly into a file.

RYAN came in with an armload of daffodils so bright and so sunny she couldn't do anything but smile. She took her grandmother's favored rose medallion vase to the kitchen and busied herself arranging the flowers. "I've made some progress, I think," she told Ryan. "I've put together some lists. I'll go get them."

"Fine." He opened the refrigerator, perused the contents. "Want a sandwich?" Since she was already gone, he shrugged and began to decide what an inventive man could put together.

"Both your lunchmeat and your bread are on the edge," he told her when she came back in. "But we risk it or starve."

She sat and aligned the edges of her papers. "Now—"

"Mustard or mayo?"

"It doesn't matter. Now, what I've done—"

"Coffee or something cold?"

"Whatever." She heaved out a breath. "In order to—"

"Milk's off," he said, sniffing the carton.

"Dump it down the sink, then, and sit down." Her eyes flashed. "Why do you purposely aggravate me?"

"Because it puts such pretty color in your face." He held up a can of Pepsi. "Diet?"

She had to laugh, and when she did, he sat at the table across from her. "There, that's better. I can't concentrate on anything but you when you're sad."

How could she possibly defend her heart against these kinds of assaults? "I'm not sad."

"You're the saddest woman I've ever known." He kissed her fingers. "But we're going to fix that. Now, what have you got?"

She gave herself a moment to regain her balance, then picked up the first sheet. "I've made a time line from the date the *David* came into our hands—for the two weeks it remained in the lab."

"You made graphs and everything." He leaned closer, admiring the work. "What a woman."

"Here are approximate times the *David* was locked in the lab vault. Getting to it would have required a key card, a combination, and a second key. Or," she added, "a very good burglar."

His gaze slid over to hers. "There would have been no reason for me to steal a copy if I'd already taken the original."

"This is a time line of the work period on *The Dark Lady*. It's very fresh in my mind, so this is completely accurate."

" 'Project terminated,' " Ryan read, and glanced at her. "That was the day you got the axe."

"Yes." It still stung. "The following day the bronze was transferred to Rome. The switch had to be made in that small window of time, as I'd run tests on it just that afternoon."

"Well, they had to be ready, the copy fully prepared. The plumber had it for a week. It took the government a week to contract Standjo. Your mother contacts you and offers you the job."

"She didn't offer. She ordered me to come to Florence."

"Mmm." He studied her chart. "Why did it take you six days between the phone call and the flight?"

"I was delayed."

"How?"

"This very large man in a mask came out of nowhere, put a knife to my throat." Her hand fluttered there. "I was just coming back from a trip. Got out of the car, and there he was. He took my briefcase, my purse."

"Did he cut you?"

"A little, just—just enough to scare me. Then he knocked me down, slashed my tires, and took off."

He was blind with fury at the thought of someone holding a knife to her throat. "How bad were you hurt?"

"Just bruises and scrapes. He took my passport, driver's license, all my ID. It took me several days, even pulling strings, to arrange for new ones."

"He was after your ID, darling, because someone didn't want you to get to Florence too soon. They needed time to get to work on the copy and couldn't afford you underfoot until they had it under way, so they hired a pro."

The explanation was so simple, so perfect, she wondered why she hadn't made the connection herself.

THERE was no place to buy a bottle on Easter Sunday. When he caught himself driving around and around looking for one, Andrew began to shake. Damn it, everybody was on his back. He was sick of it, he decided, hitting his fist on the wheel. He'd just keep driving. He wouldn't stop until he found a liquor store that was open.

He glanced down, stared at the fist that was ramming over and over into the steering wheel. The fist that was bloody and torn. It scared the hell out of him.

With his hands trembling, he jerked the car to the curb, rested his head on the wheel, and prayed for help.

The quick rap on the window had him jolting up. It wasn't until he saw Annie circling with her finger, telling him to roll down the window, that he realized he'd headed for her house.

"What are you doing, Andrew?"

"Just sitting here."

She studied his face. It was a mess, she noted. "You tee somebody off?"

"My sister."

Her eyebrows rose high. "Miranda punched you in the eye?"

"No." He touched it with his fingertips. "I slipped on the stairs."

"Really?" Her eyes focused on the fresh cuts and seeping blood on his knuckles. "Did you punch the stairs?"

He stared at his hand. He hadn't even felt the pain. What was a man capable of when he stopped feeling pain? "Can I come in?"

"You won't get a drink in my place."

"I know. That's why I want to come up."

She studied him another moment, then nodded. "Okay."

She unlocked the door, and they walked into the small apartment. She went into the kitchen and took a bag of frozen peas out of the freezer. "Put that on your hand for now. We'll clean it up in a bit. Now, what did you do to upset your sister?"

"Got stinking drunk, humiliated her in front of her boyfriend."

"Miranda's got a guy?"

"Yeah. I entertained him by falling down the stairs."

"You've been a busy boy, Andrew."

"Oh, yeah." He tossed the bag of peas into the sink so he could pace. He couldn't keep still. "We've got a lot of trouble at the institute. I'm under a lot of stress right now."

"If you're breathing, you have stress. You drink yourself blind, the stress is right there when your vision clears up."

"Look, maybe I've got a little problem. I'm going to deal with it. I just need a little time."

"You've got a big problem, and you can deal with it." She crossed to him, took his wrists so he would look at her. "You need a day, because it's only today that has to count."

"So far today stinks."

She smiled, rose on her toes to kiss his cheek. "It's probably going to get worse. Sit down. I'll doctor those knuckles."

"Thanks, Annie." He sighed. He kissed her cheek in turn, then rested his head against hers just for the comfort of it. He pressed his lips to her hair, then to her temple. Then somehow his mouth was on hers. The sheer warmth of her soothed like balm on a wound.

She had let herself wonder once if it would be the same. The feel of him, the taste. But that was long ago, before she'd convinced herself that friendship was enough. It took all of her strength of will to step back from him. He nearly pulled her back, but she held up her hands, palms out in warning.

"Oh, Annie, I'm sorry." What had he done? How could he have ruined the single friendship he couldn't live without?

"I bounced a two-hundred-pound man out of my bar last night because he thought he could buy me along with a beer. If I hadn't wanted your hands on me, you'd have been flat on your back, checking out cracks in my ceiling plaster." She turned and stepped to the refrigerator. "Want a Coke?"

"I don't want to ruin things," he began.

"Ruin what?"

"You matter, Annie. You've always mattered."

She took two Cokes from the refrigerator. "You've always mattered too. I'll let you know when you ruin things."

"I want to talk about . . . before."

She set the bottles on the counter, forced herself to turn, to meet his eyes. "It's painful for me, Andrew."

"You wanted the baby." He'd never spoken of the baby before. "I could see it in your face when you told me you were pregnant. It scared the hell out of me."

She closed her eyes. "Yes, I wanted the baby. I had this fantasy that I'd tell you, and you'd be happy and just sweep me up. Then we'd . . . Well, that's as far as it went. But you didn't want me."

His mouth was dry as dust. He snagged one of the bottles off the counter and gulped down the soda. "I cared about you."

"I was in love with you, Andrew, but I knew you weren't in love with me. Andrew Jones of Jones Point and Annie McLean from the waterfront? I was young, but I wasn't stupid."

"I would have married you."

"Would you? Your offer didn't even hit lukewarm."

That was something that had eaten away at him for fifteen years. "I know. I didn't give you what you needed that day."

She picked up her own Coke. "Looking back, I can't blame you. I'd have ruined your life." The bottle froze halfway to her lips as he stepped toward her. He snatched it out of her hand, set it down, then took a hard grip on her shoulders.

"Maybe I wasn't in love with you. I don't know. But making love with you mattered to me. However badly I handled things afterward, that night mattered. And damn it, Annie, you might have made my life."

"I was never right for you," she said in a furious whisper.

"How do you know? We never had a chance to find out. You tell me you're pregnant, and before I can absorb it, you had an abortion."

"I never had an abortion. I lost the baby. I had a miscarriage."

His grip relaxed, and he stepped back. "You lost it?"

"I told you, when it happened."

"I always thought"—he turned away—"I thought you told me that to make it easier on both of us. I figured that you hadn't trusted me enough to stand by you, to take care of you and the baby."

"I wouldn't have done that without telling you."

"You avoided me for a long time afterward. We never talked about it, never seemed to be able to talk about it."

"You"—she had to swallow—"you wanted the baby?"

"I don't know. But I've never regretted anything more in my life than not holding on to you."

"It hurt me. I had to get over it. Over you."

Slowly he turned back, his eyes level on hers. "Did you?"

She shook her head. "It's not a fair question just now. I'm not going to start something with you that's based on what was."

"Then maybe we'd better take a look at where we are and start from there."

MIRANDA went back to work on the computer. Ryan had given her a whole new line of worry. If he was right, the daylight robbery hadn't simply been a matter of chance, hadn't been some itinerant thief looking for fast cash. It had been a well-planned, carefully orchestrated part of the whole. Yet it hadn't begun with the attack, but with the forgery and theft of the *David*.

Miranda had seen the acquisition of the *David* as another step in her career and had used the authentication as the basis for one of her papers. She'd gotten quite a bit of attention for that, she recalled, in the academic and scientific world. The Fiesole Bronze would have sent her reputation rocketing.

Both pieces were hers. Both pieces had offered her a solid boost up the reputational ladder. And both pieces had been forged. What if they hadn't been the target at all? What if she was?

She jerked as the phone rang. She picked it up. "Hello?"

"Miranda, I have some difficult news."

"Mother, what is it?"

"Sometime on Thursday night the lab was broken into. Giovanni was killed."

"Giovanni." She shut her eyes as tears began to swim.

"The police are investigating, but they have no leads to date. The funeral is tomorrow."

"Tomorrow?"

"I thought it best you hear it from me. Please inform Andrew. I realize you were fond of Giovanni. We all were. There's no need for you to fly in for the services. They're to be simple and private."

"I could fly out tonight."

"That's neither necessary nor wise. The press is well aware that you worked together on the Fiesole Bronze. Your presence here would only stir it all up again."

She closed her eyes and tried to keep her tone even. "Do the police know why the lab was broken into? Was anything stolen?"

"It doesn't appear anything was taken. A great deal was destroyed. The authorities believe it's possible Giovanni knew his assailant."

"I'd like you to keep me informed of the progress."

"I'll see that you're kept up to date. Good-bye, Miranda."

"Good-bye, Mother."

She replaced the receiver, then sat staring at it until she realized Ryan had come in and stood behind her. His hands came to her shoulders, but she nudged him aside. "I'm going for a run."

She didn't often run, but when events and emotions built up to a high inside her, she ran. She chose the beach below the cliffs. As her muscles warmed, she tugged off her light jacket and tossed it aside. No one would steal it.

Orange buoys bobbed on the surface of the dark blue water. Farther out, boats skimmed and sailed as people took advantage of the hint of spring and a Sunday holiday. She followed the curve of the beach. A lobster boat swayed on the current while the waterman in his bright red cap checked his pots. He waved, and she waved in return. Then she stopped, bending over, hands on knees, while her breath screamed out of her laboring lungs.

She sat on the smooth dome of a rock, brought her knees up to rest her head on them. An oystercatcher stalked up and down the shoreline looking important. It made her smile a little. Look at me, he seemed to say, I'm very cool.

"We'd see how cool you are if I'd brought some breadcrumbs," she told him. "You'd be scrambling to gulp them all down before your buddies got wind of it."

"I've heard people who drink too much start believing in talking birds." Andrew laid her jacket in her lap. "You dropped this."

"I came down here to be alone for a while."

He sat on the rock beside her. "Miranda, I'm sorry. I had too much to drink. I embarrassed you. It won't happen again."

"Won't it?"

"No, it won't. I know I've got a problem. I'm trying to come to terms with that. I'm—I'm going to a meeting tonight. A.A."

He saw the flicker in her eyes, of hope, of sympathy, of love. "I'm going to stay at Annie's place for a few days. Give you some privacy with Ryan, give you and me a little space."

"Annie's? You're going to stay with Annie McLean?"

"I'm not sleeping with her. Annie and I . . ." He wasn't sure how to explain it. "We've got a history. Maybe now we're going to see about having a present."

"I didn't know you were anything but friends."

He stared down the beach, thought he could almost pick out the spot where two reckless teenagers had lost their innocence. "I'm sleeping on her couch for a couple of nights. I'm going to get my feet under me again, whatever it takes. But the odds are I'm going to disappoint you again before I do."

She'd read everything she could get her hands on about alcoholism. She knew about backsliding, starting over, failure. "You're not disappointing me today." She held out a hand, linking fingers tight when he took it. "I've missed you so much."

He picked her up off the rock. "Don't give up on me, okay?"

"Tried. Can't."

He laughed. "Okay. Since we've made up, how about a pot roast?"

"It's too late in the day to start one. I'll make you a very manly meat loaf."

"Good enough."

As they started back, she braced herself, knowing she would have to tell him. "Andrew—" She stopped. "Mother called a bit ago. Someone broke into the lab in Florence. Giovanni was there. He was murdered."

"What? Giovanni's dead? Murdered? What is going on?"

She couldn't risk telling him. His emotions, his illness were too unstable a mix. "She said the lab had been vandalized. Giovanni was working late, and someone came in. She said she didn't think anything had been taken."

"It makes no sense." His face was grim. "Someone breaks into the gallery here, takes a valuable bronze, and doesn't squash a fly. Now someone breaks into the lab at Standjo, kills Giovanni, wrecks the place, and takes nothing? What's the connection?"

He didn't expect an answer, so she was spared from lying. "I'm going up to call Detective Cook," he said. "Give him something to chew on besides his Easter ham."

"I'll be there in a minute"—she smiled—"to start your Easter meat loaf."

He spotted Ryan on the cliff path. "Boldari."

"Andrew." Ryan stepped aside.

"Maybe you think since she's a grown woman and her family's screwed up that there's nobody to look out for her, but you're wrong. You hurt her, and I'll break you in two." His eyes went to slits when Ryan grinned at him. "You hear a joke?"

"No. It's just that the last part of that statement is very similar to what I said to my sister Mary Jo's husband when I caught them necking in his Chevy."

Andrew rocked on his heels. "You're not my sister's husband."

"Neither was he at the time." The humor blinked out of Ryan's eyes, and discomfort blinked on. "What I mean to say is—"

"Yeah?" Andrew nodded. "What do you mean to say?"

"I have a great deal of affection and respect for your sister. She matters to me. Is that what you want to hear?"

"Yeah. That'll do. By the way, I appreciate what you did for me last night." Andrew turned and started up the path. "We're having meat loaf," he called back. "Go make her put her jacket on, will you?"

"I'll do that." Ryan started down, skidding a bit on rocks. Miranda started up. He caught her against him. "Your arms are cold. Why don't you have your jacket on?"

"The sun's warm. Andrew's going to an A.A. meeting tonight."

"That's great." He pressed his lips to her brow. "It's a good start."

She drew in a breath. "There's something else. I told him about Giovanni. He's made the connection between the break-in here and the one there. He's going to talk to Detective Cook about it."

"Great. Bring in the cops."

"It's the reasonable thing to do. I can't go on lying to Andrew for much longer."

"Then we'll have to work faster." He draped an arm around her as they walked up the path. "I heard a rumor about meat loaf. In some cultures it is considered an aphrodisiac."

"Really? That was never covered in my anthropology courses."

"It only works if you serve it with mashed potatoes."

"Well then, I guess we'll have to test that theory."

"They can't be instant."

"Please. Don't insult me."

"I think I'm crazy about you, Dr. Jones."

THE PRICE
Chapter Seven

WHAT do you mean you're going to call my mother?" Ryan sat on Miranda's desk, facing her. "I'm going to call her to tell her my conditions for the loan of the Vasaris and a Raphael and a Botticelli."

"Raphael and Botticelli? You never agreed to loan us anything but the Vasaris."

"New deal. Five paintings—a three-month loan. The reason I'm choosing the New England Institute of Art History is because I was very impressed with the facility when I was here a few weeks ago and I was particularly intrigued by Dr. Miranda Jones's idea of creating a display of the history and progress of the Italian Renaissance."

"Were you?" she murmured. "Were you really?"

"I was riveted." He picked up her hand and noted she'd taken off the ring he'd put there. "And then you brought up the idea of holding a fund-raiser at the institute, benefiting the National Endowment for the Arts. As Boldari galleries are staunch supporters of the organization, I was caught. It was clever of you to dangle that lure."

"Yes," she murmured, "wasn't it?"

"But having been told that Dr. Jones is on leave, I'm quite concerned. I can't possibly work with anyone else. The delay has me considering working with the Art Institute in Chicago instead."

"She won't care for that."

"I didn't think she would." He played with her hair. "We need you back inside the institute. We need whoever's behind the forgeries to know you're back on the job. Then we need everyone who was connected to the two bronzes here, together in one spot. We're going to throw a hell of a party."

"A party? The fund-raiser?"

"That's right. And we're going to have it in Giovanni's name, a kind of memorial."

"Giovanni." It turned her blood cold. "You'd use him for this?"

"You can't change that he's dead, Miranda. But we'll arrange it so that whoever killed him comes." He took out his cell phone. "What's your mother's number?"

"That's her home number," she told him after she'd recited it. "With the time difference that's most likely where you'd find her."

Ryan punched in the number, the connection was made, and he began his pitch to her mother.

"Please, call me Ryan. I hope I can call you Elizabeth. I'm sure you know how brilliant and delightful your daughter is, but I must tell you what a tremendous impression she made on me. When I learned she'd taken a leave of absence, well, disappointed is a mild term."

He listened for a moment. "Oh, yes. I have no doubt there are staff at the institute who could implement the basic idea. But I'm not interested in working with the second line. Lois Berenski at the Chicago Art Institute is quite interested in . . ."

It took forty minutes, during which he allowed Elizabeth to wheel and deal until she gave him exactly what he wanted.

He hung up and said, "Miranda, answer the phone."

"What? The phone's not ringing."

"Wait for it," he told her, then grinned when the phone pealed. "That'll be your mother. Act surprised and just a little reluctant."

"Hello? . . . Hello, Mother."

Her leave was to be terminated immediately, and she was to contact the Boldari Gallery and make arrangements for the gala. The display would be completed the second weekend in May.

"It's done," Miranda murmured after she said good-bye and replaced the receiver. "Just like that."

"I didn't mention Giovanni," Ryan told her. "That can't come from me. You'll have the idea for this tomorrow, and after running it by me and securing my agreement, you'll send her a memo. All key staff members from all Jones organizations will attend the event in a show of unity, support, and respect."

"I don't see what good this does."

"Logistics. Everyone connected in one place, at one time." He smiled. "I'll be flying in from New York tomorrow."

"Oh, will you?"

"Yes. It's going to be a pleasure to see you again, Dr. Jones."

"IT'S good to have you back." Lori set a cup of coffee on Miranda's desk and touched a hand to her arm. "I'm so sorry about Giovanni. I know you were friends. We all liked him so much."

"I know." *His blood's on your hands.* "I need to work, Lori, to dive in."

Lori poised her pencil over her notebook. "Where do we start?"

"Set up meetings with carpentry—get Drubeck. He did good work on the Flemish display a couple of years ago. I need to talk to legal, and we'll need to pull someone out of research. I want to be notified the moment Mr. Boldari arrives. Arrange for lunch in the VIP lounge at one o'clock and see if Andrew can join us. I'll need measurements of the South Gallery. Oh, and I want to see a decorator."

Lori's busy pencil paused. "A decorator?"

"Yes. I have an idea for atmosphere." Miranda drummed her fingers. "Send a memo to Andrew requesting that I be copied on publicity. Mr. Boldari is to be put through at any time."

"Of course."

"I'll need to talk to security."

"Check."

"In four weeks ask me for a raise."

Lori's lips curved. "Double check."

IT WAS good to be back in the saddle, to have specific tasks and goals. She was in restoration, checking out the progress of the Bronzino personally, when she spotted Detective Cook wander in. "Detective? What can I do for you?"

"This is some setup you've got here, Dr. Jones." He dug into his pocket and came up with a pack of Juicy Fruit. "Gum?"

"No, thank you."

"Quit smoking." He took out a piece and unwrapped it. "Still driving me nuts. An addiction's what it is. An addiction can take over your life, make you do things you wouldn't do otherwise."

He knew about Andrew's drinking. She could see it in his eyes. "I never smoked," she said. "Would you like to go to my office?"

"No, no. I won't keep you long." He drew a breath of air that smelled of paint and turpentine. "I'd been told you were out on leave. Took a little vacation?"

She started to agree. Instinct stopped her. "I'm sure you're aware that I was told to take leave due to the break-in here and some difficulties that came out of my trip to Florence last month."

She was quick, he thought, not easily tripped. "I heard something about it. Another bronze piece, right? You had some trouble authenticating it. Two bronzes. Funny, don't you think? And I heard about your man in Italy. The murder. That's a rough one."

Distress came into her eyes. "He was a friend. A good one."

He spread his hands. "I came in because your brother's got a theory on how maybe the two incidents are connected."

"Yes, he told me. Do you see a connection?"

"Sometimes you don't see it until you're on top of it." He flipped through his notebook. "You also authenticated the bronze *David*. Nobody can seem to lay their hands on the paperwork."

"I assume the thief took the documents as well as the bronze."

"That makes sense, but he'd have to know just where to look, wouldn't he? Camera blips only put him inside for"—he flipped some pages again—"about ten minutes. He'd have to be fast as greased lightning to have added a trip to the lab for records."

"All I can tell you is the records are missing."

"You have many people work alone here at night—like you and your brother coming in the week after the burglary?"

"Excuse me?"

"I got a statement here from your night security. He says that on March twenty-three, about two thirty a.m., you and Dr. Andrew Jones came in to do some lab work. That's late hours you keep."

"Not habitually." Her heart was stampeding in her chest. "We decided to get some work done while it was quiet. Is that a problem?"

"Not for me. Just keeping it tidy." He scanned the room. "You know, it's hard to find a paper clip out of place here. I bet you put everything in the same place every time. A routine, a habit."

"You could call it an addiction. Detective, I have an appointment very soon, and I'm pressed for time." She glanced at her watch. "I really—" She broke off when Ryan came through the door.

"Miranda, how nice to see you again." He took her hand, brought it to his lips. "I'm sorry. I'm a bit late. Traffic."

"That's all right. I've been tied up for a while. Detective Cook—"

"Oh, yes. We met, didn't we?" Ryan offered a hand.

"I'm glad to hear you're not put off by the theft here, Mr. Boldari. Not everyone would loan a gallery all that art after its security was breached."

"I have every confidence in Dr. Jones and the institute."

"Still, it wouldn't hurt to add on a few men. I could give you the names of a couple of good cops who moonlight in private security."

"That's very kind of you," Miranda said.

"No problem, Dr. Jones. Mr. Boldari." There was something between those two, Cook thought as he headed out the door. And there was definitely something about Boldari. Everything about him checked out neat as pins in a cushion, but there was something.

WITH THE MOST RECENT PLANS for the exhibit still crowded in her head, Miranda slipped out of her jacket and hung it in the foyer closet at the house. As she walked into the parlor, she felt the beginnings of a headache creep in behind her eyes.

She lowered herself into a chair as Ryan poured her a glass of wine. "Try this," he said. He sat on the arm of her chair and began to rub her neck and shoulders. "How's your work?"

"I chose some fabric for drapings and worked with the carpenter on some platforms. The invitations came in."

"Good. We're on schedule. I've got to go out of town a few days."

"What? Where?"

"New York. I have to deal with the transport of the pieces for this exhibit."

"When are you leaving?"

"First thing in the morning. I'll be back in a week or so. You might want to see if Andrew will move back in so you're not alone."

"I don't mind being alone."

"I mind." He picked her up, slid into the chair, and settled her on his lap. He took the glass of wine out of her hand and set it aside. "But since he's not here at the moment . . ."

He'd meant to leave it at a kiss, a nuzzle, a quiet moment. But when her arms tightened around him and her mouth moved urgently under his, he lost himself. "I can't get enough of you." His words were more irritated than pleased. "I always think I have, then I only have to see you to want you."

And no one had ever wanted her—not like this. She felt herself falling. Just feelings, no thoughts, no reason. Just needs, basic as breath. She let herself go, because a part of her didn't believe he'd come back.

HE WAS gone when she awoke, leaving only a note on the pillow beside her. "Good morning, Dr. Jones. I made coffee. It'll be fresh unless you oversleep. You're out of eggs. I'll be in touch."

Though it made her feel foolish as a lovesick teenager, she read it half a dozen times, then tucked it into her jewelry case.

The ring he'd pushed onto her finger, the ring she'd kept foolishly in a velvet-lined square box in the case, was gone.

His plane landed at nine thirty, and Ryan was uptown at his
gallery by eleven. It was a fraction of the size of the institute, more
like a sumptuous private home than a gallery.

He spent three hours at his desk, catching up on work with his
assistant, in meetings with his gallery director, and arranging for the
transportation of the pieces to Maine.

Next was a call to his travel agent cousin. "Joey, it's Ry. Can you
book flights for my family to Maine?" He gave the dates.

"No problemo. All first-class, right?"

"Naturally."

"Always a pleasure doing business with you, Ry."

"Well, that's nice to hear because I have a favor to ask."

"Shoot."

"I'm going to give you a list of names. I need to find out what
traveling these people have been doing. For the last three and a half
years."

"Look, Ry, I love you like a brother, but this kind of thing is
dicey. Airlines aren't supposed to give out that info."

"I've got season tickets to the Yankees. VIP lounge."

There was a short silence. "Give me the names."

"I knew I could count on you, Joey."

When he was done, he kicked back in his chair. He took the ring
he'd given Miranda out of his pocket. He thought he would have
his friend the jeweler pop the stones and make them into earrings
for her. Women, even bright, practical woman, could get the wrong
idea about a ring. He'd have the earrings shipped to her when he—
and the bronzes—were a comfortable distance away.

She was going to get what she needed, he reminded himself.
They would prove her bronze had been genuine. They'd uncover a
forger, a murderer, and she'd be haloed in the spotlight, with her
reputation glinting like gold.

He had several clients who would pay a delightful fee for a prize

like *The Dark Lady*. He could start a new gallery in Chicago or Atlanta or . . . Maine.

No, he'd have to stay clear of Maine after this was done.

A pity, he thought. He'd miss it. He'd miss her.

It couldn't be helped, he told himself. He had to neatly close out
one area of his life and start a new one—as a completely legitimate
art broker. He'd keep his word to his family, and he'd have kept his
word to Miranda. More or less.

But he felt a nasty little ache around his heart.

MIRANDA was about to shut down for the day and take the rest of
her work home, when her computer signaled incoming E-mail under
the header "A Death in the Family."

Uneasy, she clicked on READ. "You have *The False Lady*. There's
blood on her hands. Killing becomes her."

Miranda stared at the message, reading each word over and over.
Struggling for control, she studied the return address. The URL was
the standard route all Standjo organizations used for electronic
mail. She hit the REPLY button. "Who are you?"

She left it at that and hit SEND. It took only seconds for the message to flash across her screen, denying her. "Not a known user."

"SO, HAVE you heard from Ryan?"

Miranda supervised the maintenance crew in the removal of selected paintings from the wall in the South Gallery. "Yes. His office
faxed the details of the transportation schedule. All items will arrive
next Wednesday."

Andrew studied her for a moment, then shrugged. They both
knew that wasn't what he'd meant. Ryan had already been gone a
week.

He dug into the bag of pretzels he'd taken to eating by the pound.
They made him thirsty, and he drank gallons of water. He'd worked
it out in his mind that the liquid was flushing toxins out of his system.

"I'd like you to take a look at the menu before we sign the final
contract with the caterer. It's really your show."

"It's *our* show," Miranda corrected. She rubbed her eyes.

"You've been putting in a lot of hours on this."

"There's a lot to do. Anyway, I like being busy."

"Yeah." He rattled his pretzels. "Neither one of us is looking for loose time right now."

"You're doing okay?"

"Is that the code for 'Are you drinking'? No, I'm not drinking."

"I'm glad you came back home, but I don't want you to feel you have to be there with me if you'd rather be with Annie."

"The fact that I've figured out I want to be with Annie makes it a little rough to stay there sleeping on her couch. If you get the picture."

"Yeah, I get the picture." She crossed over to dip into the pretzels herself.

Chapter Eight

THE buzzer on Miranda's intercom sounded. "Yes?"

"Mr. Boldari is here," Lori said. "He wonders if you have a moment to see him."

Ryan. "Would you ask him to wait, please."

So he was back. He'd been gone nearly two weeks, and not once had he called her. Oh, E-mail and faxes—she smoothed her hair, added lipstick—all sent by some office drone and signed in his name.

He wouldn't have the satisfaction of knowing she'd needed him. Had needed him every day and night of those two weeks. She steadied herself, then went to the door.

"Ryan." She sent him a polite smile. "Sorry to keep you waiting. Please, come in. Would you like some—"

She never finished. As she closed the door, he pressed her against it and crushed his mouth to hers in a hungry kiss.

She kept her arms at her sides and gave him nothing back, not even the passion of resistance.

When he drew away, his eyes narrowed in speculation. She shifted aside. "I'm sure you want to see the final design. I think you'll be pleased." She moved to a drawing board and began unrolling a large sheet of paper.

"That can wait."

She looked up. "Did you have something else in mind?"

"Entirely. But obviously that can wait as well." He crossed to her and cupped a hand under her chin. "I missed you." He said it with a hint of puzzlement in his voice. "More than I intended to, expected to. More than I wanted to."

"Really?" She stepped away. "Is that why you called so often?"

"That's why I didn't call."

She turned aside. "If you'd wanted to end our personal relationship, Ryan, you could have done it less cold-bloodedly."

He laid his hands angrily on her shoulders. "Do I look like I want to end it?" He dragged her toward him, covering her mouth with his again. "Does that feel like I want to end it?"

"Don't play with me this way. I didn't think you were coming back. People have a remarkably easy time walking away from me."

He didn't think or plan or calculate the odds; he just spoke. "I'm halfway in love with you. Maybe more. And nothing about it is easy."

Her eyes went dark; her cheeks went pale. "I . . . Ryan . . ."

"No logical response for that, is there, Dr. Jones?" He took her hands. "What are we going to do about this situation?"

"I don't know."

"I'm not willing to shift back and make it only business between us. If you think that's an option here, you're mistaken."

"However I feel, I won't be pressured, and I keep my options open."

"We'll see about that, Dr. Jones," he murmured.

"Whatever our personal relationship, we have priorities. I think we should give all the information we have to the police. It's what should have been done from the start. I let my feelings for you—"

"You haven't told me what those are. Are you going to?"

She looked away. "I've never felt for anyone what I feel for you.

I'm nearly thirty years old, and I've never had a serious, long-term relationship. I don't know if I'm capable of maintaining one."

"First you have to be willing to find out. Are you?"

"Yes."

He took her hand, held it. "Then we start from there. I'm as much out of my element as you are."

"You're never out of your element," she murmured. "You have too many elements."

He laughed and gave her hand a squeeze. "Why don't I tell you about my trip?"

"You saw your family."

"Yes, my brother and his family will fly in from San Francisco for the gala. The rest of the family will come in from New York. I should warn you, you're going to be checked out thoroughly."

"Wonderful. One more thing to be nervous about."

"Your mother's coming. And your father—which is a small dilemma, as he thinks I'm someone else."

"Oh, I forgot. What will we do?"

"We won't know what in the world he's talking about." Ryan grinned when she gaped. "Rodney's British. I'm not. And he's not nearly as good-looking as I am either. He'll be confused, but he's hardly going to stand there and call Ryan Boldari a liar."

"I don't see what choice we have, and my father certainly doesn't pay close attention to people." She tugged her hand free of his.

Ryan noticed there was something jittery in her eyes. "What?"

"I've been getting . . . communications."

"Communications?"

"Faxes, for the most part. For some time now. Faxes, one E-mail, here and at home."

His eyes were narrow and cool. "Threats?"

"Not exactly."

"Why didn't you let me know this was going on? Don't tell me you weren't frightened. I can see it in your face. What do they say?"

"Various things. One said Giovanni's blood was on my hands."

"If you believe that, you're giving them what they want."

"I understand that, Ryan. But I know it's someone who knows me well enough to use what would hurt me most."

He wrapped his arms tightly around her. "Hold on to me. Come on, hold on. You have copies of the faxes?"

"Yes."

"I want them." When she started to pull away, he held her in place, stroked her hair. "The E-mail. Did you keep it on your machine?"

"Yes."

"Then we'll trace it." Or Patrick would, he thought. "I'm sorry I wasn't here." He drew back. "I'm here now, Miranda, and no one's going to hurt you while I am."

When she didn't answer, he looked at her carefully. "I don't make promises lightly, because I don't break them once I do. I'm going to see this through with you. Do you still want to talk to Cook?"

She'd been so sure that was the right thing. So sure, until he'd made her believe, against all common sense, that she could trust him.

"We'll see it through, Ryan. I guess neither one of us could swallow anything less."

"PUT the base directly over the mark." Miranda watched the two men haul the marble stand to the center of the room. "Perfect."

She narrowed her eyes, envisioning the Donatello bronze of Venus bathing in place on the column. This gallery was devoted to work of the Early Renaissance. She'd had the tall windows draped in deep blue fabric shot with gold. Tables of varying heights were also spread with it, and on the glittering fabric were the tools of artists of that era. The chisels and palettes and brushes. It was a pity they had to be closed under glass, but even with such a rich and sophisticated crowd, fingers could become sticky.

On an enormous carved wooden stand a huge Bible sat open to pages painstakingly printed in glorious script by ancient monks. There were embroidered slippers, a comb, a woman's ivory trinket box. Huge iron candlestands flanked the archway.

"Very impressive." Ryan stepped between them.

She gestured to a large map, dated 1454, on the wall. "Florence,

Milan, Naples, Venice, and the papacy. The birth of a new school of thought in art—humanism. Rational inquiry was the key. Have you seen the other areas?"

"I thought you'd walk me through."

"All right. But I'm expecting my mother within the hour."

She walked with him through the room. "The next gallery, the largest, represents the High Renaissance."

He strolled over to study a table artfully crowded with religious artifacts. Silver crucifixes, chalices, relics. "You've done an amazing job here, Dr. Jones."

"I think it works well. The Titians will be the major focal point of this room, along with your Raphael. It's a magnificent piece."

"Yes, I like it quite a lot."

"I'd have put *The Dark Lady* there. Where everyone could see it."

"We'll get it back." He stepped to her. "Patrick's been working on tracing that E-mail you received."

"Did he manage it? It's been more than a week. I thought he must have given up."

"The user name was attached very briefly to an account. Put on and taken off, and buried under computer jargon."

"What was the account?"

He laid his hands on her shoulders. "Elizabeth Standford-Jones, and under her password. I'm sorry."

"It can't be." She pulled away from him. "She couldn't do this. She couldn't hate me this much. I can't accept that."

"She had access to both bronzes. No one would question her. She sent for you. Then she fired you and sent you home. She pulled you away from the institute. I'm sorry."

She closed her eyes and let his arms come around her.

"Excuse me."

She jerked in his arms as if they were bullets and not words at her back. Very slowly she turned. "Hello, Mother."

Elizabeth didn't look as though she'd just spent the last several hours flying across an ocean. Her hair was perfectly coifed, her steel-blue suit showed not a single crease or wrinkle.

"I apologize for interrupting your . . . work."

Miranda nodded. "Elizabeth Standford-Jones, Ryan Boldari."

"Mr. Boldari"—Elizabeth put warmth in her smile—"how nice to finally meet you."

"A pleasure." He crossed the room to take her hand. "I hope your flight was uneventful."

"It was, thank you. I hope the project is progressing as you'd anticipated, Mr. Boldari."

"Ryan, please. And it's already exceeded my expectations. Your daughter is everything I could wish for."

"You've been busy," she said to Miranda, scanning the room, impressed and pleased. "You have work to do yet, of course. Several of Standjo's staff members flew out today and others will be here tomorrow. They know they're at your disposal. Elise and Richard are here now." She turned to Ryan. "I'd like to see your Vasaris."

"Yes, Ryan, show her the Vasaris. They're in the next area."

"I feel obliged to tell you, Elizabeth," Ryan began when they left Miranda, "that this very impressive exhibit wouldn't have been possible without your daughter."

"I'm well aware of Miranda's talents."

"Are you?" He said it with a slightly mocking lift of brow. "I assumed since you didn't comment on the results of four weeks of intense work on her part, you found them lacking in some way."

Frost lined her voice. "My relationship with Miranda isn't your concern, any more than your relationship with her is mine."

"Odd. I'd say the opposite, since your daughter and I are lovers."

Her fingers tightened briefly on the strap of the slim leather attaché case she carried. "Miranda is an adult. I don't interfere with her personal affairs."

"Just her professional ones, then."

"Elizabeth?" A group of people came in, with Elise in the forefront. Ryan saw a small woman with pixie hair and big, brilliant eyes. One step behind was a balding man he tagged as Richard Hawthorne. Hovering over them was John Carter.

Elizabeth made introductions.

"It's so nice to meet you," Elise told Ryan. "I was in your gallery in New York only last year. It's a treasure. And this"—her eyes shone as she turned a circle—"this is glorious. Richard, get your nose away from that map and look at the paintings."

He turned. "It's an excellent exhibit. You must've worked like dogs."

"Miranda had us jumping through hoops." Carter smiled sheepishly. "Every department head's been chugging Maalox for the past two weeks."

"She's done a brilliant job." Elise glanced around again. "I, um, I thought I'd see if Andrew's free for a few moments."

ELISE hesitated outside the open door of Andrew's office.
She rapped lightly on the jamb.

"We're expecting five hundred guests," he said into the phone, then glanced up and froze.

It all flooded back. The first time he'd seen her, in a lab coat, when she'd taken over the job as assistant lab manager at his father's recommendation.

The way she'd laughed and told him it was about time when he'd finally worked up the nerve to ask her out.

The way she'd looked on their wedding day, radiant, delicate. The way she'd looked when she'd told him it was over, so cold and distant. And all the moods in between that.

The voice on the phone was buzzing in his ears. His hand fisted under the desk. He wished there was a drink in it.

"I'm sorry, Drew," she began when he finally hung up. "Ms. Purdue isn't at her desk, so I thought I'd take the chance."

"It's all right." The foolish words scraped at his throat.

"I know this is awkward. The last time we saw each other was—"

"In a lawyer's office," he finished.

"Yes. I was hoping by now we could at least be—"

"Friends?" He let out a bitter laugh.

"No, not friends. Just something less than enemies." It wasn't what she'd expected, this hard-eyed, cynical look.

"We don't have to be enemies, Elise. We don't have to be anything anymore."

"All right. This was a mistake." She spun around and rushed out. By the time she got to the elevator, tears were stinging her eyes. She punched the button with her fist.

He waited until the click of her heels had echoed away before lowering his head to the desk. She was so beautiful. How could he have forgotten how beautiful she was? She'd belonged to him once, and he'd failed to hold her, to hold their marriage.

He had to get out. Get air. He used the stairs, avoiding the wing with all the bustle of work. He left his car in the lot and walked.

And when he stopped in front of the liquor store, when he stared at the bottles, he told himself he could handle a couple of drinks. Not only could he handle them, he *deserved* them. He'd earned them for surviving that face-to-face contact with the woman he'd promised to love, honor, and cherish. Who'd promised to do the same.

He stepped inside and bought a bottle of Jack Daniel's. Good old Jack. Dependable Jack Black. He could taste it on his tongue, feel the heat slide down his throat.

As the sun set toward twilight, he went into the park. The yellow daffodils were a small ocean of cheer backed by the more elegant red tulips. The first leaves were unfurling on the oaks and maples. The fountain trickled. Over to the left, swings and slides were deserted. Children were home being washed up for supper. He'd wanted children, hadn't he? Imagined making a family, a real family where those in it knew how to love, how to touch each other. Laughter, bedtime stories, noisy family meals. He'd never pulled that off either.

He sat on a bench, running his hand up and down the shape of the bottle in its thin paper bag. One drink, he thought. Then none of this would matter quite so much.

Two pulls, and you'd wonder why it ever had.

ANNIE drew two drafts while the blender beside her whirled with the fixings for a pitcher of margaritas. Happy hour on Fridays was a popular sport for the business crowd and college students.

She saw Andrew come in, saw what he had in his hand. She watched him walk to the bar, take a seat, set the bottle on the bar. Their eyes met over the brown paper sack.

"I didn't open it."

"Good. That's good." Annie signaled to her head waitress, then tugged off her bar apron. "Let's take a walk, Andrew."

He nodded, but he took the bag with him when he followed her out. "I went to a liquor store. It felt good to be in there."

The streetlights were shining now, little islands of light in the dark. End-of-the-week traffic clogged the streets.

"I thought I could just take a couple of pulls from the bottle. Just enough to warm me up," Andrew said.

"But you didn't."

"No."

"It's hard. What you're doing is hard," Annie said. "And tonight you made the right choice."

"I saw Elise. She's here for the exhibit. I knew she was coming. But when I looked up and saw her, it just slammed into me."

Annie jammed her hands into her pockets and told herself she was insane even pretending she and Andrew stood a chance.

He walked to a park bench, sat, and set the bottle beside him.

"I can't tell you what to do, Andrew, but if you could make your peace with it and with her, you'd be better for it."

Because he needed it, she leaned forward and kissed him.

He picked up the bottle, handed it to her. "There, that's a hundred percent profit for you." There was a relief in it—the kind a man feels when he whips the wheel of his car just before plunging off a cliff. "I'm going to go to an A.A. meeting." He puffed out a breath. "Annie, about tomorrow night. It would mean a lot to me if you'd come."

"Andrew, you know I don't fit in with all those fancy people."

"You fit with me. Always have."

"Saturday nights are busy." Excuses, she thought. Coward.

"I'll walk you back." He rose. "Annie, come tomorrow."

"I'll think about it," she said. The last thing she wanted to do was go up against Elise on the woman's turf.

RYAN TOOK MIRANDA HOME and persuaded her to go to bed early. The fact that he barely had to bully her into it only proved to him that she was running on fumes now.

When he was certain she was asleep, when Andrew was closed off in his own wing, Ryan changed into his dark sweater and jeans, slipped his tools into his pocket, and drove to town.

He'd stayed in the same hotel on his first trip and knew the layout perfectly. He'd also taken the precaution of getting the room numbers for all the parties he intended to visit that night.

No one took notice of him as he crossed the lobby and walked to the elevators like a man in a hurry to get to his bed. Elizabeth and Elise were sharing a two-bedroom suite on the top level. He saw no lights under any of the three doors of the suite, heard no murmur of voices or television from inside. The seven-hour time difference from Florence could be a killer the first couple of days.

He was inside the parlor in just under two minutes. He stood still, in the dark, listening, judging, letting his eyes adjust. Then he got to work. He searched the parlor first, though he doubted either woman would have left anything vital or incriminating in that area.

In the first bedroom he used the penlight, keeping it away from the bed, where he could hear soft, steady breathing. He took a briefcase and a purse back into the parlor with him to search.

It was Elizabeth in the bed, he noted as he flipped through the wallet. He went through every scrap of paper and her datebook. He found a safe-deposit-box key and pocketed it. He checked her passport against the dates his cousin had given him. It was Elizabeth's first trip back to the States in more than a year, but she'd taken two quick trips into France in the last six months.

He put everything but the key back where he'd found it. Then while she slept, he searched her closet, the dresser, the cosmetic case in the bathroom. It took him an hour before he was satisfied and moved on to the second bedroom.

He knew Andrew's ex-wife very well by the time he was done. She liked silk underwear and Opium perfume. She favored the top designers. Expensive tastes. He made a note to check her income.

She'd brought her laptop. The contents of her purse and brief-case were orderly. The small leather jewelry case he found contained a few good pieces of Italian gold and an antique silver locket con-taining a picture of a man facing a picture of a woman. They were faded black-and-white, and from the style he judged them to have been taken around World War II. Her grandparents, he imagined, and decided Elise had a quietly sentimental streak.

He left the two women sleeping and moved down the hallway to Richard Hawthorne's room. He too was fast asleep.

It took Ryan ten minutes to find the receipt for a storage facility in Florence, which he pocketed.

It took him thirteen to find the .38. That he left alone.

In twenty he'd located the small leather notebook hidden inside a black dress sock. Scanning the cramped handwriting with his light, Ryan read quickly. His lips tightened in a grim smile.

He tucked the notebook into his pocket and let Richard sleep. He was, Ryan thought as he slipped out, in for a rude awakening.

"Excuse me, you broke into my mother's bedroom last night?" Miranda sat behind her desk, the first time she'd been off her feet since six that morning. It was now noon, and Ryan had finally shoe-horned her during her meeting with the florist.

"Nothing was broken," Ryan assured her. "There was hardly any point in getting them all here if I wasn't going to do something. I got a safe-deposit key out of her purse. It's a Maine bank—with a branch in Jones Point. I'll check it out."

He waited until Miranda opened her mouth, shut it again with-out saying a word. "I didn't find anything in Elise's room except for her laptop. If I have time, I'll go back in and see if I can open it up while she's out of the room. Now your father—"

"My father? He didn't even get in until after midnight."

"You're telling me. I nearly bumped into him in the hall. In any case, my doing the other rooms first gave him time to settle in. He was out like a light. Did you know he's been to the Cayman Islands three times in the last year?"

"The Caymans?"

"Popular spot the Caymans. Good for scuba, sunshine, and money laundering. Now, all that is speculation. But I hit gold in Hawthorne's room. I found this." He took the storage receipt out of his pocket. "He rented this space the day after the bronze was brought to Standjo."

"People rent space for all sorts of reasons."

"They don't generally rent a small garage just outside of the city when they don't own a car. Then there was the gun."

"Gun?"

"The handgun. Why would a nice, quiet researcher need a gun to attend an exhibit?"

"I don't know. Richard and a gun. It doesn't make sense."

"I think it might once you read this." He took the notebook out of his pocket. "It describes a bronze, ninety point four centimeters, a female nude. It gives test results on said bronze, dating it late fifteenth century in the style of Michelangelo."

He watched her cheeks drain of color. "The time of the first test is at 2000 hours on the date *The Dark Lady* was accepted at Standjo. I imagine the lab's closed at eight most nights."

"He ran tests on it on his own?"

"It lists them, step by step. And it adds the documentation. He found something he didn't tell you about. An old baptismal record from the Convent of Mercy, written out by the abbess on a male child, infant. The mother's name was recorded as Julietta Buenodarni. The child was baptized Michelangelo." He saw when the idea struck home. "One might speculate, after his papa."

"Michelangelo was, by all accounts, homosexual."

"That doesn't make him incapable of conceiving a child." But he shrugged. "Doesn't mean the kid was his either, but it does make the theory that they had a close personal relationship highly possible, and if they did . . ."

"It helps support the likelihood that he used her as a model."

"Exactly. If they were lovers or if they had a close enough platonic relationship that she would name her only child after him, it goes a long way toward concluding that he created the bronze of her."

She could see the sense of it now. "Richard stole the bronze and copied it. And the *David,* he had to have taken that as well." Her fisted hand pressed against her midriff. "He killed Giovanni."

"It wouldn't be proof," Ryan said. "But it would add weight."

"We need to take this to the police."

"Not yet. I'd feel a lot more confident of the outcome if we had the bronzes in hand before we talk to cops. I'll go to Florence tomorrow, check out his storage space. Once we've got them, we'll work out what to tell the cops."

"He has to pay for Giovanni."

"He will. Give me forty-eight hours, Miranda."

She pressed her lips together. "All right. But tonight . . . how can we possibly go through with tonight? He'll be there."

"Tonight goes as scheduled. We don't know if he acted alone. Hawthorne's made a mistake. Now we'll see if someone else makes one. When I have the bronzes, we'll give him to the cops. I have a feeling he won't want to hang alone."

She jumped to her feet. "Hang."

"It's an expression."

"But—prison or worse. If it's one of my family, I don't know if I can live with knowing I helped put them behind bars."

"Just a minute." He grabbed on to her before she could evade. "Whoever's responsible for this put your life on the line. What's your alternative? To let them walk? To leave *The Dark Lady* wherever she is? Forget what's been done?"

"I don't know. There has to be a middle ground."

He held the book out. "You take it. Keep it."

She stared at it, taking it gingerly as if the leather would burn. "How am I going to get through tonight?"

"With that Yankee spine of yours? You'll do just fine. I'll be with you. We're in this together."

She nodded, put the book in a drawer, and locked it. Forty-eight hours, she thought. That was all the time she had to decide whether to make the book public or to burn it.

IT'S GOING TO BE PERFECT. I know exactly how it will work now. It's all in place. All those people will be there, admiring the great art, drinking champagne. Miranda'll move among them, gracious and cool. The brilliant Dr. Jones. The perfect Dr. Jones.

The doomed Dr. Jones.

Her star's rising again. Tonight it falls.

I've planned my own exhibit for tonight, one that will overshadow hers. I've titled it Death of a Traitor.

I believe the reviews will be very strong.

Chapter Nine

NO ONE knew her stomach was alive with butterflies. Her hands were cool and steady, her smile easy. The unflappable Dr. Jones. She wore a long column of midnight blue with a high banded collar and sleeves that ended in narrow cuffs.

She watched her mother, elegant as an empress in a gown of petal pink, working the crowd. Her father was beside her, of course, dashing in his tuxedo, the well-traveled adventurer with the interesting air of a scholar. How handsome they looked together, how perfect the Joneses of Jones Point appeared on the surface.

"You belong in one of those paintings behind you." Ryan took her hand. "You look magnificent."

"I'm absolutely terrified. I always am in crowds."

"So we'll pretend it's just you and me. You need champagne." He handed her one of the flutes he'd taken from a roaming waiter. "To the very successful results of your work, Dr. Jones."

"It's difficult to enjoy it."

"Fall into the moment." He touched his lips lightly to hers, causing more than one eyebrow to raise. "I find your shyness endearing and your skill in masking it admirable."

"Were you born with that talent or did you develop it?"

"Which? I have so many."

"The talent of knowing exactly the right thing to say at precisely the right time."

"Maybe I just know what you need to hear. There's dancing in the Center Hall. You've never danced with me."

"I'm a terrible dancer."

"Maybe you've never been properly led. Let's find out." He kept a hand at her back as they maneuvered through the crowd. At least a dozen times she was stopped, congratulated.

"There's Mrs. Collingsforth." Miranda nodded to a woman with an amazing stack of white hair in a gown of maroon velvet.

"Of the Portland Collingsforths?"

"Yes. I want to introduce you. She's fond of attractive young men."

Miranda wound her way through to where the widow was sitting. "Mrs. Collingsforth, I hope you're enjoying yourself."

"Lovely music. It's about time you put some punch into this place," she said. "Places that house art shouldn't be stuffy. Who's this?"

"Ryan Boldari." He bent down to take her hand and kiss the gnarled knuckles. "I wanted to thank you for lending the institute so many wonderful pieces from your collection."

"If the girl threw more parties instead of burying herself in a laboratory, I'd have lent them to her sooner."

"I couldn't agree more." He beamed at Mrs. Collingsforth, making Miranda feel superfluous.

"Keeps herself glued to a microscope."

"Where one often misses the big picture."

Mrs. Collingsforth narrowed her eyes. "I like you."

"I wonder, madam, if I could impose on you for a dance."

"Well"—her eyes twinkled—"I'd enjoy that, Mr. Boldari."

"Please, call me Ryan." He tossed Miranda one wolfish grin over his shoulder as he led Mrs. Collingsforth into the music.

"That was smooth," Andrew murmured at Miranda's shoulder.

"As grease on a tree limb. It's a wonder he doesn't slide off and break his neck. Did you meet his family?"

"Are you kidding? I think every other person here is related to him. His mother collared me, wanting to know if we held art classes for children here, and why not, didn't I like children? She's great."

Andrew's hands were fiddling with his tie. Miranda took one of them and squeezed. "I know this is hard for you. All these people—Elise."

"Sort of a trial by fire. Elise, the cases of free booze." He glanced toward the entrance again. Annie hadn't come.

"You need to keep busy. Do you want to dance?"

"You and me?" He dissolved in easy, genuine laughter. "We'd both end up with broken toes." Then his smile stiffened. Miranda didn't have to shift her gaze to know he'd seen Elise.

She came up to them, a sleek fairy in filmy white. "I just wanted to congratulate both of you on a wonderful and successful exhibit. You've done a fabulous job." She seemed to take a deep gulp of air. "Andrew, I know my being here is awkward for you. I've decided to go back to Florence tomorrow."

"You don't have to change your plans for my benefit."

"It's for mine too." She looked at Miranda then. "Your parents are very proud of what you accomplished here."

Miranda goggled before she could control it. "My parents?"

"Yes. Elizabeth was just saying—"

"Annie." Andrew said the name almost like a prayer. "Excuse me." He made his way toward her. She looked so lovely. Her red dress glowed like a flame in all the sober and conservative black.

"I'm so glad you came." He caught her hands like lifelines.

"I feel ridiculous." The dress was too short, she thought, too red. "Why don't I just grab a tray? I'd fit in better that way."

Ignoring the raised eyebrows, he kissed her. "You fit in fine. Come over and talk to Miranda." But when he turned, his eyes locked with Elise's. She only shook her head, then hurried away.

"Your wife looked upset," Annie commented.

"Ex-wife," Andrew reminded her, grateful to see Miranda making her way toward them.

"Annie, it's so good to see you." It was rare for Miranda to follow impulse, but she did so now, bending to press her cheek to Annie's.

"He needs you," she whispered, then straightened with a smile. "I see some people I think you'd enjoy. Andrew, why don't you introduce Annie to Mr. and Mrs. Boldari?"

He grinned. "Yeah, thanks. Come on, Annie, you're going to love these people."

It had lifted Miranda's heart to see that warm glow in Andrew's eyes, but then Elizabeth found her. "Miranda, you're neglecting your duties. Several people have said they've yet to have a word with you."

"Of course. I'll do my duty. But just once tonight you might have said to me that I'd done a good job." Miranda turned, walked up the stairs to mingle with the guests on the second level.

"Is there a problem, Elizabeth?"

She glanced at her husband as he came to her side, then looked back up at Miranda. "I don't know. I'll have to find out."

"Senator Lamb would like to see you. He's an NEA supporter."

"Yes," she said. "I'll be happy to speak with him."

And then, she thought, she was going to deal with Miranda.

FOR an hour Miranda concentrated on her role as hostess. When she finally slipped off into the ladies' room, she leaned against the counter. Too many people, she thought. She just wasn't good with so many people. But everything was perfect. The exhibit, the gala, the press. She reached into her bag for her lipstick.

The explosion of sound had her hand jerking. The slim gold tube clattered onto the counter. Her eyes went wide with shock.

Gunshots? Impossible. Even as the denial raced through her, she heard the high, horrified sound of a woman's scream.

She rushed to the door. Outside, people were shouting. She ran for the steps just as Ryan rounded the lower landing.

"It . . . from upstairs. It came from upstairs."

"Stay here."

He might have saved his breath. She hiked up her skirt and was pounding up behind him. "You check that way. I'll look down—"

"The hell you will. If you won't stay put, then you'll come with me." He took a firm hold of her hand.

More footsteps sounded on the stairs behind them. Andrew said, "Miranda, go downstairs. Annie, go down with her."

"No."

Since neither woman was going to listen, Ryan gestured to the left. "You check that way. We'll go down here." He cautiously nudged open a door. "Stay behind me."

Miranda reached in under his arm and flicked on the light. He shoved her back and stepped into the room. Satisfied it was empty, he strode down the hall to the next room.

They worked their way down until he spotted light under the door to her office. "Did you leave your light on?"

"No. And the door should be locked. It's not quite closed."

He eased to the side of the door, nudged it. It opened another two inches, then bumped into an obstruction.

"Oh, my God." She recognized the filmy white gown, the silver shoes. Dropping to her knees, she pushed at the door until she could squeeze inside.

Elise lay crumpled, facedown. Blood trickled from a wound at the back of her head. "She's alive," Miranda said quickly when she pressed her fingers to Elise's throat and found a fluttery pulse. "Call an ambulance. Hurry."

"Here." He shoved a handkerchief into her hand. "Press that against it. See if you can stop the bleeding."

"Just hurry." She folded it into a pad and applied pressure.

"Miranda, what—" Andrew pushed in the door. "Oh, no! Elise." He was on his knees.

"She's alive. Ryan's calling for an ambulance on my phone."

"She needs to be covered. Do you have a blanket?" Annie asked.

"In my office. There's a throw. Just through there."

Annie stepped quickly over Andrew.

"I think she's coming around." Andrew gently touched a bruise on Elise's temple. "She must have hit her head when she fell."

"Miranda." Annie stepped back into the room. "Ryan wants you. We'll take care of her. Brace yourself," she murmured.

Miranda got to her feet and stepped into her office. On her desk, flung onto his back, with red spreading over his frilled white shirt, was Richard Hawthorne.

MIRANDA gave her statement again and again, going back over every step. And lying. No, she had no idea why Richard or Elise would have been in her office. No, she didn't know why anyone would have killed him. When they finally told her she was free to leave, she walked downstairs on legs that felt as fragile as glass.

She looked over her shoulder as she heard footsteps on the stairs. Ryan came down, brought her into his arms.

"Oh, God, oh, God, Ryan. How many more?"

"Shh." He stroked her back. "It was his own gun. Someone shot him with his own gun. There was nothing you could have done."

"Nothing I could have done." She said it wearily, but pulled back to stand on her own. "I want to go to the hospital, check on Elise. Andrew's there. He shouldn't be alone."

But when they got there, he wasn't alone. Miranda was surprised to see her mother in the waiting lounge, staring out the window, a paper cup of coffee in her hand. Andrew stopped pacing when they came in.

"Is there any word?" Miranda asked him.

"They stabilized her in emergency. The resident thought concussion, but they want to do a CAT scan. She was out a long time. She lost a lot of blood." Some of it, he noted, had stained Miranda's dress. "You should go home, Miranda. Ryan, take her home."

"I'm going to stay with you, just the way you'd stay with me."

"Okay, okay."

Elizabeth turned from the window. "There's coffee. It's neither fresh nor palatable, but it's strong and hot."

"Excuse me, Dr. Jones." All three of them turned, made Cook's mouth twitch. "Guess that's pretty confusing."

"Detective Cook," Miranda said. "I hope you're not ill."

"Oh, no. I came to talk to Dr. Warfield once the doctors clear it."

"To Elise?" Baffled, Andrew shook his head. "I thought you were with robbery. Nobody was robbed."

"Sometimes these things are connected. Maybe you can tell me what you know before I talk to Dr. Warfield."

Elizabeth moved forward. "Is it really necessary?"

"I'm sorry for your distress, ma'am. Dr. Jones."

"Standford-Jones."

"Elizabeth Standford-Jones. You're the victims' employer."

"That's correct. Both Richard and Elise work for me in Florence. Worked for me," she amended. "Richard worked for me. He was a brilliant art historian."

"And Dr. Warfield?"

"She is my lab director in Florence."

"She used to be your daughter-in-law."

"Yes. We've retained a good relationship. I don't allow family difficulties to interfere with work. I'm quite fond of Elise."

"Anything going on between her and Hawthorne?"

"Going on?" Elizabeth said with frigid disgust. "What you're suggesting is insulting and inappropriate."

"They were both single adults. They were in a third-floor office together. The party was downstairs."

"I have no idea why either of them was in Miranda's office, but obviously they weren't alone."

A doctor in green scrubs came to the doorway. "She's doing well," he told them. "She has a concussion, but the CAT scan was clear."

Elizabeth said, "I'd like to see her."

"I cleared the police in. She became agitated when I suggested they wait until tomorrow. It seemed to ease her mind to talk to them tonight."

"I'm going to want some time with her." Cook took out his badge, then nodded toward Elizabeth and Andrew. "I'll wait. I've got plenty of time."

He waited over an hour; then he saw a fragile woman swathed in white bandages. "I appreciate you talking to me, ma'am."

"I want to help." Elise winced as she shifted.

"I'll try to make this fast. Can you tell me what happened?"

"Richard. He shot Richard."

"He?"

"I don't know. I didn't see. I saw Richard." Her eyes filled. "He's dead. They told me he was dead. Poor Richard."

"What were you doing upstairs with him?"

"I was looking for him. He'd said he'd go back to the hotel whenever I wanted to leave. Richard's not much on parties. We were going to share a cab."

"Dull party?"

"No. It was a wonderful exhibit. But Andrew and I used to be married, and it was awkward. He had a date there."

"So you went looking for Hawthorne."

"Yes. We'd agreed to leave around ten thirty, so I tried to find him. I thought he might have gone upstairs to the library. He wasn't there." She closed her eyes. "I saw the light in Miranda's office. Then I heard Richard shout something—something like 'I've had enough.' I walked over. There were voices. But I couldn't hear what they were saying."

"Was it a man's voice or a woman's?"

"I don't know. It was very low, only a murmur really. I thought he and Miranda might have come up to discuss something, and I didn't want to interrupt."

"Miranda?"

"It was her office, so I just assumed. And then . . . I heard the shots. I was so shocked, I didn't think. I ran inside. I think I called out. I— It's just not clear."

"That's all right. Just tell me what you remember."

"I saw Richard lying over the desk. The blood everywhere. I must have screamed. Then someone . . . something hit me." She was crying openly now.

"When you went into the office, you didn't see anyone?"

"Only Richard." She closed her eyes, so that tears squeezed through her lashes.

IT WAS nearly dawn when Annie opened her door and found Andrew still in his tux, the tie loose around his neck.

"Elise's going to be all right. I needed to tell you."

"I know. Come on in, Andrew. I've made coffee." She was bundled in a robe and had washed the makeup from her face.

He closed the door, watched her walk to the kitchen.

"Annie"—he took her by the shoulders, turned her around—"I needed to go with Elise tonight."

"Of course you did."

"I needed to go to make sure she was all right. I owed her that. While I was waiting for the doctor to come out and tell us how she was, I thought about that and what I might have done differently to make it work between us. The answer is nothing. The marriage just failed. I didn't. She didn't. It did."

He bent to kiss the top of her head. "I waited until I was sure she was going to be all right. Then I came here because I had to tell you."

"I know that, Andrew." She patted his arm.

"I haven't finished. I haven't started to tell you."

"Tell me what?"

"My name is Andrew, and I'm an alcoholic." He seemed to quiver once, then steady. "I've been sober for forty-one days. I sat in the hospital tonight, and I thought about drinking. It just didn't seem to be the answer. Then I thought about you. You're the answer. I love you."

Her eyes went damp, but she shook her head. "I'm not your answer, Andrew. I can't be."

"I love you," he repeated. "Part of me always has. The rest of me had to grow up enough to see it. I know what I feel, and I know what I want. If you don't have those same feelings for me and don't want what I want, then you tell me straight. It's not going to send me out looking for a bottle."

"What do you want me to say? You're a Ph.D. I'm GED. You're Andrew Jones of the Maine Joneses, and I'm Annie McLean from nowhere." She put her hands over his. "I run a bar. You run the institute. Get a grip on yourself, Andrew."

"I'm not interested in your snobbery right now."

"Snobbery?" Her voice cracked.

"You didn't answer my question. What do you feel for me, and what do you want?"

"I'm in love with you, and I want a miracle."

His smile spread slowly. "I don't know if it'll qualify as a miracle. But I'll do my best." He buried his face in her hair. "You'll probably turn me down when I ask you to marry me."

"You—you could ask me now and save yourself the suspense."

"I want to build a life and a family with you."

"We both really screwed up the first time."

"We weren't ready."

"No." She touched his face. "It feels like we are now."

"Belong to me." He kissed her. "Let me belong to you. Will you, Annie?"

"Yes." She laid her hand over his heart. "Yes, Andrew. I will."

RYAN stood in the doorway of Miranda's office, trying to picture the crime. How far would the bullet have propelled Richard's body? How close had he and his killer been standing? Close enough, he thought, for the bullets to have left powder burns on the tuxedo shirt. Close enough for Hawthorne to have looked into his murderer's eyes. Ryan was sure of that.

"You shouldn't be in here, Mr. Boldari."

"They've taken the tape down," Ryan said without turning.

"Better we keep it closed off awhile yet." Cook waited until Ryan moved out of the doorway, then shut the door.

"I wanted to see if I could get it all clear in my mind. There doesn't appear to be any sign of a struggle, does there, Detective?"

"No. Everything tidy. He knew who pulled the trigger, Boldari. You'd met him, hadn't you?"

"Briefly, on Friday and again the night he died."

"Never met him before that?"

"No, I hadn't."

"I wondered about that, seeing as you're in art, he was in art."

"Do you think I came up here last night and put two bullets into Richard Hawthorne?"

"No, I don't. We've got several witnesses who put you downstairs when the shots were fired."

Ryan leaned against the wall. "Lucky I'm a sociable guy."

"Yeah. Of course a few of those people are related to you, but there were those who weren't. Nobody can seem to say where Dr. Miranda Jones was during the time in question. You two have gotten very friendly."

Ryan came off the wall quickly, almost violently. "Friendly enough that I know Miranda's the last person who could kill."

Idly Cook took out a stick of gum and unwrapped it. "It's funny what people can do with the right motivation."

"And hers would be?"

"I've done a lot of thinking about that. There's the bronze—the one from here, the one that got lifted out of a display case. I tracked a number of burglaries with that pattern. Somebody's darned good at their job. Somebody has connections."

"So now Miranda's a thief—an expert art burglar?"

"Or she knows one or is friendly enough with one," he added. "Funny how the paperwork on that piece went away too. Then I start thinking about that big-deal bronze in Florence—the one that turned out not to be such a big deal. I found out somebody went right into the storage area at the national museum over there and took it, slick as spit. Now why would somebody want to risk that kind of theft for something that isn't worth more than the price of the metal?"

"Art's a subjective mystery. Maybe someone took a liking to it."

"Could be, but whoever did it was a pro. Pros don't waste their time, unless they've got good reason. You'd agree with that, wouldn't you, Mr. Boldari? Being a professional yourself."

"Certainly." Damned if he didn't like this cop, Ryan mused. "I detest wasting time."

"Makes me wonder what that bronze is worth to somebody."

"If I see it, Detective, I'll do an appraisal and let you know. But I can tell you, if that bronze was real, if it was worth millions, Miranda wouldn't kill for it. And I think you agree," Ryan added. "Being a professional yourself."

Cook chuckled. Something wasn't square about the guy, but you had to like him. "I agree. Woman's got integrity pasted on her fore-head. That's why I know, in my gut, she's hiding something. And if you're friendly enough with her, Boldari, you should convince her to tell me before somebody decides she's expendable."

SHE was asking herself just how much she could tell, could risk telling. In the South Gallery, surrounded by the art of the masters, she sat with her hands over her face. When her mother came in, she let them fall into her lap.

"I thought I might find you here. I haven't been able to find your brother."

Miranda rose. "I hope he's sleeping. It was a difficult night." She didn't add that he hadn't been sleeping, at least not in his own bed, when she'd left the house that morning.

"Yes, for all of us. I'm going to the hospital. Your father's meet-ing me there. Hopefully Elise will be released this afternoon. It was fortunate she wasn't hurt more seriously."

"I know you're very fond of her. Fonder, I think, than you ever were of your own children."

"What a ridiculous thing to say, and what an inappropriate time to say it. If this stems from the business in Florence—"

"Oh, it goes back much farther than what happened in Florence. You didn't stand by me. All of my life I've waited for that moment when you'd finally be there. Why weren't you ever there for me?"

"I refuse to indulge you in this behavior." With an icy stare Eliz-abeth turned and started out.

Miranda grabbed Elizabeth's arm, whirling her around with a violence that stunned both of them. "You will not walk out on me until I have an answer. Why couldn't you ever be a mother to me?"

"Because you're not my daughter," Elizabeth snapped out, her eyes flaring to a blue burn. "You were never mine." She wrenched her arm free. "Don't you dare stand there and demand from me after all I've sacrificed, all I've endured because your father elected to pass his bastard off as mine."

"Bastard?" Her world tilted. "I'm not your daughter?"

"No, you are not. I gave my word that I would never tell you." Infuriated, Elizabeth strode to the window, stared out. "Well, you're a grown woman, and perhaps you have a right to know."

"I—" Miranda pressed a hand to her heart because she wasn't sure it continued to beat. "Who is my mother? Where is she?"

"She died several years ago. She was no one," Elizabeth added, turning back. "One of your father's . . . short-term interests."

"He had an affair."

"His name is Jones, isn't it?" Elizabeth said bitterly. "In this case, he was careless and the woman became pregnant. She insisted he deal with the child. It was a difficult situation."

A stab of pain lanced the shock. "She didn't want me either."

With the faintest of shrugs Elizabeth walked back and sat. "I have no idea. But she demanded that Charles raise you. He came to me and outlined the problem. My choices were to divorce him, lose what I had begun to build here at the institute, and give up my plans for my own facility. Or—"

"You stayed with him. After a betrayal like that."

"I made the choice that was best for me. It was not without sacrifice. I had to go into seclusion, lose months while I waited for you to be born. When you were, I had to present you as mine. I resented the fact of you, Miranda," she said evenly. "You were a reminder of my husband's lack of marital integrity. For Charles you were a reminder of a serious miscalculation."

"Miscalculation," Miranda said quietly. "It's hardly a mystery now why neither one of you could ever love me."

"I'm not a maternal woman. After Andrew was born, I had no intention of having another child. Ever. You were given a good home, a fine education." Elizabeth sighed, got to her feet. "You were never harmed, never neglected."

"Never held."

"I gave you every opportunity to prove yourself in your field. Up to and including the Fiesole Bronze. I took your reports, the X rays, the documents home. After I'd calmed down, I wasn't quite sure you could have made such blatant mistakes or that you would skew test results. Honesty has never been something I doubted in you."

"Oh, thank you very much," Miranda said dryly.

"The reports, the documents were stolen out of my home safe. I might not have known, but I wanted to bring your grandmother's pearls here and put them in the safe-deposit box I keep at a local bank. I was going to give them to you before I left."

"Why?"

"Perhaps because, while you were never mine, you were always hers." She picked up her bag. "I have to meet your father."

When she was gone, Miranda walked to the window. The storm that had been threatening all day was rolling in.

"You okay?"

She leaned back as Ryan laid his hands on her shoulder.

"How much did you hear?"

"Most of it."

"Eavesdropping again," she murmured. "I feel . . . relieved. For as long as I can remember, I've been afraid I was like her, but I'm not." She turned and laid her head on his shoulder. "I don't ever have to worry about that again."

"I'm sorry for her. For closing herself off to you. To love."

Miranda knew what love was now, the terror and thrill of it. Whatever happened, she was grateful that part of herself had been opened. Even if the lock had been picked by a thief.

She held on one last moment, then drew away. "I'm going to go to Cook with Richard's book."

"Give me time to get to Florence. I'll leave tonight if I can manage it. Thirty-six hours should do it."

"I can't give you more than that. I need this to be over."

"It will be."

She smiled. "No sneaking into bedrooms, no rifling through jewelry boxes or safes."

"Didn't I resist those pearls of your grandmother's? All that gold of Elise's? The pretty locket I could have given one of my nieces?"

"Your nieces are too young for lockets." She let out a sigh. "I didn't get mine until I was sixteen. My grandmother gave me a very pretty heart-shaped one."

"And you put a lock of your boyfriend's hair in it."

"I didn't have boyfriends. She'd already put her picture in it anyway, and my grandfather's. It was to help me remember my roots."

"You'll have her pearls now."

"Yes, and I'll treasure them. I lost the locket a few years ago." She straightened. "Broke my heart."

"I'll meet you back at the house later," he murmured. "Go straight there, will you, so I don't have to search you out."

"Where else would I go?"

Chapter Ten

ANDREW whistled as he walked into the house. He knew a grin was plastered on his face. He was in love. And Annie loved him back. They'd spent the day together and talked until his throat was raw. So many thoughts and feelings bursting to get out. He'd never been able to talk to anyone the way he could talk to Annie. Except Miranda. He couldn't wait to tell Miranda.

They were going to be married in June. Not a big formal wedding. Something simple and sweet, that's what Annie wanted. He was going to ask Miranda to be his best man. She'd get such a kick out of that.

He stepped into his bedroom. He wanted to get out of the wrinkled tuxedo. He shrugged out of his jacket, tossed it aside.

He was still grinning when out of the corner of his eye he caught a blur of motion. Pain exploded in his head. His knees buckled as he tried to turn, tried to strike out. The second blow had him crashing into a table and falling into the black.

THE storm broke. Miranda was a mile from home when the rain flooded over her windshield. Lightning slashed so close that its companion burst of thunder shook the car. It was going to be a mean one.

To narrow her concentration, she switched off the radio, shifted forward in her seat. But her mind played it all back.

The call from Florence, then the mugging. John Carter flying out while she was delayed. Richard had run tests. Who had worked with him? Who had brought the gun to the institute and used it? John? She tried to imagine it but kept seeing his homely, concerned face. Could he have pumped two bullets into Richard, have struck Elise? And why in her office? Why at an event with hundreds of people wandering the lower levels? Why take such a risk?

Because it had impact, Miranda realized. Because it once again put her name in the paper in a scandal. It was personal; it had to be. But what had she done to create that kind of animosity? If she was forced to resign from the institute, John would be the logical choice for her replacement. Could it be that simple?

Who else was left? Giovanni and Richard were dead. Elise was in the hospital. Elizabeth . . . Could that lifetime of resentment have bloomed into this kind of hate? Leave it for the police, she told herself when she pulled the car to the front of the house. In less than thirty-six hours she would pass this nasty ball over to Cook.

She picked up her briefcase, holding it over her head as she made a dash to the porch.

Inside, she called out for Andrew. She hadn't seen him since she'd left the hospital the night before. It was time, she'd decided, she told him everything.

She called out again as she started upstairs. "Andrew?" His door wasn't quite closed. The room was pitch-dark, and she reached for the light switch that would turn on the floor lamp. She muttered an oath when the lamp stayed dark. He hadn't replaced the bulb again. She started forward, and tripped over him.

"Andrew!" In a brilliant flash of lightning she saw him at her feet, still wearing the tux. It wasn't the first time she'd come across him passed out in his clothes and stinking of liquor.

"How could you do this to yourself again?" she murmured. She crouched down, hoping that she could rouse him. It struck her suddenly that she didn't smell whiskey. She laid a hand on his head. And felt the sticky warmth. Blood.

"Oh, God. Andrew. No. Oh, please." Her smeared and trembling fingers probed for a pulse. And the bedside lamp switched on.

"He's not dead. Yet." The voice was soft, with a light laugh at the edges. "Would you like to keep him alive, Miranda?"

RYAN let himself into Elizabeth's suite. The rooms were silent and empty.

In one of the bedrooms he took out the jewelry case precisely as he had two nights ago. And removed the locket.

It was only a hunch, but he'd learned to follow his instincts. He studied the old photographs, saw no particular resemblance. Using a small probe, he popped one elegant little oval out. She'd had it inscribed under her photo. "Miranda, on the occasion of your sixteenth birthday. Never forget where you come from or where you wish to go. Gran."

"We've got you," he said quietly, and slipped the locket into his pocket. He was already pulling his phone out as he hurried back out to the corridor.

"ELISE." Miranda forced herself to speak calmly, to keep her eyes on Elise's face and not on the gun. "He's badly hurt. I need to call an ambulance."

"He'll keep for a while. It's amazing how quickly you can bounce back from a good bash on the head." Her eyes glittered with delight. "Don't worry. I didn't hit him nearly as hard as I hit Giovanni. But then, Andrew didn't see me. Giovanni did."

"Giovanni was your friend. How could you have killed him?"

"I wouldn't have had to if you'd left him out of it."

Miranda curled her fingers into her palm. "And Richard."

"Oh, Richard. He killed himself." A faint line of irritation dug between her eyebrows. "He started falling apart right after Giovanni. No one was supposed to die, he said. Well, plans changed. The minute he sent you that ridiculous E-mail, he was dead."

"But you sent the others, the faxes."

"Oh, yes. Did they frighten you, Miranda? Make you wonder?"

"Yes. You killed Rinaldi, the plumber, too."

"That man was a constant annoyance. He kept insisting the bronze was real."

"You have the bronze, but you'll never be able to sell it."

"Sell it? Do you think this is about money?" She laughed. "It's never been about money. It's you. It's you and me, Miranda, like it's always been."

Lightning shimmered against the glass of the window behind Elise. "I've never done anything to you."

"You were the prized daughter of the house. The eminent Dr. Jones of the Maine Joneses, with your highly respected parents, your bloodline, your snooty grandmother in her big house."

Elise gestured wildly, swinging the gun. "You know where I was born? In a charity ward, and I lived in a lousy two-room apartment because my father wouldn't acknowledge me. I deserved everything you had, and I got it. But I had to work for it, to beg for scholarships. I made sure I went to the same colleges as you did. I watched you, Miranda. You never even knew I was there."

"Let me call an ambulance for Andrew."

"Shut up! I'm not finished." She kicked a discarded shoe across the floor. "You talk, and everyone listens. It should have been me, and it would have been if the s.o.b. who got my mother pregnant hadn't been married to your grandmother."

"My grandmother?" Miranda shook her head even as her fingers slid slowly down to check Andrew's pulse. "You're trying to tell me my grandfather was your father?"

"The old bastard just couldn't keep his zipper up, even into his sixties. My mother thought he'd ditch his wife and marry her. Stupid, stupid, stupid." The gun swung back, its barrel aimed at Miranda, and Elise smiled. "I watched you. I planned for years. You were my goal. I went into the same field. I married your useless brother. I'm more of a daughter to your mother than you've ever been."

"Oh, yes," Miranda said with perfect sincerity. "You are."

"I'd have had your position sooner or later. Remember the *David?* That was quite a coup for you, wasn't it?"

"So you stole it, had it copied."

Elise laughed again, her expression as capricious as the lightning outside and just as volatile.

"What do you want?" Miranda demanded as she rose.

"I want you to listen!" she shouted. "I want you to do what I tell you, to crawl when I'm finished. I want it all."

"All right." How much time, Miranda thought frantically, before Elise snapped, before the gun went off? "I'm listening. The *David* was really only practice, wasn't it?"

"Oh, you're smart. Always so smart. It was backup. I knew I could put a chink in your reputation with it. But I'm patient. There was bound to be something bigger. Then there was *The Dark Lady*. I knew this would be the one. Elizabeth trusted me. I made certain she trusted me. Kowtowing to her every whim for years. Standjo's going to be mine too," she added matter-of-factly. "I'll be in the director's chair by the time I'm forty."

"*The Dark Lady*. You wanted her. I can't blame you. But you couldn't do it alone. So you had Richard."

"Richard was in love with me," she said almost dreamily. "I might have married him. We ran the tests at night. I had the combination to Elizabeth's safe. It was ridiculously easy. All I had to do was arrange for you to be delayed. I did specify that you weren't to be seriously hurt. I wanted to keep you healthy until I could ruin you."

"You leaked the project to the press."

"Elizabeth reacted exactly as expected—it didn't hurt that I gave her subtle little nudges, all the while claiming I was sure you didn't mean it. I was your champion, Miranda. I was brilliant."

The phone rang. Elise smiled. "We'll just let the machine pick that up, shall we. We have so much more to talk about."

WHY the hell didn't she answer? Ryan fought his way through the storm, tires skidding on wet pavement. Steering one-handed, he punched in information and got the number for the hospital.

"Elise Warfield," he demanded. "She's a patient."

"Dr. Warfield was released this evening."

Ice gathered in his gut. He punched the accelerator, sending the car into a violent fishtail. Going against a lifetime of habit, he called the police.

"I'M GOING to need the copies, Miranda." Elise stepped forward. "We want this all tidy in the end, don't we?"

"Why should I give them to you? You're going to kill me anyway."

"Of course I am. But . . ." She shifted the gun and stopped Miranda's heart. "I wouldn't have to kill Andrew."

"Don't." Miranda held up her hands in surrender. "Please."

"Give me the copies, and I won't."

"They're hidden out in the lighthouse." Away from Andrew, she thought.

"Oh, perfect. Can you guess where I was conceived?" Elise laughed until tears swam in her eyes. "How wonderful that it all ends where it really began." She gestured with the gun. "After you, Miranda."

With one last glance at her brother, Miranda turned. If she could distract Elise for just an instant—she was bigger, stronger, and she was sane. "If you shoot me, how will you explain it?"

"I'll put the gun in Andrew's hand, his finger on the trigger, and fire it again. You struck him. He shot you." She jabbed the gun into the base of Miranda's spine.

Miranda opened the back door and stepped out into the driving rain. Hunched against wind and rain, she walked toward the point. She could hear the waves crashing wildly. Every slash of lightning threw the cliffs into sharp relief.

"Your plan won't work out here, Elise. If you use that gun on me now, they'll know it couldn't have been Andrew."

"Shut up. What do you care? You'll be dead anyway."

"Richard kept a book. He wrote it all down. Everything."

"Liar!"

"Everything's recorded, Elise. They'll know I was right. Dead or alive, I'll still have the glory. Everything you've done is for nothing."

Hand fisted, Miranda swung around. The force of the blow struck Elise on an upflung arm and sent her sprawling. Miranda leaped on her, grabbing for the gun.

She'd been wrong. Sanity wasn't an advantage. Elise fought like an animal, teeth snapping, nails gouging Miranda as they rolled over the rocky ground toward the edge of the cliffs.

RYAN shouted her name as he ran into the house, shouting it again and again as he pounded up the stairs. When he found Andrew, terror squeezed his heart into a hot ball.

He heard the crash of thunder, then the blast of gunshots. With fear drenching his skin, he shoved through the terrace doors.

There, silhouetted by the flash of lightning, he saw two figures tangled on the cliffs. Even as he offered up the first prayer, as he climbed over the rail to leap down, he saw them go off.

HER breath was sobbing, burning her throat. She gripped the gun, tried to twist it away. It bucked in her hand—once, twice—and the fury of sound punched pain in her ears.

Someone was screaming, screaming, screaming. She tried to dig her heels in for purchase and found her legs dangling in space. In the blasts and jolts of light, she could see Elise's face over hers, contorted, teeth bared, eyes blind with madness. In them, for one horrified second, she saw herself.

From somewhere she heard her name, a desperate call. As if in answer, she twisted, shoved viciously. With Elise clawing at her, they tumbled over the edge.

She could hear a woman laughing. Rock bit at her skin as she fought to cling to the wall of the cliff. Wild with fear, she looked over her shoulder, saw Elise's white face, saw her release her hold on rock to aim the gun—and then she fell.

Trembling, sobbing, Miranda pressed her cheek against the face of the cliff. Her muscles were screaming, her fingers burning. Below her the sea she had always loved crashed impatiently.

She lifted her face to the pounding rain, stared at the edge just a foot above her head, watched the shaft of light from the old tower slice through the dark as if to guide her. She would not die this way. She kept her eyes focused on the goal and fought to find some small purchase with her feet. She clawed her way up one sweaty inch, then another before her feet slid free.

She was dangling by bloody fingertips when Ryan bellied over the edge. "Miranda, hang on. Take my hand."

"I'm slipping."

"Take my hand. Reach up just a little." He braced himself on the slick rocks and held both hands down to her.

"I can't let go. My fingers are frozen. I can't let go. I'll fall."

"No, you won't. Take my hand." While his head screamed with panic, he grinned at her. "Come on, Dr. Jones. Trust me."

She pried her numb fingers from the rock and reached for his. For a gut-wrenching instant she felt herself hang, a fingertip away from death. Then his hand clamped firm over hers.

"Now the other one. I need both your hands."

"Oh, God, Ryan." Blind now, she let go.

When her full weight locked his arms, he thought they might both go over. He inched back, cursing the rain that seemed to turn the rock into glass. But she was helping him, boosting herself with her feet. She used her elbows on the ledge, scraping them raw as he dragged her the last few inches over the top.

When she collapsed on him, he wrapped her in his arms, cradled her on his lap, and rocked them both in the rain.

"I saw you go over. I thought you were dead."

"I would have been." Her face was buried against his chest. From somewhere in the distance came the whine of sirens. "If you hadn't come . . . I couldn't have held on much longer."

"You'd have held on." He tipped her head back, looked into her eyes. "Now you can hold on to me." He picked her up to carry her to the house.

"Don't let go for a while."

"I won't."

Epilogue

B UT he did. She should have known he would. The thieving s.o.b. Trust me, he said. And she had. He'd saved her life, only to carelessly leave it in shambles.

Oh, he'd waited, Miranda thought as she paced her bedroom. He'd stuck by her until her cuts and bruises were treated. He'd stayed until they were sure Andrew was out of danger. He'd even held her hand while they'd given Ryan's slightly edited version of events to Cook. Then, without a word, he'd packed up and left.

She knew just where he'd gone. He'd gone after *The Dark Lady* and the *David*. He'd probably already passed them along to one of his clients for a fat fee.

If she ever saw him again . . . but of course, she wouldn't. She was alone in a big empty house, with Andrew being fussed over by his fiancée. He was happy and healing, and she was glad of it. And she was miserably envious.

She had her reputation, she thought. She had the institute and perhaps, finally, her parents' respect if not their love.

She had no life whatsoever.

She shoved open her terrace doors to step out into the spring night. White and full, the moon rose over the sea, cruised among the stars, and gave the seascape a mystic, intimate glow. The sea sang its rough song with an arrogance that made her yearn.

He'd been gone for two weeks. She knew he wasn't coming back. She'd get over it. And while she would never trust another man in this lifetime, at least she knew she could trust herself.

"This moment would be more atmospheric if you were wearing a long, flowing robe." He was grinning at her. Dressed in thief's black and standing in her bedroom grinning.

"Jeans and a T-shirt," he continued. "Though you fill them out nicely, they lack the romance of a silk robe the breeze could flutter around you." He stepped out onto the terrace. "Hello, Dr. Jones."

"You son of a . . ." She rammed her fist full out into his face.

It knocked him back several steps. He dabbed at the blood on his mouth. "Well, that's one way to say hello."

"You used me. You lied to me. Trust me, you said, and all that time you were after the bronzes. You walked out of here and went to Florence for the statues."

"Of course. I told you I was going to."

"Miserable thief."

"I'm an excellent thief." He smiled again, combed his fingers through the thick dark hair the breeze blew into sexy disorder. "Now I'm a retired thief."

She folded her arms. "I imagine you can live very well in retirement for what you sold the bronzes for."

"A man wouldn't have to work again in several lifetimes for what the Michelangelo is worth." While she clenched her fists, he watched her warily. "She's the most exquisite thing I've ever seen. *The Dark Lady* sings, Miranda. She is incomparable."

"She belongs in a museum, where she can be seen and studied."

"I came to offer you a deal."

"Did you really? Why would I deal with you?"

He shrugged and turned back into the bedroom. "Okay then, on to business. I have something you'd like to see." He brought out his bag, took out the carefully wrapped contents. Even before he uncovered it, she knew, and was too stunned to speak.

"Gorgeous, isn't she?" He held the figure as a man holds a lover, with great care and possessiveness. "It was love at first sight for me. She's a woman who brings men to their knees, and knows it. She isn't always kind, but she fascinates. It's no wonder murder was done for her. When I found her in that dusty garage and held her for the first time, I would have sworn I heard harpsong. Do you believe in such things, Dr. Jones?"

"Why did you bring her here?"

"I imagined you'd want to see her again."

She couldn't help herself. Moving closer, she ran a fingertip over the smiling face. She lifted her gaze from the bronze to his beautiful, treacherous face. "I didn't expect you to come back."

"Actually, to be honest, neither did I." He set the bronze on the stone table. "We'd both gotten what we'd wanted. You've got your reputation. You're quite a celebrity these days. I imagine you've had offers from publishers and Hollywood to sell your story."

She had, and it embarrassed her. "You haven't answered the question."

"I'm getting to it," he muttered. "I kept the deal. I never agreed to give the *David* back, and as to her—I never agreed to anything but to find her. I found her, and now she's mine. How bad do you want her?"

"You want me to buy stolen property?"

"Actually, I was thinking of a trade."

"A trade?" She thought of the Cellini he coveted. And the Donatello. Her palms began to itch. "What do you want for her?"

"You."

Her rapid thoughts screeched to a halt. "Excuse me?"

"A lady for a lady. It seems fair. In the past few days it occurred to me, much to my discomfort, that I want you more than I want her."

"I'm not following you."

"Yes, you are. You're too bright not to. You can have her. You can give her back to Florence or use her for a doorstop. I won't give a damn. But you'll have to give me what I want for her. I've got a yen to live in this house."

"You want to live here?"

He narrowed his eyes. "Yes. I want to live in this house. It's a good spot to raise children. Look at that, you went white as a ghost. And I love you, Miranda, beyond sense."

She made some sound—it couldn't be construed as words—as her heart staggered in her chest. Stumbled. Fell.

He crossed to her. She hadn't moved a muscle. "I really have to insist on children, Miranda. I'm Irish and Italian. What else would you expect?"

"You're asking me to marry you?"

"I'm working my way up to it. Take the deal, Miranda. You won't regret it."

"You're a thief."

"Retired." He molded her hip with one hand, reached into his pocket with the other. "Here, let's make it official."

She jerked her hand free when he started to slip the ring onto it. The ring he'd given her once before. He took her hand and pushed the ring into place. "Take the deal."

Now she recognized the pressure in her chest. It was her heart beating again. "Did you pay for the ring?"

"Yes, I paid for the ring."

She let herself consider it, watched it wink and sparkle. And let him sweat, she thought. She hoped. "I'll give her back to Italy. Explanations of how I came by her might be awkward."

"We'll think of something. Take the deal, damn it."

"How many children?"

His smile spread slowly. "Five."

She snorted out a laugh. "Please. Two."

"Three, with an option."

"Three, final."

"Done." He started to kiss her, but she slapped a hand on his chest. "I'm not finished. No side work whatsoever."

"I'm retired," he muttered. "No side work. Fine. Next?"

"That should do it." She touched his cheek. "I love you beyond sense," she murmured. "I'll take the deal. I'll take you, but that means you're taking me. The Jones curse. I'm bad luck."

"Dr. Jones." He turned his lips into her palm. "Your luck's about to change. Trust me."

Flight of
EAGLES

Jack
Higgins

Wars are fought on many battlefields. In the steel-gray skies over the English Channel two extraordinary pilots—brothers, twins—skirmish and elude each other for only so long. Their destiny is to meet. And the final conflict that must be resolved is the one inside the heart.

✠

THE ENGLISH CHANNEL
1997

1 WHEN we lost the starboard engine, I knew we were in trouble, but then, the whole trip was bad news from the start.

My wife, Denise, and I were staying at our house on Jersey in the Channel Islands when a phone message indicated a strong interest from a major Hollywood producer in filming one of my books. It meant getting over to England fast to our house at Chichester, a staging post to London. I phoned the air-taxi firm I usually used. All they could come up with was a Cessna 310 from Brittany and an aging pilot named Dupont. Beggars not being choosers, I booked the flight, because the weather forecast wasn't good and we wanted to get on with it. I sat in the rear, but the 310 had dual controls, and my wife, a highly experienced pilot, chose to occupy the right-hand seat in front. Thank God she did.

The English Channel is subject to fogs that appear in an incredibly short time and close down everything fast, and that's exactly what happened that morning. Taking off from Jersey was fine, but within ten minutes the island was fogged out. We started for the south coast of England—Southampton. Dupont was close to sixty from the look of him, gray-haired, a little overweight. Watching him as he worked the plane, I noticed a film of sweat on his face.

Denise was wearing headphones, and at one stage Dupont engaged in conversation with air-traffic control.

She turned to me. "Bad fog down there. Southampton's out. We're trying for Bournemouth, but it doesn't look good."

Having avoided death in the army, I've learned to take life as it comes. I smiled, confident in my wife's abilities, found the half bottle of champagne they'd thoughtfully provided in the bar box, and poured some into a plastic glass.

It was exactly at that moment that the starboard engine died on us. For a heart-stopping moment there was a plume of black smoke, and then it faded away.

Dupont got into a state, wrestling with the controls, frantically making adjustments, but to no avail. We started to go down. In a panic he shouted in French to air-traffic control, but my wife waved a hand at him and took over, calmly, sweetly reasonable. "We have fuel for perhaps an hour," she reported. "Have you a suggestion?"

The air-traffic controller's voice was just as calm. "Cornwall is your best bet. It's not closed in as fully there. Cold Harbour, a small fishing port. There's an old RAF landing strip there from the Second World War. Abandoned but usable. I'll put out your details to all rescue services. Good luck."

We were at three thousand feet for the next twenty minutes. The fog swirled around us, and then it started to rain very hard. Dupont seemed more agitated than ever, the sweat on his face very obvious now. Occasionally he spoke, but again in French. The plane started to rock as a thunderstorm exploded around us.

Denise spoke on the radio, very controlled, giving our details. "Possible Mayday. Attempting a landing at Cold Harbour."

There was lots of static, and then it cleared and a voice echoed strong and true. "This is Royal National Lifeboat Institution, Cold Harbour. Zec Acland speaking. No way you're going to land here, girl. Can't see my hand in front of my face."

For Dupont this was the final straw. He gave a sudden moan, seemed to convulse, and his head lolled to one side. The plane lurched down, but Denise took the controls and slowly leveled it out.

I leaned over and felt for a pulse in his neck. "It's there, but it's weak. Looks like a heart attack."

"Take the life jacket from under his seat and put it on him," she said, still calm. "Then do the same for yourself." She put the 310 on automatic and pulled on her own life jacket.

I took care of Dupont and struggled into mine. "Are we going into the drink?"

"We don't have much choice." She took manual control again.

I tried to be flippant, a personal weakness. "But it's March. I mean, far too cold in the water."

"Just shut up! This is business," she said as we went down. "Cold Harbour, I'll have to ditch. Pilot seems to have had a heart attack."

That strong voice again: "Do you know what you're doing, girl?"

"Oh, yes. One other passenger."

"The Cold Harbour rescue boat is already at sea, and I'm on board. Give me a position as accurately as you can."

Fortunately, the plane was fitted with a satellite Global Positioning System, and she read it off. "I'll go straight down," she said.

"By Jove, you've got guts, girl. We'll be there. Never fear."

Denise throttled back, and we descended. I watched the altimeter. One thousand feet, then five hundred. We couldn't see a thing—nothing—and then, at a couple of hundred feet, broken fog, the sea below, and she dropped us into the wind. For those few moments I think she became a truly great pilot. We bounced, skidded along the waves, and came to a halt. The shock was considerable, but she had the cabin door open in an instant.

"Bring him with you," she called, going out onto the wing.

I unfastened Dupont's seat belt, then shoved him headfirst through the door. She reached for him, slid off the wing into the water, and pulled him after her. With the plane sinking, I then slipped off the wing. Denise shouted, "Oh, no, Tarquin's in there."

This requires a word of explanation. Tarquin was a bear, but a unique bear. When we found him sitting on a shelf in a Brighton antiques shop, he was wearing the leather flying helmet, flying boots, and blue flying overalls of the Royal Flying Corps from the

First World War, as well as the insignia of World War Two's Royal Air Force. He had had an enigmatic look on his face, which was not surprising, the dealer informed us, because he had flown in the Battle of Britain with a fighter pilot. It was a romantic story, but we tended to believe it, because he had the appearance of a bear who'd done things and been places. In any case, he'd become Denise's mascot. There was no question of leaving him behind.

I reached for the handle of the rear door, got it open, and dragged out Tarquin. "Come on, old lad. We're going for a swim."

Oh, but it was cold, like acid eating into the bones, and that, I knew, was the killer. You didn't have long in the English Channel. I held on to Dupont and Tarquin, and Denise held on to me. "Great landing," I said. "Very impressive."

"Are we going to die?" she demanded, gagging on seawater.

"I don't think so," I said. "Look over your shoulder."

Which she did, and found a rescue boat emerging from the fog like a ghost. The crew were at the rail in yellow oilskins. One old man stood out, white-haired and bearded, and when he spoke, it was that same strong voice we'd heard on the radio—Zec Acland. "By Jove, you brought it off, girl."

"So it would appear," Denise called.

They hauled us into the boat, and then the strangest thing happened. Acland looked at the soaking bear in my arms, his face bewildered. "Dear heavens, Tarquin. Where did you get him from?"

DENISE and I sat on a bench in the main cabin, blankets around us, and drank tea from a thermos flask while two crew members knelt on the floor and worked on Dupont, fastening an oxygen mask over his face. Zec Acland sat on the bench opposite.

Another man entered, a younger version of Acland. "This is my boy, Simeon," Zec said. "Cox of this boat, the *Lady Carter*."

Simeon said, "There's a navy helicopter landing at Cold Harbour right about now. Take you people to civilization in no time."

I glanced at Denise, who made a face, so I said, "Frankly, it's been one heck of a day. Any chance we could stay overnight?"

Simeon laughed. "Well, my dad, here, is publican at the Hanged Man pub. Usually has a room or two available." He turned and saw the very wet bear beside his father. "What's that?"

"It's Tarquin," Zec Acland said.

A strange expression settled on Simeon's face. "You mean— So you weren't lying. All these years I thought you just made it up." He picked Tarquin up, and water poured out. "He's soaked."

"Not to worry," Zec Acland said. "He's been wet before."

It was all very intriguing, and I was just about to take it further when we rounded a promontory and saw a quay on the bay beyond. The *Lady Carter* eased into the quay, and the engines stopped. In the near distance we heard a sudden roaring, and Simeon said, "That'll be the helicopter. Better get him up there."

They carried Dupont out on a stretcher, and we followed.

THE pub, the Hanged Man, had mullioned windows and timber inserts. Zec took us in and found a motherly sort of woman behind the bar, who answered to Betsy and who immediately took Denise off upstairs to a hot bath. I stopped at the old beamed bar with Zec and enjoyed a quick whisky near the roaring log fire.

He sat Tarquin on a ledge near the fire. "Let him dry natural."

I said, "The bear is important to you?"

He nodded. "And to another. More than you'll ever know." He turned. "Time you had a bath, too. What business would you be in?"

"I'm a novelist," I said.

"Would I know you?"

I told him.

He laughed. "Well, I guess I do. You've helped me get through a bad night or two."

WE HAD dinner in the corner of the bar—sea bass, new potatoes, and a salad—and shared an ice-cold bottle of Chablis with Zec and Simeon. Denise and I both wore jeans and sweaters provided by the management. There were perhaps eight seamen at the bar. The log fire burned brightly, and Tarquin steamed gently.

"My dad used to tell me about Tarquin, the flying bear, when I was a kid," Simeon said. "I always thought it was a fairy story."

"So now you've finally learned the truth," Zec said, then turned to Denise. "Tell me where you got him."

"Antique shop in Brighton. I was intrigued by the fact that he wears wings from both the Second and the First World Wars."

"Yes, well," Zec said, "he first went to war with the boys' father."

There was silence. Denise said carefully, "The boys' father?"

"A long time ago, 1917 in France, but I last saw Tarquin in 1944. On his way to occupied France. Then, all these years later, he turns up in an antique shop in Brighton." Zec seemed to brood.

My wife leaned back. "Tarquin is an old friend, I think?"

"You could say that. I took him out of the Channel once before—1943. Went down in a Hurricane. Great fighters, those. Shot down more of the Luftwaffe than Spitfires." There were tears in his eyes. "Harry, that was, or was it Max? We could never be sure."

Simeon said, "You all right, Dad?" He poured more wine. "Come on, Dad, drink up. Don't upset yourself."

"My bedroom. The red box in the third drawer. Get it, boy."

When Simeon returned with the box, Zec placed it on the table and opened it, revealing papers and photos. He passed the pictures, one after another, to Denise: the quay at Cold Harbour, a moored rescue boat—a much older model. The pub looked the same. There was a shot of an army officer, engagingly ugly, about sixty-five from the look of him, steel-rimmed spectacles, white hair.

"Brigadier Munro," Zec said. "Dougal Munro, Oxford Egyptology professor before the war. Then he joined the intelligence service. What was called Special Operations Executive—SOE. Churchill cooked that up. Set Europe ablaze, he said, and they did. Put secret agents into France, that sort of thing. They moved the local population out of Cold Harbour. Turned it into a secret base."

Simeon said, "You never told me that, Dad."

"Because everyone here had to sign the Official Secrets Act." He shook out more photos. "That was Julie Legrande. Ran the pub." There was a picture of another officer, a captain, a walking stick in one hand. "Jack Carter, Munro's aide. Left his leg at Dunkirk."

Next came a large brown envelope. He hesitated, then opened it. "Official Secrets Act. What the hell. I'm eighty-eight years old."

If the photos before had been interesting, these were astonishing. One of them showed an airstrip with a German Junkers 88S night fighter, a swastika on its tail. The mechanic wore black Luftwaffe overalls. There were two hangars beyond.

"What on earth is this?" I asked.

"The airstrip up the road. Night flights to France, that sort of thing. You foxed the enemy by being the enemy."

"Not too healthy if they caught you," Denise observed.

"Firing-squad time if they did. Of course, they also operated RAF stuff like this." He passed her a photo. "Lysander. Ugly beast, but they could land and take off in a plowed field."

Another photo showed the Lysander, an officer, and a young woman. He wore an American uniform, the bars of a lieutenant colonel, and a string of medal ribbons. But the fascinating fact was that on the right breast of his battle-dress blouse were RAF wings.

"Who was he?" I asked.

He examined the photo. "Harry, I think, or maybe Max. I could never be sure."

There it was again, that same comment. Simeon looked as bewildered as I did. Denise said, "And the young woman?"

"Oh, that's Molly—Molly Sobel, Munro's niece. Clever girl, a doctor. Used to fly down from London when a doctor was needed."

He seemed to have gone away to some private place of his own. We said nothing. The fire crackled; rain battered the window.

Denise leaned forward and put her hand on Zec's. "The pilot," she said. "Harry or Max, you said?"

"That's right."

"Which doesn't make sense."

"Dear girl, all the sense in the world." He leaned back, laughing, then opened another envelope from the box. "Very special, these." They were large prints. The first was of an RAF flight lieutenant, the same man we'd seen earlier in an American uniform.

"Yank in the RAF," Zec said. "He'd flown for the Finns in their war with the Russians, and when that caved in, Harry got to England and joined the RAF."

"Harry?" Denise said gently.

"Harry Kelso. He was from Boston." He took another print out—Kelso in American uniform again. "Nineteen forty-four, that."

The medals were impressive. A Distinguished Service Order and bar, a Distinguished Flying Cross and two bars, the French Croix de Guerre and Legion of Honor, the Finnish Gold Cross of Valor.

I said, "This is incredible. I've a special interest in the Second World War, and I've never heard of him."

"You wouldn't. As I said, the Official Secrets Act."

"But why?" Denise demanded.

Zec Acland took another photo from the envelope and put it on the table—the showstopper. "Because of this," he said.

The photo was in color and showed Kelso once again in uniform, only this time that of the Luftwaffe—baggy blue-gray trousers with large map pockets, and flying blouse with yellow collar patches. He wore a silver pilot's badge, an Iron Cross First Class, and a Knight's Cross with oak leaves.

"But I don't understand," Denise said.

"It's quite simple," Zec Acland told her. "The Yank in the RAF? That was Harry. This is the Yank in the Luftwaffe, his twin brother, Max. American father and German mother, a baroness. So Max, being the eldest by ten minutes, was Baron Max von Halder. The Black Baron, the Luftwaffe called him." He put the photos away and smiled. "I'll tell you what I can. Make a good story for you. Not that anyone would believe it."

By the time he'd finished, Simeon, I think, was as astonished as Denise and I were. Again it was Denise who spoke. "Is that it?"

"Of course not, girl." Zec smiled. "Lots of pieces in the jigsaw missing. I mean, the German end of things. Top secret there, too." He turned to me. "Still, a smart chap like you might know where to pull a few strings."

"A possibility," I said.

Pieced together from what a German cousin of mine uncovered and from what Zec told me and from some researches of my own, this is what we found out about the true and remarkable story of the brothers Kelso.

 AUGUST 1917. At ten thousand feet over the lines in France, Jack Kelso was as happy as any human being could be. Twenty-two years old and the scion of one of Boston's finest families, he could have been doing his final year at Harvard, but instead, he was in his second year with the British Royal Flying Corps.

The aircraft he was flying was a Bristol fighter, a two-seater with an observer-gunner in the rear. Kelso's sergeant, who had taken shrapnel the day before in a dogfight, had been hospitalized, and Kelso, a hotshot pilot with fifteen German planes to his credit, had illegally taken off on his own. Well, not quite on his own, for sitting in the bottom of his cockpit was a bear called Tarquin in leather helmet and flying jacket.

Kelso tapped him on the head. "Good boy. Don't let me down."

At that period the British War Office still banned parachutes on the argument that their use made cowards out of pilots. Jack Kelso, a realist and a rich young man, sat on the very latest model of parachute, his private possession.

The weather was bad—wind and rain—and in the noise and confusion Kelso wasn't even aware what kind of plane it was that made his luck run out. There was a roaring, a shadow to port, machine-gun fire ripping through the Bristol, a bullet tearing into his left leg, and then he descended into the safety of heavy cloud.

He turned back toward the British lines and was aware of a burning smell. He made it down to five thousand feet, then three thousand, flames flickering around his engine. There was the briefest glimpse of the trenches below, the battlefields of Flanders. Time to go. He unbuckled his seat belt, stuffed Tarquin inside his heavy leather coat, then turned the Bristol over and dropped out. He pulled his rip cord and floated down. A khaki-clad British infantry patrol, half plastered in mud, reached him in a matter of minutes.

The field hospital was in an old French château, which stood in glorious parkland. Jack Kelso had lapsed into unconsciousness, thanks to the morphine the infantry patrol had administered. He awakened to a fantasy world—a small room, white sheets, French windows open to a terrace. He tried to sit up and cried out at the pain in his leg. The door opened, and a young nurse in a Red Cross uniform entered. She had blond hair, a strong face, green eyes, and looked to be in her early twenties and was the most beautiful thing he had ever seen in his life. Jack Kelso fell instantly in love.

"No, lie back," she said, pushing him back against the pillows.

An army colonel entered the room. "Problems, Baroness?"

"Not really. He's just confused."

"Can't have that," the colonel said. "Taken a rather large bullet out of that leg. A little more morphine, I think." He went out.

She charged a hypodermic and reached for Kelso's right arm.

"Your accent," he said. "You're German. He called you baroness."

"So useful when I deal with Luftwaffe pilots."

"I don't care what you are, as long as you promise to marry me, Baroness," he said drowsily, starting to fade. "Where's Tarquin?"

"Would that be the bear?" she asked.

"No ordinary bear. He's my good luck."

"Well, there he is, on the dressing table."

And so he was. Jack Kelso got one clear look. "Hi there, old buddy," he called, then drifted into sleep.

BARONESS Elsa von Halder had been trapped in Paris when the war began. Her father was a general killed on the Somme. At twenty-two, she was from fine old Prussian stock, with a decaying mansion and no money. As the days passed, Kelso filled her with tales of his privileged life in the States, and they found they had something in common—both had lost their mothers to cancer.

Three weeks after he arrived at the hospital, sitting in a deck chair on the terrace with many wounded officers and taking the sun, Kelso watched her approach. She held out a package to him.

"Open it for me," he said, and she did.

Inside was a leather box and a letter. "Why, Jack, it's from headquarters. You've been awarded the Distinguished Service Order." She took it out and held it up. "Aren't you pleased?"

"Sure. But I already have a medal," he said. "What I don't have is you." He took her hand. "Germany is going to lose the war. All you have to go back to is an old house and no money. Marry me, Elsa. Trust me, I'll take care of you. You know I'll keep asking until you give in."

So she did, and they were married two days later. After all, he was right. She *did* have nothing to go back to.

The honeymoon in Paris was fine, not the greatest romance in the world, but then, he was always aware that she hadn't married him for love. She became pregnant very quickly, and Kelso insisted that she go to the States. So she sailed for America, where Abe Kelso, Jack's father, received her with considerable enthusiasm. She was a big success on the social scene, and nothing was too good for her, especially when she went into labor and produced twin boys. The eldest she named Max, after her father; the other Harry, after Abe's.

On the western front Jack Kelso received the news by telegraph. He was by now a lieutenant colonel, one of the few old hands still around, for losses on both sides had been appalling that last year of the war. And then suddenly it was all over.

GAUNT, careworn, old before his time, Jack Kelso, still in his uniform, stood in the boys' bedroom and looked at them sleeping. Elsa stood at the door, a little afraid, gazing at a stranger.

"Fine," he said. "They look fine. Let's go down."

Abe Kelso stood by the fire in the drawing room. He was taller than Jack, with darker hair, but had the same features.

"Honestly, Jack." He picked up two glasses of champagne and handed one to each of them. "I've never seen so many medals."

"Loads of tin." His son drank the wine down in a single gulp.

"It was bad this past year?" Abe inquired as he gave him a refill.

"Bad enough, though I never managed to get killed. Everyone but me." Jack Kelso smiled terribly.

"That's an awful thing to say," his wife told him.

"True, though." He lit a cigarette. "I see the boys have fair hair. Almost white." He blew out smoke.

"They *are* half German."

"Not their fault," he said. "By the way, my personal score there at the end? It was forty-eight."

She saw then just how damaged he was, but it was Abe who spoke with forced cheerfulness. "Now Jack, what are you going to do with yourself? Back to Harvard to finish that law degree?"

"You must be joking. I'm twenty-three years old, and I've killed hundreds of men. I've got the trust fund my mother left me. I'm going to enjoy myself." He emptied the glass and limped out.

Abe Kelso poured a little more champagne into Elsa's glass. "Look, my dear, he's been through a lot. We must make allowances."

"Don't apologize for him. That isn't the man I married. He's back there in that godforsaken war. He never got out."

Which wasn't far from the truth, for in the years that followed, Jack Kelso acted as if he didn't care if he lived or died. His exploits on automobile-racing circuits were notorious. He still flew, and crash-landed on three occasions. His capacity for drink was enormous. For her part Elsa played the good wife, elegant hostess, affectionate mother. She was always Mutti to Max and Harry, taught them German, and they loved her greatly. Yet their affection for their drunken war-hero father was even greater.

He'd managed to buy a Bristol fighter and kept it at a small flying club outside Boston that was owned by another old RFC ace, named Rocky Farson. The boys were ten the day Jack strapped them into the rear cockpit and took them for a flight. Their birthday treat, he called it. Elsa threatened to leave him if he ever did it again. Abe, as usual, was the man in the middle, trying to keep the peace, on her side because Jack had been drunk.

Disillusioned with her marriage, Elsa had only her sincere friendship with Abe and her love of the boys to sustain her. They were totally alike: their straw-blond hair and green eyes, their high German cheekbones, their voices, their mannerisms. No birthmarks set them apart. Most times even she couldn't tell them apart. It was a constant sport for them to change roles and make fools of everyone. They were totally bonded, and the only thing they ever argued about was who owned Tarquin. The fact that Max, as the eldest by ten minutes, was legally Baron von Halder never bothered them.

It was the summer of 1930 when the tragedy happened. Jack was killed when his Bentley spun off a mountain road in Colorado and fireballed. What was left of him was brought back to Boston, where Abe, now a Congressman, presided over the funeral. The twins, in black suits on either side of their mother, seemed strangely still, frozen almost, and older than their twelve years.

Afterward, at the big house, when everyone had left, Elsa sat in the drawing room, elegant in black, and sipped a brandy. Abe stood by the fire.

"Now what?" he asked. "It's a bleak prospect."

"Not for me," she replied. "I've done my bit. I was a good wife, Abe, and put up with a lot. I want to go back to Germany."

"And live on what? Most of the fortune his mother left is gone, Elsa. You know that."

"Yes, I know," she said. "But you've got millions. More than you know what to do with. You could help me, Abe. Let me go home. I'll restore the estate. I'll restore the family name."

"And take my grandsons with you? I couldn't bear that."

"But they're my sons, too. They belong with their mother. And Max—Max is the Baron von Halder. You can't make him give that up, Abe. It wouldn't be right. *Please,* I'm begging you."

Abe Kelso sat for several long moments, the air thick with regret and loss. Finally he spoke. "I've often worried about it, you know— what would happen when Max was old enough to appreciate the title. Would he move away to claim it, leave us all here? But with Jack dead and you wanting to leave, there's not much *us* left, is there?" He smiled sadly. "You're right, Elsa. Max does deserve that chance. And so do you, for putting up with Jack all these years. So I'll give you what you need. But on one condition—Harry stays with me. Are we agreed?"

She didn't even argue. "Agreed, Abe."

Later, before dinner, when she went down to the drawing room, Max and Harry were surprisingly calm, but then, they'd always been like that—alone, cool, detached, on the outside looking in.

She kissed them in turn. "Your grandfather has told you?"

"Of course," Abe said. "The only problem, it seems, was who was to take possession of Tarquin, but he stays here. That bear sat in the bottom of the cockpit on every flight Jack made." For a moment he seemed lost in thought; then he straightened up. "Champagne," he said. "Half a glass each. You're old enough. Let's drink to each other. We'll always be together one way or another."

The boys said nothing, simply drank their champagne, old beyond their years, as usual, as enigmatic as Tarquin the bear.

THE Germany to which Elsa von Halder returned was very different from what she remembered—unemployment, street riots, the Nazi party beginning to rear its head. But she had Abe's money, so she put Max into school and set about regenerating the von Halder estate. One of her father's oldest friends, Hermann Göring, the fighter ace from the war, was a coming man in the Nazi party, a friend of Hitler's. All doors were open to him. And Elsa, beautiful and rich, was an asset to the party and the toast of Berlin society.

Hitler assumed power in 1933, and in 1934 Elsa allowed Max to go to America for six months. Abe, who was a U.S. Senator by now, was overjoyed to see him, and as for the brothers, it was as if they'd never been apart. On their birthday Abe gave them a special present. He took them out to the airfield their father used to fly from, and there was Rocky Farson, the old fighter ace.

"Rocky's going to give you a few lessons," Abe said. "I know you're only sixteen. Just don't tell your mother."

Rocky taught them in an old Gresham biplane. He discovered

they were natural-born pilots, just like their father. And just like their father, whoever was flying always had Tarquin in the cockpit.

Rocky took them way beyond normal pilot skills. He gave them lessons in dogfighting. *Always look for the Hun in the sun. Never fly below ten thousand feet on your own. Never fly straight and level for more than thirty seconds.* He taught them the famous Immelmann turn—you dive in on the opponent, pull up in a half loop, roll out on top, and come back over his head at fifty feet. By the time Rocky had finished with them, the boys were experts at it.

"They're amazing, truly amazing," Abe said to Rocky in the canteen at the airfield.

"It's like being a great sportsman," Rocky said. "You either have it or you don't—that touch of genius—and the twins have it."

"I think you're right, but to what purpose? I know there are rumbles, but there won't be another war. We'll see to that."

"I hope so, Senator," Rocky said, but in the end, it wasn't to matter to him. Rocky had an old Bristol refurbished, took it up for a proving flight, and lost the engine at five hundred feet.

At the funeral Abe looked at the boys and was reminded, with a chill, that they looked as they had at their father's funeral: enigmatic, remote, their thoughts tightly contained. It filled him with a strange foreboding. But there was nothing to be done about it, and the following week he took Max down to New York and saw him off for his return to the Third Reich.

MAX sat on the terrace of their country house with his mother and told her all about it—the flying, everything. "I'm going to fly, Mutti. It's what I do well."

Looking into his face, she saw her husband, yet, sick at heart, she did the only thing she could. "Sixteen, Max—that's young."

"I could join the Berlin Aero Club. Göring could swing it."

Which was true. Max appeared by appointment, with Göring and the baroness in attendance, and a Heinkel biplane was provided. A young Luftwaffe lieutenant was there, who would one day become a Luftwaffe general. His name was Adolf Galland.

"Can you handle this, boy?" he asked.

"I think I can manage."

Galland laughed out loud and stuck a small cigar between his teeth. "I'll follow you up. Let's see."

The display that followed had even Göring breathless. Galland could not shake Max for a moment, and it was the Immelmann turn that finished him off. He turned in to land, and Max followed.

Standing beside his Mercedes, Göring nodded to a valet, who provided caviar and champagne. "Took me back to my youth, Baroness. The boy is a genius."

Galland and Max approached, Galland obviously tremendously excited. "Fantastic. Where did you learn all that, boy?"

Max told him, and Galland could only shake his head.

"So what do we do with this one?" Göring said to Galland.

"Put him in an infantry cadet school here in Berlin, just to make it official," Galland said. "Next year, at seventeen, grant him a lieutenant's commission in the Luftwaffe."

Göring nodded. "I like that."

Max said, "A pity my twin brother, Harry, isn't here, Lieutenant Galland. We'd give you hell."

"No," Galland said. "Information is experience. You are special, Baron, believe me. And please call me Dolfo."

It was to be the beginning of a unique friendship.

IN AMERICA, Harry went to Groton prep school and had problems with the discipline, for flying was his obsession, and he refused to sacrifice his weekends in the air. Abe Kelso's influence helped, of course, so Harry survived and went on to Harvard at the same time his brother was commissioned as a lieutenant in the Luftwaffe. Harry ground through college; Europe ground onward into fascism; the Third Reich continued its remorseless rise; the world stood by.

When the Spanish Civil War came, Galland and Max took HE51 biplanes over the front, Max flying two hundred eighty combat missions. He returned home in 1938 with the Iron Cross Second Class and was promoted to Oberstleutnant.

For some time he worked on the staff in Berlin and was much sought after on the social circuit, where he was frequently seen as his mother's escort and the favorite of Göring, now become all-powerful. And then came Poland.

During the twenty-seven-day Blitzkrieg that destroyed that country, Max consolidated his legend, shot down twenty planes, received the Iron Cross First Class, and was promoted to captain.

In those euphoric days Max had his own image—no white dress jackets, nothing fancy. He would always appear in combat dress: baggy pants, flying blouse, a side cap, and all those medals. He went to top functions with Göring, even Hitler, and always with his glamorous mother. They christened him the Black Baron. There was the occasional woman in his life, no more than that. He seemed to stand apart, with that saturnine face and the pale straw hair, and he didn't take sides, was not a Nazi. He was a fighter pilot—that was it.

As for Harry, just graduated from Harvard, life was a bore. The war in Europe had started in September 1939. One day, in November, Harry went into the drawing room and found Abe sitting by the fire reading a magazine.

"Get yourself a drink," Abe said. "You're going to need it."

Harry poured a Scotch and water. "What's the fuss?"

Abe passed him the magazine, a close-up of a taciturn face under a Luftwaffe side cap. Then he passed him a copy of *Signal,* the German armed forces magazine. "The Black Baron," he said.

Max stood beside an ME109 in flying gear.

"Medals already," Harry said. "Isn't that great? Just like Dad."

"I thank my stars they call him Baron von Halder instead of Max Kelso. Can you imagine? My grandson the Nazi?"

"He's no Nazi," Harry said. "He's a pilot. He's there, and we're here." He put the magazine down.

Abe said, "Harry, it's time we talked seriously. You graduated last spring, and since then all you do is fly and race cars, just like your father. What are you going to do? What about law school?"

Harry smiled and shook his head. "Law school? Did you hear Russia invaded Finland this morning?" He took a long drink. "The

Finns need pilots badly. I've already booked a flight to Sweden."

Abe was horrified. "Damn it, Harry, it's not your war."

"It is now," Harry Kelso told him, and finished his whisky.

THE war between the Finns and the Russians was hopeless from the start. The weather was atrocious and the entire country snowbound. On both sides the fighter planes were outdated. But Harry soon made a name for himself flying a British Gloucester Gladiator, and as always, Tarquin sat in the bottom of the cockpit, in a waterproof zip bag Harry had purchased in Stockholm.

Finally the Finnish air force managed to get hold of half a dozen Hurricane fighters from Britain. Already an ace, Harry flew the new aircraft in snowstorms and high winds, was promoted to captain, and decorated, his score in downed targets mounting rapidly.

A photojournalist for *Life* magazine turned up and was astonished to discover Senator Abe Kelso's grandson and hear of his exploits. Abe was now very much a coming man, a member of Franklin D. Roosevelt's kitchen cabinet. So Abe once again found a grandson on the cover of a magazine—Harry in a padded flying suit standing beside one of the planes and holding Tarquin.

Finland surrendered in March 1940, and Harry flew out illegally in a Hurricane to Stockholm. He was on a plane to England before the authorities knew he was there.

When he reported to the Air Ministry in London, an aging squadron leader examined his credentials. "Very impressive, young man. There's just one problem. You're an American, and that means you'll have to go to Canada and join the RCAF."

"I shot down twenty-eight Russians, twelve of them while flying a Hurricane. I know my stuff. You need people like me."

"A Hurricane?" He examined Harry's credentials again. "I see the Finns gave you the Gold Cross of Valor. Nice piece of tin."

"Aren't they all?" Harry told him.

The man pushed a form across. "All right, fill this out. Country of origin, America. I suppose you must have returned to Finland to defend your ancestral home?"

"Exactly."

"Ah, well, that makes you a Finn and that's what we'll put on your records. Bloody clerks. Always making mistakes."

OPERATIONAL Training Unit was a damp and miserable place on the edge of an Essex marsh. The CO was a wing commander called Teddy West. He examined Pilot Officer Kelso's documents and looked up. "All right, let's see what you can do."

Those in the curious crowd that assembled were never to forget it—at five thousand feet West chased Harry Kelso, Hurricane to Hurricane. They climbed so close that some gasped in horror, but Harry evaded West, looped, and settled on his tail. West banked to port and rolled, and Harry, once again finding West on his tail, dropped his flaps and slowed with shuddering force. West heaved back on the control column and narrowly missed him. Then Harry was on his tail again.

The ground crews actually applauded as the two of them walked back. The station warrant officer took West's parachute and gestured toward Kelso. "Who the blazes is he, sir?"

"A lot of men I knew in the Flying Corps all rolled into one," West said. "I'm posting him to 607 Squadron in France immediately."

THE 607 in France was only halfway through its conversion program to Hurricanes when the Blitzkrieg broke out on the western front on May 10, 1940. The savage air war that followed took many casualties.

Harry, flying a Hurricane, put down two ME109s above Abbeville, France, and although neither of them was aware of it, his brother shot down a Hurricane and a Spitfire on the same day.

The 607 was pulled back, what was left of it, to England. Dunkirk followed, with retreating British troops in Belgium taking heavy losses. France fell, and Harry, awarded a DFC and promoted to flying officer, was posted to a special pursuit squadron in West Sussex code-named Hawk. Only there was nothing to pursue. The sun shone, the sky was incredibly blue, and everyone was bored to death. On the other side of the English Channel, Max and his comrades were just as bored.

And then, starting in July, came attacks on British convoys in the Channel: dive bombing by Stukas and Junkers, protected by the Luftwaffe's finest fighter planes. Their objective was to close down the English Channel, and the RAF went up to meet the challenge.

So Harry Kelso and his brother, the Black Baron, went to war.

The air battles lasted through July, and then came the true Battle of Britain, starting on Eagle Day, August 13.

Hawk Squadron was based at a prewar flying club called Farley Field, and it was hot, very hot, and the pilots were lounging in deck chairs, chatting or reading magazines, when they heard a loud roaring noise nearby. Only Harry Kelso was on his feet, jump bag—with Tarquin—in hand, running for his plane as the German Stukas, high in the sky above, banked and dived. He lifted off, banking to port, as the first bombs hit the runway. Banking again, he found a Stuka in his sights and blew it out of the sky. There were four more, and he went after them, shooting them down over the sea. He returned to a scene of devastation and six dead pilots. He'd been the only one to get off the ground.

On the same day, Max and his squadron, flying ME109s, provided cover for Stukas attacking a radar station near Bognor Regis, West Sussex. Attacked by Spitfires, he downed one, but nearly all the Stukas were shot down, as well as three 109s. Max scrambled across the Channel to refuel and was back again an hour and a half later.

That was the pattern day after day, a war of attrition. Max and his comrades flew in, providing cover to Dornier bombers, and Harry and his friends rose to meet them. On both sides young men died, but the Luftwaffe had more pilots.

On August 30, Biggin Hill, the pride of the British Fighter Command, was attacked by a large force of Dorniers. Over the sea near Folkestone, Harry shot down two Dorniers, but a burst from one of the rear gunners hit his engine. He sent out a Mayday and dropped his flaps. The English coast was ten miles away. He reached for Tarquin in the jump bag and attached the bag with a special clip to his belt, then parachuted out, landing in a reasonably calm sea. A klaxon sounded, and he turned to see an RAF crash boat coming up fast.

When Harry was delivered back to Farley Field, a pilot officer told him a group captain was waiting to see him. Harry opened the door to his office and found Teddy West sitting behind his desk.

"What a surprise, sir," said Harry. "Congratulations on your promotion."

"You've done well, Kelso. Anxious couple of minutes when we heard where you were, but all's well that ends well. Congratulations to you, too. You're promoted to flight lieutenant."

Harry asked, "Are we winning, sir?"

"Not at the moment. We will in the end. America will have to come in, but we must hang on." West stood up. "I need you for a day or so. We've got a German ME109 at Downfield, north of London. Pilot had a bad oil leak and decided to land. Tried to set fire to the thing, but a home-guard unit was close by."

"That's quite a catch, sir."

"Yes, well, be a good chap. Have a quick shower and change, and we'll be on our way."

Downfield was surrounded by barbed wire, with guards at the gate. The 109 was on the apron outside one of the hangars. Three RAF and two army officers were examining the plane. A Luftwaffe lieutenant, no more than twenty, stood close by, his uniform crumpled. Two RAF guards with rifles watched him.

Harry walked up to the lieutenant and held out his hand. "Rotten luck," he said in German. "Glad you got down in one piece."

"*Mein Gott,* are you German?"

"My mother is." Harry gave him a cigarette and a light.

The older army officer was a brigadier. He looked about sixty-five, had an engagingly ugly face. white hair, and steel-rimmed spectacles. "Dougal Munro," he said, introducing himself to Harry. "That's excellent German, Flight Lieutenant."

"Well, it would be," Harry told him. "My mother taught me."

"My aide, Jack Carter." Munro introduced the man at his side. Carter was a captain in the Green Howards. He leaned on a walking stick, for, as Harry learned later, he'd left a leg at Dunkirk.

The senior RAF officer, a group captain, asked West, "Look, Teddy, why the delay?"

West turned to Harry. "Show them. Five minutes only. We don't want to get you shot down."

Kelso went up to three thousand feet, banked, looped, strafed the airfield at three hundred, turned into the wind, and landed. He taxied toward them and got out. "Excellent plane," he said. "Marginally better than a Hurricane and certainly as good as a Spitfire."

The RAF group captain turned and said to West, "Very interesting, Teddy. I think I'd like a written evaluation from this officer."

"Consider it done."

The group captain and his two officers went to their staff car and drove away. Munro held out his hand to Harry. "You're a very interesting young man." He nodded to West. "Many thanks."

He went to his car, Carter limping after him. As they settled in the back, he said, "Everything you can find out about him, Jack."

"Leave it to me, sir."

The staff car drove away, and Harry lit a cigarette and turned to West. "I asked you were we winning and you said not at the moment. What do we need?"

"A miracle."

"They're a bit hard to find these days."

But then it happened. London was accidentally bombed by a single Dornier, the RAF retaliated against Berlin, and from September 7, 1940, Hitler ordered the Luftwaffe to turn on London. It was the beginning of the Blitz and gave the RAF time to repair its damaged fighter bases in the south of England.

IN A café in France, Dolfo Galland was playing jazz on the piano and smoking a cigar when Max came in and sat at the bar. "That's it, Dolfo. We had the Tommies beaten, and our glorious Führer has just thrown it all away. So what happens now?"

"We get drunk," Galland told him. "And then we go back to work, play the game to the end."

3 THE Blitz on London, the carnage it caused, was so terrible that the red glow in the sky at night could be seen by Luftwaffe planes taking off in France, and by day the sky seemed full of bombers.

The Knight's Cross was awarded to those who shot down more than twenty planes, and Galland already had it. Max got one on September 10, although by then he'd taken care of at least thirty planes.

Harry and Hawk Squadron engaged in all the battles, six or seven sorties a day, taking heavy losses until Harry was the only surviving member of the original squadron. And then came the final huge battles of September 15: four hundred Luftwaffe fighters over England against three hundred Spitfires and Hurricanes.

In a strange way nobody won. The Channel was still disputed territory, and the Blitz continued. Hitler's grandiose scheme for the invasion of England, Operation Sealion, had to be scrapped, but Britain was still left standing alone, and the Führer could now turn his attention to Russia.

IN BERLIN in early November it was raining hard as Heinrich Himmler, dressed in his black Reichsführer SS uniform, got out of his car and entered Gestapo headquarters in Prinz Albrechtstrasse. A flurry of movement from guards and office staff followed him as he passed through to his palatial office. Behind his silver pince-nez his face was as enigmatic as ever. He gave an order to his secretary, went into his office, put his briefcase on the desk, sat down, and extracted some papers. There was a knock at the door, and it opened.

"Ah, Sturmbannführer Hartmann."

"Reichsführer. In what way can I be of service?"

Hartmann wore an unusual uniform, consisting of Luftwaffe-style flying blouse and baggy pants, but in field gray. His collar tabs were those of a major in the SS, although he wore the Luftwaffe pilot's badge, and on his sleeve was the SD badge of Sicherheitsdienst—SS intelligence. He was thirty, almost six feet, with a handsome craggy face and closely cropped reddish brown hair. A Luftwaffe fighter pilot, he'd been badly injured in a crash. Later posted to the air courier service, he was transporting Himmler when his Fieseler Storch had been bounced by a Spitfire. Hartmann had saved the day, and the upshot was that he was transferred to the SS to be Himmler's personal pilot and also his personal aide in SS intelligence.

Himmler said, "The Blitz on London continues. I've been with the Führer. We will overcome in the end, of course. Panzers will yet roll up to Buckingham Palace."

With reservations Hartmann said, "Undeniably, Reichsführer."

"However," Himmler said, "I've spoken to Admiral Canaris about the military intelligence situation in England, and frankly, it's not good. All his agents there have been taken."

"Not quite, Reichsführer. Our Department Thirteen, which I've taken over, recruited a few deep-cover agents before the war."

"Really? Who would these people be?"

"Irish mostly, disaffected with the British Establishment. Also various neutrals—some Spanish and Portuguese diplomats."

Himmler got up. "You are telling me we have, in the files, deep-cover agents that military intelligence doesn't know about?"

"Exactly."

Himmler nodded. "Good. Make sure they are still in place."

"At your command, Reichsführer."

Hartmann returned to his own office, where his secretary, Trudi Braun, forty and already a war widow, looked up from her desk. She was devoted to Hartmann—such a hero and a tragic figure besides, his wife having been killed in the first RAF raid in Berlin.

"Trouble, Major?" she asked.

"You could say that, Trudi. Come in, and bring coffee."

He sat behind his desk, and she joined him two minutes later with a cup for her and a cup for him. She sat in the spare chair.

"Trudi, our esteemed Reichsführer still believes Operation Sealion will take place. You worked for Department Thirteen. So that list you told me about—give me a full rundown on it, particularly the Spanish and Portuguese on our payroll."

"There's a Portuguese man named Fernando Rodrigues, who has actually passed on low-grade information from time to time. He works at their London embassy."

"Really," Hartmann said. "And who else?"

"Some woman called Dixon—Sarah Dixon. She's a clerk at the War Office in London."

Hartmann sat up straight. "Are you serious? Get me the files."

Fernando Rodrigues was a commercial attaché at the Portuguese London embassy. His brother, Joel, was a commercial attaché at the Berlin embassy. Hartmann read the files and recognized the two of them for what they were: greedy men with their hands out. Sarah Dixon was different. She was forty-five, the widow of a bank clerk who'd died of war wounds from 1917. She was born in London of an English father and Irish mother, and her grandfather, an Irish Republican Army activist in the Easter Rising against the British in Dublin, had been shot. She lived alone and had worked at the War Office since 1938. She had originally been recruited by an agent who was later shot dead in a gunfight with Special Branch policemen.

Hartmann looked up. "So she's still waiting?"

"So it would appear, Major."

"Good. Get this Joel Rodrigues here. Tell him to contact his brother in London by diplomatic pouch. He's to link up with Mrs. Dixon, make sure she's still available if we need her."

"Very well, Major."

THAT evening Hartmann accompanied Himmler to a reception at the Adlon Hotel ballroom. The Führer held court, his entourage hovering. There was Goebbels, Admiral Canaris, von Ribbentrop.

"The only one missing is that fat fool Göring," Himmler said acidly, waving away a waiter with glasses of champagne on a tray, much to Hartmann's regret. "He should be ashamed to show his face after the failure of his fighters over Britain."

Truly angry, Hartmann contained himself by lighting a cigarette, because he knew Himmler could not abide smoking. Before Himmler could comment, however, Göring entered.

"The woman on his arm," Himmler said. "Isn't that the Baroness von Halder?"

"I believe so," Hartmann said.

"Is she his mistress?"

"My information is that she is not, Reichsführer."

"She had an American husband, did she not?"

"Died years ago."

"Interesting. So are her diamonds. How does she manage?"

"Her late husband's father is an American Senator, a millionaire. He set up a trust fund for her in Sweden. We have a file on her."

"And who are the two Luftwaffe officers?"

"The one in the white dress jacket is Major Adolf Galland, the highest scorer in the Battle of Britain. The captain is Baron von Halder, the baroness's son. They call him the Black Baron."

"How theatrical."

"A brilliant flier. We flew together for a while. He has a twin brother, who flies with the RAF."

Himmler frowned. "Is that true?" He stared across the room. "Make sure you keep the file on the von Halders open. I smell something I don't like here."

At that moment Göring called for silence and turned to Hitler. "My Führer, Baron von Halder's score of enemy planes now stands at sixty, and for this he has been awarded oak leaves for his Knight's Cross." He held out a red leather box to him. "I beg you, my Führer, to honor this brave officer personally."

Hitler gazed at Max with that strange penetrating look, then nodded gravely. "You are wrong, Reichsmarschall. The honor is mine." Göring handed him the medal, and Hitler in turn presented it to Max. "The Reich is proud of you, Baron." He turned to Elsa, "And you, Baroness, like all mothers, honor the Reich."

The entire crowd burst into applause. The Führer nodded, then, seeing Himmler, beckoned, and the Reichsführer joined him.

"WELL, THAT WENT WELL," Elsa von Halder said.

"Yes. You must be proud of your boy here," Göring told her. He thumped Max on the shoulder, then saw Hitler beckon him also. "Duty calls," he said, and left them.

Hartmann appeared. "Dolfo . . . Max," he said.

"My God, it's Bubi." Galland laughed.

Max shook Hartmann's hand. "You old dog. We thought you were finished after the crash."

"Himmler made me his personal pilot, only he insisted I be transferred to the SS."

"Well, you can't have everything." Max turned to his mother. "Mutti, this is an old comrade, Bubi Hartmann."

"Sturmbannführer," she said. "What a pretty uniform."

"I am, alas, Baroness, but a poor player." He kissed her hand. "May I add to your pride in your son here? I am told that your other boy was also decorated last week."

"My goodness," she said.

"You see, our intelligence sources are very good." He turned to Max. "The Biggin Hill attack, August the thirtieth? He had to bail out over the Channel off Folkestone."

Elsa looked at Max. "He's as bad as you, as bad as your father. You all have the same death wish."

"Never mind, Mutti." Max waved to a waiter. "Champagne for all of us, and let's drink to Harry."

IT HAD been raining in London. Harry and Group Captain Teddy West were sitting in the corner of the bar at the Garrick club, enjoying a whisky and soda, when Brigadier Dougal Munro came in.

"Dougal," West called, "join us." Munro came over, and West added, "Harry, you remember Brigadier Munro?" He smiled. "He was at Downfield when you tested the 109 for us."

Munro sat and offered Harry a cigarette. "Actually, you could do me a favor, old boy."

"And what would that be, sir?"

"Oh, don't call me sir. I was a simple professor of archaeology before the war," he said. "Same favor as last time, only this time a Fieseler Storch plane. Tomorrow morning? Downfield again?"

"My pleasure."

"Good. I've got a treat for you. My niece is joining us. Molly— Molly Sobel. Half American. Her father's a major general at the U.S. War Department. Brilliant girl, a surgeon at Guy's Hospital at the moment. Sad, though—her mother was killed in the bombing two months ago."

"I'm sorry," Harry Kelso told him.

"Aren't we all," Dougal Munro said, and then Molly Sobel entered the bar, hesitantly, for by tradition it was men only. "Molly, my love, let's go to the dining room."

She was twenty-three, a few months older than Harry—a small girl, around five feet four or five, with fair hair, blue eyes, and a determined and rather stubborn face. Introductions were made, and they all had shepherd's pie with a bottle of hock.

"A German wine. That's ironic," she commented.

"Nothing wrong with a good German wine," Harry said.

"I thought you were a Yank in the RAF," she replied.

"Sure I am. But I also have a German mother in Berlin right now and a twin brother, who's a captain in the Luftwaffe." He grinned when he saw he'd left her speechless.

"And doing very well," Munro said. "His score is sixty."

"And how would you know that?" Harry asked.

"Oh, I run that kind of department." He stood up. "Got to go. Got a place to stay tonight?"

Harry shook his head no.

"I have a flat in Haston Place, near my office at SOE headquarters. Molly stays there. Plenty of room." Munro patted her on the shoulder. "Take care of him, my dear."

He went off, and West lit a cigarette. "Listen to me. With more of you Yanks arriving, the powers that be are forming the Eagle Squadron—all Yanks. You'll want to transfer, I imagine."

"Not particularly." Harry stood and said to Molly, "I'm sure you're busy. If you give me the address, I'll show up this evening."

"I haven't had a break in forty-eight hours, so I've got the rest of the day off. What do you want to do?"

"I'd just like to walk," he told her. He turned to West. "I'll see you in the morning, sir," he said, and went out with Molly.

They walked through the city, smoke hanging in the air from the bombing. "It must have been rough for you, all this," he said. "Thousands killed, death, destruction. Your hospital must be overflowing."

"Most nights are pretty rough, but we get by."

"Munro told me your father is a major general."

"That's right. A flier, like you. Bombers."

"And your mother was killed in the Blitz. That was rough."

"I didn't have time to mourn. Too busy in the emergency room."

They reached the Embankment and looked out at the river, the boats passing up and down. "What's all this about your brother being in the Luftwaffe?" she asked.

"My brother, Max. Our father was American. I'm sure Munro has given you all the gory details about my mother, the baroness."

"And your brother, the baron."

"The Black Baron. A real ace—Max."

"But so are you. Doesn't it bother you?"

"Max over there and me over here? Same difference. If I'd been born ten minutes earlier, I'd be over there and he'd be here."

"No. It's not the same. Your brother was in Germany. He didn't have a choice where to fight, but you did. You chose to be here."

"Don't imply noble motives. I fly. That's what I do. I flew for the Finns. Now I fly for the Brits. Fliers are fliers." He turned. "Let's go."

She took his arm. "You look tired."

"Tired?" He laughed. "I'm exhausted. We all are. Those left, anyway. You're walking with a ghost, Doctor."

It was early evening when they reached Haston Place, a pleasant old square with a central garden. The house was Georgian, the flat spacious and pleasant. A fire burned in the grate in the sitting room. There were many antiquities on display, most of them Egyptian.

"Let me get you a drink." She poured whisky from a decanter into two glasses and toasted him. "I'd like to say one thing. You told me your brother was an ace. Well, so are you, and one half Yank to another half Yank, I'm very proud of you."

She swallowed her whisky, tears in her eyes, and Harry put his hands on her shoulders. "Molly, my love, that shell that's kept you whole—don't let it crack. Death night after night, then your dear mother. You've been to hell and back."

"Still there."

"Not you. A soldier's daughter and a real trouper. You'll survive. Now, could I see my room? I'd really appreciate a shower."

MOLLY was sitting by the fire, reading the *Times,* when Munro appeared, his aide, Jack Carter, limping behind. "There you are, my dear. Interesting afternoon?"

"You could say that." She folded the newspaper. "How are you, Jack?" She kissed his cheek warmly. "Any problems with the leg?"

"Well, it hurts like the devil on occasion, but so what?"

"You're a lovely man, Jack Carter."

"Enough of this mild erotic byplay. Find out anything that we didn't know, Molly?" Munro said.

"Not much, and I wish you wouldn't pull me into these devious schemes of yours, Uncle Dougal. We spoke about his past, his brother. If you want a doctor's opinion, he loves his brother, admires him. A real ace, he called him."

Harry, having heard some of this on the stairs, came in, smiling. "Well, here we are. What delights have you got in store for tonight, Brigadier?"

"Dinner at the River Room at the Savoy."

The dinner was superb: smoked salmon, Dover sole, salad, champagne. The band was playing—Carrol Gibbons and the Orpheans. Molly said, "Well, isn't anyone going to ask me to dance?"

"I'm too old, and Jack's not up to it anymore. Your turn, Flight Lieutenant," said Munro.

So Harry took her to the floor, and they danced to "A Foggy Day in London Town."

"Very apt. Make it smoky for foggy," he said.

"Ah, but this is good," she said. "I feel alive for the first time in weeks. Do you feel alive, Kelso?"

Before he could reply, the headwaiter moved toward her through the dancers. "I'm sorry, Dr. Sobel. Guy's called. They want you back as soon as possible."

They returned to the table. "The hospital?" Munro asked.

"I'm afraid so."

Munro nodded to Carter. "Send her in my staff car."

She picked up her purse, and Carter helped her into her coat. She smiled. "Take care, Kelso."

He didn't reply, and she went out, Carter limping after her.

 IT WAS two weeks later that Sarah Dixon left the War Office and walked quickly through the winter sleet. Christmas wasn't too far away, not that it meant much these days. She caught the tube at the nearest station. It was overcrowded, everyone was tired and wet, and she was unaware that she was being followed.

Fernando Rodrigues was darkly handsome, thirty-five, of medium height, and wore a trilby hat and trench coat. The details his brother had forwarded in the diplomatic pouch had included a photo. He'd checked her address—a flat off Westbourne Grove.

She was unaware of his presence as she took out her key for the front door. He loomed behind her, and she turned in surprise.

He said, "Mrs. Sarah Dixon?"

"Yes. What do you want?"

"I have a message for you: The day of reckoning is here."

It was the code given her in 1938, and her response was astonishing. "Good Lord, you have been a long time. Come in."

He followed her inside. The flat was very small, just a bathroom, kitchen, sitting room, and bedroom. She took off her coat. "Who are you?"

"Before I answer, tell me one thing. Are you still anti-British?"

"Of course. They shot my grandfather like a dog. I'll have my revenge for that."

Rodrigues was amazed by her control and also strangely excited. So middle-class, so neat and orderly in her tweed suit.

"So what is this about?" she asked.

"Look, there must be some restaurants near here. Let me give you a meal."

They found a small Italian family sort of place on Westbourne Grove and sat in a secluded corner. He ordered a bottle of red wine and lasagna for both of them. It was incredible how he warmed to her, ended up telling her everything. "My name is Fernando Rodrigues. I'm a commercial attaché at the Portuguese embassy. I communicate by diplomatic pouch—which is, of course, inviolate— with my brother, Joel, who has a similar post at our embassy in Berlin. It's all very convenient and foolproof."

"And lucrative. A nice suit you're wearing."

"Life should be for pleasure, senhora." He smiled.

"I think you're a rogue, Mr. Rodrigues, but I like you."

"Fernando, please. Tell me, are you in or out?"

"Of course I'm in. I'm a secretary-clerk in accounts at the War Office. I don't have access to anything of great interest."

"Who knows? Things change." He took a card from his wallet. "There's my address and phone number."

IN NORTH Africa, the Italians had made a mess of their attack on Egypt, and so in February 1941 Hitler gave General Rommel command of the newly created Afrika Korps, which soon took everything before it. The British then sent General Montgomery to take command of the British desert forces, and Harry was posted to one of the two British Hurricane squadrons in Egypt.

The battles waged back and forth, but Montgomery began to turn things around. In September 1942 Harry was awarded his third DFC. El Alamein followed only days later, the turning point of the war in North Africa. Harry was transferred to Halifax bombers, engaged in flights across the Mediterranean to Italy. In January 1943 he was supposed to have attacked installations at Taranto, but bad weather had dispersed the squadron. Going down hard through mist, he'd come across the Italian cruiser *Orsini* and attacked it, scoring two direct hits that caused the cruiser to break up and sink. Badly damaged, with one engine out and two of his crew dead, he managed to nurse the Halifax to a crash landing on the Egyptian coast. He received the Distinguished Service Order and promotion to squadron leader.

As for Max, he'd been promoted to major and transferred to the Russian front after the German invasion of Russia in June 1941. At first there were great victories in Russia. Then came the hell of war in winter, and the defeats began. Though the German armies ground to a halt in the snow, on the whole the Russian pilots were no match for their Luftwaffe adversaries. Max's score rose rapidly, until he'd downed sixty planes on the eastern front and was awarded the swords to his Knight's Cross for his work at Stalingrad, which he finally left a week before the German surrender in February 1943.

BACK in Berlin, Göring decided Max had done enough, and pulled him out of Russia. Elsa waited for him in her suite at the Adlon. She looked well, not a day older, but she was shocked at his appearance. "Max, you look terrible."

"So would you, Mutti. Russia was a terrible place. The bottom of the heap. What Hitler wants it for, I'll never know."

There was a knock at the door, and Elsa's personal maid, Rosa Stein, came in. "A message, Baroness. General Galland will meet you at seven." Galland had been promoted to major general in November 1942 and was now in command of all fighter aircraft.

"We're meeting Dolfo?" Max said. "That's good."

"You need a decent dinner," she said. "So let's just enjoy ourselves and forget our beloved Führer and his damned Nazi party."

"You *have* changed," Max observed. "There was a time you thought they were rejuvenating Germany."

"That time is long gone, Max. You know the old joke about who's running the lunatic asylum? I think I know."

"Don't say it out loud, Mutti. Come on, let's find Dolfo." As they went downstairs, he added, "Rosa looked worried."

"She has a right to. Her husband, Heini, is Jewish. They haven't sent him to one of those camps, because he's an electronics wizard. But lately the SS have been making noises."

"Isn't it ever going to end?" Max said wearily.

They went into the bar and sat on a couch in the corner. "Any news of Harry?" Max asked.

"Not really. He sank that Italian cruiser in January. Göring told me about it, but of course, I wrote you about that."

"I wonder how he is. I'd love to see him," Max said.

A moment later Galland entered. Max jumped up and embraced him. "You've done well, Dolfo." He touched the Knight's Cross.

"I've done well?" Galland held him at arm's length. "You look terrible. Some time on staff, Colonel, is what you need."

"Colonel?" Elsa said.

"Lieutenant Colonel will do for a start. He was offered the appointment in Russia and tore the order up."

"I fly for a living, Dolfo," Max said. "I can't fly a desk."

"All right. Staff for a while, and then I'll let you fly. France if you like, the Channel, just like the old days."

"Good," Elsa said. "Now that's settled. Shall we eat?"

IN LONDON that evening, Sarah Dixon entered the little Italian restaurant on Westbourne Grove where she and Rodrigues had had their first meal. Sitting at a table, he rose to meet her. "How are you?"

"I've got rather startling news," she said as she sat down. "I'm being transferred to Special Operations Executive in Baker Street."

"That's hot stuff," he said. "SOE handles all undercover work in Europe, parachuting agents in, and so forth."

"So it would appear. Mind you, I'm not being posted to anything special. Same boring office routine, but it's more money."

"The possibilities are limitless."

"Well, it would be nice to come up with something important after all the low-grade rubbish of the past couple of years." She squeezed his arm. "I'm so excited, Fernando."

"You should be." He leaned over and kissed her.

IN AUGUST 1943 Sicily was occupied, and in September, Allied troops landed on the Italian mainland. In Cairo, Harry reported to a transportation officer based at Shepherd's Hotel.

"England for you, sir," the officer said. "Dakota to Malta to refuel and then Gibraltar. Thing is, one of the pilots is sick. Would you mind being backup?"

"My pleasure," Harry told him.

At the airport, he met the pilot in the crew room, a flying officer named Johnson, who was all over him. "Why, you sank the *Orsini*, sir. What a job that was."

Harry ignored that. "Do you envision any problems?"

"The Luftwaffe's based on their part of the Italian mainland now. Milk run, really. Half a dozen passengers."

"Anyone special?"

"Oh, some brigadier or other. They're all in the lounge."

Harry went into the lounge and found Dougal Munro there. Harry asked, "Would there be anything devious behind this meeting, Brigadier?"

"Now, do I look like that sort of chap?" Munro said.

"Actually, you do."

"Well, you're wrong. You have been covering yourself with glory since we last met, as has that brother of yours."

"Max? What about him?"

"Shot down who knows how many Russian planes. He's on staff in Berlin. Moved up one—lieutenant colonel."

"Good for Max."

"Did you know Teddy West is now air vice marshal?"

"I didn't." Harry was genuinely pleased. "How's your niece, the good doctor?"

"Molly? Worked off her feet. She liked you, Harry."

"I'm no good for her, Brigadier. I'm no good for anybody. It's a miracle I'm here at all, and that can't last forever."

"All right, Harry, never mind," Munro said cheerfully. "I've just been with Eisenhower. Your name came up."

Harry hesitated. "Is that so?"

"He's surprised you haven't switched to your own people."

"And who would my own people be?"

"Three Eagle Squadrons in the RAF, Harry. In September '42 they were transferred to Eighth U.S. Air Force."

"I know about that," Harry said. "And those who transferred were rotated to America as instructors. Who needs that?"

"The American air force is filled with greenhorns, Harry. They know nothing."

"Who cares?" Harry said. "Where were they when we were fighting the Battle of Britain? Playing games while Britain stood tall."

"Eisenhower seems to think you're letting the side down."

"Well, tough," Harry said. "I started RAF, and I'll finish RAF. It's what my old man did the First War."

"By September last year, all Americans had to transfer, Harry."

Harry considered it. "Let's see what Teddy West has to say."

IN ENGLAND, Harry had two weeks' leave and went to a small cottage he'd bought near Farley Field. He walked on the shingle beach and remembered the air battles over the Channel. When he was hungry, he ate at the Smugglers Inn, not far from the cottage, never in uniform, always in a sweater and pants.

On one day of cold rain in late September he was throwing pebbles into the sea when he heard the noise of a vehicle drawing up above the beach. He turned and found an RAF staff car. A sergeant jumped out, put up an umbrella, and opened the rear door.

Teddy West emerged, resplendent in air vice marshal's uniform. "Harry!" He waved. "Good to see you."

Harry hurried over and shook hands. "Great to see you, sir."

"Munro told me you looked a bit rough. You seem fine to me."

"Sea air, pub grub, lots of sleep."

"Good. Get in and let's go to your cottage. Lots to discuss."

Harry joined him in the rear seat. "Work, sir?"

"You could call it that. The Americans still want to get their hands on you, Harry. I've tried to lose you in the files. You're still officially Finnish, of course, but it can't last forever. I do have a suggestion."

"What would that be, sir?"

"Munro has a secret base at a place called Cold Harbour in Cornwall. They drop agents into France, pick people up, and so on."

"You'd like me to join?"

"You could be useful."

"So what would my duties be?"

"A run to France by night. More test flying of captured planes. Plenty of odd jobs. A sort of aide to me, and that means appropriate rank for the times you need a little muscle." He opened a bag he'd brought and took out a new uniform. "Forgive me, Harry, but I went to your Savile Row tailor. He's put the new uniform on your account. You are now a wing commander. That makes you the equivalent of your brother—a lieutenant colonel, I hear."

"Good Lord," Harry said. "I don't know what to say."

DURING October, Harry worked for West, visiting squadrons and assessing readiness for what everyone knew was bound to be ahead during 1944—the invasion of Europe. It was boring but necessary work. Strangely enough, Max was doing similar things for Galland in France, although he spent time in Berlin. Like Harry, he chafed at the bit, but Galland urged him to be patient.

One person who wasn't patient was Baroness Elsa von Halder. Earlier in the year there had been a Gestapo roundup of Jewish men with German wives. SS soldiers and Gestapo agents marched into laboratories, offices, and engineering plants and arrested Jews on the spot. Over three hundred German women gathered in protest outside Gestapo headquarters, and at the very front stood Elsa beside her maid, Rosa Stein, whose husband, Heini, had been arrested. Himmler, looking from his window with Bubi Hartmann, was not amused.

"Decent German women making such an exhibition and supported by a baroness of one of our oldest families. Disgraceful. Even more so that they married Jews in the first place."

Bubi Hartmann had absolutely nothing against Jews. In fact, his dark secret was that his maternal great-grandmother had been Jewish. Thankfully, it was so far back that it had never come out.

"Of course, the industrialists have all protested at the arrest," Bubi said. "All highly skilled, an asset to the Reich. I remember you recently pointed out their usefulness to the Führer."

Himmler nodded gravely.

"A great pity," Bubi went on, "that the minister of propaganda didn't listen. This is the direct result of his order."

"That fool Goebbels! Always the stupid thing."

"The Führer won't be pleased. If I may suggest, Reichsführer, a word from you. Good sense, as usual? It would leave Goebbels with egg on his face."

"You're right, Hartmann, and it's an excuse to see the Führer. I have other matters to discuss as well."

As Hartmann turned to go, Himmler said, "One more thing. Baroness von Halder out there is mixing with the wrong company."

THAT same evening, at the White House, the Oval Office was in half darkness, with only a table light on the desk. There were papers everywhere, and the air was heavy with smoke. Roosevelt sat behind the desk in his wheelchair, a cigarette in his usual long holder.

"Mr. President," Abe Kelso said, "you sent for me?"

"There you are, Abe. How do you think the war's going?"

"Up and down. Poorly in Italy."

"Well, Abe, top secret, but the Allies will land at Anzio, south of Rome, in January."

"The German army in Italy is one of their best. It could be tough."

"I expect it will be. Eisenhower and Montgomery will move to London in January to prepare for the invasion of France. I want you to go over, Abe, as my private fact finder."

"At your command, as always, Mr. President."

"Good. Now, what about your grandsons? How are they?"

"Well, the one we don't mention is now a half colonel in the Luftwaffe. Medals up to his eyes."

"And the other? Harry, isn't it?"

"A wing commander. Also medals up to his eyes."

Roosevelt frowned. "You mean he's still in the RAF? Abe, don't you think he should be with our air force?"

"He doesn't seem to see it that way."

"Then I think you should change his mind, Abe. Speak to him when you're over there. Tell him it's the presidential wish."

"As you command, Mr. President."

"Excellent. Now push me into the sitting room, and I'll mix you one of my celebrated martinis before you go."

SARAH Dixon found life considerably more interesting at Baker Street with SOE than at the War Office. For one thing, and in spite of the fact that her duties were administrative, she did get to see who was who—Munro, for example, Jack Carter, and others. One day West came in with Harry Kelso.

"That wing commander," she said to a woman called Madge Smith in the canteen. "I heard him speak, and he sounded American, but the badges on his uniform say Finland."

"Oh, that's Harry Kelso. A real ace. He sank the *Orsini,* and you're right. He is a Yank. He's Air Vice Marshal West's aide, and he does courier work for Munro."

"Courier work?"

"Special duties flights out of Cold Harbour in Cornwall."

"How interesting," Sarah said.

Even more interesting were the events of the following day. Madge said, "Be a love. Take this file to Nelly in the copying room. Five copies. ASAP."

On her way through the downstairs corridor Sarah had a quick look. There was a covering letter to the War Office, a map of Cold Harbour, details of aircraft normally there, drops to France, flights from London's Croydon Airport to Cold Harbour, with pilots listed. Harry Kelso was mentioned.

She couldn't believe it, went into the copying room, and found Nelly, a middle-aged gray-haired woman, stacking sheets.

"They want this fast, Nelly. Five copies."

"What a morning I've had! Run off my feet. I haven't even had a chance to go you-know-where."

"Well, go now. I'll start this lot for you."

"What a dear you are."

She rushed out, and Sarah ran the sheets through, folded them, and put them inside her pocket. Then she started on the five copies. She was almost done when Nelly appeared.

"Bless you. I had a smoke while I could." Nelly clipped the copies. "There you are, dear, and give Madge my love."

It was four days later that Joel Rodrigues delivered the report to Bubi Hartmann's secretary, Trudi, who took it to her boss at once.

"We've struck gold," Bubi said. "Read that."

She went through it quickly. "Did you note the name of one of those pilots?"

"Harry Kelso, the Baroness von Halder's other son."

"Will you tell the baron?"

"Of course not. But Himmler, yes, if only to show what great work we do. Tell Rodrigues to inform Mrs. Dixon we must have all information possible. And put the Rodrigues brothers on double pay."

MAX was flying a Junkers 88S solo from Berlin to a coastal base called Fermanville in France. At 0200 hours Max crossed the coast in scattered cloud with a half-moon. Visibility was fair as he called Fermanville and gave his position.

"Who are you?" the ground controller's voice asked.

"Colonel von Halder, delivering a new black bird."

"Have you a gunner?"

"No."

"What a pity, Baron. I have a target."

"Give me the position, and I'll take a look."

"Steer naught six seven degrees. Target range, five kilometers."

The Junkers moved out of the cloud, and Max saw the prey, a Lancaster bomber, smoke feathering from a starboard engine.

He called in, "I have visual sighting." Then he closed in.

It was very badly damaged—so badly that the rear gunner's turret had disappeared. Max went down five hundred feet into cloud and came up below. The JU88S had a pair of twenty-millimeter cannon mounted to aim upward. If Max fired, it would rip out the belly of the bomber.

He looked up and thought of the carnage he would cause—the cold wind whistling through the gaping holes in the fuselage, the dead and the dying. And for some reason, surprising even to himself, he thought, No. Enough. He banked across, aware of the pilot over there, clear in the moonlight, raised a hand in salute, then flew away.

He landed at Fermanville, taxied to dispersal, and got out as the ground crew came forward. He walked away, depressed, weary, and disturbed. A sitting duck, and he'd let it go. Why? He'd never done such a thing before, always gone for the kill.

"What's happening to you, old boy?" he asked himself softly.

THE first time Munro asked Harry to fly him and Carter down to Cold Harbour in a Lysander, it was a bad flight. The new year was starting, and slate-gray rain was slicing across the Cornish landscape. They went in at a thousand feet, and below was the inlet of Cold Harbour and the quay with a naval craft moored beside it.

"Isn't that a German E-boat?" Harry said.

"That's right," Munro told him cheerfully. "Nothing to do with you. It's a mind-your-own-business sort of place, Harry. You'll see."

"What about the villagers?" Harry asked, starting his descent.

"Moved them all out, old boy," Carter told him. "Still use the pub—that's the Hanged Man—for base personnel. A lady called Julie Legrande runs it for us. Ah, there's Grancester Abbey."

Gray stone, a couple of towers, all very imposing, with a walled garden running down to the river. A lake. "Nice," Harry said.

"We keep the agents we deliver to France there overnight."

Harry skimmed across the abbey and dropped down onto a grass runway. There were two hangars, several huts, and two aircraft on the apron, both German fighters. Harry switched off, opened the door, and he, Munro, and Carter got out.

Munro said, "To assuage your curiosity, dear boy, it's useful on occasion in our line of work to use enemy aircraft."

A jeep appeared, driven by a woman in her early thirties. She wore a sheepskin coat, and her blond hair was tied back. She had a calm and sweet face. "There you are, Brigadier." She smiled.

"Julie Legrande . . . Harry Kelso, Air Vice Marshal West's aide."

"Oh, the wing commander's reputation goes before him."

"Enough of that. We'll take the jeep." Munro turned to Harry. "Straight back to London for you. Get him a sandwich or something in the canteen, Julie, then see him off."

The canteen was simple enough: a few tables and chairs, a bar counter, a kitchen. The place was empty.

"Coffee?" she said.

"No. I'm a tea man now," he said. "The Brits make the worst coffee in the world."

He sat down and waited, and she appeared with a pot of tea and a plate of sandwiches. As he ate, she lit a cigarette and watched. "The great Harry Kelso. That Italian cruiser was something."

"Luck," he said. "One of the handful of times I was flying a bomber. I'm a fighter pilot."

"But what does that mean?" she said. "Flying fighter planes is a temporary job. Wars come and go, but they always end. What happens after?"

"Philosophy on a wet morning in Cornwall? I don't think I'm up to that." He finished the last sandwich. "Time to go."

"I'll see you off."

As they walked to the Lysander, he said, "Munro's niece, Molly—do you know her? She's a doctor."

"Yes. She comes down from London if there is an emergency. Sometimes people arrive from the other side in poor condition."

"I see." He took her hand. "Nice to meet you."

"And more often in the future," she said.

He climbed into the Lysander, switched on, and taxied away. As he rose up through the heavy overcast, it suddenly came to him, with a sense of shock, that she was right—he never thought it *would* be over, not in his heart.

5 EISENHOWER and Montgomery reached England in January 1944. In that month the Luftwaffe started to bomb London again. The Little Blitz, as it was called, wasn't as bad as the first time around, but bad enough. JU88S pathfinders operating out of Chartres and Rennes pinpointed the targets, and Max flew one of them. But soon the bombing ended.

One day Max reported to Galland at Luftwaffe headquarters in Berlin and found him in the canteen having sandwiches and beer. Galland looked up, genuinely pleased. "Good to see you, Max."

"I thought we should talk." Max sat down. "Our latest escapade over London has run its course, it seems. I'd like to return to 109s. The Junkers isn't my cup of tea."

Galland frowned, then nodded. "I'll make you my personal aide on the French coast. You'll have your own ME109. What you do with it when my back is turned is your business. Is that acceptable?"

"Perfectly."

"Good. I must go. By the way, I hear the Gestapo picked up Generals Prien and Krebs the other day, also some junior people. The whisper is, there was a failed bomb plot against the Führer. They were all members of that bridge club at the Adlon Hotel."

"So?" Max said.

"Doesn't your mother play there?"

Max was thunderstruck. "I'm not certain."

"I think she'd be advised to go to another club," Galland said. "These are troubled times." He turned and went out.

Max rang Bubi Hartmann at his office, but he was out, Trudi Braun said. He told her he wanted to meet him in the Adlon bar at six. She put the phone down, and Bubi replaced the extension.

"This is bad," he said. "It could be about the bridge club. His mother plays with them."

"But Max is your friend."

"So what do you want me to do? Put my head on the block?"

She shook her head. "You're a good man, Bubi, in entirely the wrong job."

"All right." Bubi straightened his uniform. "Give me that report on French Resistance activity. It will give me an excuse to talk to Himmler."

REICHSFÜHRER Himmler examined the report and nodded. "Very thorough. All these terrorists will be rounded up and shot."

"Certainly, Reichsführer."

"And now I have to meet with the Führer in the bunker."

"Anything in particular?" Bubi Hartmann asked.

"I'm not sure, although he is hardly pleased by that attempt on his life the other day. Naturally, we arrested all involved. A bridge club—can you believe it? They were all executed at once: Prien, Krebs, some junior officers, and two women."

Bubi turned pale. "Firing squad, Reichsführer?"

"Too honorable a way out for such scum. No. The Führer's orders were clear—execution with piano wire. And no, Colonel, your friend's mother, the good baroness, was not among them. At the moment there isn't enough proof."

"I see, Reichsführer."

Bubi made for the door, and Himmler called, "I'd advise you to consider your friendship with the baron, Hartmann. You are valuable to me, but no one is indispensable."

In the bar at the Adlon, Max sat drinking cognac to steady his nerves. He was afraid, but not for himself, only his mother. How stupid she had been, how incredibly stupid. Hartmann came in.

"Bubi, thank God you came," Max said.

"Just this time, Max. I can't take chances. This is very bad."

"Tell me."

Which Bubi did, in graphic detail. "So now you know."

"Merciful heaven, that they can do such things."

"They can, believe me. Your mother must take care." He stood. "We won't meet again, Max. Himmler himself has warned me off."

ELSA was in her suite, sitting on the couch by the fireplace, enjoying a drink, when Max came in.

"My darling boy, how marvelous. Just in time for a cocktail."

"Never mind that. I've news for you. Your friends Generals Prien and Krebs and the others, plus a couple of women, all members of your bridge club? Does this mean anything to you?"

"I heard a whisper that there had been some difficulty."

"That's one way of putting it. The difficulty was an attempt to blow up the Führer, which failed. Your friends are all dead, Mutti, hung by the neck by piano wire."

She was visibly shaken. "That can't be true."

"Hartmann risked his own neck to warn me. The only reason Himmler hasn't had you arrested is that he lacks solid proof."

"Damn him!" Elsa said, and there were angry tears in her eyes. "They can't do this to me."

The dressing-room door flew open, and Rosa appeared. Her eyes were swollen with weeping, and Max said, "What is wrong?"

"They've sent Heini to Auschwitz," Elsa said.

"How could that be, Mutti? You just told me 'They can't do this to me.' Wasn't that your phrase?"

"Damn you, Max."

She hammered at his chest, and he took her wrists. "You think being Baroness von Halder matters? Not in the Third Reich. You think Göring will help you when you're in a mess like this? You were always window dressing, Mutti, just like me."

"Max, please."

"I've had it. You carry on down this road, and you'll take everyone with you." He turned to Rosa. "So they took Heini? Never mind. The way my mother's behaving, they'll have you, too, before long. Perhaps even me." He walked to the door.

Elsa called, "Max, listen."

He turned. "And it was for this that we left Boston? It was to support the arrogance of a von Halder that I lost my brother?"

He went out the door, and she collapsed in tears on the couch.

HIMMLER'S Mercedes turned into Vosstrasse and drove toward the Reich Chancellery and the Führer's bunker—his underground headquarters. It was protected by thirty meters of concrete, proof against any bomb the Allies could drop on Berlin.

The Mercedes drew into a car ramp, and an SS sentry saluted. Himmler got out and went below. Walking through dim lighting, endless corridors, he finally came to a door manned by another SS sentry. He passed inside to find Goebbels, von Ribbentrop, Hitler's personal secretary Martin Bormann, and Admiral Canaris standing at the general map table. He could hear the angry sound of the Führer's voice coming from his private study.

"What's going on?" Himmler asked Bormann.

"He isn't pleased."

The door opened, and Field Marshals von Rundstedt, Rommel, and von Kluge emerged, the Führer behind them. "Go on, get out. Come back to me with common sense or not at all."

They went out in confusion, Rommel looking grim, and Hitler turned to the others. "This map," he said. "The Channel, France. All they can talk about is where the enemy will land. Calais or Normandy—who cares? We will crush them on the beaches."

"Naturally, my Führer," Bormann told him.

"So why can't they come up with something useful, these clowns?" He slapped his thigh and laughed. "Do you know what would be useful, gentlemen, really useful?"

They all stared nervously. It was Himmler who said, "What would that be, my Führer?"

"For a bomb to fall on Eisenhower! He's the leader, the brain. With him out of the way they'd be in total disarray."

"You are right, as always," Himmler said. "There are, of course, many ways to skin a cat. A simple assassination."

Hitler turned to Himmler. "What a pleasing prospect, Reichsführer. It lifts my heart to think of it."

Later in his office Himmler said to Bubi Hartmann, "Is there anyone among our agents who could accomplish such a task?"

"I regret to say no one, Reichsführer. Can you imagine the security around Eisenhower?"

"Still," Himmler said, "bear it in mind, Colonel."

IT WAS a day later that Senator Abe Kelso crossed the Atlantic in a Flying Fortress and moved into a suite at the Savoy in London. One of the first things he did was to track down Harry, which led him to a phone conversation with Teddy West.

"I understand my grandson is your aide?" Abe said.

"In a manner of speaking, Senator, but it's more complicated. He operates with a special duties squadron."

Abe said, "Are you telling me I can't see him?"

"It's not that. The fact is, he isn't here. He's in Scotland supervising the inspection of a captured German plane. I wish we'd known you were coming."

"Top secret. Trouble is, I'm due back in six days. I've plenty to do, but Harry was a priority. I last saw him in '39."

"I'll speak to him and see if we can hurry things along."

Abe met with Churchill and Eisenhower, listening patiently. Even when generals like Patton and Bradley were disagreeing, they were worth listening to. He had an uncomfortable lunch with Montgomery, when the field marshal made no secret of his belief that he and not Ike should be in supreme command.

THE following morning Harry flew a JU88S down to London. As he landed, an RAF staff car rolled up, and West got out. "Thought I'd pick you up, Harry."

"That's good of you, sir." Harry followed him into the car.

"Your grandfather's at the Savoy. I'll drop you off." West offered

Harry a cigarette. "By the way, I've got a flight for you tomorrow."

"And what would that be?"

So West told him, then dropped him off at the hotel.

Abe, standing by the window of the sitting room of his suite, was enjoying a cigar and looking out over the Thames. There was a knock at the door.

"Porter, sir."

"Come in. It's not locked," Abe bellowed.

The door opened, and the porter entered with two bags.

"What's this?" Abe demanded, and then Harry stepped in.

"Hello, Abe," he said, and it was as if the years had melted away.

Abe, overcome by emotion, flung his arms around him and wept. A few minutes later, sitting by the window, he said, "For heaven's sake, Harry, this is unbelievable. Look at all those medals."

"Remember what Dad used to say? Nice bit of tin. Any news of Max and Mutti?"

"No. My connections have dried up."

"I might be able to find something out."

"How could you?"

"I work for a Brigadier Munro. The intelligence field."

"I've heard of him. He's heavily involved with Ike."

"He would be," Harry said. "I'll see what I can do."

Abe nodded. "Harry, we've got a problem. The President wants you in the U.S. Air Force, and so does Ike."

"Oh, for goodness sake!" Harry exploded. "I've had enough of this! What are they going to do? Court-martial me?"

"Harry, you're being stupid."

"How come? I mean, do they think Max should transfer in from the Luftwaffe?" He got up and took a deep breath. "Enough. I need a bath. What are you doing tonight?"

"I've booked a table in the River Room."

"Excellent." Harry opened his jump bag and put Tarquin on the table. "There you go, Abe. Doesn't that take you back? Every flight I've done, he's been there." He picked up his other bag. "I'll use the spare room." As he opened the door, he added, "I hear you're flying down from Croydon to Southwick House with Ike tomorrow."

"How do you know that?"

"Because I'm the pilot."

The River Room was busy early, but then, everywhere in London was these days. Abe and Harry were seated at a table for four. Abe ordered champagne cocktails, and Harry said, "Who are the others?"

"Oh, I decided to invite your Brigadier Munro while you were in the bath. When I asked him to join us, he suggested bringing his niece, a Dr. Sobel. I understand you know her."

"Yes, we've met, but it was some time ago."

At that moment Munro arrived with Molly. He was in uniform. She wore an evening suit in some sort of brown crepe. Her hair was tied back with a brown velvet bow.

Harry and Abe stood up, and Munro said, "My niece, Molly."

Abe looked at her with considerable approval. "I understand you know my grandson."

She smiled at Harry and shook hands.

"Last time I saw you, you looked tired," he said.

"And now?"

"Good enough to dance with," he said. "Let's leave the older generation to talk."

The Orpheans were playing a slow fox-trot, "Night and Day," and she moved into his arms. "Here we are again," he said.

"And here you are covered in glory, as usual."

"What about you? Still at Guy's?"

"I'm a senior surgeon now."

"That's great. Do you still do work for Munro? I mean as the flying doctor to Cold Harbour."

"Now and then." She frowned. "You mean something more."

"That time you and I took a walk after lunch at the Garrick—I overheard Dougal asking you what you could get out of me."

"Oh, rats," she said. "I'd make a rotten spy."

"That's okay. I enjoyed the walk. Are you spying tonight?"

"If you must know, my uncle told me he was seeing you and your grandfather for dinner and I asked if I could come."

"Did you, now? I wonder why?"

"Don't be a pig, Harry Kelso. You know why."

For a moment she was close to tears, and he was immediately contrite. "Okay, I'm sorry."

The orchestra moved on to "A Foggy Day in London Town," and Molly inched closer.

"Any man in your life?" he asked.

"Yes, but he isn't doing much about it."

He held her even closer, and at the table, Munro said, "I might as well tell you, Senator, the poor girl has fallen for the wretch."

"And I might as well tell you, that suits me just fine," Abe said.

Molly and Harry sat down, and the waiter suggested the evening's main dish: a haddock-and-potato pie. They all took it.

"That's war for you—real food." Munro raised his glass. "To us and to hell with Hitler."

"Speaking of the Führer," Harry said. "Any news of Max?"

"None that you'd like to hear. During the Little Blitz he was in a pathfinder. I believe he made fifteen or sixteen raids."

"That must have been tough," Harry said calmly. "The south of England is no place for Luftwaffe these days."

There was a slight pause. Molly said, "Tough? Harry, he was bombing London. A hundred people died in a single tube station."

"The cruiser *Orsini* had a crew of eight hundred and twenty men," Harry replied quietly. "Only seventy-two survived." He shrugged. "Like they say, war is hell. A tube station, a cruiser . . . People die, Molly. We kill them. That's what we do."

Silence reigned for a few uncomfortable moments before Munro changed the subject. "You're going down to Southwick tomorrow with Ike?" he said to Abe.

"That's right, and Harry's our pilot."

"Have you met Ike yet, Harry?" Munro asked.

At that moment the waiter came over. "I'm terribly sorry, but it's the hospital, Doctor. You're wanted immediately."

"Oh, dear, here we go again. May I use your car, Uncle?"

"Of course."

"I'll see you to the door," Harry said.

They went out of the entrance and stood on the pavement while the porter went to get the driver. When the staff car drew up, Harry opened the door for her. "It was nice seeing you again."

"Oh, you fool." She reached up and kissed him on the mouth. "I suppose you'll go to hell your own way." And she got into the car.

HARRY found Munro and Abe deep in conversation. "What are you two up to?" he said as he sat down. "Winning the war?"

"The war *is* won, Harry," Abe said. "Just a matter of time."

"Bloody battles to come both in Russia and Europe," Munro said, "but at the end stands victory. More champagne, Harry?"

"Better not. I'm flying in the morning."

Abe said, "Brigadier Munro's mentioned one item of news out of Berlin that isn't too comforting. There was a bungled attempt on Hitler's life. A number of officers and two women were executed. They were all members of Elsa's bridge club."

Harry turned very pale, his face like stone.

CROYDON Airport was thick with mist, and heavy rain was falling as Abe waited in a rather bare Nissen hut and drank bad coffee. The Lysander, that squat and ugly high-wing monoplane, was on the apron being checked by two mechanics. A staff car drew up, and the driver got out and opened the door for Eisenhower.

Ike walked to the hut. "Morning, Abe," he said. "Is that coffee?"

"The worst in the world, but it's hot."

"That'll do me." He took the cup a sergeant offered him. "All that mist and rain, Abe. Do you think we're going anywhere?"

"I'm not sure. Better ask the pilot."

Harry came out of the map room at that moment and turned to Ike. "No problem, sir. Heavy rain, but otherwise clear in the Southwick House area. I'll have you there in forty minutes." He took a flying jacket from a peg.

Ike said, "You're American?"

"Harry Kelso, sir."

Ike held out his hand. "At last we meet, Wing Commander, and it's a privilege."

HARRY, as good as his word, landed at the airstrip right on time. A staff car was waiting. Ike insisted that Harry come up to Southwick House with them for a meal.

Fort Southwick was of nineteenth-century construction, with a maze of tunnels, and it was being used as combined underground operations headquarters for Operation Overlord, the invasion of France. All signal traffic concerned with the coming invasion passed through it, and at its heart was the Naval Plotting Room, one of the best-kept secrets of the war. Southwick House had been chosen as Overlord HQ because of its proximity to the fort.

Over roast beef and Yorkshire pudding Eisenhower said, "Wing Commander, I've got to be frank with you. The time has come for you to move to our air force."

Harry suppressed his impatience. This was Eisenhower, after all. "I'm happy as I am, General. I'd like to finish what I started."

"I believe your grandfather has told you it's the President's wish, and it is also mine as your Supreme Commander. Now let's finish our meal in harmony. The beef is really excellent."

Later that night Munro phoned Harry at the Savoy. "How did it go with Ike?"

"To use a grand old English phrase, he put the boot in. He's given me a week to decide of my own choice. After that I don't have a choice. Do you know if Teddy West is around?"

"I'll see, but I can offer you something to take your mind off it for the next two days."

"Anything. What is it?"

"A big man in de Gaulle's organization, a Colonel Jobert, needs to be picked up in France by Lysander operating from Cold Harbour. I need you to shadow the mission in a Hurricane. Will you do it?"

"Absolutely."

"Such a mission means you will be starting an official tour with my special duties squadron, and as you're aware, such tours extend to sixty operations. I may just have saved your bacon." Munro rang off.

"Everything okay?" Abe asked.

"I'm back on duty tomorrow. Sorry, but that's the way it is."

"Will it be rough?"

"I'll be flying over there, but hey, I've been doing that for years. You'll be going back the day after tomorrow anyway."

"True." Abe nodded. "I can't tell you how much it's meant to me to see you." He was very emotional.

After Abe went to bed, Harry switched off the lamps. He lit a cigarette and looked out over the Thames in the half-light, then turned and saw Tarquin peering at him out of the gloom.

"Well, here we go again, old buddy," he said.

 HARRY reported to Croydon at ten the following morning and found a Hurricane waiting for him, parked on the other side of the Lysander. As he went into the operations room to check conditions, he saw a staff car drive up outside. Munro and Jack Carter emerged. The surprise was Molly Sobel.

They came in, and Munro said cheerfully, "Ah, there you are."

Harry said to Molly, "Are you coming with us to Cold Harbour?"

"So it would appear."

"Just a precaution," Munro told him. "A hazardous mission. Better to have Molly on hand."

Harry turned to Carter. "Major now? Congratulations."

"And you." They shook hands, and the Lysander pilot came in.

"Flight Lieutenant Grant," Munro said. "He's done umpteen drops for me. Really knows his business."

Grant was twenty-two or -three and had a ginger mustache. "I say, this is a first, meeting you, sir," he said to Harry, then went off to the ops room.

The orderly sergeant provided tea, and Harry took out a pack of cigarettes. His jump bag was on the table, and Molly said, "Is the famous Tarquin in there?"

"Oh, you know about him?"

"Of course. May I look?"

"If you like."

He lit a cigarette, and she unzipped the bag and took Tarquin out. Munro and Jack stopped talking. "My word," Jack said.

"Oh, he's wonderful." Molly held Tarquin close.

"He did every flight over Flanders with my dad. That's why he wears RFC wings. The RAF wings come from me."

"Every flight?" Munro asked.

"Every flight."

Molly replaced Tarquin in his bag and closed it.

"Ah, well, let's get on with it, then." Munro turned to Harry. "We'll see you at Cold Harbour."

RAIN was already driving in from the sea as Harry took the Hurricane down for a landing and taxied toward the hangars. A flight crew came out to meet him.

He got out and stretched. As he lit a cigarette, Julie Legrande drove up in the jeep. "Hello there. Jump in," she said. "The Lysander won't be here for an hour. I'm sure you could do with something to eat."

"That suits me."

At the Hanged Man, Julie led the way inside. A log fire burned brightly in the open fireplace. There were eight men, a rescue-boat crew, in there—four playing cards, one by the fire reading a newspaper, the others drinking beer at the bar.

"Come on, Julie, we're starving," someone called.

"Don't fuss. The pies are in the oven."

The man reading the newspaper said, "You leave her be, or I'll belt you one."

The crew laughed. Someone said, "You tell him, Zec."

They all looked curiously at Harry. Julie took him over to the fire. "Coxswain Zec Acland . . . Wing Commander Harry Kelso."

Acland was thirty-four, an intensely attractive human being, full of energy and with a tanned seaman's face. He looked what he was—a fisherman bred to the sea from childhood.

"Ah, the Hurricane pilot." Zec held out a hand as hard as granite. "My, my, boy, is there any medal you're missing there?"

"I bought them all on sale in Camden Market," Harry said.

The crew laughed, and Harry put his jump bag carefully on the table and sat down.

Zec was immediately curious. "Something special in there?"

"A bear," Harry told him, and lit a cigarette.

Everyone stopped talking; then someone laughed. "A bear?"

"I see. A mascot?" Zec said.

"No. More than that. He's flown with me every mission."

Again someone laughed. Julie went behind the bar and pulled two pints.

"I was a navy man," Zec said. "No room for mascots on torpedo boats."

Julie put the two pints on the table. "The wing commander sank the *Orsini*."

The room went quiet, and everyone was looking at Harry. Zec said, "You did that? A lot of sailors went down in that one."

"Seven hundred and forty-eight." Harry tasted his pint. "Something wrong?"

"Sailors are sailors, Wing Commander. Irrespective of their country, the sea has always been the common enemy."

"The war, the war, the bloody war," Julie said.

"That's about it. Not your doing, Wing Commander. The war's doing. Let's have a look, then."

Harry took Tarquin out, got up, and put him on the bar. No one laughed. There was silence, and then one of the sailors, built like a brick wall, with tangled hair and beard, spoke. "Why, he's marvelous. I declare, I've never seen the like."

They crowded around, and Julie leaned across the bar. "What a darling. Can we leave him here for a while?"

"Sure," Harry said. "As long as he's back in the bag for the flight tonight." At that moment the door opened, and Munro, Molly, Carter, and Grant, the Lysander pilot, entered.

"Wonderful smell, Julie, my love," Munro said. "Just in time for the pies, are we?"

LATE that evening they gathered around the map table in the library, a large chart before them. Munro said, "There's the target, Grant, two miles outside this village—Grouville. One pickup: Colonel Jobert. Forty-five-minute flight over there. You'll have a clear moon fading into dawn." He turned to Harry. "That suit you?"

"Absolutely," Harry said. "But I would point out that it will be dawn, which means we'll be highly visible."

"That's what you're there for," Munro told him.

At the airfield, Grant took off first, the Lysander lifting up into the sky and turning out to sea. Unarmed, he would fly below radar height. Harry gave Grant fifteen minutes, then took off, leveled the Hurricane at two thousand feet, closed in upon the Lysander in no time at all, and took up station.

They passed the French coast, moved inland, and there was the target—flashlights laid out in an L shape. Harry circled as Grant landed, the dawn already coming up.

AT THE airfield at Fermanville, twenty miles away, Max and two other duty pilots on night shift were playing cards when the alarm sounded. The controller said calmly, "We have traffic. Two targets. Scramble at once, and I'll give you the coordinates."

Max and his friends were out the door and running across the apron to where their ME109s were waiting. A moment later Max, as flight leader, took off first, and the others followed fast.

AS THE day dawned, gray clouds swept in, and rain hammered against the Hurricane's canopy. At two thousand feet Harry flew through broken clouds, turning in wide curves, aware of Grant far, far below. Then a couple of miles away an ME109 emerged from low clouds and pounced on the Lysander.

Harry went down. The Hurricane could do four hundred miles an hour in a dive. He came up behind the ME, his four Hispano cannon thundered, and he blew most of the tail off the plane. At the same time a second ME came in from starboard and raked the Hurricane from stem to stern. Part of the cockpit and the windshield disintegrated, and a splinter ripped Harry's cheek. He banked, rolled as the second ME flashed past, fired his cannon instinctively, and the Luftwaffe plane simply blew up.

The Cornish coast was fifteen miles away, the Lysander at eight hundred feet making for home. Grant, looking up, had seen it all. The Hurricane was trailing smoke, and a third ME had appeared.

"A miracle!" Colonel Jobert cried. "I've never seen such flying."

"He'll need more than a miracle now," Grant told him, and called Cold Harbour over the radio.

MAX, on the outer edge of the sweep, had seen the action from afar and knew great flying when he saw it. He watched one, then two go down. Then he swept around and came in for the kill.

As the smoking Hurricane slowed, Max throttled back and took up station to port. He had a secondary channel designed to eavesdrop on the RAF frequency and used it now. "Hey, Tommy, you fought a great fight, but it's time to go, or you'll end up like burnt steak."

Harry, hanging in there, didn't need to recognize the voice. Every instinct told him who it was. "Hello, Max. It's been a long time."

"Harry! It's you," Max said as the Hurricane started down. "Do you think you can make the coast?"

"It's not likely, but I'll give it a try. How's Mutti?"

"For heaven's sake, Harry."

"Tell her to take care. Himmler's just waiting for his chance."

"Watch it, Harry! Watch it! Your fuselage is breaking apart. I can see flames!"

Zec Acland's voice came over Harry's radio. "This is rescue boat *Lively Jane*. We're on our way, Kelso. Give me your position."

Harry's radio started to smoke and went dead. He snapped on

the jump bag to his belt, pulled back his canopy, and unfastened his seat belt. The smell of burning was terrible, and fire was licking around his boots. He flipped the Hurricane over and fell out.

Zec Acland's voice came over the radio channel again. "Are you there? Can you give me your position, Wing Commander?"

Max cut in. "Listen to me. This is your friendly local Luftwaffe pilot here. He's just jumped." He gave the position and went into a steep dive, following the parachute as it descended to port.

The heaving carpet of waves and foam below was terrible to see. He's had it, Max thought. They'll never see him. And then it came to him, the one chance, and he reached for the linen bag on his left knee containing a dye, which, if you went into the sea, spread in a huge yellow patch. He pulled the bag free, then yanked back his canopy and went down.

HARRY plunged into the waves, went under, inflated his Mae West, surfaced, and fought to get rid of his parachute. He went into a trough, the waves so high that he couldn't see beyond, then rose on a crest to see the ME109 over to the left. He wondered what his brother was playing at, and then Max throttled back to virtually stalling speed and came in, incredibly, at a hundred feet, leaned out of the cockpit, and dropped the dye bag. It fell to the side of Harry, and the yellow stain started to spread.

Harry struggled toward it, and Max increased speed, pulled back the column, and climbed to a thousand feet, and there, only a mile away to the north, was the *Lively Jane.*

Some of the crew shouted in dismay as the black plane with the Luftwaffe crosses and the swastika flew overhead.

Max called over the radio, "*Lively Jane,* he's a mile due south. I dropped my dye bag, so look for the yellow stain. I'll circle him till you get there. And get it right, or I'll blow you out of the water."

"All right, you devil. I don't know what your game is, but we'll be there," Zec replied. He was so involved in the hunt that it took a moment for the penny to drop: Was that Luftwaffe pilot speaking *English?*

COLD. IT WAS SO VERY COLD. Harry went down in the troughs, bounced up on the waves like a cork, the jump bag on its strap following him.

"Not good, old buddy, not good at all," he said, pulling the bag close, and then he was aware of a roaring engine and looked up.

Max came in low, waggled his wings, and circled.

"Crazy fool," Harry whispered. "Go on, get out of here, Max, while you still have enough juice."

The yellow stain was enormous now, and Harry floated almost in the center. As he was tossed high again, he saw the *Lively Jane* a hundred yards to his left. He went down, was thrown high, and the rescue boat was suddenly there, turning broadside.

Oh, but he was tired. He tried to strike out, and then the boat was on top of him. Hands reached down and hauled him over the rail. A moment later he was on his knees, vomiting salt water.

Molly was there, crouched beside him. "Your face—it's bad. Let's get you below."

A voice crackled over the radio. "Hey, you got him?"

"Yes, thanks to you," Zec said. "Whoever you are."

Harry put up a shaking hand. "Give me the mike." He grabbed it. "Max, it's me."

"I love you, Harry."

"And I love you. Remember, tell Mutti to take care."

The ME109 turned away, climbed high into the somber sky, and fled like a departing spirit.

One of the crew pulled Harry up, and Molly put an arm around his shoulders. "Who was that?" Zec demanded. "He sounded American." He frowned. "In fact, he sounded like you."

"Well, he would. That was my brother, Max, my twin brother."

IN THE medical room at the abbey, Harry, in a robe, sat back, the morphine injection Molly had given him taking effect as she examined his left cheek.

"Just keep still while I stitch you up. Ten should do it. You'll end up with an interesting scar, Harry. The girls will love it."

"Get lost," he told her.

"I've no intention of getting lost. Now shut up, and keep still."

The door opened, and Munro looked in. "Can I join you?"

"Look and learn," Harry said. "Grant and Colonel Jobert made it back?"

"They certainly did and proceeded on to London. The colonel was ecstatic. Said you were a hero extraordinaire and intends to ask de Gaulle to make you a chevalier of the Legion of Honor."

"Oh, no," Harry groaned.

"Brace yourself. I've just spoken to Teddy West and gave him the full details. He told me he's recommending you for the immediate award of a bar to your DSO. He's proud of you, Harry." Munro went to the door and opened it. "And so am I. We're on your side. I'll see you later."

"You see?" Molly said as she placed the final stitch. "You always act as if you're alone. It's not true. Today you had Max and Zec, Munro and West."

"And you."

Before she could reply, the door opened, and Julie came in. "How's the boy wonder?"

"Ten stitches, and he's as good as new. Except for his uniform."

"Let's see what we've got in the supply room," Julie said.

Harry and Molly followed her out and along the corridor, and Julie opened a door at the far end and entered. It was an Aladdin's cave, handguns and automatic weapons laid out in rows on a huge table, British and German uniforms, French civilian clothes.

"Just give him a nice comfortable sweater and some slacks," Molly said. "A decent meal. Then I'll tuck him up in bed."

Julie shrugged. "Help yourself, Harry. There's everything you could want here. Underwear, shirts, shoes, and socks."

"We'll see you in the library." Molly followed Julie out.

They went down to the kitchen, where Julie busied herself with the meal. Molly said, "Can I help?"

"Not really." Julie checked the chicken in the oven. "He's not for you, *chérie,*" she said without turning.

"He's not for anyone," Molly said.

"Then why bother? He's always been on borrowed time."

"There's a war on, Julie. You take what you can. Except I don't really have a choice."

LATER, in bed, the curtains drawn against the light, Harry lay propped up against a pillow and smoked a cigarette. The door clicked open, and a moment later Molly slipped into bed beside him.

"Grant will be back with the Lysander in late afternoon."

"Good." He put an arm around her.

"What's going to happen to us, Harry?"

"Who knows?" he said, and held her close in the soundless dark.

7 IN LONDON two days later, staying at Munro's flat on Haston Place again, Harry caught a taxi to Guy's Hospital to keep an appointment Molly had arranged. He reported to reception, and a nurse led him to a surgical theater. Molly, in a white coat, was inside. "There you are." She ripped the surgical tape away from his face in one deft movement and examined his wound. It was healing nicely, so she didn't tape it up again, just sprayed it with antiseptic.

"What now?" he said. "Do you have time for lunch?"

"I'm free, actually, but I had a phone call from my uncle. He wants you at the flat. Air Vice Marshal West wants a word with you."

At Haston Place, they went upstairs to the flat, and when Molly rang the bell, it was Jack Carter who opened the door. He shook Harry's hand. "It's wonderful to see you in one piece."

Laughter came from the sitting room, and Carter led the way in. There was Munro and West and an American major general. The big surprise was General Eisenhower, sitting on the window seat.

Molly moved to the major general and kissed him. "Hello, Dad."

Eisenhower got up and held out his hand. "Wing Commander,

you're extraordinary. Have you met Molly's father—Tom Sobel?"

Sobel was of medium height, with a black mustache and hair. His handshake was firm. "It's an honor to meet you, son."

"Fine. So now we've got the pleasantries over, to business," Eisenhower said. "I gave you a week," he said to Harry.

"I told you how I feel, General."

"Listen to me," Sobel said to Harry. "You've served magnificently with the RAF, but it's time to put on your country's uniform."

There was a silence. Ike said, "I can make it a direct order."

It was West who said smoothly, "The agreement has been that anyone into a tour with the RAF would finish that tour. I believe Wing Commander Kelso has a wee bit of tour left to go."

Eisenhower gave him a sharp look. "Okay, tell me the worst."

"Wing Commander Kelso has just started a tour with our most important special duties squadron. He has fifty-nine missions to go. Some of these are flying you, sir, for the courier service."

Eisenhower stared at West for a long moment. Then he burst out laughing, and even Sobel smiled. "You sly fox," Ike said. "And you, Brigadier. Okay, you win, but I want him in American uniform today." He turned to Harry. "That's an order, Colonel."

Munro smiled. "Actually, it's all taken care of, General. Air Vice Marshal West and I spoke to Wing Commander Kelso's tailor in Savile Row yesterday. They agreed to do a rush job. As you know, he's due at the Connaught Hotel at three to receive the Legion of Honor from General de Gaulle."

"Oh, dear," Harry groaned.

"Then tomorrow morning at eleven, Buckingham Palace for his second award of the DSO."

Eisenhower grinned and said to Harry, "That just about takes care of you, I'd say."

Munro said to Molly, "If you've got time, go to Savile Row with him. We want him to look good for de Gaulle. He's very particular."

"You can all go jump in a lake," Harry said, and walked out, Molly hurrying after him.

Ike called, "Keep an eye on him, Doctor."

When Harry emerged from Savile Row, he was wearing cream slacks and the brown battle-dress tunic favored by many U.S. Air Force officers. The silver wings of a pilot were over his left breast, above the medals. RAF wings were on his right breast.

"You look lovely," Molly said. "Terribly dashing." She glanced at her watch and took his arm. "We must get a move on."

They arrived at the Connaught Hotel and waited at the reception desk.

A young French captain appeared. "Colonel Kelso?" He looked uncertainly at Molly. "The young lady is with you?"

"Yes. On General Eisenhower's orders. This is Dr. Sobel."

"Ah, I see." The captain gave her his most charming smile. "If you would follow me." As they went upstairs, he added, "Colonel Jobert is waiting in the suite to thank you personally."

When they reached the suite, the captain opened the door and led the way in. De Gaulle was seated next to a coffee table by the window, and there was a box in Moroccan leather on the table.

Jobert, in uniform, stood close by, and he rushed forward and embraced Harry. "I will remember your heroism all my life, for it was my life you saved."

"May I introduce Dr. Sobel? She's here at the Supreme Commander's request."

"Excellent." Jobert turned to de Gaulle, who was lighting a cigarette and seemed indifferent to the whole business. "With your permission, General?"

General de Gaulle nodded, and Jobert opened the box, took out the insignia of the chevalier of the Legion of Honor, and pinned it on Harry's tunic. He kissed both cheeks, stepped back, and saluted.

De Gaulle spoke. "The republic thanks you, Colonel, but now you will excuse us. There is much to do."

Harry gave him a perfunctory salute. The captain opened the door, and Molly and Harry exited, made it to the stairs, and collapsed into laughter.

"The republic thanks you," she said in a deep voice. "He doesn't like anyone, that man. He's not even grateful."

Harry was trying to unpin the medal. "The thing is stuck."

"Here, let me. It's very nice. Give me the box." She replaced the medal, snapped the box shut, and offered it to him.

"You keep it," he said. "Souvenir. After all, I'm getting another at the palace in the morning. Will you come? Guests are allowed."

"Harry, I'd love to. But I'm going to leave you." She took his arm as they reached the pavement. A cab pulled up to drop somebody off, and she waved to the driver. "I'm due at the hospital, and the evening shift often drags on very late." She kissed his cheek, got into the cab, and was driven away.

THE next morning, at Haston Place, Harry came into the sitting room perfectly dressed for the occasion. "My, you do look pretty," Munro said. "But bad news from the medical front. Molly can't make it."

"Really?" Harry shrugged. "Serves me right for falling for a doctor. I might as well get going."

He put on a trench coat and went out. He smoked a cigarette and wandered about rather aimlessly, aware of being alone, and that made him think of Max and the dogfight over the sea. Max must have told his mother by now. He was certain to have done that, which made Harry think of Elsa. She'd have loved to turn up at the palace this morning.

He flagged down a cab. "Buckingham Palace," he said.

IT WAS raining hard when he came back out through the palace gates. The policeman on duty saluted. Harry saluted back, and just then a staff car drew up. It was Munro. Harry scrambled in and closed the door.

"Tried to get here earlier," Munro said, "but I got held up at the War House. Come on, let's see it."

Harry took out the box and opened it. "Same as before."

"It's never the same, Harry. What did the King say?"

"He said, 'This is getting to be a habit,' and then the Queen said, 'I see you've changed sides.'"

"Well, that was nice."

"How many people know how Max saved me?"

"Only my people, dear boy. I prefer to keep it that way. It isn't even mentioned in my official report. You parachuted down, and the *Lively Jane* saved your bacon. End of story."

THE destruction of the two ME109s by Harry in the Hurricane had been so instantaneous that the German air-traffic controller back at Fermanville had no idea what had happened, and the secondary channel wasn't monitored, which meant that Max's conversations with Harry and Zec Acland had gone unrecorded. On his return Max's story had been simple. They had undertaken a sweep search; his two comrades had made first contact. He'd seen them go down and also the Hurricane. He made no mention of the Lysander. The story was accepted. After all, who would think to question the Black Baron?

Back in Berlin, he discovered that Elsa was at the country house, and he drove out there. As usual, she was overjoyed to see him and fussed a great deal.

"No, Mutti. Please, just listen. I've something to tell you."

When he was finished, she sat there, looking astounded. "Oh, my goodness. What a miracle!"

"Yes. He came out of it in one piece, and that's all that matters, but what he said about Himmler . . . What do you think?"

"How would he know?"

"I can only guess. He was covering a plane called a Lysander that drops and picks up Allied agents in France. That means a special duties squadron, and that means intelligence."

For the first time she actually showed panic. "What do I do?"

"You take care, Mutti, very great care. See Göring, be charming to the others, and if the Führer speaks to you at any function, show how much you're dazzled by his greatness. It's as simple as that."

There were tears in her eyes. "I'm sorry, Max, so sorry."

"That's all right, Mutti. We all got it wrong. We helped create the beast, and now it threatens to devour us."

IT WAS DARK THREE DAYS LATER when Bubi Hartmann flew down to Wewelsburg in a Storch, piloting himself. A Mercedes and driver were waiting. He didn't know why Himmler wanted to see him. The Reichsführer had been in retreat at Wewelsburg for almost a week. He'd had the castle developed into a center for all true SS values. It was also a center for racial research. As the Mercedes approached, the towers and battlements became clear. Lights shone at the windows and flaring torches at the drawbridge. It looked like a set for a historical movie. Bubi loathed it.

In the entrance hall the sergeant of the guard took his coat and relieved him of his Walther pistol. "The Reichsführer is in his sitting room, Colonel. Do you need an escort?"

Bubi shook his head and went up the stairs. The place was festooned with Nazi flags; there were even swastikas on the ceilings. He came to the sitting room, knocked, and went in.

There was a log fire, more flags. Himmler sat behind the desk. He looked up. "So you finally got here?"

"Fog in Berlin, Reichsführer. How may I be of service?"

"I've gone through the mail you sent yesterday. Of particular interest was your most recent report from London."

"Yes, Reichsführer."

"The information about the Baron von Halder's brother shooting down two of our planes while on some covert mission for Munro, then parachuting into the sea, where a convenient rescue boat saved him, is melodrama of the finest quality."

"I agree." Bubi couldn't think of anything else to say.

"And now Kelso becomes a lieutenant colonel in the U.S. Air Force as a special duties pilot ferrying Eisenhower. Bizarre, isn't it?"

"I suppose so," Bubi said lamely.

"Even more bizarre—I've discovered something you missed, Colonel. The third plane, the one that survived? Would you be interested to know who the pilot was?"

Bubi felt cold, very cold, and swallowed hard. "Reichsführer?"

"It was Baron Max von Halder—a remarkable coincidence. But then, I understand life to be full of them."

Bubi managed to control his breathing. "What would the Reichsführer like me to do?"

"Why, nothing, Colonel. Nothing at all. There is another matter I wish to discuss. You'll recall the Führer raised the question of a possible assassination of Eisenhower. Would there be no chance of us putting in one of our own people? A trained specialist?"

"I don't think so, Reichsführer. I have a few people in England, but they don't constitute a network. To drop such an agent in by parachute would be very hazardous. It just wouldn't work."

"Really? Well, try and think of something, Colonel. I don't want to disappoint the Führer."

For Harry, things took a kind of steady turn. He did general courier work and frequently flew Eisenhower on the London-to-Southwick run. Just as frequently, he flew to Cold Harbour with Munro and Jack Carter, and Molly sometimes came. Things were heating up, as everything converged toward D-day, Munro putting more and more operatives into France.

The weather was good, and when Molly was at Cold Harbour, she and Harry would walk on the beach, eat at the Hanged Man, and fool with Zec Acland and the rescue-boat crew.

It couldn't last, of course, and one day, landing at Croydon after bringing a couple of returning agents back to London, Harry found a message asking him to report to SOE headquarters in Baker Street. When he got there, Munro had a large-scale map of the Channel on a table.

"What's it all about?" Harry asked.

"Morlaix, twenty miles in from the French coast. Forty-five minutes in the Lysander, would you agree?"

Harry had a quick look. "Depending on weather."

"I've a major agent to drop there at midnight. An in-and-out job, no one to bring back. It's vitally important. A Frenchman named Jacaud, the leader of the Resistance in that whole area. There's a lot happening, and he must be there."

"So what's the problem?"

"Harry, at such short notice it needs somebody of your caliber."

"No need for soft soap, Brigadier. When do I leave?"

JACAUD was not what Harry had expected at all. He was no more than five feet six in height, wore round steel spectacles, a tweed suit, and a trilby hat, and looked like a schoolmaster. At Croydon they spoke in French.

Jacaud said, "This story of you and your brother, Colonel—if I may say—it is like something out of a novel."

"I think it was Oscar Wilde who said that life at its most remarkable resembled a bad novel," Harry told him.

"Terms such as bad and good mean very little in the life I lead." Jacaud lit a Gitane cigarette. "Is the weather prospect okay from Cold Harbour?"

"Excellent."

At that moment a staff car drew up, and Munro and Jack Carter got out.

"There you are," Munro said. "Sorry about the delay. We'll get straight off if that suits you, Harry."

"Certainly, Brigadier. Ready to go."

"Message from Molly," Carter said. "She wanted to see you off, but there are the usual emergencies at Guy's. You know how it is."

"She worries too much," Harry said. "I'll take her to the River Room tomorrow night. A decent meal, the right kind of music—who could ask for more?"

"Molly could," Carter said.

"Yes, well, the ways of women are a mystery. Let's get moving."

THERE were broken clouds, a quarter moon—excellent conditions for low flying. The flight across to France at four hundred feet—below enemy radar—posed few problems. It was quite pleasant, with Tarquin, as usual, in the bottom of the cockpit, and then the unexpected happened.

Suddenly there, to port, were two torpedo boats of the Royal Dutch Navy operating out of Falmouth Naval Base. They opened up with everything at once—machine-gun bullets, cannon shell.

Harry went up fast into broken cloud and lost them. He turned to Jacaud and shouted, "Sorry about that. The Dutch don't seem to know which side they're on. ETA, fifteen minutes."

At Fermanville, air-traffic control picked Harry up at the greater height, and the controller alerted the night patrol. Max was enjoying a three-day leave in St.-Malo when the three ME109s rose into the night sky in search of his brother.

At Morlaix, the dropping zone was clearly marked on the heath. Harry made a perfect landing. Jacaud scrambled out to meet the people running toward him and slammed the door. Harry roared down the heath and started to rise, when disaster struck.

Two MEs came in low and shot up the heath, where the landing lights were still visible, and as Harry lifted, the third ME chased him, cannon fire tearing his wings apart. His nose dipped, and he went down. At the far end of the heath were trees. Harry pulled back on the column, but his wheels clipped the trees, and a moment later flames erupted into the night.

Jacaud and his men started to run toward the fire. They came to the wood and started through, and then, outlined against the flames, they saw two armored personnel carriers. One of the men, a local farmer named Jules, grabbed Jacaud's arm. "SS panzer unit. There's nothing we can do."

"All right," Jacaud said. He crawled to the edge of the wood with the others and watched.

Harry had managed to get the door open, reached for Tarquin in the jump bag, and scrambled to the ground, his flying jacket on fire. When he tried to stand, his left ankle refused to support the weight. He started crawling, dragging the jump bag with him, but the pain in his ankle was so intense that he released his grip. And then soldiers were beside him, tearing the burning jacket off.

The SS carried Harry to a personnel carrier, put him inside, and drove away. There was little of the airplane left now, as it burned fiercely. When the flames subsided, the men in Jacaud's group got up and moved close.

Jacaud lit a cigarette and said to Jules, "What a man. He was a really top man—Legion of Honor, everything."

One of the men came back with the jump bag. "I found this near the plane. Crazy thing—it's a bear in flying clothes."

"Really?" Jacaud said. "Well, bring it with you to the mill."

At the old mill, sacks of grain were stacked everywhere, and in the loft a secret door in the wooden wall opened into a back room, the control center for the Resistance in the Morlaix area. A young woman stirred coffee over a stove.

Jacaud said, "It's Cold Harbour I need, Marie. Leave that."

"I can't contact them for another thirty minutes," she said. "We're on a fixed schedule. Meanwhile, coffee will do you good."

"Right, as usual." He took the mug she handed him. "Where would the Germans take a prisoner?"

"Château Morlaix, just outside the village. The SS have appropriated it as their headquarters."

"No way of getting to him?"

"Only if you're intent on committing suicide."

He nodded. Jules came in with the jump bag, opened it, and sat Tarquin on the table. "There's a label. It says 'Tarquin's bag.' "

Jacaud said, "It must have been some kind of mascot."

"Daft I call it," Jules said. "A bear with wings."

Marie picked Tarquin up. "He's special. You can tell. Jacaud, can I have him? My daughter will fall instantly in love."

"Why not?" Jacaud looked at his watch. "But get me Cold Harbour now."

MUNRO left the radio room, got into a jeep, and drove down to the Hanged Man. Jack Carter and the rescue-boat crew were there, Julie behind the bar. Munro stood just inside the bar, his face saying it all. As people glanced at him, they stopped talking one by one. It was Julie who said, "What is it, Brigadier?"

Later, sitting by the fire with Jack and Zec, he said, "At least Jacaud made it safely. I know that sounds callous, but it's the name of the game. Jacaud is of primary importance. You agree, Jack?"

"I suppose so," Jack said. "But to be frank, what seems of primary importance to me is who's going to break this to Molly?"

Munro took a deep breath. "Leave it with me." And he got up and went out.

IN THE doctors lounge at Guy's Hospital, Molly was grabbing a coffee and sandwich. There was a knock at the door. She got up and opened it to find her father standing there.

Molly smiled. "Why, Dad, what brings you here?" And then her smile disappeared. "Just tell me the worst. Don't dress it up."

Sitting there minutes later, smoking a cigarette, her face haggard, she said, "So he could still be alive?"

"From what the Resistance leader Jacaud says, yes, but from all accounts it was a very bad crash."

"But he survived." She nodded and smiled a strange, cold smile. "If Harry Kelso was dead, I'd know it, Dad."

AT CHÂTEAU Morlaix, Kelso was very much alive as he lay on a bed in a room that the SS had turned into a surgery, propped up against pillows, smoking a cigarette. No burns—that was the incredible thing—though his face was bruised and the left ankle hurt like hell. The SS guard wore a panzer uniform.

The door opened, and a young SS Hauptsturmführer called Schroeder, the unit doctor, came in holding an X ray. "As I feared, Colonel. The ankle is badly broken, but the break is clean. My commanding officer, Major Muller, is on his way."

"Thank you, Captain," Harry said. "Your English is excellent."

At that moment a Sturmbannführer in black uniform festooned with awards entered the room.

Schroeder got his heels together. "Major Muller."

"What's the story here?" Muller asked in German.

"This is U.S. Air Force colonel Kelso. His ankle is broken."

"Yes, but what was he up to?"

"Flying one of those Lysander planes the English use to bring secret agents in. Our ME109s shot him down as he was taking off."

"Which means he dropped somebody off. You'll have to translate for me."

It might have been the clever thing to stay quiet, but Harry said in German, "That's not necessary, Major, but what is necessary is that I get a shot of morphine and something done about this ankle."

Both the SS officers were astonished. Muller said, "I congratulate you on your grasp of our language, Colonel."

"Thank you, but what about the ankle? I've complied with the Geneva Convention—name, rank, and serial number."

Muller frowned, then walked across to where Harry's tunic hung on a chair, noting the medals. "My goodness, Colonel, you have had an interesting war." He took out a silver cigarette case, offered Harry a cigarette, and gave him a light. "Captain Schroeder will see to you at once. We are all soldiers here, after all. I'll speak with you later."

He beckoned to Schroeder, and they went out. Schroeder said, "It's a bad break, but I can fix it."

"Anything he needs," Muller said.

"One thing, sir," Schroeder said. "We haven't informed Luftwaffe headquarters at St.-Malo that he survived."

"And we won't." Muller was excited. "The colonel's medals are extraordinary. This man is a big fish, Schroeder, very big."

"But, Major, Luftwaffe regulations—"

"Stuff regulations," Muller said. "I'm sending a signal to SD headquarters in Berlin right away. I'm going to the top." He slapped Schroeder on the back. "Your best work on this one!" And he hurried away.

LIKE most people these days at Gestapo headquarters in Prinz Albrechtstrasse, Bubi Hartmann didn't bother going home, because of the regularity of RAF raids. He had a cot made up in the corner of his office. He'd slept well, until three in the morning, when the RAF had struck. Half an hour of hell, and then they were gone. He got up, splashed cold water on his face, then went to his desk. He started to go through some papers, and a moment later Trudi came in. She was holding a signal flimsy in one hand. "I'm not sure how you'll feel about this. You put a red flag out on anything to do with Lieutenant Colonel Harry Kelso." She held out the flimsy. "The signals unit just received this."

After he read it, she said, "Are you going to notify the baron?"

He shook his head. "I can't afford to, Trudi. This goes to the Reichsführer. Fetch me an orderly." After she went out, he wrote a brief note, put it in an envelope with the flimsy, and sealed it.

It was nine in the morning when Himmler summoned him. The Reichsführer was standing at the window looking out. "Another night of terror bombing, Colonel, and that fat fool Göring swore that if a single bomb fell on Berlin, he would eat his hat. So much for the Luftwaffe helping us win the war." He turned. "So it is left to the rest of us to help the Führer fulfill his glorious mission." He walked to the desk and picked up the signal flimsy. "And this, Colonel, presents us with our opportunity."

Bubi was totally mystified. "Reichsführer?"

"God sometimes looks down through the clouds, Colonel, and he has this morning. I've found your assassin for you."

"I'm afraid I don't understand."

"It's simple enough. We have in our hands one rather damaged Lieutenant Colonel Kelso of the U.S. Air Force. According to your reports, he does special flights for Eisenhower. So we allow him to escape and fly back to England, where at the first opportunity he disposes of Eisenhower."

For a moment Bubi was convinced he was going mad. "But Reichsführer, why should he? Besides, he has a broken ankle."

"But his brother doesn't." Himmler smiled. "They can't be told apart, or so I'm informed. A simple change of uniform is all that's needed. We arrange for him to conveniently escape from Château Morlaix, steal a plane. He flies back, and even if he doesn't get to fly Eisenhower, the good general is certain to want to see him."

Bubi Hartmann struggled to come to terms with all this. "But Reichsführer, for Baron von Halder to impersonate his brother, he would need to know everything about him, which presupposes that Colonel Kelso—and the baron—would go along with the plan."

"Oh, but he will. They both will, especially after you've arrested their mother, which you will this morning. Discreetly, of course."

Bubi felt sick.

"You seem upset," Himmler said. "I would have thought you would have welcomed this chance to serve the Reich, Colonel, for it has served you well, in fact, given you unequal opportunities for one with Jewish antecedents." Bubi was numb with horror, and Himmler smiled gently. "How could you imagine that I wouldn't know? The taint affects your whole family. Your father is still alive, I believe, and his sister. And there is, of course, the question of your secretary, Frau Braun, an intimate relationship."

Bubi took a deep breath. "What do you require of me?"

"Good. I've always admired your pragmatism. Now, the man at the Portuguese embassy here, Joel Rodrigues, will be transferred to Lisbon today, joining the courier service, carrying diplomatic bags by air to London. You will see him this morning, write a report for his brother and the Dixon woman outlining the operation and telling them to expect the baron in a matter of days. Tomorrow Rodrigues will fly to London with the usual embassy bag. I don't see how we can fail. Do you?"

Bubi's mouth was dry. He coughed. "I agree, Reichsführer."

THE first thing Hartmann did was to tell Trudi to get hold of Joel Rodrigues and order him to report at once. Then he told her to come with her shorthand book. He dictated a letter of instruction for Fernando Rodrigues and Sarah Dixon, the project in complete detail, as Himmler had outlined it.

When he finished, Trudi sat there, her face white. "What a swine. And you'll go through with it?"

"I have no choice. There's Jewish blood in my family, Trudi. I didn't think anyone knew, but he did. My father's under threat, my old aunt. Even you, as my secretary."

She sat there staring at him.

"Type up the letter," Bubi said. "Quickly. Then find out where Max is and order a plane for me. I'll fly myself."

AT THE ADLON, ELSA WAS seated by the fire, reading a magazine, when Rosa admitted Bubi Hartmann into the suite. Elsa held out her hand, and Bubi kissed it.

"What a surprise, Colonel."

"I bring you rather momentous news, Baroness. Your son Colonel Kelso was shot down on a mission last night. He is now in our hands."

She said calmly, "Is he well?"

"A broken ankle. He's at a place called Château Morlaix in Brittany. I'm under orders to fly down there to interrogate him."

"Does Max know of this?"

"No. But he'll be informed. Himmler has given me permission to take you with me if you should desire."

"May I bring my maid?"

"Naturally. I'll have a car pick you up in an hour." He put on his cap, saluted, and left.

As Rosa hurriedly packed, Elsa told her of the conversation.

"It would be strange, Baroness," Rosa said, "to perhaps see both of your sons together."

"A long time since that happened, a long time." Elsa put her jewelry in its usual box. "Put that in my large handbag. Oh, and this." She produced a Walther PPK pistol from a drawer, checked the weapon expertly, and put it in the handbag. She smiled serenely. "It's well to be prepared."

 AT FERMANVILLE, Max was enjoying a drink in the officers mess in the early evening when Bubi Hartmann walked in. Max excused himself from a group of officers and went to greet him. "Bubi." Then he frowned. "Is there a problem?"

"In the corner," Bubi said. "We need privacy."

Max said, "What is this?"

Bubi waved the waiter away. "Do you know a place called Château Morlaix, about forty miles from here?"

"Of course. There's a Luftwaffe feeder station there."

"I landed there early this afternoon. Flew down from Berlin in a Storch with your mother and her maid."

Max looked anxious. "Is she under arrest?"

"Not in the way you think. Read this, Max." He took a letter from his pocket and passed it over. It was quality paper, and the heading was embossed in black.

DER REICHSFÜHRER—SS   Berlin, April 1944
The bearer acts under my personal orders on business of the utmost importance to the Reich. All personnel, civil and military, must assist him in any way he sees fit.

Heinrich Himmler

It was countersigned by the Führer.

Max handed it back. "Bubi, what do we have here? I heard an SS panzer unit had taken over Château Morlaix."

"Yes. Under my direct orders. A ring of steel."

"Because my mother is there? Come on, Bubi."

"No. Because your brother is there."

"Harry at Château Morlaix?" Max was very pale. "Look, what is this? Himmler isn't into happy families. What does he want?"

"Later, Max, later. If you could collect your things, we'll be off."

AT MORLAIX, Harry was propped up in bed, his left leg in a plaster cast across a pillow, flicking through a magazine, when the door opened. "Colonel," Major Muller said, "I have your mother here."

Elsa stepped into the room, and Muller withdrew, closing the door. Harry looked at her and smiled. "My goodness, Mutti, you haven't aged at all. It's incredible." He dropped the magazine and held out his arms, and she ran to him.

Later she sat beside the bed.

"So you've no idea what's going on here?" he said.

She shook her head. "I've told you all I know—Bubi Hartmann,

Himmler. Max, of course, told me of your warning when you went down in the sea. Where did you get your information?"

"I do special flights for British intelligence. The people I deal with have contacts in Berlin."

"I see." She lit a cigarette. "So you haven't married?"

"Mutti, I'm still only twenty-five years old."

"Your father was twenty-two when he married me."

"Well, I have been rather busy."

She nodded. "Is there a girl in your life, a proper girl?"

"Perhaps. Her mother was English, and her father's an American general. She's a brilliant surgeon."

"She sounds promising. I'm impressed."

"Don't be, Mutti. She deserves better."

Before she could reply, the door opened, and Bubi appeared. "Another guest for you, Colonel." He stepped back, and Max moved into the room.

DINNER was served in the château's magnificent dining room. Harry was carried down in a chair by two SS orderlies. Muller, Schroeder, and two young lieutenants joined the party. The food was excellent: turtle soup, mutton roasted to perfection, an excellent salad, good champagne, and a fine prewar claret.

Elsa said, "I must say, the SS does know how to do things well, Major Muller."

"Anything else for you would be totally unacceptable, Baroness," he replied gallantly, and raised his glass. "To Colonel Kelso and the Baron von Halder, brothers-in-arms."

Everyone stood except Elsa and Harry and drank the toast. Bubi said, "And now, Major, if you could excuse us."

"Of course, Colonel."

After Muller and his officers left, Max said, "All right, Bubi, what's the game?"

Bubi stood by the fire. "Everyone thinks that the important question about the invasion is where the Allies will land. The Führer doesn't agree. He thinks we should put our efforts into something really worthwhile." He paused. "Such as assassinating Eisenhower."

There was total astonishment on every face.

"But that's crazy," Max said.

"It is, but unfortunately, Himmler agrees with him. Through my agents in London, Colonel Kelso, I know all about Brigadier Munro, Major Carter, Cold Harbour, and the SOE in Baker Street. I know you have a lady friend, a Dr. Sobel, whose father is a general on Eisenhower's staff. I know you often fly Eisenhower as a courier pilot. Your falling into our hands has led to the Reichsführer coming up with, in his opinion, a brilliant plan."

He paused, and Max said, "Go on, Bubi."

"It goes something like this. Colonel Kelso escapes, steals the Storch on the landing strip, and flies back to a hero's welcome. Eisenhower will wish to see him. If not, he is certain to fly the general on some occasion. At a suitable moment he assassinates him."

There was a profound silence; then Harry laughed out loud. "And how do I accomplish all this on crutches?"

"It wouldn't be you," Bubi told him. "It would be Max."

Elsa said, "Oh, my God."

Max drank a little claret and put down the glass. "And why would I do such a thing? I fly fighters, Bubi. I'm no assassin."

Bubi came to the table and poured more wine, considerably agitated. "I'm just an errand boy. I've got Himmler's hand on my throat, too. This is none of my doing."

"All right," Max said. "Just tell us the worst."

"The baroness, regrettably, has enjoyed entirely the wrong circle of friends. Eighteen arrested, twelve executed, two of them women. It's called guilt by association. If you don't cooperate, you two, it will be very much the worse for her."

Elsa tossed wine into his face. "You swine!"

Max jumped up and caught her arms. "Don't be stupid. He's got just as much choice in this as we have."

"Ridiculous," Harry said. "To do this, you'd need my cooperation. My life in detail, my girl Molly, my friends at Cold Harbour." He shook his head. "I won't do it."

Bubi wiped his face, and Max said, "Give us some time."

"Tomorrow morning," Bubi said. "That's the best I can do."

ELSA had retired, and the SS orderlies carried Harry back to his room and helped him onto the bed. After a while the door opened, and Max came in. "Two sentries. They are taking good care of you," he said in English.

"I like the uniform," Harry told him. "Very handsome."

Max crossed to the chair where Harry's tunic hung. He examined the medal ribbons. "You're not doing too bad yourself." He pulled a chair forward and took out his cigarette case. "So here we are, brother, together again." He gave Harry a cigarette and a light. "The only thing missing is Tarquin. How is the old boy?"

"Don't ask. Every mission I flew, he was there."

"What happened this time?"

"They shot me up real good. I clipped trees coming down." Harry shrugged. "The Lysander came apart, then flamed. I remember grabbing at his jump bag as I dived out, but my jacket was on fire. As the SS guys dragged me away, the Lysander blew up."

"And Tarquin went with it?"

"So it would appear. He was my good luck. Now he's gone."

"Don't talk nonsense. You were your own good luck. A great pilot." Max smiled. "Almost as good as me. I'll ask Bubi to have some men search the area."

"Speaking of Bubi, where exactly does he fit into all this?"

"Oh, we flew in France in the old days." Max told him the story. As he concluded, he said, "It's true what he said. He's just as much in Himmler's power as the rest of us." He went to the window and peered out.

Harry said, "What happens now?"

"I don't know. We'll see what he has to say in the morning."

"You mean you'd actually go through with it? Kill Eisenhower?"

"He's nothing to me. He's the other side. I've killed a lot of people, and so have you. It's called war." Max went to the door and turned. "This young woman, the doctor—do you love her?"

"She loves me. I don't really know what love is. I didn't seem to have the time. You know how it is?"

"I'm afraid I do." Max opened the door. "See you in the morning."

AT LISBON Airport, Joel Rodrigues took a one a.m. flight to London as an embassy courier. The flight was not good. There were thunderstorms. The plane was crowded, every seat taken. Many people were airsick. Somehow Joel survived, helped by a half bottle of brandy he'd had the forethought to put in his pocket.

At Croydon Airport, he waited in a queue to pass through customs and security, and was suddenly aware of his brother on the other side, waving to him. Joel waved back.

"Passport, sir," the security officer said.

Joel passed it across. "Diplomatic immunity. Portuguese embassy."

"I see, sir." The officer examined the passport.

How often in life small things carry the seeds of disaster, for Joel Rodrigues had committed a serious blunder that others—Himmler, for one—should have foreseen. His passport carried arrival and departure stamps for Berlin.

Special Branch from Scotland Yard always had a presence at the airport. By chance that morning, Detective Chief Inspector Sean Riley was standing not too far away—a tall, thin Irishman.

The security officer nodded, and Riley stepped forward. He didn't take the passport, simply glanced at it, saw everything, looked up, and smiled. "Welcome to London, sir."

Joel moved through and embraced his brother. As they headed off, Riley beckoned to a young man in a shabby raincoat. "You follow those two to the ends of the earth, Lacey."

"My pleasure," said Lacey, and went after them.

AGENTS of the British secret intelligence services have no powers of arrest. This is why they always work closely with Special Branch. As it happened, Riley serviced SOE's Section D, and its head, Munro. It was eight thirty when he phoned Baker Street. Munro took the call. Riley explained about Joel Rodrigues. "The thing is,"

Riley said, "there was a Portuguese embassy car waiting, and my lad Lacey heard the chauffeur call the other man Rodrigues, too."

"Really?" Munro said. "Anything else?"

"Yes. They stopped off at a flat near Kensington Gardens, then carried on to the embassy. Lacey drove back and checked out the flat. It's in the name of a Fernando Rodrigues. I've already looked him up. He's chief commercial attaché."

Munro sighed. "They always are, Sean, but I think this is a good one. The Berlin stamps in the passport—that's the thing. I want full surveillance—photos, the whole business."

"I'll get right on to it, Brigadier."

BREAKFAST at Morlaix was a private affair. Harry made it down the stairs, assisted by crutches, and sat at one end of the table. Elsa was on his left, Max on the right. Bubi sat at one end. They ate in silence—scrambled eggs and bacon, toast, excellent coffee. Finally Bubi looked at his watch. "It's nine thirty," he said. "I'll be back at ten. I'll expect your answer then." And he went out.

"He can go to hell," Elsa said in English, and nodded to the orderly, who poured more coffee.

Max said, "It isn't that simple."

"Remember who you are, Max—Baron von Halder, the Black Baron, Germany's greatest ace. What can they do to you?"

Max shook his head. "You still don't see it, Mutti, do you? In the hands of people like Himmler we are nothing."

Harry said, "He's right. We're in a real fix here."

"You mean you'd go along with this ridiculous notion?" Elsa said. "I despair of both of you." She stood up.

Max said, "Mutti, we have to think of you."

She drew herself up. "I am Elsa von Halder. Reichsmarschall Göring is my friend. They wouldn't touch me."

She went out like a ship under sail, the door banging behind her.

IN THE sitting room, Bubi supervised the setting up of a sixteen-millimeter projection camera. He dismissed the orderly who'd helped him, took a reel of film from a tin can, and carefully threaded it through the projector.

"All right, now, Bubi," Max demanded, "what is this?" He was standing by the window, and Elsa and Harry occupied the couch.

"Early in the day for a film show, I'd have thought," Elsa said.

Bubi said, "Before we start, let me say again that I'm only obeying orders. I have no choice in this matter."

At that moment a plane roared overhead, obviously descending. Bubi looked out the window. It couldn't be possible, and yet in his heart he knew it was. "Wait here," he said, and went out.

It was ten minutes later that the door opened. Bubi Hartmann led the way in. Reichsführer Himmler walked in, wearing black uniform and cap, his eyes glittering behind the steel glasses.

"And so, Hartmann, is this matter resolved?"

"I'm afraid not, Reichsführer."

"As I feared, so let's get on with it." He turned to Max, Harry, and Elsa. "Colonel Hartmann has told me he has explained the purpose of your presence here. It seems you are being difficult."

Elsa, proud to the last and close to tears, said, "You can't treat me like this. I'm Baroness von Halder and—"

"You are a traitor to the Reich," Himmler said tranquilly. "Many of your wretched associates have already paid the price for their treachery. If I'd had my way, you would have gone down the same road. However, you do serve a purpose."

Max was on his feet. "Damn you!"

"Conspiracy against the Führer carries only a summary sentence—death by hanging with piano wire, the execution to be filmed as a record to, shall we say, encourage the others?" He nodded to Bubi, who started the projector.

The film was absolutely horrific, one wretched victim after another brought in by SS guards, all rank insignia removed from their uniforms. With piano-wire nooses around their necks, they were lifted up to be suspended from meat hooks. The final convulsions were appalling to see. Particularly harrowing were the executions of the two women, one of whom appeared to be at least seventy.

When the film ended, there was a stunned silence. Suddenly Elsa gagged, got to her feet, lurched to the fireplace, and was sick.

It was Himmler who spoke first. "I deplore violence of any sort, but when confronted with treachery, the Third Reich must protect itself. All traitors must accept the same punishment." He turned to Max and Harry. "In your case, you have the chance to perform a great service. In return, your mother's life will be spared. If you persist in being difficult . . ." He shrugged.

Elsa lurched back to the couch, a handkerchief to her face, and Himmler looked at Max. "You intend to be sensible, Baron, I trust."

"Yes, blast you!" Max told him.

Himmler looked at Harry. "And you, Colonel?"

Harry remained silent, his face white.

Himmler leaned in and spoke quietly. "I need hardly point out that if your mother has to pay the ultimate penalty, then so shall Baron von Halder. You will sacrifice them *both,* Colonel?"

"You lousy little bastard," Harry said, but Himmler saw that he had won.

"Excellent." Himmler turned to Bubi. "I'll be on my way. I leave this matter in your capable hands, Colonel."

He nodded, then walked out of the room. Elsa sobbed quietly, while Max lit a cigarette and Harry stared at the wall.

"Do you really think I can carry this off, Bubi?" Max asked.

"With your brother's assistance. You've got twenty-four hours."

"You swine," Elsa said. "How can you be a party to this?"

"I told you, Himmler had me by the throat," Bubi said. "I'm part Jewish. I didn't think he knew, but that devil knows everything."

Max said with genuine compassion, "I'm truly sorry."

"So am I," Bubi said. "But we're stuck now." He took a deep breath. "First things first. We must do something about your face."

"My face?"

"Yes. Your brother has a prominent scar on his left cheek. We'll have to take care of that. I'll let Schroeder tell you."

"Let's get on with it, then," Max said, and let Bubi lead the way.

When the others had gone ahead, he put his hand on Harry's arm. "We'll figure something out, brother."

Harry nodded grimly.

DR. SCHROEDER charged a hypodermic. "This is a local anesthetic. It will freeze your face for a couple of hours."

Max winced as the needle entered his cheek. "Now what?"

Schroeder was examining Harry's left cheek. "Good work, and comparatively recent. Am I right?"

"Yes."

Schroeder turned to Max. "Let's say you banged your face in the crash, leading to external bruising on the left side. As your brother's scar is recent, it would be reasonable to assume it would burst."

"If you say so." Suddenly Max couldn't feel his face.

"It would therefore be necessary to stitch it up again." Schroeder nodded. "Which is what I shall do."

"But he doesn't have a scar," Harry pointed out.

"True, but he soon will."

ELSA was horrified at the sight of Max's face. "What have they done to you?" she asked as they sat down to lunch.

"It's necessary, Mutti. Harry has a scar, so I must have a scar."

She was beside herself. "But your beautiful face!" She turned to Bubi. "Listen to me. I've thought of something. Even if this works, even if Max does what he set out to do, how does he get away?"

Bubi, spooning potatoes onto his plate, said, "Well, he has access to aircraft. He could conceivably fly back."

"And if that isn't possible?"

"We have agents in London at the Portuguese embassy. We should be able to arrange passage to Lisbon by boat."

"Passage to Lisbon?" Harry snorted. "With the whole country locked up tight after Eisenhower's death?"

There was a pause. Elsa glared at them. "You mean you intend to go through with this madness?"

"I don't see we have much choice, Mutti. I'm thinking of you."

"No," she cried. "Don't put this one on me. I won't have it." And she got up and ran out.

In her bedroom suite, Elsa sat on the window seat, smoked a cigarette nervously, and told Rosa Stein everything.

Rosa said carefully, "But with Reichsführer Himmler in total control, what can be done?"

"I'll go to Berlin. I'll appeal to the Führer."

"Baroness, I must say this. In the first place, we are prisoners here, so Berlin is out. In the second place, the Führer will listen to Himmler, not you." She shook her head.

Elsa stared at her. "There must be something I can do."

Rosa gazed sadly at her. "No, there is nothing you can do."

A knock came at the door. Elsa opened it, and Bubi and Major Muller entered. She stared at them coldly.

Bubi took a deep breath. "I regret to tell you that by direct order of Reichsführer Himmler, you are to be transferred to the hunting lodge at the other end of the estate."

"I refuse to go." She stood there, defiant.

"Then my further instructions are to have you returned to Berlin, by force if necessary."

She seemed to age then and sat down. "No. You win. I'll go, but may I please see my sons? Just once?"

"After Max has gone, you can see Harry. That's the best I can do." Bubi turned to Muller. "See to the Baroness, Major."

"Of course, Colonel."

Outside in the corridor, Bubi lit a cigarette, his hands shaking, his thoughts full of self-disgust. "Where does it all end?" he whispered.

He walked to the library, where Harry and Max were looking at photos. "That's Molly and me," Harry said, "at Cold Harbour."

"Very good. She looks nice."

Bubi was making notes. He said, "I've got files from Berlin. Let's see what we need—details on Dr. Sobel, Cold Harbour, Eisenhower, his headquarters at Southwick." He sighed. "We've got a long day ahead of us, gentlemen."

Grimly the brothers set to work.

THE HUNTING LODGE WAS comfortable enough. There was a log fire and beamed ceilings in the sitting room and another log fire in the main bedroom. Rosa unpacked the suitcases, and Elsa prowled from room to room, unable to be easy.

There was a liquor cabinet in the sitting room. She had a large brandy, but instead of calming her, it seemed to make her worse. She went back upstairs to her bedroom. Rosa was unpacking the smaller bags now, laying out jewelry on the dressing table. She produced the Walther PPK. "Where shall I put this, Baroness?"

Elsa held out her hand. "I'll take care of it."

She went back downstairs and put the Walther on the couch beside her. Max was as good as dead, and they'd finish off Harry afterward, and all because of her—it was the only reason the boys were doing this. She knew what she must do.

She called, "Rosa, come here."

Rosa appeared a moment later. "Yes, Baroness?"

"Phone the château. Ask Colonel Hartmann to come at once."

THE lodge had a man at the entrance, and there were guards in the vicinity. Elsa, peering out the window, saw the staff car approach, went to the couch, and sat down. She had secreted the Walther between the cushions, and now she called to Rosa, "After you've admitted the colonel, go to the kitchen and stay out of the way."

"As you say, Baroness."

The doorbell rang. Rosa went and opened it, and Bubi entered, followed by Muller and Schroeder. "There you are, Baroness. Is there a problem?" Bubi asked.

"Only the existence of you Nazi mongrels," she said. "And the problem of my own existence. After all, without me you've got no hold on my sons."

Her hand came up clutching the Walther, and Bubi, seeing it all and realizing what she intended, cried, "No!"

He threw himself to one side, and Muller, behind him, took the first two bullets. Schroeder found his Mauser and instinctively fired three times, hammering Elsa into the back of the couch.

Bubi stood up and crouched over Muller. "Dead."

Schroeder, leaning over Elsa, said, "So is she." He looked at the Mauser. "I never killed anyone before." He seemed dazed.

"It's not your fault. She wanted to die."

There was pounding at the door, and Bubi opened it. A sergeant stood there, aghast.

"Major Muller and the baroness are dead," Bubi said, and turned to Schroeder. "I'm putting you in charge of this. Keep it all under wraps. Neither the baron nor Colonel Kelso must know."

Schroeder looked baffled, then nodded. "I'll get on with it." He paused. "What about the maid, Colonel?"

Bubi swore and went to the stairs on the run, but of Rosa Stein there was no sign. He spoke to the sergeant. "There was another woman here, the maid. Tell the guards to look for her."

IN THE kitchen, the door partially open, Rosa had witnessed the whole appalling scene, had heard everything. Terrified out of her mind, her only thought was to get away. Grabbing an old raincoat from a peg, she pulled it on and opened the outside door.

It was then that she had her first piece of luck, for the guards, attracted by the sound of gunfire, were running around to the front of the house. She hurried across the lawn to the gate in the brick wall, took a deep breath, and ran for her life.

MAX and Harry were still in the library when Bubi went in. He forced a smile. "Still at it? Are you feeling confident?"

"You must be joking, Bubi," Max said. "This is a lot to expect."

"I know, I know, but with luck it could be over very quickly. You could be in and out, Max, a couple of days. These Portuguese diplomats I'm using—I've already given them instructions to check on shipping." He opened a file and took out a sheet of paper. "It's all there."

Max nodded. "When do I go?"

"About four o'clock in the morning. You steal my Storch, and it's not much more than an hour to Cold Harbour."

"A couple of bursts of machine-gun fire in the fuselage would be a nice touch," Harry said sarcastically.

"Actually, an excellent idea." Bubi stood up. "We could dine at nine if you like."

"And say good-bye to Mutti," Max said to Harry.

"That's not possible, I'm afraid," Bubi said. "Your mother has been difficult, to say the least. Himmler left explicit orders that the moment the operation began, she was to be held separately. You can't see her, Max, and that's final."

"Come on, Bubi," Max said.

"Once you've gone, I'll let your brother visit her." Bubi almost choked on the lie. "That's the best I can do." He went out.

Harry said, "Time's running short, Max. Do you really think you could do it?"

"You saw that film," Max said. "Those two women kicking on the wire, their eyes bulging. I'd go to hell to get the devil himself before I'd let that happen to my mother."

AROUND the same time, in London, Fernando and Joel Rodrigues presented themselves at Sarah Dixon's flat. Lacey and an expert photographer, a constable named Parry from Scotland Yard, were in close pursuit and got pictures of them going in and coming out. They then followed them along Westbourne Grove to the Italian restaurant Sarah and Fernando had used for years.

"There's something funny about this," Lacey said. "I've seen that woman before. I'll be back in a moment."

He entered the restaurant, which was reasonably busy. He stood at the end of the bar and ordered a glass of wine. As the headwaiter passed, he pulled him over, produced his warrant card, and asked the names of the two men and woman at the table by the window.

"The lady is Mrs. Sarah Dixon. The taller one is Senor Rodrigues from the Portuguese embassy. I've never seen the other."

Lacey patted the waiter's shoulder and went out. He found Parry on the other side of the road. "Everything okay?" Parry asked.

"Fine. Let's take the film out and get it processed at once." Lacey paused. "Well, what do you know," he said. "I've just remembered where I've seen her."

IN HIS flat at Haston Place, Munro sat by the fire, enjoying a hot toddy, when the phone rang. He picked it up. "Munro."

"Carter, sir. We have a problem, Brigadier."

It was a phrase they only used in the most extreme situations. Munro said, "Bad?"

"Very bad, sir. Chief Inspector Riley and one of his men are with me. I think you should see us."

"Soon as you can, Jack."

In five minutes they were there—Carter, Riley, and Lacey. Riley described the arrival of Joel Rodrigues at Croydon, the blunder of the Berlin stamps in the passport. He went into Lacey's involvement and brought things right up to date. He snapped a finger, and Lacey passed him a cardboard file. Riley opened it and extracted black-and-white prints. "The Rodrigues brothers and the lady, Brigadier."

"Mrs. Sarah Dixon—she's on the staff at Baker Street, sir," Lacey said.

Carter took over. "Detective Constable Lacey recognized her, sir. His duties with Special Branch take him into SOE headquarters."

"Dear Lord," Munro said. "Didn't anybody screen this woman?"

Carter sighed. "She may simply have been . . . overlooked."

Munro shook his head. "This could be serious."

WHEN Bubi went into the dining room to join the brothers for dinner, he received a shock. For a wild moment he thought it was Harry standing by the fire in an American uniform, then realized that Harry, seated next to him, crutches on the floor, was wearing the Luftwaffe flying blouse. "It's unbelievable," Bubi said.

"You'd better believe it," Max said. "Isn't Muller joining us?"

"No. He was called to St.-Malo. And Schroeder is busy." He turned to the orderly by the door. "Right now we eat."

"Yes. Go to a good death, but do it on a full stomach." Max sat down at the table. "Is there anything I've forgotten, Harry?"

"Just take it easy. There are still people you won't recognize. General Sobel, for example. Relax, let them come to you."

"I'll do my best." Max glanced at the window. "Listen to that rain. Pity poor sailors at sea on a night like this."

"Pity poor pilots, more like." Harry picked up a glass of wine. "I can't think of an appropriate toast."

"What about heaven help us all?" Max said.

ROSA, trudging through the forest, was miserable and thoroughly soaked. It was so dark now that she blundered into trees. Lightning crackled in the sky and momentarily lit things up. There was a track and some sort of hut. She staggered toward it, found a door, and opened it. It seemed warm in there, and when the lightning crackled again, she saw piles of hay. She lay down on a pile, and it smelled good. She closed her eyes and was instantly asleep.

THE Storch stood outside in the rain, and Max, a military raincoat over his shoulders, lit a cigarette as an SS sergeant major with a Schmeisser fired a burst into the fuselage, close to the tail, then another burst into the port wing.

"Excellent." Bubi turned to Max. "This is it, I suppose."

"The moment of truth." Max held out his hand. "Give me your Walther, Bubi, and the spare clip. I'll say I took it from the guard I knocked out and then shot another."

Bubi took the Walther from his holster and the spare clip and handed them over. "Off you go." Bubi held out his hand. "I'm sorry."

"Not your fault, Bubi. I'll be off."

He walked to the plane and climbed in. The SS sergeant major closed the cabin door for him. Max switched on. A moment later the prop started to turn, then quickened. Rain hammered against the windshield, but as always, what he called the plane feeling enveloped him. This was what he'd been born to do—to fly.

The Storch moved forward and turned into the wind. Max roared down the runway, pulled back on the column, and lifted into the darkness.

9

A HEAD wind slowed Max down, but the flight was no trouble at all. He kept radio silence for the first forty minutes and then called in. "Cold Harbour, Cold Harbour, are you receiving me?"

There was an almost instant reply. "This is Cold Harbour receiving you loud and clear. Who are you?"

"Colonel Harry Kelso getting out of Brittany in a Luftwaffe Storch. ETA, twenty minutes."

"Stand by." The RAF corporal on radio duty was shocked, reached for his telephone, and rang through to Julie Legrande's room.

DAWN suffused the sky. The light was very strange and the dark sea angry and storm-tossed below him. Max was totally exposed now, a perfect target for any wandering Spitfire or Hurricane. He wouldn't stand a chance—blown out of the sky in seconds. He laughed. What an end that would be to the whole sorry business, but it wouldn't help his mother or Harry or even poor old Bubi.

Julie spoke over the radio. "Harry?"

"The coast's coming up. Yes, it's me, Julie."

"It's a miracle!"

"I'll be with you in ten minutes," he said. "Battered but unbowed."

"I'll be waiting. I'll phone Munro in London."

"Yes, wake the old fellow up. Over and out."

"GOOD heavens, Julie, are you sure?" Munro said.

"I've spoken to him myself, Brigadier."

"I'll be with you as soon as possible."

He went downstairs to the basement flat, where Jack Carter lived, shook him awake in bed, and told him.

Carter said, "I can't believe it."

"Let's get moving, Jack. Phone Croydon and book a Lysander."

"I'll get right on it." Carter sat up and reached for his false leg. "Does Molly know?"

"Of course not. I'll tell her now."

He went back upstairs, knocked on the door of her bedroom, and went in. She'd been awake for some time, but then, she'd slept badly since the news of the crash. She sat up. "Uncle Dougal? What is it?"

"Some rather astonishing news, my dear." And he sat on the bed.

MAX swept in from the sea, and there it was below, Cold Harbour, exactly as Harry had described—the rescue boat tied up at the quay, the pub, the cottages, and, finally, the abbey and the lake. He dropped down on the grass runway and taxied toward the hangar. Half a dozen ground crew ran forward.

"Bloody marvelous, Colonel," the flight sergeant said, and they all crowded around. "Your face doesn't look too happy, sir."

"Oh, I'll survive. Banged up when the Lysander went down." Max pretended to examine the fuselage. "You'll need some repair work here. I took off under fire, so to speak." He reached inside the Storch for the German military raincoat.

Julie drove up in the jeep, braked to a halt, got out, and flung her arms around him. "You'll never know how good it is to see you, Harry Kelso. But my goodness, your face."

"Which is why I won't kiss you. It hurts." He managed a grin. "But I can still eat and you know what? I'm starving."

"I'll take you down to the Hanged Man. Come on, get in."

He sat in the passenger seat. There was a pack of Senior Service cigarettes and a lighter in the glove compartment. "You don't mind if I help myself?"

As he opened the pack, she said, "I always thought you hated those things. I've only seen you smoke Players."

He recovered quickly. "Julie, my love, after what I've been through, I can smoke anything."

She smiled. "Yes, I can imagine."

Max, the first hurdle safely passed, leaned back, the adrenaline flowing, everything sharp and clear.

Zec Acland knelt at the fire, placing more logs, when the door opened and Julie stepped into the bar, followed by Max. Zec hadn't been so astonished in his entire life. "Well, bless my soul, Colonel, and us thinking you were maybe dead and gone."

"Almost, but not quite. I managed to steal a Storch and made a run for it. I had to shoot one of the guards." Max took the Walther from his raincoat pocket. "The name of the game."

Zec looked grim. "What happened over there?"

Max stuck to the facts as closely as possible—the successful dropping of Jacaud, how he'd been bounced by the ME109s, how the SS patrol had saved his bacon. "They took me to Château Morlaix. My face was battered in the crash, but a doctor there stitched me up again."

"Then what?" Julie asked as she headed toward the kitchen. "I can hear you from there."

"They had word that I was to be shipped out to Berlin." He was warming to his story. "I realized once that happened, I was finished. The escape was an absurd chance and very simple. I'd been dining late with the commandant. There was a guard at my door, of course, and I pretended to go to bed. I decided to make a break sometime after three. The bathroom was very old-fashioned, with a French window. I climbed down, turned the corner, and there was a staff car, the driver beside it, smoking a cigarette. I picked up a brick from a flower bed and struck him from behind. That's where I got the Walther. I slipped on his raincoat and side cap and drove away."

Julie brought a dish of eggs, bacon, and toast to one of the tables. "Come and get it." She sat down. "What happened then?"

"I drove up to the airstrip." He was eating now and enjoying the eggs and bacon. "There was a Storch parked on the apron. It was raining heavily, no sign of guards. I drove up, got out, and opened the door. Then the sentry appeared, so I shot him. I did the quickest takeoff of my life. Two other sentries sprayed me with their Schmeissers, but no great harm, and here I am." He finished his breakfast and sat back. "All I need now is a great cup of coffee."

"Coffee?" Julie said. "I thought you'd switched to tea."

Mistake number two.

Max grinned. "All I've had since last Friday is coffee, Julie. The SS has never heard of tea, but you're right. Back to tea it is!"

UP AT the abbey, he played it carefully and allowed himself to be taken by Julie to Harry's room. He put the military coat on the bed.

She looked at him. "Your slacks aren't too good. There's a rip in the left leg. Let's see what I've got in the supply room."

Supply room. Yes, Harry had mentioned that.

Max said, "I'll come with you."

He was astonished by all the uniforms, the weaponry, but managed not to show it. Julie found a pair of khaki slacks and handed them to him. "British army, officers. They'll do until you get to Haston Place. You must have a spare uniform there. See you in the library."

Haston Place. Number Three. Basement flat with Carter. Munro's bedroom on the right, top of the stairs. Molly next to him, and Harry third door along. SOE headquarters ten minutes away in Baker Street.

Max descended the broad stairs ten minutes later. Library to the left, dining room to the right, kitchen through green baize door. He found Julie by the fire, piling on logs. She had a look at him.

"That's better. I've got to go to the pub and put the pies in the oven for the crew's lunch. I suppose you'd like to take it easy?"

"I've never taken it easy in my life, Julie. I could do with a stroll."

"I've just had a call from Munro. He's about to leave in a Lysander. He's got Jack with him. Molly wanted to come, but she has a heavy operating schedule this morning."

Strange, the feeling of relief.

Max said, "I'll see her soon enough."

"That's no way to be, Harry Kelso. You should be straining at the leash. Men!" She shrugged. "I don't know. No romance at all."

LATER, back at the abbey, Munro and Jack Carter sat opposite Max in the dining room and listened intently as he told them the same story he'd given Julie and Zec.

When he was finished, Munro said, "Amazing, Harry. But there's no rest for the weary. Croydon's your next stop. I rang Teddy West."

Air Vice Marshal West and no photo.

"How is he?" Max asked.

"Ecstatic. I've left it to him to break the good news to the Supreme Commander." Munro stood up. "Great to have you back, Harry, even if you do look as if a truck's run over your face. Molly sends her love. I thought we'd dine at the River Room tonight, invite her father. Celebrate your return from the dead."

WHEN they landed at Croydon, it was early afternoon. Again Max was saved by chance, for as he assisted Jack Carter out of the Lysander, Carter said, "Air Vice Marshal West over there."

Max turned. West actually hugged him. "Don't you ever frighten me like that again."

"I'll do my best, sir," Max replied.

"Looks like we'll be running out of medals."

AT HASTON Place, Max found Harry's bedroom with no trouble. He dropped his military raincoat on the bed and checked the wardrobe. The extra uniforms hung neatly there, shirts and socks on the shelves, spare shoes.

There was a knock at the door, and Carter looked in. "The brigadier's asked me to drop you off at Guy's. He wants Molly to check your face over. You could have a hairline fracture."

"Fine. Let's go, then."

At Guy's, the emergency room was busy, as usual. Max lay on the X-ray table and did as he was told. Jack Carter sat in the corner. A young man in a white coat took X rays, whistling cheerfully. Then he escorted Max down the corridor and opened a door. "In here."

Molly, a stethoscope around her neck, sat behind a desk. She jumped up, came around the desk, and flung her arms around him. "Harry, don't do that to me again. Never again. I've been in hell."

He held her close. "I'm sorry." He kissed her forehead gently.

She pulled away. "What's this?" There was a slight frown on her face. "Tenderness, romance from the great Harry Kelso?"

Max said smoothly, "You know what they say in the movies? It was hell out there. Perhaps it's produced a new me."

"I'll believe that when it happens." Just then the X rays arrived. She put them on the screen and switched on the light. After a while she nodded. "No fracture." She turned. "Tell me what happened."

Which he did.

AT THE River Room, they had a circular table at the window, and Munro ordered champagne for himself, Max, Carter, and West while they waited for Molly and her father.

"To you, Harry." Munro raised his glass. "I should think you've used up your nine lives."

"We'll see," Max said.

"No, we won't," West told him. "You're grounded by Ike's direct order. You're finished in the air."

"He told you that?"

"Yes. He wants to see you, but I'm not sure when. I'm flying Ike down to Southwick tomorrow morning."

"You're flying him?" Max said.

"Well, there's life in the old dog yet, and it keeps my hand in."

At that moment Molly and her father weaved their way between the tables. Max had no problem this time, for this had to be General Sobel, and he was smiling broadly. He pumped Max's hand. "I can't tell you what this means. Ike was thrilled." He seated Molly. "He wants to see you, Harry, but couldn't manage it tonight. He'd like you to join him at seven in the morning at Croydon."

"Sounds good to me." Max reached for his glass, his hand steady and yet nothing but turmoil in his head.

Oh, no, so soon?

ROSA Stein had slept for at least twelve hours, the sleep of utter exhaustion. When she finally awakened, the light had faded. She left the hut and followed the track, her mind numb, and within fifteen minutes she came to a farm. Smoke drifted from the chimney; cattle lowed from the barn. A young woman emerged with a pail of milk. It was Marie, Jacaud's radio operator. "Who are you? What do you want?" she called in French.

Rosa burst into tears. "Help me. Please help me," she cried. Great sobs racked her body. Marie gestured to the door, and Rosa followed.

MAX and Molly danced on the crowded floor, but he wasn't anywhere near as expert as his brother. The fact that there were so many people provided an excuse for clumsiness. After one bump too many, he said, "I'm sorry. I'm not doing too well."

"That's all right. You've been through hell, Harry." She held him close. "Uncle Dougal told me you lost Tarquin."

"Afraid so. He must have fireballed in the crash."

The headwaiter appeared on the edge of the floor and beckoned. Molly said, "I don't believe this. Every time I come here with you, the same thing happens." She pulled away, went and spoke to the waiter, and returned. "Good old hospital again."

"I'll wait up for you," he said as they went back to the table.

"Don't bank on it. If it's after midnight, I'll stay at hospital."

Molly went off in Munro's staff car, and West offered to drop off the others in his. Outside, Max said, "Look, I feel like a walk, Brigadier. I'm kind of wound up."

"Perfectly understandable, dear boy," Munro said. "Have a saunter, enjoy yourself."

Sobel said, "I'll see you in the morning at Croydon."

"I'll be there."

They all piled into West's staff car, which drove away. Max flagged down the first taxi that came along and climbed inside.

The taxi dropped him off in Westbourne Grove. Max found the side street leading to the block of flats with no trouble. He paused at the entrance, checked the names, and pressed the buzzer. After a while Sarah Dixon said, "Yes?"

"Mrs. Dixon? The day of reckoning is here."

She said calmly, "Come up. Second floor."

He pushed open the door and went in. From the doorway opposite, Parry had caught him twice, one of forty-eight people he'd photographed that night. He was bored, and he was cold. "Bloody Yank," he said softly. "Here for a whore, I suppose."

IT WAS three in the morning when Jacaud arrived at Marie's farm. They went into the kitchen, and Jacaud sat at the end of the table while Marie left to get Rosa. Tarquin the bear sat at the other end, and Jacaud gazed at him morosely. "It's all right for you." He'd once been a university professor of philosophy, but all notions of philosophy had gone out the window. He didn't believe in people anymore.

Marie brought Rosa into the room.

Jacaud spoke in good German. "Listen. No one will hurt you if you tell the truth. Tell me who you are and what this is all about."

Fifteen minutes later he sat there frowning as she finished. It was Marie who said, "This is crazy. One brother impersonating another to kill Eisenhower? I can't believe it."

"I've had a thought," Jacaud said. "We arranged for Helene, that friend of Jules's, to sleep with the SS doctor, Schroeder. Have Jules go round to her place. If the German is there, bring him to me. He can confirm this woman's story."

Twenty minutes later Captain Schroeder, fast asleep and entwined with the delicious Helene, awakened to find the barrel of a Colt automatic under his throat and Jules at the side of his bed.

"Get up and get dressed, or I'll blow your brains out."

Helene sat up in alarm, and Jules grinned. "Not you, darling. You've served France well. Go back to sleep."

SCHROEDER, convinced that he was faced with death, was most cooperative. He sat at the end of the table and talked. "You must understand, she wished to die," he said when he finished.

Marie said to Jacaud in French, "Was he any help?"

"Oh, yes," Jacaud said. "He knows enough. I'll write a report. You must transmit it to Munro at Baker Street at once."

She shook her head. "Not possible. They're not on channel for me until seven o'clock."

"All right, seven, then."

AT CROYDON, MIST DRAPING the airfield, Tom Sobel drank coffee and looked out with some gloom at the weather.

Max came in from the operations room. "It's fine at Southwick. No real problem landing there."

"Well, that's a blessing, but where on earth is Teddy West?"

At that moment two things happened. A staff car drew up outside, and Eisenhower got out; then a flight lieutenant hurried in from operations with a signal flimsy, which he handed to Sobel.

Sobel read it and looked up as Eisenhower came in. "Bad news, General. Teddy West's staff car was in an accident on the way here. Not too serious, but he needs hospital treatment."

"Damn!" Eisenhower said. "We have an important conference, Tom, as you know. Can you find another pilot fast?"

There was an inevitability about it—Max saw that. "You've got one, General. I'll fly you down."

Eisenhower turned and held out his hand, that famous smile in evidence. "Glad to see you again, Colonel. What extraordinary happenings. Are you really up to flying? Your face looks terrible!"

Max held out his hands. "Steady as a rock, General."

Ike glanced at Sobel. "What do you think, Tom?"

"If Colonel Kelso says it's okay, it's fine by me, sir."

Ike nodded. "Right, Colonel. Let's move it."

Max went into the anteroom, took off his raincoat, and helped himself to a flying jacket. He transferred the Walther and the spare clip from the raincoat to one of the pockets and went outside.

MUNRO and Jack Carter decided to sign in early at SOE headquarters. They arrived at a quarter to seven. Jack made his way to his office, while Munro went upstairs to his own. He found Detective Constable Parry sitting on the bench outside.

"You're early."

"Lacey told me to make sure you had each evening's surveillance photos on the Dixon woman first thing."

Munro led the way inside his office. "Let's see."

Parry dropped one photo after another on the table. "Pretty ordinary, on the whole." He laughed. "Mind you, they've probably got their quota of whores there. Here's a nice one of some American officer. That's the entrance to Sarah Dixon's apartment block."

Munro looked at the photo, stunned. "Oh, no. No!"

There was a knock at the door, and Carter came in, a flimsy in one hand. "Just received from Jacaud, Brigadier. Plain language, marked utmost priority."

Munro read it, then said, "That isn't Harry Kelso in the photo. It's Max, his brother, and he's here to assassinate Ike." He reached for the phone. "Get me Croydon." A moment later he was talking to operations. "General Eisenhower's flight—has it left?" He listened, then replaced the phone. "Book me a plane to Southwick, Jack. Utmost priority."

"But Brigadier, what if—"

"What if he shoots Ike and Tom Sobel and flies off to France? We'll just have to hope he doesn't, because there's nothing we can do about it. I'll follow them down. You hold the fort. Pull the Rodrigues brothers in and get Riley to arrest the Dixon woman." He got up. "Tell her we don't intend to hang her as long as she cooperates."

IN THE Lysander, Max flew at five thousand feet, through broken cloud. Eisenhower and Sobel sat behind, shouting to each other above the roar of the engine.

Max was prey to conflicting emotions. He'd met the Supreme Commander, shaken hands, recognized the face, and yet the man himself meant nothing. It would be simple to draw his Walther, turn, and shoot Eisenhower between the eyes, but that would mean Sobel as well, Molly's father, which would make her also a victim in this whole sorry mess. How would Harry feel if he flew into Morlaix with two dead bodies, one of them the father of the woman he loved? For he did love her—Max knew that now, having met her.

On the other hand, what about Mutti? If he didn't kill Eisenhower, she was dead. So what should he do? Fly to Southwick and wait for another opportunity? Turn around now, get it done? Max had never felt this way in his entire life. He'd told Harry he would go to hell itself to save his mother, so why this strange paralysis?

The decision was taken out of his hands a moment later. There was a sudden roar, and the Lysander rocked in the slipstream of a black shadow that passed overhead and banked to port.

"What is that?" Eisenhower demanded.

"A Junkers night fighter," Max said. "Over from France trawling around in the south country. Hang on, gentlemen."

Every pilot's instinct in Max's body was on full alert as he dropped almost a thousand feet and the Junkers came in on his tail and fired, a shell puncturing his left wing and shattering the windshield. The Junkers banked away in a wide circle.

Max yelled to the back, "He's too fast for us. But, on the other hand, we're too slow for him." The Junkers was a quarter of a mile away, turning, and Max called over the radio, "Lysander One en route for Southwick under attack over South Downs."

The Junkers came in again. Max banked steeply, and the stream of cannon fire missed. The flying took control of him then. He went down, faster, two thousand feet, one thousand, the wooded slopes of the Downs looming below. The Junkers overshot, banked, and came in again. Max took it to six hundred and then, without warning, dropped his flaps—the old trick he'd used so many times before. The Lysander almost lurched to a halt, and the pilot of the Junkers, banking frantically to avoid hitting him, lost control and went straight into the forest below. Flames mushroomed as Max pulled back the control column, climbed, and leveled at one thousand feet.

He turned. "Are we okay back there?"

Eisenhower and Sobel looked stunned, and suddenly Max knew—this was the time. He could still pull his pistol, shoot them both, and be off to France.

But he wasn't going to.

Something had changed in the last few minutes, a decision had been made without his even having to think about it. As the adrenaline of the air duel coursed through his blood, he knew—he was a pilot, not an assassin.

He called Southwick. "Be with you in fifteen minutes."

A HUNDRED YARDS FROM THE Portuguese embassy Jack Carter sat in the back of a staff car and waited. The gray-haired man in the blue suit who hurried along the pavement was Colonel da Cunha, head of embassy security. Carter opened the door, and da Cunha joined him. "A long time, Jack. You said it was urgent."

"It is. Fernando and Joel Rodrigues—they're in the pay of the Nazis in Berlin." Da Cunha opened his mouth, and Carter raised a hand. "It's definite. I can give you proof."

Da Cunha took a cigarette from his case and lit it. "They'll claim diplomatic immunity, Jack."

"You mean you will. Fair enough. They're of no further use to us. Get them on tonight's flight to Lisbon and tell them not to come back, ever."

"Thank you, Jack. You're very kind."

"I can afford to be. We're winning the war." He reached over and opened the door, and da Cunha got out and walked away.

When Jack got back to the office, Sarah Dixon was signing a statement sheet, Riley seated beside her, Lacey by the window.

"Have you got everything?"

Riley nodded. "It's the German twin, all right."

Sarah Dixon said, "What happens now? A trial?"

"Heavens, no," Carter said. "You're no longer important. We'll put you in detention, of course. As for after the war, we'll see."

She smiled, and Riley and Lacey took her out.

AT THE Southwick airstrip, the Lysander rolled to a halt, and a large group ran forward—officers of the General Staff and RAF personnel.

Eisenhower raised his arms and waved them back. "I'm fine, and so is General Sobel, thanks to the finest bit of flying I've ever known." He turned to Max. "Colonel Harry Kelso, by the authority vested in me as Supreme Commander, I intend an immediate award of the Distinguished Service Cross." He shook Max's hand and turned to Tom Sobel. "We'd better get moving."

Tom Sobel put an arm around Max's shoulders. "I'm proud of

you, son, and Molly will be even prouder. Look, why don't you get something to eat in the officers mess? Just take it easy."

"Fine," Max said. "I might just do that."

Sobel moved away, following Eisenhower, and Max lit a cigarette, his hands shaking. What would happen now to Mutti, to Harry? Rain started to fall, and a Royal Military Police major moved to his side and raised an umbrella. "Got to keep you dry, Colonel, for Brigadier Munro. He'll be arriving soon."

In that moment Max knew they were onto him. "What is this?"

"My name's Vereker. The two corporals over there are my men." Max looked across and saw them, wearing the distinctive red cap of the Royal Military Police. "I don't know what's going on here, but I've been ordered to arrest you under the Defence of the Realm Act."

"Sounds interesting," Max said.

"I know you're carrying a weapon, Colonel. If you could just pass it over discreetly, I'd be obliged."

"Oh, I'm always discreet." Max took the Walther and the spare clip out of his flying jacket and passed it over. "What do we do until the brigadier gets here?"

Vereker slipped the Walther into his pocket. "How about a drink in the mess? I think I can trust you. After all, where can you go?"

"Never a truer word said, Major." Max smiled. "So lead on."

Vereker and Max sat in a window seat, enjoying a whisky and a cigarette, and waited. What was it Munro had discovered, and how? Max wondered. Not that it mattered. It was all over, and heaven help his mother and Harry.

When Dougal Munro finally entered the mess, he hesitated, then came toward them. "Major," he said to Vereker, "from this moment you are bound by the Official Secrets Act. We'll use your office."

Moments later Munro sat behind Vereker's desk and handed him a folded document. "Your warrant for this arrest, Major."

Vereker examined it and looked up, bewildered. "But this is in the name of Oberstleutnant Baron Max von Halder."

"Quite right. It seems Colonel Harry Kelso crash-landed in Brittany last week and escaped to fly back in triumph in a stolen Luftwaffe Storch. Only it wasn't Harry Kelso—it was his twin brother."

Vereker was dumbfounded. "But why?"

"To assassinate General Eisenhower."

"But that's crazy, Brigadier. He's just saved Ike's life."

"Yes, bizarre, isn't it?" Munro turned to Max. "When it came to it, you couldn't do it, could you?"

"Oh, I was thinking about it. Then the Junkers turned up. Strange, that. If I was a fatalist, I'd have just let it happen, and the three of us would have gone down together. A perfect solution."

"You're not a fatalist?"

"Never have been. And when that guy came in on my tail . . ." He shrugged. "I'm a fighter pilot. I did what came naturally. I may be a killer, but not *that* kind of killer."

"I think I understand."

"Which leaves my mother and Harry in deep, deep trouble." He frowned. "But wait. You haven't told me how you caught me."

"We were shadowing Sarah Dixon. We had a police cameraman checking everyone calling at her block of flats, and there you were. Foolish, that."

"Well, I'm just an amateur at this kind of thing."

"And then we had a report from my chief agent in Morlaix, and now I know everything—Bubi Hartmann, your mother, Harry, the dreadful dilemma Himmler put you in."

"How could you know all this?"

"Your mother's maid, Rosa Stein, was found wandering in the woods and, thank God, fell into the hands of my agent."

"Rosa? Wandering in the woods? What on earth are you talking about?"

So Munro told him.

MAX sat there, haggard and drawn. Vereker opened a cupboard, poured brandy into a glass, and handed it to him. Max gulped it down and looked up at Vereker, a dreadful smile on his face. "So now you know the kind of people you're fighting against. Just make sure the good guys win."

"I'm sorry, Max," Munro said.

"Our own fault. Hitler took over, and we sat back and went with the flow. We weren't Nazis. We kept telling ourselves that, only I ended up shooting down over three hundred planes for them. And what really hurts is that it isn't over. They still have Harry."

"And Bubi Hartmann lied to you."

"Yes, Bubi lied. But I think I understand him a bit. He's part Jewish, you see, and Himmler found out. Bubi was as much under the thumb as the rest of us."

Max took out a cigarette, his hands shaking. Vereker gave him a light. "What happens now?" Max asked. "The Tower of London?"

"Cold Harbour," Munro said. "This has gone on long enough, and I want you out of here before Ike sends for you." He turned to Vereker. "Tell Ike that I needed to inspect the remains of that Junkers with Colonel Kelso's expertise. And remember, this never happened."

IT WAS early afternoon when they drifted across Cold Harbour and bounced down rather uncomfortably. Julie drove up in the jeep and got out. "Nice to see you back. There's still time for lunch."

Munro said, "Why not? That suit you, Max?"

"As you say, why not?"

Julie said, "Max? What is this?"

"Let's get out of this rain, and I'll tell you."

Zec was the only person in the bar, sitting by the fire, reading a book. He looked up and smiled. "Good to have you back."

Munro said, "Let me introduce you. Oberstleutnant Baron Max von Halder, Harry Kelso's brother."

"Dear me," Zec said.

Max went behind the bar and helped himself to a pack of Players cigarettes. He lit one and gave a tired smile as he came back. "Get it over with, Brigadier. I'll go for a walk, if that's all right with you. I'll eat later."

The door closed behind him, and Munro turned to the others. "It's a rotten story, but here goes."

When he had finished, Julie said, "Dreadful. His poor mother."

"I never heard the like," Zec observed. "But what are you playing at here, Brigadier? You should have taken him to London."

"True, and the answer is, I've no bloody idea." Munro sighed. "This job makes one such a liar. I can't help feeling there is someway we can use this. I'll let it bubble around for a while."

The door opened, and Max came in. There was more color now to the unbruised section of his face. "I could murder one of those pies right now. I'm starving."

"And a pint of ale," Zec said. "I'll join you."

"And me," Munro added. "An active morning, to put it mildly."

Julie produced steak-and-kidney pies and potatoes, and as they began to work their way through them, they heard a roaring overhead. Julie went to the door and looked out. "Lysander," she said. "Now, who would that be?"

"Whoever it is will show themselves soon," Munro said.

It was perhaps fifteen minutes later that the door opened, and Jack Carter limped in, followed by Molly. "Don't blame Jack, Uncle Dougal. I made him bring me," she said.

"There was a signal from Southwick, sir," Carter told him. "General Eisenhower is trying to find you."

"Well, I didn't receive it, and for the moment I stay lost."

Jack turned to Max. "That was some flying this morning."

"Runs in the family," Max told him. "Just like Harry. The only thing we do well is fly."

Molly said, "I'd like to talk to you. Is that all right, Uncle?"

"I think we can bend the rules."

She went out, and Max followed her. They walked to the end of the quay, and she sat on a bench and he leaned on the railing. There was a strange intimacy between them.

"Jack told me everything about the whole rotten business. I'm so sorry about your mother."

"So am I. I'm also sorry about Harry, still stuck over there."

"Tell me how he was."

"You love him a lot, don't you?"

"Oh, yes."

"Nothing but grief there for you. I know, because there's nothing but grief there where I'm concerned."

"It doesn't matter. Love doesn't look for reason. Love is beyond reason. So tell me."

"He was in fair condition. A smashed ankle, but Captain Schroeder did a good job there, just like he did on my face."

"Terrible, the whole thing." She shook her head. "But to kill Eisenhower . . ."

"If you'd seen the film Himmler made us watch of the executions of so-called traitors . . . It was past belief."

"I understand. I really do. The irony is that if anyone else had been piloting Eisenhower's plane, the general would be dead by now." She stood up. "There must be something we can do."

"Send in the commandos?" Max shook his head. "Things like that take time to organize. The Rodrigues brothers will be back in Portugal fast. They'll report in, if only for the extra cash."

They walked along the quay. "This is terrible," she said, tears in her eyes. "I feel so helpless, and there's nothing to be done."

Max put an arm around her shoulders. "Oh, I don't know. I've been thinking. Molly, what if I became the pride of the Luftwaffe again? Changed into the right uniform in Julie's supply room, sneaked up to the airstrip. There are two Storchs there. I'd be at Morlaix in an hour, land at the airstrip, and play it by ear."

"It's madness," she said. "Certain death for you."

"Certain death for Harry now. At least we'd be together."

"It's fantasy. It's not possible."

When they reached the pub, Jack Carter was outside with Julie in the jeep, ready to take Max up to the house. Max climbed in, and Julie drove away. Molly entered the pub, where Munro was leaning on the bar, talking to Zec over a whisky. The brigadier turned.

"So you've no ideas about how to help Harry?" Molly said.

"No. It's impossible."

"Max doesn't think so."

Munro frowned. "Tell me," he said, which she did.

10 MAX spent the afternoon brooding in the locked bedroom Jack Carter had shown him to. There was nothing to do except think, and finally he'd had enough of that. Lying on the bed, he drifted into sleep. It was six thirty when Jack came for him. "Time for dinner, old son. We don't like to leave you on your own."

"That's very civil of you," Max said, and followed him downstairs to the library, where he found Munro with Zec Acland, and Molly seated by the fire.

"There you are," Munro said. "What'll it be? Whisky?"

"Actually, a brandy and soda would go down nicely."

Carter got it for him, and Max said, "So what now?"

"I'm not sure," Munro told him.

"I always thought the Tower of London was de rigueur for people like me."

"Dear boy, there's never been anyone quite like you." Munro was exasperated. "Blast, Max, I keep thinking you're Harry."

"Inconvenient, isn't it? What does Eisenhower have to say?"

"He doesn't know yet. This whole affair is dynamite, as our American friends would say. Publicity is the last thing we need, with the invasion due in a matter of weeks."

Julie looked in. "Dinner is on the table."

Zec was the first to stand up. "I always think better on a full stomach myself." He led the way out.

They sat around the table and enjoyed Julie's carrot soup, Dover sole, and sautéed potatoes. Conversation was sporadic.

Finally Munro said, "Let's adjourn to the library."

"Frankly, I've had enough." Max stood. "When you decide what to do with me, let me know, but I think I'll go to my room. Jack?"

Carter stood up. "Certainly, old boy."

The rest gathered in the library. When Jack came in, they were all sitting quietly. He went to the sideboard, poured a whisky, and raised his glass. "Cheers, everybody. And if you'll excuse me saying this, he's an absolutely smashing fella even if he's a Luftwaffe ace. War is war, a bloody stupid game over which we have no control."

"But we do have control," Molly said. "Uncle Dougal?"

"All right, I'm defeated. Give me a brandy, Jack, and I'll tell you about an interesting conversation Molly had earlier with Max."

When he was finished, it was Carter who said, "And you believe that, sir, that he would really try to save his brother?"

"For goodness sake, Jack, use that fine brain of yours," Molly exploded. "This is a great man, a fine man, who had everything. They blackmailed him and his brother into a terrible act. Then they butchered his mother."

"And now there is Harry at that blasted château awaiting the outcome," Julie put in. "Himmler will have him executed without a second's thought. You are talking evil walking the earth here."

"While we sit and do nothing," Molly said.

There was silence while Munro brooded. It was Zec who spoke. "They're good boys, Brigadier. They deserve a chance."

Munro nodded. "You're right, of course, all of you. I'm not making excuses, but I'd like to think that in my heart I've known all along why I brought Max here instead of taking him to London."

"So what do we do, sir?" Carter asked. "Will you tell him?"

"Goodness, no. That's far too simple. We'll let him escape."

AT CHÂTEAU Morlaix, Bubi Hartmann and Harry were finishing dinner. Neither one had said a great deal. Bubi was preoccupied, waiting for news from England and also concerned at the disappearance of Schroeder. Finally Harry reached for his crutches.

"I'll see you up to your room," Bubi said.

They mounted the stairs, and Bubi nodded to the SS guard, who opened the door.

Harry said, "What about my mother, Bubi? When do I see her?"

"Tomorrow, Harry. I think I can promise that." Bubi turned, and Harry went into the room. He felt strangely uneasy, went and peered out through the barred windows, wondering about Max and what was happening to him. Finally he lay on the bed and slept.

Downstairs, Bubi sat in a corner of the drawing room, drinking more brandy than was good for him. He was reaching for the bottle when the phone rang. He checked his watch, frowning: ten o'clock. Who could it be?

He picked up the phone, and the operator said, "I've got a call for you, Colonel."

"Who is it?"

"Well, he's obviously French, though his German's good. He insists on speaking to you personally."

"Put him on."

Jacaud said, "Colonel Hartmann?"

"Who is this?"

"Oh, I run what you call your opposition in this area. A friend of mine, a Brigadier Munro, has been in touch with me."

Bubi almost choked. "What do you want?"

"Nothing," Jacaud said. "I'm simply here to impart information. I understand the following names will mean something to you. The Rodrigues brothers are winging their way back to Lisbon. Sarah Dixon is in custody, and so is Baron von Halder. Here's a good one for you—the baron was actually flying Eisenhower down to Southwick when a wandering JU88 bounced them. Would you believe the baron made the joker crash? He saved Eisenhower's life."

"Damn you!" Bubi groaned.

"You're the one who's damned. The great day's coming soon. Oh, by the way, thanks for Schroeder. We'll need a decent doctor when the real fighting starts."

He rang off. Bubi sat there, clutching the phone, horror on his face. It was all over. He was finished. He had no illusions about the price of failure over this business. He lit a cigarette nervously. There was one thing he could do. At least he had a priority line to Berlin.

He rang through to his secretary. "Trudi, it's me."

"Colonel, what is it?"

"Just listen. The whole thing's a failure. The Rodrigues brothers, the Dixon woman, and Max—all arrested. Get out of there, Trudi. Use your authority as my secretary while it's still worth something and run for it. If you could warn my father, I'd appreciate it."

She was in tears. "This is terrible."

"Run like hell, my love."

Bubi felt a strange kind of relief. What the devil, he thought. Let's get it over with. He called Himmler's office.

A few moments later Himmler said, "So, Colonel, you have good news for me?"

Bubi, suddenly past caring, said, "On the contrary, Reichsführer, all bad."

There was a pause; then Himmler said, "Tell me."

Which Bubi did, experiencing a perverse enjoyment by going into the finer details, such as Max's actually saving Eisenhower's life. When he was finished, there was silence.

Finally Himmler said, "An ill-judged venture from the start, Colonel, but I must confess to having been carried along by your enthusiasm. The death of the wretched baroness showed a deplorable lack of leadership on your part, and now we have the embarrassment of Baron von Halder in British hands. You'll have a plane at the château tonight with Standartenführer Fassbinder on board. Tomorrow he'll take charge and bring Kelso to Berlin."

"And myself, Reichsführer?"

"You might as well come with them. We'll discuss the future."

He rang off, and Bubi put down the phone. He'd just received his death sentence, and so had Harry Kelso. The coffin lid had closed. Bubi picked up the brandy bottle and went upstairs to his room. He drank another large one. He took off his belt and holster, withdrew his brand-new Mauser, and grinned. Standartenführer Fassbinder could be in for a surprise. Bubi had never liked the swine, and it was better to go down fighting. He lay back and plunged into a drunken sleep.

MAX was lying on the bed and smoking a cigarette when the door creaked open. He glanced at his watch. It was two o'clock.

"Max, it's me." Julie switched on the light.

Max sat up. "What is it?"

"It's a bloody mess. No one seems to know what to do, except Molly."

"What are you talking about?"

"After you'd gone, Molly told us what you'd said to her on the quay—about stealing the Storch and flying off to get Harry."

"And what did Munro say?"

"He thought it was crazy." She shrugged. "But I don't. I fought the Nazis with the Resistance. I don't like them, Max, but so help me, I like you, and I'm probably a little bit in love with Harry, though don't tell Molly. Anyway, you deserve a chance—you and Harry. If you want to go, I'll help. I checked that Storch you came over in, and the tank is full. The ground crew are in bed. So let's go."

In the supply room, Max changed into a Luftwaffe uniform. Julie even found him a Knight's Cross to wear. He selected a Walther, slipped a magazine into the butt, and screwed a silencer on the end. He slipped a spare magazine into the large map pocket in the pants. "Loaded for bear—that's what my grandfather used to say."

"If you're ready, I'll take you up there."

Max followed Julie down to the back door and across the yard to the jeep. As she switched on and drove away, she said, "I've checked the weather report. About four this fog is due to clear, and you'll have a full moon up there."

As they approached the airstrip, he said, "This is the second time in a week that I've taken on an impossible task. My mother thought the Eisenhower thing was madness, that I was going to my death."

"You're still here."

"Only just. Is this madness, Julie?"

"Heaven help me, but I don't know."

He lit a cigarette. "Okay, I could be back here by five if the duty controller at the Morlaix airstrip accepts the famous Black Baron. They never knew what I was up to, you see. I think I stand a chance as long as Bubi has kept the lid on things."

The Storch was on the apron. Julie pulled up, and they got out and walked toward it. All was quiet. Max opened the door, then kissed Julie on the cheek. "God bless you."

"God bless you, Max."

He got into the pilot's seat. "Where's Munro, by the way?"

She was taken by surprise. "I don't really know."

"Come on, Julie." He smiled, closed the door, and switched on. A moment later he lifted into the night.

IN THE Hanged Man, Zec stirred the fire into life. Jack Carter and Molly sat in the inglenook, and Munro stood at the bar. The rescue-boat crew were scattered around the room.

One of them spoke. "What's it all about, Zec? You said something special."

At that moment there was the sound of the Storch passing overhead. Another man said. "What was that?"

Zec looked at Munro, who said, "That was Colonel Kelso on his way to France to attempt a pickup, probably the most hazardous mission ever undertaken from Cold Harbour. Positively suicidal. If he's successful, we may see him at five. On the other hand, he may need assistance at sea."

"Which is why I want you on hand," Zec said. "Any objections?"

One of the men laughed. "Come on, Zec, build up the fire, shut up, and let's get the cards out."

Zec took a pack of cards from his pocket. "What's your pleasure, Brigadier?"

"Poker," Munro told him. "I've always had a weakness for stud poker. Unfortunately, I only play for money."

There was a roar of laughter. Someone joined two tables together, and everyone crowded around.

MAX left his contact with Morlaix until he was five miles out. His trip across from Cold Harbour to Brittany had been made at five hundred feet. He felt calm, totally in charge, no fear at all.

"I'm coming to get you, Harry," he murmured softly.

At the château, Harry stirred, came awake as if from a dream, stared at the ceiling, and then the dream receded. He lay there, for some reason very alert and excited, and reached for a cigarette.

The duty controller at Morlaix was Sergeant Greiser. There was nothing to do, no traffic since Standartenführer Fassbinder's arrival at midnight. Greiser sat there yawning when at three thirty Max's voice sounded over the radio. "Come in, Morlaix. Are you receiving me?"

Greiser reached for the mike. "Loud and clear. Who are you?"

"Baron von Halder on special assignment. I'll be with you in five minutes. You will notify no one of my arrival. I act directly under the orders of Reichsführer Himmler. Over and out."

Greiser, incredibly excited, switched on the landing lights, went out of the radio hut, and ran through a light rain to the hangar that housed Fassbinder's ME109. A young sentry stood there, his Schmeisser slung over one shoulder. "What's the flap?" he asked.

"Storch coming in."

"At this time in the morning? Who is it?"

"Mind your own business," Greiser told him.

The Storch made a perfect landing, taxied in, and halted. Max switched off, got out, and approached. "You are . . ." he asked.

"Greiser, Herr Baron." The sergeant clicked his heels. "A great honor."

Max lit a cigarette. "I'll take you into my confidence, Greiser. This is a special duties flight. I'm due at the château to pick up a passenger. Have you a vehicle I can use?"

"A staff car, Herr Baron. I'll drive you myself."

"Not necessary. I'll be back within thirty minutes. Show me." Greiser led him to a second hangar, and there was the car. Greiser saluted, and Max drove away.

At the château, a young SS guard huddled in the sentry box. Max pulled up to the swing bar. "Raise this thing! It's Baron von Halder. I've just flown in, and I'm tired."

The boy never even queried him. He took in the Luftwaffe uniform, the Oberstleutnant's tabs, the Knight's Cross, stumbled to the swing bar, and raised it. Max drove through, moved along the drive to the main entrance, and stopped. There was a guard at the door.

Max said, "Baron von Halder. I'm expected."

This guard was older and harder, a different proposition. "Your pass, Herr Baron."

"Certainly." Max took the silenced Walther from his map pocket and shot him between the eyes.

He dragged the corpse into the shadows, then opened the front door and stepped inside. A young SS corporal sat at the table. He glanced up, and Max shot him twice in the heart.

It was very quiet. He stood there for a moment, then mounted the stairs. It was strangely dreamlike, as if not happening at all, and yet it was. He had never felt so purposeful, so strong in his life. He moved with total certainty, almost like a cat, his feet quiet as he drifted along the carpeted corridor to his brother's room.

The guard was seated, reading a book, his Schmeisser on the floor. He looked up, and Max put the silencer against his forehead and fired, then turned the key in the door and moved inside.

"Harry, it's me."

Harry, lying on the bed, couldn't believe it. He sat up. "Max? What in the world is happening here?"

"Just listen. It all went wrong. I was arrested, and Munro took me to Cold Harbour. I stole a Storch and flew over. I'm taking you back to England. Do you think I'd leave you here? To Himmler?"

"But what about Mutti?"

"Mutti's dead. She was shot to death before I even left. They lied to us, Harry. Bubi lied. Let's go."

"Oh, no!" Harry moaned. He pulled on his right shoe, picked up his crutches, and struggled after Max, his mind in a turmoil.

At the head of the stairs a bathroom door opened, and Bubi came out. "Max, it's you!"

Max could have shot him. Instead he struck him twice across the side of the head, and Bubi went down like a stone.

"Come on," Max said to Harry, and they descended the stairs. "Let's get out of here."

He helped Harry into the staff car, slid inside, and drove away. At the gate, the sentry was out in a flash. They passed through, and

Max increased speed and drove back to the airstrip. He pulled in beside the Storch, then helped Harry in, closed the door, and went around to the pilot's side. As he climbed in, Greiser ran across the apron. "Is there anything I can do, Herr Baron?"

"No, thanks. You've done splendidly," Max told him.

He taxied to the far end, turned into the wind, and thundered down the runway. A moment later the Storch lifted and faded into the dark.

At the château, Bubi staggered to his feet, blood on his face, then ran along the corridor to raise the alarm. Five minutes later he rushed down the château steps and jumped into the back of his car. "The airstrip," he told the driver.

It had to be the airstrip, the only way Max could have got here. Both of them together once again. Enough to make even Himmler happy. It could change everything.

ZEC threw down his cards. "That's it, Brigadier. I reckon you've cost us ten quid."

"I can't help superior play," Munro told him.

"Yes, and I can't help my nose. Out there at sea I smell things, Brigadier, things on the wind. I can't sit here. I've a feeling we're better off fifteen or twenty miles out there and waiting."

Munro didn't even hesitate. "I bow to your superior judgment."

"We'll leave now." Zec turned to the crew. "Move it!"

AT THE airstrip, Bubi jumped out of the staff car and ran across the apron. He opened the door of the radio hut.

Greiser turned, surprise on his face. "Colonel."

"Baron von Halder—he was here?"

"Why, yes, Colonel. He landed in a Storch, said he was on a mission for Reichsführer Himmler, and borrowed a staff car. Twenty minutes ago he and a passenger took off again."

"You imbecile!" Bubi turned and ran toward the ME109 in the hangar. The Storch was slow, but the 109 was very fast indeed. He could still retrieve the situation.

JULIE'S WEATHER REPORT PROVED totally accurate, for as the Storch moved out over the sea, the cloud cover cleared and the moon appeared, a hard white light. Max turned and spoke to Harry, who was wearing the spare headphones and mike. "You okay?"

"I've never felt better."

Max smiled. "We made it, brother. I'm sorry for Bubi, but I'd love to see Himmler's face."

"So would I." Harry checked the instruments. "ETA, thirty minutes, I'd say."

There was a sudden roaring, and the Storch rocked in turbulence as the ME109 banked to take station to starboard. Bubi's voice crackled on the headphones. "Turn back, Max. The jig's up. I can't let you do this. It's a death sentence for me and those close to me."

"What about our mother, Bubi? You lied."

"That wasn't my fault. I swear it."

"Too bad," Max told him. "But it's a fact of life. Come on, Bubi, you seriously want me to turn around?"

"If you don't, I'll shoot you down."

"Bubi, I always liked you, but you were never very good. What do you say, brother?"

"Tell him to take a hike," Harry said.

"You heard, Bubi. If you fancy trying to blow us away, go for it. It's a lot quicker than dangling in a noose from a meat hook."

He went down fast, and at fifteen hundred feet Bubi came in on the Storch's tail. Pieces flew from the fuselage and wings. Max kept on going down, and Harry said, "Not that old trick?"

"It saved Eisenhower the other day. I'll tell you about it sometime."

At seven hundred feet Bubi came in again, the Storch staggered, and Max groaned at a hammer blow in the back. He dropped the flaps, the Storch almost stopped dead, and Bubi Hartmann, with nowhere to go, plowed into the sea.

"It never fails," Max gasped. "Don't you find that?"

"Takes me back to those first lessons," Harry said. "Where would we have been now?"

"Long gone." Max choked, and blood poured out of his mouth.

"Oh, no!" Harry said.

"Call Cold Harbour," Max said. "We're losing power fast."

Harry called. "Cold Harbour, come in. Colonel Kelso here, plus brother, in one badly damaged Storch."

It was the rescue boat that answered. "Zec here, Colonel. We're twenty miles out in the *Lively Jane.* Give me your position."

Harry did. Then he said, "My brother's been hit."

"We'll be there, boy. No more than three miles away."

The Storch descended, clear in the bright moonlight, the sea black below. Dawn was touching the sky to the east. On the *Lively Jane,* it was as if all the crew saw the plane at the same moment. Molly, in the stern cockpit, leaned on the rail with Munro as the boat raced on over the waves. The Storch was clearly visible now, a mile to port, smoke trailing.

At four hundred feet the engine died and the propeller stopped. There was silence, only the sound of the wind, and Max coughed again. "Get your life belt on."

Harry did as he was told, then pulled another from under the seat. "Now you, Max."

"No point. I'm drowning in my own blood."

A hundred feet, then lower, skimming the wave tops, and Max swung to port and landed parallel to the crests. The Storch settled, water pouring in. Harry opened the door and unfastened his seat belt. The Storch was already sinking. He tried to unfasten Max's belt, but it seemed jammed.

Max coughed, another gush of blood erupting from his mouth. "I'm finished. Get out of here."

"Max," Harry cried. "No!"

Baron Max von Halder summoned up every last atom of strength and punched him in the mouth. Harry went backward through the open door. A wave caught him and pulled him away. Behind him the *Lively Jane* swerved in broadside, but Harry only had eyes for the Storch—the port wing under the water, the aircraft tilting—a last glimpse of his brother in the cockpit. Only a shadow, and then the plane went under the waves, disappearing forever.

TWO CREW MEMBERS TOWED Harry in, and willing hands reached down and pulled him up. He slumped to the deck, and someone draped a blanket over his shoulders.

"Harry, it is you, isn't it?" Munro demanded. "What happened?"

"Max got me out. Bubi Hartmann chased us in an ME109. Shot us up good. Max took a cannon shell in the back. Then he made Bubi crash back there. End of story."

Molly had an arm around him. "Come on. Let me examine you."

"What for? To tell me I should be dead? I've known that for years. I believe my brother knew the same. Now he's gone." Harry's face was like stone. "You know what, Molly, my love? My luck ran out with Tarquin. I'm a dead man walking." And he stood up and went below.

COLD HARBOUR
1998

IT WAS almost a year to the day when my wife, Denise, and I returned to Cold Harbour, and what a year. My hunt for the truth about Harry and Max Kelso had taken me to many places—files at the Pentagon, the Public Records Office in London, Luftwaffe files in Germany, Portugal, and Madeira. I traced a wonderful old American of eighty-three who'd flown with the RAF and had ended the war in the U.S. Air Force. He'd known Harry Kelso well, and his information about the man was invaluable.

The prime movers were all dead, needless to say—Brigadier Dougal Munro, Jack Carter, Teddy West. General Eisenhower was long gone, and Major General Tom Sobel, who disappeared over the English Channel en route to Normandy two weeks after D-day. One incredible piece of luck concerned Major Vereker of the Royal Military Police. He'd died in 1953, but his daughter was kind enough to give me an envelope she'd found among her father's effects all those years ago—a meticulous account of the events of that day at Southwick when he'd arrested Max on Dougal Munro's orders.

Why the island of Madeira? Simple enough. Fernando and Joel Rodrigues were finished with the Portuguese diplomatic service. They opened a bar in Alfama, the old quarter in Lisbon. With the end of the war in Europe, Sarah Dixon was released from detention. A happy ending for someone. She went to Portugal and married Fernando. In 1950 they moved to Madeira and opened a bar and restaurant. She was long gone, but not Fernando, who was still around at eighty-nine, incredibly active. He listened to what I had to say and laughed when I'd finished. "I read your books in Portuguese—do you know that?—and this is a good plot."

"Just like my other good plots?" I asked.

"Except that this one is true." He laughed again and proceeded to put me straight on a few points. He died a few months later.

THE plane Denise hired was an Archer, a single-engine job. The reason for the trip was simple. I'd sent a typescript of the story to Zec Acland at Cold Harbour. I'd had a phone call the previous day asking if we could come down.

So here we were, flying west, the sky dull, a hint of rain. Immersed in the facts of the book, as I had been for so long, I thought of 1940—the Luftwaffe flying in, the RAF rising to meet them, the Battle of Britain, Harry and Max, the brave young men on both sides, more than fifty percent of whom had died. It was a depressing thought—all those planes on the bottom of the Channel, and in one of them were the remains of Oberstleutnant Baron Max von Halder.

Thunder rumbled on the horizon as Denise banked and took us over Cold Harbour. The village was spread below—the Hanged Man, the cottages, *Lady Carter* tied up at the quay. We drifted over the abbey, the lake, and dropped down on the runway. Denise taxied toward the wartime hangars, where an old Land Rover waited, Zec Acland leaning against it. We got out.

Zec came forward, and Denise kissed him on the cheek. "You don't look any older."

"You have a way with the words, girl. You've got Tarquin in there, I suppose?"

"Oh, yes," she said.

"Bring him along. We'll take a run down to the Hanged Man, have a sandwich and a drink." He got behind the wheel, and we joined him, Tarquin in his new waterproof jump bag, and set off.

A few minutes later he pulled up outside the pub, and we got out and went in. There was no one else there, but then, it was only eleven o'clock. The fire burned brightly, though, and I was filled with a strange sense of déjà vu, not just because Denise and I had been here before in dramatic circumstances. It was everything that had happened here—Dougal Munro, Jack Carter and Molly, Julie Legrande and Max and Harry.

"Betsy?" Zec called.

She looked in from the kitchen. "Hello, there."

"We're ready." He turned to Denise. "Can we have a look at him?"

"Of course." She unzipped the bag, took Tarquin out, and sat him on the bar.

Zec sat down and stared for a long moment. There were tears in his eyes. "You wonderful little scamp."

Betsy came in with a mound of sandwiches. "How about a drink?"

"Tea for me," Denise told her. "I'm flying."

Zec said, "Open that bottle of champagne I put in the fridge, and I'll have some, too."

We tucked into the sandwiches, which were delicious. I said, "The typescript I sent you—what did you think?"

"All right as far as it went." He suddenly guffawed. "No, damn it, it was bloody fascinating. A few gaps, though."

"Such as?" I drank some champagne.

"I'll let Lady Carter fill you in. She's expecting us."

Denise stopped eating. "Lady Carter? But that's what the rescue boat's called."

"It would be. Her husband paid for a new boat ten years ago, before he died. The Royal National Lifeboat Institution named it after her."

"Lady Carter?" I asked.

"Jack Carter's wife. Sir Jack Carter, after his father died. Ended the war a colonel, Jack did. Came down here and bought the abbey."

"And Lady Carter?" I asked, although I already knew the answer.

"Lady Molly people call her around here. Molly Sobel as was. She was a doctor in these parts for years. A saint."

Denise looked at me, a query in her eyes, then turned back to Zec. "Were there any children?"

"No. Jack was blown up at Dunkirk and lost his leg, but he was damaged, if you follow me. Not that it mattered. Not after Harry."

"What happened?" I said.

"I'll let her tell you that. She's waiting. And bring Tarquin."

At the abbey, he didn't bother with the front door but led the way around a corner and followed a terrace above a wonderful rose garden. French windows stood open, and there she was, sitting in the library on the couch by the fire.

She was eighty years old, her white hair a halo, the face still young, good cheekbones. She looked up from the typescript, my typescript, and put it to one side. "I recognize you from those photos on the backs of books."

"Lady Molly." I took her hand. "My wife, Denise."

She pulled Denise down beside her. "They tell me you're an excellent pilot."

"Thank you," Denise said.

"I've been fascinated by the book. So many things I never knew." She hesitated. "Could I see Tarquin?"

Denise unzipped the bag, took him out, and offered him. Lady Molly gazed at him. "Oh, Tarquin." She held him close, and there were tears in her eyes. "Where did you get him? Harry thought he was destroyed in the Lysander crash."

"Apparently, Marie took him for her daughter," I said. "Marie was killed fighting with the Resistance after D-day. The child was adopted by relations, and that was the last heard of Tarquin."

"Until we found him on the top shelf of an antique shop in Brighton," Denise said. "How he got there, we'll never know. His name had traveled with him, though."

There was a pause. I said with some diffidence, "There's one gap. What happened to Harry afterward. I had difficulties there."

Lady Molly smiled. "Well, Eisenhower had to be told. It was decided to put top secret on the whole thing. I mean, the idea that the Supreme Commander had been in hazard before D-day was unthinkable. Harry continued to do occasional courier work for Munro. He always had to go back for more, even after they made him a full colonel. After the Channel crash and what happened to Max, he was never the same. He said he was a dead man walking. I think he wanted to prove it. I think he wanted to be with Max. They were one, you see, interchangeable in a way you don't appreciate. Was Max, Harry, or was Harry, Max?"

Denise took her hand and said gently, "What happened?"

"So stupid, so bloody stupid. Almost the end of the war. My uncle had this thing going with some German general. Harry volunteered to make the flight from here in an Arado, wearing Luftwaffe insignia. He landed, picked the man up, flew back across France. They were attacked by an RAF Mosquito and badly shot up."

"And went into the Channel?" I asked.

"Oh, no. The weather was lousy, but he made it to Cold Harbour. I was here with my uncle and Jack. The Arado rolled to a halt, and when we opened the door, the German general was gibbering in the back seat and Harry was dead at the controls."

She stared into the past, anguish on her face, and Denise hugged her, Tarquin between them. Finally Lady Molly pulled herself together. "It means so much to see Tarquin again."

"He's come home," Denise said. "He rightfully belongs to you."

"Oh, no. I'm very grateful." Lady Molly hesitated. "If I could borrow him. Would that be all right? Temporary loan only."

"Of course," Denise said.

Molly nodded. "I'm so grateful." She stood. "Now I'd like you to come with me. There's something you should see."

Light rain was falling. She put a raincoat over her shoulders and cradled Tarquin in her left arm. Zec took two umbrellas from a stand, gave us one, and walked to one side, holding the other over Lady Molly. Denise and I followed.

There was a flintstone wall, an old gray-stone church on the other side, cypress trees, and a clump of beech trees. Zec opened a gate, and we passed through into the graveyard. We followed a narrow path between gravestones, many obviously very ancient. Finally we stopped in the far corner, under a cypress tree. The grave there was well tended. There were fresh flowers, the grass carefully cut. The headstone was a slab of Cornish slate and the inscription cut into its face was stamped in gold.

"Here we are." She smiled and held Tarquin tightly.

It said MARCH 1945. IN LOVING MEMORY OF COLONEL HARRY KELSO AND HIS BROTHER, OBERSTLEUTNANT BARON MAX VON HALDER. TOGETHER AT LAST. BROTHERS-IN-ARMS.

The rain increased, and Zec moved close, holding the umbrella, something indomitable about him as he stood there, an arm about Lady Molly. Denise was fighting to hold back the tears.

Lady Molly turned. "Don't be sorry, my dear. It was a long, long time ago, and now that it doesn't matter, I'm going to tell you something that even dear Zec here never knew."

Zec frowned, puzzled, and we stood there and waited.

"As you discovered, back in 1930, when their father died and the boys were twelve, Elsa struck a bargain that she would return to Germany with her eldest son, Max the baron, and Harry would stay with his grandfather."

"That's right," I said.

"Harry gave me a different version. He told me just before he died. I've always felt he saw death coming. He told me that when the decision was put to the boys, they didn't like the idea. And there was a further problem—Tarquin, the bear who'd flown in France with their father. Who got Tarquin? All this was between the boys. Abe and their mother knew nothing of it."

"What did they do?" I asked.

"Decided that Tarquin must stay in America in the house their father had been born in. Then they tossed a coin to see who would go to Germany with their mother."

Zec looked stunned, and Denise said, "Oh, no!"

"Yes, my dear," Molly said. "Harry Kelso was Baron von Halder, and Max was Harry Kelso."

It was the most astonishing thing I'd ever heard. It took my breath away. It was Denise who said, "Together at last. But in a way, they always were."

"Exactly." Lady Molly smiled. "We'll go back now." And she walked ahead of us, Zec holding the umbrella over her.

WE SAID our good-byes, and Zec drove us to the airstrip. He shook hands and kissed Denise on the cheek. "Take care, girl."

We got into the Archer. Denise sat on the left-hand side, and I locked the door. As she switched on and the engine rumbled, rain lashed across, and there was mist out there on the sea. "We'd better move it," she said. "It'll get worse before it gets better."

We roared down the runway and lifted into the gray sky, climbed to a thousand feet, and then suddenly she banked to port.

"What are you doing?" I asked.

"I just want a last look."

But as we turned over the sea and moved back to the land, the mist had already rolled in. Of Cold Harbour, there was no sign. It was as if it had never been.

LaVyrle Spencer

Then Came Heaven

*B*rowerville, Minnesota.

It's a caring, close-knit town. So when a tragic accident leaves Eddie Olczak to raise his two little girls alone, friends and neighbors take care of everything.

Everything, that is, but the loneliness.

Chapter 1

CYRIL Case was making the daily run from St. Cloud to Cass Lake, sitting up high on his box seat in engine number 282. Beside him, his fireman, Merle Ficker, rode with one arm out the window, his striped denim cap pushed clean back, so the bill pointed skyward. It was a beautiful morning—sunny, the heavens deep blue, farmers out in their fields taking in the last of their crops, most harvesting with tractors. They'd passed a country school a couple miles back, where the kids, out for recess, waved from the playground and their teacher, a slim young thing in a yellow dress, had stopped gathering wildflowers and fanned her handful of black-eyed Susans over her head as she watched them pass. It was days like this that made driving a freight train the best job in the world—green woods, gold fields, and the smell of fresh-cut alfalfa blowing straight through the cab.

Cy and Merle were having another one of their friendly disagreements about politics. "Well, sure," Merle was saying, "I voted for Truman, but I didn't think he'd send our boys to Korea!"

"What else you gonna do?" Cy replied. "Those Communists go in and start bombing Seoul. Can't let 'em get by with that, can we?"

"Well, maybe not, but you ain't got a nineteen-year-old son, and I do! Now Truman goes and extends the draft till next year. Heck,

I don't want Rodney to get called up." Merle pointed. "Whistle post up ahead."

"I see it."

Ahead on the right, the arm of the white marker shone clear against the pure blue sky. Cy reached up and pulled a rope. The steam whistle battered their ears in a long wail: two longs, a short, and a long—the warning for a public crossing.

The whistle post flashed past, and the long wail ended, leaving them in comparative quiet.

"So," Cy continued, "I suppose your boy's gonna go to work for the railroad if he doesn't get—" He stiffened and stared up the track. "Good Lord, he ain't gonna make it!"

A car had turned off Highway 71 and came shooting from the left, trailing a dust cloud, trying to beat the train to the crossing.

For one heartbeat the men stared; then Cy shouted, "Car on the crossing! Plug it!"

Merle jumped and hit the air brakes. Cy grabbed the Johnson bar and squeezed for dear life. With his other hand he hauled on the steam whistle. Machinery ground into reverse, and the brakes grabbed. From the engine through the entire train, everything locked in a deafening screech. Steam hissed as if the door of hell had opened.

"Hold on, Merle. We're gonna hit 'em!" Cy bellowed.

"Jesus, Mary, Joseph," Merle chanted as the train skated and shrieked and the puny car raced toward its destination.

At thirty yards they knew for sure.

At twenty they braced.

At ten they saw the driver.

"Dear God, it's a woman," Cy said. Or thought. Or prayed.

Then they collided.

Sound exploded and glass flew. Metal crunched as the gray '49 Ford wrapped around the cowcatcher. Together they cannonballed down the tracks, the ruptured car folded over the metal grid, chunks of it dragging along half severed, tearing up earth, strewing wreckage for hundreds of yards.

Slower . . . slower. All those tons of steel took forever to decelerate while the two terrified railroad men rode it out and listened to the fading squeal that dissolved into a whine.

Then a whimper. Then silence.

Cy and Merle sat as rigid as a pair of connecting rods, exchanging a shocked, silent stare. Number 282 had carried the Ford a good half mile down the railroad tracks and sat now, calmly chuffing, like a big old contented whale coming up for air.

Merle finally found his voice. "No way that woman's gonna be alive."

"Let's go!" Cy barked.

They scrambled from the cab, bellies to the ladder, free sliding down the grab rails. From the caboose, twenty cars back, the conductor and a brakeman came running—two bouncing dots in the distance—shouting, "What happened?"

Running alongside the locomotive, Cy yelled to Merle, "Look there, the engine's hardly damaged," but when the two men rounded the snout of the engine, they halted dead in their tracks.

It was a sickening sight, that car flattened as if for a junkyard. The coupler at the front of the cowcatcher had actually pierced the automobile and protruded like a shining silver eye. Some broken glass remained in the driver's-side window, jagged as lightning.

Cy moved close and peered in.

She was brown-haired. Young. Pretty. Or had been. Wearing a nice little blue-flowered housedress. Surrounded by broken fruit jars. Cy closed his mind to the rest and reached in to see if she was still alive. After a minute he withdrew his hand. "I think she's dead."

"You sure?"

"No pulse that I can feel."

Merle was as colorless as whey. His lips moved silently, but not a sound came out. Cy could see he'd have to take charge.

"We're gonna need a jack to get her out of there," he told Merle. "You better run to the highway and flag down a car. Tell 'em to run to Browerville and get help"—Merle was already hustling off at an ungainly trot—"and have 'em call the sheriff in Long Prairie."

At that moment the conductor and brakeman reached Cy.

"He dead?" one of them asked.

"She. It's a woman. Couldn't feel any pulse."

They stood motionless, absorbing the shock.

"Better get the fusees out," Cy told the brakeman.

"Sure thing." The brakeman headed up the track to the north to set out the warning for any southbound trains. Another brakeman walked a mile off the rear of the train and did the same.

"Her license plates are gone, but she's got a purse," Cy said dully. "I saw it under her—" He quit talking and swallowed hard.

"Want me to get it, Cy?" asked the conductor.

"No, that's—that's all right. I will," he said as Merle returned.

Cy steeled himself and retrieved the purse of the dead woman. He wiped it off on the leg of his blue-and-white striped overalls.

They all looked down at it in Cy's oversized hands. It was a little wedge-shaped white plastic affair with hard sides.

Cy opened it and looked inside. He picked things out very gingerly, then set them back in with the greatest care: a clean white handkerchief, a rosary with blue glass beads, a pack of Sen-Sen. And a small black prayer book, which he examined more slowly. Stuck into its pages was a recipe for Washday Pickles, written on the back of an envelope. A name was written on the front of the envelope, with its canceled three-cent stamp and its simple address of Browerville, Minn. The same name was written on the inside cover of the prayer book and on a Social Security card they found in a small pocketbook, which also held some school pictures of two little girls.

Her name was Krystyna Olczak.

EVERYBODY in Browerville knew Eddie Olczak. Everybody in Browerville liked him. He was the eighth or ninth kid of Hedwig and Casimir Olczak, Polish immigrants from out east of town. Eighth or ninth, they said, because Hedy and Cass had fourteen, and when there are that many in one family, the order can get a little jumbled. Eddie lived half a block off Main Street, in the oldest house in town. He had fixed it up real nice when he married that cute little Krystyna Pribil, whose folks farmed just off the Clarissa

Highway out north of town. Richard and Mary Pribil had seven kids of their own, but everybody remembered Krystyna best because she had been the Todd County Dairy Princess the summer before she married Eddie.

The children around town knew Eddie because he was the janitor at St. Joseph's Catholic Church and had been for twelve years. He took care of the parochial school as well, so his tall, thin figure was a familiar sight, moving around the parish property, pushing dust mops, hauling milk bottles, ringing the church bells at all hours of the day and night. He lived a scant block and a half from church, so when the Angelus needed ringing, he ran to church and rang it.

The bells of St. Joseph's pretty much regulated the activities of the entire town, for nearly everybody in Browerville was Catholic. Folks passing through often said how amazing it was that a little burg with only eight hundred people boasted not just one Catholic church, but two! There was St. Peter's at the south end of town, but St. Joe's had been there first and was Polish. And St. Peter's lacked the commanding presence of St. Joseph's, with its grandiose neo-baroque structure, onion-shaped minarets, Corinthian columns, and five splendid altars.

At seven thirty each weekday morning Eddie rang what was simply referred to as the first bell: six monotone clangs to give everyone a half-hour warning that church would soon start. At eight a.m. he rang all three bells in unison to start Mass. At precisely noon he was there to toll the Angelus—twelve peals on a single bell that stopped all of downtown for lunch. During summer vacation every kid in town knew that when he heard the noon Angelus ring, he had five minutes to get home to dinner or he'd be in big trouble! And at the end of each workday, though Eddie himself was usually home by five thirty, he ran back to church at six to ring the evening Angelus, which sat the entire town down to supper. On Sunday mornings, when both High and Low Mass were celebrated, he rang one additional time, then again for Sunday vespers. And on Saturday evenings, for the rosary and benediction, he was there, too, before the service.

Bells were required at special times of the year as well. It was also

Polish Catholic tradition that whenever somebody died, the death toll rang once for each year the person had lived.

Given all this ringing, and the requirement that sometimes a minute of silence had to pass between each pull on the rope, Eddie had grown not only regimented but patient as well.

Working around the children had taught him an even deeper form of patience. They spilled milk in the lunchroom, dropped chalky erasers on the floor, licked the frost off the windowpanes in the winter, clomped in with mud on their shoes in the spring, and stuck their forbidden bubble gum beneath their desks.

But Eddie didn't care. He loved the children. And this year he had both of his own in Sister Regina's room—Anne, nine, in the fourth grade and Lucy, eight, in the third. He had seen them outside at morning recess a little while ago, playing drop the hanky on the rolling green playground. Sister Regina had been out there with them, playing too, her black veils luffing in the autumn breeze.

They were back inside now, the drift of their childish voices no longer floating across the pleasant morning as Eddie did autumn cleanup around the grounds. He was a contented man as he loaded a wheelbarrow with tools and pushed it over to clean out the goldfish pond in Father Kuzdek's front yard. It was an immense yard, situated south of the church, with the rectory set well back from the street. Sometimes the Knights of Columbus helped him mow and trim the lawns. They had done so last Saturday, the same loyal workhorses showing up as they always did.

Eddie was on his knees at the fishpond when he was surprised to see one of those workhorses, Conrad Kaluza, coming up Father's sidewalk. Eddie sat back on his heels and waited.

"Well, Con, what the heck are you doing up here at this time of day? Come to help me clean out this slimy fishpond?"

Con looked pale and shaken. He squatted down beside the pond. Eddie noticed the muscles around his mouth quivering.

"What's the matter, Con?"

"Eddie, I'm afraid I got some bad news. There's, ah . . ." Con paused and cleared his throat. "There's been an accident."

Eddie tensed and looked southward, toward his house. His backside lifted off his heels. "Krystyna . . ."

" 'Fraid so," Con said.

"She okay, Con?"

Con cleared his throat again and dragged in a deep breath.

"I'm—I'm afraid not, Eddie. A train hit her car at the crossing out by her folks' place."

"*Yezhush, Maree-uh,*" Eddie said in Polish, and made the sign of the cross. He made himself ask, "How bad is it?"

When Con failed to reply, Eddie shouted, "She's alive, isn't she, Con?" He gripped Con's arms. "She's just hurt, isn't she?"

Con's mouth worked, and when he spoke, his voice sounded wheezy and unnatural.

"This is the hardest thing I ever had to say to anybody."

"Oh, God, Con, no."

"She's dead, Eddie. May her soul rest in peace."

Eddie's face contorted, and he began rocking forward and backward. "She can't be. She's"—Eddie looked north toward his inlaws'—"she's out at her ma's house, canning pickles. She and her ma were . . . Oh, Con, no, no. Not Krystyna!"

Eddie started weeping. "Not my Krystyna," he wailed.

Con waited awhile, then urged, "Come on, Eddie, let's go tell Father, and he'll say a prayer with you."

Eddie let himself be hauled to his feet but turned toward the school building on the far side of the church. "The girls . . ."

"Not now, Eddie. Let's go see Father first, okay?"

Father Kuzdek answered the door himself, a massive, balding Polish man in a black cassock. He was in his early forties, with wire-rimmed glasses like President Truman's denting the sides of his round pink face.

"Con, Eddie . . . what's wrong?"

"There's been an accident, Father," Con told him. "It's Krystyna. Her car was hit by the train."

Father went still. "*Kyrie, eleison,*" he whispered. Lord, have mercy. "Is she dead?"

Con could do no more than nod.

Father Kuzdek caught Eddie around the shoulders with one beefy arm. "Ah, Eddie, Eddie, what a tragedy. This is terrible. So young, your Krystyna, and such a good woman."

Father made a cross in the air over Eddie's head and murmured in Latin. He laid both of his huge hands on Eddie's head and went on praying, ending in English, "The Lord bless you in this time of travail." Father dropped his hands to Eddie's shoulders and said, "I ask you to remember, my son, that it's not ours to question why and when the Lord chooses to take those we love. He has His reasons, Eddie."

Eddie, still weeping, bobbed his head.

Father dropped his hands and asked Con, "Where?"

"The junction of County Road 89 and Highway 71, north of town."

"I'll get my things."

Father Kuzdek came back wearing his black biretta, carrying a small leather case containing his holy oils. They followed him to his garage. He backed out his black Buick, and Eddie got into the front, Con into the back.

Father turned left onto the highway. When he said, driving toward the scene of the accident, "Let us pray," they did.

THEY spotted the red warning clouds from the fusees long before they saw the train itself. They passed the caboose—even it had cleared the crossing—and paralleled the train until they saw, up ahead on the shoulder of the highway, a gathering of vehicles: Constable Cecil Monnie's Chevrolet, a truck from Leo Reamer's D-X station, the sheriff's car, and Iten & Heid's hearse. Browerville was too small to have a hospital, so when the need arose, Ed Iten used his hearse as an ambulance.

As Father slowed down, Eddie stared. "It pushed her all this way?" he said, dazed. Then he saw his car, flattened and ripped and peeled off the locomotive in sections. Beside the train a body was laid out on a stretcher.

He left the Buick and stumbled through hip-high grass, down a ditch, up the other side, with Father and Con close on his heels. The conductor, with his clipboard, stopped gathering accident data for the railroad company and stood in silent respect, watching the party of three arrive.

Never again would Eddie Olczak fear hell, for on that day, while he knelt beside Krystyna's body, he experienced a hell so unmerciful that nothing in this life or the next could hurt more.

"Oh, Krystyna." He wept, as the souls in purgatory surely wept, to be set free from the pain and the loss. With his face contorted, he looked up at those standing above him and asked, "How am I going to tell my little girls? What will they do without her? What will any of us do without her?" They didn't know what to say, but stood by, feeling the shock of mortality come to stun them, too. Father Kuzdek kissed and donned his stole and dropped to one knee to pray.

"*In nomine Patris . . .*"

Eddie listened to the murmuring of Father's voice as he administered extreme unction. He watched Father's oversized thumb anoint his wife's forehead with oils and make the sign of the cross.

Krystyna's parents came and her sister Irene, and they clung to Eddie in a forlorn, weeping band and fell to their knees on the cinders, keening and rocking while Eddie repeated the same thing over and over. "Sh-she was on her way out to your house, Mary. That's where she should be right now. She should be at your house." And they stared through their tears at the wreckage of the fruit jars strewed along the railroad tracks, reflecting the noon sun like waves on a lake.

When they'd had time for weeping, Father gave a blessing to Mary, Richard, and Irene, and the stretcher was borne to the hearse, trailed by the bereaved. When the doors of the hearse closed, Mary asked her son-in-law, "Have you told Anne and Lucy yet?"

"Not yet." The thought started Eddie crying again, dully, and Krystyna's father clamped an arm around his shoulders.

"Do you want us with you when you do?" Mary asked.

"I—I don't know."

"We'll come with you, Eddie, if you want," Irene put in.

"I don't know," he repeated with an exhausted sigh.

Father Kuzdek stepped in and said, "Come, Eddie. We'll tell the children together, you and I, and then you and Mary and Richard and Irene can all take them home."

"Yes," Eddie agreed, grateful to have someone tell him what to do next. "Yes, thank you, Father."

The little group dispersed to the various cars, a new dread spreading through them. They all knew that as difficult as the last hour had been, the next one would be worse, telling the children.

Chapter 2

SISTER Regina rang the brass handbell and waited beside the west door for the children to come in from recess. They came barreling down off the hilly playground and gathered on the narrow sidewalk that connected the schoolhouse with the convent. Double file they lined up, the obedient ones doing so quickly while the troublemakers jostled and aggravated. When all of them were in rank and file, she led the way inside. Some children detoured to the bathrooms while Sister placed the brass bell on one end of the parapet where it remained while not in use—and woe to the student who touched it without permission! She waited beside the drinking fountain outside her room, her hands hidden inside her sleeves, monitoring their return to classes.

St. Joseph's Parochial School was laid out symmetrically, with three rooms on either side of a central gymnasium, divided from it by a thick parapet topped with square columns that created a hall on either side. Each hall had two classrooms holding two grades apiece. At the northwest corner was the lunchroom, at the southwest corner the flower room, where the nuns raised plants for the altar.

At the east end the gym gave onto a storage room. At the opposite end was a stage with an ancient canvas curtain sporting a tableau of a Venetian canal and gondolas. Countless piano recitals had been held on that stage, for musical training was so vital a part of the curriculum at St. Joseph's that the gym had been named Paderewski Hall, in honor of Poland's famous composer.

Sister Regina held her classroom door open for the last straggler, who tested her patience by continuing to guzzle water at the hall fountain. "That's enough, Michael. Come along."

He took three more gulps, then swiped his face with the back of a hand as she swept him inside her room with the closing door.

She clapped her hands twice, then folded them. "All right, boys and girls, let's stand and begin our afternoon with a prayer."

The shuffling subsided, and the room grew quiet.

"In the name of the Father, and of the Son and of the Holy Ghost . . ." Thirty-five children made the sign of the cross with her. When the prayer ended, they took their seats with a sound like a flock of geese landing while Sister walked around her desk to face them. She was a tall, thin woman with pale skin and kind hazel eyes. Her eyebrows were the light brown of summer corn silk and her lips as prettily curved as the top of an apple. Even when she was displeased, her expression never grew grim, nor did her lips lose their forgiving lift. When she spoke, her voice was filled with patience and quietude.

"Third graders, you're going to work on your spelling." Her two rows of third graders occupied the right half of the room. She passed out work sheets and got them busy. She had gathered her fourth graders around her desk to work on their arithmetic tables, when someone knocked on the door. The interruption signaled a swell of chatter, and she shushed the children as she moved to answer.

In the hall Father Kuzdek stood with Eddie Olczak.

"Good afternoon, Father. Good afternoon, Mr. Olczak." She could tell immediately something was terribly wrong.

"Sister, I'm sorry to interrupt your class," Father said. "Could you shut the door, please?" Father was recognizably distraught, and Eddie had been crying. When the door closed, Father said, "We've brought some very bad news. There's been an accident. Eddie's wife was killed by a train this morning."

Sister Regina gasped softly, and her hand flew to her lips. "Oh no." She made the sign of the cross, then broke a cardinal rule by touching a layman. "Oh, Mr. Olczak," she whispered, laying a hand on his sleeve. "Not your lovely wife. I'm so sorry. What—what happened?" She looked to Father for an answer.

"She was driving," the priest replied. "It appears that she was, ah"—he swallowed and bumped his glasses up to clear his teary eyes—"she was trying to beat the train to the crossing on her way out to her folks' house."

Sister felt the shock rush through her. Of all the women in the parish, Krystyna Olczak was the one the nuns relied on the most for help. One of the most cheerful, pleasant ladies in town. "Oh, dear me, this is so terrible."

Eddie tried to speak, but his voice was choked. "I have to . . ." He had to clear his throat and start again. "I have to tell the girls."

"Yes, of course," Sister whispered, but she made no move to return to the classroom and get them. She found herself reluctant to watch their happiness be shattered. They were such lovely children, Mr. Olczak's girls—carefree, polite, above-average students, with Krystyna's sweet disposition, who never caused problems in the classroom or on the playground. They were children who were fussed over at home, clothed in pretty dresses that their mother made herself and kept starched and ironed to perfection. Many days Anne and Lucy came across the school grounds holding hands, their hair fixed in ringlets or French braids, their shoes polished and their hot-lunch money tied into the corners of their cloth handkerchiefs. Their mother had taken pride in them, sending them off looking like little Shirley Temples, and when the Olczak family walked into church together on Sundays, everybody watched them and smiled.

But now she was dead. How unthinkable.

Poor little children, Sister thought. Poor Mr. Olczak.

Eddie Olczak was a simple, diligent, easygoing man whom Sister Regina had never heard criticized for anything. He had worked as the church janitor since before she came here four years ago. Tens of times a week she heard people say, "Ask Eddie," or—if it was a nun speaking—"Ask Mr. Olczak." Whatever anyone requested, he provided without complaint. He didn't talk much, but he was always there when needed.

It felt peculiar to see this man cry, to see him needing help. Yet here he was, standing in the hall weeping, with Father's arm around his shoulders. He swiped his eyes and tried to summon the fortitude to have his children brought into the hall.

"I'll be all right," he managed in a cracked voice, drawing a red hanky from his back pocket. "I've . . ." He cleared his throat and blew his nose. "I've just got to get through this, that's all."

Father said, "Please get the children, Sister."

Give me strength, O Lord, she prayed, turning back into her classroom to carry out the hardest assignment she'd ever had.

She sent the fourth graders back to their desks, all but Anne Olczak. Anne was a thoughtful child. She had pretty blue eyes and brown hair, parted in the middle today and drawn back with matching barrettes. Her dress was green-and-brown plaid with a white collar. Sister Regina touched her shoulder and felt a welling inside such as she'd never experienced before, made up of empathy and love for this child who had bid her mother good-bye this morning with absolute trust that she'd be there at home waiting at the end of the school day.

Who would be there for her and Lucy from now on?

Halfway down the aisle closest to the windows Lucy was laboring over her spelling words, gripping her pencil and concentrating so hard that the tip of her tongue was showing. Lucy was dressed today in a starched yellow dress. She resembled her older sister but with a smattering of freckles and one dimple in her left cheek. Teachers were not supposed to have favorites, but Sister Regina couldn't help favoring the Olczak children.

Sister Regina stopped beside Lucy and leaned down to whisper,

"Lucy, your father is here to talk to you and your sister. Will you come out into the hall with me?"

Lucy looked up. "Yes, Sister," she whispered. She laid her yellow pencil in the groove at the top of her desk, slid from her seat, and led the way to the door for the three of them. Sister Regina opened it and followed the children into the hall, her heart heavy with dread.

Anne and Lucy smiled and said, "Hi, Daddy!" going to him as if he'd come to take them out of school early on some lark.

Eddie dropped to one knee and opened his arms. "Hi, angels." His little girls hugged his neck, while his face reflected torture.

Sister Regina watched their daddy's arms go around their waists and crush the bows on the sashes that their mommy had tied for the last time ever, that morning before they left for school. He kissed their foreheads hard and clung to their small bodies while Sister pressed the edge of her folded hands against her lips and told herself she must not cry. A line from the Scriptures went through her mind: *Suffer the little children to come unto me,* and she committed a venial sin by questioning God's wisdom in taking their mother. Why a good and young woman like that? Why Krystyna Olczak when she was needed here by her family?

Eddie sat back on his heels and looked into his children's faces. "Anne, Lucy . . . there's something that Daddy's got to tell you."

They saw his tears and sobered.

"Daddy, what's wrong?" Anne asked, her hand on his shoulder.

"Well, honey . . ." Against her small back his open hand looked immense. It covered the plaid of her dress while he cleared his throat, trying to make himself say the words that would alter their lives forever. "Jesus has decided to—to take your mommy to heaven."

Anne stared at him silently. Her mouth tightened slightly.

Lucy said matter-of-factly, "No. Mommy's at Grandma's making pickles. She said that's where she was going today."

Eddie forged on. "No, sweetheart, she's not. She wanted to go there, and she started to go there, but she never made it."

"She *din't?*" Lucy's eyes got wide with bemusement, still no fear. "But how come?"

"A train hit her car at the railroad crossing, and Mommy died." His last words were uttered in a ragged whisper.

"She did not!" Anne spouted angrily. "She's at Grandma's!" She turned and looked up at Father Kuzdek, the ultimate authority figure at St. Joseph's. "My mommy didn't die, did she, Father? Tell my daddy that it's not true. She's making pickles at my grandma's."

Father Kuzdek struggled to lower his considerable bulk down on one knee, his cassock puddling on the floor. "We don't know why Jesus took your mommy, Anne, but it's true. She's in heaven now with the angels, and what you have to remember is that she'll always be there looking out for you, your own special guardian angel who loved you and took care of you while she was here on earth. Only now she'll do the same thing from heaven."

Annie wheeled and flung herself against her father, who was still kneeling, burying her face against his shoulder.

Lucy asked timidly, "What's wrong with Annie, Daddy?"

Sister Regina had begun crying, her young, smooth, unlined face remaining serene while tears ran down her cheeks and wet the starched white wimple beneath her chin. She knew not for whom she felt the more pity, this father or his children. Though she had never longed for secular liberties, she suddenly wished for the freedom to open her arms and embrace them, the father included. But it was not done, of course. *The Rule of Benedict,* the book by which the nuns lived, forbade physical contact with the secular. Thus she stood in silent prayer, asking for strength for herself and the Olczaks.

Father Kuzdek drew Sister Regina aside and said, "Under the circumstances, Sister, I think we should excuse classes for the remainder of the day."

"Yes, Father."

"I'll speak to your students first."

"Yes, Father."

They left the Olczaks in the hall and entered her classroom, where some disorder had naturally taken over. Father's appearance immediately silenced the children and sent them scuttling for their seats. "Good afternoon, children," he said.

"Good afternoon, Father," they chorused in a singsong.

"Boys and girls," he began, then studied the hardwood floor where a streak of sunlight turned the boards the yellow of honey. "You all know what death is, now, don't you? We've taught you how important it is to be in a state of grace when you die. We never know when we're going to die, do we?" He went on, incorporating a catechism lesson into what he had to tell them. When he finally divulged that Lucy and Anne's mother had died today, Sister Regina sensed the change in them. Some of them contorted their faces, lifting eyebrows, biting lower lips, expressing their dismay wordlessly. Others stared at him, disbelieving.

Father Kuzdek gave them time to acclimate to the news, continuing his lecture for several minutes, then announced that school would be closing for the remainder of the day and they'd all be going home as soon as the school buses could be recalled. He ended, as always, with a prayer. "In the name of the Father . . ."

Sister Regina made the sign of the cross and folded her hands. Father asked the children to be quiet and obedient while he and Sister left the room. He asked her to go to the other three classrooms and inform the other nuns that school was being dismissed and why.

Returning to the hall, Sister was not at all surprised to find that two of Eddie's brothers and their wives had already heard the news and had arrived, along with some older nieces and nephews and one of Krystyna's sisters, Irene Pribil, who was weeping copiously in Eddie's arms. Krystyna's parents were there, too, hugging their grandchildren and weeping. Browerville was so small that it took no time at all for the word to spread that one of its young had died tragically. Krystyna Olczak was especially well loved by the women of the town. She took in sewing and gave home permanents in her kitchen to earn pin money. She contributed pies and cakes for bake sales and drove the nuns to Long Prairie when they needed their eyes checked and took carloads of children out to Horseshoe Lake in the summer to swim. She was to the town's society what Eddie was to St. Joseph's—the one you could always call on to do more than her share.

It was Eddie's brother Sylvester who said, "Nobody's rung the death toll yet. You take the kids home, Eddie, and I'll do it."

Eddie—dry-eyed now but trembling—replied, "No, Sylvester. I want to do it myself. She was my wife and now she's gone and I've rung that bell for everybody that's died for the last twelve years and now I'm going to ring it for her. I got to, see? Thank you for offering, but this"—Eddie's voice broke—"this is my job. I'd appreciate it, though, if you'd take Anne and Lucy home."

"All right, Eddie," Sylvester said, gripping his arm.

"Girls," Eddie said, dropping down to one knee. "You go with Uncle Sylvester and everybody, and I'll be there in a little bit, okay?"

"All right, Daddy," Anne said, "but I have to get my sweater first."

"Me, too," added Lucy.

Sister Regina was back in her room, leading her children in a final prayer, when the door opened and Lucy and Anne came in.

The prayer stopped, and the room fell silent.

Anne said, "We have to get our sweaters."

The two girls walked sedately, as they'd been taught—no running in the schoolhouse—to their desks and got their sweaters from the backs of their seats. Their classmates stared at them in mute fascination, unsure of what was expected of them.

On their way out Lucy stopped before her teacher, looked up, and crooked her finger. Sister Regina leaned down so Lucy could whisper in her ear. "My mommy died, so we have to go home."

Anne nudged her and whispered, "Come on, Lucy, let's go."

Sister Regina thought her heart would explode at the words of this child who still did not understand the import of today's tragedy. Again she wanted to put her arms around her—around both children—and comfort them and thereby comfort herself as well.

But Holy Rule forbade it.

Instead, she could only say, "I shall pray for you both."

Somehow, today, the promise of mere prayer felt inadequate.

EVERYBODY faded away and left Eddie, as he wished. Lucy and Anne went off with his brothers Sylvester and Romaine and their wives, Marjorie and Rose, and the rest of the relatives. The school buses came, and the students were dismissed.

Alone at last, Eddie stood in the gloom of Paderewski Hall. Tears leaked down his cheeks, but he hadn't the energy to wipe them away. Instead, he buried his hands in the deep pockets of his overalls and walked next door to the church.

He entered through one of the center doors. It closed behind him, sealing him into the vestibule with its stuffy silent smell. It was the smell of aged wood and snuffed candles and of old-country traditions brought here by his Polish immigrant grandparents, and the grandparents of his peers, before the turn of the century.

The bell ropes hung to his left, beside a radiator, three of them, suspended from an ornate tower one hundred and fifty-two feet above his head. He knew which rope played the lowest most morose note. The rope was thick as a cow's tail, worn smooth and oiled by his hands over these last twelve years.

It took a surprising amount of effort to swing an inert bell that large, but Eddie had done it so often it was second nature to him.

Today, however, when his hands gripped the rope, nothing happened. I can do this, he thought. I will do it for Krystyna.

His grip tightened. His shoulders rounded. His eyes stung.

Bonng.

The bell tolled once for the first year of her life, born on the bed in her parents' room, out on the farm where they still lived.

He waited a full minute, the longest minute of his life.

Bonng.

The bell tolled again for the second year of her life, when . . . Surely this was all a mistake. Surely when he finished and walked home, Krystyna would be there, the same as always, wearing an apron, standing at the kitchen table, setting some woman's hair in pin curls. But no more. No more.

Bonnng.

Twenty-seven times he rang that bell. Twenty-seven minutes it took him to tell the town she was gone, while he remained dry-eyed and stoic in the face of duty. And then, at the end, according to custom,

he grasped all three ropes at once, sending up a glorious tintinnabu-
lation of rejoicing—*life everlasting, amen!*—and it was then, as he
rang the bells in unison, that Eddie finally broke. Surrounded by
the deafening sound, his tears came all at once and, with them, anger
and condemnation. He hauled on those ropes as if to punish them,
or himself, or to curse a fate too cruel to be borne, sometimes hauling so hard that the weight of the bells pulled his boots several inches
off the floor, weeping and howling out his sorrow and rage where
only God and Krystyna could see him, while above his head the bells
poured forth a celebration of her arrival in heaven.

Chapter 3

EDDIE might have thought all the nuns went to the convent after the school buses left, but Sister Regina did
not; she returned to her schoolroom. She knew Mr. Olczak was going
to ring his wife's death knell. The sound of the first bell and the picture of him ringing it drove her to her knees in profound sympathy.

It was there Mother Agnes found her, with her back to the door,
her forehead on her sleeve, and her sleeve on the edge of the desk.

"Sister Regina?"

She lifted her head, discreetly wiped her eyes, and turned.

"Yes, Reverend Mother?"

Mother Agnes was in her late fifties, with a prominent chin,
ruddy complexion, and pale blue eyes that were huge and watery
behind thick glasses. "Have you forgotten matins and lauds?"

"No, Mother, I haven't."

"Ah," Mother Agnes said, then stood thoughtfully for a moment.
"We waited for you."

"I'm sorry, Reverend Mother. I beg your indulgence. I wish to stay here awhile, in the school. I feel that I need some time alone." Permission was needed for everything that differed from commonality within the religious community. Matins and lauds were the ultimate example of commonality: universal prayers being sent up by every religious the world over at the same time of day. One did not ask to be alone to pray matins and lauds when your community was doing it together. To do so was to break your vow of obedience.

A truly obedient nun would have followed her superior without a word, and this is what Mother Agnes expected. She had been a member of the Order of St. Benedict much longer than Sister Regina, and she understood the value of giving up *self* to serve God. Sister Regina had not fully learned how to give up self.

"It's the children, isn't it?" Mother Agnes asked.

"Yes, Mother, it is." Sister Regina rose and faced her superior.

"You aren't forgetting what Holy Rule says?" Mother Agnes referred to *The Rule of Benedict* by its common name.

"No, Mother, I'm not." Holy Rule said familiarity with the secular was to be avoided.

"At times such as these, when one feels compelled to offer sympathy, your concern for the Olczak girls would be better directed toward prayer than grief, and the sublimation of your own sorrow toward the greater glory of God."

Sister Regina felt a flutter of resentment. She'd had Anne in her third-grade class last year and had tried very hard not to favor her, but within her black habit beat a very human heart that could not help being warmed by the child. Now this year, not only did she have Anne again, but along came little Lucy, equally beguiling. To see them lose their mother was the most traumatic thing Sister Regina had experienced. To be told she should sublimate her feelings brought her such a piercing wish to rebel that she felt it best to keep silent.

Both nuns knew all of this as the death bell sounded again. Furthermore, they both knew that Sister Regina had taken vows of poverty, chastity, and obedience, and that of the three, obedience had always been the most difficult for her to swallow. She could not understand how subduing her grief today could do her soul or those of the Olczak children any good. What she wanted to do was weep for them and do it alone.

Mother Agnes, however, had other ideas. "So you'll return to the convent for meditation, Sister?" Meditation always followed matins and lauds.

"Yes, Mother."

"Very well, then." Sister Regina knelt to receive Mother Superior's blessing; then the two of them left the schoolroom together. While they trod the silent hall in their high-topped black shoes, the death bell rang again, and Sister Agnes said, "Remember, Sister Regina, we must not question God's will."

"Yes, Mother."

They left the yellow brick schoolhouse and walked side by side, entering the square white clapboard house thirty feet away.

They passed into the central hall and up the hardwood steps to the second story, past the row of closed bedroom doors to the tiny chapel on the northwest corner.

Inside the chapel six nuns knelt on six prie-dieus. Two other prie-dieus waited, empty. Sister Agnes knelt on one, Sister Regina on the other. Not a word was spoken. Not a veil fluttered in the absolute stillness of the chapel. At the front of the room, above a miniature altar, a pair of candles burned at the foot of an alabaster crucifix. The light from a pair of north-facing windows was muted by stretched brown lace that tinted the chapel the dim, rusty hue of tea.

Neither the elbow rests nor the kneelers of the prie-dieus were padded. Sister Regina knelt on the unforgiving oak and felt a pain telegraph clear up to her hip joints. She offered it up for the faithful departed and in the hope that she might more gracefully fulfill her vows. One of those was the vow of poverty: Austerity and a lack of creature comforts—presently, padded kneelers—were part of that poverty. She accepted this the way she accepted the sky being blue. As part of her life as a Benedictine nun, and after eleven years since entering the postulate, she no longer thought of the softness of the furniture at home or the luxury of drinking all the warm milk she wanted straight from the cow. She folded her hands, closed her eyes, and bowed her head, like her sisters.

Meditation had begun. It was a time in which it was possible to get closest to God, but to do that, one had to grow empty of self and full of His divine love.

It was while Sister Regina was attempting to empty herself of self that the three church bells began pealing in unison, signifying the beginning of life everlasting for Krystyna Olczak. At their celebratory note Sister Regina's head came up and her eyes opened. It was he ringing them, Mr. Olczak—but, oh, how could he bear it?

She found herself doing exactly what Reverend Mother had warned her not to do—questioning Krystyna's death. She longed to discuss it with her grandmother Rosella, the most deeply religious person the young Regina Potlocki had ever known. Grandma never questioned God's will. It was Grandma Rosella who had been unshakably certain that it was God's will young Regina become a nun.

There had been a moment, watching the Olczak girls leaving with their aunts and uncles and grandparents and cousins, that Sister Regina had wished she, too, could be folded into the wings of her family, just for this one day. But she had given up all temporal ties to family when she'd taken her vows. Holy Rule allowed home visits only once every five years. Her family was now these seven other nuns who lived, worked, and prayed together in this convent.

She opened her eyes, examining them as discreetly as possible.

Sister Dora, who taught first and second grades, the most animated and happy of them all. She was a gifted teacher. Although Holy Rule forbade special friendships within a community, Sister Dora was Sister Regina's favorite.

Sister Mary Charles, grades five and six, a tyrant who elicited satisfaction out of whipping the naughty children with a strip of rubber floor tile in the flower room. Sister Regina thought that what Sister Mary Charles needed was for someone to whale the tar out of *her* backside and see if she might change her ways.

Sister Gregory, the piano teacher, fat as a Yorkshire pig on market day, who declined dessert every night under the pretext of offering it up, then nipped at it after it was placed before her until it was gone.

Sister Samuel, the organist, who was pitifully cross-eyed and plagued by hay fever. Sister Samuel sneezed on everything.

Sister Ignatius, the cook, who was very old, very arthritic, and very lovable. She had been here longer than any of them.

Sister Cecilia, the housekeeper, who told Mother Agnes anything that she discovered or overheard within the community, claiming that the spiritual well-being of one affected the spiritual well-being of all. She was an unmitigated busybody, and Sister Regina was getting tired of forgiving her for it.

Sister Agnes, their superior and principal, who was very much in cahoots with Sister Cecilia in monitoring the consciences of the other nuns rather than letting them monitor their own. She taught seventh and eighth grades and was a stickler for Holy Rule and the constitution of their order.

They were all meditating in silence, each of them having been helped by Mr. Olczak hundreds of times, knowing both of his children and having relied upon their mother for her charity on many occasions. Could they truly divorce themselves from caring about the aftereffects of this tragedy on that family? Well, Sister Regina could not. Her mind was filled with images of Anne and Lucy and their father. Had he gone home to them now? Would he cry in his bed tonight without Krystyna? Would the children? What was it like to love someone that way and lose them?

When meditation ended, Mother Agnes rose and led the silent departure from the chapel, the line of women descending the steps in single file and gathering in the refectory at their accustomed places. They began with grace, led by Sister Gregory, their prayer leader this week. She called for a special blessing on the soul of Krystyna Olczak and on her family. Then their simple supper began—beef stew tonight, served over boiled noodles, with a side dish of pickled beets, grown in their own garden and pickled by Sister Ignatius.

After evening chapel the nuns retired to their rooms, locked in Nocturnal Silence until six thirty a.m. Sister Regina's cell was a duplicate of everyone else's—a narrow room with a single cot, desk, chair, lamp, window, and crucifix. No bathroom, no clock, and only a tiny closet in which hung two extra sets of clothing and a mirror no larger than a saucer, by which she could pin her veil in place. The mirror was used for little else, for vanity had been forsaken along with all other worldliness when she took her vows.

She removed her habit and donned a white nightgown from her closet. When the last bell sounded at ten p.m. for lights-out, Sister Regina lay in the dark with her arms locked over the covers, stretching the blanket binding so tightly against her breasts she hoped it would relieve the ache within. But instead, all the pain and sadness she had so dutifully sublimated came bursting forth in a rash of weeping. And while it started out as grief for the Olczaks, it permutated into something altogether different, for at sometime while she cried, she realized she was doing so for her growing dissatisfactions over this life she had chosen. She'd thought Benedictine communal life would mean strength and support and a constant sense of peace within. A strifeless valley of serenity where sacrifice and prayer and hard work would bring an inner happiness, leaving nothing more wanting. Instead, it meant silence when communication was called for, withdrawal when it was sympathy that was needed.

With the greatest of sorrow Sister Regina admitted that her religious community had let her down today.

WHEN Eddie Olczak got home, his house was overrun with family, both his and Krystyna's. Nine of his brothers and sisters still lived in the area, and five of Krystyna's as well. Most of them were in his kitchen and living room, along with assorted spouses, nieces and nephews, and, of course, both sets of parents. So many people were there, in fact, that his little four-room house couldn't hold them all, some overflowing onto the side porch and yard.

They moved toward him as Eddie came up alongside the pair of overgrown box-elder trees in his front yard. Their loving arms, reaching to comfort him, opened the floodgates again, and they shared tears as he was passed from brother to sister, father to mother.

Facing his parents was worst of all. He found them in his crowded living room and went to his mother first. She was a short, stubby woman with tightly curled graying hair that always seemed to smell like the foods she cooked. When they hugged, he had to dip his head to kiss her hair.

"*Mommo,*" he said in Polish, their arms around each other.

"Oh, Eddie, my boy . . . my precious boy . . ." They did their weeping and hugging, then he turned to his dad.

"*Poppo,*" he got out; then his dad's powerful arms were around him, strong farmer's arms with splayed hands as tough as harness leather, hauling him close. "She's gone, Poppo, she's gone."

"I know, son. I know." Cass Olczak was not an articulate man, but a loving one just the same. He could only hold his boy and suffer with him and hope Eddie understood that he'd do anything to take the pain away if he could. Cass had come straight from the fields in his striped bib overalls and smelled dusty and sweaty, with overtones of the barn. He was a thick man, a little shorter than Eddie, built low to the ground like the Cossacks from whom he'd descended.

Krystyna's sister, Irene Pribil, came up, asking in a shy, retiring way, "Have you eaten anything, Eddie?"

"No. I'm not hungry, Irene."

His mother said, "We should make coffee, though."

"Yes," Irene added, "and there's cake."

Where the cake came from so fast, Eddie couldn't guess, but he wasn't surprised: These women thought food was the antidote to any crisis. They brewed egg coffee, and before the first cake could be cut another arrived from a neighbor, followed by other foods from other neighbors—deviled eggs, sliced roast beef and gravy, some pork chops over scalloped potatoes, and poppy-seed coffee cake. The women laid the foods out on the kitchen table that Eddie had made for Krystyna as a wedding gift. He had painted it white, and she had trimmed the backs of the four matching chairs with fruit decals. They had figured that when they had more children, he'd make more chairs. But there would be only these two little girls, who now sat dutifully on the front porch with a bunch of their cousins.

Lucy ate only a piece of cake. Anne ate nothing.

Adults sat on the porch rails with plates on their knees, and on the wide porch steps, and inside the tiny living room on the piano stool and on the overstuffed maroon horsehair sofa.

Afterward the women washed dishes and the men stayed with Eddie, who asked six of them to act as pallbearers—three of his brothers and three of Krystyna's. The air grew chill as the stars came out. The children started playing starlight-moonlight, but were stopped by their mothers and scolded for their insensitivity. The older ones got sheepish, and the young ones pouted, not clearly understanding what they'd done wrong.

The hovering departures began.

The four parents, plus Irene, who had ridden with her folks, and Romaine and his wife, Rose, were the last ones remaining. Irene commandeered Eddie's arm and clung to it as the group moved toward the two cars parked at the boulevard. Eddie could feel Irene trembling as she clamped her elbow firmly around his, as if to steady herself. The tremors came from deep within her, and he understood what she was going through. She was two years older than Krystyna. The two of them had been closest, and because Irene had never married and still lived with her folks, she spent a lot of time here at the house. They had done everything together, Krystyna and Irene—given each other permanents, danced the polka together at the Saturday night dances, made matching dresses, confided secrets.

When all four parents had gotten into the cars, Irene gave Eddie the last hug. She let loose a sob and said, "Oh, God, Eddie . . ." She wept against his shoulder, and he held her head fast, knowing that out of these two vast families, nobody would miss Krystyna more than the two of them—husband, sister and best friend.

Withdrawing from his arms and turning toward the car, she said, "Anything you need, you let me know."

"I will."

She climbed into the back seat of her dad's '38 Plymouth and Romaine shut the door. The cars pulled away and left Eddie standing with his daughters and Romaine and Rose.

"The girls need baths," Rose said. "Why don't I take them inside and fill the tub?"

Eddie dropped a heavy hand on Rose's shoulder. "Thanks, Rose." To his children he added, "Daddy will be right here. You go with Auntie Rose, and she'll bring you down when your pajamas are on." He watched them go, exhausted and listless. Then Eddie and Romaine sat down on the porch step in the gathering dark.

"What'm I gonna do, Romaine?" Eddie said.

"Keep working at the church, I guess. Take care of the girls the best you can. You'll get through it one day at a time."

"I don't know how to cook," Eddie said. "How'm I supposed to do my job and come home and fix supper for them, and wash and iron their dresses like Krystyna did, and fix their hair in pin curls and do all that stuff? Heck, I got to be at church to stoke the furnace before Mass in the winter and ring the bells at seven thirty and eight, and that's just when they should be getting up and getting ready for school. How can I be in two places at once?"

"We'll work it out, Eddie. Don't worry, we'll work it out. All of us can help you for a while till we figure out what to do."

Eddie sighed. "I don't know, Romaine. . . . I don't know."

After a while Romaine and Rose went home, and Eddie closed the doors against the night chill. He turned to find the girls hovering a footstep away, looking up at him as if fearing he, too, would disappear from their lives. "Girls . . ." he said. He picked them up and carried them upstairs. At the top of the steps he passed their room and asked, "How would you like to sleep in Daddy's bed tonight?"

Another night they would have squealed, "Yes! Yes!"

Tonight Anne nodded her head without speaking a word, and Lucy asked somberly, "Will we sleep with you all the time now?"

"No," he answered. "Just for the time being."

He stood them on the bed Krystyna's folks had given them for a wedding present. He turned the bed lamp on and pulled down the covers that Krystyna had washed last Monday and put on the bed fresh off the line, the way she loved to do. "Get in, and I'll be here in a minute, soon as I get washed up, okay?"

He left them sitting on the bed, staring after him as he went into the bathroom and closed the door. Krystyna's nightie was hanging on the back of it. Her face powder had left a dusting around the faucets on the sink. On top of the toilet tank sat a bottle of her Avon perfume. He lifted it and read the label: FOREVER SPRING. He opened it and smelled it, and dropped down to sit on the closed lid of the toilet. A tornado of weeping swirled out of him suddenly, and for his children's benefit he muffled his sobs in a towel.

Later, when the worst had passed, he washed his face, hung up his overalls, and went in to the girls, dressed in his boxer shorts and undershirt.

Anne was sitting up in the middle of the bed, wide-eyed and motionless, the way she'd been so much of the time since it happened. Lucy was curled up on a pillow, awake, sucking her thumb. She popped up the minute he came out.

"We want you to sleep in the middle, Daddy," Anne said.

So he got in between them, his head on the crack between the two pillows, and got them both snuggled up at his sides with their freshly washed hair close by for kissing. He reached up and switched off the bed lamp.

Moonlight flooded in over the linoleum floor. Lucy said, "Daddy, isn't Mommy really coming home anymore?"

He smoothed her silky hair and said, "No, baby, she's not. She's already gone to heaven."

Lucy put her thumb in her mouth and considered for a full minute. Then she began to cry. Anne, meanwhile, remained coiled up in a pinwheel of hurt, her backside to her daddy and her tears wetting the sheets on her mother's side of the bed.

IRENE Pribil awakened on the Monday of her sister's funeral in the same bedroom the two had shared as girls. It was a big south room, with a high ceiling and wide white woodwork, in a farmhouse that had been built in 1880. East of the house was the garden she helped her mother plant each spring and harvest each summer. In the chicken coop beyond the garden was a flock of Plymouth Rock hens she'd raised in the brooder house and fattened all summer and which she would soon sell to Louis Kulick at his produce store in Browerville, earning herself enough cash to buy a few Christmas gifts for her folks and sisters and brothers and their kids. Ahead of her, as far as she could tell, were years and years of nothing but the same.

Irene had gone to country school through the eighth grade, like all the rest of her brothers and sisters. Then, just like they, she had gone to work—in Long Prairie, where she kept house for a family named Milka who owned the dry-goods store.

Krystyna, too, got a job in Long Prairie, operating a mangle at the dry cleaners, and on weekends the two girls always managed to catch a ride home to the farm and from there go with their brothers to one of the dance halls for a Saturday night dance.

It was at the Clarissa Ballroom that they met the Olczak boys. There were so many of them that Irene couldn't keep all their names straight. But two she remembered: Romaine, because for a while he was sweet on her and gave her her first kiss. And Eddie, because from the first time she ever met him, she was sweet on him and wished more than anything that he *might* try to kiss her.

It had never happened. Eddie had taken one look at Krystyna and gone blind to all others. Never once, in all the years since, had Irene let Krystyna know how she felt about Eddie. Eddie either.

In the spring of 1945 Irene's mother fell off a stepladder while painting the granary and broke her collarbone. Irene returned to the farm to help out while her mother recovered, and stayed.

She had always intended to leave, preferably by getting married, but with homegrown pork and beef and cream and butter plentiful, she had gotten quite fat. No young men were asking her to the dances on Saturday nights anymore. At home with her folks Irene had food, shelter, company, and love, and she grew complacent with these. But life was lonely and steeped in routine.

Irene sought social diversion primarily with Krystyna and Eddie, playing cards at their house, often eating supper there, talking gardening and sewing, spending time with their children.

Over the years that she watched the young married couple together, she grew to love them both even more. Her love for Krystyna was so pure and rewarding it would never have occurred to her to let her sister know she loved Eddie. And her love for Eddie—well, it had grown into a golden glow. In Irene's eyes he was more than ideal. He was a god.

It was through Krystyna and Eddie that Irene had lived vicariously. Her joy at being with them and the children dulled the dread she carried at the prospect of life as an old maid.

But now Krystyna was dead, and there would be no more borrowing shoes and giving each other permanents. She could not drive to town and visit in Krystyna's kitchen. Who would she laugh with? Irene sat up in her childhood bed, feeling abject and targeted, as if some preeminent force had it in for her and was showing her how simple it was to remove every vestige of happiness from her life.

She rose with an effort and cocked a hand to her head, where a swift throb reminded her of how much crying she'd done in the last four days. Downstairs, her mother was making sounds in the kitchen. Her father, she knew, was out cutting hay before dressing for the funeral: Death didn't halt the seasons.

Irene shuffled downstairs, where she found her mother taking a cake out of the oven: There would be a dinner after the funeral, at the Paderewski Hall, with the ladies of the parish providing food. Even in her grief Mary Pribil, like her husband, felt the demands of life pushing her from behind.

"Mama?" Irene said to her mother's back. "I'm going to take the old truck and go in early and help Eddie get the girls dressed. Fix their hair the way Krystyna would have liked it. Okay?"

Mary refused to turn around. She pulled up her apron and used a corner of it to wipe her eyes. "You do what you got to do. It ain't gonna be an easy day to get through, that's for sure."

Irene crossed the kitchen, kissed her mother, and left the room.

THE funeral was at eleven a.m. It was shortly after nine thirty when Irene crossed Eddie's front porch and knocked on the door. Eddie answered the door with shaving cream on one side of his face, dressed in black gabardine trousers and a sleeveless ribbed undershirt with a U neck.

"Irene," he said without his customary smile.

"Hi, Eddie," she said as he opened the screen door for her. "I thought I'd come over and fix the girls' hair and help them get dressed, the way Krystyna would have."

Eddie took a beat to register what she was offering. "That's nice, Irene. I appreciate that."

"I didn't think . . . I mean, I didn't know how you'd . . ."

"It's okay, Irene. I know what you mean. I hadn't got around to figuring that out yet, either."

He headed upstairs. Halfway to the top he turned and said, "I wanted them to wear those little pink-and-white striped dresses, the last ones Krystyna made for them."

"Sure, Eddie," she said, following him.

The children's bedroom was at the top of the stairs, Eddie and Krystyna's down the hall. One had to go through Eddie and Krystyna's room to reach the bathroom. The girls came running through their parents' bedroom into the hall, dressed in their cotton underwear. Lucy was squealing, "Daddy, Daddy, look at us!" They had painted their faces with his shaving cream. "We're going to shave!"

"Auntie Irene is here," he said. "She's going to get you dressed and comb your hair real pretty. But first come back in the bathroom with me and wash that shaving soap off."

They said, "Hi, Auntie Irene." Then he herded them away.

She stood looking after them, filled with a sense of loss, complicated by the realization that Krystyna was gone forever and Eddie was no longer married.

She went into the girls' room and made up their bed, listening to Eddie talk to them. He was the gentlest, most loving father she had ever seen, and she felt she had the capability of being the same kind of mother. How perfect it would be if she could marry him and take care of him and the girls for the rest of her life.

Guilt swept down and smothered the idea. Krystyna wasn't even buried yet, and here she was wishing to step into her place. She wiped a tear from her eye, looked up, and whispered, "Forgive me, Krystyna. I'm so sorry."

The girls were dressed and combed when Eddie came downstairs in his black suit, a crisply ironed white shirt, and striped tie, wearing his Knights of Columbus pin in his lapel. He reached the doorway just as one of his brothers rang the first bell at St. Joseph's, a reminder that in thirty minutes Krystyna's funeral Mass would begin.

"Well, I guess it's time to go," Eddie said. "The girls look nice, Irene."

She touched them on the backs of their heads. "Go see your daddy," she whispered.

They crossed the kitchen solemnly and took their daddy's hands, and he thought that without those two small hands in his, he might have sunk to the floor and refused to leave the house, refused to walk down the sidewalk and cross Main Street and see that precious face lying in the casket and watch the metal lid close over it forever.

But he did it, clutching those two small hands and listening to the pat-a-pat of their patent leathers on the sidewalk while Irene followed behind. Reaching Main Street, he found that people were funneling toward the funeral home from all directions.

The decision about whether or not to let Anne and Lucy view Krystyna was decided when the girls balked and pulled away. They were beginning to cry when Eddie left them with Irene at the rear of the funeral home and took his place up front. Father Kuzdek said prayers and performed the closing of the casket, replete with the sprinkling of holy water and the spreading of incense. The pallbearers bore the casket out to the hearse, and the lengthy procession of mourners walked the block and a half to St. Joseph's, Eddie once again holding his children's hands.

INSIDE the church Sister Regina waited with her pupils, who sat and fidgeted. There had been no eight o'clock Mass this morning. Instead, the entire student body was attending the Requiem Mass.

At last the funeral procession passed by Sister Regina's pew, an altar boy leading the way, carrying a crucifix on a long wooden pole.

Then Lucy and Anne moved past with their father, and Sister Regina caught a glimpse of Mr. Olczak's lorn face as he directed them into a front pew.

The Mass began. "Eternal rest grant unto them, O Lord . . ."

When the service was over, the exit from church started, accompanied by the intermittent tolling of the single mournful bell, which would continue until the hearse pulled away from the curb and headed for the cemetery.

Sister Regina wanted to be at the graveside to say final prayers. She needed the mingling just as Krystyna's friends and family did. But Holy Rule would not allow it.

Chapter 4

AFTER the funeral they all said, "Eddie, come out to the farm for a few days. Come to our place. Don't stay at the house alone"—his folks, her folks, his brothers and sisters. But Eddie had no desire to leave his house. Nor had he any desire to put off going back to work. Idleness only made the time pass slower.

He asked his girls, "Anne, Lucy, do you want to go out to Grandma Pribil's or out to Grandma Olczak's for a few days?"

"Will you come, too?" Anne asked.

"No, sunshine. It's time for me to go back to work. I've been off for four days, and that's long enough."

"Then I want to go home with you."

"Me, too," Lucy seconded.

Irene approached Eddie. "What are you going to do in the morning when you have to be at church before they leave the house?"

"I don't know."

"I could come, Eddie. I could come any day—every day, actually—and feed them breakfast and get them ready for school."

"Aw, no, Irene, that's asking too much."

"I wouldn't mind. I know how Krystyna took care of them, and I can do the same. I'd be happy to."

"But you'd have to drive in from the farm every day."

"Four miles, what's that? And I can take Dad's old truck."

Anne tugged on her daddy's hand. "Can she?"

Lucy repeated, "Can she, Daddy, pleeease?"

Eddie ignored the warning that sheered through his mind and disappeared with his sister-in-law's words. Physically and emotionally spent as he was, he found it easy to accept Irene's solution.

"All right, Irene. I won't be able to pay you much, but—"

"Oh, for heaven's sake, don't be silly, Eddie. I wouldn't take one red cent if you begged me. These are my nieces, and I love them." She didn't say "And I love you, too," but she thought it.

He squeezed her arm, half on her sleeve, half on her bare skin, and said, "Thanks, Irene," sending shivers clear through her.

IRENE showed up at seven the next morning. He was only half dressed and ran down to answer the door, his shirttails flying. Irene was wearing makeup and wouldn't look him in the eye.

He left her downstairs in the kitchen and closed his bedroom door when he heard her coming up to awaken the girls.

By the time he finished getting dressed and went downstairs, she had cooked hot Coco-Wheats for the girls and oatmeal, coffee, and toast for him. The table was set with a floral luncheon cloth, and his favorite oversized cup, cream, and sugar were all set out, waiting. The girls were in their places, still in their pajamas. Beside each of their cereal bowls she had put one of their daily vitamin pills.

He came up short in the kitchen doorway, surveying the perfect duplication of Krystyna's morning routine, and suddenly it struck him what she was doing. He wanted to shout, "Get out! You're not Krystyna, so don't try to pretend to be!" But he needed her.

When he stepped into the room, Irene looked at him and flushed.

"I, uh . . . I think you like oatmeal . . . um, right?" she stammered.

"Uh, yes. Yes! Oatmeal's fine." He pulled out his chair.

When he sat, she didn't, but stood near the kitchen sink. He gave her a baffled look. "Aren't you eating anything?"

"Oh, I ate at home."

"Oh," he said, unsure of how to deal with her. "Well . . ."

"If you have a nickel for each of their school dinners, I'll tie them in their hankies."

"Sure." He reached into his pants pocket for the coins. It was uncanny: The woman knew every nuance of their morning routine.

Eddie polished off his coffee and set down the cup. "Got to go ring the first bell," he said, pushing up from the table.

He hugged the girls, taking extra time today. How he hated leaving them in Irene's care, not because she wouldn't do a good job of getting them ready, but because he was stepping into a new routine without Krystyna in it. Each step he took made him feel as if he was betraying her. Yet he didn't know what else to do.

WHEN the girls were ready to walk out the door, Irene handed them their hankies with the nickels tied into the corners and gave them hugs and kisses on the cheek. "Would you like me to be here at four o'clock when you get back home from school?" she asked.

"Well, I guess so," Anne replied.

Lucy asked, "You mean you'd stay here all day?"

"No. I'm going back to the farm as soon as I wash the dishes. But I can come back when school is out, if you'd like."

Anne said, "We can be by ourselves awhile. We're not babies."

"No, of course you're not. I just thought . . ." She patted Anne on the shoulder. "Well, in any case, take your sweaters."

A minute later the two little girls started out for school, Anne dutifully taking Lucy's hand as they headed up the street.

"Is Auntie Irene going to be our new mother?" Lucy asked.

"How can she be our mother when she's our aunt?"

"I don't know." Lucy shrugged. "She's doing everything that Mommy did, so I just thought she was going to be."

"She's just our baby-sitter, that's all."

"Oh. Well, is she going to make our white dresses for Easter?"

"I don't know. You can wear mine from last year."

"I don't want your hand-me-down. Mommy promised she'd make me a brand-new dress for Easter. So who's gonna make it?"

"Well, I don't *know* who's gonna make it!" Anne was having difficulty keeping her lip from trembling.

Lucy halted, jerked her hand out of Anne's, and abruptly started to cry. "I don't want Mommy to be dead! I want her to make my Easter dress! I'm goin' back home!"

Anne grabbed her hand. "You can't go back home."

Lucy bellowed, "I want my mommeeee!"

Anne, who wanted her mommy, too, put her arms around Lucy and petted her hair the way their mother would have. "Come on, Lucy, let's go see Sister Regina, and she'll know what to do."

Sister Regina was writing on the blackboard when they came in: "September 12, Feast of the Most Holy Name of Mary." Some of her students had already arrived and were mingling around the desks.

"Good morning, Sister," Anne said.

Lucy tried to say the same thing, but it came out choppy as she cried.

"Good morning, children. Oh, my goodness, Lucy, what is it?" Sister said sympathetically, setting down her chalk.

"She wants to go back home, but Mommy isn't there."

Lucy stood rubbing her eyes, sobbing. "I want my m-mommy." Some of their classmates turned to watch in fascination.

"Come with me," Sister said, and, reaching for both of their hands, led them through the cloakroom and into the flower room. Against one wall a metal cot covered with an army blanket sufficed as a nurse's office. Sister sat down and drew the children down beside her, feeling them huddle against her, small and forlorn and trusting. In spite of the fact that Holy Rule disallowed it, she put her arms around them.

"Now what has made you cry on this beautiful new day?"

"She wants our mommy back."

"Oh, Lucy, dear, so do we all. But let me tell you something. When you came into my schoolroom a minute ago, do you know what I was writing on the blackboard? I was writing down what today's feast day is. And do you know what it is?"

Lucy looked up tearfully and wagged her head no.

"Why, it's the feast of the Holy Name of Mary. That means that if we ask the Blessed Virgin to intercede for us for anything today, we have a good chance of getting it. I think we should ask Mary if your mother is happy in heaven. Shall we do that?"

"I guess so."

Continuing to hold the children tightly, Sister Regina shut her eyes and prayed aloud, "Dear Mary, mother of Jesus, who loved and cared for Him just as Krystyna loved and cared for her children, Anne and Lucy, we wish to send a prayer that their mother's soul be happy and abiding with Jesus. They want her to know that they will do their very best to persevere here on earth."

Lucy whispered, "Sister?"

She looked down at the angelic face lifted to her. "Yes, Lucy?"

"What's a purse of ear?"

"It means to do our best even when it's hard. But just think, you'll have special help not only from Jesus but from your own mother, who lives in heaven with Him now."

"But how can she help me? Can she make my Easter dress?"

"No, she can't, Lucy, but she'll find a way for you to get one."

"How?"

"Well, your mommy's an angel now, and angels find a way."

At the nun's reassurance Lucy offered a quavering smile.

"Now, do you know what?" Sister brightened her voice. "The other children have arrived, and it's time to go to church for Mass. Your daddy will be ringing the bell. Would you like to go see him?"

Anne slipped to her feet, and before Sister could rise, she swung around and flung up her arms in a spontaneous hug. She clung, her warm cheek against Sister's cool one. Within Sister Regina a bubble of joy burst and spread its goodness, as if the angel Krystyna were, indeed, watching over all of them. It was so unexpected, that hug, the kind of thing a mother must get all the time and take for granted. But Sister Regina had never had such a hug before, and it incited her every maternal instinct, forcing it up into the light like a wildflower growing from the crevice of a rock.

Sister followed the children back to the classroom with a new, expansive feeling in her heart. What had passed in the flower room brought thoughts of the children of her own that she'd given up by becoming a nun. Funny how little she'd thought of it back then. Growing up, she had never considered another path in life than that of becoming a nun. Her grandmother had put the notion into her head, and the nuns who had taught her had furthered it by assuring her that to become a religious was more rewarding, more noble, and more privileged than any other walk of life, that she should feel very blessed that she'd had the calling to a vocation. God had chosen her.

Anyone could be a wife and mother, they intimated, but only the *chosen* could enter a religious vocation.

But look what I've given up, she thought now.

She got all the children into line and led them to church. The bell was ringing as they mounted the steps and entered the vestibule, but Mr. Olczak stopped ringing the bell when he saw his children heading toward him. He could see that Lucy had been crying. She ran the last couple of steps, and he bent on one knee and scooped her up; then he included Anne in the embrace. Sister Regina compared the love that she, as a religious, felt for her God to the love this father and his children felt for one another, and she was struck by an earth-shattering realization. They were wrong, she thought. They were all wrong. These are the chosen ones. I was the one who left life behind.

IRENE Pribil came to the classroom door to collect Anne and Lucy at four o'clock when school was out. The girls ran to their aunt gladly, and Sister smiled, relieved that they'd be cared for.

Sister then accompanied the rest of her pupils outside, half of them to be excused to walk home, the others to be marched to waiting school buses. After the buses pulled away, she returned to the schoolroom.

This was her favorite time of day. With the children gone, the room became her own. She went to the blackboard, rolled back her sleeve, and began erasing, when Mr. Olczak said from the doorway, "Afternoon, Sister."

Her heart leaped as she turned and found him standing in the doorway holding a dust mop. Beside him, a rolling bucket held an assortment of cleaning supplies.

"Good afternoon, Mr. Olczak."

"How did my girls do today?" He came in and began running the wide mop around the perimeter of the room.

"This morning Lucy had a bad spell, but Anne brought her to me and we had a quiet talk away from the other children, before they saw you. They both seemed calmer afterward."

He turned a corner and went along the back of the room. "I'll tell you, Sister, I'm sure glad they have you. I could've used somebody to talk to this morning myself."

She knew she should not encourage personal talk, so offered a small smile instead and sat down at her desk.

He went around the third side of the room, then stopped at the rear again. "Irene came in this morning," he told her. "She sort of, well, took over for Krystyna, if you know what I mean."

Sister merely nodded.

"I was glad to have her get the girls ready for school, but I kind of resented her being there, invading Krystyna's territory."

In her lifetime no adult man had ever confided in Sister this way. It was wholly unexpected, and she felt somewhat rattled by his openness. Holy Rule was wildly waving its arms for her attention, but she ignored it. After all, his children were her students: What he had to say affected them, did it not?

"That's perfectly understandable."

"I guess that was pretty selfish of me, wasn't it?"

Their eyes met across the classroom. "I wouldn't worry about selfishness for a while if I were you, Mr. Olczak."

"Irene knew where everything was—you know what I mean?— like where Krystyna kept things, and all of a sudden I had this feeling like—like she was trying to *be* Krystyna. I didn't like that very much." He was battling tears.

From outside a *ka-klunk* from the cement-block factory sounded like a heart beating when you put your ear to someone's chest, and she imagined, for a moment, it was his heart, broken, and it was her ear on his chest searching for a way to heal it.

She tried to quell the urge to approach and comfort him. Forbidden to do such a thing, she went on in the calmest voice she could muster. "It's natural that you should want Krystyna's place to be inviolate. All you can do is remember that Irene only meant to help. Just don't waste your time feeling guilty about your reaction. I don't think God would find you uncharitable, Mr. Olczak. I think He would understand what you're going through."

She could see the tension ease from his shoulders.

"You know what, Sister? There's never been a time when I talked to you that I didn't feel better afterward." He even managed a little smile for her benefit.

"Yes, well, that's"—she realized she was treading on forbidden ground and finished lamely—"that's good, Mr. Olczak."

She pulled a stack of fourth-grade spelling papers to the center of her desk and began correcting them. He emptied the garbage can, then started washing the blackboards. When he was finished, he said, "Well, Sister, I'll see you tomorrow."

"Yes. Good-bye, Mr. Olczak."

When he was gone, she sat still, recognizing the rush of feelings and the stirring of blood caused by the man who'd just left the room. It was the kind of womanly response she had denied herself when she donned this habit. And it was forbidden.

She folded her hands—a tense gripping with the fingers knit. Lowering her head to her knuckles, she closed her eyes. Dear God, she prayed, help me to remain pure of heart and immaculate of body like your blessed mother. Help me to maintain the vows I've taken and to resist these impulses toward worldliness. Let me be content in the life I've chosen, so that I may serve You always with pure heart and spirit. Amen.

When Eddie walked into the house, he could smell chicken stewing and coffee brewing. Irene was in the kitchen, lifting fluffy white dumplings out of a kettle when he reached the doorway.

She looked at him. He looked at her.

She blushed. He frowned. She recognized his displeasure and felt her stomach quiver. "Lucy wanted dumplings," she said, apologizing.

"Lucy always wants dumplings. Irene—"

She went to the back door and called through the screen to the girls in their playhouse, "Girls, time to come in for supper!"

"Irene, I appreciate your help, but—"

"No. Don't say any more. I was just going to get the food on the table; then I was going home. Honest, Eddie."

Though she tried to hide her tears, he saw them glimmer in her eyes. The sight of them made him feel small, so he relented.

"Now listen, you've made this nice supper. You might as well stay and eat with us."

The girls came barging in.

"Are the dumplings ready?" Lucy bellowed.

The meal was laid out, steaming and smelling delicious, and though Irene gave the table a longing look, she did so backing away. "Ma's expecting me," she told Eddie. And to the children, "Girls, you be sure to wash up good before you sit down. Now come and give me a hug. Bye-bye, honey. Bye-bye, dear." She hugged them both and scuttled away.

The girls dove for the sink and the bar of soap while Eddie followed Irene to the front door, feeling guilty for resenting her kindness. He remembered Sister Regina's words. She only meant to help. Furthermore, she probably needed to be near him and the girls to handle her own immense grief.

He came up behind her and laid a hand on her shoulder. "Irene."

"Eddie, I didn't mean to— Well, you know."

He squeezed her shoulder and let his hand drop. "I know."

She turned to face him. "What do you want me to do, then?"

He sighed. "I need your help, Irene," he admitted.

"Okay, then. Should I come in the morning?"

Resigned, he answered, "Yes, if you don't mind."

She opened the door and said, "I'll be here."

He watched her hurry to the truck that was parked at the curb. She got in and drove away a little fast for Irene, and he realized just how much he had hurt her without intending to.

THE meal she'd cooked was delicious. He hurried the girls to finish eating and let Mrs. Plotnik next door know that they'd be outside playing with a bunch of the neighborhood kids while he ran over to church to ring the Angelus. When he got back home, he washed the dishes, then called the girls in for their bath.

He filled the bathtub and left them with orders to stay out of their mother's dusting powder. A minute after he closed the bathroom door, it opened again, and Anne came out, bringing him a note. "Look at what I found on the clothes hamper, Daddy."

It was written in pencil, nearly illegible.

> Eddie I tuk yor close home and washd them you can coom & get them tomorr they will be irned Aunt Katy.

Aunt Katy Gaffke was his mother's sister. She lived about a two-minute walk from Eddie's house. Born in Poland, Aunt Katy had never become proficient at writing English, but Eddie understood her message and the love behind her charitable deed.

The next day, when he went to her house, he found his freshly ironed shirts hanging from her kitchen doorway and Aunt Katy in a low armless rocker on her glassed-in porch, fast asleep.

He leaned down and touched her shoulder. "Aunt Katy?"

She jerked awake, looked up, and mumbled, "Eddie, didn't hear you come in. Sit down, sit down."

He sat on her daybed, which was covered with homemade rag rugs that made the mattress nearly as hard as a church pew.

"I sure appreciate your washing and ironing our clothes, Aunt Katy," he said.

She flapped a hand. "Gave me something to do."

"I'd like to pay you."

"You might like to, but you ain't goin' to. And what's more, I intend to keep on washin' em ever Monday when I wash m' own."

He got up and kissed her on the forehead, then sat back down.
She smelled like homemade lye soap and fried Spam.

"How're them little girls doing?" she asked.

"Irene comes in the morning and gets them ready for school."

"How 'bout in the afternoon?"

"She's been coming then, too, but it's too much to ask of her."

"Tell 'em to come here. They can play around here after school
just as well as they can play around your house."

"Are you sure?"

"They'd be company. Days get pretty long since your uncle Tony
died."

"Are you really sure, Aunt Katy?"

"They ain't learned to make rag rugs yet, have they?"

"No."

"Well, they got to learn, ain't they? I'll keep their hands busy, you
can bet on that."

AND so a pattern was established. In the mornings Irene came
before school, and in the afternoons Aunt Katy watched the girls
after school. She fixed supper for all four of them and taught the
girls to dry dishes for her. On washday Eddie would run over to her
house in the late morning and help her carry out her washtubs and
empty them in the yard. On Saturdays he cleaned his own house.
The girls learned to dust the furniture and beat the rugs. On Sundays they fixed their own hair the best they could. On school days
at four o'clock Eddie need not worry.

It was a small, safe town, Browerville, and parents watched out
for everybody's children, not just their own. Every adult in town
knew not only the name of every kid in town, he knew the names of
their dogs as well. Doors were not locked, so the girls could have
walked into anyone's house and gotten whatever they needed. If
they had fallen and needed a bandage, someone would have put it
on. If they had been hungry and needed a snack, a cookie jar and

glass of milk would have been offered. If they had grown sad and needed their mother, a pair of loving arms would be there to gather them in.

Yes, his friends and neighbors and relatives took care of everything. Everything but the loneliness.

Chapter 5

SEPTEMBER moved on, and the leaves began to turn.

Every year in October the various parish sodalities combined their efforts to put on an autumn bazaar. It was held on a Sunday after the second Mass, in Paderewski Hall. The ladies cooked a hearty dinner made of foods from the fall crop: chickens, pies, vegetables, and breads. The St. Joseph Society ran a booth where fancywork was sold—doilies and dresser scarves and embroidered dish towels. The Sacred Heart Society had a bake sale, and the Altar Society was in charge of the bingo game. The Knights of Columbus operated a gambling wheel, and on the west end of the school, next to the boys' bathroom, the K.C.'s also had a beer garden.

It was there that Eddie was drinking his second bottle of Glueks when Romaine found him.

"So how goes it, Ed?" Romaine asked.

Eddie took another swig of beer. "Lonely, Romaine, lonely."

"We're going to a dance next Saturday. Want to go?"

"Nah. It's too soon."

"Okay, but I promised Irene I'd ask."

"Irene?"

"Yeah. She said if you were going, then she'd go."

"Irene," Eddie muttered to himself, shaking his head.

"She's a good egg. And she's always liked you, Eddie."

"Yeah, I know." Eddie raised the bottle again.

"She misses Krystyna almost as much as you do, Eddie."

"I just don't feel like dancing anymore," he said.

Romaine caught him around the shoulders and said, "Okay, but let us know when you do."

"Yeah, sure."

There were tables set up throughout the center of the hall, and Eddie's gaze wandered over them. Diners shifted, finishing their meals and leaving their wooden folding chairs askew. Eddie reacted like a janitor and, heading into the dining area, shoved chairs beneath tables as he went. In the far northwest corner were all the nuns. They occupied the same table every year.

He paid particular attention to Sister Regina. She'd been acting funny toward him. She was never in her room after school anymore when he went in to clean it, and he missed seeing her and chatting with her. Whenever they encountered each other in passing, she refused to meet his eye. If he didn't know better, he'd have thought she was afraid of him.

He watched the nuns as they carried their plates to their table.

When they were all seated, he headed their way and asked, "Anything I can do for you, Sisters?"

Old Sister Ignatius replied, "Yes, Mr. Olczak, some coffee for me, if you don't mind."

"Coming right up, Sister. Anyone else?"

Though Sister Gregory smiled and replied, "Yes, please, Mr. Olczak," Sister Regina refused to look at him.

"Coffee, Sister Regina?" he said, and she finally looked up.

And that's when he knew. It struck him like a broadside how she was blushing, how very red her cheeks were against the pure, stiff, white of her wimple, and how she could not hold his gaze. "Yes, thank you, Mr. Olczak," she nearly whispered, her glance skittering away self-consciously. She had always been demure in manner, keeping a proper distance, a soft voice, and a retiring attitude. But today was different. Today she shied away like he'd sometimes seen

Irene do. Just like a woman who's battling a case of lovesickness.

But that can't be, he thought. She's a nun!

The possibility rattled him so badly that he ran off to fetch their coffee, with his heart thundering in his ears. "Three coffees for the nuns!" he ordered, butting into line and forgetting to excuse himself.

What if the others saw her blush and grow flustered, and suspected the same thing he did? He didn't have any idea what they did to a nun if she got caught liking a man.

When he took the three cups of coffee back to their table, he intentionally set hers down first, then moved around the table with the others so he could look back at her.

"Now if you want anything else, you just whistle," he said.

They all acknowledged him but Sister Regina. She kept her eyes on her plate as if she didn't trust herself to catch his gaze.

Something inside Eddie went ka-wham!

And it wasn't ego. And it wasn't virility. It was just plain fear.

IMMEDIATELY after the fall bazaar Eddie began avoiding Sister Regina's classroom until he was sure she was gone after school. He thought about her often and decided his suspicion was wrong. She couldn't have a crush on him. It simply wasn't in her nature. She was the most totally dedicated nun he'd ever known. He must have done something to alienate her, and it bothered him considerably, wondering what it was.

One night, after Anne had asked at dinner why nuns couldn't be mothers, he dreamed the oddest dream. In it Krystyna stood in the stone grotto in front of the school, saying not a word, smiling at him with an expression of extreme peace. But she was dressed in a black habit of the Order of St. Benedict.

ON NOVEMBER 1, the feast of All Saints' Day, there was no school—the perfect chance for Eddie to wax the schoolroom floors. When he came to the third- and fourth-grade room with his electric buffer, he was surprised to find Sister Regina working at her desk, cutting out something made of brown construction paper. She glanced up as he appeared, then quickly back down at her work.

"Good afternoon, Sister," he said, pushing the machine inside. "Nasty day, isn't it?" he remarked, plugging in the machine.

"Yes, it is." Flurries of snow were pecking at the windows.

"Looks like we might get some real snow before the day is over."

She said nothing but went on snipping, snipping with her scissors.

"It's a holy day of obligation. What are you doing working?"

"Oh, this isn't work. I'm cutting out a cornucopia for the bulletin board. This is . . . creativity."

He stepped closer and looked at what she was doing. "Oh, that's right, Thanksgiving's coming. It's going to be hard to be grateful this year without Krystyna." When she made no reply but continued acting standoffish, he decided *something* had changed her, and he was going to find out what. "You mind if I sit down a minute?" he asked.

She finally looked up, and he detected a blush she could not hide. But she spoke with total composure. "No," she said quietly.

He sat down on the first seat of the row of desks in front of her. "Sister, have I done something to offend you?" he asked quietly.

"No."

"You seem to be going out of your way to avoid me."

"No, I haven't." She spoke as reservedly as ever.

"Yes, you have, Sister Regina. I used to come in your room after school, and we'd talk about Anne and Lucy and about Krystyna and all my feelings after I lost her. Now you make sure you're not here when I come in. I just wondered if I said something or did something that wasn't proper."

"You've done nothing."

"I miss that, you know?" he continued softly. "I suppose I could talk to the other nuns, but . . . I'm not as comfortable talking with them as I am with you."

She kept her eyes on an orange pumpkin she was cutting and said, "You may talk to me now, Mr. Olczak."

"I dreamed of Krystyna the other night," Eddie said. "She was standing in the grotto, wearing a habit like yours. I don't know why I'd dream that." He hesitated, waiting for a response that never came. "I guess it was because Anne asked one day why nuns can't be mothers, and I told her it was because you are married to Christ."

"Yes, I am," she replied, carefully setting down her scissors on the desktop. "And that's why conversations such as this are forbidden to me. Surely you know, Mr. Olczak, that in our order conversation with seculars is strictly limited to necessity."

His spine straightened slightly. "No, I never knew that."

She rose and went to stand at the window, looking out, so she need not face him. Tucking her hands into her sleeves, she explained, "The life of a nun is one of silence and reflection, which is all part of obedience. And obedience is one of the vows we take. Perhaps you're right. Perhaps I *have* been avoiding you, because I find that when I'm with you, it's easy to forget to observe the rules about ordinary silence and I talk too much."

He studied her straight back. "You mean, Sister, that every time I come in here and talk to you, I cause you to sin?"

When she made no reply, he insisted, "Do I?"

"Our vows are perpetual, and the obligations they impose bind us under pain of sin, yes."

"Why didn't you say something before this?" he asked.

"Because some of it *was* necessity, your necessity. I thought you needed someone to talk to, so I decided to be your listener. And since we as nuns are admonished to practice 'the most cordial charity'—and I quote Holy Rule—I thought, When is charity more needed than after a loss like you suffered? You and your girls. These last two months since Krystyna's death have been . . ." She couldn't finish. There were tears in her throat.

"Sister," he whispered, horrified. "I've made you cry."

"No, you haven't." She dug a handkerchief from her sleeve and tipped her head down as she used it.

"Then what is this?" He crossed the room and stood right behind her shoulder. "Please, Sister, turn around."

"No, I cannot." She sniffed once. "It's me who has made me cry, not you. I've been going through a personal crisis, and it's been a very difficult time. Please forgive me, but I must go." She wheeled around and hurried from the room at a pace that made her veil billow.

"Sister, wait! I'm sorry! I wouldn't—" But she was gone.

Left behind in the empty schoolroom, Eddie didn't know what to do, think, believe. He'd caused her to sin? And to cry? Jesus, Mary, Joseph, help me understand what I've done to her, because she's the last woman on earth I'd want to upset this way.

HE LAY awake for hours that night, going over and over that scene in his mind. Standing behind her today while she lost her composure, he had an outpouring of feelings that he'd only experienced with Krystyna. He'd wanted to comfort her, to hold her as she cried, the way he would any woman in distress. But the mere idea of it was jarring, given that she was a nun. Hold her? In his arms?

Nuns were representatives of God. They were holy creatures. They were as close to angels as it was possible to be on this earth. There was no man alive who revered nuns more than Eddie Olczak.

So what was he doing lying here in his bed thinking about holding one? He missed Krystyna, that's all. He missed her, and Sister Regina was the only other woman he felt comfortable with. It'd be a long time before he was over Krystyna. But if he was ever to marry again, it would be somebody like Sister Regina, he was pretty sure. Anne was just crazy about her. So was Lucy.

Sister Regina . . . Sister Regina . . . Oh, Sister, could it be we all love you in a way that's not allowed?

THE next day was All Souls' Day, on which a Catholic could get a plenary indulgence by going to confession and Communion, in addition to saying a number of designated prayers for the poor souls in purgatory and for the Pope.

Sister Regina pledged to herself she'd fulfill all the necessary requirements, believing it would bring about a remission of her temporal punishments for the sin she'd committed the previous day by once again talking to Mr. Olczak on such a personal level.

That morning after chapel she stopped Father Kuzdek in the front hall. "Father, may I have a word with you?"

"Certainly, Sister."

"I'd like to go to confession, please."

"Now?"

"Yes, Father, if you could spare the time."

"Very well. Get your wrap. We'll go straight to church."

Outside the convent, the air smelled like fresh laundry and the sky was still blue-black at six thirty a.m. Five inches of snow had fallen overnight, and flurries still drifted down. Mr. Olczak had already been here and cleared a temporary path. There was no escaping the distraction of Mr. Olczak, for even now his shovel could be heard from somewhere at the front of the church, scraping away at the wide, tall steps before early Mass.

Mr. Olczak! His name was on her mind altogether too much. How was she to get over her preoccupation with him when he was present in her world nearly every waking hour of the day?

Father entered the church. He led her through the sanctuary, both of them genuflecting on their way to the confessional. Inside the cubicle it always seemed to smell of must, with overtones of manure from the farmers' shoes. Sister Regina stepped into the cramped space and knelt, hemmed in by heavy maroon velvet curtains that could not stop a chilly draft. She heard Father settle himself in his chair before the partition between them slid back, and she saw the shadow of his hand make a cross in the air.

"*In nomine Patris, et Filii, et Spiritus Sancti.* Amen."

She made the sign of the cross with him and began the words she'd been taught as a child: "Forgive me, Father, for I have sinned. My last confession was two weeks ago. I've come to confess something of grave importance." She drew a shaky breath.

He heard it and said, "I'm here, Sister."

"Yes," she whispered. "This is very difficult." She fortified herself with another deep breath before going on. "I've somehow managed to become friends with a secular, just friends, but in the course of our friendship I've allowed myself to speak too freely, and our conversations have sometimes bordered on personal things. I know I'm breaking my vow of obedience by speaking to this person, yet it doesn't feel wrong when I'm doing it. How can this be so, Father?"

"This person is a man?" Father asked.

Her heart started racing with fear. "Yes, Father."

"And are you attracted to him?"

After several long beats she whispered, "Yes."

"Are your talks with him causing you to doubt your vocation?"

"No, Father. I had begun doubting it before these talks began."

The racing of her heart got worse, and she realized tears had sprung into her eyes. She had admitted for the first time to someone else that her faith in her vocation was shaken. Until the words were actually spoken, there was still time to recant, to tell herself she was wrong and these dissatisfactions were temporary.

Father took his time responding. "Have you spoken to Mother Superior about this?"

"I'm—I'm afraid to, Father."

"But Sister Agnes is your spiritual adviser. You must place your trust in her. These matters could affect you all the rest of your life."

"Yes, Father. I'll try. And, Father, you must understand, it's not just about this man. It's much bigger than that. I've begun finding fault with so much about my life within the religious community— the personal ways of the sisters: How Sister Samuel sneezes on our food at the table or Sister Mary Charles punishes the children with her strap. Then there's Sister Agnes admonishing me not to get too wrapped up in the lives of the children, and this makes me angry, yet I'm not allowed to discuss it with anybody. Holy Rule says my anger itself is a sin. More and more lately I've begun to question Holy Rule and our constitution."

"Anger is human. How we manifest it dictates whether it's a sin or not. Perhaps, Sister, you're being too hard on yourself."

"I don't think so. Time and again I've broken Holy Rule, and every time it happens, I do penance, then go on believing I was right. It's been just terrible, Father."

"Do you think, Sister, that there isn't a one of us who's doubted our vocation at one time or another?" She didn't answer, so he went on. "Sometimes when we wrestle with doubt and temptation and win out over them, we come through the test stronger than before and more certain that the vocation we chose is absolutely the right one for us. Pray, Sister. Pray good and hard for the answers, and I know they'll come to you. Do penance. Meditate as much as possible. And do talk to Sister Agnes. You may be surprised at what you hear."

"Yes, Father. I will. Thank you."

He gave her a remarkably slight penance: Undoubtedly he knew that the struggle she was going through was penance enough.

SHE decided against talking to Sister Agnes right away, thinking perhaps she hadn't prayed, meditated, or done penance enough. She would do more of all three first.

The weather stayed as somber and joyless as her reflection while November advanced toward Thanksgiving, and she called upon Christ to let His will be known to her. She devoted herself to an intense period of soul-searching, during which she prayed many hours each day. She routinely fasted from breakfast until supper, offering up her hunger as further penance for her doubtfulness. Meditation and reflection became a deeper part of each day, but they yielded little beyond continued confusion. She expected the answer to descend upon her in a nimbus of recognition, a shimmering knowledge that would suddenly light her from within.

But this did not happen. If Christ knew what He wanted her to do, He was keeping it to Himself.

During Thanksgiving week she wrote to her grandmother about the anguish she was going through. But the letter went unposted, because their constitution dictated that all outgoing mail be placed, unsealed, on the superior's desk. Sister Regina put the letter away, resenting the fact that she could never send it, adding yet another notch on her tally of repressions.

SHORTLY after the first Sunday in Advent, when the Christmas crèche was put up in church, a big snow came, followed by a period of intensely cold weather, so cold it was dangerous. The schoolchildren, shut in by the thermometer and relegated to playing in the gymnasium and the halls during recess and noon hours, became more and more rambunctious. Among the younger kids running grew rampant. Among the older ones bickering and fighting were common.

It was Monday of the last week before Christmas vacation that Anne Olczak got into a game of tag with some of her older cousins from the upper classes across the hall. They'd been racing around the parapets, and Sister Mary Charles had warned them a number of times to stop.

It was Anne who was unlucky enough to be hurtling around the stub end of the parapet toward the girls' bathroom hall when she knocked off the brass handbell. It struck the head of a first grader on its way to the floor, where it bounced, with a resounding clang, a few feet away from the black shoes of Sister Mary Charles.

"Olczak, come here!" she screamed and latched onto Anne's shoulder like an eagle grabbing its dinner. "Now look what you've done!" Anne stared up at the nun, transfixed with fear. "Pick up that bell!"

Anne picked it up posthaste and deposited it back on the parapet. The first grader was yowling, blood streaming from a slice in her forehead.

Sister Mary Charles pointed a bony finger at the floor. "You wait right here, missy, and don't you move one inch."

"Yes, Sister," Anne whispered in sheer terror.

Sister bent to attend the younger child, then took her away to her own teacher to be examined and bandaged. Poor Anne had to wait ten minutes, with her terror mounting, until Sister Mary Charles returned for her, sour-faced and bitter. "All right, young lady, march!"

Anne didn't have to ask where. She knew.

She was already crying when the flower-room door closed behind them. Through her tears she could make out the strip of rubber floor tile waiting beside the ferns.

"You are disobedient!" Sister said, rolling up her right sleeve. "And disobedience must be punished. Do you understand?"

Anne tried to whisper, "Yes, Sister," but no sound came out.

Sister picked up the rubber strip. "Hold out your hands. And while you get punished, ask God to forgive your sins."

"But it was an acci—"

"Silence!" Sister screamed so loud her voice shook the fern fronds. "Now out with those hands!"

Anne's two sweaty hands trembled forward in slow motion.

Sister raised her weapon and swung—and Anne couldn't help it, her arms retracted like window shades.

Sister Mary Charles's outrage magnified. "All right! It was going to be five. Now it's six!"

LUCY was sitting with her back against a hall wall, playing cat's cradle with the younger girls, when her cousin Mary Jean came tearing toward her and slid to a stop on her knees.

"Sister Mary Charles's got Anne in the flower room!"

"Annie? What'd she do?"

"She knocked the bell off the parapet, and it fell on some little kid's head," Mary Jean said. Lucy knew you didn't touch that bell.

"Annie?" She looked toward the flower room and got a sick feeling in the pit of her stomach. "She's in there with Sister Mary Charles?" Lucy peeled the yarn off her fingers and got to her feet.

Don't you hurt my sister, you big meanie!

"Hey, Lucy, wait!"

But Lucy was running in the hall, heading to the rescue, and she didn't stop till she got to the flower-room door. Inside, she could hear Sister screaming, "Don't talk back to me!" Lucy began crying and ran to the closest person she could think of to help.

"Sister Regina, come quick! Sister Mary Charles's got Annie in the flower room, and she's giving her a licking!"

Sister Regina had been sitting at her desk. She jumped to her feet so fast her chair tipped over as she headed for the cloakroom.

"Go play, Lucy. I'll take care of this."

She flew through the cloakroom, a dervish in black veils, and flung open the flower-room door, shouting, "Stop that this instant!"

Anne had taken four licks and stood sobbing.

Sister Mary Charles spun around. "This child has disobeyed! She must be punished!"

"Not with anger and cruelty. I will not allow it."

"*You* will not allow it. Since when is it your place to allow or disallow it when I'm reprimanding the children!"

"This is not reprimanding. This is persecution, and that is not a naughty child. A stern talking-to would do."

"We teach them that disobedience is sin, and this is the punishment. It's no worse than hundreds of others've gotten over the years, and they're all better off for it."

"God punishes sin, not you. And I cannot believe one of those children is better off for it. Anne, please go into the bathroom and blow your nose and wait for me there."

Anne ran out, leaving the two alone. Sister Regina said in her calmest voice, "I've disagreed with your whipping the children ever since I came here, but it seemed to be a tradition, and everyone accepted it. Well, not me. I see no reason why the children should be sacrificed to some bitter need you have within you."

Sister Mary Charles had thrown her strap down. "You overstep your bounds, Sister, and doing so, you break Holy Rule."

"Please, don't speak to me of Holy Rule. You might try relearning chapter six on charity, where it says teachers may not inflict corporal punishment on a pupil. What about *that* holy rule?"

Sister Mary Charles went out and slammed the door.

Sister Regina dropped her face into her steepled hands and collected herself for a moment. When the bell rang for afternoon classes to resume, she realized that Anne was still in the lavatory waiting.

The girls' bathroom had windows of stamped, textured glass, and woodwork as dark as molasses. Anne was standing with her face against a corner, crying her little heart out, and Lucy was nearby, vicariously miserable but too young to know what to do.

When their champion arrived, Lucy stated soberly, "She got 'er on the hands, Sister, and Annie won't stop crying."

Sister made Anne turn around, and Anne plunged against her, hugging hard. Sister's heart swelled with pity and love, and she disregarded Holy Rule and her own threatened vows and returned the hug, soothing the child's hair with one hand. What to do now—send her back to the classroom to face curious stares and whispers? Or give her a reprieve? She made a decision. "Come with me, girls. Let's go find your daddy."

They found him in the lunchroom, carrying out the garbage. He stopped in surprise when he saw the three of them.

"What's going on, Sister?"

She stood with one hand on each girl's neck, holding them near her protectively. "I think it would be best if Anne and Lucy left school for the rest of the day. Is there someone they could go to?"

"Sure, Aunt Katy. But why?"

"Anne had an accident and knocked the bell off the parapet. It hit a child, and Sister Mary Charles punished her in the flower room. I stopped her."

He went down on one knee, frowning. "Annie? Come here, honey. Tell me what happened."

"We were playing tag and I knocked the bell off the parapet and it hit this little girl on the head and it was bleeding, but it was an accident, Daddy. Sister said I committed a sin, but I didn't, and she hit me on my hands with the rubber strap."

Sister Regina had never seen Eddie's face suffused with anger that way. "Come on. You, too, Lucy." He rose, stern-faced and decisive, taking both girls by the hands. "We'll go get your coats, and I'll take you over to Aunt Katy's till suppertime. And don't you worry about whether or not you sinned, Annie. You didn't."

While Sister returned to her students, Eddie went into the cloakroom to find the girls' coats. Before he left, he stuck his head into the classroom and motioned Sister to the doorway. Then he whispered, "Thank you, Sister. Will you be in trouble for stepping in?"

"No, Mr. Olczak."

"Good. I'm so—" She watched him battle anger. "Nothing. I'll talk to you later."

Chapter 6

IT SURPRISED Sister Regina how calm she was now that the time was here. Her doubts had dissipated with her abrupt decision to step in and stop Sister Mary Charles from whipping Anne. It was as if that moment galvanized her decision, for she knew with calming certainty that leaving was the right thing to do and now was the right time to set the wheels in motion.

By the time she and Mother Agnes met that night in the empty community room of the convent, Mother Superior was aware of what had taken place in the flower room.

"Come in, Sister Regina," she invited in a kindly tone, "and close the door if you like."

Sister Regina did so soundlessly. She knelt for Mother Superior's blessing. A whisper, a touch on the head, and she rose, seating herself on an armchair with a stiffly upholstered seat and a straight back. The house was silent; a single dim lamp glowed on a corner table.

Sister Regina spoke first, softly. "Thank you for seeing me, Mother Agnes."

The older woman nodded wordlessly.

"Undoubtedly you think I've come to talk about what transpired in the flower room this noon, but I've come about a problem that I've been praying about." Sister Regina spoke low and slow. "I fear that I've been growing more and more dissatisfied with my life here within the spiritual community. These feelings have been growing for a very long time. I realize that I no longer belong here, and I wish to seek a dispensation from my vows."

Much to Sister Regina's surprise, Mother Agnes showed no sign of shock. She said quite calmly, "I imagine you've asked God's help in making your decision, Sister?"

"Many times."

"Good. Then let me say that it's not a sin to doubt your vows."

"In my head I know that. In my heart I feel differently, because I knew from the time I was eleven years old that this was what I wanted to be. Everybody said I should be a nun, especially my grandmother. She, above all, gave me to believe that life as a religious was the epitome of service to God."

"What has made you change your mind, Sister?"

Sister Regina had thought through her answer long before. "Though I've tried and tried to find fulfillment in my relationship with God, I can never disassociate myself enough from worldly concerns to be completely at one with Him. I've always had trouble honoring my vow of obedience. Lately I've begun to question everything—Holy Rule most of all. Today, when Sister Mary Charles took Anne Olczak into the flower room, everything finally became crystal-clear. I knew the time was here to make this change in my life."

Mother Agnes nodded. "I think the Olczak children hold a very special place in your heart. And I think that when their mother died, you wanted very much to make up for their loss."

"The death of Krystyna Olczak has had a profound effect on me. She was the most nearly perfect mother and daughter and wife and parish supporter I've ever known. When she died, I began assessing what she had given to the world and comparing it to what I as a nun give to the world." Sister Regina's voice dropped to a softer note. "Krystyna Olczak served God in as noble a way as I ever did."

"Do you feel bitter about your years as a religious?"

"No, Mother, not bitter at all. When I entered the postulate, I felt it was God's will for me, that His voice was within me. His voice is *still* within me. I believe He's guiding me in my present decision."

"That's a very powerful argument, Sister Regina. And I am the last one to try to convince you otherwise. This is your life; you must live it as you see fit."

This was not at all the response Sister Regina had expected.

"Do you mean that, Mother?"

"Of course I mean that. But let me just say there are very few nuns I've known who haven't at one time or another questioned that they made the right choice, including me."

"You considered leaving?"

"Yes, I did. But I, like you, heard the voice of God within me. Only He told me He needed me here, and I've never been sorry."

A thoughtful moment spun past, then Sister Regina said, "I would very much like to go home and tell my family about my decision. Christmas vacation starts this week. The timing seems providential."

Sister Agnes finally showed some dismay. "So soon? Perhaps if you take more time to pray and meditate . . . make a retreat."

"I made a retreat last August for exactly this purpose, Mother Agnes, and I've said so many prayers since, and meditated and done penance. I believe that God and I have reconciled ourselves to my decision. Now I need to reconcile it with my family."

Sister Agnes nodded solemnly. "Well . . . so soon."

"I understand it can take as long as six months for the paperwork to go clear to Rome and back."

"Yes, but— Oh, dear, I suppose I'm resisting out of selfish reasons because I don't want to lose you, Sister. You're one of our best teachers, and you have added much to our religious community."

"Thank you, Mother."

"Have you made plans? What will you do to earn a living?"

"I'm not sure yet, but I can always teach."

"I must warn you, the Catholic Church frowns on letting former nuns teach in their schools."

"Not even in another town?" It had been Sister Regina's plan to become a lay teacher in another parochial school.

"Very doubtful." Mother Superior's voice grew understanding. "It's my duty to inform you of the Church's stand on these things."

They'll deny me a job? When I'm a qualified teacher? The news went zinging its way through Sister Regina like an electric current. What went unsaid was that once she doffed her habit, the Church was afraid she might influence other nuns to quit.

"I'll just have to take this one step at a time," Sister Regina replied. "I thought I'd speak to you first, then my family, then whomever I must see to take the necessary formal steps."

"That would be the prioress, Sister Vincent de Paul, at St. Ben's. You would go to her, state your intentions, and fill out a form requesting the dispensation of vows. She'll forward it to the president of the congregation, who will send it to the Holy Father in Rome."

"And then . . . while I wait? What then?"

"You return here and continue as before, until the Holy Father signs the paper and it's returned to you."

"I see." There's public school, Regina thought. I could always teach in public school. But the idea was repugnant—teaching in a place devoid of prayer. She wanted to remain close to the religious structure, much the way a child swimming over his head for the first time wants a life buoy floating along by his side. "So after I see Sister Vincent de Paul is time enough to think about my future."

"Yes. I suppose so."

They seemed to have covered everything, but Regina still didn't have one important answer. "About my going to see my family?"

Mother Agnes's face had grown long and sad. Nonetheless, she found a weak smile and said, "You have my permission."

Sister Regina reached out and touched the older woman's sleeve. "Please don't be sad for me, Mother Agnes."

Mother Agnes put a hand over Sister Regina's and gave it a light pat. "Yes . . . well . . ." Their hands parted and got tucked away again. "Please kneel for my blessing."

On her knees Sister Regina felt the faint touch on her head. Mother Agnes spoke in a voice thinned to a small whisper. And though her prayer invoked the deity to guide Sister Regina in the choice she would be making, Sister Regina had already made up her mind that before she returned from Christmas vacation she would go to St. Ben's and sign the papers that would release her from her vows.

SCHOOL let out for Christmas vacation on Friday, December 15, and wouldn't resume until Tuesday, January 2. Since Eddie had to work throughout the vacation, plans were made for the girls to spend the first week at Grandpa and Grandma Pribil's and the second week at Grandpa and Grandma Olczak's. Eddie got one of his nephews to ring the evening Angelus and took the girls out to their Grandma Pribil's late Friday afternoon.

Krystyna's mother told the girls they could help her bake Christmas cookies. And out in the barn, she said, they had a mother cat with four kittens. They could choose one to bring into the house and make a bed near the woodstove for it, and when they went back home, they could ask their daddy if they could take it.

Grandpa Pribil took them out to the barn, and they chose a fluffy striped kitten with a tail straight as an asparagus sprout. Aunt Irene said it was the color of burnt sugar, so the girls decided her name should be Sugar.

They all had a delicious home-cooked meal together, and then spent a long evening playing cards. Mary threw a misshapen blue sweater over her housedress and stepped onto the porch with Eddie as he was leaving. They paused at the top of the steps and looked out at Eddie's truck. A light snow was settling on its green paint.

Eddie put his arm around his mother-in-law's shoulder and gave her a hard squeeze. "Well, better go. Angelus comes early."

They kissed cheeks and hugged good night. "Take it easy," he said.

From the kitchen window Irene watched Eddie walk to his truck, get in, start the engine, and turn around in the farmyard. She watched with a yearning that filled her throat and eyes. She was still watching when he rolled slowly out the driveway and headed off down the gravel road, leaving twin tracks in the snow.

THE next day Eddie worked in the abandoned school building taking down the Christmas trees from all the classrooms and burning them in the incinerator. With the help of Romaine's boy, Joey, he moved the wooden folding chairs out of the gymnasium storage room and washed and waxed that floor. He checked the furnace and filled the coal hopper for overnight. That's what he was doing when Romaine found him around quarter to four that afternoon.

"Hey, little brother, been looking for you. Saturday afternoon, your kids are gone to the farm. Thought maybe you'd want to stop by the liquor store and have a couple of bumps."

"Sure. Why not? Just give me a hand with this coal."

They finished filling the hopper and drove to the liquor store. Outside, it was one of those gray, murky, windy days. Inside, it was smoky, and a desultory dice game was in progress.

Romaine ordered a shot of whiskey with a water chaser. Eddie ordered a bottle of Grain Belt.

Their drinks came. They made the senseless toast, "Bumps!"

Romaine clapped his glass down. "So how goes it, Eddie?"

"It's tough," Eddie replied. "Who wants to play Santa Claus alone?"

One of the locals, Louie Kulick, walked in. He perched on a barstool next to Eddie and said, "Where's Sister Regina going?"

"What do you mean?"

"She's standing outside, waiting for the bus. Funny thing, she's all alone." Everybody knew the nuns always traveled with partners.

Eddie set down his bottle of beer and said, "Be right back."

Below the Greyhound sign next door Sister Regina was standing on the sidewalk, with a small cardboard suitcase at her ankle. She clutched a thick black hand-knit cape to her throat. She looked frozen in place, shuddering in the cold of the darkening afternoon.

"Sister Regina?" he said from behind her.

She spun at the sound of his voice and said, "Oh, Mr. Olczak!"

"Are you waiting for the bus?"

"Yes. But it's late, it seems."

"Sister, pardon me for asking, but where's your partner? Isn't anyone traveling with you?"

"I'm alone today, Mr. Olczak."

"Oh." His puzzlement showed, so she told him, "I'm going home for Christmas. My parents have a farm near Gilman."

"Oh, Gilman." He did a quick calculation and guessed it was between an hour and a half and two away—that is, if the bus went all the way to Gilman. If you considered stops, and possibly a change of bus, she'd be lucky to reach her destination by ten o'clock that night.

"Will the bus take you all the way there? To Gilman, I mean?"

"Not quite."

"To where?"

"You needn't worry about me, Mr. Olczak."

"To where, Sister? St. Cloud? Foley?" She looked away, and her veil filled with wind. He stood at her shoulder, persisting. "And from there, how're you getting to the farm? Let me drive you, Sister."

"Oh no, Mr. Olczak." He detected a note of panic in her voice.

"I can take you right to your folks' farm. Let me. Please."

"Where are your children?" she inquired.

"At their grandma Pribil's. Let me take you, please."

She wanted very badly to say yes, but could not. Glancing away, she admitted, "I'm not allowed. Not without a partner."

"I'll use Romaine's car. You can sit in the back. I'll take you right to your mother and father's door. Are they expecting you?"

She stared at the distance and refused to answer.

"Do they have a telephone?" he asked. Still no answer, so he said, "They don't, do they?" Very few farmers did.

"I have an uncle in Foley," she finally replied. "I'm sure he would give me a ride out to the farm."

Eddie's patience was growing thin. "Pardon me, but this is stupid, Sister, that you should wait for a bus that's late, in weather like this, then wander around Foley in the middle of the night, not knowing when you'll get home. Would Krystyna have let you do that without trying to help? Well, neither will I. Wait here."

He went back in and told Romaine, "Got to borrow your car. Sister Regina needs a ride to Gilman, and I better not take her in my truck. Will you ring the Angelus for me at six?"

"Sure."

"Thanks. If you need my truck, take it. Keys are in it."

Romaine's car was across the street. Eddie made a U-turn, swung back to the curb, and got out beside Sister. He put her suitcase in the back seat, let her get in beside it, then slammed the door.

When he was seated behind the wheel again, he said, "I see

there's a blanket back there. Better put it over your lap 'cause it'll take a while for the heater to warm up."

She covered her lap and watched the snowflakes parting like blown hair in the headlights.

"How far is Gilman from Foley?" he asked.

"Just a few miles, on this side."

"Good. Well then, you give me directions when we get closer."

After that he drove in silence.

She could make out the silhouette of his head against the windshield, the line of his cap, his right ear, right shoulder. It wasn't bad enough she was breaking Holy Rule with every mile they traveled unchaperoned; she was indulging in forbidden thoughts about him. The physical attraction he held for her, combined with his thoughtfulness, his loneliness, his very *availability,* put a sharp pang up high beneath her ribs. It was a heady thought that in a mere six months from now such simple pleasure as riding in an automobile with a man she liked would be hers to enjoy whenever the opportunity arose.

What if he knew she was going to seek a dispensation of vows? What would he say? How would he react to the news? She wanted to tell him why she was going home. But she was still a nun for at least another half a year, and during that time she was expected to comport herself according to the rules of the order.

At Long Prairie they headed out into flat farmland—miles of darkness lit only by the headlights, falling snow, and an occasional light on a barn. "This is it," she said after forty-five minutes of silence broken only by her directions. "Pull up next to the apple trees."

A dog started barking, and a yard light came on.

Eddie pulled up where she'd told him to, killed the lights and engine, then turned around and looked at her over the seat. "Sister, you just tell me when, and I'll come back and get you."

"That won't be necessary. I have to stop at St. Benedict's on my way home, and I'm sure my dad will take me."

"Well . . . okay, then. Merry Christmas."

"Merry Christmas to you, too. And thank you for the ride. I hope you'll be all right on the way home."

He got out and opened the rear door for her. As he reached inside for her suitcase, a woman's voice called, "Jean, is that you?"

"Yes, it's me, Mama."

"Oh, my gracious me, it *is* you!"

And a man's voice, full of sudden emotion. "Regina?"

Then they were leaving the shelter of the glassed-in back porch and hurrying down the walk. Eddie watched them hug, thinking over and over, Her name is Jean. Her name is Jean. Her father tried to wrest the suitcase from Eddie, saying, "Let me take that."

"No, sir, I've got it. I'll take it to the house."

"This is Mr. Olczak, Daddy, our janitor at St. Joseph's," Regina said. "He was kind enough to drive me on this ugly night."

"Mr. Olczak." They shook hands. Frank Potlocki said, "Come on in. Bertha will get you a cup of coffee before you head back."

The kitchen was as ordinary as field straw but spotlessly clean. There was a cast-iron wood range, a table as big as a hay wagon, and worn blue linoleum on the floor. Bertha Potlocki filled a pot from a water pail while Frank dropped firewood into the stove.

Then they all sat at the table, and Bertha asked her daughter, "How long are you staying?"

"For Christmas."

With one hand Bertha covered her daughter's hand on top of the oilcloth. The tears in her eyes told how long it had been since this had happened. "Wait till your grandma finds out you're here! Oh, Jean, how that woman misses you."

"How is she?"

As they talked, Eddie saw that Regina (Jean) Potlocki had grown up much like he, in this big drafty farmhouse, surrounded by people she loved. A mother with a face burned red from cooking on a wood range and a father who, even in the dead of winter, sported a white forehead above his hat line and a red face below. From the pantry came home-baked buns. From out on the chilly porch a bowl of butter, a pint of chokecherry jelly, and a pitcher of thick cream, straight from the separator.

Across the table Eddie watched Sister Regina fold her hands and say a quick prayer before slathering her bun with the rich memory of home. She took a huge bite and looked up, with butter in the corners of her mouth, and saw him watching her with a smile.

She blushed. And she remembered that she wasn't allowed to eat with seculars but found her mother's homemade bread and choke-cherry jelly too wonderful to resist.

AT THE door, when he was leaving, Eddie faced Sister Regina with her parents four feet away, hiding the things he was feeling. "If you know what day you'd like to come back, I can come and get you."

"Oh no, thank you, Mr. Olczak. Daddy will take me."

"You bet we will, won't we, Mother?" Frank shook Eddie's hand. "Now you have a safe trip back."

"I will. It looks like the snow's letting up."

Eddie glanced at Sister and felt the insane desire to hug her. He had the sharp impression that if he did, she'd hug him back.

"Merry Christmas, Mr. Olczak," she said quietly.

"Same to you, Sister." He backed away a step, nodded, opened the door, and said, "Frank . . . Bertha . . . nice to meet you."

"Same here," they said, and turned him out into the snow to drive home and wonder if it was a mortal sin to fall in love with a nun.

Chapter 7

THE word had spread throughout the family that Jean was home, and on Sunday, after Mass, the house filled with her grandma Rosella, her sisters and brothers, and their families. There were eighteen people around the table by the time the meal was served and, with no formal planning, food enough for all.

Regina waited to announce her news to the family until the children had left the table. When the coffee cups had been refilled and the group had grown sated and lazy, only then did she speak. "I have something to tell all of you."

With every eye resting on her, Sister Regina spoke in a soft but resolute voice. "I've decided that I don't want to be a nun anymore. I'm asking for a dispensation of my vows."

Bertha's hand flew to her lips. Her eyes flashed to Frank's. They both gaped at Sister Regina. Nobody knew what to say. Bertha was the first to speak. "You don't mean that, Regina."

"Yes, Mama, I do."

"How can you *do* this to us?"

I'm not doing anything to you, Mother, Regina thought.

Then everybody started babbling at once.

"Nobody quits the convent."

"Jesus, Mary, Joseph . . ." (whispered, accompanied by the sign of the cross).

"It's that man who brought you home, isn't it?"

"Some *man* brought her home?"

"Shh, keep your voices down! The kids will hear!"

The comments burbled on and on until Grandma Rosella stopped them by bursting into tears.

Frank got up and went around the table to her. "Ma," he said, dropping down to one knee. "It's not the end of the world."

"Yes, it is. . . . For me, it is." She lifted her ravaged face. "All I ever wanted was for my little Jean to be a nun, and now what does she do but betray me."

Regina felt a bubble of anger pop inside, but she kept her voice meek. "I'm not betraying you, Grandma."

"God, then. You're betraying God. You made a vow to Him."

"With provisions for renouncing that vow."

Rosella raised her voice. "It's a man—that's what it is! Nuns don't give up their habits unless there's a man involved!"

Her mother said, "If there's a man, Jean, you might as well go ahead and tell us. We'll find out sooner or later anyway."

Someone started reciting an act of faith, and the hubbub mounted.

Sister Regina Marie, O.S.B., who usually maintained a mien of composure that the saints themselves would envy, stood up and shouted, "Stop it, every one of you! Stop it right this minute!"

Their mouths shut like gopher traps, and they stared at her.

Her voice was trembling as she began. "I'm sorry I shouted, but that's something I haven't been allowed to do for eleven years—shout. There's a paragraph in our Holy Rule about it." She scanned the circle of faces. "Can you imagine your life without shouting? Or without touching other human beings? Or without being allowed to have a special friend or talking to acquaintances you meet on the street? Owning a wristwatch so you can check the time whenever you want, or buying your own bottle of shampoo, or writing a letter to your own grandma without someone else reading it? I couldn't write to you over the years and tell you of my growing dissatisfactions. Perhaps if I could have, it wouldn't have gotten to this point where I want so badly to be free."

They were all sitting with their chins dropped. She went on. "I made the decision to be a nun when I was eleven. Think of that—eleven! I hadn't even grown to my full height yet or been to the county fair without Mom and Dad or had a boyfriend. How can a child of eleven know what she's committing herself to?"

She glanced around the table. Some faces were lifted, their expressions softening. "And everybody said what a wonderful nun I'd make. Grandma said so. Mother said so. The nuns at school said so. So I became one, and I *was* happy for a long time. In my religious community there's the wonderful sense of belonging. There's a sense of purpose to every hour of every day, of doing good, and of changing the world in important ways. And I love teaching. . . . Some of the children have grown very special to me, and their families, too.

"And of course," she went on, "from a much more practical standpoint there's tremendous security to living in a convent. All my worldly needs are taken care of—food, clothing, shelter, company, a job, a place to go if I get sick, a home for me in my old age. When I leave my order, I'll have nothing. I'll be starting over as a . . . a displaced person. Maybe now you can understand what an agonizing decision this has been for me."

Nobody said a word, so she went on, beseeching them to believe her. "And I haven't missed the worldly things, but I want . . ." Her voice had grown tender and yearning. "Most of all I want a friend. Somebody I could talk to about all of this. And if that friend were a man, would you forgive me? Because I do have a friend who's a man, and yes, he's the one who drove me home. His wife died last September, and in his sorrow he turned to me. Oh, not physically. We talked and prayed together. He has two beautiful children, and I love them and feel such pity for them. I wanted to reach out to them when their mother died, and to their father as well. But this, you see, is forbidden to me."

Her voice landed on her family like rose petals on a lawn.

"I've taken a vow of chastity, so if I say to you that I love this man—and I think I do—you think he's the reason I'm leaving my vocation. But he came last. All the other reasons came first."

One of the children came to the doorway just then and said to the adults, "Aren't you going to do the dishes and play cards?"

Grandma Rosella moved first—an easy escape. "Come on, girls," she said to her daughters. "Dishes are waiting."

There was no card playing that afternoon. Instead, when the dishes were washed, Sister Regina's siblings left one by one, taking their families and empty roasters with them. When her grandma left, Regina walked to the car with her. The old woman gave her granddaughter a prolonged hug and said, "I don't know, Regina. I just don't know. I think you should make a retreat, make sure you're doing the right thing. Will you do that for me?"

Regina sighed. "All right, Grandma, I promise."

SHORTLY after Christmas, Sister Regina's father drove her to St. Benedict's Convent and deposited her at the portal she remembered so well. It hadn't changed since Sister Regina had studied there as a novitiate. In the chapel, dwarfed by its baroque granite arches and humbled by its stained-glass dome, she spent the next four days in prayer, open to her God, inviting Him into her heart and mind, inviting Him to change her will to suit His.

But by the end of the fourth day nothing she heard, felt, or sensed asked that she remain a Benedictine nun. Instead, she emerged feeling an unquestionable validation of her decision to quit.

Thus she came that last afternoon to the daunting oak doorway leading to the office of the prioress, Sister Vincent de Paul, to seek a dispensation of vows.

Sister Regina's heart was clamoring fearfully as she made the request. The prioress, however, reacted with calm thoughtfulness.

"I'm sure you've asked God for guidance on this."

"Yes, Sister."

"And you've spoken about it with your spiritual adviser."

"And with my priest. My family also knows."

"Well, then, your mind seems to be made up."

"It is, Sister."

"This will bring to a close a major portion of your life. But I've known a number of nuns who saw fit to leave the order, and every one of them made a strong ally for us as a lay person. So"—she found a form and passed it across the desk—"all that remains is for you to fill out the official form, which I'll pass on to Sister Grace, the president of the congregation, and she'll send it on to Rome."

Filling out the form took so little time it seemed ironic, after the years of study it had taken to become a nun.

Sister Vincent added her signature and centered the form on her ink blotter, then rested her hands beside it and looked up.

"You undoubtedly know that it can take up to six months for a dispensation to come through."

"Yes, Sister."

"During that time be reminded that you are still bound by your perpetual vows. And for obvious reasons it would be best not to disclose the fact that you're seeking the dispensation."

"Yes, Sister."

"Very well." Sister Vincent rose, tucking her hands beneath her front scapular. "May the Lord be with you, Sister Regina."

"Thank you. God bless you, Sister."

"And you."

The sense of irony continued as Sister Regina found herself leaving the grounds of St. Benedict's and walking down the street toward the bus depot, carrying her suitcase. She had expected to be put through the third degree by the prioress, to have to defend her decision the way a criminal defends himself under inquisition. Instead, the prioress deferred to her decision with the utmost respect and facility. There seemed to be an unwritten code at work that said, We don't force anyone to stay who doesn't want to.

THE winter days rolled along, doleful and dreary, with little to change the routine save Forty Hours devotion, when the church lights remained ablaze for forty consecutive hours of prayer.

It was just after Forty Hours that Eddie was uptown in Wroebel and John's one day buying some flannel for polishing brass. Passing the time of day, John Wroebel remarked, "So we're going to lose Sister Regina. Too bad, isn't it?"

Eddie's body snapped alert. "Lose her? What do you mean?"

"She's quitting being a nun. Didn't you hear? Seems she's started the procedure to get out of it for good."

John was holding out Eddie's change, but Eddie failed to reach for it. "Who told you that?"

"Father Teddy." That was John's brother, a priest at St. Mary's in Alexandria, Minnesota. He had been one of the guest priests here at Forty Hours devotion. "Here's your change, Eddie."

Eddie scarcely felt the coins drop into his palm as he turned away. He left and made a beeline for St. Joseph's, wondering all the way, Is it true?

The foremost thought on his mind was getting it straight from her. When he peered into her classroom, she was strolling the rows with her back to him while the children bent quietly over their open books.

He tapped on the doorframe and said, "Excuse me, Sister, could I talk to you a minute?"

She swung around, meeting his eyes across the stuffy classroom. He saw the hint of pleasure she couldn't quite hide.

"Yes, Mr. Olczak?" she whispered, approaching him.

"Could you come into the flower room for a minute, please?"

Her brow lifted in surprise.

"Please," he repeated, and walked across the cloakroom. He opened the flower-room door and turned, holding it open for her, waiting.

She gave a quick glance at her students; they were all quiet and engrossed in their work. Her eyes downcast, she passed him and entered the privacy of the flower room.

He shut the door behind them, then closed the hall door, too. He stopped in front of her, face to face. Closer than ever before.

"Is it true?" he said. "Are you leaving the order?"

She raised startled eyes to him. "Where did you hear that?"

"From John Wroebel. Father Teddy told him."

She averted her head, unwilling to tell a lie, yet compelled to withhold the truth.

He touched her on the stiff white cloth beneath her chin, forcing her to lift it. There his finger remained, on the immaculate starch that he had never touched before. "Is it true?"

"What are you doing? You must not touch me."

Then she touched him deliberately for the first time—knocked his hand aside so she could escape. But when she moved, he moved faster, gripping her thick black sleeves and making her stay.

"Do you know how scared I am right now?" His cheeks were flushed, and a vein stood out in his forehead. "Do you think this is easy for me?"

"Don't!" She gripped his wrists and strained to push them away, but he was so tremendously strong it made no difference.

"Sister, please, if this has anything to do with me—"

"Don't!" A plea this time, with her eyes slammed shut.

"When did you decide to leave? When?"

"Please, Mr. Olczak . . . you're hurting me."

He released her. "I'm sorry, Sister," he whispered, "but I need to know. When are you leaving? And why? Please, just tell me. Has this got anything to do with me? Because I think it does."

"I'm still a nun. This is forbidden."

"When will you get out? Where will you go?" He caught her by an arm once more.

She closed her eyes and began whispering, frantically, "Hail Mary, full of grace, the Lord is with thee. Blessed art thou amongst women—"

"I think there are some feelings between us, aren't there?"

"Please, Mr. Olczak," she whispered weakly.

"Just answer me one question then. When will you be free?"

Her mouth opened, and tears shot into her eyes.

"I have to know," he said quietly. "When?"

"It takes six months," she whispered. "Now let me go." He released her carefully and let his hands drop. "And if you have any regard for me, don't do this again, please."

"Very well. I'm sorry, Sister."

"I must get back to the children."

He stepped aside and gave her access to the door. She walked toward it briskly, went out, and returned to her classes.

It was Lent, mournful and seemingly endless. In keeping with the somber spirit of the season, Eddie and Sister Regina bore their feelings for each other like penances they could offer up: *I will practice patience. I will not succumb to my temptations. I will pray instead and do good deeds.*

So if he had to clean her room after school when she was still there, they'd stumble through that hesitation step when he appeared at her door and came inside. She'd look up from her desk and say nothing. He'd stop inside the doorway and say nothing. Usually she'd be the first to recover.

"Hello, Mr. Olczak," she'd say simply and return to work.

"Hello, Sister," he'd reply; then while he swept and emptied and erased and scrubbed, the two of them pretended an indifference that served only to make them more aware of each other. And if their hearts raced when they encountered each other in the hall, and if their breath shortened, they hid it well.

The somber mood lifted on Holy Saturday noon. Lent was over! Fasting was over! The children of the parish could eat the candy they'd given up for Lent; the adults could eat meat! And Eddie rang the bells again.

He rang them and rang them, longer than at any other time of year, and with them he felt his spirits lifting.

Still, he missed Krystyna on Holy Saturday night with an exceptionally sharp ache. Easter had always meant new clothes for all. The girls had their new coats—matching lavender ones, ordered out of the Montgomery Ward catalogue—and new white gloves and new white shoes and long white stockings and their crisp white veils for tonight's procession. But as the three of them walked to St. Joseph's in that spring twilight, the girls walked forlornly one on each side of Eddie instead of between him and Krystyna as it had always been before. The sound of their hard heels on the sidewalk brought such a lump to his throat he had to look up at the sky and force himself to think about something else to keep his eyes from welling up.

At church they helped him ring the early bell, and that cheered them somewhat when they got to ride the rope on the upswing. Then they went with him to flip light switches and illuminate the place to its fullest.

By the time they returned to the vestibule, others were arriving. Mothers were smoothing little boys' rooster tails and clamping veils on little girls' heads. Fathers were collecting coats and carrying them inside. Nuns were organizing the procession and shushing the children's whispers. The organ started playing, and the altar boys were busy lighting candles.

Someone touched Eddie's elbow. "Hello, Eddie."

He turned. "Oh, hello, Irene." She looked quite pretty tonight in a new soft pink spring coat and a hat with a fine veil that floated above her carefully curled hair. She wore eyebrow pencil and tomato-red lipstick, and she'd darkened her lashes the way Krystyna always had. She looked quite a bit thinner, too.

"Happy Easter," she said.

"Same to you."

"Happy Easter, girls."

The exchange between Eddie and Irene was observed by Sister Regina from across the vestibule, where she was lining up her students in preparation for the procession. She watched Irene touch Eddie's elbow and Eddie turn to find her there and the two of them visit. Then Irene knelt down to retie the children's bows. Irene was thinner and, since losing weight, bore a noticeable resemblance to Krystyna. Both girls smiled and flung her a hug and a kiss. When she stood up, Eddie smiled at her, too, and touched her shoulder as they exchanged some conversation. For only an instant a hint of coquettishness telegraphed itself from the angle of Irene's head and the slight tilt of her body toward Eddie's.

A powerful and foreign reaction caught Sister in the region of her chest, a hand that seized and twisted: jealousy.

Appalled at herself, she turned away. But some truths were at work and undeniable. Irene Pribil was more like the children's own mother than any other living being. She had the artistic knack to care for them with Krystyna-like flair that Sister Regina had never learned. Irene could flirt, practice her wiles on her brother-in-law, comb her hair in a perky flounce, even lose weight in an effort to win him. She could demonstrate her abilities as a substitute mother, and—who knows?—maybe wangle a proposal out of him yet.

Sister Regina, on the other hand, was forbidden to voice a word of her own feelings. She was forced to stand aloof and pretend she felt nothing for him. Maybe he was hurt by the fact that she hadn't divulged her plans to quit the order. Maybe he took that as an indication that he was nothing special to her. Maybe, before her dispensation came through, he would reconsider Irene and realize what a perfect stepmother she'd make for the girls.

How she longed to walk right up to him and say, "I do love you and your children, but I'm still bound by my vows until my dispensation comes through. Please be patient. Please wait."

But she could not do that, of course, under pain of sin.

Chapter 8

IT WAS a warm sunny Tuesday, May 8, and school had just been dismissed for the day when Mother Agnes came into Sister Regina's classroom and closed the door behind her.

Mother Agnes said, "Your dispensation has come through."

Sister Regina's heart felt as though it had leaped to her throat. "Oh! So soon? I—I was told six months."

"Three to six months. It's been five, I believe."

"Nearly . . . yes." Sister Regina stepped back and dropped into her desk chair, short of breath. "Why am I so stunned?"

"It's a step that will alter your life. And very final."

Sister Regina tried to conquer her emotions, but now the uncertainties of her future reared their heads like dragons. She sat in a state of fluster, barely listening to Mother Superior.

"Your father will be here at five o'clock this afternoon to pick you up. He'll bring clothes for you to wear. In the meantime, you may strip your bed and remake it, and pack your belongings."

"Five o'clock?" That was when the other sisters would be chanting matins and lauds. "Am I not to be allowed to say good-bye?"

"Under the circumstances, the prioress and the president of the congregation would rather you didn't."

She glanced over her empty classroom. "What about the children? I didn't get a chance to tell my pupils I'd be leaving."

"I believe that's for the best, Sister."

"I don't," she wanted to argue. Those children were not merely strangers who sat in these desks five days a week. They were young people she cared about in myriad ways. But the church saw every one as a potential priest or nun, and it would not do to be candid about a nun who was leaving. It might breed the dread question, Why?

So she must depart without good-byes. Mother Superior was waiting.

"I'll show you where we were working in our reading and arithmetic books, and I've put a marker in the novel I've been reading the children every Friday afternoon."

All the while Sister Regina marked the pages and gave Mother Agnes verbal instructions to pass along, her heart grew heavier and heavier. She'd always assumed she'd stay until the end of the school year and have a picnic on the school grounds with the children on the last day and watch them board the school bus, waving good-bye, ending the school year like any other.

But everything was orchestrated to keep this departure quick and clandestine. Pack up the traitor and pretend she has gone anywhere but where she has: toward freedom.

The moment came to walk out of her classroom for the last time. "Please, Mother, may I be alone for just a few minutes?"

"Yes, of course."

Sister Regina had not thought it would be this hard, but five years was a long time. Finally she made herself move as far as the doorway but stopped and turned with tears in her eyes. Good-bye, children, she thought. I will miss you so much.

In the hall she found Mother Superior waiting a discreet distance away. From across the auditorium she heard Mr. Olczak whistling while he cleaned. I'll write to him, she thought, and explain why I left without a word. Good-bye, Mr. Olczak. I'll miss you, too.

IN HER room at the convent she stripped and remade the bed and packed her personal belongings in her cardboard suitcase. There were pitifully few—underclothes, the black shawl that Grandma Rosella had knitted for her, prayer books, rosaries, the crucifix she'd received from her parents when she took her vows, a black-bound copy of Holy Rule, shampoo, toothbrush and toothpowder, and class pictures from the last five years.

She placed the pictures atop her personal items, then closed the suitcase just as Sister Agnes appeared with a packet of white butcher paper tied with store string.

"Your parents have arrived, and they brought these for you. And here are your dispensation papers, signed by Pope Pius." She offered a white envelope. "There's also a small amount of cash. It's not much, but it's only right and proper not to turn you out without something to fall back on. Well, Regina, how do you feel?" Not "Sister" anymore, just plain "Regina."

"Scared."

Reverend Mother offered a smile. "No need to be. God will watch over you. Now if you'll kneel for my last blessing . . ."

Regina knelt and felt the older nun's hands on her head.

"Good and gentle Savior, watch over Regina as she goes forth into the secular world. May she continue to practice obedience to You, and to offer up for Your greater glory whatever work she chooses to do in the future. May she practice charity to all, and continue to espouse the cardinal virtues so that at the end of her temporal life she may dwell with You in life everlasting. Amen."

"Amen," murmured Regina.

She rose and faced Mother Superior, whose watery blue eyes looked a little more watery than usual.

"Remember His words—*Be not afraid, for I am with you all the days of your life.* Now go in peace."

When the door closed behind Sister Agnes, Regina opened the butcher paper and found a short-sleeved white cotton blouse with buttons up the front and a pretty skirt of periwinkle blue printed with tiny pink rosebuds. The skirt, she could tell, was homemade. Tears stung her eyes as she realized how much love it had taken for her mother to cut it out and stitch it for this occasion.

Beneath the skirt she found a pair of white anklets, a very demure full-length cotton slip, and a clean but used brassiere of unadorned white. Pinned to it was a note in her mother's hand: "I couldn't guess at your size, so this is one of mine. Hope it'll do till we can buy you some."

For the very last time, Sister Regina undressed as required by their constitution, in the reverse order of which she'd dressed that morning. She kissed each piece of her habit and laid it aside, with a prayer for each. She hurried to don the brassiere, finding it too large. The blouse was store-bought and fit her fine. The skirt was tight around the waist, but she got it buttoned anyway. The white anklets looked silly with her black Cuban-heeled oxfords, but she had no other shoes.

When she was all dressed, she removed from her left ring finger the plain gold band she had donned when she became the bride of Christ. With a heavy heart she laid the ring upon her neatly folded garments on the chair.

"I'm sorry," she whispered. "It simply wasn't the life for me."

From her desktop she took a small mirror and a short black pocket comb and put them to use on her hair. It was cider blond, cut haphazardly by her own hand. As she combed it, she had a sudden fear of going out into public this way, unstyled and dumpy.

So much to learn. But she would. She would.

Downstairs in the music room her parents were waiting.

"Hello, Mother, Dad. Thank you so much for coming."

They sprang from their chairs as if caught in some illicit act.

"Sist—" Her mother shot a sheepish glance at her feet and began again. "Jean, dear. How did the clothes fit?"

"Just fine, Mother. Thank you for making the skirt."

"I didn't make it. Your sister Elizabeth did. She also sent a shorty coat for you. She wasn't sure what you'd have for outside wear."

"How thoughtful."

Her father hadn't said a word yet. He held the coat while she slipped it on, and for a moment she felt his hands squeeze her shoulders through the warm wool and shoulder pads.

"I'll bring your suitcase" were his first words.

They went out first, and she followed. Not even Mother Superior was waiting in the hall to say good-bye.

I have no regrets, Jean thought, and went out into the spring evening.

Ah, the wind. The wind in her hair! And on her legs! And in her uncovered ears! It sighed through the deep afternoon while the lowering sun clasped her bare head with warmth. Robins were singing louder than she ever remembered, so exquisitely audible without a layer of starchy white cloth binding her ears.

Then she was in the back seat of her father's car and they were pulling away from the curb, and she wondered if Mr. Olczak was in the school building, cleaning her classroom, or if he'd gone home already and who would tell him she was gone.

THREE days after Jean returned to the farm the mailman brought a letter from Anne Olczak. Her heart fluttered with excitement as she read the return address.

Dear Sister Regina,

Daddy said it would be o.k. if I wrote to you because I was very sad when you left. I never thought you would go away too and now I hate school. Sister Clement isn't a very good teacher and she falls asleep all the time and recess is no fun cause the boys are meen to us and she doesn't make them behave.

Daddy said the reason you didn't say goodby is that they make nuns go wherever they say and you have to do it. I don't think that's write so I've desided not to be a nun when I grow up. I was going to be a nun but now I'm not going to be one.

Daddy says its o.k. if I tell you that I use to pretend you were my mother after my mother dyed. I use to pretend that sometimes. That is why I felt bad when they said you were gone.

Lucy got 100 in her spelling test.

I hope you are fine Daddy says you are fine and you did not die too. Well I have to go and clean out Sugar's sand box.

Love,
Anne Olczak

Jean waited to reply until the last weekend in May, when Anne would celebrate her First Communion. Then she sent a holy card as a gift, and a letter to all of them.

Dear Mr. Olczak, Anne, and Lucy,

I shall address this to all three of you because you are all on my mind. I must first apologize for not letting you know I was leaving. I certainly would have if I'd been able. Unfortunately, I had to leave in haste and good-byes were not possible.

Although you children will probably wonder why, I have made a big change in my life, and I am no longer a nun. I requested a dispensation of my vows from the Holy Father in Rome, and it came the day I left Browerville. I am now living with my mother and father on their farm.

It's good to be back with my family again, but I certainly do miss all of my students. Anne, I was so happy to get your letter, though I felt very sad to hear that you didn't like school anymore. Next year will be better. Wait and see.

This Sunday you will be making your First Communion, Anne, and I'm so proud of you. I shall think of you in your white dress and veil and say a prayer for you that day. I wish I could be there at Mass with you, as I know it will be a glorious day in your life.

Lucy, next year it will be your turn to receive the sacraments for the first time, so you must study your catechism hard during the school year to prepare for it. Anne wrote that you received a 100 on one of your spelling tests. Good for you!

Mr. Olczak, you are a good and kind man, and I always admired how much patience you had with the children when they'd come right behind your broom and mess up the school building again. I pray for you and for the repose of Krystyna's soul. I hope by now God has given you some solace in your life.

It would please me very much to hear from all of you in the future so that I may know you are doing fine.

God bless you all,
Jean (Regina) Potlocki

EDDIE found the letter in his post-office box three weeks after Sister Regina left. It had been the longest, gloomiest three weeks of his life. He'd been in agony. But he had only to read her name on the outside of the envelope to feel his spirits soar. He stood on Main Street in front of the post office and read the letter two times.

That night at suppertime he read it aloud to the girls. When he finished, they stared at him agape.

"She's not a sister anymore?" Anne exclaimed.

"No, she's not."

"But how can that be?"

"Well, she had to ask the Pope himself to sign a paper letting her be a regular person again."

"But why did she quit? Didn't she want to be our teacher anymore?" Lucy said, her young face showing disillusionment.

"Honey, being a nun means much more than being a teacher. I'm sure there were other reasons she left."

"Like what?"

"Honey, I can't tell you that, because I don't know."

"You mean it's like a secret?"

"Sort of, yes. Her secret. Her reasons are private."

Lucy asked, a little sheepishly, "Doesn't she get to wear her black dress or veil anymore?"

"No. I suppose she dresses just like other women now."

"But—but nuns don't got no hair."

He hid his urge to laugh and asked, "How do you know?"

Lucy shrugged protractedly in reply.

Anne spoke up again, more soberly than her sister.

"Won't we ever see her again, Daddy?"

He thought, If I have my way, you will. But he decided it was best to answer, "I don't know."

HE COUNTED the weeks since she'd left, cautioning himself that he must not rush. Three weeks, and he got the letter. Another week, and the children were out of school for the summer. Seven weeks, and the bare spots on the playground were beginning to fill in with grass. How long should a man stay away from a newly released ex-nun in order to keep her free from gossip?

He waited two full months, and on July 8, a Sunday, he finally ran out of patience. But he decided it would look better if he took the girls along. After church he asked them, trying to sound casual, "How about if we all take a ride this afternoon? I thought we might go over and visit Sister Regina."

"Reeeally, Daddy?"

"Now we don't know for sure that she'll be home. We'll just drive over and take a chance."

He wasn't sure who was more impatient to see her, himself or his kids. Halfway there, Anne asked him to stop the truck so she could pick some wild roses for Sister. Then she corrected herself and said, "I mean, for Jean."

It sounded foreign to all of them.

About a hundred yards from her folks' farm he saw that they were having a family picnic. Cars and trucks all over the place and tables out on the lawn and people standing in clusters visiting and kids in shorts splashing in and out of a washtub full of water.

He couldn't drive on past. Every eye at that picnic would look up to identify who was rumbling by on their quiet country road. Besides, the girls would raise a stink.

What could he do but pull in the driveway?

He couldn't identify her at first amongst all the strangers. Some quit what they were doing and ambled over to see who it was as soon as the truck doors slammed. Then a girl who was just getting ready to pitch a horseshoe looked over and saw the familiar truck and dropped the shoe on the ground at her feet. Waving exuberantly above her head, she hurried toward them.

"Hello!" she called, smiling as she came. "Anne, Lucy . . ." She reached them and squeezed both of Anne's hands, wild roses and all, then both of Lucy's. "What a surprise! My goodness, this is just wonderful!" Her smile was brilliant as she continued to grip Lucy's hands. "You're both here. I'm so happy!"

The girls stared at her, mesmerized, trying to equate this woman with the nun they'd known. Her hair was the color of a peeled apple left out in the air, neither gold nor brown, cropped rather short and left to its own slight natural curl. She was wearing a wrinkled cotton dress of pink and white lattice design, and over it a white apron. Her feet were bare.

Finally she dropped Lucy's hands. "And Mr. Olczak, how nice to see you again." She spoke much quieter to Eddie than to the girls, offering her hand more sedately. Just a squeeze while she smiled up and he tried to catch his breath. Quickly she spun and called, "Look, Mama and Daddy, it's Mr. Olczak! And he's brought his girls!"

Frank came over from the horseshoe court, and Bertha rose from a lawn chair, where she'd been visiting with some ladies.

Frank gave Eddie a firm handshake. "Well, hello again, Mr. Olczak. Nice to see you."

Bertha lingered a step farther away, reserving her smile and enthusiasm. "Hullo." It was easier for her to be civil to the girls than to Eddie. "So these are the girls we been hearing about. Which one of you wrote that letter to Jean?"

Anne raised her hand. "I did."

"Well, that was some nice letter. Made her real happy."

Jean interrupted. "Come and meet some of the others. This is my brother George, my brother-in-law Curt, and my aunt, Bernice." Eddie lost count of the family members. "And this is my very special sister, Liz. She's closest to me in age."

Liz said quietly, "Hello, Eddie. I've heard a lot about you."

She has? Eddie thought, but hadn't time to dwell on it.

His kids stuck close, and Jean paid them much more attention than she did him. She asked if they'd like a piece of cake.

They looked up at Eddie for permission, and he said, "It's okay."

"Come with me," Jean said, and took them off to a table where white dish towels kept the flies off the leftovers.

The men took Eddie down by the big galvanized watering tank, where a cold beer was plucked from the water and put in his hand. They talked about the crops and Truman lowering the draft age and about how Frank and Bertha's granary needed a new roof and they'd all get together and put it on in the fall after the crops were in.

Eddie tried to pretend interest, but his attention kept wandering to Jean. She had a waist now and curves above and below and legs that had a bit of suntan on them. And those bare feet! Her face looked different, too, without all that stiff white starch around it.

She was organizing the whole tribe of youngsters into some running game, and only when Lucy and Anne were happily involved did she slowly cross the yard toward him.

"Would you like to sit down and talk?" she asked Eddie. "I'd love to know how the girls are doing. Anne had her First Communion, and Lucy's taking swimming lessons, she tells me."

"Sure," he said, following her, studying her spice-colored hair from behind, trying to get used to the fact that she was now as approachable as other women.

They sat on the grass in the shade of some birches, not far from where the children were playing. She settled down Indian-style, tucking her feet beneath the latticed skirt of her dress. They talked about his children and Browerville, and she asked after all of his relatives.

He sat at her left, facing the same direction as she. She wasn't even looking at him when she remarked, "You're staring at me."

"Oh!" He felt his face flare. "Sorry. You *do* look different."

"Yes, I know. It takes some getting used to, doesn't it?"

"Lucy wanted to know what we'd do if you didn't have hair."

She laughed and pulled a few blades of grass.

"Not only do you have hair, you're barefoot. Can you blame me for staring?"

"No. But my mother is watching us."

He glanced toward the women. Bertha was doing exactly that.

"Mama isn't accepting all of this very well."

"And you?"

"It's . . . taking a while. I've lived in a convent for over eleven years. At times I feel there's really no place for me anymore."

"Are you sorry you quit?"

"No," she answered without pause. "But, you see, I don't really have a routine anymore or a home. I have my family, but I feel as if I'm here on sufferance."

"I'll bet they don't feel that way."

"No, I suppose they don't. It's just me. But it's odd to be a full-grown woman moving back into your parents' house."

He considered awhile, then said, "I thought you'd teach."

"They won't let me, not in a Catholic school. Bad influence, you see."

He bristled. "You? A bad influence?"

"Not on the students. On the other nuns."

"Oh, I get it. Some of them might decide to quit, too."

"Preservation of the order, it's called."

"Pardon me, but that's stupid."

"It's why there was so much secrecy surrounding my leaving. They didn't even give me any notice. Mother Agnes just came into my schoolroom that day and said I should go and pack." She turned to meet his eyes. "I wanted to find you and—"

"Hello. Mind if I join you?" They'd been so intent on their conversation they hadn't seen Liz approaching. Eddie felt as if he'd jumped from a tree limb and caught his suspender on a branch. There he hung, suspended in midair, with Jean's emotions only half revealed.

She could do nothing but conjure up a smile for her sister and invite, "No. Please . . . sit down."

They talked and talked, and in time other family members joined them, and before he knew it, Eddie realized he should start for home.

Much to his regret, he and Jean never found time to finish their private conversation. He rounded up the girls and headed for the truck. When they were inside, with the engine started, Jean's hands were the last folded over the window edge.

"Good-bye, girls. Say hello to everybody back home."

"Bye, Sister," they both said. They had forgotten and called her by her old name. She merely smiled at the slip.

"Good-bye, Mr. Olczak. Please come again."

"I will. Good-bye." He found it difficult to say Jean.

But as he put the truck in reverse and backed out onto the gravel road, he promised himself he would. And soon. As soon as he could get back here to pay a call on her. Without the girls.

Chapter 9

ONE week passed—one hot, lengthy, impatient July week with the sun so intense it seemed to have faded the blue sky. In the garden the string beans grew so fast they needed picking morning and evening. Jean picked them and helped her mother can them. And all the while she thought of Eddie.

In Browerville, Eddie passed the week sanding and varnishing school desks and thinking of Jean. He'd made up his mind he'd drive back to the farm and visit her the following Saturday night.

On Thursday he told his sister-in-law Rose, "I need a favor on Saturday. I need to have the kids go to the movies with your kids, then sleep overnight at your house afterward."

"Oh, where you going?"

"I'm going to visit someone. It's . . . ah, Sister Regina."

"Sister Regina?" Rose repeated, her mouth and eyes widening. "You mean *our* Sister Regina who isn't a nun anymore?"

"That's right. Only her name is Jean now. Jean Potlocki."

"How long has this been going on?" Rose asked, point-blank.

"Look!" Eddie said, his patience growing short. "If I have to go through the third degree just to leave the kids here overnight, I'll find someplace else to take them!"

"Settle down, Eddie. I won't ask any more questions. Of course you can leave the kids here. Does Romaine know about this?"

"No."

"Well, I'm gonna tell him."

"I'm sure you will. And everybody else in town, too, I suppose." Eddie walked out of her kitchen, shaking his head.

HE BOUGHT NEW CLOTHES FOR Saturday night, a pair of pleated trousers, blue, and a nice light, cottony shirt with short sleeves and pale blue and white stripes. When Jean recognized his truck coming down the road, raising a cloud of dust, she thought, Oh no, why didn't I follow my instincts and take a bath and put on some decent clothes and let the beans go for just one night?

But she'd been afraid to believe he'd come again so soon. So she had slipped on her dad's barn boots, tied a dish towel on her head to keep the gnats out of her hair, and had gone out to the garden to pick beans in the evening cool.

She stood there in the bean patch, straight as a scarecrow, watching his truck approach on the other side of a band of raspberry bushes that separated her from the road. He didn't notice her there, but drove into the yard, parked, and walked up to the house.

She was fifty yards from the back door when she saw her mother answer his knock and point down at the bean patch. He turned, spotted her, and started her way. She wanted to move, but couldn't. Instead, there she stood, looking an absolute fright, while the man she loved walked straight toward her between the vegetable rows.

He stopped one bucket of beans away from her, his toe nearly touching the galvanized pail that sat between the rows, half full.

"Hello, Jean," he said, speaking her given name for the first time.

"Hello, Eddie," she replied, for the first time, too.

"I hope it's okay that I came back so soon. I would have telephoned, but . . ." He didn't bother finishing.

"And I would have taken a bath and gotten dressed, but . . ."

They both laughed. "I'm glad you didn't," he said. "I like finding you out here like an ordinary woman."

"A little too ordinary," she said. "I look a fright."

"Not to me you don't."

She dropped her eyes and said self-consciously, "No man has ever paid a call on me before. I didn't picture it happening with a dish towel on my head and my daddy's barn boots on my feet."

"Neither did I. Since last Sunday I've been picturing your hair the way it looked when we were talking under the birch trees."

She lifted her eyes. "My hair is very plain."

"I like the color of it. Do you mind?" he asked, reaching toward the dish towel.

Her stillness became acquiescence. When he'd swept the towel from her hair, they stood in place, letting him get his fill of her. She felt her color rising but made no objection as he studied her openly.

Finally he said, "There are so many questions I want to ask you." He glanced over his shoulder at the house. "Can we walk?"

"For miles and miles," she replied, and turned away from him, leaving the bucket of beans where it was. They walked side by side along two adjacent vegetable rows, in the opposite direction from the house. The sun disappeared behind them, and when they reached the end of the garden, she turned left onto the road and said, "What was it you wanted to ask me?"

"Last Sunday, remember when we were talking and Liz interrupted? You were about to say that the day you left Browerville you wanted to find me and . . . and what?"

"I wanted to find you and tell you that I was leaving. I wanted to tell you good-bye. I wanted you to know where you could find me."

"I found you anyway, but I went through hell before I got your letter and realized you were prevented from saying good-bye."

"I believe we've both gone through a lot of that since Krystyna died, haven't we?"

"Yes."

"How are you doing in that regard?" she asked.

"Without Krystyna? Going through some guilt since I started having feelings for you. How are you doing in that regard?"

"About the same. I loved Krystyna."

"Everybody loved Krystyna."

"I think both you and I will always love Krystyna, and I think that's a lovely note on which to start our friendship."

"Friendship?" he repeated, and stopped walking. "I asked you this once before, but you refused to answer, so let's clear it up right now. Do you—do you have feelings for me?"

"Yes, Mr. Eddie Olczak, I do." She smiled and tilted her head.

"But it would have broken about a dozen Holy Rules, not to mention my vow of chastity, if I'd answered you then."

He took her hands and held them. "Then there's one other thing I have to know. Am I the reason you quit?"

"No. You were a part of it, but certainly not what started it."

"Then why did you quit?"

She told him, going clear back to the year before Krystyna died. She spoke of all her misgivings with life in the religious community and the anguish she'd gone through while making the decision and the role his children had played in making her realize she wanted children of her own and her fear of the feelings she was having for him. She told him about the scene at Christmas dinner when Grandma Rosella had burst into tears, and of going to St. Ben's.

"I was so afraid, Eddie."

In the midst of Jean's recital the afterglow of sunset had streaked the western sky like smeared fruit, but already it began to fade as he studied her downturned face. "So was I. I'm still afraid."

She looked up in surprise. "Of what?"

"Lots of things. Starting rumors by coming over here too soon. What my kids might say. Kissing a nun for the first time."

Jolted by shyness, she immediately dropped her gaze again. His voice fell to a softer tone. "Tell me, how do I get over the notion that if I kiss you, I'd be kissing Sister Regina?"

"The last time I was kissed I believe I was something like ten years old, so you're not the only one who's scared, Eddie."

He put his hands on her face and beckoned her to lift it. When she did, he held it like a chalice. "Then let's get this over with," he whispered, lowering his head and touching his lips to hers with a pressure so slight they made no demands. Her lips remained closed, her body stiffly angled toward him from one step too far away, and he realized she didn't know any better.

He drew back only far enough to whisper, "Want me to teach you a way that's more fun?"

"Yes," she whispered, terrified, intrigued, and eager all at once.

He placed his warm open lips over hers and encouraged her to enjoy it. He smiled against her mouth and waited patiently for her to lose her inhibitions. Then, reaching between them, he captured her hands. "It's okay to put your arms around me. There are no Holy Rules now."

He placed her arms around his neck and held them there as a new kiss began, and she became a willing student, curving against him like the new moon against the eastern sky. And at last the kiss flowered.

They stood beneath that rising moon, ushering out the tired day with a ceremony as old as time. First kiss, standing between the ditches where the wild evening primroses opened their yellow petals and perfumed the air like vanilla. Second kiss, with his strong arms lifting her free of the road and her big black overshoes dropping off her feet to the gravel. Third kiss, ending when he lowered her down to stand on his shiny black shoes, and some frogs started croaking in a pond they hadn't noticed was there.

Standing on his shoes, she hid her face against his crisp striped shirt, which smelled of factory starch. "Oh, my goodness," she whispered, breathing hard, "it's much different when you're thirty."

"Is that how old you are? I was thirty-five in March."

They were comparing ages like people with serious intentions. To leaven the seriousness, she said, "Well, you know what they say, a person is never too old to learn."

He smiled and asked, "So what did you think of it?"

"I liked it very much. You're a very good teacher."

"And you're a very good pupil."

She stepped off his shoes, back into the black boots. "You're teasing me because I'm so ignorant of these things."

"No." He joggled her up close and made her lift her chin. "I'd never tease you because of that."

"All right, then, you're forgiven. For everything but catching me in my boots and babushka."

"What can I do to make it up to you?"

"Let me think," she said, turning westward and starting slowly for home. Full dark had arrived by the time they reached her driveway, and she informed him, "I thought of something."

"What?"

She drew a deep breath. "I've never been on a date."

"You haven't!" He grinned in the dark. "Funny thing you should mention it, because I was trying to work up the courage to ask for one next Saturday night, but I didn't know what you'd think of me showing up here three weekends in a row. I don't want any talk to start. Your dispensation was only granted two months ago."

"The same goes for you. It's less than a year since Krystyna died. What will the people in Browerville say?"

"We'll find out soon. Next Saturday I'll have to tell whoever baby-sits the girls. Three weeks in a row I drive clear over to Gilman to see you. They'll all guess why."

She said a most profound thing. "Our strength, Eddie, is in our truth, and our truth will render gossip impotent."

He did not kiss her good night—they were too close to the house. Approaching it, he observed that only the front-room lights were on. The kitchen, directly off the back porch, was dark.

They stopped at the steps and turned to face each other.

"Seven thirty, then, next Saturday night?" Eddie asked.

"I'll be ready. And I won't have my daddy's boots on."

EDDIE got there ten minutes early, and Jean was waiting on the back step.

In the truck, Eddie said, "Well, where do you want to go?"

"I don't know. I've never done this before."

"Well . . . do you want to go to a dance?"

"Oh no," she said with a fleeting frown. "I don't know the first thing about dancing."

"Well, then, how about a movie?"

"Yes! A movie! Oh, I'd love to see a movie."

"There's a theater in Little Falls. We could drive that way and see what's playing."

"Take me anywhere! I'm having the time of my life just riding in my new dress!"

He couldn't help chuckling at her and eyeing her askance. The dress had a V neck, cap sleeves, and made her look thin as a buggy whip. "I thought it looked new."

"I made it," she said, "especially for tonight. Blue, because that's your favorite color."

"How did you know that?"

"You wear blue suits a lot and blue ties. Last Saturday night you wore a blue-and-white striped shirt. I liked it."

He was falling in love so hard it felt like a dogfight in his gut.

"Come over here," he said, catching her hand and tugging. "I'll bet you never rode in a truck with a guy's arm around you."

"No, I haven't." He could tell his teasing flustered her.

"Well, now you have." He dropped an arm around her shoulders and let it lie lightly, rubbing her bare right arm.

She sat very still. He could tell she was absorbing the newness of having her arm stroked. It gave her goose bumps he could see.

When they were halfway to Little Falls, he had an idea, but decided he'd better quit stroking her while he suggested it. He removed his arm and told her, "There's a drive-in theater at Little Falls, too."

She wasn't *that* sheltered! She knew what happened at drive-in theaters and why the Catholic Church spoke out against them.

"A drive-in theater?" she repeated, sitting up more erectly.

"Look," he said, "you know me. If you think I'd take you to a drive-in theater just to get you in some compromising position, you're wrong. I just thought you maybe never went to a drive-in before and you'd like to try it."

He watched her struggle with some remaining misgivings, but she conceded, "All right, then. I'll try the drive-in movie."

So they went to the Falls Drive-in and watched Doris Day and Gordon MacRae fall in love and sing their way through a musical courtship in *On Moonlight Bay*. Jean's eyes glowed with delight all through the movie, especially when the two stars harmonized together. When they sang "Cuddle Up a Little Closer" and kissed on-screen, Eddie watched Jean and wished he could kiss her, too.

But he was as good as his word, keeping himself squarely behind

the wheel, glancing at Jean only when she'd laugh or whisper a remark about Doris Day's pretty clothes. When the movie ended and
the beams from a hundred car lights blanched the big screen, they
stayed, discussing the story, and how much she'd loved it, especially
the singing and the pretty dresses. Soon the second feature was
starting, but he turned down the sound, and they kept talking. It
seemed there was no end of subjects they had to talk about.

Then somehow they found themselves lounging with her hand in
his and their eyes on each other instead of the screen.

"Jean?" he whispered, and that single word tore them loose from
their moorings. They met in the middle of the seat, kissing hungrily
enough to scatter good intentions to the four winds.

"Oh, mercy, how I missed you," he breathed as the kiss ended in
a powerful embrace. "I thought this week would never end."

"Oh, me too." She squeezed him hard. "Me too."

They kissed again, running their hands over each other's backs,
feeling the awesome power of temptation. It was a renewal for him
and a discovery for her. When the kiss ended, she said breathlessly
at his ear, "Oh, Eddie, is this what I gave up when I went into the
convent? I never felt like this before. Never."

"I want you."

"Shhh, Eddie, don't say it."

"But I do. I want more than this, more than just holding you and
kissing you. I wanted you when you were still a nun. I went to confession and confessed it, but it didn't stop. And it's *not* just because
I've been without a woman for a long time, and it's *not* because I'm
missing Krystyna. It's you. I love you, Jean, and I'm afraid it's too
soon to say it, but what else can I do?"

She calmed him with five words. "I love you, too, Eddie."

"You do?"

"I've loved you since right after Krystyna died."

"I love you, you love me, my kids are nuts about you, and if I'm
not mistaken, you're nuts about them. Will you marry me?"

She let their embrace wilt. "And live where?" She waited a beat,
then added, "In Browerville?"

He knew how preposterous it sounded, but what else could he offer? "I live there. My house is there. My work is there."

"I was a nun there. How can you expect people to accept me as your wife?"

He spoke with barely suppressed anger. "They're supposed to be Christians! Good Catholic ones! And what was it you said? Our strength is in our truth, and our truth will render gossip impotent. Maybe it'll do the same to any of their . . . their *blame opinions!*"

"Let's think about it for a while. We've only been seeing each other for three weeks."

"But I've known you for four years—five, come September. I'm not going to change my mind."

"Nevertheless, let's think about it for a week. Please, Eddie . . . just come next Saturday. Same time. I'll be ready. Now I think I'd better get home."

It was a difficult good-bye at her door. He drew her to him, full length, and kissed her with his throat already constricted from the thought of driving away and not seeing her for seven days.

He walked backward away from her, his arm extended till their fingertips no longer touched. Only then did he turn away.

Chapter 10

THE next Saturday was only the fourth day Eddie and Jean had spent together. They stayed away from the drive-in theater and remained at her folks' farm instead. He said, when he got there, "Could we just sit in the yard and talk?"

She squelched her disappointment and replied, "Sure, if that's what you want."

" 'Cause I hope that before I leave, we might need to have your parents come out here so we can talk to them, too."

They sat on a pair of Adirondack chairs out near the apple trees, and Eddie asked her again, "Will you marry me, Jean?"

She got tears in her eyes, pressed eight fingertips to her lips, and nodded repeatedly until she could get control.

"You will?" he said, amazed no further wheedling was needed.

She nodded again, for she still couldn't speak.

Eddie let his eyes sink shut and whispered, "Thank you, God."

He bent forward and took her hands. She tried to say, "Oh, Eddie, I'm so happy," but little came out, so he leaned forward and kissed her softly. When their lips parted, she said, smiling through her sniffles, "Just think, I get to be Anne and Lucy's mom."

"You mean I can tell them at last?"

"Oh yes."

"And maybe we'll have a couple more someday. What would you think of that?"

"Just thinking of having your babies makes me happy."

"Well, then"—he fished in his pocket—"I have something for you." He came up with a modest diamond ring and put it on the finger that had once held a plain gold band.

"Oh, Eddie," she said, admiring her extended hand. "Eddie." She leaned forward and hugged him. "I love you so much."

"I love you, too, Jean."

They sat like that awhile as evening cooled the yard and the frogs started a pulsating serenade down in the ponds.

In time he asked, "Should we go get your parents now?"

She nodded against his shoulder.

"How soon should we tell them we want to get married?"

"Soon. Please." Her voice was muffled.

He smiled and rubbed a hand down her hair, gave her neck an affectionate squeeze, and whispered, "Let's go, then."

Their announcement brought a stolid acceptance from Bertha and a statement from Frank: "You can have the wedding reception here. No daughter of mine is going to get married without a proper send-off. Mother will butcher the chickens, and your sisters can come over and help with all the cooking. It's no less than we did for every one of them." So the law was laid down.

When Eddie kissed Jean good-bye beside his truck, she said, "Tell me what Anne and Lucy say. And tell them I can't wait to be their mom. Or should we say stepmother?"

"Mom is fine. It doesn't take anything away from Krystyna."

WHEN he told the girls he was going to marry their ex-teacher, Lucy's face scrunched up in delighted surprise.

"You *are?* Can I wear my white dress and be your flower girl?"

"Well," he chuckled, "I hadn't thought of that. Maybe."

"Annie could be one, too, couldn't she?"

"Maybe. If she wants to."

"Is Sister Regina gonna live with us, then?"

"Her name is Jean now, and yes, she's going to live with us."

"And take care of us like Mommy did?"

"And take care of you like Mommy did."

Lucy clapped her hands and said, "Goody."

He rested a gentle hand on Anne's back. "So is it okay with you if I marry her and she comes to live with us?"

Anne moved closer and nestled against him. "If I can't have my real mommy, she's the next best thing."

With a lump in his throat he kissed Anne's forehead, then Lucy's.

THE banns were announced for three weeks, and they were married in St. Peter and Paul's in Gilman on a sparkling Saturday in late August, one week shy of the anniversary of Krystyna's death. Half the town of Browerville was there, including Father Kuzdek, and so many Olczak relatives it looked like a family reunion. All of Jean's family attended, too, including Grandma Rosella. Richard and Mary Pribil came, too, but not Irene. Irene, they said, wasn't feeling well that day and had decided at the last minute to stay home.

Anne and Lucy did, indeed, act as flower girls. They were outfitted in long dresses—petal pink and pouffed over crinolines—

lovingly stitched by their aunt Irene, who sent a note via her parents telling the girls how sorry she was not to see them march down the aisle, but that she'd be thinking of them all day long.

The bride wore a white dress, for the second time. And a white veil, for the second time. But today her betrothed waited at the front of the church, a real, flesh-and-blood, beloved man, withheld, at her insistence, from viewing her until the moment she appeared at the foot of the aisle and moved toward him.

She did so while the pipe organ shook the floor with Mendelssohn and his children strewed flower petals grown in their grandparents' gardens. Ahead of Jean, her sister Liz moved—step, point, step, point—gowned in pink a shade deeper than the children's. Beside Eddie, his brother Romaine waited with two rings in his pocket.

Eddie, in a new blue worsted suit, waited with his hands joined, stiffly motionless but for one knee that kept locking and unlocking nervously. His face bore a telltale flush beneath its summer tan as he watched his bride approach, her face screened by a short veil, while an immense one trailed behind.

Jean's father squeezed her hand and passed her to Eddie. When she touched his sleeve, he covered her hand, felt it trembling, looked down at her, and smiled. He did not remove his hand from hers until the ceremony forced him to.

"*In nomine Patris* . . ." the parish priest, Father Donnelly, began, and Eddie had to make the sign of the cross. But the minute it was made, he covered Jean's hand again.

They bowed their heads; they were prayed over. Finally the priest murmured instructions for Liz to turn back Jean's veil, then to the bride and groom, "Would you join right hands, please?"

With hearts in one accord they heard, "Repeat after me . . ."

"I, Edward Olczak, take thee, Jean Potlocki, to be my lawful wife, to have and to hold, from this day forward, for better, for worse, for richer, for poorer, in sickness and in health, until death do us part."

Then Jean spoke in her sweet voice. "I, Jean Potlocki, take thee, Edward Olczak . . ." She felt the tears form while she repeated the phrases that tied her to Eddie for life, ". . . until death do us part."

Father made a cross in the air and sanctified their union. He asked for the rings, blessed them, and Eddie repeated, "With this ring, I thee wed." Holding his wife's thin hand, he slipped the band where another had been only four months ago.

She, too, whispered, "With this ring, I thee wed," and slid his new ring over the place where Krystyna's used to be.

The others to whom they'd been wed were with them in that moment as surely as the guests filling the pews behind them, blessing this union and granting it peace.

The organ boomed, and they strode from St. Peter and Paul's, burst into the sunlight where, on the high church steps, he kissed her politely, reserving his ardor for later. But he smiled in jubilation as their mouths parted and their smiling eyes met.

"Mrs. Olczak," he said.

"Oh, the sound of it!" she replied.

Then they turned and submitted themselves to six hours of social obligation: receiving line, dinner in the farmyard, hugs from well-wishers, perusing the gifts, spending time with Anne and Lucy, and giving special attention to Grandma Rosella.

Perhaps the most touching moment of all came when Richard and Mary Pribil congratulated them as they prepared to leave. Mary captured Eddie and, an arm around his neck, began to cry.

Lucy, who was departing with her grandparents, pulled on Jean's hand and said, "Why is Grandma crying, Jean?"

Jean answered, "Because she's both happy and sad."

"But why is she sad?"

Jean cupped Lucy's sunburned cheek and said, "Because she misses your mother, and so do I." Anne stood close by. Jean beckoned her over and took a hand of each child in her own. "I was very proud of you today, and I want you to know that I love you both and I will be the best mother I know how. I don't have much experience, so sometimes you might have to help me and tell me what I'm doing wrong, but you had the best teacher of all in your own mother, so I'm quite sure we'll muddle through. Now you be good at Grandpa and Grandma Pribil's house and say your prayers at night, okay?"

"We will."

"And if you want to come home before Wednesday, you just tell them to bring you." The plan was, the girls would come home Wednesday afternoon, giving the newlyweds a four-day honeymoon, only they'd be spending it at home in Browerville, where Eddie could settle her in the house before the new school year began next week.

After seeing the children off, there were final good-byes, and while Jean changed clothes, Eddie's brothers loaded the wedding gifts onto the bed of Eddie's pickup.

She came out of the house at last, wearing the pretty blue dress she'd made for their first date. He put her in the pickup, and then finally . . . finally . . . Eddie was starting the engine and they were waving good-bye as they pulled out of the driveway and raised a dust cloud down the road.

It was around six in the evening, the sun still high and the red-winged blackbirds bobbing in the marsh, their songs whistling in the open truck window. Eddie and Jean had the rest of the night to themselves. He peered at her and she peered back, and they laughed for their freedom. He said, "Let's go home."

HE PARKED in front of his yellow brick house beneath the box elders and walked her to the back door, holding her elbow. He had decided to take her in through the back, which was out of sight of the street, giving them more privacy. He swung the door open, picked her up, and carried her inside.

She had never been inside his house before. From his arms she surveyed the kitchen—wood range, white cabinets, running water, and the table and chairs he'd made for Krystyna.

"Put me down, Eddie," she requested quietly. Looking up at him she said, "It's a very nice kitchen. Did you make all this?"

"The cabinets and the table, yeah."

"I thought so. Show me the rest."

The sun was setting through the west living-room window as she took in the maroon horsehair furniture and the upright piano, too big for its corner.

"There's a sewing machine out here," he said, pointing to it in the tiny front entry. "You're welcome to use it anytime."

She passed near him, went to the machine, and touched it lightly with her fingertips, giving him the impression she might have said a word to Krystyna while doing so.

"And there's an upstairs, too."

"Yes." When she mounted the bottom step, a metal washer bumped the wall on the end of its long string. "What's this?" she said.

"It's a string so the kids can turn on the light before they go up to bed. Krystyna put it up."

He chided himself for mentioning Krystyna, while Jean pulled the string and looked up as the light came on in the upstairs hall ceiling. She started up the steps, and he followed.

"This is the girls' room," he said at the top. She stepped into the sunlit room and smiled as her eyes wandered over the wallpaper and the rosettes on the window frames. Sugar, sleeping on the bed, woke up and stretched all four feet out in front of her, squint-eyed and stiff.

"This is Sugar," he said. "I'm sure you've heard about her."

"Hi, Sugar," Jean said, giving the cat a cursory scratch before Eddie led her to the other end of the hall.

"And this is our room."

They stood just inside the doorway.

"Oh my, it has a door to outside. Isn't that lovely."

"We sleep with it open a lot in the summer." He realized too late that he'd said "we."

"May I?" she said, unfazed, glancing up at him.

"Of course."

She crossed the linoleum and opened the east door, letting in the sound of the neighborhood children playing running games outside and the green whisper of the box-elder trees.

"There's a bathroom," he said. "I put that in, too."

"I think I'll be lucky, married to a handyman." She came near him and peered into the bathroom. "I don't think there's anything you can't do, Eddie."

"There's a dressing table. I cleared it all out for you. The closet's awful tiny, but whatever you have, we'll make room for."

"Thank you, Eddie."

He took off his suit jacket and hung it in the closet. "I'd better get those wedding gifts inside," he said, heading for the stairs.

She was standing uncertainly near the dressing table when Eddie returned, bearing with him her suitcase.

"I brought you this," he said, and put it on the foot of the bed.

"Thank you." She opened it and took out a white plissé nightie, at odds with the time of day. The sun hadn't even dropped below the horizon. It streamed across the blue scatter rug beside their bed.

"Eddie, there's something that I want to say." She turned and found him close behind her. "I understand that this was Krystyna's house, that she shared your life here. And it's okay when you mention her name and when you tell me this was hers or that was hers or that she did whatever for Anne and Lucy. Memories of her will be here for many years to come, but because I love you, and because I know you love me, it takes nothing away from our marriage. So, please, Eddie, don't look so guilty when you mention her name."

In the beat before he scooped her into his arms, she saw relief flood his face. "How I love you," he breathed.

"I love you, too," she told him gently.

"I think, Jean Olczak, that you're a saint."

"Oh no, I'm not. I'm so very mortal that I'm scared out of my wits right now."

"Don't be scared." He eased his hold and repeated, softer, into her eyes, "Don't be scared."

"What should I do?"

"Go into the bathroom and put your nightgown on."

When she padded back into the bedroom, her suitcase was on the floor, the bed was turned down, and Eddie was wearing nothing but trousers, leaning against the doorframe with one shoulder, looking out at the twilight. The children's voices had disappeared. Purple shadows were stealing over the town.

Sensing her return, Eddie sent a glance over his shoulder and opened his free arm. It closed around her when she reached him; then he shifted her over and settled her comfortably against his front. It was hard to believe that what she wanted to do with him was no longer a sin.

She reached back and rested her hands on his trouser legs, and he started kissing her neck. She turned in his embrace and kissed him, folding her arms up his bare back, following her instincts. Touching him, tasting him was the best thing she ever remembered. It grew easier and easier while minutes stretched on.

Abruptly he lifted his head, found her hand, and whispered, "Come with me." To the bed he led her, and sideways across it so they could see each other. He kissed her eyes, cheeks, nose, mouth, and covered her breast with an unhurried caress.

She fell still beneath it, wonderstruck by discovery.

She murmured once, his name, he thought—"Oh, Eddie"— before sensations silenced her again.

He whispered something to her, something to calm whatever fears she held, called her "Jean, darling Jean."

He taught her things he'd learned with Krystyna, and there, in the lessons, Krystyna brought them another gift. For it *was* a gift and wondrous and deserved. They had waited, done the pure, right thing, postponed every pleasure till they'd earned its right through marriage. And when that marriage was consummated, there in the dark of that warm August night, they emerged resplendent—loved and loving.

SHE said afterward, with wonder in her voice, entwined with him still, "Isn't God wonderful, thinking up such a thing?"

Eddie kissed her forehead and rested his cheek against it. "I think He's pretty wonderful for giving you up to me."

"I do, too," she said, and fit her foot into the snuggliest place on him, and her hand and one bent knee. "I hope you like sleeping all snuggled up, because I know I'm going to want to be like this a lot. I've slept alone too long."

He wriggled deeper and spread his hand wider on her flank.

Jean said, "Eddie, could I ask you something?"

"Sure."

It took her a while to work up the courage. "How often—how often do men and women, um, do this?"

He laughed heartily. "Ah, my adorable virgin bride."

"You promised me you wouldn't laugh at my ignorance."

"I'm not laughing at you, darling. You just tickle me."

"All right, then, how often *do* they?"

He decided to have some fun with her. "Well, let me see—tomorrow is Sunday, and after Mass, we've got the whole day to ourselves, so we could do it, say, thirty, forty times. But then on—"

"Thirty or forty!"

"But then on workdays we'd have to cut that down some."

"Oh, Eddie, you're teasing." She gave him a punch through the soft bedspread.

They kissed, and afterward he told her, in the voice of a patient teacher, "We can do it every day if you like. Usually at the beginning, when people first fall in love, they want to do it more than once a day; then after they're married awhile, they do it less often. Maybe a couple times a week, maybe more, maybe less. When women get pregnant, they don't feel much like doing it; then toward the end they're not allowed to do it at all."

They thought about that awhile, and she said, "Just think, I could be pregnant right now."

"And what would you think?"

"I said a novena asking that it would happen soon."

He reared back and looked down at her, surprised. "You did?"

"Yes, I did. I'd take as many of your babies as I could get."

"Oh, Jean . . ." He hauled her up from the crook of his shoulder and kissed her softly. "I'm so lucky."

They thought about the children they might have, the ones they already had, and a future of loving them all, working hard for them and for each other. At the foot of the bed they felt Sugar jump up and pick her way tentatively up the bedspread.

Eddie's hand went down and found the cat. "Hi, Sugar."

Jean scratched Sugar's soft fur. "I like cats," she said.

The cat started purring. They were getting blissfully sleepy.

Suddenly Jean sat up and threw the covers back. "Oh my gosh, I forgot my prayers!"

She scrambled from the bed, got to her knees, and joined her hands, naked as a jaybird, while he grinned to himself in the dark. He didn't interrupt her, but neither did he join her. He'd had enough prayer for one day during their long wedding ceremony. Besides, what they'd done together seemed like a prayer to him.

Pretty soon she finished and climbed back in. He held back the covers for her, and she found her old spot on his shoulder.

"Do you kneel down and pray every night?" he asked.

"It's an old habit, hard to break."

"Ah." He understood.

"Eddie?"

"Hm?"

"I'll need to get a driver's license, but first I'll have to learn to drive. Will you teach me?"

"Of course. Why?"

"So I can take the nuns to St. Cloud or Long Prairie to get their eyes examined or their teeth filled. Like Krystyna did."

"Oh. Like Krystyna did."

"Yes."

He smiled. There would always be a little touch of Sister Regina left in his wife, Jean. But that was okay with him. After all, it was the nun he'd fallen in love with.

When he was growing woozy, he mumbled above her ear, "G'night, Sister."

But she was already asleep, dreaming of having his babies.

ABOUT THE AUTHORS

DAVID BALDACCI

After years of writing fiction while also working as a trial lawyer, David Baldacci became literally an overnight success when his first novel, *Absolute Power,* was published in 1996. As he recalls, "The book went out on Monday, Warner Books snapped it up, and I was wealthy on Tuesday." With the success of his next efforts, *Total Control* and now *The Winner,* Baldacci has been able to give up his law career. He and his family live in Virginia.

NORA ROBERTS

Nora Roberts started writing in 1979, when her sons were young. Now, almost twenty years and one hundred–plus books later, this best-selling novelist still writes during school hours, even though one son is in college and the other has graduated. Roberts says of work and family, "You're always juggling balls, and the trick is to realize that some balls are glass and some are rubber and just to make sure you don't drop the glass ones. There are plenty of balls that can be dropped and picked up again later. And family just isn't one of those."

JACK HIGGINS

With *Flight of Eagles,* Jack Higgins returns to the World War II era of *The Eagle Has Landed,* the 1975 best seller that first brought him fame and fortune. A string of hits followed for the Belfast-born author, who also writes under his real name, Harry Patterson. A high school dropout, he served in the military, then worked as a circus roustabout, a laborer, and a truck driver before going to college and becoming a teacher and author. He has dedicated *Flight of Eagles* to his wife, Denise, "pilot *extraordinaire.*"

LaVYRLE SPENCER

LaVyrle Spencer returned to her hometown, Browerville, Minnesota, for the setting of *Then Came Heaven,* her last novel. "I am retiring, but leaving my many loyal readers with a glimpse of my early life," she says. Though her story is fictional, Spencer used the names of some real people she recalled nostalgically from her childhood, among them her father, Louie Kulick. "I had family love, a safe little town, and the grounding of church and parochial school," she says, all of which "set me off on the right foot."

The volumes in this series are issued
every two to three months. The typical volume
contains four outstanding books in condensed
form. None of the selections in any volume has
appeared in *Reader's Digest* itself. Any reader
may receive this service by writing
The Reader's Digest Association, Inc.,
Pleasantville, N.Y. 10570
or by calling 800-234-9000.

Visit our Web site at
http://www.readersdigest.com

ACKNOWLEDGMENTS

Pages 6–7: photo © George Kamper/Tony Stone Images.
Pages 178–179: photo by McConnell Studios Ltd.
Page 338: illustration by Robert Hunt.
Pages 466–467: illustration by Donna Kae Nelson.